CW00741043

The Nightwing's Quest

Stirling Davenport

Jigsaw Press
Sun River, Montana

For information address: Editor, Jigsaw Press, P.O. Box 136, Sun River, Montana, 59483.

ISBN: 978-1-934340-33-2
Library of Congress Control Number: 2007942989

This is a work of fiction. Names, characters, places, and incidents are products of the author's imagination and/or are used fictitiously. Any similarities to actual events, locales, persons, or worlds, either living or dead, is purely coincidental.

Proudly manufactured in the United States of America

For the missing pieces of your reading puzzle...

Jigsaw Press
Sun River, Montana
www.jigsawpress.com

Acknowledgements

I wish to thank firstly my co-creators Miles Ballew and Herman Davenport. Before there was even a book, they inspired me to make up the story—and listened to each new chapter as it unfolded, giving their feedback. Thanks also goes to Dan Schupack for his early input on the characters.

Next I want to thank my wonderful writing group, who got to read and critique all those hundreds of drafts that came out week by week and year by year—that would be the Six Foot Ferrets Writing Group which back then was composed of Dawn Rosner, Ann Wheeler, Mary Beth Miller, Bret Taylor and Tom Kobak. They're all fine writers and they made me a better writer. I also want to credit Senthil Subramanyam for pushing me to finish the book, and Tsering Dorjee for encouraging me in the last days of editing.

I am also grateful to my friends and family for being patient with me, and special thanks to Barbara Hugo for editing the photo of my watercolor illustration.

And finally, thanks to Mari Bushman and Jigsaw Press for making my dream a reality.

*I dedicate this book to my son and granddaughter, my parents,
and the fairies at Rockdale.*

Part One

Prologue

History of Nightwing Seran

In the days when women were the slaves of men, the High Kings were in power, supported by their champions, the Siadhin Lords. Each of the twelve Siadhin Lords ruled the Great Houses of the cities. And each Lord was aided by a priest-magician. Thus there were twelve houses of dark-elven magic to protect the realm from the goblins, demons, trolls and ogres who besieged it from the vast underground called the Merimn'a.

It was said that the caverns of the Merimn'a had yielded rich ores of silver and precious stones. But from the deepest netherworld, the Kolkondor, Demon of Destruction, learning of their wealth, had sent his minions to steal the treasure from the dwarves who mined it.

Then, there had been such battles that the very heart of the earth trembled. Cave-ins and earthquakes resulted, killing the dwarves, and leaving only foul creatures.

Since that time, it was up to the Siadhin Lord's great army of warriors and priest-magicians to protect the dark-elven cities from the terrible horde of the underworld.

Thus, the cities of that time became centers of warfare and each day the army went forth to battle the creatures of the Merimn'a. All the wealth of the people went to make weapons, and the wailing of the hungry filled the streets.

Assisting the High King and the Siadhin Lords were the priest magicians serving Gantalor, the god of war and magic. The wizards who worshipped this god drew circles of chalk in front of each Great House and said incantations for the victory of the elves over the fell creatures of Kolkondor.

In each city a priest-magician resided, whose duty it was to chose two females to be sacrificed to Gantalor. Each time the moon above was full, the mushroom called the moonteller turned silver. Then, these two would be brought from the pits where they were chained and thrown into a chasm leading to the Merimn'a.

These women and girls were considered by the Alvarran rulers to be a small price to pay for safety. And yet, in the hearts of the females of the realm, rebellion festered, fed by the callous disregard of generations of Alvarran men, from the High King himself to the Lords of Siadhin, his henchmen, and all who used their women like animals for the slaughter.

Thus it was that the female, Sonner, pregnant with her first born, escaped from her owner, and secretly followed the army to the very edge of the Underworld. There she saw the great secret so terrible that it shook her to her soul: there were no ogres or trolls or demons. Only a great sea covered the once wealthy mines of the dwarves. It was all a lie, to keep the women enslaved.

It is a common dark-elven saying that a pregnant woman has the sight. So it must have been with Sonner, for she was blessed with a vision. The Goddess Miralor Herself spoke—She who comes to women in labor, She who blesses the newborn ones and sees to the dying ones who enter the realm of invisibility. Miralor stood before her, clothed in a veil of dark light, and said:

"Sonner, brave and good woman of Alvarra, in your womb is a daughter, whom you have named Seran. Is it not so?"

The poor woman nodded, overwhelmed.

"Seran will be next ruler of Alvarra, newly cleansed of the evil that now runs through it like a poison. You will call her Nightwing and all will bow down to her."

Sonner was too frightened to speak. The vision disappeared. In a rush, she scrambled back, eluding guards and lords and wizards. And in the days that followed, the news was whispered from woman to woman and town to town, from the slave pens to the pits of the doomed.

The revolution was born.

The most beautiful flowers grow in darkness.

—Alvarran proverb.

-1-

THE RABBIT SNIFFED the piquant mist of early morning. A faint breeze made her ebon fur a glossy ripple, and stirred the leaves of the ironwood tree. The rabbit's ears flexed backwards toward the sound. The tree's curved trunk obscured the small opening of a tunnel.

A figure emerged. The rabbit's nose quivered, her body still.

The figure straightened with precision, grace and something more. A gleam of basalt caught the first glimmer of sunlight.

The rabbit's body moved in one fluid leap, prelude to a dash for the bushes, but the knife was quicker. With a piercing squeal, the squirming animal was pinioned to the ground, and the hue of its fur underwent a metamorphosis— from deep black to light brown with white patches. Her pink nose twitched in her death throes.

The hunter strolled to retrieve his weapon, snorting with a vicious disappointment. His dark skin matched dark cloth, a wholly black silhouette against the trees and the blush of dawn on the horizon. His breath came in taut bursts as he scanned the trees. His pointed ears twitched with feral excitement. His mouth watered and yet he did not feed on the slain brown rabbit.

The dark elf sheathed his blade in the deep pocket of his legging. With a wary glance at the rising sun, he melted back into the shadows, staring at the body of the rabbit, in the vain hope that it might change again. The tree sighed, and a raven lighted on a low-hanging branch, ready to make a meal of the fallen creature.

A swoop to the ground, claws extended, ended in frustration. Before it had reached the corpse, there was not a single whisker, nor a drop of blood, nor an indentation in the sandy soil. The startled raven flew away.

The hunter frowned, examining his blade. The blood had disappeared from that, too. Disappointment congealed into rage as he hurried down the endless steps leading to the caverns and lands below.

When he reached the first inner door, he was greeted by his lieutenants, who sang his praises. He bore their congratulations with a stern, impatient dignity.

"Child's work," he said, letting the cold drafts of air fill his nostrils and calm his nerves.

"But, Lord, you dared the Scourge," said one.

"You're not even burned," said another.

"Sunlight is the least of my enemies," he insisted.

"We are eager to destroy them, My Lord."

"When do we fight?" asked another.

"When I say it is time," said the hunter.

A sweet voice said, "Dekhalis, My Lord, let me take your hood." A woman emerged from a lighted doorway. Crystalline jewelry reflected the quartz ceiling above her.

"Ah, Priestess Theowla," said the hunter. "Queen Theowla, they will call you, when I am crowned."

She smirked, sliding next to him, her tufted ears soft with desire. "The Goddess Drimma will be pleased that she is worshipped, instead of that weakling Miralor."

"Truly. Better the wine of revenge than the milk of compassion. Leave us," he told his lieutenants, and they obeyed with alacrity. Dekhalis pressed a spot on the granite wall, causing a slab of stone to slide open. He and the woman entered, activating a warm shower of light that illuminated a down-filled pallet.

The woman's chest was warm against his own. "Did you get the Nightwing's rabbit?" she breathed, her lowered eyes filled with guile.

"No. My mother's magic is strong. But she cannot watch my sisters every moment. First Ombra, then Tiala, and the others. When the last of them is dead, I will be King. I will avenge my father and all other men who have been exiled under the Nightwing's tyranny these last twenty-five hundred years." He looked at Theowla. "And you will have your revenge for being passed over by my mother as High Priestess of the House of Drimma."

A large, white spider on the wall observed that Dekhalis's glance upon his consort was not soft and though his body showed desire, his expression resembled the stone-edged blade he pulled from his leg sheath and laid upon the green marble table by the bed.

-2-

IN THE royal death chambers of Alvarra, deep beneath the earth's surface, sixty-seven dark elves assembled for the funeral of Ombra Denshadiel, the Nightwing's oldest daughter.

Like statues, they kept vigil beside the shimmering Lake of All Souls, their ebon faces flickering with the blue light of the phosphorescent water. The sound of water dripping off stalactites echoed in the immense chamber. Nobles, friends and royal family were dressed in the sacred black of the Nightwing. The men wore long robes, the women a variety of garments, ranging from pants and tunics to flowing gowns.

As the eldest daughter of the Nightwing, Ombra would have become the next ruler of Alvarra. Her mother, the Nightwing Avenwyndar, was too old to attend, but the new heir, the second daughter, Tiala, was present, her chin held high.

By custom, only the royal daughters participated in the rites, while royal sons obediently watched. There was a son, the Nightwing's youngest child, Dekhalis. Tall and athletic, his face was hard as he looked down on his sister's bowed head. He put his arm around her and whispered, "She slipped."

Tiala stared at him, frowning over tear-filled, green eyes. Anguish marred her delicate features. "How could that be, Dekhalis?"

He blinked and looked away, but she dug her nails into his arm. "Ombra was used to the crystal mines. She even slept there. She wouldn't have fallen from a bridge she used every day."

Dekhalis pointed at the ceiling. The ritual was starting.

Birth and death were the most sacred of events in Alvarra, and, of the accompanying ceremonies, a royal funeral was the most hallowed of all. First, the body was lowered into the Lake of All Souls, which was believed to be bottomless. Next, the royal daughters tossed starflowers into the water as symbols of their bond with the departed. Then the time of mourning would officially begin. To ensure the safe journey of the departed from this life to the next, no elf in the entire country would be allowed to wear armor, use arms, or employ magical artifacts or spells for three moons.

Tiala looked up at the ceiling of the cavern, then at the thrice-woven silken rope hanging down and encircling her sister's bier. As the dark crystal casket descended toward the Lake of All Souls, the bards began playing *The Endless Dream*.

Only a fully trained bard could play the sixty-three-stringed dreaming harp. The notes rose to the top of the glowing, flickering cave and enfolded the celebrants. There was a hush over the crowd, and envy surged within Tiala. Someday, if she were good enough, she could play one of those harps. She would be the first bard Nightwing.

She stooped to pluck a single starflower from the bunch at her feet. She tossed it over the lake, and its pink, translucent petals took on a shimmer of blue as it spiraled down and dipped beneath the water. Her sisters came forward and did the same, each tossing a long-stemmed starflower into the lake to join their sister Ombra's body.

First the spirited Eleppon, taut and angry in the uniform of the Swift Legion. The pants and short tunic with billowing sleeves were better suited for riding horses than attending ceremonies of state. With a look of compassion at her older sister, she hurled the starflower into the lake.

Next, tiny Noth, dressed in a black velvet blouse and hose, fingering a necklace of multicolored stones. She disliked crowds and ceremonies, and she scowled as she tossed her flower.

Last, the youngest, willowy Inuari, whose robe bore the black rabbit insignia at the collar denoting her rank as chelate to Miralor. Sobbing and sniffling, she threw her flower with such a weak arm that it barely cleared the bank. Tiala supported her sister to keep her from falling.

As each of the sisters tossed her flower, Dekhalis stood at a discreet distance, along with the other males, watching the rippling circles spread across the placid lake.

Above the crowd, a ledge jutted out from the slab of stone, and the ancient priestess Kalista stepped onto it. Her centuries-old face was covered with a spiderweb of lines in the ghostly light. As the last shimmering note faded from the dreaming harps, all eyes lifted to her shadowed figure. The quiet resonated with the dripping water, and the crone waited until the echoes of the music were swallowed by the cavern. When she spoke, her ageless voice was tinged with nuances of sagacity.

"The time of mourning is at hand." There was a murmur of assent from the Nightwing's daughters. The High Priestess tossed a last starflower into the lake and said, "Our beloved Nightwing's oldest daughter has descended. Name her with your wishes."

"For Ombra...for Ombra," whispered the crowd, accompanied by the dreaming harps, as each person added a wish for the royal daughter.

The priestess finished, "We send her wise counsel and profound love as she joins her revered ancestors. May she soon grow accustomed to the deeper life."

There was only the *plop* of dripping water until the hollow cavern was pierced by the sound of a low, melancholy bell, whose somber tones echoed mournfully through the area. Each tufted ear reverberated with the sound, as did the entire country of Alvarra, from the depths of the Royal City to the grotto of the poorest farmer above.

The priestess spoke, "The death bell has rung from the Temple of Miralor and the emissaries of the Goddess will now gather our possessions of power. Thus, we put ourselves at Her mercy, knowing that life and death are in Her hands. You may approach, Appointed Ones."

A tall figure entered the cavern from the far exit. She wore a body suit of bright red and a matching mask, and carried a large toad-skin bag. As she circulated among the celebrants, each elf woman deposited carefully wrapped weapons and magic artifacts into the leather sack. Most had nothing to consign, but many a noble woman trained in weapons play as a form of sport and exercise.

Forbidden to possess such items for centuries, the men stood quietly with arms folded into their robes. Their expressions ranged from resentment to resignation. Before the emissary's bag was full, a similarly garbed figure entered with another bag. The muffled thud of metal and wood echoed in counterpoint to the renewed music of the harps.

Tiala placed a small crystal music box and a silver dagger into the bag. Likewise, Eleppon solemnly surrendered her long sword, wrapped in a sheath of pink silk. Noth dropped a small pouch into the sack, and it made a faint clinking sound; she liked to keep her weapons a secret.

The masked one looked for Dekhalis, but whenever she saw him, he disappeared again into the crowd. Tiala also watched his movements with increasing anxiety. As a favored royal son, he had not been prohibited from weapons play like other men. She herself had assisted his training.

Tiala noticed an elf woman whose smirk seemed out of place. She recognized this one as Theowla Twomothers, standing with a small group of priestesses from the House of Drimma. There was a place for revenge, Tiala well knew. It was a part of her history. But Tiala had never trusted Theowla. She was a woman in whom bitterness and ambition lurked beneath a net of seductive beauty.

At last, the emissaries from the temple had collected items from everyone except Dekhalis. Looking around, the woman in red saw him standing by the exit with folded arms.

All eyes followed her as she walked up to him and held out the bag. The harps sang.

From a side slit in his robe, Dekhalis withdrew a needle-sharp stiletto and suspended it over the neck of the bag, a smile lurking at the corners of his mouth. He laid the edge of the stiletto under the chin of the masked elf woman, and she held her breath.

"I hereby challenge the time-honored traditions of Alvarra." His bitter tone shattered the peaceful stillness, and the people whispered, staring.

Immobilized, Tiala watched his malicious expression. Eleppon took a step forward, fists clenched, while Noth hovered in the background, more curious than upset. Inuari clasped her hands so tightly that her dark knuckles paled.

Dekhalis looked around, pleased with the reactions he was receiving. His green eyes sought those of Kalista on her ledge. "I refuse to go into mourning," he announced, his voice echoing like a shout.

"Brother—don't!" Tiala cried.

Dekhalis narrowed his cat-like eyes at her, and she shrank back at the newly revealed hatred. Tiala identified Theowla's soft chuckle from the shadows.

Kalista's voice cut through the tension. "Since you are in contempt of our traditions, you no longer deserve to live among us. In the name of our ruler, the Nightwing, I hereby exile you to the Purple Moors of Forgetfulness."

There was a gasp from the crowd. Tiala felt a knot in her stomach. *Oh, my brother.*

The vast purple moors were enchanted in such a way that once a creature set foot on them, all memory was wiped away forever. For the long-lived elves, such a fate was a prospect second to death. Whatever his crimes, no elf honestly wished that agony on another.

But Dekhalis's cruel laugh cut through their sympathy. "Do you expect me to abide by your judgement? I have never been one of you, neither able to rule nor to enjoy the innocent pleasures of the common man. I care nothing for your traditions." His stiletto glinted in the velvety light and those around him drew back in shock. "Who will oppose me?"

"Don't," Tiala said again. Inuari covered her face in her hands.

"What do you mean to do, brother?" asked little Noth, her face a mask of guile.

"I will live, dear sister, whereas *you*..." he shrugged and pointed to Tiala, and then to each of his sisters in turn. "Who knows what might happen to all of you? After all, wasn't Ombra's death a tragic accident?"

A group of women close to Dekhalis moved in to encircle him, but he waved his weapon at them with obvious meaning. His well-knit body rippled with muscular zeal as he stalked the weaponless would-be attackers. One by one, they withdrew.

Eleppon moved to Tiala's side and murmured, "Should I send for the guards?"

Even without weapons, their personal guards, the Ladies of Skill, were formidable. With weapons, they would prevail.

Tiala's clear voice entreated the priestess on the outcropping. "May the Ladies of Skill be spared the prohibition, Mouth of Miralor?"

Eleppon admired her sister's resourcefulness. She had used the spiritual title, not the secular one. Maybe it would allow for a change of policy.

Dekhalis hesitated, too, and looked up with his first uncertainty.

The crone held out her hands, and many could see they were shaking. In a voice that no longer seemed ageless, she croaked, "My daughter, we are a proud race, an ancient people. We must not let the actions and threats of a diseased one infect our way of life and our traditions. The full three moons will be observed."

Dekhalis chuckled with a soft cruelty; then, leaping to the exit, he turned and glared once more at his sister Tiala. "Be very careful, sister—you are next," he said.

Tiala darted forward and her sister Eleppon moved with her. But Dekhalis ducked into a hidden passage. Tiala knew she could find it, given time, but by then, he would be gone. Such passages were one of the features of underground life, where privacy—especially the royal kind—was a treasure well-guarded by stone.

Over the excited whispers of the assembly, Kalista addressed Tiala by her formal title, "Tiala na'a Nightwing, you must continue the ceremonies."

Tiala's voice shook as she strove for calm. "Yes, your Reverence." She spread her arms. "Please—you are all invited to the feast at the Royal House in honor of my sister, Ombra. Let us celebrate her entrance into the life of the dead." Tiala could not continue, as fear clogged her throat.

Eleppon took her arm and together they watched the guests move through a high archway that opened to a wide tunnel with crystalline walls warmed by the saffron glow of phosphor-stone lamps. One by one, the bards packed up their harps and joined them.

Peering at every shadow, Tiala led her sisters through a narrow tunnel known only to herself, back to the Royal House. The tunnel ended in a concealed door behind a fountain in the great hall.

She was greeted by a tall, dark-elven woman dressed in the livery of the Nightwing. A deep blue body suit with a silver emblem of a rabbit as a breastplate and chased silver gauntlets identified her as a Lady of Skill. Tiala whispered, "Guard my sisters well. See that no food or drink touches their lips before it is tasted—and search for Dekhalis. He must be found."

"Yes, na'a Nightwing."

Seeing Tiala stride off, Eleppon protested. "Where are you going?"

"To see our Mother," said Tiala. "Ombra wouldn't want you to miss her feast."

Tiala had no stomach for the delicacies being served in the banquet hall, and went instead to an inner set of rooms, well hidden from the common area. She nodded to the priestesses who stood watch and entered the central chamber.

The cavern contained an ornate, white marble cabinet, two lizard skin chairs set against the wall, and a giant sea shell with thistle down coverlets. In this bed was the thin, fragile body of a 497-year old elf. Tiala pulled one of the chairs closer to the bed and sat down.

The Nightwing Avenwyndar was so old she was becoming transparent, in the way that the ancient elves did as they departed their lives. No one knew how much longer she could last. Her body seemed small, nestled in the down-filled bed. She looked asleep, though she occasionally stroked the long fur of her familiar, the black rabbit curled at her side.

Tiala wondered what world the Nightwing visited and hesitated to disturb her. She said, "I know you are aware of everything, Mother—even when you are not here. Please tell me what to do about Dekhalis."

She waited, but there was no change in the Nightwing's soft breathing.

"The High Priestess has decreed that we cannot break the time of mourning for Ombra, but I must do something." Tiala's voice broke. "By the end of the three moons, he can raise an army. You know the sort of charm he has and how many admirers are already close to him. My mother, I have been a fool. Dekhalis must have planned this for a long time. Who knows how many warriors he has trained?"

The silence reverberated after her hurried speech. She swallowed. "Years ago, a traveler brought us news of a place in the surface lands where upworld fighters go to prove themselves. Remember? He said it was a fortress called the Manor, ruled by one named Mischa—surely some powerful woman like ourselves."

Tiala peered at her mother's face, but the diaphanous features were relaxed and remote. "You see? There I might find champions who are not subject to our rules, and who can help protect us from…" A tear escaped, running from the corner of her eye into her long, tufted ear. She brushed it away in irritation. *Why is this happening to us, Mother? What deeds have we done to deserve this betrayal?* Into her mind came a voice—not paper-thin like the figure in the bed, but strong like the wind that barreled down the central flue of their cave in winter.

If it is your destiny to travel to the upworlders, my daughter, then it is there you must go. I have seen this day coming, as I watched your brother's heart grow hard with envy and hatred.

Tiala stared. *You knew? We had no warning…*

Perhaps I was not meant to bear a son. My first one was kidnapped, born long before you or your sisters. That is why Dekhalis is so precious to me. But I let it blind me to the truth.

Tiala wanted to say something comforting, but could think of nothing.

Some things must take their course. Go, my child, and have courage. I give you my blessing.

Tiala leaned down and kissed the Nightwing's face. "I will not fail you. Spirit of the foremothers be with us," she murmured, and went to the arched doorway of the small cavern.

Tiala's own room was not far, and she hurried there, closing and locking the round door behind her. With shaking fingers, she lit a lumpy green candle and took a sheet of dark parchment made of thin, supple bark. She dipped a raven's quill pen into the inkstand on her desk. In a few moments, she had written in pale, luminous ink: "Mischa, May darkness light your way and beauty surround you in the land of Terrarg."

Quickly, she outlined her plight, and asked for safe passage to the upworld stronghold. In return for help in finding champions Tiala would pay any sum of *z'a*—dark-elven gold—that Mischa might name. She was sophisticated enough to know that the upworld worked on a gold standard, not the silver—or *luaavh*—favored in Alvarra.

The dark elf tossed back her glossy hair and blew out the candle, then arose, rolling the parchment. She wet her fingers and pinched off a piece of the soft green wax to seal it.

-3-

FAR FROM Alvarra, in the upworld called Terrarg, the sun beat down with the harsh, white glare of mid-morning, making the Manor appear like a glistening diamond on the sand. The Outland Territories stretched for leagues in all directions.

Inside the practice halls and enclosed arena, the guests huddled with an air of expectancy, protected from the heat by a roof and thick walls of stone. High, slotted windows let in only a few rays. The stadium was illuminated by torches set into the walls. The fifty circular rows of seats were graduated around a stone pit. Hundreds of spectators murmured with mingled excitement and fear. Most of them knew they might be called to fight.

A white-garbed herald mounted a high platform and announced, "Yellow Thirteen—three contestants." In the Manor, as elsewhere, the local dialect was augmented by Terrargian, a language of traders—with words borrowed from the human, elven and dwarven tongues.

Each of the potential combatants wore an armband of colored silk, with a numerical symbol written in the universal fighter's code. Not all of the guests could read, but most had enough experience to recognize numbers.

An usher moved into the rows of seats, and chose three fighters whose yellow armbands bore the symbol for thirteen. He then led them to the arena floor, depositing their armbands into a pouch at his waist.

The fighting pit was of smooth stone, covered with a thin layer of sand that failed to hide the stains of recent battle. Circling the pit was a slotted trough from which drifted the smell of the sewers below. A high wall prevented the crowd from touching the combatants. As usual, the arena was filled to capacity. Various banners hung from the high ceiling, belonging to champions from years past who had lent their names to the Manor for posterity.

A very large young man was one of the chosen. He wore brown leggings and a short robe, and his long, brown hair was drawn into a monk's clasp on the top of his head. On his back were strapped two butterfly knives made of metal alloy. They looked almost new. A muscle twitched around his mouth, the only mark of his nervousness. He strove for calm as he breathed deeply, eyes half closed.

The second contestant was older, a well-muscled blue elf, who smirked with self-confidence, shrugged off the aid of the usher, and strode with purpose to the stone floor. He was girded with two weapons, one a long, ruby-hilted sword which had an iridescence to its silver blade, the other a well-worn bastard sword made of steel. He also carried a small javelin on his back, and daggers hidden in his boots and sleeves. He folded his arms and smiled at the crowd, turning his handsome, battle-scarred face this way and that.

The third was a stout, middle-aged dwarf, who also shook off the usher's arm and stomped toward the pit, amid shouts and cheers from the crowd. He had a great axe strapped to his back, and carried a long spear decorated with dwarven runes in silver and bronze.

"Bejo, the Mighty!"

"Victory be yours, Bejo."

The dwarf's face grew comical as he bestowed a gap-toothed grin on his admirers.

The herald announced, "Obsidian, novice from the lands to the east…Six Stixopholous, veteran of the Seven Years War…and Bejo of the shining axe… will fight…" the crowd was hushed in anticipation "the three ogre brothers of Ddor."

The crowd cheered, not only for the favorite, Bejo, but because the ogres were infamous criminals who had been sought for years. They had terrorized the desert and wilderness beyond, looting, raping, and burning whole villages.

"Good luck," said the elf to his tall companion. Obsidian nodded, his brown eyes focused on the huge double doors at the far end of the arena. He strove to ignore the bloodstains on either side.

Bejo the dwarf and Six Stix the blue elf scowled at each other. Six Stix spat and turned his back on him. They moved away from each other, putting the monk between them. Bejo had not fought in the Seven Years War against the elves, but it was clear he wished he had.

Bejo raised his axe and planted himself in a battle stance, while Six Stix drew his bastard sword, gripping it before him with both hands. Obsidian stood, knees slightly bent.

A gasp went up from the assembly as the doors opened and three huge, exceedingly ugly humanoids emerged. The smallest of them was three times the size of Six Stix. Their leathery skin had a greenish cast and was covered with boils. Their hair looked like the branches of stunted trees, and they gave off a hideous stench. They carried spiked clubs, and growled, fanning out, with heavy, stomping tread.

When the ogre nearest Six Stix got within arm's length, the blue elf whirled his bastard sword and sliced through the hide of the ogre's chest. Howling, the ogre crashed his club down with the force of a falling tree.

Six Stix leapt to the side and raised his sword a second time. He deftly severed the tendons in the backs of the ogre's knees, sending him to the floor.

Seeing the defeat of his brother, the second ogre attacked Six Stix with his spiked club, ramming the elf's shoulder with a terrible blow. Six Stix fell to one knee, clutching his shoulder, his dark blue eyes wincing with pain.

The third ogre lunged at Bejo with a gloating howl. The dwarf brought his axe down on the ogre's arm, but the monster deflected the blow and swung his club, hitting Bejo in the belly. The dwarf sat down heavily, in great pain, but managed to thrust his spear into the ogre's side. With a horrible wail, the ogre fell on the dwarf, who was crushed under the monster's dead weight. The crowd screamed, "Get up, Bejo."

Obsidian, who had been casting his brown eyes back and forth between the two contests, decided that the elf was in greater need of help. The lamed ogre was struggling to his knees while his brother was raising his club for another blow. The monk reached behind him and in one graceful movement, drew the butterfly knives from their sheaths. Before the ogres could further damage the elf, Obsidian wielded his knives against the ogres in a flurry of motion so swift that no one could follow it.

But the ogres felt all the power of the fifty slicing strokes. Turning in pain and terror, they fled to the edge of the floor, one of them hopping on one foot, both dripping green blood from shallow cuts.

The crowd was on its feet.

"Did you see that monk? He's amazing."

"I don't believe it."

"Finish them."

"Kill them."

Many had lost family members to the terrible ogre brothers in past years and some had even worse tales to tell. It was said that the ogres roasted and ate even their own young.

Those nearest the pit hollered, "Bejo! Get up, Bejo." But the dwarf lay still.

It was the ogre who staggered to his feet. He plucked the lance from his side and tossed it onto the dwarf's body. As the throng hurled obscenities at him, he roared back at them and shook his noxious fists, green blood pouring from his side. The monster lumbered closer to his brothers.

Obsidian crossed his butterfly knives in front of him, eyes locked on the ogres. He panted, infused with a new fear.

Six Stix waited for the monk to strike, then shrugged. He leapt up, unsheathing the elegant long sword, his shoulder muscles bulging against the leather vest. Swiftly, he attacked one of the ogres, goring him neatly through the belly. The ogre fell to the stone floor, and his skull cracked open like a nut, spilling green viscous liquid toward the sluices at the edge of the pit. The other ogres moved forward, growling and circling the elf as he taunted them with his blade held high.

Obsidian still did not move. He glanced at the lifeless body of his fellow fighter, Bejo, and narrowed his eyes at the ogres.

Six Stix stepped back a pace and grated at Obsidian, "Do I have to do all the work?"

The youth replied, "It's against my principles to kill without provocation."

Six Stix's slanted eyebrows shot even higher, "Provocation? Do I have to die to get your help?"

Obsidian frowned with uncertainty. "At least you kill fast; that is merciful."

Six Stix grunted an obscenity. He reached behind him for his javelin and sent it squarely into the heart of the second ogre as the fiend advanced with filthy claws. Then, stooping over Bejo's sprawled body, Six Stix grasped the exquisitely carved spear and raised it to his good shoulder, aiming squarely at the third ogre's forehead.

The spectators were on their feet now, their hoarse cheers drowning out even the roar of the ogre's battle cries.

The last ogre brother gave a ghastly scream, his eyes bulged out, and dark spittle drooled from his mouth. The cries of the audience and the sight of his own blood spilling on the floor had driven him to the very brink of madness.

The spear glided through the air with a purpose, slicing into the ogre's forehead like a hand into a glove. The bronze point embedded itself deep into his flesh. The ogre grabbed the handle and wrestled with it, attempting to dislodge it, howling with each movement.

Six Stix's vision clouded over. Disoriented, he was vaguely aware of the ogre's struggle. He strove to hide his exhaustion, but his shoulder felt dislocated.

He stumbled to one knee and watched as the ogre broke the shaft of the spear. The weapon splintered into pieces, the runic writing obliterated forever, the point embedded in his forehead. Six Stix let out his breath as the ogre finally collapsed.

When it was obvious that the monster was dead, the crowd cheered with abandon and tossed coins into the arena floor. Six Stix heaved to his feet and bowed, showing his dimpled smile. Ignoring the pain in his shoulder, he gathered all the money, and Obsidian left by the exit passageway that had opened behind them.

Four gnomes wearing purple livery wrapped the body of the dwarf in a scarlet cloth, and carried him off on a stretcher. The spectators maintained the respectful silence that followed the death of a fellow contestant.

Once out of sight, the monk doubled over and took a deep breath. He had survived his first real battle. He hadn't expected it to be so terrifying. The monks had trained him well, but not for the revulsion and terror the ogres had evoked. *Not for the death of a comrade.* Bile rose in his throat.

Six Stix soon joined him, still stuffing money into his bulging waist band and under his mail shirt. With his good arm, he slapped Obsidian on the back, grinning up at him. "Good fight, little brother."

Obsidian stared at the fighter. "How can you be so jolly when you've just killed three fellow creatures—and seen your own comrade die at their hands? Look at your shoulder. It's bleeding."

Six Stix noticed the youth's pallor. "Not your first battle, is it?" The monk didn't reply. "Well, well. You religious ones always seem to be your own worst enemies. Can't drink, can't wench, and now, can't even eat, I'll wager." He laughed at the youth's greenish complexion. "Your appetite will return, though you may not believe it. As soon as I get this shoulder seen to, we'll eat."

Obsidian swallowed. *This elf interests me. I would like to feel his confidence, his lust for life. But I want to be in control of myself—shaping my body and mind until I am one with the Master of All...* He was vaguely aware of Six Stix relating some battle story as they walked up the stairs toward the common rooms. He admired the indigo scars on the fighter's body, but wasn't sure he wanted to know their history.

-4-

THAT EVENING, in one of the guest rooms of Mischa's manor, an elven wizard sat brooding. One candle cast its light from a wall niche above his shoulder, illuminating his bluish skin. Another candle flickered on the table before him. Embaza was tall and angular, even when seated with his dark blue cloak around him. His handsome face seemed ageless, a mine of elven shadows, strained and haunted.

He gripped the candle and dripped several drops of wax into a small dish. He blew on the wax to hasten its drying and began to work it with his long fingers until the mass bore a close resemblance to himself. He then drew a long steel needle from a hidden pocket of his cloak and pushed it gently into the wax of the figure's neck.

He leaned his head back, and the cloak slipped down his shoulders, revealing a necklace of rare firestones that sparkled blue, then white, in the candle's glow. His mouth opened in a silent scream of both torture and ecstasy. The darker skin at his lower neck had an ebony hue quite different from the deep blue of his face and hands. Soon he would have to reapply the dye.

Tears brimmed in his green eyes, and he withdrew the needle, his body slumping like a marionette whose strings had just been cut. When he straightened, he returned the objects to the recesses of his robe. He sighed with relief and a smile curved his lips. *Pain is my friend.*

He stood and surveyed the room. It was small and plain, but comfortable. The bed was made of hardwood, the tall chest furnished with a lock as he had requested. The floor was bare. He donned the hood of his cloak, entered the closet, and slipped into the darkness, closing the door behind him. He had excellent night vision and soon found a slight crack in the back wall.

Embaza pressed on one side of the crack and the wall swung open to a dark corridor beyond. He took a small strip of cloth from inside his cloak. Onto it he had glued eight very fine needles with dried sap. Now he pressed the cloth over the spot that opened the secret passage, his nimble fingers avoiding the needles. Then he side-stepped the doorway and released his hand. The hidden passage closed as silently as it had opened.

The hallway was cool and damp, dimly lit by chips of silica worked into the stone walls. The material was said to be older than the desert, from a time when the earth itself was hot. It was rare to find such stones nowadays, but Mischa's grandfather had purchased them at high cost from greedy tribal chiefs.

With his night vision, Embaza didn't need the light. His soft boots made little noise as he crept along to the southwest. He ignored two doors for a third, where he stopped and listened for a few moments.

Ah, she is asleep. Examining the door, he found a small piece of thread to one side, two feet from the bottom. He tugged it gently, and the door came open, revealing another closet as black as his own.

He pressed through the garments that hung to the right, causing a slight rustle in the stillness of the cramped chamber. Soundlessly, he opened the door to the adjoining bedroom.

A diminutive female was in the down quilted bed. Her flaming red hair glistened even in the darkness. The woman's sleep was troubled by his presence and she sniffed the air like an animal.

Undaunted, Embaza approached and peered at her sleeping figure. *Polah. You have a secret, too, and I will know it.*

She gave a slight moan. Embaza's sensitive ears discerned a note of torment. He tried to imagine what she must be dreaming. He sent a tendril of consciousness out to her, but then she seemed to fall into a deeper sleep, not moving, barely breathing, as if she were in a coma. Embaza waited for many minutes, watching her still form, then decided to leave.

As he stepped back into the closet, he stumbled over a tiny wire caught on the soft leather of his boot. Polah was instantly awake, and she sat up in the bed, peering at the closet as if she could strip away the darkness like a skin. She covered her upper half with the blanket. "Who's there?" she murmured, a seductive growl in her voice that underlay her peculiar lilting accent. *A southern accent,* she had said at dinner.

Embaza shuddered, reminded of wolves and foxes roaming the woods of his youth—or someone's youth. He never wanted to think about childhood and never lingered long on the reasons why.

But now, he could see the red-haired Polah as if she were that first remembered woodland animal, outlined against a full, silvery moon, standing proud and fearless on a mound of earth. The scent of moss and fur overwhelmed his senses as he let his imagination have its sway.

All this took but a moment, after which Embaza flattened himself to the wall of the closet and cultivated quiet, his green eyes peering softly into the darkness of the bedroom where the woman sat with feral alertness, her red hair crackling with electricity around her small, heart-shaped face.

The invisible thread being woven between them grew stronger, like a hollow log filling with rainwater.

"Little fox," Embaza whispered in a low, caressing voice.

Polah sat transfixed, her shining, black eyes darting to the corner of the room. Her skin flushed, she reached up to touch her cheek. She looked back toward the closet and something in her body had softened, yet her voice was bitter.

"Do you think you know me?" she asked.

"I will always know you," answered Embaza. There was a long silence.

"You frighten me," she said. "Please leave." *Before you are sorry.*

Embaza backed away from the menace in her voice, opened the door, and left without a word. Exhilaration filled his breast and every step seemed like a sparkling pool amid the shadows of the night. He made his way to his own closet door and entered his room, taking no notice of the needles sticking into his palm or the taste of the sticky sap as he absentmindedly licked his fingers. In his mind, he smelled only moss and fur.

-5-

High above the arena floor, the half-gnome Prince Mischa leaned his arms on the balcony, holding his spyglass and enjoying the illusion of height he could never have on the ground. His three-and-a-half foot frame seemed taller in the high stool, and he kicked his dangling feet against the lower rungs. Mischa brushed back his sun-bleached hair with a pudgy hand. His plump figure was poured into a gold and red brocade robe, but his slippers were encased in the purple of his own livery. A glass of ale sat nearby, attesting to his conservation of the precious water from his deep wells far below.

The aerie was hidden from view by means of clever masonry and the slotted windows melted into the design of the ceiling when seen from below. Mischa had just witnessed three battles and was feeling excited and, as always, full of interest and sympathy for all the contestants. He was a great believer in the nobility of battle and its inherent justice.

Although many of the participants would disagree, Mischa believed those who were meant to die did so. The arena provided the set of circumstances that made it possible. And in the devising and manipulation of these dramatic events, the Prince imagined himself a representative of the God of the Desert. He noticed those who were worthy and gave their all, and also those who were without mercy or used unfair tactics. He laughed to himself. How cleverly a battle could be manipulated by a slight shift of light or wind. *Child's play,* he thought as his gaze strayed over the instruments of magic in his aerie.

He could force a gust of wind or a well-placed pebble from the blow-pipe in his lap. He also had a plain, gold ring that produced myriad effects when he pointed it at an individual. He believed in justice, yes—but not in that alone. When his ring could place a sudden cramp or flash of blindness into the path of justice, then what was he, he reasoned, but an agent of fate?

He scanned the crowd with his spyglass, and wrote some numerical symbols on a sheet of parchment. A discreet knock on the door interrupted his concentration. "Enter," he said, sitting as tall as he could in his chair.

A small bearded creature, half Mischa's size, wore a purple, peaked hat and matching uniform that stretched over his large belly. The gnome's voice was squeaky and shrill as he asked, "Have you chosen the next battle mates, your Highness?" He was careful to keep his distance from the Prince, and his knees trembled as he glanced with undisguised fear at the various artifacts.

"Here," said Prince Mischa, handing him the parchment on which he had written the symbols for "Red Twenty, Yellow Thirty-One, White Eighty-Eight." The little man bowed and left, nearly tripping in his haste.

Mischa forgot the gnome and squirmed in his chair with anticipation. He always enjoyed seeing a fighter's first battle in the arena. Yesterday's had been delightful. The monk's reluctance to kill had pleased him. Just as worthy had been the desire of the other two to dispatch justice to the ogres. The natural antipathy between the dwarf and elf could have been manipulated, but he had felt no urge to interfere, even when Bejo had fallen. It had been a fair contest.

He was hoping that he had chosen the next three candidates as well when the herald made the announcement, interrupting his reverie.

A tall blue-elven wizard, an athletic blonde acrobat, and a small redheaded woman descended to the pit. Mischa's excitement rose at the way the redhead avoided touching the wizard and the wizard's dark eyes bored into her back. Conflict within conflict, just as he had hoped. *To bring out the best—and the worst—in them.* His bright blue eyes darkened to the color of steel.

Both of the women are lovely, and the wizard is a sensitive soul beneath that veneer of cold mystery. What drives these people to test themselves so? He had asked himself the question a hundred times.

The Prince admired the gait of the acrobat. Anebra was another of the crowd's favorites. As usual, she was dressed in pants and jerkin made of triangular patches of leather covered at the waist by a long cord wrapped around several times. Mischa remembered that costume from previous bouts in the arena. Each triangle of leather contained a hidden pouch in which there might be a weapon or distraction of some kind. The waist cord was a noose. He squinted his eyes, training the spyglass on her agile form.

Anebra's hair was cut like a boy's, and shone in the torchlight. She glanced at the wizard with a flirtatious smile, but for all her obvious charms, Embaza had eyes only for the redheaded woman.

The wizard is new at this. How will he fare? Mischa studied Embaza. *What tricks are up your sleeve, my friend?* Mischa's spies had reported that Embaza carried powerful artifacts hidden under his robe. Mischa didn't always trust these reports. The simple gnomes were easily fascinated by items that were merely unusual to a desert dweller. However, the spies also had said the wizard studied scrolls filled with arcane symbols. The Prince smiled. Those would be nice to get his hands on.

Mischa had circulated rumors that the elven wizard was a penniless exiled king, that he was a great sorcerer gone mad. He enjoyed stirring up the other guests, but this proved unnecessary. Embaza himself told a different story every time he was questioned about his origins. "From the Land of Othrit…from the mountains where lions dwell…from the Blue Desert…across the Zanderif Sea…"

As to the redhead, Mischa had no illusions. Polah Fennwarren was a very dangerous female. He had researched her, excited by her potential. *A woman alone, without a single friend.* She could be tamed by the right person. He would have to tread carefully. Nervously, he twisted the ring on his pudgy finger.

Best of all, he had a potential bride at last. A royal bride, exotic, beautiful and heir to a dowry of unimagined magical wealth. Mischa well knew that dark elves frightened ordinary mortals who had no knowledge of their sun sensitivity. He chuckled to himself. "Just what I need to help me keep order, but patience, patience…"

-6-

IN THE Royal City of Alvarra, in the vast crystal caverns that housed the royal family, it was long after third bell. For the second time, Inuari begged Eleppon to sit down and finish her kumquat rind soup, but the tall dark elf continued to pace, reaching for her scabbard again and again. She was obviously annoyed that she couldn't get accustomed to its absence. Yet, she still cut a dashing figure in her plain black uniform with the divided skirt and long, fitted jacket.

The sisters had met for dinner on the terrace in Inuari's private garden where the young novice performed her daily devotions to the Goddess. Inuari was still robed in the black satin she had worn to the funeral. The rabbit insignia on the collar was worked in velvet threads that melted into the shadows of her graceful neck. She was oblivious to the familiar surroundings, the lavender smell of flowering nightshade, the creepers of blind jasmine along the stone walls, and the sweet call of the sorrow-bird.

Phosphor-stone globes hung from the ceiling on long filaments of spidersilk, illuminating the area with a soft glow. Inuari's little glass shrine of Miralor gleamed among the shadowy ferns and mosses. A smaller replica of the ancient temple itself, through its walls Inuari could see the chipped onyx rabbit worked into the tiled floor. Now she strove to regain the sense of peace the shrine had always given her. She absentmindedly ate her soup, surprised when it was gone.

Eleppon plopped into one of the graceful satinwood chairs and pushed her bowl aside. Chin on her hands, she surveyed the attractive scene with a brooding stare.

They had agreed that this would be a safe and quiet place to talk about their plight. Although she wore the sacred black of the royal family, Noth had covered her loose black pants and shirt with a rich jerkin of long, tawny goat hair. Another of her necklaces peeped out from the collar of her shirt, an ostentatious emerald on a black silk cord. Her dainty, long-fingered hands played with the silver spoon as her soup grew cold.

Noth loved kumquat rind. Its tart flavor was one of her favorite culinary pleasures, but she, too, had no appetite and envied Inuari's ability to eat. "Well," she said, folding her hands in her lap, "where is Tiala?"

Eleppon stared intensely at her sister, her hawklike features tinged with irritation. "Inuari and I received the same information you did, Noth. If she'd wanted us to know where she was going, she would have taken us with her."

Inuari blinked thick lashes over large, frightened eyes, her pupils mere pinpoints of black in a sea of emerald. Noth looked unconvinced and leaned forward. She narrowed her eyes and the planes of her delicate face were sharp. "You aren't keeping secrets from me?" she asked.

Eleppon pursed her lips and shook her head. "You're the one who keeps secrets." A sorrow-bird sounded from the elder bushes, and they all froze for a moment, nerves frayed by fear.

Inuari reached into her black velvet gown for a crumpled parchment with red satin ribbon sewn around its borders. "Here." She gave it to Noth.

Noth unfolded it and read aloud, "Little One, I've gone to bring champions...don't try to follow. Pray to Miralor. I'll come back soon with help. love, Tiala." She squashed the parchment with tense fingers, and tossed it back across the kunzite table.

Eleppon got up and resumed pacing, her velvet boots making no sound on the blue marble terrace. "She must have been crazy to try this." Her outburst startled Inuari, who began to cry.

"Stop it," said Noth and Eleppon in unison.

Noth said, "Look, Eleppon, just because she didn't take *you*, you're all upset. She knew the risks—and besides, she was the one in the most danger."

"You don't think Dekhalis will hurt you because you're his favorite," blurted Inuari.

Noth jumped up and snatched Inuari's collar, nearly ripping the dainty embroidery of the black rabbit. "How dare you say that?"

Eleppon intervened, separating the two with her superior strength. "Now, stop it. We're getting as bad as our brother. Could you please remember that we're in mourning?"

"I didn't do anything," Inuari said.

"You liar—," exclaimed Noth, but Eleppon clapped her hands.

"Stop it. Sit down. Please. I'd like to have one sisterly meeting where we don't fight amongst ourselves."

"As you wish," Noth appeased, sliding her tiny form back into the curve

21

of the satinwood chair. Although she acknowledged that Eleppon was trying hard to fill Tiala's slippers, she missed Tiala's easy charisma. Even dreamy Ombra had let Tiala keep the peace at meetings.

Inuari sent a modest plea to Miralor that she could keep from annoying her sisters. She looked up at the ceiling high above, and a droplet of water fell from a stalactite onto the lavender bluets that lined the terrace.

"Back to business," said Eleppon. "I have something to report. I was asked to attend the High Council as our mother's representative. They wouldn't let me speak, but I was appalled at how lightly they are taking our brother's threats. There are rumors that riots have broken out in some of the villages, and even murders." She looked at each sister before continuing. "He is reviving the old Swords of Siadhin, which shouldn't surprise any of us. He has always been eager for any lore about the Siadhin Lords and their armies."

Inuari said, "We know how...malicious he can be. But do you think he is really serious? I mean, if somehow he can be caught and contained..."

Eleppon shook her head. "Already he has stirred up dissent. People are grumbling that the Nightwing has lost her power because Dekhalis has not been captured. If we don't do something soon, he will be making allies in the big cities of Douvilwe and Aeryinne."

Inuari moaned and covered her mouth.

Eleppon continued. "In Council, someone raised the old argument that succession should take place before the death of the ruler. I know we cannot take this step, especially with Tiala's absence. But, I wonder...can we afford to sit and do nothing?"

Noth shook her head. "I didn't want to tell you, but... "

"What?" snapped Eleppon.

She slid a very thin parchment from her sleeve. "I stole this from Dekhalis's private desk. I know it was wrong, but I was afraid." Noth spread the paper upon the table. "Look at these numbers. He is raising an army! He already has 100 followers in the village of Kolar, near the entrance to the uplands, and 75 in Treevon, outside of Douvilwe. Can you imagine how many others will join?"

"But surely the priestesses must know," said Inuari breathlessly.

Noth shook her head. "They're as bad as the High Council. They will pray and do ceremonies. In mourning, they can't even use wands and crystals. What good are mere words?"

Fresh tears filled Inuari's eyes. "You call into question my beliefs, sister."

"Belief is irrelevant," said Eleppon, spreading her dark hands over the smooth, rosy surface of the table. "We must face facts. We are in peril and hampered by the very traditions we're trying to protect. You know that the Nightwing only holds trials for soldiers once a year. Even then, only a few children enter the training in hand-to-hand combat, and fewer still are taught to use weapons. We have grown soft."

"Then how can our brother find men who can fight us?" asked Inuari.

"They make their own weapons, and he trains them himself," said Eleppon. "Since I'm the oldest, I could go and speak to the representative from Tskurl. Maybe the dwarves can help us."

The others looked skeptical, and Noth said, "Come on, Eleppon, you don't seriously think those knot-headed dwarves care what happens to us, do you? They don't even have a royal lineage. Their primitive society is nothing more than a bunch of tribal families and barrows. Anyway, the latest treaty says they'll only protect us from an outside threat."

"Fine," said Eleppon. "Do you have a better idea?"

"Well," said Noth, stroking her dainty jaw line, "what of the enchanters? The fox-people of Comrhae Deip are led by a good woman, I am told. We could send for the Comrhae Mother, Swano'dar."

Eleppon shook her head. "If the priestesses cannot use magic, there's going to be a lot of objections to our involving the shape-changers."

Noth said, "We could appeal to our mother. As Nightwing, doesn't she have secret resources?" Her expression was animated with curiosity, despite the dangers they faced. Someday, she, too, might know what those resources were.

But Inuari opposed this plan. "Our mother is dying. Would you want to be the one to interrupt her meditations, to interrupt her conversations with the Goddess?"

Noth regarded her in a sideways glance. "What do you know?"

Eleppon shook her head, "Tiala talked to her the day of Ombra's funeral. In private, remember? Maybe our mother is doing more than we can imagine."

Inuari nodded. "We must have faith in Miralor." The others were silent. Miralor had not prevented Ombra from falling to her death.

Thoughts of Ombra's murder brought home the shocking reality of Dekhalis's threat. Noth shivered and crossed her arms, burying her fingers in the goat hair vest. Maybe Tiala was better off away from home, but this raised another fear. "I'm worried about Tiala. You know what they say about the surface...the Scourge..."

"She must have made careful plans," consoled Eleppon. "I cannot believe Tiala could have left me behind on impulse. We've always done things together."

"Nonsense. Listen to this..." Noth snatched Tiala's missive from across the table and unfolded it again. With her forefinger, she found the sentence she wanted, "She says, 'I will bring help.' What help? She doesn't even say how long she'll be gone."

"She couldn't have known that yet," said Eleppon. "Be reasonable,

Noth."

"I've been thinking," said Inuari, "what if she just waits the three moons—until the mourning period is ended? Then our brother—," she stopped and swallowed, still uncomfortable with the idea of Dekhalis as an assassin.

Noth looked at her with interest, "That's not a bad idea, little sister. Why didn't she think of it herself? Why not just go into hiding?" She looked at Eleppon for confirmation, but the young officer was gazing at the fitted marble stones in the floor, working at a crack with her boot.

"If I were Tiala," said Eleppon, "I don't think I would do it that way." She looked at her sisters. "What would it accomplish? Only a bloody battle when the mourning ended. No, if Dekhalis's assassins and rogues are as numerous as our spies would have us believe, then she wouldn't want to risk starting a war."

Dejected, the three sisters were silent. If Dekhalis wanted to start a war, could anyone stop him? Noth's stolen parchment proved the truth of the rumors of Dekhalis's popularity. Inuari whispered, "Why do you think he's doing this?"

No one answered her, but they all remembered little private incidents that made them feel a bit guilty. Each had at one time or another done something to make him angry.

Eleppon had beaten him at wrestling, and when he had asked to learn the holds she had used, she had scoffed, "Why bother? You're just a boy. You'll never command the army."

Noth could recall many episodes where she had cheated her brother in various childhood games. Although she didn't like to admit it, she was probably responsible for at least part of his highly developed guile. And because she was female, she had also enjoyed more freedom, and though he begged her repeatedly, she had never let him come with her on her rooftop escapades. She had always taken for granted her superiority, knowing it rankled him.

Inuari could only remember one incident, when she had seen him for the first time. He was a few days old and the nurses said he had just opened his eyes that morning. She remembered the hour because third bell had rung, sending its clarion sonnet through the crystal caves of her mother's private rooms. Inuari had been angry at not being the baby anymore, and she had run up to Dekhalis and shaken her fist at him, saying, "You'll never be loved as much as I am." She had been so ashamed afterward that she had never told a single soul, but she was sure that in some way, her brother had understood her and was punishing her now.

Noth said, "I've always wondered if that time he nearly died from the spider poison, he might have been changed somehow. Maybe his mind was permanently poisoned."

Inuari murmured, "You always make excuses for him."

"Whatever the reason," said Eleppon, "our problem remains the same. Dekhalis has not been seen since the funeral. The Swift Legion has posted bulletins in every tavern and hall outside the Royal City, but there's been no sign of him."

Noth said, "He has as many hiding places as a cave worm—and more friends."

"He's probably hidden near the upworld, where a disguise would be least noticeable. Even now, we still admit travelers looking to view Alvarra's wonders."

Inuari said with a burst of compassion, "It's not unusual for one who is exiled to the Purple Moors of Forgetfulness to try to escape. He could be really frightened."

Eleppon snorted, pacing anew. "He's too busy to be frightened. There is talk of strikes among the canal workers and street-sweepers. Men are becoming more and more emotionally unstable."

Inuari said, "Our mother always allowed Dekhalis to manage this."

Eleppon snarled. "He was always so good at it."

"Have either of you gotten any more notes from him?" Noth asked.

"Yes," said Eleppon. "It was pinned to the stable door. Like the others, it was in our secret family code—I couldn't even show it to my Captains."

"Mine was under my plate at dinner," said Inuari. "It read, 'You looked quite lovely in that green frock you wore last night, little priestess.' I'm still trembling about the night the new court minstrel sang that awful warning to you and then disappeared."

Noth leaned her chin on her hands. "I found one in the lichen gardens when I was gathering moss for supper."

"What did it say?" asked Eleppon.

"'Dear Noth, Did you know that it takes ten hours to die from the venom of the Samanthian spider?'"

Inuari said, "I'm afraid in my own bedroom, checking under my pillows before I sleep at night."

"Me, too," Noth said.

The distant chittering of a bat from high in the cavern startled them from their dour thoughts.

Eleppon said in her most commanding voice, "We can't give up. I'm going to talk with the other members of the Swift Legion. Maybe we can devise something. At least we still have our horses." She longed for the sword she had so carefully wrapped in pink satin and placed in the bag at the funeral. She knew it was safely guarded now in the Temple of Miralor, in a locked room. Even if she could have retrieved it, she would not. For a Nightwing's daughter to break mourning was unforgivable.

Noth, too, yearned for her weapons and had fewer scruples than her sister. But, although she considered herself an accomplished burglar, she could not imagine stealing them back, using them, and then returning them so skillfully that the items were never missed. The priestesses, she knew, kept meticulous records of every weapon that was tendered during a period of mourning and counted them daily. Of course, she might steal a kitchen knife.

She stood also, a head shorter than Eleppon. "I'll send more spies into the cities and the cultivated lands. Somehow, we'll find out what he is planning. We don't need weapons to outwit him."

Inuari said, "I will get an audience with Kalista and talk with the other priestesses in my Order. Maybe they know what our mother is doing."

"Good," said Eleppon.

Noth looked skeptical. She hadn't much faith in their little sister's ability to get useful information.

They hugged each other with more confidence than they felt, and Eleppon admonished the other two to be careful. Noth enjoined them to set the traps at bedtime. She had devised elaborate alarms for each. Eleppon reminded them that the Ladies of Skill, their palace guards, were experienced hand-to-hand fighters.

With these farewells concluded, Eleppon and Noth passed through the high, arched doorway that led to Inuari's sitting chamber and the common rooms beyond.

When they were gone, Inuari felt very young and alone. The familiar beauty of her garden failed to reassure her. Lifting her skirt, she stepped between the ferns and flowering nightshade, and entered the glass shrine. She knelt on the onyx floor and extended her arms to welcome the spirit of the place. "Help us, oh Miralor, Mother of all," she entreated.

As if in answer, drops of water splashed from a stalactite onto some ferns, and she gazed up into the darkness, breathing in the fragrant mist. For the first time since Ombra's death, she felt comforted. A moment later, a fragment of bark fell into her lap from somewhere high above. She picked it up, wonderingly, then gasped and dropped it in fright. On the bark was a message, hand-printed in their family code, "I wouldn't pray alone if I were you, Inuari."

-7-

EMBAZA WAS delighted that Polah had been chosen to fight beside him. *Now, perhaps I'll discover your secret, little fox. I can never resist a mystery.* He was also intrigued with the acrobat, Anebra. He took a deep breath and recited a spell of calming, while the usher waited. Then he unfolded his long body and walked to the aisle to join the women.

Anebra joked with the audience as she continued downward to the pit. She was jaunty and graceful, and many envied Embaza the chance to fight beside her. Anebra was, however, a little afraid of him and clowned without getting too close. *He's so weird. Always trying to act mysterious. That Polah is strange, too. There's something about her accent, her way of laughing with all her teeth showing. Such pointed teeth.* Anebra's light blue eyes darted sideways at her, even as she smirked to hide her discomfort.

Polah noticed Anebra's avoidance. *The acrobat dislikes me. Why am I so cursed? And why was I paired with the wizard? I wish he would stop staring at me.* Her face did not betray her, and the spectators saw only a calm fighter with the loose-jointed walk of the natural athlete, comfortable and competent. For such a small woman, there was something powerful in her physical confidence. She wore a loose tunic, belted with a strip of hide, and boots that were fashioned for quickness and maneuvering. A hunting knife was sheathed at her side.

When the three reached the pit, there was a hushed anticipation in the stands. Whispers about Embaza rippled through the rows of fighters, while whistles and catcalls greeted Anebra and Polah. Women always got special treatment in the arena. Although they accepted an occasional veteran like the famous female dwarf known as the General, most men were fascinated by women who chose possible death in the arena over the gentle arts of home and hearth.

Embaza raised an eyebrow for the benefit of those who were watching. He was a natural showman, and his show had started. First he withdrew the necklace of blue firestones from beneath his robe and let it fall softly on his chest. Those nearby gasped at its stark beauty. The gems glowed and sparkled against his dark robe. Embaza turned back his sleeve to reveal three long needles threaded into the cuff. Then he flexed his fingers like an athlete or actor warming up before a performance. In truth, he was both.

Some looked for hints of muscle beneath the robe of this handsome blue elf. His hand gestures thrilled others unaccustomed to seeing magic performed under pain of death. He drew a piece of wax from his robe and began kneading it, all the while staring at the double doors ahead.

Anebra glanced at him with grudging admiration, sensing the crowd's mood, but Embaza didn't seem to notice. His face remained in shadow. One sunbeam from the high, slotted window above lanced the floor of the pit, and Anebra danced into it.

In an obvious attempt to outshine Embaza, she began doing deep lunges from side to side. Her buttocks nearly touched the ground. The leather patches moved like a skin over her splendid body. The onlookers feasted on her youthful beauty. Many of them bore hideous battle scars or had a missing eye or ear, hand or arm. Some cheered and others were silent.

Meanwhile Polah swayed on her feet, her eyes unfocused, her mind drifting to a place outside the arena. Her trance-like posture was in such contrast to the others that it was eerie. One of the men in the stadium tossed a coin at her to get her attention. She didn't even look down.

Then the herald announced, "Embaza from the…Embaza of…" There was much laughter at the herald's confusion. Many were aware of Embaza's seeming lack of origins. The tension mounted as the herald paused, regaining his power over the audience. "Embaza the mysterious, Polah the small, and Anebra the quick…will fight…" He peered at the parchment as if in some doubt. When the crowd's eagerness was at fever pitch, he said, "seven…ah, no…eight, ah…" He teased them with expert sensitivity, sensing the moment when impatience might degenerate into rage or, worse, disinterest. At length, the herald announced, "Eight giant rats…and a sand demon."

A great gasp echoed around the arena. Giant rats were commonplace. The Manor's foundations were full of them. But sand demons were rare in the desert, unknown outside of it. Little was known about their fighting tactics, but many myths were told of their lightning speed, huge bodies, overwhelming stench, sharp fangs and long claws. Some insisted that they employed magic. One thing all agreed upon: no one had ever survived a fight with one. There were excited murmurs among the rows of both seasoned and unseasoned fighters.

"How did the Prince's hunters catch it?"

"Must have used witchcraft or potions."

"My uncle was killed by one."

"My mother, too."

"It's not fair. Aren't there any rules to this?"

"Can they be hurt by spells?"

"Look at the magician. He seems nervous."

"Wouldn't you be?"

"I'd give my sword to be in his place."

"You're crazy."

The opening of the double doors silenced all conversation. First came the rats. Five as big as large dogs rushed out in all directions, only prevented from charging the crowd by the high stone wall that surrounded the fighting pit.

Anebra was the first to react, her reflexes like springs. She leapt over the back of the nearest rat and onto another. In a flash, she had whipped a stiletto from a slit in her leggings and speared the rat in the back of the neck. It rolled its head and tried to bite her, but she leapt away, somersaulting into the air and dropping to the ground by the stone parapet.

28

While the onlookers cheered, the wounded rat darted back at Anebra, sensing its attacker, and bit her on the leg as she leapt again. She landed awkwardly and looked pale, but drew two daggers from inside pockets of either forearm and crouched, ready. The rat bared its fangs, crazed by the taste of her blood.

Still in the shadows, Embaza had kneaded the wax into a crude figure, and was eyeing the rats with intense concentration. His necklace winked with brilliance, and the rats snarled, squinting at its light. Then Embaza drew one of the needles from his sleeve, and inserted it into the waxen form in his left hand. One of the rats fell down with an ear-splitting screech.

Something terrible was happening to Polah. She writhed and squirmed as if poisoned. The audience cried out to her, horrified that she would be eaten by the rats before she had a chance to defend herself.

"Is she ill?"

"Was she bitten?"

"I didn't see it…"

The rats were more afraid of her than of either Embaza or Anebra. They avoided her like sunlight. Sure enough, her reddish hair gleamed as if from within.

Dizzy, Anebra got to her feet, the pain in her left leg a genuine nuisance. The rat she had wounded lay quiet at last, blood matting its thick, spiky coat.

As that one fell, another rushed at Embaza, but he halted it with the thrust of a second needle. The rats gave off a horrible stench, redolent of the sewers below. There beneath the pit they thrived on the blood that dripped into the drains from the continuing battles of the men and monsters above.

This blood lust was evident now in the red-rimmed eyes of the two remaining rats that edged around the pit. One of them bared its teeth at Polah, whose small face was now hidden by a mass of red-gold hair, but still it did not advance.

"Get up, girl," cried a man in the front row.

The other rat attacked Anebra. Its huge, yellow teeth dripped venom, and her vision blurred. She shut her eyes and jumped blind, landing on the rat's tail. Before it could turn, she had buried a dagger into its back. But Anebra was now so lightheaded she couldn't regain her footing. Wailing, she fell onto one hand. The cheering of the throng rang in her ears and dulled her pain.

The last rat turned and hissed at Anebra, worrying back and forth in a sort of frenzy. Its drooling fangs were almost a blur to the acrobat in her weakened state. Embaza pulled a dagger from the scabbard under his robe and squinted at the rat, but it remained a moving target.

Polah's muscles tore within, as if some powerful force opened her, folding her skin, laying her racing heart open to the air. Pain seared her helpless body, and her lungs hurt. She envisioned herself in shreds and then somehow, a gathering began. New strength poured back into her ripening form, filling her solar plexus, her chest, her throat.

As the onlookers gasped, Polah rose out of her crouch and lifted her head, threw back her mane of hair, and in a dazzling splendor of surprise, showed the crowd a face that was not human. Belt and tunic fell away, torn into shreds; the hunting knife clattered on the stone floor. She dropped to all fours, and before all eyes, human melted into fox as large as any great wolf.

Her needle-like fangs and black eyes glinted dangerously. Thick fur the color of firelight gleamed along her back to the brush of her tail, and down her legs to black paws. The delighted cheers of the onlookers dimly penetrated her pointed ears like the roar of the ocean in a shell.

With a glance behind him, the rat screamed in terror and rage. Polah swiftly closed upon him and went for his throat, ripping out his jugular in one bite.

There was a gasp, and then a roar from the assembly as the onlookers crowded each other for a better look.

Anebra sat stunned, very near shock.

Embaza took a deep, shuddering breath as he stared at Polah. *I knew it.* Grasping his dagger, he circled the two combatants, looking for an opening. He was careful to avoid the sunbeam, keeping it in the rodents' eyes.

With a strength derived from terror, the rat clamped its hideous teeth into the fox's tail. Somewhere within the wild mind of the fox, the spirit of the woman crouched, wanting to let go, lie down, sleep. But the instinct of the predator swelling her breath, flowing in her veins, drove her teeth into the rat's soft underbelly. Oblivious to the blood spurting from her tail, she tightened her jaws to prevent the desperate rat from rolling away. One last shudder and the rat lay still.

The fox released her prize and raised her head. Her dark eyes appeared wounded, confused. She turned and stared straight at Embaza. Their gaze held for a long moment, and wordless understanding passed between them.

To Polah, everything now had a dreamlike quality. *It's as if all my life was false—and this—this dream—is real.* Could she be both fox *and* woman?

Embaza's mind was calm and clear as a lake. He'd been waiting for this. *Yes, little fox, come into my mind. There is plenty of room for you...* He welcomed his burgeoning powers, expanding his chest as if he might fill the arena with his breath alone.

Anebra was dressing her wound with a strip torn from her leggings. All three combatants were dimly aware of the cheering mob, whose screaming approval soured quickly to warning when out of the doors rushed three fresh giant rats—and behind them, a menacing shape that filled the doorway.

-8-

IF THERE were ever a moment when magic was needed, this was the time. Embaza thrust his dagger into a scabbard beneath his robe and reached for a small bit of smooth gray stone from a hidden pocket. Standing in the center of the pit, he muttered beneath his breath: *Dakshan Ogondeesif Zmandelastra Cadrith Rluthammbahl...* The words were old and the odor of mold emanated from him as he spoke. His voice shook with unaccustomed fear. The shadowed silhouette in the doorway grew, but ventured no nearer.

Kneeling, Anebra freed the hemp rope from her waist. Anger fueled her courage. *You won't make me afraid.* As Embaza's voice grew louder, Anebra tossed a loop over the neck of the nearest rat.

The rodent hissed at her, lips drawn back over filthy teeth, and charged. Hand over hand she took up the slack, periodically jerking the line to keep the rat off-balance while simultaneously tightening the noose. A death match ensued, a race to strangle the beast before it tore out her throat.

Embaza's voice continued unraveling the ancient words, but there was still no apparent effect except for the primeval smell.

From the back of the pit, Polah's black eyes glistened as she measured the space between herself and the rats. The bite wound in her tail was not deep, the blood already dried upon her matted fur. She was more interested now in the shape in the doorway, and made no move toward the smaller creatures. A protective membrane settled about her mind and she sent a tentacle of awareness into this invisible lake. *It is I,* said the voice.

Embaza. What are you doing in my mind? But there was no answer from the wizard. *Chanting a spell. And yet here.* The bond between them frightened her.

The rat's talons were inches from the acrobat's face when its eyes began to bulge. With her last ounce of strength, Anebra gave a final desperate jerk on the rope and the rodent's eyes rolled up, showing a hideous yellow. Its loathsome body fell on top of her, and a scream escaped her as rat spittle drooled onto her neck, searing her skin with sizzling white trails of acid. Tears of pain blinded her as she rolled away from the rat and struggled to focus on the doorway. She could just discern Embaza's dark form in front of her; the fox was a vague red ball of fur.

The other two rats cowered before Embaza as if they were being crushed, their gaze glued to the small gray stone in his hand.

The fox advanced with caution, eyes still on the doorway.

Embaza continued his measured chanting, like a ship riding out a storm.

Anebra listened to Embaza's words, as mesmerized as the spectators. Polah saw, or rather felt, the words fall into the clear inner lake of her mind like huge raindrops. Yet, her senses were alert. She was peripherally aware of Anebra, hurt in the corner, and she moved instinctively to shield the acrobat. It was a strange sensation for one used to being a loner, but the urges of her animal side were too powerful to ignore.

From the doorway, a shape hurtled toward Embaza. Moments afterward, no one could remember what it looked like. A streak of teeth and claw and golden fur, a foul-smelling cloud that encircled the wizard and dashed back through the doorway.

Embaza staggered, but by some inner strength, continued to speak the secret words of the spell. The firestones of his necklace gleamed against the dark blue of his skin. The audience was subdued, straining for a clear glimpse of the creature.

The great fox took a few steps forward until she was beside the wizard. Anebra rested on one knee and tried to stand, coiling her rope into her hand. But she was too weak from the rat's poison and collapsed on the stone floor. Terrified, she tried to compose herself for death as her consciousness ebbed.

In his aerie, Prince Mischa twisted his ring and waited. He rang a small brass bell and in a few moments, three women in brown robes came up next to his chair. He pointed down to the pit and said, "Attend to the woman when it is over."

Then, to the crowd's amazement—and Embaza's relief—a dim, gray-blue mist swirled around the floor in front of the doorway. His voice grew more resonant as he continued, *"Omaygazi Wodiszgorjana Nugozid…"*

Parting the mist, the demon moved out of the shadows of the doorway. The color of shaded sand, as large as a bull, it had the feline agility of a panther. Its teeth were like a wolverine's, except for the double row of huge fangs on either side. Its movements were deliberate, and intelligence lurked in its pupil-less eyes as it paced back and forth. The monster's silence was more menacing than the snarling and hissing of the rats, and its horrible smell preceded it, stinging Embaza's eyes. The sound of its claws scratching the sand along the stone floor made an unnerving counterpoint to the chanting of the wizard.

As the mist rose, the sand demon continued to pace, staring at Embaza. Polah felt her heart beat faster, an animal pulse she could not ignore. *I must attack now while it is still intent on the elf.* A force like an iron band abruptly throttled her windpipe, a physical blow that widened her eyes.

Not yet, said the voice inside her mind.

*How dare you interfere with me like this? How **dare** you tell me what to do?*

Filled with rage, only the invisible restraint at her neck kept her from rushing forward with tooth and claw.

Quiet, little fox, let me concentrate.

The mist reached the monster's underbelly and esper trails undulated in the air. The sand demon emitted a low growl. Then, in a matter of seconds, it encircled Embaza for a second time, knocking Polah to one side. As before, the demon returned to prowl in the doorway.

"What did it do?" said a spectator.

"Some kind of magic. Remember the story of Objon?"

"Oh, when the demon encircled him thrice…" He made a throat-cutting gesture.

Embaza fell to his knees, but his voice did not waver as he continued to recite the spell. The lone sunbeam embroidered the edge of his robe. *I must finish before the demon makes its third circle.*

A brand of burning sparks fell into the lake of Polah's mind. She watched Embaza, her head cocked to one side. *Are you all right?* She moved back to his side, keeping an eye on the rats who cowered at her feet, still immobilized.

The mist was now up to the sand demon's neck, but the monster never stopped pacing. Anebra lay unconscious at the edge of the pit, her breathing ragged. Polah stood ready to attack, while Embaza came at last to the final words of his spell …*Mob dorova zanithwyn.* There was a momentary pause as spectators and fighters alike waited to see if the beast would fall.

The monster turned and snarled, opening its huge mouth and terrifying fangs. Something that could have been a laugh emanated from it. High above, even the Prince shuddered, the golden ring in his fist.

Embaza waited, assailed by doubts. *What did I leave out? Why isn't it working?* He took the third needle from the cuff of his robe and readied his wax. The sand demon's eyes were contemptuous as they raked over the wizard.

Embaza recited to himself, *Pain is good. If I have pain, nothing can hurt me…* He thrust the needle into the wax and fixed the monster with a glazed stare, while one by one, the rats screamed in agony and died.

When the last rat had stopped twitching, the sand demon gathered its massive hind quarters and rushed towards Embaza. The crowd watched in horror as the creature encircled the wizard for the third time.

Embaza dropped like a stone.

Undisturbed by the screaming crowd, the demon headed for the doorway, but a furry red body hurtled into its path. The monster's massive jaws fastened onto Polah's left hind leg, and with one savage bite, tore it in two.

Bleeding and in shock, the fox clamped the corded throat of the demon in her sharp teeth. Tendrils of gray-blue smoke clouded the pit. The scent of fresh blood mingled with the musty odor of the arcane mist. Those near the pit covered their eyes and mouths. The Prince was kneeling on his chair now, peering at the scene below. *Where are they? I can't see,* he fumed.

The sand demon whirled and bucked, rolling over and over, trying to shake the fox from its throat. Again and again, it turned to reach for another leg, her tail or neck, but the fox was in an awkward position, and the monster could not reach her.

Polah knew only blind instinct now. This was no rat; this was her death. She held on because there was nothing else to do.

Embaza lay as if he were dead. Yet, even in Polah's torn and bloody mind, the lake still shimmered and the voice spoke, *The demon's counter spell has stopped me—but you must not give up, Polah. Our magic is strong. Let me work through you...* The frenzied spectators roared, and two or three tried to climb the slippery stone wall of the pit, failing because of the steep angle.

To the fox, victory didn't seem likely. She was near death herself, bleeding from the hideous stump of her leg. *I can't go on. I won't make it. Sorry, so sorry...* Despite the urging of the onlookers, it seemed her life would slip away. High above, Mischa pounded his fists in frustration, unable to get a clear view.

From the floor of the pit, the blue mist rose in the air and fashioned itself into long fingers that crept into the demon's eyes, ears and mouth, filling every orifice and every pore with the magic of the most ancient of elves.

In desperation, the creature turned toward the wizard with unseeing eyes, claws extended. Then, it gave one last, soul-chilling howl and tumbled to the floor.

Polah's jaws opened by reflex and she lay panting on the slick stone.

The crowd erupted as if awakened from a dream. People cheered, stamped and clapped their tribute to the courage and perseverance of the three champions.

From all sides of the arena, voices took up the Heroes' Lament, the ultimate tribute to fallen warriors. Most believed that all three fighters were dying or dead. The single beam of sunshine lit Polah's glossy coat like a torch.

As the last chord sounded, Embaza raised his head to shouts of surprise. He lurched to his knees and looked at his comrades. He drew his dagger once more from the scabbard in his robe, and crawled through the gore of the stone pit until he hovered over the sand demon. Then with a savage thrust, he sliced the heart out of the monster and tossed it into the trough at the edge of the pit.

Ignoring the screaming praise of the multitude, he lifted the body of the mutilated fox and carried it to the edge of the pit, then searched for an exit. From a door cleverly hidden in the rounded wall, three women dressed in brown entered the arena.

"The Prince sent us. Is she still alive?" asked the tallest of the three women.

"Yes, but she is not for the likes of you to heal," said Embaza. None of them questioned him. "See to the other one—quickly. She is wounded and, I think, poisoned." As the healers moved forward, he detained the third one with his eyes. "Show me where I can take the shape-changer." It was the first time he had spoken the term aloud and it gave him a wry satisfaction.

The young woman led him into the corridor and up a short flight of stairs to a room with a linen-covered cot, table and chair. Limestone walls offered a window through which the desert could be seen, unadorned by any living thing. The afternoon sun from the opposite side of the Manor cast long shadows cooling the unbroken expanse of sand. He turned back the sheet, and laid Polah on the bed.

"This will do," he said, "leave us now."

When the healer had gone, he dragged the chair to the side of the bed, sat down and took a black velvet pouch from his robe. From the pouch, he withdrew a plain silver ring. He then held the ring to the stump of the fox's leg and chanted, *"Gosuvidna, blenatl witherna..."*

Soon the smell of green herbs pervaded the arid room. Exhaustion finally overcame him. His fingers loosened on the ring, he fell back into the chair and closed his eyes.

-9-

THE NIGHTWING Avenwyndar Denshadiel lay dying. But this was nothing out of the ordinary; she had been dying for years. She had long since ceased to yearn for the use of her limbs, or even the clarity of her senses. What she had gained in other abilities more than made up for the physical powers lost to aging.

Amid the swan's down quilts, she lay motionless, her body so frail that to touch her was dangerous. She so rarely spoke, that when she did, one would have thought it was the wind. Near her was a sleek black rabbit which she occasionally stroked very gently, the only movement that did not tax her.

In the cavern that formed the Nightwing's room, all was space and air. Transoms were cut into the crystal walls, connecting with skylights that reached tens of leagues to the surface. The diluted sun or moon beams trickled into the room and intersected the floor around her bed in the pattern of a star. Two chairs formed from giant sea turtle shells matched the bed. Other than these, the room was empty of furniture. The Nightwing no longer needed such things.

Around her bed were three dark-elven women. The first was the ancient High Priestess Kalista, dressed in a black velvet robe, a unicorn embroidered in white silk on the collar. The second wore the white homespun robe of a nurse, the stark uniform softened by a belt of dark blue, and the third was the Nightwing's youngest daughter Inuari, clothed in a simple black satin robe with the black rabbit insignia of the royal novice on her collar.

The nurse bent over the Nightwing holding a small bottle of a sticky, golden liquid. She let one drop of the liquid fall onto Avenwyndar's lower lip where it shimmered like a bead of amber before slipping into the wizened mouth. The Nightwing gave no sign of acknowledgement.

The other two women sat in the chairs nearby. The older one spoke, "You may leave us now, Moura," and the nurse bowed and withdrew.

Inuari whispered to the crone, "Do you think my mother knows we are here, your Reverence?"

Kalista nodded, resting her hands on her knees. "She is aware of everything."

Inuari couldn't help staring at the old priestess' black knuckles, so knotted and wrinkled. She still considered old age romantic, and wondered if she would ever be as wise and respected as the High Priestess. Death had a romantic aspect, too. Even Ombra's passing, tragic and violent though it had been, carried a certain mystique unrelated to the question of murder or, in this case, outright assassination.

Enthralled as she was by what might lay beyond life, Inuari could not imagine life without the Nightwing to guide her. Avenwyndar Denshadiel was her mother, true, but also the head of her order, the Sisterhood of Miralor.

It had been a long time since Alvarra had enjoyed a Nightwing so gifted in the mystic arts. Inuari felt honored to be sitting with Kalista and her mother. Only Tiala was allowed the same latitude. Inuari supposed that her other sisters were considered too rowdy.

The ideal of self-modesty was not a part of the priestly training in Alvarra. Inuari wondered why. In her studies of the cultures of other lands, she had found this intriguing concept of humility prevalent.

She was proud that her own culture had evolved from barbarity to its present height of civilization. Still, her mother's time had been exciting. A few men had been employed in unusual positions. One of the Nightwing's own husbands was said to have dabbled in science, keeping a secret laboratory in the Merimn'a, that mysterious place beneath the Royal City. That new laws had passed each century to prevent such abuses only made Inuari more curious.

She asked the priestess, who jerked awake, "Why are we not allowed to travel beneath the City—to the Merimn'a? What's down there, your Reverence?"

"It's nearly deserted, child, the result of so many cave-ins. Originally, you know, there were rich mines of silver and gems—," she stopped, and Inuari nodded. "Well, at that time, it all belonged to the dwarves and they sold the ores to our people. As they became rich, they wanted to become richer. In their greed, they overworked the mines. The collapse that followed was inevitable, but it was a disaster of unimaginable proportions. Water from the center of our world surged in, drowning the miners and creating a vast, raging sea."

Seething with questions, Inuari recognized the finality of Kalista's tone and knew it was wise not to challenge. If the High Priestess wanted to continue, she would.

"Of course, some survived, and some land masses remained above water. There were even cave beds that could be used as homes, but those who remained in the Merimn'a were few, and they intermarried. Eventually sea creatures came up on land, and they intermarried with the survivors. What lives down there now is a hybrid of strange creatures that have almost no resemblance to any civilized people." Kalista stopped again and closed her eyes, dozing.

"I've heard that the Merimn'a is a prison, filled with our society's outcasts," Inuari interjected, unable to resist a question.

The old priestess was alert. "Where did you hear that?"

Inuari caught her breath. "I read it in a book, your Reverence." Kalista glared at her, and reluctantly, Inuari admitted, "My page let me read it—I know it wasn't on my assigned list…"

"You were inquisitive." The crone shook her head. "You'll learn not to bother with the fashionable nonsense they write in Douvilwe and Aeryinne. You're free to explore and find out for yourself, of course. You were chosen for the honor of joining our order, Inuari, because we thought you were special. I hope you won't disappoint us." She patted the novice's knee, causing Inuari to flinch.

Nightwing Avenwyndar heard this conversation and approved. The High Priestess was just doing her job, shielding Inuari from the truth. In spirit, Avenwyndar visited the Merimn'a regularly. True, there were some strange creatures, as new life often evolved on the heels of a natural disaster, but there were also outlaws and exiled wizards. Her heart went out to her daughter. If only she could tell her the truth, but Inuari's mind was not yet ready to receive direct information. She planted what seeds she could while the child slept.

Unaware of her mother's concern, Inuari turned her mind to other dilemmas to dull the sting of Kalista's rebuke. What had become of Tiala? And what were they going to do about Dekhalis?

The priestess, seeing that her words had taken root, decided to channel the novice's curiosity elsewhere. "My child, the Nightwing has communicated with us. At fifth bell, while we were in prayer."

Inuari's eyes lit up. She'd been waiting for a sign that her mother was yet alive and working on the inner planes. "What did she say?"

"She has sent one of the priestesses to aid your sister, Tiala. Even now, the Priestess Zelwyn of the Order of Loote is near her."

"Oh," cried Inuari, clasping her hands together. "Will she weave a circle of power around her?"

"No," said Kalista, "There are certain limitations in that cruel climate. Besides, as a priestess, she must observe mourning even there." She sighed. "But she is a healer and will try to see that Tiala is protected from the Scourge of Elves."

"Ah," said Inuari, awed that the crone could speak of it so casually. Curiosity practically devoured her now. "Pardon me, your Reverence...I know it is presumptuous..."

"Speak, child," said the crone.

"What is it like to dance in the moonlight?"

The old woman heard the awe in the young elf's voice and hoped she could retain it. All too soon, the magic of the experience would be replaced by fear. *Wait until she is spied upon by the children of the upworlders.* The priestess smiled, "You will see," and left it at that.

Kalista saw the Nightwing's hand move a fraction of an inch, and the rabbit's fur rippled in ecstasy. The old priestess silenced her own thoughts. A familiar voice in her mind said, *Sister of Miralor,* and Kalista greeted her monarch.

Take the child to the priestess Jetta, who lives by the waterfall, said Avenwyndar. *Tell Inuari to pray there and fast for three nights. At eleventh bell, she must watch for spirits. Tell her Miralor has spoken.*

Yes, Nightwing, answered Kalista. *May I ask what is your intention?*

I want her safe. She is too young and her mind too unformed to be of use. I will send instructions in her dreams, and she will grow in the practice of listening.

It will be done, my Liege.

Avenwyndar withdrew from the mind of the priestess. Even Inuari, whose sensitivity was not very advanced, suffered a chill.

For the novice, the pressures of her situation were almost unbearable anywhere outside of this room. The riots and demonstrations in the cities had produced a menacing atmosphere, and the strikes by male servants were becoming a great nuisance as well. There was nothing to do now but let nature take its course. At least, when the period of mourning was over, they could use troops if they had to, though the thought sickened her.

The conditions in Alvarra baffled Inuari. Most of her learning had been confined to philosophy and law, and she liked it that way. Politics were for Tiala and Eleppon. In the Royal City, she had always felt safe from the tumult in the cities above, but she was increasingly afraid for her sisters and their way of life. Dekhalis was doing more than just making trouble. He was brewing a revolution. She wished the Sisterhood would do something.

Kalista was worried too, but like the other priestesses, she had seen upheaval before. It never lasted. The only thing to do was to retire behind the walls of the temple and wait it out. This time, though, the rabble rouser was a royal son, and that spelled real trouble.

Kalista wished she had asked the Nightwing more about Zelwyn's situation. The Sisters of Loote were healers who traveled in many strange and dangerous lands. Zelwyn was one of the more successful ones, having attracted followers among the upworlders themselves. Kalista hated to think of her friend in the Outland Territory, where if she weren't careful, she would be roasted alive by the Scourge.

It was bad enough that young Tiala had left in this way. What a foolish thing to do. Some were sure to say she had abdicated. The old priestess shook her head and sighed. Keeping the royal daughters in line was a chore that needed younger bones. She was tired of it. The royal novice was good, though, she had to admit. Very good. It was wise to keep her sheltered from the danger—and the longer they could keep her out of politics, the better.

Kalista cleared her throat and said, "Inuari, I have a message for you... from Miralor."

-10-

IN A locked bedroom on the second floor of Mischa's manor, Tiala Denshadiel considered her plight. Had she been mad to come? She recalled her first meeting with Mischa—Prince Mischa. Never had the thought occurred to her that he might be a man. She examined the room, a sense of danger closing around her.

The walls were fashioned of white marble, the floor a carpet of woven reeds, softened and dyed a rich shade of blue. The chairs and tables were carved with the images of wild animals, claws and hooves inlaid with silver.

Tiala sat in the largest chair, her fingers restlessly exploring the raised designs of desert elk on its arms. Behind her was a pale green marble fireplace, and above it, a long bell-pull. Playing the old tunes and ballads had somewhat restored her spirits. She had fallen asleep with her travel-harp in her lap. Now she was stiff and sore, but full of energy. She rose and paced.

Like most of her kind, Tiala had black hair, chiseled features and deep green eyes. She wore her hair long, knotted at the ends and tucked into the back of her sash. Her traveling gown was of pale yellow spidersilk, embroidered in violet that had faded over time. The divided skirt fell to her ankles and enhanced rather than concealed her tall, shapely body.

Although her dwarven guard was not well-educated, and very much in the pay of the Prince, Tiala decided that talking with the General was preferable to boredom. At least here was a deepworlder. *Someone civilized.* She laid the harp on a table, and went to the door. She put her ear to it and listened, but there was no sound. She knocked softly, and after a few moments, tried again. There was still no answer. She was feeling more like a prisoner than a guest, and she was unused to inactivity. This was not an efficient way to search for champions.

In answer to her original missive, the Prince had sent three guards led by a dwarven warrior of impeccable reputation. As Tiala had expected, the trip across the desert had been terrifying. She gritted her teeth, remembering how she had been wrapped in water-soaked robes and laid in the bottom of the cart. The heavy cloak had protected her at first, but a few hours after moonset, the strains of dawn had penetrated the very boards of the cart. As the Scourge of Elves rose, the cloth had dried, and Tiala's skin had crawled with the energy of madness.

Initially wracked with tremors and uncontrollable itching, she had cried out as a raging fever coursed through her body. The guards had talked and sung to her endlessly and, at nightfall, had tenderly fed her and bathed her aching skin. Tiala was chagrined at recalling the way she had tried to strangle the leader—the one called the General—as the Scourge sickness wormed its way into her very mind. Better not to think of that now.

What a fool I was to ask for sanctuary here. The elven fighter who had first told her about the Manor had boasted of his battle exploits, but said little about Mischa. Few upworld blue-elves visited the Royal City since it was so far underground. They had superstitions about the "demons and devils" of the underworld, and indeed, this one had worn talismans around his neck and sigils embroidered into his belt which the upworlders thought were powerful against goblins and other such riffraff.

Tiala could not remember the stranger's name, but she had been impressed with his bravery and battle scars, no matter how ridiculous his superstitions. The last thing she remembered him saying was, "Only the best go to the Manor." She only wished she had learned more about Mischa.

She shivered, remembering her first impressions of the Prince. Behind the smiling face of the rotund little man lay a cold, calculating mind that flashed from impenetrable blue eyes—eyes that had witnessed too much violence.

Tiala glanced at the braided cord hanging above the mantelpiece. Prince Mischa had pointed it out, saying, "When you wish to leave my establishment, simply tug that bell cord and I will be notified." Her host had added, "You may not change your mind once you have signaled, so be very sure."

Anger fueling her thoughts, she paced faster. Dark elves were not welcome here. That had been plain in the murderous looks of the giant guards attending the Prince. During the day, she was forced to remain in this sheltered room, and at night, the door was locked against her wandering the halls. It was unlikely she'd have the chance to watch an actual battle.

She wondered about the General's background. Since she worked for the Prince, she must have been tried in the arena. She had the look of an old warrior, maybe a veteran of the Seven Years War. *A worthy champion—but can I trust her?* Although they lived in the same deepworld conditions under truces that had been unbroken for a thousand years, there were vast differences between dwarf and dark elf. Could the lands of Tskurl and Alvarra be truly bridged?

Tiala decided to tap on the door again, but before her hand touched the polished wood, she heard footsteps coming up the hall. She held her breath, hoping.

The footsteps stopped in front of the door, and a deep female voice said, "Na'a Nightwing Tiala, are you in?"

The General's formal greeting made Tiala shake her head. *Where else would I be?* "I'm here," she snapped, despising the dialect that everyone spoke in the Manor. It was a hybrid between elven and some human tongue. To Tiala's ears, it made them all sound like pigs.

A key clicked in the lock and the door was opened by a stout dwarven woman with a round, dimpled face, a wisp of beard and curly, brown hair flecked with gray.

What a beauty, thought the General, as her brown eyes met Tiala's green ones. The dwarf was always protective of those she considered worthy. Beautiful dark-elven women certainly qualified. She knew the high-born elf didn't particularly like her, yet the General had too much self respect to care.

"I thought you might be thirsty so I brought you some sweet ale," said the dwarf, holding out a chased silver flask.

Tiala took the flask, surprised and a little embarrassed—both by the gift and the fact that the General had switched into a quite acceptable dark-elven patois. "Thank you. Won't you sit down?"

The General noticed a gameboard and playing pieces for *Rogues & Rascals* on a small writing table in the corner. *Another form of competition. Typical of Mischa to place it in a guest room.* Instead of sitting in the chair by the door, she strode over to the gameboard and gestured to the elf, "Would you like a match?"

Tiala wasn't very good at this game, at least not among Alvarrans, who were believed to have created it. After all, she had stopped playing when she reached her first hundredth birthday. But she was suddenly filled with fond memories of sitting in the stalactite garden with her brother, Dekhalis. How happy they had been. She could see him now, laughing at her straightforward playing-style as he announced in a childish voice, "I will beat you, Sister. Wait and see." Had the signs of his megalomania been evident even then?

A memory thrust itself into her mind—one she would have preferred to avoid. At the age of ten, Dekhalis had lured his bodyguard into a spider pit for a mock duel in which he managed to gore her in the belly with his toy sword. Claiming to be afraid, he fled in panic, leaving the bleeding Lady of Skill to be mauled by spiders. Because of his age, everyone had assumed it was an accident. Now Tiala wondered.

With a lift of the chin, she said, "By all means, let's play, General. I'm bored to tears." The General sat down in the chair with a military precision, flicking her sword to one side. Tiala admired the weapon. It was indeed finely-wrought, like so many dwarven arms. She hesitated to ask, but curiosity overcame her restraint. "What an unusual sword. Is it a family heirloom?"

The dwarf sat up straighter and blushed. "It belonged to my ancestor, Dragonbane of Estenhame, my Lady. It came to me by my mother, Kurn of Faithborn."

Tiala nodded. Estenhame was the tribe or village. Dragonbane was a common name for a female warrior. Faithborn may have been Kurn's mother, or the mother of her husband. Tiala asked, "Are your weapons always passed from mother to daughter?"

"It's a tradition in Estenhame," said the dwarf, pushing up the sleeves of her mail shirt.

"I heartily approve." Tiala wondered at the dwarf's relaxed manner. If she was her keeper, why was she allowing such familiarity? Was this a possible champion? The thrill of destiny prickled her spine. "Let's begin—are you a rogue or a rascal?" She held up one of each, the *rogues* silver, the *rascals* gold.

"Oh, I'm a rascal," said the General, a smirk on her face. "You start."

Tiala almost smiled, then moved one of six small minion-pieces forward two spaces on the board. The first game continued for an hour, during which Tiala and the General developed a healthy respect for each other. Their respective styles of playing were similar, each using carefully planned campaigns.

The General used her lizard minions to harry Tiala's flanks of wildebeest. Tiala's plan of attack was similar except that she favored mounted toads and carrion birds (which could move diagonally). Her rogue queen, a silver muskrat, stayed in the background, traveling east to west as the occasion warranted, while the General's golden lion, the master rascal, hovered behind the lizards, waiting for the kill.

Tiala said, "I know a bit about this barren land, but can you tell me more about it?"

"Terarg is isolated. Most of it is a wasteland called the Outland Territories.

Under a loose organization of tribes, the desert is home to various peoples," said the dwarf, stroking her beard and frowning at the board.

"Can you describe them to me?"

The General said, "There are leather-garbed gnomes, a handful of giants with blackened front teeth and white turbans, and various visitors including elves and humans from the northern mountains, and my own people. Many veterans of the wars come to the arena, seeking past glories."

"And who rules here – the Prince?"

"Actually, the whole Outland Territories is governed by a Patriarch."

"Another man in a ruling position," spat Tiala.

The General chuckled. "The obscurity of the location is ideal for the Prince's purpose. He has one passion, which draws hundreds of guests year after year, a few by special invitation. It is said that he is addicted to fighting—or, to be more specific, to watching others fight. And if someone dies out here in the middle of nowhere…" She spread her hands. "The desert tells no tales."

Tiala watched her guard with interest. She had to admit the General was impressive. She had shown great poise and resourcefulness in the desert. Not many would have known what to do with a dangerously ill dark elf. So far, she had displayed none of the prejudice or cruelty hinted at by the Prince and other guests.

However, Tiala knew the General must be loyal to Mischa, else why would the Prince have sent her? And yet there were moments in the desert when Tiala had felt safe with her.

The General moved her wolf piece.

Tiala said, "I have heard that many a warrior will pay dearly for the chance to win fame in Mischa's arena."

She lifted her head proudly. "Those who survive are the elite."

"Surely, there are others like you here. They all can't be like the Prince."

The General laughed. "There is no one like the Prince, my Lady. Thank the Gods of the Forge for that."

Tiala frowned. "I'm not used to being cooped up like a cricket in a box— and even less to being in a keep ruled by a man."

The General sipped her ale, uncertain how to comfort this monarch. "You play very well, my Lady."

Tiala smiled in acknowledgement, "You're kind to say so, but surely your skill is greater than mine in the arena. The Prince said that you were once unbeatable. Is that true?"

The General stroked her beard and thought a moment. "Well, I don't recall doing anything out of the ordinary," she said, moving her golden buffalo vizier in a diagonal streak across the board to stand before the rogue king, a silver crocodile. "Of course, there was a fight today that caused a lot of talk. Two women and a wizard faced a sand demon." She described the monster in graphic detail for Tiala's benefit, drawing heavily on the tales told in the barracks.

"Did they defeat it?" Tiala countered the rascal vizier's challenge with her rat page.

"I heard the wizard used some sort of foul spell and one of the women turned into a weird-creature, some kind of fox, I think." She grimaced. "But what with poison and other wounds, they aren't expected to live. No one sings the Heroes' Lament for survivors."

Tiala focused on the game, and strove to calm her disappointment.

"Tell me of your life, my Lady," said the General.

Tiala draped her legs over an arm of the chair. "I was trained in the tradition of second royal daughter, learning the warrior craft and serving my required years in the army. I'm accustomed to an active life, composed of study, physical practice, poetry—and music." She examined her nails. "I discovered I had a liking for it."

"What sort of music?" asked the dwarf.

"Everything from the owl song of the world above to the crystal chimes of the caves below. At my coming of age ceremony, I might have announced my decision to follow the Way of the Bard, but now those plans have been suspended." Tiala's eyes held a faraway look.

"You are brave, my Lady."

Tiala said, "Or rash. How will I find my champions? And will they be what I need? Surely, there are some here who are cunning, intelligent and strong…but what if they are also ruthless?" She pursed her lips. "Well, maybe they will have to be ruthless. My brother is so twisted now, he is no longer elven."

She had a sudden image of Ombra's smashed and broken body. "No dark elf who spent all her life exploring the amethyst caves could fall from a sturdy archway." Tiala remembered her first suspicions and clenched her fists at the memory of Dekhalis's deadly behavior at Ombra's funeral. Tears filled her eyes. *Ombra had been such an artist…crystal chimes that sang in the wind, mirrors that reflected one's youth.*

The images faded, replaced by a picture of Dekhalis as he had once existed in her heart, a tall, handsome elf with the dusky black skin of the deepworlder, long tapering ears that blended with his blue-black hair. His features were so dear to her. She longed to go back to childhood when he tagged after her and questioned her about everything. She had opened her books to him and taught him weapons play…and now, he wanted to be king. The unfamiliar word was bitter on her tongue.

Play continued as the two women touched on various topics. The General noticed the way Tiala sipped her ale, conserving it with a habit that the dwarf interpreted as good army discipline. She wondered what the elf's training had been. Although the General won the first game, Tiala learned by watching, and developed an astute defense that earned her the second.

As they talked, Tiala overcame her original prejudice against the dwarf, even glimpsing the fact that she might have been a little jealous of the General's fighting reputation. As the time wore on, she offered a confidence or two. "Have you ever used a ranseur tempered in an orange flame?"

"No," replied the General. "how does it handle?"

"Splendidly," said Tiala, "It can cut through bone as well as flesh." She was relaxed and missed the look on the other's face.

There's more to this monarch than meets the eye, thought the dwarf.

"Indeed," said Tiala, as if she could read minds. "My weapons-master always told me not to waste sympathy on my enemies. She often said, 'They're not wishing you long life when they raise their swords.'"

The General chuckled. "True," she said, "but tell me, na'a Nightwing, do you ever question your role as executioner?"

"What an interesting word 'executioner.' In my mother's house, we were always taught to value life. Our own and those of others. But we revere death as well. Death is a release, an outpouring of self not into oblivion, but into a state of peace. Nightwing Mhorgiana taught: 'Once a soldier has chosen to dance with death, do not blame yourself for playing the tune.'"

"Profound," said the General, "but I know a poem that suits me better:
> *Come embrace me, my lover, my friend,*
> *Empty my mind of all its care,*
> *Fill me up with your dreams and desires,*
> *And I'll go to battle with your scent in my hair.*"

Tiala hummed. "I can almost hear the melody. Perhaps you could teach it to me."

The General nodded. "It's better in Tskurlan."

With a pang of longing for the magical beauty of her own country, Tiala picked up her small harp and played a sad tune. It was a very old folk song about a soldier far from home, recalling the beauties of her simple cave. The General looked down at the dyed carpet, embarrassed by the feelings aroused in her.

Tiala thought, *I've got a lot to learn about music and poetry. I hope I will live long enough to become a true bard and not just a novice with a common travel-harp.* She looked at the gameboard. *What was the General doing with that wolf piece?*

The sweet ale had done its work, and not long after they had begun the third game, Tiala dozed in her chair. The General quietly left the room.

She had barely locked the door behind her when she heard a scuffling on the stairs ahead. She hoisted her broadsword into both hands and squinted in the direction of the noise.

A rat scurrying across the landing brought a smile to her face. *I miss my homeland, too. Being with the Alvarran has reminded me of that. Hearing the music…perhaps someday I'll tell her that I, too, know the songs of cave and crystal.*

She sheathed her sword and bit into the desert pear from her pocket. Its sweet juice dribbled onto her beard and she dabbed at it absently. *Perhaps I shall join this Alvarran on her quest and see my barrow again.*

-11-

AFTER THEIR ordeal in the arena, Obsidian and Six Stix spent much time together. The young monk wanted to learn from the older, more seasoned warrior. Obsidian listened to Six's tales of lust and bravery, interrupting only to protest the elf's tendency toward profanity. He was never sure how many of the stories were true, but he liked them nonetheless.

For the second night, the two were sitting in one of the small common rooms in their particular guest wing. Due to the exertions of the day and other distractions reputed to be found in the Manor, this room was usually deserted late at night. Six Stix rested heavily in a deep stuffed chair. Beside him on a small oaken table was an almost empty flagon of ale.

Obsidian was comfortable on a wooden bench, his large frame unconfined. The strong, young planes of his unlined face glinted in the lantern's soft light. He practiced extending his peripheral vision while simultaneously concentrating on his new friend.

Six Stix toyed with the flagon, reluctant to drink the last drop. His fine-boned elven face was ruddy with the spirits, and he was in high humor. The old indigo scars along his cheek seemed to fade in the light. To Six Stix, the chance to entertain—and train—a young fighter reminded him of the Seven Years War when he had held rank. Like many a blue elven fighter, the arena at the Manor provided a temporary sense of belonging that recalled lost glories.

"Obsidian, my boy, never cross a dragon—especially a female one." He winked.

Obsidian took no offense to Six's patronizing. He was too clever to miss the point of a story by taking issue with details.

"Why is that, Sir?" he said.

Six Stix laughed again, as if at some private joke. "Well," he said, "dragons only mate once every 73 years." He chuckled some more. "And the female gets…restive. A wee bit irritable." Here, he leaned forward and looked straight at Obsidian, then right and left, as if the shadows might be listening.

"So?" asked Obsidian, restraining a smile.

"They have a peculiar way of killing a man," he said in a conspiratorial whisper.

Obsidian started mentally chanting, beginning a long series of relaxation techniques. *If he draws this out any longer, I'll have to go into a trance.* Leaning forward, his arms resting on his knees, he raised his eyebrows. "How?"

Six Stix's head turned to one side, his chin jutted out, his dark blue eyes twinkled, snaked back and forth, then pinned Obsidian. "They lick him to death." He waited.

Obsidian could not help himself and burst out laughing. "To be licked by the foul, scaly, and no doubt fiery tongue of a dragon is beyond imagination, but to be licked to death is beyond belief."

To his surprise, Six Stix slapped his knee and joined him. In a moment, both were hooting with merriment. A pudgy gnome, dressed in the ubiquitous purple livery under a grimy white kitchen apron and carrying a tray of bottles, appeared at the door.

"Like a refill?" she asked.

"No, no," said Obsidian, waving her away before Six Stix could protest. The monk smiled at the elf, thinking, *I'm really getting fond of the old fibber.*

"Well, my boy," said Six Stix, "think I'll get a little rest. I doubt we'll get a chance to fight again for a few more days, but it's always good to be prepared."

Obsidian knew the value of rest; he practiced it like religion. But he only nodded and checked the impulse to help Six Stix out of the sunken armchair.

"Well," said Six again, "I'm off…" He seemed to be waiting for Obsidian to leave.

Obsidian nodded to him, "Good night," and went down the hall to his room.

Six Stix smiled. The glazed look of liquor was gone from his eyes. *Time to finance this little adventure.* He reached into his pocket for a set of small lock picks. He whistled and left the room, walking nonchalantly down the corridor.

Obsidian leaned against his door, convinced that Six Stix had not gone to bed. When he heard light footsteps heading toward the kitchen, he waited until the noise receded before opening his door to follow.

Six Stix reached the kitchen and peeped into the large room. A row of cooking pots sat drying on the draining racks. The air was cool and clean. No smell of food; no steaming punch or honey mead. The workers had retired.

He tiptoed quickly to a cabinet, half hidden by a rack of towels. The narrow door was loose on its hinges and swung toward him with a slight creak to reveal a crude, circular staircase leading upward.

The elf moved quickly for his size and brawn. In moments he was halfway up the stairs. At a noise from above, he plastered himself against the curved wall, hidden from sight.

To his dismay, voices and a scuffling noise arose from the kitchen below. He strained to hear more. *I wonder how the Prince rewards a guest who goes roaming around. The gnomes all act deaf and dumb when I ask them. Why the secrecy? I haven't found anyone who's actually met the Prince. Lizard's breath, he could be a giant parrot for all we know.*

Suddenly, he glimpsed a large shadow coming from below—and not the shadow of a gnome, even allowing for distortion. The angle of the stairs left no room for swordplay. He eased a dagger out of his wrist sheath, waiting, ready to spring.

Whoever was coming made very little noise. This both impressed and worried him. When the familiar face of a certain monk rounded the corner, Six Stix almost knocked him down.

"Do you want to get yourself killed?" he hissed.

"Sorry," said Obsidian, "I was curious." *Besides, you might need me, the way you've been drinking.*

"Well, come on," Six whispered, "no sense in standing here talking." He led them up the staircase. Both moved with stealth.

When they reached the landing, Six Stix gestured for Obsidian to wait, then peered into the corridor ahead, relieved to find it deserted. *All good little gnomes should be asleep.*

After a quick glance to either side, he motioned Obsidian to join him, pointing to the end of the hall where they made a quick right. They reached the next turn with no trouble, their progress stopped by a door. Six Stix pressed his ear to the polished wood, yet heard nothing.

He tried the latch, but it was locked.

"Curses," whispered Six Stix.

Obsidian smiled at the modified obscenity. *I'm having an effect on him.* He watched with interest as Six Stix took a short length of wire from his pocket, and inserted it into the grooves around the latch. The blue elf opened the door, and both cried out as the floor collapsed beneath them. They hurtled through an inky blackness to a painful landing on a hard wood floor.

The last thing either of them saw before losing consciousness was a beautiful woman leaning over them.

"Paradise," Six Stix murmured.

Obsidian thought, *I doubt it.*

-12-

Six Stix opened his eyes to a veiled elven maiden with shiny black hair and enchanting hazel eyes. He was lying on a pile of soft furs and carpets, nutmeg flowers perfuming the air. He reached out to touch the woman and, to his delight, she smiled and caressed his hand.

He then noticed Obsidian in a sunken pool of lilies, being bathed by two more ladies—one, a golden-skinned elven beauty with silver hair and the other a dusky, blue-eyed human with pure white hair. Both wore veils and the flimsiest of clothing. The monk seemed to be dozing, eyes closed in ecstasy. Although Six Stix had a tendency to be suspicious in unfamiliar surroundings, he saw no harm in this pleasant scene. He chuckled to himself. *The Prince sure knows how to entertain his guests. Or perhaps we've dropped into his harem.*

Just then, Obsidian opened his eyes and started up, splashing water in the face of the elven woman who had been washing his neck. She yelped and tumbled backward into the pool. The other woman giggled and said, "What's the matter with you? You might have hurt Rha." Her soft blue eyes shone with a teasing beauty.

His suspicions aroused, heat inflamed his face and he guessed he might be blushing. "I don't need a bath," he said, rolling over to his knees to leave the pool, his hairlock dripping water down his back.

Six Stix called out from his couch, "Oh, have some fun for a change, lad. When will you see so much water again in this desert?"

Rha took Obsidian's arm and said, "Yes, relax. You've been hurt, see?" She touched a thin cut on Obsidian's back. He winced and actually felt quite weak. He sank back into the pool and the golden elf with the silver hair continued to bathe his back and shoulders with a soft sponge. "The water has healing properties, you see," she said in the sweetest of voices. "It comes from the Oasis of Cloves, the only one of its kind in the world. That is where my people dwell."

Meanwhile, the human woman slipped into the pool with them. Rha said, "Here is Cinna—she will massage your shoulders, young warrior."

However soothing their words, the lack of exits in this circular room troubled Obsidian, but not nearly so much as the seductiveness of the place—the veiled women, the pool, even the water. Something wrong with the water...a sweet, sickly smell. Seemingly against his will, his muscles relaxed and his eyes closed.

As he sank into unconsciousness, he was oblivious to Rha pushing on his shoulders or his body sinking deeper into the water.

Cinna murmured through her veil, "He is quite heavy. Do you think we can handle him alone?"

Rha whispered, "The water is working on him at last. It will be easier now." She glanced over her shoulder at Six Stix, but he was occupied.

Six Stix luxuriated in the lap of the lovely elven woman, who combed his curly hair with her fingers and crooned, "So big and strong you are...you want to fall asleep in little Sefer's lap? Hmmm?"

He was unaware of Obsidian's inert body slipping deeper and deeper in the pool nearby. All he knew was that the woman who held him had on the most striking scarf he had ever seen, shimmering with a silvery sheen that captivated him.

Six Stix liked to manhandle his females in a tender way, preferring to be the one in charge. However, at this moment he was content to remain passive and allow the graceful Sefer to minister to him. A languid sensation began in his toes and moved up through his body. Soon, he was tingling all over as the woman massaged his tired muscles, smoothing a tangerine-scented oil over his rough skin and into his short, black curls.

Naturally, as his pleasure mounted, so did the overwhelming urge to mate with this woman. He pulled her down on top of him, and she matched his desires with her own. As the seconds stretched into moments, he lost all track of time. It seemed to Six that they made love for hours.

Finally, when he had indeed spent himself, the woman urged him to continue. Although he tried to stop her, he was forced to repeat his performance over and over, like a puppet. Eerie at first, the sensation soon became excruciating.

As exquisite pleasure turned into overwhelming pain, her true intentions became clear and he marveled at how stupid he had been.

He wrestled with the woman, ripping off her veil, and she laughed, showing perfect teeth. Sefer's beauty mocked him, stealing his will to resist. Her musky scent, her silken hair, the unearthly luminescence of her scarf...*The scarf*...In a final burst of energy, he tore the sheaf of silk from her neck. With an outcry, she collapsed in his arms, unconscious.

Dizzy and exhausted, Six Stix pushed her away and crawled onto the floor. He shook his head to clear it, alarmed the next instant to see Obsidian in trouble. The young man lay in the pool, eyes closed, surrounded by lilies. The white-haired woman and the golden elf were pressing him down into the water. Only the monk's head was visible, his expression slack.

Before Six Stix could scramble to Obsidian's aid, a needle-like pain on his left wrist turned his attention to a large iridescent silver snake coiling on the floor nearby. *Where did that come from?* At least five feet long and big around as his neck, Six lunged for its head, but it reared back, opening its cruel jaws, exposing its deadly fangs.

Six Stix gritted his teeth as the pain in his wrist lanced up to his shoulder. He readied himself as the creature writhed closer. The snake struck with the speed of lightning, but the elf snatched it behind the head with his right hand. The undulating reptile hissed and tried to spit venom at the fighter, then coiled its tail about Six's leg, cutting off the circulation.

They rolled across the floor. His wrist burned now, a torment that traveled up his arm and seared through the shoulder damaged by the ogre in the arena the day before. With his injured left hand, he pried the serpent's tail free of his leg, then struggled to his knees.

The snake was maddened, hissing and spitting, its wicked teeth snapping the air. Six's entire left arm seemed about to dissolve, his grip on the tail slipping away. In a desperate move, he whipped the snake above his head, cracked its body to the floor, and the enraged monster inadvertently struck its own tail.

Bent double and gasping for breath, Six Stix dropped the snake when it went limp, the silvery skin shriveling into the dazzling scarf that had enchanted him so. By some miracle, the pain in his wrist and shoulder subsided. His heart thumping his rib cage, he sat back on his heels in relief.

Obsidian's head was now submerged. Six Stix shot to his feet and, under the glares of the women, dove into the pool, surfacing with a fistful of Cinna's white hair. Obsidian came to life with a mighty kick, sputtering for breath as his chin cleared the water.

The four grappled now, a seething mixture of arms, legs and hair. Amid curses and shouts, Six Stix and Obsidian dragged the outmatched women from the pool, the blue elf left with arduous task of sitting on their squirming would-be assassins to contain them while the monk unceremoniously ripped silken cords from the wall hangings to bind their wrists behind them.

"Please," said Cinna, "don't hurt us. It's not our fault."

Obsidian said, "You did harm enough to a monk of—" He stopped before he could make the ultimate blunder of revealing his order to an outsider—and a woman. *I've never been so off-balance.*

Six Stix said with a velvet sarcasm, "Why don't we just let you sleep now, Ladies? You must be tired from your exertions." He inspected the bonds to be sure they were tight. "We'd better find our clothes and weapons or you'll be sorry."

Both Six Stix and Obsidian soon discovered that the only clothing in the room belonged to the women, neither adventurer the least bit inclined to masquerade as a harem girl.

Six Stix grasped Rha by her silver hair, wrenching her head back. "Where did you put our weapons and clothes?" he demanded.

"Ouch. I don't know—I swear it. Sefer must have taken them."

Six Stix twisted her hair until she shrieked and squirmed. Obsidian said, "Maybe she's telling the truth. Let her be, Six."

Six Stix said, "For now." He released Rha, who cried, "Monster." He looked at her in disgust. "The Prince has some explaining to do."

He knelt beside Sefer, the black-haired woman who had fainted on the pillows, and slapped her, but she couldn't be roused.

At last, Obsidian yanked down a curtain of green cloth, tore two holes for his arms, and wrapped it around him like a robe, which he belted with another silken cord.

Six Stix split the seams of the black velvet covering one of the larger pillows. He ripped a hole for his head, fashioning a crude tunic that he belted with a braided cord. A second pillow case served as a breech cloth, and he tossed a third to Obsidian.

The loss of their weapons, however, was a serious matter for both.

Obsidian's butterfly knives had been wrought especially for him, weighted and honed to perfection. He had never been without them. Six's most prized possession was his jeweled sword. He wished he had left it in his room, where the rest of his wealth was under triple lock.

Six Stix squared his shoulders and scanned the circular walls for cracks and concealed doors. The room was beautifully appointed and the elf could not resist prying an amber gem from one of the hanging lamps, which he rolled in a fold of his makeshift tunic and thrust under his corded belt. When he saw the shimmering magic scarf, he was tempted to take that, too, but stifled the impulse.

Obsidian studied a tapestry woven of metallic threads depicting a caravan laboring its way across the desert under a fiery sun. Carts filled with gems were drawn by great lizards with glistening golden scales. *What strange beasts of burden.* He admired the workmanship. *Almost as if it were...alive?*

He whipped a corner up and away from the wall. A low, arched doorway led to a dark stairway beyond. "This way out," he cried.

The elf exclaimed over Obsidian's good fortune, and together, they escaped the room.

Obsidian glanced behind him, and the wall hanging fell back into place, concealing their passage. Although it was dark, the stairway curving up and out of sight appeared to be empty.

"Here we go, again," murmured Six Stix.

"After you," said the monk.

"This hasn't put you off women, has it, lad?"

"Hasn't changed my mind at all."

-13-

IN ALVARRA, the twelfth bell had rung, and according to the ancient folk tales, the elven spirit of sleep was at its deepest. Dekhalis lurked outside the secret passage to his room in the royal complex. Concealed by a roseglove bush behind him was the tunnel through which he had crawled, all the way from the Thieves' Quarters in Douvilwe. He rather enjoyed the feeling of being a snake, but now he needed to stand and release the stiffness in his joints.

The passage vented onto a tiny garden, one of those marvelous sights in Alvarra that added to its aura of enchantment, whether viewed from the ground or glimpsed from an escarpment above. Such gardens were usually only a few yards wide, but could extend half a league upward, distracting the eye from the maze of crystal that formed the Royal City.

An owl hooted from a tall cedar-birch. The smell of moss and lichen blended with the five-petaled nightshade and fragrant snowblossoms. On the other side of the garden was a doorway, hidden by trumpet vines. The nest of bats living just beyond was one of Dekhalis's favorite traps. The bats warned him of any intruder and kept the other birds and animals from disturbing him.

To avoid alarming the bats, he quietly leapt to the trunk of the cedar-birch, and from there to a crouch on a ledge just beyond the door. Dressed entirely in black, he appeared to be a mere shadow.

He shimmied along the ledge until he reached a hidden skylight, little more than a stone plug in the roof to keep water from dripping in. Like all the royal masonry, it fitted seamlessly. Using his stiletto, he removed it carefully.

He dropped down on silent feet into his bedroom, the spacious cave which he had not visited in a fortnight.

The dark elf smiled at the instruments of torture—ropes, blades, tongs, bits of hair, feathers and fur—that decorated the walls, reminders of early experiments with the small animals that frequented the garden. A white marble writing desk next to a matching fireplace gleamed in the darkness.

A very large, four-poster bed of the finest petrified teakwood dominated one corner of the room, a matching chest at its foot. Over the bed were hand-drawn icons of famous men, most of them criminals who had been exiled or executed. In each of the bedposts, a needle dart trap would kill anyone who lay down on the bed without disarming them. Several personal guards had discovered this fact, as revealed by the telltale stains on the headboard.

On a prominent ledge was a large bust of himself made by his dead sister, Ombra. Pleasure burned within him at the memory of her death.

At the chest near the bed, he deactivated more needle traps, opened the lid, and rolled back a blanket of white silk. He sifted through leather garrotes, bone and steel knives, stilettos, barbed hooks tipped with poison, spiked pebbles, and various articles of clothing for a pair of thin black silk gloves, which he stashed in his pocket. He selected two of the bone knives and slid them into thin leather sheaths sewn into the quilted vest, each a perfect fit. Other sheaths were already tenanted.

Dekhalis closed the chest and went to the desk, unlocking it with a key from among those around his neck. Under the lid was a maze of cubbyholes, drawers and shelves. He pressed a spot at the back of one drawer to access a metal box in a hidden niche, alarmed to find the box unlocked. *Noth, you little toad.* Letters from various thieves and assassins, correspondence that went back to his childhood had disappeared. His anger boiled into a seething core of hatred. *Just one more score to settle.*

Anxious now that Noth had tampered with more than just the metal box, Dekhalis sought the smaller box of wormwood he had glued to the back of the niche with sap. The clink of glass reassured him. *My poisons are safe.* In one of the tiny bottles the milky liquid resembled a common medicine for indigestion. He had tested it on one of the servants, delighted with the swift and agonizing death it produced. The bottle he deposited under a flap tied over another sheath sewn into his vest.

He restored both the metal and wormwood boxes to the niche, then turned to the true purpose of his visit.

Inside the fireplace was a chimney that reached up many leagues. Too narrow for use as a tunnel, it was a perfect place to hide his most precious treasures, the artifacts he had stolen from the royal treasury. At an early age, he had decided his destiny. That day in the spider pit, when he knew by the expression on his bodyguard's face that she had accepted her doom, he had realized his power, thrilled to it in fact, and vowed there and then not to live in the shadows like the men before him.

So cleverly that no one ever suspected, he had stolen one thing at a time, arranging a wealth of evidence to ensure that someone else was blamed. He waited no less than ten years between thefts, his most difficult task fooling his mother and her priestesses, whose intuition was deadly. He considered every wile and blandishment used to confuse them as his training.

Years of vigilance had paid off. His charm was honed even finer than Tiala's, and he had a wellspring of guile to match.

He climbed into the chimney as far as he could, then reached into a hidden recess to grab a soot-covered bundle. He descended like a spider, one step at a time, then brushed himself and the hearth clean with a feather broom hanging from the fireplace mantle.

Seated on the floor, he unveiled the lacquered chest, unlocking it with another key from the cord about his neck. With trembling fingers, he removed the red velvet covering of three objects nestled on cushions of black silk. He ignored the large crown made of golden crystal and a plain silver mirror to examine the crooked wand.

The runic gashes in the dark wood had been stained with witchvine juice, the purple liquid identified by its bitter, aromatic smell. Dekhalis did not know how to activate the Wand of Disguise, an artifact so holy that when its theft was discovered, his mother the Nightwing had assembled the heads of every Sisterhood to pray to the goddesses for an entire moon.

During this time, he had eaten a poisoned mushroom, just enough to put him into a coma but not kill him. By the time the poison had worked its way out of his system, his scapegoat had confessed to the crime, been tried and sentenced to the Purple Moors of Forgetfulness.

When I am King, I will learn how to use this Wand to spy on those witches and their allies.

He laid down the Wand for the heavy crown, a relic of ancient days, carved from a single piece of citrine. Although no longer used for the investiture of Alvarran rulers, it matched the antique initiation chair in the Great Hall. He put the artifact on his head, pleased with the fit. When they saw him wearing this, who among the people would dare fail to recognize Dekhalis as the ruler of Alvarra?

The plain, oval mirror with its silver handle was about two handspans long, its mate—a large, gray crystal orb—missing by design. He tilted his handsome face this way and that, admiring his likeness, the crown a halo of golden light across his brow.

Abruptly his image rippled and dissolved, as if a stone had been tossed into his reflection. The silvery veneer became a palette of many colors lit from within, then another face materialized.

Dekhalis smiled. "Brother Zhido," he said to the hideous dark elf staring back at him from the mirror. Zhido might have been handsome otherwise, but his ears curved around the front of his face like horns, giving him an evil expression. It was no joy to be an ugly member of a long-lived race so dependent on beauty. Dekhalis found the existence of such creatures convenient. No one made a more loyal follower.

"I have watched and waited, Master—where have you been?" whined the afflicted Zhido. His deep green eyes glittered from below his grotesque brow of ears.

"Do you have the locket?" Dekhalis demanded, ignoring his minion's distress.

"Yes, your Highness," said Zhido, displaying the thong about his neck from which dangled a glass locket bearing something dark and shiny inside. According to his master, it was a lock of Tiala's hair. Zhido clutched it jealously, a visible symbol of his closeness to Dekhalis.

"And have you learned how to use it? Has it led you to her?"

"No, my Lord," answered Zhido, blinking his eyes under the repulsive overhang of his hairy ears. "But I followed your plan and found someone to assist us, named Morbigon."

"Tell me about him," snapped Dekhalis.

"He is an albino who came up from the Merimn'a, where he learned magic from the outlaw wizards. He is rumored to be mad. If so, this madness is useful. He sends his mind into the future and brings back the knowledge to make wonderful artifacts. We found him selling them in the center of the city of Aeryinne."

"From the Merimn'a? There are powerful sorcerers there. He could be our key to them." Dekhalis thought of his father Rozadon, the Nightwing's last consort and, it was rumored, one of her favorites. His heart ached with the longing for a father he had never known. Surely Rozadon would want his son to avenge his father's exile to the Merimn'a.

Zhido frowned and his ears touched, forming a straight line above his eyes. "I doubt he is from the Merimn'a, Master. They kicked him out. He says the Brotherhood there is pledged to its own cause. We can't trust them."

Dekhalis sneered at what he regarded as cowardice. "I would use goblins if it furthered our liberation." Yet, maybe his lieutenant had a point. "Have you tested this Morbigon?"

"Yes, Master. He is yet another man whose talent has been scorned by the witches."

"And the wenches, too, I should imagine."

"I wouldn't know," said Zhido with bitter dignity.

"Well, what good is his talent to us?"

"I have set him the task of finding Tiala the Usurper's location. He scries the future and says she will recruit allies. The albino promised to send phantom creatures from the forbidden realms to combat them. He is powerful, my Lord."

"And you rely on this crackpot to do your work?" asked Dekhalis, resolved to meet this Morbigon, and pull his fangs a little.

"No, your Highness. I have spies in every part of the Territories. We'll find her, and when we do, we'll destroy her."

"Do not fail me," said Dekhalis, his eyes glittering like emeralds. "I want her killed, and her body brought to me before the next moonteller turns silver." These abundant mushrooms were already tinged pale pink. A day or two more, and the moon above would be full.

Dekhalis wasn't worried, not yet. Three moons was ample time. With luck, he would keep Alvarra in mourning for a year or more. But there was no sense in letting his followers become lax.

The dark elf in the mirror was too frightened to answer, but Dekhalis knew that for all his apparent cowardice, Zhido was an accomplished rogue. He had hand-picked and trained him in the use of the gray crystal orb. The poor wretch couldn't know that whoever held the mirror enslaved the user of the orb.

"Zhido," said the would-be king, "if you fail me, count on my extreme displeasure."

The henchman lifted his eyebrows, and the strange ears rolled up, displaying tufts of hair. It always frightened him when Dekhalis spoke in that soft way. "My Lord, she will not escape us."

"I'll believe that when I see her body lowered into the Lake of All Souls," said Dekhalis. "Begone. The next time we speak, you'd better have good news."

The grotesque image shimmered and disappeared, Dekhalis startled briefly by the sight of his own face with its graceful ears, high noble forehead and winged brows.

He replaced the artifacts and restored the wrapped lacquer chest to the cache in the chimney. They were safer here than in the Thieves' Quarter. In a few moments he was gone, leaving no trace of his visit.

When he reached the garden, the owl was no longer in the cedar-birch tree.

-14-

EARLIER THAT afternoon, Prince Mischa was in his private suite, studying the rules of a new game. Laid out on his desk were several small, mismatched pieces of red glass and two thin wires, the object to restring the pieces of glass in gradations of size before the opposing side could do so. The resulting item made an interesting garrote.

He was so occupied that he didn't notice a slight breeze behind him, the door to his study opened by a wrinkled, ancient gnome, three feet high, wearing a leather apron that covered his knees. A jeweled dagger protruded from one boot. He was intensely proud of his beard, black as ink, that nearly reached his toes. His name was Rearguard, an old and honorable name. The vast numbers of his tribe had roamed the desert long before the Manor had been built, as many an upstart lord had discovered. He wore the Apron of the Patriarch and the Knife of the Elder with the ease of one who is no longer even challenged.

He advanced with measured tread on the thick, multi-colored carpet, admiring its unusual pattern and beauty. He remembered when Mischa had added this to the other treasures in his private rooms. When the Prince still did not look up, the old gnome put his hands in his pockets and cleared his throat.

"Oh," said Mischa, startled from his reverie, "it's you, Grandfather." He dropped the pieces of red glass to the blotter on his desk and turned around in his chair. "It's been a long time since you paid me a visit."

"I wouldn't have come if it weren't of the utmost necessity...*Highness,*" said Rearguard, on a sarcastic note. He glanced around for a place to sit. Although in many ways still untouched by his venerable age, he did have a spot of rheumatism. He saw a small leather hassock in the corner, but made no move to fetch it. He believed strongly that the duty of the young was to cater to the aged.

When the Prince showed no concern for the elder's physical well-being, Rearguard strode to the stool and, with a display of nonchalance that fooled neither of them, brought it over to the desk. He sank down gratefully and took a few deep breaths, wiping his brow with a frayed yellow handkerchief.

The Prince was always nervous around his grandfather, although he could not admit it to himself. Being the grandson of the Patriarch was awkward, at best. He turned his chair to face the old gnome and folded his arms in his lap in the manner of a polite child.

Rearguard was somewhat mollified with this display. "Now, Mischa," he said, "I want to make you aware of some goings-on in the East Wing."

"Oh?" said the Prince. "I thought that was your province." It still rankled him that his grandfather kept certain parts of the Manor off limits even to him. *Why give me the title of Prince, if he withholds the power that goes with it? When will I get my proper legacy?* He eyed the knife and the apron with envy.

"It remains my province," said the gnome, "but there's been a rash of theft. A looking-glass here, a cufflink there. And then it was a silver goblet, a string of blue pearls, and just last night, a sack of gold from right under the bursar's desk." He pounded his small fist on his knee. "This has got to stop."

"The bursar, eh? Well, what about your own people, Grandfather?" His grandfather's face grew redder and Mischa spread his hands. "You know what I mean. They may be the soul of loyalty, but still, occasional mistakes are made."

"I didn't come here to be insulted," said Rearguard, leaping to his feet. "None of the tribes would do such a thing—we don't steal from each other, as you ought to know. Look at the riffraff you invite here, and you have the gall to accuse the Brotherhood of Gnomads?" His beard was quivering.

"Please. Sit down," said the Prince, trying for a soothing tone of voice, "I'm sure there's some other explanation." He thought a moment. "Nothing missing from the store rooms?"

"Of course not. Don't you think I checked? And what about you? Have you lost any of your playthings? It might be a good thing if you did. You know how I feel about your dabbling in magic."

"I can handle it." The Prince quickly steered the conversation away from this sore topic. "Couldn't the robberies be the result of some personal squabble among the servants?"

"I considered that possibility," admitted the gnome, folding his arms, "until last night. If it hadn't been for the bursar's room, I wouldn't even have bothered you."

"Well, Grandfather, it's simple. We'll activate the traps."

"Too dangerous," cried the gnome. "We have children running about. Just because you have no offspring, you forget—." He trailed off in a bitter tirade that continued under his breath.

Prince Mischa raised his eyebrows and shrugged a shoulder. "What else can I do? We can't let this get out to the guests. There might be panic. *You* forget, Grandfather; they're our livelihood."

The gnome stroked his beard thoughtfully. "What about lending me a spy?" he asked.

"No," said the Prince, waving his hands nervously. "I never trust anyone I can buy. Besides, intrigue makes people uncomfortable. I wouldn't like to destroy the lovely atmosphere of camaraderie for our guests, eh?"

"You and your ideas," scoffed the old gnome, "It's madness to rely on traps instead of people. I should never have let you become educated outside the tribes. If your mother hadn't been so headstrong, you wouldn't even have been born."

"Well, you'd better be glad I was," retorted the Prince, a bit hurt now. "Haven't I built you a luxurious home and filled our coffers year after year with fine treasures? Why, I've made you rich, Grandfather."

The gnome squinted his bright, blue eyes and looked up under shaggy eyebrows, smiling at last. "You're right about that, Mischief. You've done well with your inheritance—so far. But you'll learn that there's more to power than money."

"Please don't call me by that childish name," said the Prince, drawing himself up. "I've got a reputation to uphold."

"It does you good to be reminded of your roots," scolded the old man. He got up to leave. "You'd do well to remember the day I invested you and the promises you made to me. *And* to the tribes. You've taken many a wife, but have nothing to show for it. 'No chick, no wick,' as they say. Time is running out, Grandson."

The Prince controlled his temper. The last thing he wanted was another of Rearguard's scalding diatribes. "You will see to the traps, Grandfather?"

"Well, I admit, I did take the precaution of activating the false floor in the servants' quarters. But that's all I'm going to do for now. The others are unsafe. Pure nonsense."

"Fine, do what you wish," said the Prince, impatient now that the matter was settled. "Let me know how it turns out…No need for you to come personally, just send me a message."

The gnome gazed at him in mild disgust and shook his head. "A pox on all humans and their offspring," he grumbled, and carrying his beard, walked out of the room with all the bearing of a king.

The Prince looked after him resentfully. The old man always disconcerted him, though it was refreshing to deal with someone who wasn't afraid of him. *He certainly is a covetous old goat. He has more money than he'll ever need—and never spends a talent.* He considered the purpose of the gnome's visit. A thief among the guests was nothing new. The old man was right; the trap door rarely failed. If the thieves could resist the slave girls, they deserved their freedom.

Maybe I do have some scruples. The Prince chuckled at his own cleverness and turned back to the new game.

-15-

POLAH WAS *running in the forest. Wild trees groaned in the wind. Branches caught in her hair. As she pushed them away, they whipped back, tearing and scratching her face. The wind howled, and she heard far off voices calling her… "Where are you going?…Who are you looking for? Follow us …" She stumbled on through the thickening woods, toward the sweet voices.*

While Polah dreamt, Embaza wakened to pitch blackness. Gradually, his eyes adjusted, aided by the faint moonlight illuminating the room. Polah slept on the cot beside his chair. She had regained her female form, and despite admiring her nakedness, he was disappointed that he had not been awake to witness her transformation. Then, he remembered her mangled leg, and gasped. The limb was straight and whole once more.

Gently, he probed for the wound, but found no trace, not even a scar.

His hand brushed something beneath her calf—his silver ring. Puzzled, he returned the ring to the velvet pouch in his shirt. He didn't remember falling asleep, but he was sure he hadn't finished the spell of mending. Could it have worked? He had only used it once before—on a broken table leg. Musing, he covered Polah with the linen sheet.

When she reached the clearing, she saw a cliff. The wind was all around her now, pushing her down. The voices called out again, "Come to us, follow us." She braced herself and, step by step, neared the edge of the precipice. Below her a river raged. She put her arms up in front of her as a shield, but the wind swooped her up like a giant hand and tossed her into the roiling water. "Welcome," it whispered.

As Embaza gazed at Polah's face, he noticed that her skin had the faint sheen of sweat, and that she was breathing raggedly. Every few moments, she moaned. *What is it, little fox?* He sent his energy out to her, seeking her inner pulse. Instead of the usual rhythm, he discerned a churning, erratic thread that worried him. He closed his eyes, and allowed himself to enter her mind.

Suddenly, he was dragged into a torrential river, his body folded, crushed, dashed and battered along a rocky river bed. *What is this, Polah? What's wrong?* The answer was distorted, like talking underwater. She seemed insistent, her voice reaching out to him in this dream—or nightmare. The river carried him away, onward, over a huge waterfall. Down, down, down…

Embaza had experienced many a vision gone awry. As in most apprenticeships, he had fought a host of the invisible forces that plagued sentient creatures. He had wrestled imaginary demons, devils and all kinds of monsters, so he knew that when it came down to it, most of them could be seen as reflections of himself.

In the process of learning this, his masters had occasionally entered his visions, monitoring him, ready to banish his conjurings if they seemed to be doing him serious harm. None of his teachers had ever been affected by his creations. But this communion with Polah—perhaps it was beyond even Sargothian experience.

He plunged into the churning river. Polah swam toward him like an otter, grabbed his hands, and together they rose by sheer willpower. The moment their sleek heads breached the surface, they heard a loud pop.

Embaza trembled with shock and anger. *I've been overpowered by hallucination.* His hands curled into fists. *Am I not Embaza?* To earn a name of power, he had braved many terrors in his years of ascension. His teachers had assured him that he was worthy. *But were they right?* The question profoundly disturbed him.

When Embaza opened his eyes he saw that Polah had also awoken. Lying ghostlike on the cot, she seemed to be looking straight through him, and he shuddered.

As her mind settled back into the room, Polah tucked the sheet around her and sat up. She accepted her return to human form and her healed leg as natural.

Embaza said, "You and I will have to learn the truth of this."

"Mm," said Polah. She knew that she had been caught up in some sort of power that was well beyond her experience. But she still didn't understand her connection to Embaza, or why the wizard was as helpless as she in the face of this outside force. She shook her head. *If you hadn't interfered in the first place...* But she said nothing more, and with her strange, animal grace, she wrapped herself tighter in the sheet and got up from the cot.

Embaza half expected her to fall. *Such a wound...* But she walked over to the window and looked out at the moonlit desert. "How peaceful," she said.

Embaza looked at her and thought, *You're still a mystery, Polah, but not as completely as before.*

She turned from the window, and lifting her chin, said, "Lead me upstairs to my room."

Embaza smiled and bowed slightly upon leaving his chair. He walked to the door, glancing at the deserted hallway before beckoning her to follow. They ascended to her room, and although he was reluctant to leave Polah by herself, she firmly insisted and left him standing outside her door.

From the quiet around him, he deduced that it was around midnight, but he felt too keyed up to sleep. After a few moments, he decided to go down and discover what had happened to Anebra, the acrobat who had fought so valiantly with him in the arena.

When he reached the bottom of the stairs, a faint glow led him down a branching hallway and around a corner. The source of the light emanated from a doorway up ahead.

Hearing the soft murmurs of a person chanting, he instinctively slowed his pace, not wanting to interrupt in accordance with an unwritten rule at the Universities of Magic. His curiosity prevailed, however, and inside the room, he glimpsed three women in hooded robes of various shades of blue standing around a bed where someone lay under heavy quilts.

Healers usually dressed in brown, not blue. Who were these women?

One of them held a bowl of steam which she steadily rotated over the bed. A fine mist descended, obscuring the figure beneath the coverlet. The second woman chanted at the head of the bed, her hands out and eyes closed. The third, a tall figure at the foot of the bed with her back to him, suddenly pivoted, her appearance startling.

A stately-looking dark elf with deep, green eyes, her skin was almost purple in its blackness. A frown creased her forehead and, with crooked fingers, she beckoned him to join the other two dark elves at bedside.

Embaza approached hesitantly, his eyes drawn to the wizened face of the crone who had issued the invitation. Her voice emerged as a whispered croak.

"Do you know this woman?" she asked, pointing to the wan face on the pillow.

"Anebra," he said. "She fought beside me in the arena today."

"Impossible," replied the crone. "She's been like this for two days and nights."

Embaza's mind reeled. His dream activities with Polah had taken *two days?*

The old woman took his hand and placed it atop Anebra's. *So cold.* "Is she dead?" he asked, feeling foolish even as the words left his mouth.

The woman with the bowl answered, "Not quite, but the poison is strong. Do you wish to help?"

The pungent leaves in steaming water gave off a medicinal smell that permeated his senses. "How?" he asked.

"Help us guide her into the world she would choose," said the crone.

An icy shiver prickled Embaza's spine. This was not a task he relished. He had as little to do with the afterlife as possible. His masters had taught him not to grant the darkness any more attention than was necessary. Life was perilous enough.

The woman at the head of the bed stopped chanting, and the room became deathly quiet, Anebra's skin as ashen and lifeless as one of Embaza's waxen figures.

A cold premonition stole over him, but the impulse to loose Anebra's hand was curtailed by the crone's fingernails digging into his arm.

"Relax," she hissed. "You must accompany her to the crossing."

A strange calm followed, and a familiar comfort. He began his litany: *Pain is good...*

The old woman shattered his reverie: "Silence," she said. "Let there be respect for the spirits of the dead and of the living."

Not a sound breached his ears, not even the insect buzzing in the limp netting over the open window. The light from the candle flickered with a weak radiance, and Embaza willed his mind to be still.

His eyelids were heavy, but he forced them to stay open in a bid to gain mental control. He chose a focal point and stared at Anebra's pale face, as if she might awaken at any moment.

A black vortex surrounded him, emanating from the three dark elves. His breathing labored over air grown thick as honey. Presently, the waking vision sucked him into a deep cavern. On one level, he knew he was still standing in the room at Anebra's bedside, just as previously he had been sitting at Polah's.

However, his earlier experience with Polah had shaken his confidence. A lick of fear curled within him, a fear he would not allow to materialize in words, although its meaning was inescapable. The crone at his right hand sensed his incipient panic and lifted his chin with her wrinkled fingers, her voice clear within the vision.

"You have complete control of all your faculties. You may walk and talk quite naturally, but you may do no magic here. This place belongs to Loote."

Embaza abruptly recalled his studies at the University. The great bird Loote was the principal deity of a secret sect of dark-elven women. He had occasionally seen representations of her dressed in deep purple feathers with a golden beak and ruby eyes. He understood now that this secret sect were healers, and filed the information away for the future.

The vision did not last long. In the cavern of his mind, water dripped from the eaves and fell onto the cliff's edge, echoing loudly. Beyond the overhang, the depths were shrouded in darkness.

Embaza saw Anebra's linen clad body laid out on the edge of the cliff. He sensed the crone move next to him.

Around him, many eyes, feral and bright, glowed in the palpebral darkness. Out of the shadows emerged two other healers in blue robes who went to either side of Anebra and raised her to a sitting position. Then, she opened her pale, blue eyes.

Embaza almost spoke, but the crone squeezed his arm tightly, and gave him a warning glance.

With the help of the two women, Anebra rose and crossed her arms in front of her, standing like a statue. One by one, the glowing eyes converged out of the darkness and the cave filled with birds of every size and color. Wings beating the air, they circled Anebra's motionless body, then settled on her shoulders and around her feet.

A loud cawing reverberated throughout the cave from deep within its heart, and there appeared a human-sized bird in royal purple feathers. Loote's ruby eyes burned bright with the twin fires of love and compassion. The women knelt on the rough stone of the cavern floor, leaving Embaza and Anebra standing.

Loote's advance on Anebra steeped Embaza in an awe he thought relegated to his childhood. Then the Goddess spoke. her voice layered with infinite kindness, yet tinged with a note of warning.

"Choose, daughter."

Anebra's face radiated an inner light, and for a moment, Embaza saw her spirit rise like a warrior facing an unseen challenge. His heart somersaulted when she looked directly at him.

"You fought well by my side," she said. "But, there is a time for battle and a time for dying." Before he could think to stop her, she stepped off the precipice and disappeared into the dark depths of Loote's cave.

Rooted to the spot, the sound of the dripping water nearly startled Embaza out of his skin. Then Loote cawed again. Her magnificent neck reared back and purple under-feathers glistened with their own unworldly light. With a voluminous flap of wings, she rose into the ceiling of the cave, and her flock followed. The cacophony of their flight filled the cavern, rippling through Embaza and the healers.

Silence returned, and the crone's sharp nails bit his arm. He gasped, and the vision dissolved.

He opened his eyes to the woman who had formerly rotated the bowl, now standing near the window and blowing out the candle. The room was dry and close after the cool dampness of the cave. Anebra's body lay exactly as before, the other woman wrapping it tightly in the linen sheet.

The aged priestess turned a smile upon Embaza. Her face was transformed, and for a moment she seemed almost young. "We thank you for your presence," she said. "You honored her."

Pride warmed him, and he was oddly comforted by both the experience and the behavior of these women. Although he had lost a fellow warrior, it seemed somehow more than fitting that she had been granted this special rite.

"Might I know your name?" he asked the crone.

"I am Zelwyn, and these are the Sisters of Loote."

He flinched at the old woman's touch upon his sleeve. "Before you go, a word of advice." He met her eyes and she said, "Don't be ashamed of your origins. You may regret it."

She offered Embaza a small silver jar from beneath the folds of her robe. He twisted the cap and recognized the spicy smell. Sunbane was a secret known to only a few dark elves. The rare herbal preparation could not protect him fully from the open desert, but it would help.

Embarrassed, he bowed to the crone and, with one last glance at the faded beauty of the acrobat, sought the privacy of his own room.

-16-

DEKHALIS DISLIKED the bow and arrow. First of all, it lacked the compactness of an in-fighting weapon. And, more importantly, he missed the feel and smell of death that only intimacy with a victim produced. As a result, all the shadowmen carried knives, daggers, garrotes, stilettos, and barbed needles. If they wanted a bow and arrow too, that was their own business.

Today they traveled light, weapons strapped out of sight in favor of the ropes and grappling hooks of the climber. They ascended an almost perpendicular slab of crystal, guided by Dekhalis himself. Unerringly, his hands and feet found the crevices that led most easily to the top. It was one of his rules: he would not ask them to do what he could not.

Yet, many of the assassins in his inner circle were already experienced. A few called themselves Death Masters, a title no longer used. Their great-great-grandfathers had performed executions for the Siadhin Lords, those ancient ones who had served the High Kings. Dekhalis knew only what the legends told of these lords, that they ruled the Great Houses instead of the women who presided there now, and that they maintained a vast army to support the High King and his court. Dekhalis swore that his reign would rival them in power and grandeur.

"Will women really be our servants?" a recruit had asked at one of his meetings. A heated debate had ensued, with a contingent of older men arguing against the excesses of long ago.

"We should serve each other."

"The Nightwings have brought peace, if nothing else."

"Our ancestors were tyrants."

Dekhalis and his followers had no patience with soul-searchers who wrung their hands over the cruelties of their progenitors. His charismatic voice had sliced into the furor, commanding silence. "Maybe they went too far," he cried, "but surely we can forgive our ancestors for their zeal. After all, glory has its price. What price would you pay? And you?" The young recruit had blushed.

At a signal, one of the shadowmen had shouted down the soft-spoken elders. "Look at the way you're forced to live. How long will you endure it? Another hundred years?"

The assassins, who now climbed with such sure-footed diligence, aspired to more than military prowess. They craved power, a wine that more deeply addicted with each tantalizing sip. Death was its vintage; danger, its cup.

Dekhalis called to the shadowman below, "You—Chaemmor—fasten your rope. Pos, get in line." They watched their leader inch his way up the narrow crack in the crystal. The slippery slab gave off a spectral light in the gloom. One elf looked down to the cavern floor shrouded in mist, hundreds of feet below. It had taken hours to get this far.

Chaemmor observed, "He climbs like a centipede."

"So will you," said Pos with a grin. "There's no other way."

It was true. All sixteen eventually wriggled along the crack, one hand and foot at a time. At the top, Dekhalis waited, his face unreadable in the dim light. There was barely room for all to stand on the compact mound of rock without nearly touching noses.

When everyone had gained the atoll, Dekhalis announced, "We are the first men to scale the most treacherous pinnacle in all of Alvarra. Few women have even done it." Impassive faces, stoic in satisfaction, pleased him. He wanted them to know what they were up against.

He pointed to a gleaming stalactite, a few feet over his head. A droplet of water coalesced on its tip, then slid free.

"Next, we'll climb that."

One of the shadowmen grumbled, "You're mad."

Whip-fast, Dekhalis's gloved hand snaked out and grazed the shadowman's midsection with a miniature dart. The elf looked down at the drop of blood from a tiny scratch that had pierced his bright green body suit. His nervous laugh ended abruptly as a caustic aroma reached his nostrils. For a moment, he wobbled on the precipice of the needle-shaped cliff. Then, his stiffened body hurtled down the canyon, his ghastly scream echoing off the crystalline walls.

"Such a pity," commented the would-be king, with a measuring look at his other henchmen. A nerve jumped along his jaw line. "Give me your grappling hook." Dekhalis took the implement from the nearest man and, with an expert swing and a clink, snagged the high stalactite. Checking the rope with a tug, he said, "Ready?"

When no one dared an answer, he swung up, scampering hand over hand along the line into the darkness above.

"Come, shadowmen," he called, contempt dripping from his voice. One by one, they followed, several thinking, *mad he might be, but he makes things happen.*

-17-

POLAH SANK gratefully onto her bed, exhausted and elated from her first real test. *I'm truly strong and powerful.* In the darkness, her black eyes glistened with pride. For the first time, her animal abilities seemed unique rather than grotesque.

When the stirrings of her fox self began to manifest the year before, she had been afraid to show herself to a living soul. She knew better than to expect help or sympathy from friend or family. Her mother had taught her that. She had deliberately chosen to stay in a rural inn, far from her home village. Safe behind the barred door of her room, she had endured the first agonizing sensations of transformation—the aching joints and dizzy spells. Even before her coming of age, there had been other signs—the reddish glint to her hair, the needle-like incisors. Her aunt and schoolmates had suspected nothing. But Polah had been warned by her mother.

Day after day, she had waited for full transformation to occur, but when it did not, she traveled on from inn to inn, town to town. Finally, upon hearing about the arena, she made the decision to let that be the test—the catalyst.

The full metamorphosis had been gratifying. She only wished there had been someone to share it with. Unfortunately, she had stopped seeking friendship at an early age.

They killed my mother. The familiar rage welled up in her as she remembered the townspeople, brandishing weapons, cursing, shouting, drawing blood. Tears filled her eyes, but she shut off the feelings. She thought instead of the fact she had discovered. *I can heal myself.* This was the part she had only suspected. *Mama had hinted something of this before she died.*

Polah went to the wardrobe, pulled on a woolen sleeping shift and padded over to the bed.

Her mind drifted to the wizard. *Embaza.* A strange man—an enemy, she had thought at first, but now some kind of bond had developed, one she didn't understand. She was sensitive to kinship, she who had no family left. *He tried to heal my wound.* She smiled. *He probably thinks he did it himself.*

And he was in my mind—or was I in his? She shrugged, for the moment accepting the riddle as she had accepted others. *It's rather nice not to be so alone. Maybe with him, I'll find out who I am. At least I'll have new questions.* She stared at the carpet for a moment. *I can't trust him, though. That's the rule.*

If only she could gain control of her shape-changing. Nothing forewarned her that it was coming—save for the unnatural calmness of mind a few seconds before the actual change. This time it had been a lake.

Fear stabbed her when a memory from the vision returned with a vengeance. *Who were they?* The voices of the vision had been terrifying. *There's always so much to learn.* She suddenly realized how exhausted she was from the ordeal, crawled into bed and wrapped herself in the thick coverlet. Soon, she fell into a deep, dreamless sleep.

The room was still for a long time, the only sound her breathing. Dust settled, and spiders spun their silent webs.

After a while, the girl sat up in bed. Slowly, she slid her feet to the floor and stood shakily. Her hands probed the darkness ahead of her, but her eyes remained closed.

She shuffled to the back of the room and entered the closet. There, she fiddled with the wall mechanism until a door swung open. Her small form moved purposefully down the dark, narrow corridor to her left. Around a corner, she faced a stairway. Frightened mice squeaked and scurried out of the way with each bare-footed step upon worn stone.

A dark shape trailed the sleepwalker up the stairs.

In his austere chamber, Embaza was soaring through the clouds on a flying lion until a lighting bolt impaled him and his mount. He woke suddenly, covered in sweat, nauseated by the fall.

Worry scratched at his mind with persistence, as if a presence watched, but what or whom lay just beyond his mental grasp. Frowning, he slipped out of bed, lit a candle and quickly threw on leggings, robe and boots. Then from his pocket, he withdrew a tiny brass key and unlocked the tall chest. Inside were scrolls bound with silken cords of many colors.

Offense spells were red, utilizing the elements. Healing and illusionary magic were blue. Green for mind enhancement. He fished through sundry others in purple, black and yellow for the one he needed.

He glanced hurriedly at the sole parchment bound in a silver thread, mumbling to himself. Nodding once, he retied the scroll and returned it to the chest, which he then locked and further protected with his personal seal.

Embaza blew out the candle, formed the soft wax into a ball and dropped it into his pocket. Through the secret panel in his closet, he tiptoed down the lightless corridor toward Polah's room.

Foreboding told him before he entered that she was not there. After checking the other door to be sure, he returned to the secret corridor with a growing sense of dread. Movement to his left directed him to a stairway, his soft boots making no noise on the smooth stone, his body pressed against the wall as he climbed.

A shape in the shadows ahead alerted him. *A source of evil.* He unconsciously drew out the ball of wax, kneading it, his ascent gradually shortening the distance to his quarry. His throat tightened at each step closer to the menace.

He began working a needle from his sleeve slowly into the wax. The shape ahead seemed to falter, but the curve of the stairway moved the figure out of sight. Embaza stepped up his pace, pushing the needle deeper into the wax, and caught the shadow directly behind Polah. She was moving too slowly. *What's wrong with you, little fox?*

At the top of the stairs, the shadow pursuer staggered, reared up, and stabbed her in the back. Embaza ascended the last few stairs and grabbed the shape from behind. With a scream, the attacker twisted out of his hands and spiraled to the stone floor to dissolve into a vapor. Not even a rag remained. Embaza scooped his needle and wax from the step, and sped to the landing where Polah had fallen, a stone shard protruding from her back.

He dropped to one knee, gritted his teeth and removed the rough weapon, not surprised when the shard shimmered to nothing. The wound didn't look fatal, and safety became paramount. The landing was wide, exposing them to three corridors branching out in an inverted T.

Embaza lifted Polah's limp body, but her muscles contracted, and she whipped her head around to him, baring pointed teeth, raw terror in her eyes. Embaza let her fall to her feet and stood back.

Polah gave an animal-like growl, keeping her distance, and Embaza's knees wobbled in the face of this new threat. He suddenly realized how little he had slept and how desperately he needed rest to perform even the most minor of spells. If one became necessary, would he have the strength?

From the left branch of the corridor, a stout-looking dwarf brandished a two-handed sword, her chain mail shirt gleaming in what little light there was. "Who's there?" she demanded.

Polah leapt toward the voice, and Embaza collapsed against the wall in exhaustion, watching with fascination the tranformation of fox-woman into the ferocious animal that had, in the arena earlier, saved his life.

-18-

SIX STIX and Obsidian had barely begun their ascent of the stone steps leading from the harem rooms when they were stopped by the faint sound of chanting. Glancing behind, Obsidian saw only darkness. His bare feet were chilled by the cold stone stairs, worn down in the middle. *Who uses this route? Where are we?* The chanting droned on.

Defenseless without his weapons, Six Stix had done his share of street brawling. "Interested in another battle?" he whispered.

"I don't fight without a good reason," Obsidian replied in the same soft tone.

The blue elf chuckled. "Reason? You can protect me." Six Stix led the way, humming softly to himself. In their makeshift clothes, and without boots or armor, they made little noise. Soon a faint glimmer of light from above became the steady glow of torches.

At the top of the stairs, an arched doorway revealed a well-lit sandstone corridor that branched left and right. The clear reverberations gave the place an eerie feel. To Six's ears, it sounded almost like a baritone singing. Spells were common in the woods of his homeland, Graymere. He could identify some of the simpler ones, but this had the sonorous urgency of a major incantation. He whispered to Obsidian, "Cover your ears and stay back."

Obsidian obeyed. "Humility is learned," an elder had once told him, an elder who had lost an eye in a confrontation with a sorceress.

Six Stix tuned out the words of the spell by humming, a childhood trick he had perfected. Like most elves, his pointed ears were not easy to cover, but by singing softly, the noise of the spell was reduced to a mild buzzing, and he mentally recited the first five verses of the classic ode *Lay of the Lady* while he waited for the enchanter to finish.

When the buzzing ceased, Six Stix stopped humming. A deep growl that might have been a wild beast was followed by soothing words from the sorcerer. Six Stix motioned for Obsidian to unplug his ears and follow. Together, they edged along the wall to the left, toward the spell caster.

As they reached a turn in the corridor, the almond-scented air reminded Obsidian of silverfoil, the aromatic flowers that grew on the shady side of mountains. He strove to master his senses, unnerved as yet by the monotonous chanting even though it had stopped.

At the corner, Six Stix peeked around to see a tall, blue elven wizard dressed in a midnight blue robe flanked by a very large red fox. Six Stix and Obsidian recognized the pair who had been the talk of the Manor since their battle with the sand monster.

Slumped against the far wall of the corridor was a female dwarf clad in a fine mail shirt and purple leggings, her sword dangling from one hand. She was snoring loudly, chin on her breast.

So, it was a sleep spell, thought Six Stix. He knew better than to tangle with a wizard. He motioned to Obsidian, and they retreated until they were out of earshot.

"They didn't see me—too preoccupied with each other," whispered Six Stix.

"They're the heroes Embaza and Polah," said Obsidian.

"Sssh," cautioned the elf. "She's in her fox disguise, or whatever it is. She looks dangerous enough, so let's go the other way." *Wish I could get that dwarven sword, though.* He cursed under his breath.

Six and Obsidian retraced their steps and followed the branch to the right, the corridor seemingly endless, unbroken by doors, until they passed under another archway and the stone changed color.

Obsidian's stomach tightened and he took a deep breath upon recognizing the hard, white stone of the uplands called spar. This was the richest kind and difficult to mine. *I am a monk now, not a slave to the foreman.* Once in the relative comfort of the monastery, he had never looked back to his days in the Tuval mines. Memories of the lash and the giant foreman had been displaced by the chanting and a new stillness of mind. He ran his hands over the rock wall in a grudging kinship with the masons who had built this place.

Six Stix noticed the gesture. In their talks, the young man's reluctance to divulge his past had frustrated him at every turn. Six Stix discerned a spark of emotion in Obsidian's face, and quipped, "Spend your thoughts; buy peace of mind."

Startled out of his reverie, Obsidian stared into the now-familiar face of the warrior, creased with its indigo battle scars and mellowed by hardships.

"If you could see the beauty of the Tuval Mountains, you would understand.

It is the only thing that tempers life in the mines. From the time I was able to walk, I went with my father into the caves. I brought him his midday meal, and I still remember his smile when he found my mother had made him *palagri*, which he loved."

"What is that?" Six scanned beyond a corner for guards, and finding none, motioned Obsidian to follow.

"Leaf-wrapped barley meal, spiced with clove-berries." The monk's eyes glazed as he walked. "When my mother got the fever, there was no more *palagri*, only fried barley cake and tea. It was her loss that killed my father. They said it was a cave-in, but I knew he could have gotten out if he'd wished."

"So you weren't able to say goodbye? That's a pity."

"I nearly lamed myself in the struggle to get him out, tearing my foot in the rubble just as the last strut gave way. Orphaned and poor, I had no calling and no wish to follow my father, but the foreman gave me no choice. He could have freed me, but instead, citing an old law, he made me his slave. I worked in the mines for three years before escaping to the valley below."

"How did you become a monk, then?"

"The monks who found me, raised me. They said I showed potential, although I could not imagine why."

Six Stix smiled at that. The lad's willingness to learn, keen intelligence, and obedience attested to the monks' wisdom.

"It is said in the monastery that we who join are reincarnated warrior priests whom the spirits have called by mysterious means."

Six Stix asked, "Do you not miss your homeland at all?"

Obsidian shrugged. "I have few pleasant memories. Besides, I was but a child when I slipped out of my leg irons and escaped."

The surroundings became more and more luxurious. The arched doorways were embellished with increasingly ornate carving, and beyond them were richer carpets and more exquisite wall hangings.

"This must be the Prince's domain," whispered Six Stix. He noted the occasional concealed door along the hallway, such architecture common in great houses. He wished he had his tools.

Obsidian said, "We're probably trespassing. Shouldn't we be getting back to our rooms?"

"What? Look at this tapestry—it's priceless," hissed the elf, "and feel the abundance under your feet. What would be the point of the Prince owning all this if his guests never had a chance to appreciate it?"

"I'm not so sure," muttered Obsidian, more and more ill at ease. He remembered another proverb: *Know where each footfall is placed and why you place it.* He grabbed Six's arm and shook his head with a worried frown. "I'm going back. We shouldn't be here."

Six Stix stared in disbelief, then raised an eyebrow and cocked his head. "If you want to go back, go. I'll meet you in the parlor tonight." He grinned mischievously. "Just make sure they have plenty of my favorite ale, will you?"

The two friends were prevented from further disagreement by the sudden opening of a door nearby. They both turned in surprise at the haughty gnomad stomping toward them, flanked by two guards in full armor, carrying long metal staves ending in hooked barbs.

Obsidian was used to being the tallest man in a crowd, but these fellows towered even over him.

"Stay right there," bellowed the gnomad.

Two more giants in full armor, toting the same kind of weapons as their counterparts entered the corridor from a side door.

"Go on. Move and you'll be skewered like a rat," snapped the gnome. He looked grotesquely small next to the giants, but he swaggered in his leather apron, his ink-black beard trailing to his knees. "Follow me," he said to the guards, and led the way down the corridor.

"Who's that?" whispered Obsidian to Six Stix.

The giant answered instead, baring blackened front teeth. "He is Rearguard, the Patriarch of the Outland Territories—and shut up or you'll be sorry."

Pinioned by the arms, Six Stix and Obsidian were escorted through two more arched passages and down a corridor that ended in a finely carved oaken doorway, decorated with chips of emerald. A bronze keyhole sat very low on the door.

The gnome chose a matching key from a neck cord and turned the lock, then stepped aside. One giant pushed open the heavy door and thrust Obsidian into the enormous chamber. The monk nearly doubled over, but caught his balance before tumbling onto the thick snowbear carpet. Six Stix was also pushed into the room, but as he cleared the doorway, he fell against a huge gong suspended from the wall amid tapestries of red and blue wool, embroidered in gold thread. The booming undulations shattered his nerves. Trying to cover his ringing ears, Six Stix fell onto one knee. Flaming torches in golden wall sconces illuminated massive furniture carved from oak, poplar and hawthorn.

The elf's breast heaved with appreciation, despite his discomfort. The giant pulled him roughly to his feet and shoved him to Obsidian's side.

Obsidian nudged Six Stix. Behind a large table at the back of the room sat a very short man with pale skin and piercing blue eyes. "You may approach," he called out in a commanding voice.

Using their spears, the giants propelled the guests forward. The gnome swaggered up to the table, took a chair and propped up his feet. He gestured at Obsidian and Six Stix, and then, to their further surprise, said, "Here they are, your Highness."

The little man behind the table adjusted his red silk tunic over his round stomach and studied them, a menacing intelligence lurking in his icy blue eyes.

Could this be the Prince? Six Stix wondered. If so, the rumors were false. He wasn't a giant. He was very short for a human and he didn't even look like a warrior. Six Stix said, "Your Highness, I think there's been some—."

The giant muzzled him with a large, meaty hand.

The gnomad stood up, hands on his hips, and said, "There's little doubt, Mischa. These trespassers are the thieves."

The sharp poke of the spear at his back curtailed Obsidian's retort.

Although the Prince recognized the material of their makeshift garments, he pretended to be unconvinced. "How do you know?"

The gnomad snapped his fingers. "Search them," he ordered the giant guards.

In a moment, one of the guards found an object in the elf's improvised tunic, which he handed to the gnome. Six Stix tried again to speak, silenced once more by the giant's hand.

"So," crooned the gnomad, gloating, "look what we have here…" He held up a glittering amber gem, and the Prince lifted an eyebrow.

"Well, Grandfather," he addressed the gnomad, "I suppose you're right. I wonder where the rest is, eh?" The Prince disliked torture, although it was sometimes necessary. Where was the sport in it? *How can I have some fun out of this?* He found the open arena much more to his liking, although he was quite certain his grandfather, Rearguard, disagreed.

"I want to ask a question," Mischa said to the captives.

"Your Highness," Six Stix tried again, but with no more luck than before.

"Now, now," said the Prince, "*I'm* asking the questions, and if you answer nicely, I'll let you go."

Six Stix shut his mouth.

"Have you fought in the arena today?" asked the Prince, knowing well the answer.

"No," they said in unison.

"Well, then," the Prince purred, "I think you're due for another battle."

Obsidian's hackles rose in concert to his dislike for this person. For the first time, he resented being sent here for his initiation.

Six Stix blurted, "We've lost our weapons—they were stolen."

"Stolen?" said the gnome. "You've got a lot of nerve."

"Now, now, Grandfather," soothed the Prince, "fighters must be properly equipped. What kind of implements did you have, gentlemen?"

Obsidian said, "My butterfly knives were made especially for me—and my friend had several weapons—one was a jeweled sword."

The Prince snapped his fingers. "Morzig, bring me the gopher-wood case." The giant strode behind the table, jerked the tapestry aside, and entered a door. The curtain fell back into place, concealing his movements. In moments he returned carrying a large sand-colored case inlaid with tiles depicting carnivorous gopher-wood trees chopped down by Mischa's distant ancestors.

"Now," he said, opening the case, "let's see what we can find." He withdrew a handsome pair of butterfly knives, two swords and a dagger. "Satisfied?" he asked.

Obsidian's mahogany eyes gleamed at the sight of his knives, though he strove to remain calm. His estimation of the Prince took a swing toward the better.

Six Stix was elated to see his weapons once again, but remained more alert than ever. His hands twitched at his side. He could almost feel the ruby hilt of his sword once again.

The Prince ran his plump, delicate fingers over the naked blade of one of the butterfly knives. "First, you'll please return *my* things to *me*," he said with a silken snarl.

Obsidian was surprised when he saw the gnome frowning at the Prince's order. Was there dissension between him and his grandson?

Six Stix said, "You have the amber, Sire, and my apologies—."

"This trinket?" The Prince selected a large, bell-shaped ebony paperweight from the shelf behind him.

"Don't," protested the elf, but too late. Chips of golden fire flew, the jewel crushed to powder in a single blow. With great effort, Six Stix contained his horror at the destruction of the precious object.

Obsidian noted the gnome's scowl when the Prince smashed the gemstone, but Rearguard kept his silence. He rose instead to his feet with a dignity befitting a much taller man and began to pace before the captives. Glaring from beneath black brows, he counted on stubby fingers the many things that had been stolen the past week from his section of the Manor.

When Rearguard finished, Obsidian said, "Our movements can be accounted for—besides, I'm a monk. I took a vow against stealing."

"Why, then, do you keep company with such a rascal?" The Prince pinched a bit of the crushed amber between his fingers. "Aren't you a little annoyed with him for getting you into trouble?"

Obsidian's protest was cut off by the Prince's fist slamming the table. His eyes glittered dangerously. "Enough," he said. "If you insist on pleading innocent, then you'll have to demonstrate the truth in the only place where truth can't be hidden—the arena."

At least, he's right there, thought Six Stix.

"I'll fight an army if I must," said Obsidian with dignity.

"Nothing that demanding," said the Prince and pointed to Six Stix. "You'll fight him."

The gnome laughed out loud at the surprised registered by both captives' faces. *This is better than torture. That grandson of mine is a genius.*

The two adventurers watched with chagrin as the giant called Morzig closed the case and carried their weapons back to the niche behind the curtain. They were then ushered roughly into the hallway by the giants. Six Stix hung his head, as if subdued, yet with each step, carefully memorized every imperfection in the carpet, every nick in the floor.

-19-

EMBAZA LEANED against the wall, near the unconscious dwarven guard, her chin still on her chest, her hand folded yet about the hilt of her broadsword.

He needed rest himself, having completed the spell. Standing in the dim torchlight, Polah regarded him with glistening hostility. He noted that the wound in her back had stopped bleeding. *Do you still think I stabbed you? The creature who did that was a sending.* He frowned. *Only who sent it?* A creature from the phantom realms was nothing to be called forth lightly.

Embaza reached out to Polah mentally. *Why are you acting so strangely? The assassin is gone, the dwarf is no threat now—and I certainly wouldn't hurt you.*

The fox merely growled in response, Embaza vaguely discomforted by the animal's emotions. She whimpered every so often, looking to all sides of her, then snarled again as if at an unseen danger. He knelt and held out his hands, palms up, but she retreated, baring her teeth.

The fox stared at the other end of the hallway, an older part of the Manor where the occasional draft penetrated cracks in the stone walls, and spiderwebs covered the ceiling. Embaza thought, *maybe she'll calm down if I leave her alone,* and shifted his attention to the dwarf.

Her sword looked well used. He had little interest in weapons in the normal course of affairs, but squinting, saw a faint eldritch light radiating from the blade.

He squatted for a closer examination. Delicately he touched the blade and nearly screamed when it burned his fingertip.

So, it's yours alone, my bearded friend. He wondered if it was an anti-elven blade. Such things had been forged during the Seven Years War and older wars that preceded it, and judging from the battle scars and flecks of gray in her hair, the dwarf was a veteran campaigner.

Embaza studied the silken runes etched into the fantastic blade, practically worn away with use. *Too old to be anti-elven. And these pictoglyphs—I don't recognize a single one. Must be some ancient dwarven tongue.*

He stood up, regarding the fighter with new respect. Unlike the blue elves, he felt no antipathy for her race. During the hostilities, he had been closeted away in the marble towers at the edge of the Sargoth Sea, studying the arts of wizardry rather than warfare. And besides, he knew there were other elves who had not participated—the dark elves, for one. Living side by side with the dwarves in their underground caves and mountain strongholds, dependent on the same mines, the same food supplies, it would have been madness.

The dwarf's tough, sun-splotched skin left no doubt she was a creature of the underground. *Yet she has no trouble with sunlight. I wonder how I would have fared if I had not had the wizards of Sargoth to train me. Though I've learned to survive here, maybe I really belong in a velvety cave with other dark elves...* He rubbed the blue sheen on the back of his hand. Whenever he thought of his origins, a wall came up in his mind. The more he tried, the less he could remember, as if someone had stripped his memory and left in its place a blank mask through which he must view his life. His earliest recall involved the magic towers in the wasteland of Sargothas. His teachers had steadfastly refused to tell him more.

The old priestess Zelwyn the other night had upset him with her parting words about not denying his heritage. *What did she expect from me? How can I embrace something I have never known?* He looked at his stained hands again, thinking it was almost time to reapply the thin blue dye. It had been his disguise for so many years, he had almost convinced himself that he was a woodland creature. But that old healer had suggested there were depths in his origins that he might want to explore.

While he was busy with the dwarf, the fox had been exploring. Embaza was startled from his reverie by her whimpering and scratching at a section of the wall. When he came to investigate, he saw a doorway artfully hidden from casual view by the random placing of stones along its seams. After a few moments, he discerned a keyhole. *The dwarf's room?*

Sure enough, a quick search of her garments furnished him with a small silver key that turned smoothly in the lock. And no traps, which was odd. Usually dwarves were more careful.

The door opened, and he was face-to-face with an elven woman whose beauty stunned him. Dark hair to her waist, eyes as clear as emeralds, skin the color of ebony. Suddenly ashamed of his disguise, he bowed to her.

Tiala looked at Embaza with shining eyes. "Thank the Foremothers, you've found me."

Behind Embaza, the great fox regarded the elf woman with dark, slotted eyes, then bared her teeth and growled with antipathy. Tiala stared back and automatically reached for her missing dagger, then remembered she was in mourning. *What kind of champion is this?*

Embaza held up his hand, "Don't fear—she is not what she seems. Her name is Polah."

"Oh, and that explains it," said Tiala sarcastically, yet with a hint of humor in her voice. "Stay back, Fire-Fur, or you'll regret it."

The fox showed Embaza her needle-sharp teeth and the wizard stepped aside, holding up his hands. "You know what I can do to you, little fox—take care," he murmured.

"Since you are on speaking terms with this beast, can you control her?" demanded Tiala. "And where's my guard? What have you done to her?"

"Don't be alarmed. She's at her post," Embaza replied, knowing the dwarf might remain asleep indefinitely, although he saw no need to admit that just yet. Once again, he regretted using the Spell of a Hundred Dreams on her. What a luxury it would be to have the time to meditate on some of the newer spells. Such things were possible only when he was rested and safe from harm.

Tiala looked at him suspiciously, but she was inclined to trust him. After all, she had given the General strict instructions not to interfere. She recalled a scrap of conversation over *Rogues & Rascals*. *Didn't the General tell me about a battle? What was it? A woman, a wizard and a shape-changer—against...some sort of demon. But they aren't dead.* Tiala looked at the wizard and the fox with new respect. "Please assure your companion that I mean her no harm," she said in a commanding tone rarely refused in her homeland. "Come in so we can become acquainted."

She watched the tall elf squat and hold out his hands to the fox. "It was not I who stabbed you, Polah," he said.

With a whimper, the splendid animal came toward him and plaintively licked his fingers. Embaza was secretly surprised as well. *My dear,* he said silently, *are you coming to yourself again?*

The fox blinked, and Embaza felt a dull sympathy.

Curious, Tiala came a little closer. Obviously in her prime, the fox's back reached Tiala's hips. The elf woman took a piece of fowl wrapped in grain from the plate on her table, and offered it to the fox, saying in her most soothing voice, "Here, Fire-Fur."

The fox sniffed, hesitated, and approached warily.

Tiala looked deeply into eyes that flashed with human intelligence. She said to Embaza, "She is an enchanter."

He lifted his chin, but his eyes were hooded. "She is Polah," he said.

"And who are you?" she said imperiously, half-hoping he was a shape-changer, too. Why did he seem so familiar?

Compelled to tell this woman the truth—or at least some of it—he rose to his feet and said, "I am Embaza, a wizard of Sargothas. I came here to enhance my powers and, in the process, I befriended this shape-changer. But why are you here?" This was the second time in two days he had met a dark elf here in the keep and he was intrigued by the coincidence.

Tiala said, "There is nothing like Sargothas in Alvarra, since only priestesses wield the earth magic. My name is Tiala Denshadiel, heir to the Nightwing's throne of Alvarra—but you may not have heard of the deepworld. How I miss it." She stopped in surprise at the pain that crossed the wizard's face. "Embaza, do you have memories that torment you?"

If you only knew, he thought in dismay. Even the name, Alvarra, tantalized him with possibilities. *Was it my birthplace?* "It's just an old wound; it will pass."

Tiala's sense that he was holding something back spurred her to disclose her own need. "I am fulfilling a destiny I cannot escape. My family and my people are in grave danger—and I seek champions who will return with me to fight my enemies."

Embaza's eyes lit and he drew a deep breath. "I have always been curious about your land."

"It will be perilous, but if you agree to help me, you will travel through fields of yellow root blossom and velvet roseglove, into the crystal walls of the under-city, and through the caves of silver slime, where the snails never sleep. No matter what road you take, you cannot escape the enchantment of Alvarra. It is the most magical of places." She hoped magic would appeal to this wizard. She had never met one before, and took pains to hide her revulsion.

He drank her words like bitter mead. The great fox settled at his feet and closed her eyes.

"But why here, Tiala Denshadiel?" he said. "Surely you could find champions of your own in Alvarra."

"Time is precious. While the country is in mourning for my sister, no Alvarran may use weapons or magic. My enemies will use it to their advantage, but they must act with speed, for the mourning period is only three moons."

"And who are your enemies?" asked Embaza. *As a dark elf, my hands would be tied—but as a blue...*

Tiala looked at him closely, then down at the floor, her voice dropping to a whisper. "Dekhalis, my brother, is the youngest of my family—and the only male. He has threatened to assassinate us—one by one—until he is the only Denshadiel left. Then he plans to rule Alvarra." She lifted her head and stared at him with flashing eyes.

Her tone disturbed him, though he wasn't sure why. "You say he is young—how do you know that he is not merely fantasizing?"

"He killed our older sister, Ombra." Her voice trembled. "And bragged of it at her funeral. Something or someone has poisoned him against us."

Embaza folded his arms. "Before I risk my life for you, I must know more about him."

The resolve and intelligence in his voice lessened her suspicions. "He is young, but he has great charm and cunning. He is recruiting men of every description, whom I fear he will train as warriors, as he has been trained. As a royal son, he had every freedom."

"Does he use magic?"

She frowned. "Probably. He's not above stealing artifacts. Many women have such items. Fairy webs, chimes, incense, even wands made from enchanted trees. Not everyone knows how to use them, but my brother has always been interested in magic." She hesitated before adding, "Certain things have even disappeared from the Treasure House. Why do you ask?"

Embaza's eyes narrowed. "Strange things have been happening, things that make no sense at all unless someone knows we were fated to meet. Where I come from, old men look into crystals and see the future. Some can even manipulate events from far away with these items of power."

"The Nightwing and her priestesses prevent this sort of misuse of power." She crossed her arms. "It's not possible in Alvarra."

Embaza's intuition told him she was mistaken, but he allowed her to hold onto her reassurances. Whoever these priestesses were, they didn't sound equal to the task. Besides, he could see that this fellow was well-loved by those he wished most to harm. This would make any opposition even harder—love was a powerful protector. He had a sudden glimpse of the loneliness of his own life, but shook his head. *Love is not part of my plans. Pain is a more dependable companion.*

"Tiala, how did you manage to come here?" he asked. "That is—how did you prevail against the Scourge sickness?"

"Oh, that," said the dark elf with a trace of bitterness. "I'm surprised you are so well informed. Most people think we dark elves are an evil breed who are prone to insane acts of violence." She looked vulnerable for a moment and raised her eyes to Embaza. His shuttered face could not hide an expression of deep sympathy.

She said, "I was escorted by dwarven warriors who were familiar with both the upworld and the underground realms. They wrapped me in dark robes soaked in water and transported me in the bottom of a wooden cart. Even so, I became so ill that I attacked the General."

"The General?" asked Embaza. "I have heard of her."

"Yes," said Tiala, "she became famous in the Seven Years War. She is my guard—and jailor—the one you met in the hallway." Embaza started, but Tiala was studying the floor, pondering the loyalty she had seen in the General. *Do I earn such devotion?* She looked at Embaza, the charisma of a ruler blazing in her green eyes. "Will you help me?"

Embaza saw the fear and need beneath the surface, but mistrusted her charm. "I'll consider it."

Tiala mastered herself, unused to being disobeyed by a man. "I would thank you from the bottom of my heart," she said. "The very roots of our civilization are trembling at this villainy—and you…you have the opportunity to save our world."

Embaza was touched by her sincerity, in spite of himself. *Why not? She could be my own sister.* "If I do accompany you, Tiala Denshadiel…" She beamed with triumph, but he held up his hand. "First, I think you should know that I am not all I appear to be, just like my friend here. I have my own reasons for taking on your cause and one of them is that I suspect your enemies have already interfered with me—and Polah." He stroked the fox's ear.

"For that I am sorry, but I believe the Great Goddess Miralor sent both of you to me," said Tiala.

The fox lifted her head and gazed steadily at Embaza. "If she could speak," he said, "I think Polah would agree that this is an undertaking worthy of her abilities."

Tiala could hardly contain her excitement. "At last. I have champions."

Embaza frowned. "What good is a handful of fighters? Would you not do better with an army?"

The dark elf shook her head. "An army would never enter Alvarra unchallenged."

"I nearly forgot," said Embaza. "Last night, I met a healer from your land. Her name is Zelwyn. Perhaps you should talk with her."

"Zelwyn—here? Thanks to Miralor," Tiala exclaimed. "I will ask the Prince to summon her to me."

She turned to the mantelpiece to gaze at the silken rope hanging from the ceiling and recalled Prince Mischa's instructions to use the bell cord when she was ready to leave. Then he would be paid, and she would be glad to see the last of his odious hospitality.

Before she signalled her intentions, she wanted to have a small party ready to accompany her. She would certainly try to convince the General to return with her to Alvarra. *She doesn't belong with these ruffians, anyway. She's a woman of character.* "Call in the General. I must discuss the crossing with her before I settle with Prince Mischa."

Embaza held his breath. What if he couldn't awaken the dwarf? He hesitated, looking to Polah as if awaiting an answer, but she merely continued to gaze up at him, her muzzle draped on black velvet paws. Her wound was healed, only a thinning of fur to mark the place.

Tiala noticed the wizard's discomfort and said, "What's wrong?"

"Nothing," he said, and exited to the corridor, Tiala trailing him, and Polah trotting softly at her heels. The dwarf remained propped against the wall, snoring away.

Tiala said, "Is this your doing?"

Embaza showed the dark beauty his back and said, "Even with the mildest of spells, she will need time to recover." He shook the dwarf by the shoulder to no avail, and Tiala came closer.

"General?" she called, but the General slept blissfully and Tiala turned on Embaza. "You must restore her." In Alvarra, they might have used an herbal concoction or called on Miralor to stir her life force.

Embaza glanced at her. "I can try a counter spell, but I'm not as fresh as I was earlier. It may not work."

Tiala lifted her chin. "In Alvarra, we say, 'What I conceive in my heart enchants the wind.'"

She sounds like a leader, thought Embaza, braced by her confidence. He composed his mind and knelt before the General, touched her temples with his fingertips, and said, "*Nadayziah.*"

The fox watched from behind them.

"*Grandiseranim,*" said Embaza. "*Nim Esklasoria.*" The dwarf stopped snoring and the wizard sighed in exhaustion. "That's it," he said.

The General promptly slid down the wall to the floor, curling up on her side like a cat.

"Oh, no, you don't," said Tiala, "this is no time to get comfortable."

The General opened her brown eyes and regarded Tiala with a smile. "It was a glorious dream, Alvarran," she mumbled, then remembering herself, scowled and groped for her sword.

Tiala helped her up. "It seems I have escaped. I beg you not to turn me in."

"You are safe with me, my Lady," said the dwarf, who flinched upon recognizing the fox from the arena. She tightened her grip on the sword. Such creatures were unnatural and she had no liking for them. "What are you doing here?" she asked the wizard, but Embaza ignored her for Polah, who stood with a glazed look in her black eyes.

The fox stared straight ahead in the dim torchlight of the hallway, and calm descended over all, as if this moment were suspended in time. Then, as naturally as the shimmer of sunlight on a placid lake, Polah's fur turned to skin, her claws to nails, and a small, well knit woman with fiery red hair was standing naked before them.

"Splendid," Embaza cried in his awe. To witness magic like this was the pinnacle of mystic ecstasy

For Polah, it was painful. Her eyes adjusted to the change of light, and her nostrils to the air. Her head reeled. The heat of a now familiar blush warmed her face at her own nakedness. At the General's almost comical stare, she laughed uneasily and said, "Haven't you ever seen a woman before?"

"No," said the General. "That is, I—."

"Forgive us," said Tiala, recovering her poise, "enchanters usually give warning before they change shape." She motioned the fox-woman to her room where she dug out some extra garments from her travel bundle to give to the grateful Polah, then retired to the corridor to wait with the wizard and the dwarf.

Polah swiftly put on the over-sized leggings, rolling up the waist several times, and knotting the sleeves of the fine tunic around her thin wrists. The woven socks were a good fit, and she finished by wrapping the sash around her waist four times.

Tiala noticed with amusement that as Polah rejoined them, she kept her distance from the wizard, a glint of mistrust in her tenebrous eyes. *Can't say I blame you,* she thought. *He acts like he owns you.*

She said, "Polah, the wizard spoke for you, but I prefer you choose for yourself. I would be honored if you joined my cause."

The redhead looked up at Tiala and asked, "Are there creatures like me in your world?"

She nodded. "Many."

"Then I wish to travel with you to seek them out. And if I can help you along the way, I will." She glanced at Embaza. The fox in her trusted him, but her female half was not so sure.

Tiala said, "And you, General, are you going to stay with Mischa or follow me?"

The dwarf glanced between the wizard and the shape-changer. "These are your heroes, my Lady?" A sideways glance at Tiala, a sniff, and she said, "I think you're going to need my assistance."

Embaza's back stiffened and he crossed his arms. Polah made an angry little noise akin to a growl.

Tiala patted the dwarf's shoulder. "Rogue Queen salutes Rascal Knight," she said, and the two burst into laughter.

-20-

THE NEW allies contemplated the journey ahead. Some had to gather their belongings, while all needed rest.

"We'll meet back in the tower tonight and then I will notify the Prince that we are leaving," Tiala said. "It will be safer to travel in darkness." She shuddered at the thought of even that much exposure to open desert.

Polah scampered ahead of Embaza as he descended the stairway to the corridor below. He called her name mentally and a slamming door answered. Resigned, he headed for his own room on the same floor.

The General refused to let Tiala out of her sight, and invited the elf to her room while she gathered her things. Curious about the General's quarters, Tiala supposed they would be standard issue for a guard in the Prince's employ. Mischa had not impressed her as being generous.

The dwarf led the way down a long corridor. Tiala shortened her long-legged stride to match.

"What part of Tskurl do you come from?" she asked, careful to pronounce the difficult name correctly.

"My family are root cutters in the Lesser Barrows. Since I was the oldest daughter, I went into the army."

"They must be proud of the rank you've attained," said Tiala.

"I was only following tradition. There are many generals in my family."

"Did you enjoy the fighting life?"

"I've known little else, my Lady," said the General. "The war was hard, of course, but it's a good life, independent, plenty of comrades. The occasional travel, the excitement of combat."

"I hate formal titles," said Tiala as they descended a short flight of stairs, "I'll have enough of that when I am Nightwing. It's bad enough the others call me Princess, not even Na'a Nightwing, which would be accurate. Couldn't you just call me Tiala—at least in private?"

"I'll try, but I can't promise to change my habits that easily." The General cleared her throat. "My real name is Gudrun. Gudrun of Estenhame. But don't tell the others."

"Is Estenhame your tribe?"

"My tribe and my birthplace. The name passed down by the Foremother. Our traditions are different from yours, I know. You see, my Lady—sorry, Tiala—when a woman is unmarried like me, she takes the name of her foremothers. But a married woman like my mother takes the name of her husband's foremothers. This way, we bind the tribes."

"That's reasonable," said the elf, "but if you're unmarried, how will you carry on the name of Estenhame?"

"My daughter will bear the name of Estenhame, unless of course she marries…"

Tiala appreciated the long hallway unrelieved by doors or windows. "You have a daughter?"

"Yes, when I was very young. We Estenhames are known for our fertility. She's all grown up now, most likely still in the barrow. She wasn't too interested in learning to fight." Gudrun shrugged, then smiled. "That's all right. She'll be a happy root cutter."

Tiala had spent her life in the bosom of her family, even her seventeen years in the army. She envied Gudrun's independence and anonymity. *Daughters of the royal family would never be allowed to bear children and then roam around like vagabonds.*

"How did you come to work for Prince Mischa?" Tiala asked.

"After we lost the war, I was down in my luck and the Manor offered good pay, good food and good company," Gudrun replied. "Fighting in the arena brought a lot of us a pride we needed to regain."

"But you were already a well-known hero," Tiala said.

From a door nearby, three young men in purple uniforms marched toward them, and Tiala regarded them with great interest. She was not surprised that they looked frightened of her, showing the usual superstition. However, she noted with approval that they looked afraid of the General.

They stopped to salute the dwarf, who gave them a steely gaze and said, "You're late for maneuvers."

"Yes, General. We're on our way there now," said one of the men. He had great difficulty keeping his eyes off Tiala. The dark elf noticed with chagrin that all three had crossed their fingers in the ancient warding sign.

"You'd better go, then," Gudrun said. When the men had passed from view, she gave Tiala a dazzling smile. "Most of my so-called heroism is hearsay. Tales that strengthened the spirit when wine wasn't enough. But there's one particular song—perhaps you know it—'The Brave and Noble Girl.'"

More curious than ever, Tiala asked, "Can you sing it?"

Gudrun winced. "No."

"Then, what is it about?"

"It tells of a terrible battle, toward the end of the war. We were ambushed by an elite troop of blue elves who attacked us from behind. We were vastly outnumbered and I was sick with fever. Though I am ashamed to say it, I spent most of the battle leaning on my sword. Of course, the song doesn't tell it that way. At least I managed to scar the leader's cheek." She drew a wavy line in the air. "I would know him anywhere."

Tiala was stunned by the hatred in Gudrun's voice. "You lost the battle?"

"I lost my sisters." She averted her eyes. "When I first came to the Manor, I hoped I might meet him in the arena, so I could take my revenge." She raised a cold, calculating gaze to Tiala and added, "Perhaps he is here even now. I cannot watch every contest."

"Who is he?"

"Who knows? There are songs about him, too, but they don't name him. Those elite troops kept their names a secret. This gave them more freedom to do as they pleased. If he was anything like the others, he took advantage of the war to enjoy himself."

Silence accompanied them to the end of the hall, then Gudrun briefly forgot all else when the elf began softly humming a tune designed to lift the cloud of depression weighing their spirits.

At the bottom of a short flight of stairs, the dwarf worked her fingers into a tiny niche on the left side of an unmarked door. With a scraping sound, she wiggled a key beneath the upper bolt. "Stay back," she said. Standing to one side, she turned the lock and released the key, all in one smooth motion. A very thin knife blade snicked out of the keyhole. Gudrun half smiled. When it came to traps, she liked them simple but effective.

Tiala watched with respect. She knew that dwarves were jealous of their possessions, and it seemed this poor root cutter was no exception.

Gudrun went into the room and left the door ajar. Accepting the unspoken invitation, Tiala eagerly peeked through the doorway to what was little more than a closet: just a hanging bed, a small table and chair. Gudrun took a sack of clothes and personal items from a hook behind the door, and slung it over her shoulder. Taking a last look around, she said, "This is it. I guess I'm ready."

Tiala hesitated. "As long as we're here," she said, "could I see the barracks?" Her stint in the Nightwing's army had been less than ordinary, and she had often felt ostracized by privilege. The cameraderie of the typical soldier had been denied her.

"Over here," said the General, walking to the end of the hall. Tiala allowed Gudrun to make her usual survey of the area before leading her into a large room filled with empty cots, each with a small chest at the foot. One wall was dotted with windows all along its length and through them, the gray sky showed the first pink streak of dawn.

"Only the Prince's personal staff have their own rooms," said Gudrun with a hint of satisfaction. To her, privilege was never a burden.

Tiala recalled her doubts about Gudrun's loyalties. "So, where are the others?" she asked, marveling at the number of beds that could be crammed into one room. Few were dwarf-sized, most human, and none giant-sized. "Tell me something," she said to Gudrun. "Is it possible I might recruit some of these giants who work for the Prince? They don't seem to be treated very well."

The General shook her head. "They are completely loyal to the Patriarch and will do only what he tells them. The gnomads rule this entire territory. Also, the giants are superstitious and have all sorts of odd beliefs about dark elves and magic."

Tiala shuddered. Nervous in a room with so many windows, she still could not bring herself to look outside.

"My men are up before the sun rises," Gudrun said. "It's still cool in the desert and they can practice weaponry before the morning meal." She glanced through the window to the pink stain of sunrise spreading over the dunes. "We ought to leave before they get back."

"Then let's go," Tiala said. "The Scourge is making me sick."

Gudrun glanced at the elf, alarmed at the terror on her face, and said, "Take a deep breath—easy, now." She pushed her gently toward the door.

<h1 style="text-align:center">-21-</h1>

IN THE dim light of one candle, Embaza unlocked the chest in his room. He had few clothes with him and these could be rolled up into his blue cloak. He put on the gray one and opened his leather saddle bags, preferring them to a common pack because they slipped quite easily over his shoulders when he traveled. He wouldn't carry them tonight, however, and took from one side three extra candles, which he thrust into his inner pockets. He might need to make a waxen figure. Rest he needed though, or he would exhaust himself doing one spell.

When the chest was locked and sealed, and he was certain he had left nothing of himself behind, he extinguished the light and went through the corridor to Polah's room. Just outside her door, he saw a dark shape. *Not another one.*

Dagger in hand, he raced up the hallway. The closer he came to the shadow, the weaker he felt, as if his very energy was being drained. He tried to call out, to warn Polah, but a pressure in his chest allowed only a weak whisper.

As the shadow grew more distinct, Embaza saw what appeared to be a very thin wraith of a man with goat-like horns and cloven feet. *A gargoyle.* It writhed and twisted, not presenting not enough target for a dagger. He had read about these horrors in the Book of Myths, though he had never actually seen one. He struggled to remember the words of a black—*no, a purple*—scroll.

But the glowing red eyes of the monster suddenly pinned him to the wall, while the gargoyle's body seemed to meld with the darkness.

The consumptive eyes burned Embaza's will like hot coals. He couldn't move. To draw so much as a breath was torture. Then the muscles in his stomach and legs locked up as if turning to stone.

-22-

WHILE POLAH packed, she reflected on the things she was learning about herself. Her senses had become hyper-aware since she had begun shape-changing. She knew danger, love, fear, hunger, both in herself and in others. Animals had more talents than she had suspected—not just of the body, but of the spirit. Could this explain her ties to Embaza?

She shuddered with fear. *I've got to get control of myself. He communicates too easily with me. What is my bond with this wizard?* Perhaps she would find the answers in Alvarra. Every whispered tale of the underground included a reference to magic. Stories of shape-changers were not uncommon. What had the dark elf called her? *Enchanter.*

The fact that she didn't recall everything that happened to her in fox form vaguely worried her, as if patches of her memory were buried forever in primordial worlds. And these events were like beings that cast no reflection on the mirror of the mind. There was no language to describe them within herself except in the present moment. *Is this what an animal realizes? The eternal present moment? The wizard's philosophy? Now, where did that thought come from?*

She pressed her cheeks with her hands. *Who am I?* She had asked this question a million times since childhood. She removed the little rag doll from under her pillow. This she had carried around with her since she had first left home, unwilling to part with this remnant of normal life.

Embaza confused her. Sometimes she hated him for what he was, for the way he came unbidden into her mind, and yet—he could be gentle, too. Sometimes she felt a need to be near him, to warm herself at the fire of his wisdom. Her head ached with questions.

She suddenly had the vision of a shining sword, implanted in soft ground, quivering, waiting. *Why this symbol?* she wondered. Then she knew. *Embaza. Something is wrong, isn't it?* The answer was affirmative, though not in words. Polah dropped the doll. A calm stole over her body like a caress.

Even amidst the now-familiar pain of transformation and the new danger ahead, she was exhilarated by the gathering of power, thrilled with the taut young muscles of the fox, the heightened smell and hearing. Dropping to all fours, she padded into the closet and activated the secret door with her nose. For the first time, she sensed cooperation between her human and her animal senses, her mind capable and clear, without any need for thought.

In the hallway, she sniffed something unfamiliar. Her animal instinct told her to flee, an impulse her human courage dismissed. She caught a sudden movement out of the corner of her eye, and leapt aside to avoid three savage talons aimed at her back. The flapping wings were deafening, and the foul wind ruffled her fur.

Above her, an enormous owl with fierce, glowing eyes raked the opposite wall, its talons gouging a perch in the loose mortar and stone. As the bird readied itself for another pass, a larger shape emerged from the shadows to the left, a greater menace even than the owl.

A familiar voice in her mind said, *That is a gargoyle, Polah. It has no soul. Find the weakness of the man who called it here and you destroy it.*

Polah bared her teeth and growled a warning at the shape carrying a large axe. A kind of animal—half-man, half-goat—the nauseating stench choked Polah before a sweeter scent, one she recognized, had her pivot on her haunches. *Embaza.* She saw him immobilized, pressed against a wall, and bounded toward him. The owl screeched, lancing her sensitive ears with pain.

He spoke to her mind. *Polah, can you hear me?* She sent a ray of understanding to the wizard. In the wilds, where nothing was ever wasted, there was no time for idle reflection and she was a creature of action now. She could communicate only with feelings, yet she retained some human ability to comprehend his words. Although Embaza knew nothing of this, he had received her concern as clearly as if it had been translated into words. *Look out,* she had said.

The owl darted toward Embaza's head from its perch and Polah intercepted, leaping into the air and sinking her teeth into one of its huge wings. Her arc brought her down across from Embaza, and the gargoyle hurtled toward her. *Look behind you.*

Polah spun toward the gargoyle, and the screeching owl swooped in a dizzy trail, its ragged left wing flapping awkwardly, its talons just missing Polah's neck. A claw caught her ear, a screaming agony, and blood spattered her left eye. Through a haze of crimson-coated fear, Polah reared and attacked the gargoyle raising its axe to strike.

Her jaws closed about a sinewy leg, her nostrils filled with the nauseating stench. She bit down hard, then tore away a piece of the noxious flesh in an effort to get behind the monster.

Horrified, Embaza watched the gargoyle shake off the fox like a troublesome insect, then turn, axe high above the fox. The wizard checked his thoughts for fear his words might distract her.

Polah circled out of reach, one eye on the owl landing in the shadows, the other curtained in red, then faced the gargoyle. *Careful,* said Embaza. *Find its weakness.*

Flames burned within the soulless eyes behind a blistering stare, but the fox side of Polah dominated, a side wise with ancient experiences imprinted in her genes. Beyond a doubt her enemy had fear, and therefore could be killed.

The woman half of her observed the gargoyle cock its head in confusion at the fact that its adversary refused to retreat.

Polah sprang for the gargoyle's throat, and her teeth found their mark the instant the monster brought its axe down on her neck. She heard Embaza's scream, her flesh sliced like an apple, but she ripped out the gargoyle's ligaments, jugular vein, and vocal chords in her fall. There was no sound, only a horrible smell as the monster toppled to the stone floor, gurgled, gasped and died.

Perhaps it was a merciful death. Polah did not care. She was up on all fours and limping down the corridor, blood streaming from her neck. She stepped on something pulpy and looked down at a mass of feathers, black with caked blood. As she stared at the owl, her blood congealed and her wound knit closed in the strange, wonderful chemistry of her own supernatural being.

As she panted to catch her breath, enthralled by her experience, Embaza, too, watched in wonderment. His limbs like leaden weights, finally, he could move. His legs were stiff, his knees buckled suddenly, and he squatted, resting his hands on the floor and gulping deep breaths.

Polah suffered little as fur turned to skin, claws to nails, and fangs to small white teeth. She realized that for once she was relaxed, open to the experience, and still on all fours, her red hair covering her face, she missed the owl's rise from the floor. The bird of prey came at her from behind, outspread talons aiming for her naked back, its left wing hanging raggedly by a gruesome sinew, its eyes crazed with vengeance.

Embaza crawled toward Polah on pained and stiffened joints, and the owl turned on this new opponent.

The hooked beak was inches away from Embaza's face when he plunged his dagger into its feathered breast. The owl smacked the floor and lay helpless on its back, but Embaza did not remove the weapon until the bird was completely still, his hand wet with gore.

He gritted his teeth at the sight of the bloody furrows on Polah's back. Quickly, he removed his gray cloak to wrap around her. She turned her head up to him, and they gazed at each other for a long moment, the bond so palpable neither could speak, not even mentally. Polah rested her hand on Embaza's shoulder, and her head dropped to her chest, then she leaned into him.

Embaza encircled Polah in his arms, and together, they stood quietly in the hall, their minds pooling in mute understanding.

-23-

WHILE THE adventurers slept in preparation for their trip, Prince Mischa watched the sun drop behind the dunes. Perched on a leather stool under a canopy of sky-blue silk set on four poles in the desert, he sucked on a sweet lime and fanned himself with a large date leaf. He was covered from head to toe by a striped burnoose in purple-and-green silk, and his waist sash was dotted with diamonds.

"Where is Grandfather?" he grumbled. He wished he hadn't dismissed his servants so hastily. The canopy, large enough to shelter twenty men, was furnished with a soft, multi-colored carpet and bright pillows. However, the sand gave off a palpable heat, and not a single tree decorated the sere landscape.

Several yards to the east, the Manor squatted like a lord over the desert. Mischa admired the gleaming fortress, the three broad turrets of different shades of stone that formed a triangle enclosing the rest of the structure. From the outside, the arena was impossible to see. Two massive archways in the stone wall opened onto the desert, wide enough for six camels to pass under side-by-side.

Out of the nearest arch strode Rearguard, dressed as usual in brown tunic and leggings, his black beard tucked into his shirt to protect it from the harsh sun. The leather apron flapped with each step and his jeweled dagger winked in the waning light.

When he reached the canopy where the Prince was resting, the gnomad stretched out on the carpet and rested his elbow on a white satin pillow. "It was thoughtful of you to provide some furniture," he said, "but out here, I don't care for such trappings."

"Why pretend to be humble, Grandfather," said the Prince, "you had your share of luxury during your empire." He spread his arms wide. "From horizon to horizon, your tents were spread, and from sun to moon, you imposed your will upon a spineless, ignorant people."

"Merely a defenseless people who needed a protector, Mischief," said the gnome. "It never fails to amuse me the way you twist our history. You were a pint-sized little nobbin when the fate of the desert was decided, so what can you remember of it?"

"I've listened to my guards talk behind our backs. The Blacktooth tribe resents the tithe they pay to you. If their numbers were larger, they might have challenged you long ago."

Rearguard laughed. "You're forgetting, it was I who persuaded them to work for you. I know their loyalty. I'm all that stands between them and your dangerous love of magic, my boy."

Mischa scowled. "Well, Grandfather, I didn't come here to argue with you. Our bargain still stands. You agreed to get me a new harem, and I agreed to pay you one thousand and one hundred diamonds of the finest quality."

"Let me see them," said the gnome, holding out his hand.

The Prince removed one sparkling gem from the stash in his belt. "They're all of this quality." He squinted his eyes, drilling them into the gnomad's. "I trust the women are as beautiful—and as valuable."

Rearguard chuckled softly and replied, "Just wait and see. I've surpassed myself this time. These ravishing beauties are unique, each in her own way."

"Oh? They'd better be. I was pained to have to dispose of the others, but they failed to catch your thieves. Sefer is ruined—a halfwit—and the other two, Cinna and Rha, were just as useless in the end. I was lucky to find a buyer for them. I didn't even recover my original bride price. Now maybe you'll see why I insist on getting magic in the dowry."

Rearguard shook his head. "In the old days, a bride was a bride. None of this haggling over sorcery. Besides, desert families hold onto their heirlooms. They have little else. Why don't you return to the old ways and hire some real bodyguards to watch your treasure?"

"Don't waste my time, Grandfather," said the Prince. "I'm your only heir. Whether you like my methods or not, you're stuck with them. You're too old to survive alone out here."

The gnome's laughter was almost sinister. "How little you know of my resources." He sat up, raised his arm and gave a distinctive whistle. From the crest of a dune to the west rose a cloud of dust, and over the hill rode a party of gnomads on horseback. As they approached, the Prince sat up straighter and grasped the edges of his stool, counting twelve riders. Behind them, three camels carried large palanquins on their backs. The Prince's mouth watered, then another group of riders followed the camels, but he lost count at twenty. He looked to the gnome. "You didn't tell me to expect a whole tribe."

"You didn't ask," Rearguard replied, spreading his hands and chuckling, his shoulders shaking with glee.

The Prince seethed with anger at the gnome for bringing him out into the desert where he would be defenseless, unable to negotiate the terms of the deal. Why had he expected this to be a friendly piece of business? But still, he was not without his own secrets. From under his burnoose, he withdrew a small piece of crystal, held it up to the setting sun, and the prism made rainbows on the sand.

"What's that?" said Rearguard, blinking at the object.

"Nothing, just a toy," said the Prince in a soft voice, closing his hand around it.

Cold dread knotted Rearguard's stomach at the sight of another dangerous magic item in his grandson's hands, but it was too late to turn back now.

Amid clouds of dust, the riders halted within ten yards of the lone canopy. At a signal from Rearguard, one of the gnomads dismounted and handed the reins of his horse to a lieutenant. He wore a handsome desert cloak embroidered with a half-circle, symbol of the rising sun, and two scimitars in his belt. The weapons looked razor sharp.

Rearguard leaned over to Mischa and whispered, "Remember, this is a very proud chieftain. You must observe all the forms. And above all, if you insist on bringing it up, don't talk too much about magic. He'll consider it an insult to the spirits."

The Prince looked down and fondled the crystal in his lap. "Superstitious idiots," he muttered under his breath.

When the gnomad chieftain reached the canopy, he saluted Rearguard and remained at attention out of obvious respect for the old gnome.

"Be at your ease, Lord Amra. The Prince and I never stand on ceremony," said Rearguard.

"Thank you, Patriarch." Lord Amra sat cross-legged on the rug and uncovered his face. He was middle aged with a grayish beard and weathered skin, but his eyebrows were deep black.

The Prince tossed a lime to the lord from a basket on the table. Amra caught the fruit handily, grinned and bit into its juicy pulp with his strong white teeth.

"Lord Amra is head of the tribes in the west now," said Rearguard. "His daughters are the most sumptuous maidens in the territory. Unfortunately…" he made a dour face, "the poor man has thirty-four."

The Prince laughed and turned to the chieftain. "That must keep you quite busy."

"Yes, it does, Sire," said the lord and spat out a lime seed. "I don't suppose you'd take three of them off my hands?"

"Well, that depends," said the Prince. "I have…certain needs."

Amra looked him over. "Nothing my girls can't handle," he said. "Unless you're equipped with something new."

When the laughter subsided, Mischa leaned forward and said in a conspiratorial tone, "Perhaps you've heard, Lord Amra. I need a woman who combines two unique qualities…complete loyalty and a priceless dowry."

The desert lord almost laughed, but decided this was not a joke when he saw the seriousness of the glittering eyes. He tossed the remaining pieces of the lime to the sand, and wiped his hands on his thighs. "Sire," he said, "I bring you three women whose loyalty is unquestionable—and whose virtue is above price."

The Prince clenched the crystal so hard that the faceted points almost pierced his hand. "He does not mention magic," he muttered to Rearguard through clenched teeth.

"Patience," whispered the gnome. "Keep an open mind. Lord Amra's daughters are very special. Trust me."

Sensing the Prince's displeasure, Lord Amra rose to his feet, a glower on his face. "Have you changed your mind without even seeing them, my Prince?" His scimitars gleamed in the waning sunlight.

Rearguard hastened to his side. "You misunderstand," he said, "the Prince is just a nervous bridegroom." He glared an unmistakable warning at Mischa.

The Prince rose to his full height, a head taller than the other two. "I am hardly that," he said. "But I am eager to see your daughters, Lord Amra." He gestured for the chieftain to lead the way, and the three left the shelter of the canopy for the palanquins that had been removed from the camels and placed in the sand. The sun had shrunk to a sliver of gold along the western dune, its last ribbons lighting the gaily-striped gauze of the tents.

The old gnome scrutinized his grandson. *I wonder if he brought all the diamonds with him.* He rubbed his hands together. *Let's see, that's a hundred for Amra and a thousand for me. This is a good lesson in respect for Mischa.*

The Prince waited with folded arms while Amra went into the first palanquin and led out a young gnomad girl of perhaps fifteen, dressed in a white robe and flimsy veil. The rest of the tribe kept a respectful distance. The girl peeped at the Prince with eyes the color of hazelnut juice. Her soft skin burnished gold, her delicate face was framed by tawny, satin curls. "This is Delyra," said her father and raised an eyebrow. "A tender virgin."

"If you say so," said the Prince. "What else does she have to show me?"

What a cold bastard, thought Amra. He pushed Delyra gently back through the flap of the palanquin.

Amra said, "Sire, these are my daughters, not some cattle. You may be a great man, but have a little respect."

The Prince smiled, genuinely amused. "By all means. Forgive me if I have offended you."

The second daughter had a mischievous face and intelligent, black eyes. Her red hair caught the setting sun as she tossed her head, hinting of the other beauties beneath the golden threads of her desert robes. She lifted her skirt enough to show a plump and dimpled ankle, her laughter like the tinkling of little bells.

Her necklace of tiny silver scimitars with drops of genuine rubies hanging from the tips caught the Prince's eye and he motioned her closer to hook the silver chain with one finger. "What's this?" he asked her father.

Lord Amra said, "Show the Prince your necklace, Saramba."

Carefully, the girl undid the clasp and laid it in Mischa's hand. He lifted his crystal to an eye to examine the stones, turning the necklace this way and that in his palm. The rubies were perfect, each holding an inner flame of red within red, yet disappointment clawed his throat. The gems had no power, no light beyond their inherent beauty. He handed the necklace back to Saramba, with a pointed look at Lord Amra. "Cheap finery is such a bore," he said.

The chieftain narrowed his eyes and, with an air of great dignity, dismissed Saramba, then pivoted on his heel, heading for the last palanquin where he moved the curtained doorway aside. "My daughter, Azali," he said.

The diminutive gnomad girl who stepped onto the sand was no fainting maiden. Her eyes were the color of the sky at moonrise, her hair a mass of blue-black ringlets. Her sureness of movement Mischa recognized as athletic, fueling his excitement. Dressed in a traditional fighting outfit of cotton gauze, dyed in dazzling shades of blue, the tightly bound garment revealed her curvaceous body.

She stood with feet apart and hands on her hips, then tilted her head back and smiled up at Mischa, with dazzling white teeth like her father's.

She reached behind to grab three knives from her waist, then fanned them before her and, without moving her hands, arched her back until her forehead touched the sand. A flick of both wrists sent the knives flying in three directions.

Azali straightened back up with a fluid grace and called out, "Bring them to me." Three tribesmen hurried to her bidding and she held the knives out for Mischa's inspection. At first, he saw nothing out of the ordinary, but upon examination, each blade had a long hair adhering to the edge—split perfectly in half. With a surge of hope, he drew out his crystal and peered at the knives through it. Disappointment twisted his mouth.

"You have quite a talented offspring, Lord Amra. If she is half as skilled in bed as she is with cutlery, I shall be old before my time."

This witticism garnered its share of laughs, but the Prince stopped smiling. He bowed to the company and walked back to his shelter.

Sensing trouble, Rearguard snapped his fingers at the tribal lord and said, "Come. Time to close our bargain." The chieftain obeyed with a lack of enthusiasm that bothered the old gnome even more.

When the three had regained their seats under the canopy, the old gnome produced a curved wooden pipe with a smooth bowl into which he packed fragrant herbs from a pouch in his robe. He made a great ceremony of lighting and presenting it to the chieftain. "To seal the agreement," he said.

Amra drew a polite mouthful of smoke and passed the pipe to Mischa. The Prince dashed it to the sand and scrambled to his feet, shaking with fury.

"Do you think I'm an idiot? You know what I expected from this meeting."

Rearguard rose with Lord Amra, who scowled at Mischa. "I don't care what you expected. I've offered you my flesh and blood. Would you rob me of my wealth as well?"

"I care nothing for wealth," said the Prince, waggling a forefinger at Rearguard. "There's your man if you're looking for someone who loves gold and diamonds. But in return for keeping these lands free of vermin, I require a tribute now and then. A thing of power and rarity—something magical." He paused for breath. "And yes—throw in a maiden or two. I'm a man, after all."

Amra's hands moved to his sword hilts. "From what I can see, you're not a man—you're a monster. I've changed my mind. You can't have my daughters—for any price." He addressed Rearguard. "I won't forget this, Patriarch."

As Amra stalked to his party, the old gnome slid the jeweled dagger from his boot and faced Mischa. "It's about time you were taught a lesson." He tested the point with his finger. "Our people fought and died for the right to rule these lands, and you're throwing away your own legacy. Desert dwellers have old and respected traditions, and yet you grind them under your heel like sand. You'll be sorry, Mischief."

The Prince snorted. "I am master of that castle over there," he pointed to the Manor, the sun's last ray painting the tops of the towers burnt gold, "where I rule over life and death. My power is greater than yours ever was, old man."

"Just as I feared; you are stupid as well as pompous. What battle have you ever fought—you spectator in the arena of life?" He lunged with his dagger, slicing a clean line across the striped burnoose over the Prince's rounded belly.

The Prince raised the crystal to the gnome's face, and a reddish-gold light flared within. "Try to move, Grandfather," he said, chuckling.

Rearguard was horrified, held fast by the piece of quartz. Try as he would, not even an eyebrow might be twitched until the Prince closed his fist over the crystal, and dropped his hand to his side. The gnome staggered in his fright, and Mischa said, "Never forget, Grandfather. You can laugh at me, but don't cross me again."

The muffled sound of hoofbeats on the sand turned the gnomad's head and, with the barest trace of his former pride, he said, "He's leaving, taking those beauties with him. And whatever you do, he'll make sure no one else will trade with you in bride flesh."

Mischa said scornfully, "I have other means of finding women. But you, Rearguard, where else can you get diamonds such as these?" He tossed a handful of gems at the angry gnome and turned for the Manor.

Rearguard watched until the Prince was well inside the walls, then grimacing in distaste, he collected the diamonds and stuffed them into his belt.

The sun was below the dune now, and the old gnome sat down on the sand to watch dusk turn the cobalt sky to star-filled night. The wind began to stir; soon the desert would be cold. He pulled his beard out of his shirt and stroked it, the image of Azali in a backbend a pleasant, if temporary, diversion. *Ah, to be young again, what I could do with a girl like that.* Rearguard looked to the Manor, the lighted windows giving the three towers a multitude of scattered eyes. *That grandson of mine is a fool.*

-24-

SIX STIX paced back and forth, working himself into a state of nervous rage while Obsidian sat in deep meditation, effectively ignoring not only his companion, but their surroundings as well. The dungeon was little more than a garbage bin, a foul hole next to the sewers. The stench was overwhelming, the floor covered with rotten oranges, fermented beans and scraps of roasted desert rat.

Through the latticed metal grate that formed the ceiling of their prison, slivers of light were periodically obscured by the feet of a passing guard. Six Stix wasted no opportunity to hurl insults and imprecations at anyone marching overhead, but the retorts of the guards were little more than a reflex. These were doomed men after all—why bother?

At last, Six Stix dropped to a seat on the cold floor and sighed in dejection. "It's not fair. All my life, I've lived by my wits. Sure, I've stolen a bauble here and there." He glanced at Obsidian's impassive face. "But, damn it all, never anything people would miss—not the sort of thing we've been accused of. I wouldn't take a man's drinking cup. Or the coins from under his very nose. Maybe a nice sword—if I was in danger. Or food." He waited for Obsidian to comment on this self-disclosure.

The monk sat cross-legged in serene contemplation. He could hear Six Stix, and in a distant sort of way, he understood what his friend was saying, but his greater consciousness was roaming free, gathering strength, just as he had been taught to do.

Drawing each breath deep into his belly allowed energy to circulate unhindered up his spine and throughout his body. "Become like the leaf upon the wind," Master Tolimane had said. His childhood had prepared him for just such a teaching. As a boy in the Tuval mines, he had sent his mind far, far away. The brutal beatings…the hunger. He knew how to ride the wind.

As Obsidian prepared himself, he remembered an incident at the monastery, toward the end of his training. The sound of birdsong celebrating sunrise had greeted him when his master led him to one of the inner courtyards. The quiet had soon been shattered by the intonation of a large brass gong and the chanting of deep voices in unison. Sixteen monks stood in a semicircle around a pile of stone slabs, each a foot thick and stacked one atop another.

His master had said, "Listen to the voices of your brothers. They are forging harmony upon harmony, layer upon layer of spirit and oneness. With its power you will break through these stones." As Tolimane spoke, the monks had droned on, building, gathering, strengthening with hypnotic power. When the moment felt right, when he knew without question he should, Obsidian had plunged his fist into the pile of stone slabs, splitting them into two neat halves.

As the chanting hushed into one last reverberating chord, Obsidian had felt the immense power drain from him and ease away into oblivion. He experienced the awe, the humbling reverence anew, just remembering. The scene dissolved in his mind, and Obsidian swallowed, wondering if he could summon that power alone. He recalled the words of Tolimane, "When you call upon Power to vanquish your enemies, your are a little ant before a great throne. Greet the Power. If It is generous, victory will be yours. If not, you may learn a valuable lesson."

Well, Master Power, I greet you. I hope you feel inclined to help a poor monk who has gotten himself into a mess.

"Obsidian, lad," said Six Stix, "have you gone deaf? It's all well and good to do this…meditation, as you call it. But we've got to devise a plan of action. Wake up, will you?" The elf knew better than to touch a monk while he was thinking. He had once seen a fellow make this mistake, and Six's hand went to his own jawbone, as if to be sure he had all his teeth. Loudly, he said, "What do you want to do, lad, sit around and wait for them to execute us?"

Obsidian opened his eyes and silenced Six Stix in a glazed and penetrating stare. "Just a moment," said the monk, holding up one finger. He looked at the grate above, then squatted and took a deep breath.

Six Stix saw the knotting of the monk's powerful muscles. "What—?" began the elf.

Like a coiled spring, Obsidian leapt with his arms upraised and hung by his fingers from the metal latticework. His bare feet dangled in front of Six Stix, but an instant later he kicked and planted them on opposite walls like a mountain climber.

Six Stix smirked. "What are you doing?"

Using his strong feet as a base, Obsidian pressed his massive body upward, and raised the iron ceiling an inch. The sound of metal grating on stone sent a shiver down his back, but he gritted his teeth and raised the latticework higher. "Out, quickly," he ordered Six Stix.

"Right," said the elf, and with superb agility, climbed the slippery wall and inched his body through the narrow opening. He rolled away from the yawning metal crisscross of bars, then got to his feet and grabbed the latticed cover. Lifting up with all his strength, he cursed the pain in his shoulder where the ogre had hit him. The grate did not budge.

Anxious, Six Stix glanced hurriedly about and noticed an old wall sconce that had once held a torch. In this part of the Manor where repairs were not often made, the fitting had been allowed to remain broken. Six Stix pried it away from the wall to use as a lever to open the grating wide enough for Obsidian.

Six Stix caught his breath in admiration as the monk dropped to one side of the pit and, in a mighty leap, propelled himself up and out like a cork. He then grabbed the grate, kicked the broken sconce into the cell below, and lowered the metal ceiling back into place with a heavy *clink*.

They traded grins, and Obsidian said, "You look like a rag picker."

"You smell worse," said Six Stix. "We'll have to get some real clothing. Shall we risk a trip to our rooms?"

Obsidian laughed softly and Six Stix bowed with a flourish, saying, "After you, honored guest."

For the first part of their journey, luck smiled on them. The steep narrow stairs leading up to the guest quarters were not guarded and they passed no one on the ascent to their wing. They tiptoed from doorway to doorway like children playing hide-and-seek, and in passing room after room, caught wisps of conversation amid preparations for the evening meal.

"I wish I had my knives," whispered the monk.

"Don't worry, I have a few things stashed away," said Six Stix.

The door to Obsidian's chamber was ajar, and they froze with their backs against the wall. The monk listened at the crack, but hearing nothing, eased into the room, leaving Six Stix on watch in the hallway.

Obsidian's few belongings were gone, the bedchamber apparently cleaned in anticipation of the next guest. With faint hope, he went to his closet and his heart pounded with gratitude. *The Power smiles again.* On the floor lay his gray, hooded robe. He dropped the filthy velvet curtain that had served as a robe, dressed quickly, and tiptoed out to the hallway.

Six Stix led the way up the hall to his own room, passed his hand across the door, and then shook his head. "Someone's been here, too," he muttered. He pushed open the unlocked door with a growing sense of dread.

The room was a shambles. His traps were sprung, covered with congealed blood, clothing strewn around, and a canteen lay dented on the floor. Cursing, Six Stix surveyed the mess, hands on his hips. Obsidian eased the door shut and whispered, "Quiet, Six."

Six Stix searched the discarded clothing for a leather jerkin and leggings, then added soft boots. He tossed a second pair to Obsidian, but the monk simply grinned and shook his head at the narrow footcovering inches too short for his large feet. The monk did spot a long leather belt, however, that he wrapped around his waist.

Six Stix went to his closet and knelt inside, peering at the floor. Anxiously he ran his finger over the stone surface, and to his excitement, found the tiny scratch of his own making. Working his thumbnail into the crack, he pried the piece of loose mortar free to retreive a small leather bag from the cache beneath, the contents clinking like metal or coins.

He grinned at Obsidian and stuffed the leather pouch into his jerkin, then quickly went to the poster bed and reached inside the pillow. "Dwarf piss," he said, "the weapons are gone." He motioned to Obsidian to follow, then stopped at the doorway long enough to whisper, "I wish I knew where the armory was. Any idea?"

The monk shook his head.

"Well then, we'd better find our own. Without weapons, we'll never get out of here."

Obsidian started down the hall after the elf, then heard the tramp of feet. "Guards," both whispered in unison.

Six Stix ducked into a doorway, the monk on his heels like a shadow, until the footsteps had passed.

Hearing the sound of artless whistling, Six Stix tiptoed to the next doorway, where he saw the back of a female gnome briskly stirring a steaming pot on the hearth.

The promising aroma of the evening meal hit them like a physical blow. The monk inhaled deeply of the tantalizing food as he had often done when fasting, taking the nourishment into his lungs. Six Stix grimaced as hunger clenched his stomach, but motioned for Obsidian to follow with a quick wave of his hand.

The gnome's cheerful whistling and the clatter of the spoon against the iron pot masked their passage to the back stairs that led to the upper floors of the Manor.

"The halls will soon fill with people coming to dinner," whispered the elf. The two adventurers hurried along the corridor until they reached the trap in the hallway. Six Stix leapt over the false floor and Obsidian followed suit. Though he knew he should disapprove, Obsidian could not help being amused at the obscene gesture Six directed toward the hidden chamber below.

The increasingly rich carpets and tapestries betrayed their closeness to the sumptuous room where the Prince had received them. It was easy to be quiet here, the thick carpets muffling their footsteps to mere whispers. When they reached the handsome door, Obsidian looked with dismay at the ornate doorknob. He whispered to Six Stix, "That old gnome used a special key to get in. I can break down the door, but it'll make a lot of noise."

Six Stix shook his head, produced the leather pouch from his jerkin and extracted a small piece of wire, which he inserted into the keyhole. Under Obsidian's keen gaze, he wiggled the metal strand this way and that, but frowned after a few moments, and returned the wire to his pouch. He then withdrew a small, curved metal tool, which he introduced into the keyhole. The tumblers fell into place at a sudden click and the door opened. Six Stix shrugged at Obsidian's hiked brows and said, "Just a little skill I picked up during the war."

They entered the room with grim bravado, Six Stix the first inside. If the Prince and his guards were here, there would be nothing to do but fight.

Their eyes adjusted to the dim light of the full moon rising over the dunes and streaming through the finely wrought windows. It cast a gleaming ripple over the lustrous snowbear carpet, turning the large gong into a luminous disk. They were relieved to see that aside from the furniture, the room was empty.

"Well," said Six Stix. "Let's get reacquainted with our belongings." He hurried to the tapestry at the back of the room, while Obsidian remained near the outer door to listen for visitors.

Six Stix whipped the curtain aside. The vault set halfway up the wall did not appear to have a lock. He ran his hands along the edges, and his fingers traced the door seams, until he found an area where the crack seemed a bit wider, not quite natural. Extracting a thin metal strip from his pouch, he jim-mied the tool into the gap and pressed the other side. Nothing happened. He applied similar pressure to a number of other places, working his tool further into the seam in hopes of prying the latch. Just as he feared the tool would snap, the door popped open. The vault's interior was dark as pitch, but Six Stix swung up inside and waited for his eyes to adjust, the tapestry hiding the entire operation from view.

Obsidian watched the curtain with increasing hopefulness. The moonlight poured over the fur rug, and he was calmed by the almost magical beauty of the evening. The desert would be cold under such a moon, and he shivered in the thin gray robe. *What will happen when we get away from here? Will the Prince send guards to hunt us?* He tried a simple deep-breathing exercise to release his anxiety. Master Tolimane had taught, "Never waste your thoughts on a situation that is yet to be. Save your energy for the present." But another teacher, Master Inota, had said, "Look to the future. Reel it toward you by a thread." The contradictions were confusing. How did one decide which to apply when?

While Obsidian wrestled with the questions, Six Stix scanned the contents of the vault for the teakwood cases in which the Prince had stashed both his and Obsidian's weapons. He opened three of the long boxes before he saw a familiar glint of metal. He raised his jeweled sword and kissed the blade, then thrust it back into its scabbard to grab Obsidian's butterfly knives. He left the safe, dropped to the floor, and girded his weapons, but not before he lifted a matched pair of daggers from another case to add to his collection of arms. One of the pilfered blades he tucked in his belt, the other he slipped into his boot.

Six Stix had just opened a fourth case when Obsidian hissed for quiet. He froze at the muffled conversation taking place in the hallway, just outside the door. Six Stix closed the teakwood cases and returned them to their places, then soundlessly shut the vault door and allowed the curtain to hide it once again. He skittered across the carpet to Obsidian, who slid his harness over his shoulder, the butterfly knives sheathed and ready at the small of his back.

The two melted behind a large tapestry near the front door, listening for footsteps on the padded carpets outside the room. A key turned in the lock and a muscle twitched in Obsidian's cheek. Six Stix pressed himself into the wall, visions of old campaigns flitting through his thoughts. His hand tightened on the hilt of the dagger riding his hip.

-25-

SIX STIX and Obsidian held their breaths when the huge door opened.

Obsidian closed his eyes, training his ears on the scuffles of slippered feet entering the room. He heard six pair of heavily shod feet, and then the flare of torches being lit.

"Make sure we were not followed." The two intruders recognized the chill tones of their host, Prince Mischa. "You two, guard the door."

Footsteps receded, and Six Stix studied slices of the room through a sliver of separation in the tapestry's weave. In the combined illumination of torch and moonlight, details leapt out at him. Three giants stood near an ornate cabinet along the back wall. *Gods, but they're huge. And what do they eat that rots their teeth?* Then, that nasty little Prince strutted back and forth on the lush white carpet, his ringed hands clasped behind his back. His silk robe was woven with golden threads, embroidered with blue-and-silver axes.

Even from a distance, with his tiny field of view, Six Stix admired the paneled back wall carved with fire breathing dragons and other hideous reptiles. A fantastic stream gushed into the mouth of a sand serpent, while a desert caravan made its way over the dunes beyond. The wood was inlaid with fine jewels that winked behind the Prince as he paced.

"Turn your backs," said Mischa to the three giants. Six Stix watched the Prince press the panel between the emerald eyes of the green dragon with his left hand, then with his right, he pressed the nearest tooth of the sand serpent. To Six's delight, a whole section of panel slid open with a soft whir. The Prince entered the secret chamber behind the burly guards, who waited impassively.

Oh, glory, thought Six Stix. *That must be the main treasure vault. I knew it was around here somewhere.*

Obsidian and Six Stix remained immobile for what seemed like an age, listening to the Prince poke around in his treasure room. The monk carefully lifted first one foot and then the other, to ease his cramped legs. When Six's shoulder began to ache, he wondered, *What was I trying to prove, lifting that heavy grate?*

From time to time, the Prince muttered a curse that echoed about the vaulted chamber before drifting into the room. "One hundred forty-nine, one hundred-fifty—another bag missing. That rascal, wait until I get my hands on him…Ah, here it is—my demongaze."

Demongaze? Obsidian looked at Six Stix, who shrugged. A knock on the massive door startled both.

"Who's there?" shouted a guard, displaying a slight tribal accent.

"It is I—Squint Nose, steward of the East Wing," piped the answer.

Six Stix turned his head toward the door, but a giant blocked his view.

"The Prince is busy and can't be disturbed," said the guard, holding a large, spiked polearm.

The reply resembled a squeaking mouse. "His Highness *does* want to be disturbed. He said to report to him no matter what time it was…if you don't let me in, you'll be sorry."

Six Stix watched the giant swagger to the vault and hail the Prince, "Sire, pardon the interruption, but there's a steward in the hallway. Should we let him come in?"

"Who?" called the Prince.

"He says he is Squint Nose," replied the guard.

"Admit him."

A small, nervous-looking gnome dressed in a faded purple uniform hurried with small steps past Six Stix's hiding place to the vault at the back of the room. "Sire…your Highness…" he said between gasps for air.

"What is it?" said the Prince, coming out of the vault and trying to block the gnome's view of the treasure room.

"The dark Princess has rung the bell." The little gnome's blue eyes were feverish with self-importance. "You said to let you know immediately." Six Stix and Obsidian hung on every word.

"At last," proclaimed the Prince. "Tell the captain of my guard to have five of his strongest meet me at her door. Hurry, now. Go." He gave the gnome a shove and then kicked him in the seat to put him on the run.

At the malignant inflections in the Prince's words, Obsidian thought, *I feel sorry for this Princess.*

Six Stix watched the red-faced gnome scurry from the room, then turned his attention back to the vault where Mischa stood in the entry, rubbing his hands.

"What are your orders, Sire?" asked a giant.

The Prince displayed a most evil grin and said, "I plan to treat her well, if she behaves. And if she fails me," his leer swept the room, "well, there are those in the dungeon who would fancy a treat. To them, she'd just be a tasty morsel of used bride-meat ..." He gave a wicked laugh and disappeared inside the vault.

Obsidian's nostrils flared in outrage and his blood raced. Six Stix strained to see from his vantage point behind the curtain, his shoulder growing more painful by the minute. He wished the Prince would hurry up.

As if he'd read Six Stix's mind, Mishca left his treasure vault and casually touched the golden dragon between the eyes with his left hand and the peak of the farthest mountain with his right. The secret panel swung shut with the same gliding whir as before.

Six Stix sighed audibly and Obsidian pinched him. Then Six saw the Prince thrust what looked like a child's top into his waistcoat. In the other hand he carried a silver stick or maybe a wand, then moved out of sight.

"I don't trust that scoundrel," said the Prince, "the insufferable little tyrant. Who knows what else might be missing? Mustadd, defend this chamber well while I am gone. Report to me if anyone enters—anyone, you hear?"

There was a mumbled, "Yes, Sire," as the smallest of the giants trudged to the door.

The Prince walked into Six Stix's line of sight and said to a second bearded giant with folded arms who leaned down to listen, "She will be a captivating spider to preside over my web, eh Nordoom?" He laughed hideously and added, "Or, alas, maybe just another insect?"

Obsidian flushed with anger. *I must warn the Princess.* He strove to tame his flaring temper by a series of slow breathing exercises that only made him feel worse.

Six Stix thought, *Poor lass. I've seen men do monstrous things to women, but our host is a different sort of fiend, judging from his harem.* He tried to get a better look at the item the Prince carried, that silver stick or wand carved with some sort of runic designs.

The guards following shielded the Prince from view, then the heavy door slammed.

Six Stix peered around the curtain to see torches still lit. Leaning beside the door, a scimitar cradled in his arms, was the twelve foot giant named Mustadd. He wore padded, scaled armor made of a tough hide. His clothing was coated in a fine dust, and his skin was cracked and leathery from the desert. On his back was a folded pack.

As Six Stix speculated on the pack's contents, he inadvertently riffled the curtain. Noticing the movement, Mustadd hefted his scimitar and, frowning, advanced on the tapestry.

When the giant was almost upon him, Six Stix stepped clear of the curtain and drew his ruby-throated sword. The blade sang as he whipped it back and forth. The elf growled, baring his teeth. His pointed ears twitched.

In reply, his adversary merely bared his chipped and broken teeth in a grin, the two front ones blackened.

"Successful with the ladies, eh?" said Six Stix.

Obsidian relieved his butterfly knives of their sheaths and he, too, stepped from behind the curtain.

Mustadd's eyes showed momentary surprise, then he attacked Six Stix with fury, his scimitar slicing the elf's jerkin open with a vicious blow. "Die, intruder," bellowed the giant in his deep voice.

The elf resisted the urge to look down and slit the giant's forearm, exposing skin and muscle, blood and bone. "Was your mother a tree?" he taunted.

Inarticulate with rage, Mustadd raised his scimitar in one hand, then struck the elf's injured shoulder with the other fist. Six heard a 'pop' and his shoulder screamed with pain as he sailed through the air. The edge of a table opened a ragged cut in his forehead and blood temporarily blinded him.

Obsidian planted his foot in Mustadd's midsection, forcing the giant to drop his weapon, then knocked the giant's knees out from under him with the blunt edges of his butterfly knives. With his opponent at eye level, Obsidian made quick work of the altercation by slapping the hilt of his knife against the giant's temple. Mustadd hit the floor like a boulder.

"Is he dead?" asked the elf.

"No, but he'll lie still for awhile," said Obsidian.

Cupping his own forehead to cover the cut, Six Stix lurched to his feet. "Just how did you do that?" he asked.

"It's called a pressure point. I know three others, but I've never used them in battle." Obsidian approached Six Stix eagerly, "Shall I demonstrate?"

The elf shrank back. "Some other time, maybe."

"What's wrong with your shoulder?" asked Obsidian. "I know a little healing. Let me help."

Six Stix allowed Obsidian to perform the painful process of realignment, unable to stifle a cry when the joint popped back into place. When Obsidian tried to examine the cut on his forehead, Six Stix brushed him away. "It's just a scratch, don't bother." Still protecting the cut with his hand, he wrestled the giant's pack from under him and rummaged inside.

He put aside several pieces of stout rope for some dried meat that smelled too good to resist. He broke the jerky in half and bit into it, then offered some to Obsidian, who saved it in his belt.

Six Stix then found five old gold coins and a length of white cloth, a strip of which he used to bandage the cut on his head.

Obsidian examined the wound on the giant's forearm, determined that it was bleeding cleanly, and bound it with some of the same cloth.

Six Stix turned his back on Obsidian in order to examine the coins. Worn with use, each was decorated with two wavy lines, the universal symbol for water. *That Prince will never miss them.*

Obsidian snatched the rope and said, "I'll bind his hands and feet—you gag him with that." He pointed to the remnant of cloth.

Six Stix faced him and drew his bastard sword. "Don't be soft, boy. We'd be fools to leave him alive."

"No." Obsidian unsheathed his knives. "I'll not allow you to kill him while he lies here undefended."

"Do you mean to say, you'd fight me—a friend—for the miserable life of an enemy?"

Obsidian rocked back on his heels. "Six Stix, real friendship can't exist without respect. Your age and experience are far beyond mine, it's true. But you must understand that I have taken certain vows, and they come first."

Six Stix sighed. "I see you're going to be hardheaded about this. But I'll wager you'll regret it." He sheathed his sword. "We have a saying in the military, you know. 'Vows are made to be broken.'" Obsidian opened his mouth to interrupt, stopped by Six's upraised hand. "I know. They're just words to you now, but experience may tell a different tale."

Obsidian sheathed his knives, retrieved the rope, and while he bound and gagged the giant, Six Stix methodically searched his body. "Where are your maps and provisions, old fellow?" He caught Obsidian's eye and said, "This brute has next to nothing of value. Says something for the way his people live, lad. Take note of it, for we may need such knowledge later. From what I can see, he hasn't been with the Prince long."

When Obsidian finished, he rose and started toward the door, but Six Stix grabbed him by the sleeve. "Wait a minute, boy. I have business in the back room." The elf's head-wound had bled into the bandage, a grisly sight.

"We have our weapons, Six," said Obsidian. "Now, we've got to save the Princess."

"Oh, we do, do we? This is no time to be romantic." Without waiting for an answer, Six Stix hurried to the back of the chamber, placed one finger between the emerald eyes of the green dragon, another on the tooth of the sand serpent, and the secret panel slid open.

"And just how did you do that?" asked Obsidian, not sure he wanted to know.

Six Stix laughed on his way inside the chamber, then held his breath in awe. Before him were open caskets overflowing with fine jewels and loose gems amid tapestries, vases, portraits, and tubs of gold and silver coins. Some smaller, locked wooden chests lined the far wall.

While Obsidian weighed ethics versus friendship, Six Stix investigated, finally emerging from the vault. He placed one finger on the carved gold dragon and another on a distant mountain peak, and the panel slid back into place.

With a shrug, the elf said, "Not much to see, really. The usual odds and ends." He walked with a decided jingle of metal.

Obsidian also noticed that Six Stix had replaced his soiled bandage with a headband of pale green, brocaded silk. He frowned at the elf. "I'm no thief even if you are. I refuse to associate with you if you're going to steal."

Six Stix searched the young man's face. "Look," he said patiently, "I'm an old campaigner and you're just a young buck. Rules aren't everything, Obsidian. Your teachers aren't here now—I am. Trust me and I'll keep you out of trouble."

Though unconvinced, Obsidian sensed his friend's sincerity. Six Stix continued, "As for rescuing some wench, you don't know what a mistake that would be. The thing for us to do is to collect our supplies and get out of here."

Obsidian stiffened his spine. "Now, look," he said, "if you want to be a rogue and an unfeeling scoundrel, go ahead. Leave if you will. I have a duty to uphold the teachings of my order."

Six Stix stared at the youth, who stared right back, then said finally, "Very well, lad, if it means that much to you. No doubt it will be an adventure." *There might even be money in it.* He vaguely recalled that dark elves traded on a silver standard. He made a mental note to find out more about that.

Obsidian scouted the hallway and Six Stix took a last look at the trussed guard whose oozing wound had stained red the lustrous carpet.

"I ought to dispatch you...that's the general rule. You're lucky I'm in such sentimental company." Shaking his head, he nearly tripped over Obsidian, who had dropped to all fours.

In the hallway, Obsidian pressed his ear to the floor and despite the thick carpet he could hear the Prince's guards tramping down the corridor to the west. He pointed in that direction, and Six Stix nodded, allowing the young monk to lead as they proceeded single file, their weapons ready.

Six Stix threw a glance behind every few minutes. *What the lad hasn't learned yet is that every princess isn't beautiful—or even rich. And the fact that she's a woman makes her dangerous.* His aching shoulder put him in a bad humor. He reached in his pocket to keep the coins from jingling, letting their presence soothe his frayed nerves.

-26-

IN THE east tower of the Manor, Tiala sat in the large chair before the fireplace, her travel-harp in her lap. She looked around her room, satisfied with the small group that had come together a couple of hours before midnight as planned.

Several minutes had passed since Tiala had tugged the bell cord over the mantel. Now that her vigil had ended, she hoped her business with the Prince could be settled, and her party would soon be traveling by the light of a full moon over the cool desert. Resigned to that part of it, her trek would be no less than a nightmare journey.

She noted the others wore traveling garb in muted colors to better blend with the desert. Her own cloak was a dull green, but that couldn't be helped, its triple-thickness all she had to protect her during the dangerous hours of sunlight.

She glanced at Embaza, seated at the game table. He had stowed his midnight blue cloak into his saddlebags for another robe, the color of the little gray stones that flecked the dunes. It looked almost as thick as Tiala's and she wondered why. *He's a blue elf—he doesn't need protection. But there's something…fragile about him…and attractive. Maybe it's his air of mystery. Is that what draws me to him? I wish I knew.*

Seated on the floor near Tiala's feet, Polah wanted to be as close to the dark elf as she could, as if in this way she might be nearer the answers to her own deepest questions. She wore a soft shirt under her light brown cloak. The owl's scratches had not completely healed, a fact that worried her. Unbeknownst to Polah, it worried the General, too.

Gudrun had been watching the shape-changer, and noticed her shallow breathing. She also knew the rigors of the trip they faced and the strength they would need to make the crossing. *What if the woman turns into a fox again? Will she need to hunt? Is she strong enough?* It was one more thing to worry about. Gudrun had put on a thin hide tunic that covered her fine mail shirt. Her leggings and boots were well worn to a nondescript hue. Her unassuming garb was her own mark of professionalism. She leaned on the back of Tiala's chair, her pack on the floor behind it.

Tiala experienced her first real sense of relief. *Now we can truly begin.* She took up the small harp and her fingers roamed the strings at random, sending peals of harmony through the room and into the hallway beyond. For the first time since she'd arrived, she felt optimistic. *I will rescue my sisters and my dear land.*

She smiled, remembering when she'd gotten this harp. How happy and proud she'd been. Her mother had told her, "This is a travel-harp, Tiala. Although you're very young for such an adult gift, I think you'll treat it well."

She admired the graceful curves of its triangular shape. Black poppies in bloom decorated the blue cherrywood. The intricate golden pegs formed five perfect triangles strung with fifteen silver wires. *Fifteen, the lowest number of the bardic harps.* If she were accepted as a beginning bard, she would learn to master this and then the talking harp, a twenty-four stringed instrument. There were thirteen more harps, but she didn't know all their names. *So many instruments to learn. Drums and flutes, pipes and mandolins...* As her nimble fingers plucked the strings, she dreamed of her future.

At Tiala's feet, Polah closed her eyes, entranced by the music that evoked visions of the underground. *What a lovely place it must be.* With each shining note that fell from the harp, she imagined swirls of vibrant colors floating in a velvety blackness that turned to silver foxes leaping into space.

The General leaned on the back of the stuffed chair, listening to Tiala play, her mind less on the music than the near future. *Soon I will be home again. I wonder if I'll see my daughter, 'Leece, how she has been, if she's married now, or traveling.* She glanced at the wizard from time to time. Embaza sat very still in the chair by the game table, staring into space. *He has a dark look about him,* she thought. *Not like a blue elf at all. I wonder if he's of mixed blood. I'm not surprised no one's asked him about it. What a dangerous-looking fellow. It's the quiet ones you have to watch out for. He may have a temper I'll need to tame.*

For his part, Embaza was far away, the music triggering a host of unfamiliar feelings. He glanced at Tiala, and something about her harp tugged at his memory. *Have I seen that instrument before?* He noticed the black poppies painted along the cherrywood. *Poppies,* he thought. *Black poppies. For easing a woman's labor and inducing sleep.* His eyes swiveled left and right. *Now, where did I learn that? Not at the university.* The music apparently triggered some deeper remembrance than his conscious mind might readily access.

As if a membrane in his mind opened, his imagination flooded his thoughts with flowers, the colors intense, deep and vibrant. He started and sat forward in his chair at an image that might have been his father. The others were intent on Tiala's playing, but Embaza stared at the wall as if seeing a ghost. *Father...*

This *was* a childhood memory, he reckoned, submerged until now. Before him was an arresting dark-elven wizard, lines of power and wisdom etched into the crevices of his face. His kind, green eyes were penetrating and hypnotic. Embaza felt the sting of tears. *Why did you abandon me?* The old hurt flared within him, a hurt he thought he had buried in childhood.

The General's attention had strayed back to Polah, whose rapt expression seemed almost spiritual. *The fox-woman is attracted to the music.* Gudrun rubbed her bearded chin. *That could be useful. It'll make her more protective. I wonder how far she'll go in that protection, though.* She inhaled deeply. *At least, the Alvarran will have no complaints about my loyalty. It's high time I left the employ of this unstable Prince. Besides, she is of the deepworld, a sister in darkness. If all elves were so civilized, the war would never have started.*

Gudrun thought back to the early days when she had first come to the Manor. The Seven Years War had just ended, and many of her kind had needed something to soothe a battered morale.

Mischa...they're calling him Misfit now in the barracks. He's been losing their respect for a long while. Is it the magic? Maybe he's playing with things he doesn't understand. One should leave magic to the gods. That's what the gnomes say and they ought to know. Now, there's a proud old race who knows better than to dabble with the supernatural.

She looked down with affection at the hilt of her sword, its beauty and power hidden within the scarred and humble ox-hide sheath. *The forger who made this was found worthy. If he had not been so blessed, it might have had a sharper blade, but never a soul.*

The sweet notes of the harp stopped at three rapid knocks on the door. A harsh voice shouted, "It's Prince Mischa. Open up." Gudrun touched the hilt of her sword. Several days had come and gone since last she had seen the Prince. He sounded more disturbed than ever.

Tiala left the chair and trembled with excitement, suppressing her irritation with this insolent male. She slipped the travel-harp back into her baggage and, assuming a regal dignity, crossed the room to open the door.

The little man strode in with a proprietary air, ignoring the occupants for a look about the room as if he wanted to be sure the furniture had not been damaged.

Tiala glanced at Gudrun, who raised her eyebrows to reassure her that she cared not for him and his affectations. She hoped the future Nightwing had no doubts where her loyalties now lay.

The Prince snapped his fingers and beckoned to one of his giants who was forced to stoop to enter the room. More giants could be seen standing at attention in the hallway, their weapons held before them.

Polah's eyes widened, Gudrun's sword arm twitched, and Tiala's muscles knotted in readiness for flight or battle.

The Prince pointed to the chair opposite Embaza and the giant sat down, squeezing his great bulk into the man-sized chair. The gameboard gleamed on the table between the giant and the wizard, and the Prince twirled the silver muskrat queen between his fingers. He hiked his pale brows at Embaza's contemptuous scowl.

Tiala wasted no time in planting herself firmly in front of the Prince. Two feet taller, she towered over him. "Prince Mischa," she said, deliberately speaking in Terrargian versus the elven she knew he understood. "My business is finished. And these adventurers are leaving with me. Are you ready to name your price for my stay here?"

The Prince smiled, and Tiala glimpsed the guile that lay beneath his charm. "So-o-o," he said, examining the muskrat piece in his hand, "the Nightwing's daughter is tired of my hospitality?"

Tiala suppressed her annoyance. "My stay has been uneventful. Your accommodations are comfortable, and I am grateful to you. Name your price in gold, and I will send for a legion of elves to transport it here to you."

"Oh," said the Prince, feigning a pout, "but why must you leave so soon?" He looked up at Tiala with an almost maniacal boyishness. "I have grown fond of you." The threat in his voice was unmistakable. As if to underline it, he dropped the silver muskrat piece to the carpet and kicked it under the table.

Polah's black eyes flashed with anger and she moved to the side of her new mistress.

Tiala was not used to being disobeyed. She eyed the giants in the hallway and considered her options, hoping the Prince would betray some weakness she could exploit.

The Prince regarded Polah with a haughty smirk, the redhead much nearer his own height. "And you, my foxy beauty," he said, satisfied with her angry flush, "don't be so modest." He licked his lips. "I would very much like to have your company awhile longer."

Lifting her chin, Polah said, "I'm sorry, Your Highness, but we must be leaving you. We have urgent business elsewhere."

In answer, Mischa strode for the open door, beckoned the other four guards to enter, then stared at the General. "Even you, my loyal retainer? Are you going to desert me after we've had such a long and pleasant association?"

The Prince's voice carried a timbre of insanity Gudrun had never heard before. Whether from magic or some rare disease, he was changed from the man she used to know. "Your Highness," she said with a formal bow, "I have at times found you to be a fair and generous employer. But, being an adventurer at heart, I am moved to pity by this woman's tale and cannot in all good conscience abandon her."

"My, my," mocked the Prince, "such a long speech for an uneducated cow from the burrows."

The General allowed a deep frown to knit her brows. "It's barrows."

His patience at an end, Mischa rubbed his hands and said, "Let me outline the plan, and then we can get down to business, eh?" Without waiting for an answer, he pointed to the scowling Tiala. "You aspire to be a minstrel, I suppose."

Her eyes flashed, but she held her tongue.

"Oh, don't bother to deny it, everyone on this floor has heard your paltry attempts at melody," said the Prince. "So why not play a real instrument?" He withdrew the exquisite silver flute from beneath his coat and offered it to the dark elf.

Tiala's anger washed away and her emerald eyes widened. *The Glammalee.* She sensed its power the moment she saw it, and her hands opened to take the ancient instrument in her quivering fingers. "But—where did you get this? It is a thing of legend."

"So they say. And I have been waiting for just the right person to play it."

"What is it, my Lady?" asked Gudrun.

Mischa folded his arms. "Tell them."

Tiala took a breath and scanned her comrades' faces in turn.

"The Glammalee is the legendary flute made by the first elves, the children of those who mated with the fairie folk. It was said they placed all song into it—the sound of the wind, the ripple of the streams, the call of each forest creature. Then they threw it into the Valley of Mist and said that only a bard—a bard of great ability would be able to find and play it."

"And what else? Tell the rest," urged the Prince, a cunning gleam in his eye.

"There is a prophecy that someday it will be found and played again. And on that day, the ancient elves and fairies will return to dance in the Valley of Mist."

"Yes, yes—finish it," snapped Mischa impatiently.

Tiala ignored the Prince at the shudder that nearly wilted her. "Whoever hears the playing of the flute will live forever."

"There, now," said the Prince, his sweeping gaze seeking confirmation. "You hear the Alvarran? We all want her to play the flute—don't we?"

"No," said Tiala resolutely. "I won't play it. I am no great bard, and I will not be responsible for the consequences."

Mischa scowled. The General moved forward, stopped from advancing by the arm of a giant. Embaza reached into his robe for a ball of wax, which he surreptitiously began to shape, smiling all the while at the giant sitting like a stone across the gametable from him.

Two giants took up positions directly behind Tiala and Polah, heightening the tension in the room. One of the giants crossed his fingers in the warding sign behind Tiala's back. The remaining giant stayed by the door.

"Well, my lovely Nightwing," said Mischa, "that is a great shame. For you see, that's the only little thing I wanted. That's my price."

"But, surely you understand," said Tiala. "I could bring great harm to you all if I played the Glammalee."

"What do you mean?" asked Polah.

"The secret side of the story is this. Only a real bard—and one of great renown—can play the flute without catastrophe. All true bardic instruments, especially one as old and valuable as this, are protected by deep magic from unskilled hands." She glanced at the Prince. "Who knows what might happen? We could all drop dead—or be turned into butterflies."

"Enough," shouted the Prince, holding up his hand. "Give me back that flute."

"This artifact belongs to the elven people. Where did you get it, anyway?" Tiala cried, tightening her grip on the Glammalee.

"A gift from the King of Amascera," retorted the Prince. "For services rendered."

Certain he was lying, Tiala replied, "He had no right to give it to you. I'll take it to my people in Alvarra, to be revered and admired by many, as it should be."

"Nonsense," snapped the Prince, "I'll keep it and wait for the bard of great renown. I warn you, Alvarran, I'm not a man to be trifled with." The giant behind her moved closer.

She glanced at the General, heartened when the dwarf gave her an almost imperceptible nod.

Yes, thought Gudrun, *we'll find a way to get it back, my Lady.*

Tiala narrowed her eyes and handed Mischa the flute, her voice the embodiment of command as befitted the heir to the Nightwing's throne. "So, let me ask again, Prince. What price will you require for the use of this room?"

Mischa adopted the look of a man worried and confused. He would have been comical had he not been so sinister. "I've got it," he said and snapped his fingers twice. The giants behind Tiala and Polah grabbed them both by the arms, the giant with the General pinning her arms behind her back.

The fourth giant knocked over the gameboard, scattering the gleaming pieces across the rich blue carpet like stars across a night sky. In an instant, he had Embaza by the throat, lifting him to his feet, and the wizard thrust a needle into the wax. The giant doubled over, clutching his stomach in pain, and Embaza's fall caused him to lose the wax, which rolled out of reach under a chair. Before he could take a breath, a new set of strong arms had imprisoned him, bringing him to his feet.

The Prince drew himself up to his full height of three-and-a-half feet. "Dear lady," he said to Tiala, "I have an alternative plan that is sure to please you, for I find myself in the unhappy state of having no female counterpart—no loving wife to keep my fires burning on a lonely desert night."

Tiala stood open-mouthed, too appalled for words.

"What a pity," cried a voice from the hallway, and into the room leapt a very large man dressed in a gray robe, who whirled about, his glittering blades slicing the air in an intricate series of moves. He saw the dark-elven Tiala first. *Is that beauty the Princess?*

Startled by Obsidian's entrance, the giants redoubled their holds on their captives. The Prince backpedaled into a purple brocade chair, sitting down with a thump.

Near the door, the giant who held the General suddenly collapsed, and Gudrun turned in time to see a powerfully-built blue elf in his late prime, dressed in leather armor and wielding a jewelled sword. A distinctive scar on one cheek stood out amidst the sundry others lining his face.

"You," she cried, drawing her sword. "Forget trying to save *me*. You're going to die right here, Knave."

"Bitch," spat the elf, "you're the one who deserves death." They circled each other, ignoring everything else, even after the monk shouted, "Six Stix. We're here to save the Princess."

"Spirit of Night," cried Tiala in utter astonishment. "Who *are* these people?"

-27-

OBSIDIAN SLASHED and leapt around the room, hoping to keep the giants distracted long enough to form some sort of escape plan. He stole the occasional glance at Six Stix, confused by the elf's battle with their ally, the dwarf. Above all, the monk was determined not to kill. He must not fail his teachers.

Obsidian saw the way the giants watched him. *They're impressed with my form. That's odd—we don't even use this one for fighting. It's our morning dance.*

While the giants had eyes only for the dancing monk, Embaza managed to slip one arm free of the iron grasp. Bending his fingers nearly to his wrist, he slid one of his needles out of his sleeve. When he had a good grip on it, he thrust the needle as deeply as he could into the thick, ropy thigh of the guard behind him.

Leaving the guard hopping with pain, Embaza snatched the embedded sliver out of his skin and then snaked between fighters, carefully avoiding the whirling monk. He slid to his knees in front of Mischa seated in the purple chair, opened the neck of his robe to reveal the necklace of fire gems, and focused a deep, hypnotic stare on the Prince.

But Mischa was sensitive to magic, and had seen Embaza before. He knew better than to look into those eyes—or at that necklace—and with great difficulty, controlled his gaze. Fingers shaking, the Prince reached into his pocket for the sphere of metal with holes cut into the sides. Suspending it by the piece of copper wire soldered at its top, Mischa flicked the object with a pudgy finger into a slow spin, directly in front of Embaza's face.

"This is the demongaze," said the Prince softly. "The sphere of pain."

The wizard ignored him, concentrating instead on the ball of wax in his hands that he had already fashioned into a crude representation of the Prince. Sliding yet another needle from his sleeve, he probed the waxen image.

Mischa yelped at the blazing fire burning in his stomach and dropped the metal orb to his lap, his grandfather's words taunting him. *What battle have you ever fought?* Gritting his teeth, he grasped the demongaze again and twirled it before Embaza's eyes.

If it was magic, Embaza was interested, and against his better judgment, he took the Prince's bait. Two things occurred, one after another. First, in a quick study of its manufacture, he recognized how the demongaze worked, and then the soles of his feet seemed to be peeling right off. He began his antidote: *Pain is good...*

With a silent prayer to her dead sister, Tiala stomped on her guard's instep, and momentarily freed, pivoted and leapt on his back. The guard reached behind and got nothing but thin air, then dodged back back and forth to throw her off. She kicked him without mercy while raining a barrage of well-aimed blows up and down his spine. The padded armor was thick, however, as she discovered when she bit into it with her teeth.

The giant lurched forward, bent abruptly, and Tiala fought to keep her balance. He shot to his full height, shaking the polearm he had plucked unnoticed from the floor, and roared, "Insect. Ready your wings—you're going to fly." He shook himself violently, but Tiala hung on.

Meanwhile, Polah had sunk her sharp teeth into her captor's hand. He brought his fist down on the back of her neck, dropping her to her knees, but she grabbed his huge calves and curled tight around his legs.

The giant flexed his legs as if to take a step and when that didn't shake the squirming, clinging Polah, he went for the club he'd left at his feet. He swung the huge weapon clumsily about his head and brought it down, narrowly missing her, but rather connecting with his own knee. Howling with fury, he staggered and nearly fell, raising the club for a second try.

Obsidian decided the giant's fate with a leap and a solid kick to the chin that slammed him back to the wall and sent Polah rolling out of the way.

The giant recovered himself quickly and lunged at Obsidian, his club forgotten. Obsidian's butterfly knives flashed back and forth, creating a diversion for his feet to strike blows at the waist, ears, insteps and back of the neck. The giant responded too slowly, his fist sailing past Obsidian into a red swan figurine. Splinters of glass exploded in all directions, littering the dark blue rug with a fine scarlet spray.

Embaza was feeling pain in a hundred places. If he hadn't known better, he could have sworn his face had been sliced to ribbons, his eyes gouged out, his knees mashed into pulp, his ears ripped to shreds, and every muscle and joint an exquisite agony.

In her corner under the couch, Polah, too, suffered a searing pain in the soles of her feet. She grabbed them, gasping, as the pain traveled up, gnawing her ankles, excoriating her calves and ripping into her thighs. She watched Embaza in horror, and cursed the bond uniting them.

The Prince thrilled to the terror—terror such as he had never known before while the necklace held him in thrall. Even as the brilliance of its pale blue light stung his heart and lungs with beauty, he cringed at the sensation of wet knives carving his entrails. *I must have it,* he vowed.

One of the giants limped toward Embaza, thinking, *this coward stuck me with a needle.*

Polah cried out a warning as the giant raised his clasped hands above Embaza's head and brought them down. The wizard never knew what hit him. The torment riddling his body ceased.

In that same moment, Polah went slack. The wounds on her back stung with an inner fire. *Embaza?* She continuously probed with her mind, but heard only the thumping of her own heart. Her eyes swept the room, registering the various battles around her. Embaza lay motionless at the foot of the Prince's chair. She tried to send her healing ability toward him. Her mouth formed his name, but no sound could she force past her lips. Tears stung her eyes and she battled an inner fatigue. All she wanted to do was sleep.

The Prince dropped the demongaze in his lap and breathed a sigh of relief. He looked down at the device, which had seemed of little use against the wizard. "Worthless piece of trivia," he muttered, tossing it under the chair.

He bent over for the wizard's necklace, gleaming on his neck. *Here's the tool worthy of my talents.* But the moment he touched the necklace, his fingers burned with a blue-hot fire. "Ow," he cried, sucking the injured digits. One look at his scorched flesh made him nauseous. The first two fingers of his right hand were almost welded together with a melting black crust.

"Get him out of my sight," ordered Mischa.

The giant leaned over and grabbed a fistful of Embaza's long black hair, bringing his face closer. There was barely any sign of life, and he let the fine head drop to the floor with a thud. Using his foot, he rolled the wizard's inert body to the edge of the room and turned to see where else he might lend his efforts.

Polah lay dazed in her corner. Tiala clung to her assailant's back. The giant's brother grabbed the dark elf from behind and tossed her to the floor. After a few disoriented moments, she scrambled up and launched herself anew at the giant's back.

Near the door, Gudrun and Six Stix circled each other, swapping taunts and oaths. Wary of the other's ability, neither had struck a blow. As Gudrun feinted with her sword, Six Stix parried and accidentally sliced off a lock of her hair.

"Now, you truly insult me, slime," Gudrun cried. "I will avenge my sisters once and for all."

She swung her sword, cutting his leather waist band an inch deep, and Six Stix stabbed her in the chest, the chain mail under her jerkin preventing his sword from taking her life. Her boot slammed into his armpit and he taunted, "Filthy dwarves fight dirty wars."

Gudrun spat in his face, Six Stix spat back and they resumed circling one another in a ritualistic exercise of defiance.

At last, Obsidian wore down his opponent, rendering the giant unconscious by a well-placed heel to the solar plexus, another pressure point. *Now to help Six Stix,* he thought, but when he tried to intervene, the elf shouted, "Leave us alone!"

"But—."

"This is my fight," bellowed Six Stix and Obsidian backed away. When he saw a second giant advancing on Tiala, he dashed to her aid, neutralizing the guard with a swift kick to the back of the head. Although he had been warned about dark elves, this one was a princess. She didn't look evil...

Obsidian leapt on the back of the giant pinning Tiala. She wrestled valiantly, squirming in her captor's substantial arms, giving the monk enough time to reach around the massive neck and press his fingers against the windpipe.

The Prince slid a letter opener from his boot, a sharp dagger-like gift received in lieu of payment for a night in his harem—which reminded him: he needed this princess.

He threw the opener as hard as he could, his wayward aim certain to miss the open space beneath the monk's knife harness, but by chance the giant staggered, lurching forward for lack of air. Obsidian stiffened, arched and thudded on the floor, the sharp blade embedded in his back just where the Prince intended.

Tiala whirled into the arms of the giant, who was still gasping for breath.

The Prince left the purple chair to retrieve his letter opener, fascinated by the blood spurting from the wound.

Tiala cried out, "Don't let him bleed to death."

"But that's the whole idea," said the Prince and looked around. "Where is the fox cub?"

Polah's black eyes snapped open at the evil voice. A giant hoisted her up by the hair. She winced and clawed his hands, then tried to growl. *Why can't I change when I wish to?*

The Prince laughed. "Such animal spirit is good in a concubine." Now that he had the women, he was content. He said to Tiala, "My talented wench, you *will* play the flute, whether you want to or not."

The dark elf kept her head. "I'm no upworld maiden to be toyed with," she said. "You have no idea the danger you are in if you try to hold me here. My mother will send..." *Who could she send?*

"Oh, yes, your mother—who is *dying.*" The Prince laughed again.

Tiala was silent. *The priestesses are all busy watching over her. And Eleppon hasn't had much experience in commanding troops. Could she make it across the desert? Oh, no, please—it must not come to that.*

The Prince pointed to Obsidian's inert body and said to Tiala, "I can be merciful. Bind his wounds. I want to see him fight again in the arena."

She tore a strip of fabric from her under-tunic and wrapped it around the monk's massive chest, hurrying in case the Prince changed his mind. When she was done, the guard holding Polah by the hair hefted the monk with one arm and slung him over his shoulder like a sack.

Tiala wondered briefly what brought the giants here. *It can't be pleasant working for such a worm.* Her guard reached out with vise-like fingers and held Tiala fast, but averted his head and whispered something unintelligible.

Tiala sensed dark elf superstition—his fear was contagious—and felt defiled by it.

The Prince took a look at the General. *What a great fighter. Too bad she defected.* She and Six Stix were still exchanging light blows in their ritual, a contest Mischa found boring after his own skirmish with death.

He nudged the giant holding Tiala by the arm and muttered, "Gaf, do you fancy a roll with the bearded lady?" The giant stared as if he was crazy, and Mischa laughed. "Come on," he said, "we'll leave them."

He started to lead his party past the two fighters when another giant stumbled into the room. He had a bloody rag tied around his forearm.

"Mustadd," cried the Prince. "What happened to you?"

Ignoring the Prince, Mustadd stepped between Six Stix and Gudrun, knocking the dwarf into the fireplace. As she fell, her sword swept the mantelpiece and a slender crystal vase crashed to the floor with a peal of perfect clarity.

Mischa was intent on the altercation between Mustadd and Six Stix.

Six Stix ducked the giant's blow and said, "You're the last person I wanted to see. I knew I should have silenced you when I had the chance." He glanced at the monk, who moaned, draped as he was over Nordoom's shoulder.

Mustadd raised his club to reshape the elf's skull when the Prince cried, "Don't kill him!" The weapon glanced off Six Stix's head, stunning him. He staggered and the Prince laughed. "I have plans for him," he said, "and the old cow, too. Disarm them."

Exhausted, Six Stix tried and failed to remember the last time he had slept. When the giant grabbed his swords, it felt like someone lightening his load.

The General came out of the fireplace, a handful of ashes secreted in her hand, and twisted her body to protect her sword. Mustadd reached out to disarm her and Gudrun threw the ashes in his face. He roared and grabbed her, spitting soot from his mouth. She landed several painful blows, but Mustadd got her dagger and tore the belt that held her scabbard.

As he bent to retrieve the sword, Mustadd discovered its powers; a white hot hole burned through the ox-hide sheath, scorching his fingers. Holding the General's wrist with his other hand, he forced her to look at his singed flesh. "You'll be sorry," he muttered.

"Leave the weapon," ordered the Prince.

Gudrun gazed at her sword with deep despair. *The sacred blade of my ancestress. I might as well be dead.*

The Prince addressed the dwarf, "You—I'll spare your life if you wish to take a job in the dungeons. I need someone to clean the swill."

Gudrun glanced at Tiala and said, "I'll go where my Lady goes."

Mischa snorted. "Oh, yes, go with my new bride. Shall I dress you in silks and satins? No, my rustic beauty, the dungeons will suit you just fine."

Tiala's voice sliced his self-satisfaction in two. "Your bride? I'll drink poison first. You disgust me, maggot."

Gaf tightened his hold on the dark elf, betraying his nervousness. She was nervous, too. What a fool she had been to signal her readiness to depart.

Mischa had enough self-esteem to be hurt by Tiala's outburst. He sniffed with a shred of his old dignity and said, "Fine. Nordoom, take them to the dungeons. Find a cell large enough to hold them all. I want to see how well they like each other after a few days without food."

Mustadd hefted Six Stix under his arm and Nordoom pinned Gudrun's arms behind her, shoving her in front of him.

The Prince looked at Six Stix. "What's that on your head?" he said, snatching the bloody rag from the blue elf's forehead. "This looks like the brocade for my new vest." He frowned. "And I liked you."

Mischa told the guard, "Search them, then report to me." Straightening his tunic, he stomped out of the room.

Tiala was marched into the hallway bearing her grave disappointment. *My mission will bring no deliverance for my people now.* When Mustadd dragged the dwarf from the room, Tiala whispered to Gudrun, "I am deeply sorry, sister."

Gudrun replied, "Don't grieve, my Lady. It's not over yet."

-28-

To AN Alvarran priestess—or someone as sensitive—the chamber would have held an aura of relief after the frenzied battle that had taken place. Although the room torches had sputtered out, the great door was ajar and light from the hall spilled over the jamb.

The strong smell of blood and sweat was beginning to wane, but shadows of the animals carved into the chairs and fireplace moved in the torchlight as if in silent protest. Blood stained the priceless upholstery and carved wood. Shards of red glass covered the floor. The fine blue rug was bunched in disarray, chairs overturned, and pieces of crystal littered the hearth.

The unconscious bodies of three giants lay sprawled in unnatural positions, and near them the wizard lay hidden under a light gray cloak.

The figure on the floor stirred. A motion of cloth and fingers. The sound of half words, ancient rhythms, archaic vowels. Whatever they were, the shadowy forms of unseen watchers ducked down and slithered away across the shards of glass, the humps in the rug and the broken furniture, like waves of water over sand.

Embaza sat up. As his eyes adjusted to the light, he realized he was not alone. He could hear the stentorian breathing of the two giants who lay on the other side of an overturned table. He got up gingerly, feeling for his necklace, and checking his hidden pockets for needles and wax. Everything seemed to be in place.

He noticed the chair where the Prince had been sitting, and sought the demongaze so carelessly discarded on the floor beneath the seat. *This is a fine piece of work, similar to my necklace. An intensifier that works on one's deepest fears.* He tested the pronged mechanism on the side, a thin sliver of metal that should be pressed to the body of the sphere until it clicked. *If the Prince had known how to use this, I would be dead now.* He hid the demongaze in one of his pockets. *Who knows what other artifacts you've misused, my Prince? Be careful, the price is high.* The effects would be unpredictable, eventually rebounding on the user—a random, uncontrolled energy, fueled by his own intent. Embaza thought that a fitting retribution.

He took a deep breath, surveying the room for anything of value, and finding very little. *It seems like a long time since I've felt so good. And yet, I should be exhausted. Something is fueling my energy in a different way.*

He thought of this new quest. The Nightwing's daughter. *Beautiful. Intriguing. A talented woman with a strong fiber.* He looked to no avail for a clue to tell him where the others had gone. He had a sudden image of Polah, pale and determined, curled about the legs of the giant. *I must find her.* He closed his eyes and recited softly, *"Wovera Shoudoth."* A dark, ugly cell came to mind. Vague shapes moved within, but one had hair like flame. *Dungeon.*

Embaza glanced at the giants, then smiled. "Sleep well."

If he'd had the additional strength, he would have added a spell to deepen their dreaming. Padding to the door, he looked out into the hallway, shading his eyes against the illumination from the walls. He shook his head. *Here is a man who loves magic, who uses an artifact as rare and advanced as a demongaze—and yet he can't even work a simple long-light spell.*

Embaza worked his way down the hall until he recognized the stairs leading down to the arena. *The Prince always has convenient villains for his visitors to slaughter. The dungeons should be near.*

He wondered how many of the inmates were guests who had fallen out of the madman's favor.

-29-

ALL THE way down to the dungeon, Tiala resisted—scratching, biting and calling for help—until one of the giants finally cuffed her senseless. When she awoke, Tiala beheld a scene of horror beyond her imagination. The large, filthy cell had iron bars on three sides and a blackened stone wall at the back.

The moans of other prisoners added to the atmosphere of doom. A tormented shriek sparked a wave of eerie howls that assaulted her ears from every direction. Across from her cell, she had a clear glimpse of the stairs down which they had come, before it curved out of sight again.

What a hellish place. Her senses reeled, and despair crashed down on her. Despite this, she raised her chin. *I am the Nightwing Avenwyndar's daughter.*

She stood in quiet dignity, therefore, when the guards opened her cell door and deposited Obsidian's body onto the greasy floor. The monk slid several feet across the rotting slime before coming to rest against the blackened stone wall. He curled into a ball.

Polah was pushed into the fetid cell, barely able to wobble to the nearest corner. Her pallor gleamed in the dim light. She turned aside and retched, then rested her head against the bars.

Lastly, the General and Six Stix were hurled into the cell. Both were bruised and sore, not seriously hurt. They sat up, cursing each other, as if each were the source of the other's misfortune.

Tiala began to scold them, stopped by a fresh round of shrieks from prisoners in other cells. Crouching, she clapped her hands over her ears and squeezed her eyes shut. She had never imagined such misery.

Six Stix and Gudrun had no weapons, but this did not deter their antagonism. Nor did the misery and terror that surrounded them. Oblivious to the fact that they were united in their predicament, they resumed their warfare using the only tools at hand.

"Demon spawn," said Gudrun. She rose and brushed off her leather tunic.

"Rotting turd," rejoined Six Stix, getting to his feet, flexing his hands and knees. The scab on his forehead oozed a little blood, but he ignored it.

Although the General's head was level with the elf's chest, size was no deterrent either. Gudrun glared up at Six Stix, and he scowled down at her. Shifting from one foot to the other, they circled each other like wrestlers as the ritual resumed.

Polah, drained and wan from exhaustion and nausea, sat on a pile of rags, acutely aware of the conflict and catastrophe that were brewing. "Don't fight," she rasped. "Please." Both combatants ignored her.

"Stop. Listen to me," she cried. It made no difference. They were deaf to all but each other's insults. She looked over at Tiala, who crouched in private agony, and sensed the dark elf's confusion and anger.

"Princess Tiala, are you all right?" Polah asked without response.

Polah grew more and more annoyed with herself. *I'm no stranger to hardship.* Most of her childhood she had spent alone: cold, wet, hungry and motherless. However wretched, she had always had an inner strength, a well of resourcefulness to bring her through any situation. *I was never this weak before I met the wizard.*

She looked around. Tiala was beyond reach; Obsidian had not gained consciousness. Six Stix and Gudrun were hopelessly wearing a circle in the floor. There was no one to depend on but herself. She struggled to her feet.

Taking a deep breath, she reached for that inner core of strength that was her birthright—her animal self. But what she found instead was the alien voice in her heart of hearts. Her stomach knotted in defense, and fresh nausea assailed her. *Please, no.* Suddenly, she knew the voice—Embaza alive! Relief soon turned to anger.

You invade me again, Embaza. Am I not mistress of my own soul?

It was you that called me, fox woman. Besides, there are other forces here.

It made no sense, but her outrage lessened the tiniest bit. *Yes, perhaps I did. I'm tired and ill. I need your help.* The implications of asking the wizard for help bothered her. *Why am I not healing?*

Because you have been lending me your fox energy. We've used it together, to create a web of power. Such use of magic drains the ones who make it. The voice fell silent, waiting.

Polah steadied herself with one arm against the wall. *But I'm not a wizard.*

No, you are not a wizard, not trained. You are raw magic, an enchanted one. Your magic was born, not learned. Together, we are indeed a new thing. I have made you new, and you have changed me, also.

While she grappled with the new knowledge, she remembered. *The fighters.*

The elf had the dwarf by the neck and she was twisting his ears. Even in the early stages of this ritual, the two were causing each other obvious pain, yet they continued the taunting that tradition required.

"Your beard needs trimming, troll," said Six Stix.

"Try it, and I'll trim you," croaked the General.

They'll kill each other, Polah agonized.

Concentrate, ordered Embaza. *Focus all your senses on them and transmit it to me. Make your mind blank. I'm going to try something.*

Bracing herself against the wall, Polah did what he asked and saw them through both her human and animal eyes. She saw their heat, their anger and fear, smelled their sweat, their excitement, their need to win. She heard their words, though the meaning did not penetrate her thoughts. She had become a perfect lens.

As she watched, Embaza said, *Keep your concentration, no matter what happens. Remain steady.*

The General choked, the dwarf trying to speak, but the elf had such a grip on her throat that her vocal chords were failing. Suddenly, Six Stix loosed his hold and gently stroked her throat with his thumbs. Gudrun caught her breath and released his ears, grasping his hands instead and pressing them to her lips.

Polah almost laughed with relief, but remembering Embaza's words, she kept her mind centered on the two. Was it a love spell? Should she let him know it was working? Chagrined, she realized when it came to manipulating magic, she didn't know the rules. Like a fox hunting in unfamiliar territory, she remained focused on the target.

Six Stix clasped the General's hands and said, "Help me pick the lock on this cell. We have to get out of here." He led her to the door where both studied the lock as if they had been lifelong friends. It struck Polah that the same spirit animated them, whether on opposite sides of a battle or not. *Together, they make a whole.*

Yes, said Embaza. *You learn fast. The schools of Sargoth teach that the ability to accept paradox is the first lesson of magic.*

Magic. I don't choose to learn any more magic, said Polah.

The magic will choose you, because it seeks its own kind.

Polah raised her black eyes to the ceiling. She missed her privacy. She disliked this cold, bossy, intellectual wizard, but she hid these feelings deep in her animal self before the thoughts were exposed to her new ally.

-30-

LAYERS ABOVE the Royal City, the great borough of Douvilwe thrived, a testament to the harmony that could exist between nature and elves. Although boasting fewer parks than its rival, Aeryinne, it had more lawyers—or *voranas* as they were called in Alvarra—than the other eleven cities put together.

The Houses of Law were larger and more numerous even than the Houses of Diplomacy, although the latter enjoyed the advantage of being beside the only lake in Douvilwe. To the long-lived elves, lawsuits and the writing of new laws were an inevitable source of entertainment. Frivolous suits were discouraged officially, but privately, they flourished.

In one of the chambers of law, a vorana was working late. Even though the tenth bell had rung and her stomach rumbled, Faelua Erdhiann pored over the large sheaf of notes on her latest case. It was common knowledge that she kept odd hours, often working after others had gone for the day. Yet, all in all, she was no better nor worse than her sisters.

Her office was in one chamber of a much larger, multi-layered complex. Perhaps because of the sameness of the caverns, or the plain gray uniforms they wore, each attorney prided herself in distinctive touches to her personal quarters.

Faelua had decorated hers with bright, artistic rugs, a small statue of the Goddess Ordala, patron of voranas, and an unusual stained glass window, back-lit by phosphor-stone.

Her latest assignment was the case of a young thief accused of brutally murdering a known criminal named Zhido. She did not believe he was guilty, notwithstanding the deluge of evidence to the contrary. The death had been more like an assassination. There had been a rash of them, doubly shocking for a country in mourning.

Faelua was one of the few voranas who insisted these killings were related, that they portended some sinister purpose. To her experienced eye, similarities in the methods of execution showed the unmistakable signature of a single perpetrator.

The vorana was in her middle years, with a friendly, round face and plump figure. She had folded back the wide gray sleeves of her tunic and removed her slippers.

She was so absorbed in the study of her case that she did not hear the footsteps on the soft rug.

A young dark-elven male dressed in black crept up behind her, obscuring the light from the stained glass window.

Faelua ignored the interruption long enough to finish reading the sentence, then one hand covered her mouth, and the other grabbed her by the back of the neck. She gasped once before the intruder expertly snapped her neck with his powerful hands. Her body slid down in the chair, and one sleeve caught on the arm, shearing the gray silk.

Her murderer propped her body back up into a sitting position. Then he took out a colorful handbill and pinned it to her chest using her own quill. The parchment depicted the profile of a handsome dark elf in black silhouette on bright yellow. On his head was a crown. Beneath the picture, hand-lettered in bright red:

MEN OF ALVARRA

YOUR HOUR OF FREEDOM IS AT HAND.

STAND WITH US AND TAKE YOUR PLACE IN THE NEW REALM.

LORD KING DEKHALIS'S REIGN HAS BEGUN.

...SWORDS OF SIADHIN

125

The assassin squeezed through the narrow aperture he had cut in the back wall of her coat closet. Once outside, he was soon lost amid the mild pandemonium in the streets.

Even at mealtime, riots and demonstrations had become a regular feature of life in the cities. The eleventh bell still rang for curfew, but the peacekeepers could not enforce it.

Strikes were becoming more prevalent, too. The Great Houses where the noble families lived were in the southeastern part of the city, nestled like jewels in luxurious personal gardens. Not only were the noblewomen inconvenienced by the loss of municipal services, but they were outraged by the rebellion of their own servants. Even old retainers like gardeners and cooks had deserted them.

In the emergency, young women had been hired to sweep the streets—a scandal. These city folk were laughingstocks among the farmers who felt that, for once, their neighbors "to the deep" had debased themselves beyond redemption.

While most elves past a hundred years were culinary experts, these sheltered citizens knew little about marketing and even less about housekeeping. Their male consorts were pampered, hardly more useful than pets.

Because of the peculiarities of the natural configuration of these ancient caverns, the groundskeepers had a difficult time maintaining the fragile ecosystem. The soil was so old that plant life grew more and more sparse each decade, and water had to be pumped in from the city's lake. While the strikes and riots continued, noblewomen were seen watering and weeding their own grounds. Male citizens jeered at them through the bars of their ivy-covered gates.

In the Thieves' Quarters, life was the most unchanged, populated as it was by predominantly male malcontents, eccentrics and misfits. These citizens prided themselves on being independently employed free-thinkers.

It was here that Dekhalis had found his first converts. Starting with the intellectuals, whose idealism was always ready tinder, he had enflamed them with visions of power. "In my reign, there will be a man in every key post in the land," he told them. "You—all of you—counselors, sages, generals."

Privately, he made other, more personal promises to key individuals who became willing ringleaders. They easily initiated the more wretched and underprivileged into the cause.

Dekhalis called his group the *Swords of Siadhin*, evoking the name of their forefathers—those long-ago masters of Alvarra. His followers spread rumors of their exploits in every town and hamlet, and posted colorful handbills sporting his aristocratic profile. Although his lieutenants were impassioned speakers, his own orations filled the hearts of these unhappy outcasts with hope, guaranteeing almost instant devotion. In short, this son of the Nightwing was an overnight success, a romantic hero.

While he could have his pick of hideouts, he guarded his privacy. Using a maze of secret passages throughout Alvarra, he had installations hidden in all the cities, already prepared and provisioned. He was intent on developing a reputation for mystery and liked popping up at meetings of the Swords of Siadhin unannounced. Yet, he always had time for the "shadowmen," as he called them, assassins with whom he had corresponded for years. They were the invisible core of the organization, initiating riots, performing swift and silent executions, and carrying secret messages for Dekhalis hidden in their sleeves. Each wore a black silk armband embroidered with a black spider. And each had been given real weapons.

In the Thieves' Quarters at Douvilwe, in the corresponding Quarters at Aeryinne and in some of the Great Houses, Dekhalis also had friends. They never knew when he might appear or what favor he might ask. Even those on the fringe of his cause were intrigued; particularly those consorts of the nobility who, although they might not agree with his methods, were curious to see whether he would prevail. It was sure to benefit them if he did, since most of them felt like decorative chattels.

-31-

THE NIGHTWING herself was not without knowledge of these things. While she lay on the border between life and death, she followed the movements of her son with concern. *Dekhalis, my youngling, when will you find peace?* His mind was closed to her, that she knew. Years ago, when he had been capable of loving and being loved, he had already been too stubborn to open his mind to another. She had seen the flaw, but being a mother, found it hard to condemn him with her own hands. Dekhalis was especially dear to her for another reason. She had lost her firstborn son years before.

Her mate at that time, a powerful wizard named Valedd, had tried to console her, but both had been stricken with guilt and sorrow when their son was kidnapped. They had prayed together in the Temple of Miralor, with a hundred priestesses and wizards to attend them.

She missed Valedd. Of all her husbands, he had been her favorite. It was a shame he had become so ambitious. Her mind searched for him on the inner planes, but every time she found him, he disappeared. It was as if he laid a string out for her to follow, then jerked it away. She thought of it as a kind of game and wondered if he did it out of love or hatred.

Her hand, after all, had signed the order exiling her beloved Valedd to the Merimn'a. At least, there, he could have the power he desired. In her innocence, she had imagined them meeting on the steps between worlds, trysting in the romance of their youth. But Valedd had not seen it that way. When the last wizard had been expelled from Alvarra, and he had said goodbye, he had not kissed her. Not even on the hand.

Her other husbands had been chosen with more care and less wisdom, taken out of duty to her realm first and affection second. Ombra's father had been an artist, Tiala's a musician. None of them had lasted more than a hundred years, although they had given her five beautiful heirs and a handsome son to spoil. The last of her consorts, Rozadon, had fathered Dekhalis.

Rozadon had not been content to act as her companion and squire. When the boy was an infant, his father had willingly gone the way of Valedd, descending to the Merimn'a where his ambition no doubt served him well. She had no desire to know what had become of him. After Rozadon, she had lost interest in male companionship.

The Nightwing considered the bitter fact that when it came to the men in her life, she had been most unlucky. Or did she perhaps have some flaw of her own that prevented her from handling them correctly?

Her reverie was interrupted by a telepathic summons, one of those humble greetings that alerted her of a message from priestess to priestess. *Yes?* she asked of Alyanthus, a priestess from the woods near the Purple Moors.

Your Highness, said Aylanthus, *we have word from Zelwyn's followers. The healer has been killed—most mysteriously. Those who were with her said they saw creatures that had no business in our world. She used every bit of strength protecting the others from the demons who destroyed her. She was not able to make contact with your daughter.* The narrative stopped.

You are holding something back. What is it? asked the Nightwing.

The sisters say there was a wizard at the Manor, one who participated in a death rite. Zelwyn told them he was a dark one in disguise. In a dream, she saw him with your daughter Tiala. Zelwyn was killed before we could find out anything else, your Highness.

The Nightwing's heart beat faster. A wizard? A dark-elven wizard? How could that be? *Thank you, Aylanthus. I will do prayers and purification rites for Zelwyn tonight. Notify the other Orders, first the Sisterhood of Loote. Tell the Priestess Evendove that I will visit her in spirit at the ceremonies. Be sure the bards play in every temple. Zelwyn was a great lover of music.*

Yes, your Reverence, said Aylanthus, reverting to the Nightwing's spiritual title out of habit.

The Nightwing had much to consider in light of this new information.

Who would have the effrontery to call a phantom being from the forbidden realms? Perhaps Tiala needed the kind of help that priestesses could not give her. Was there a wizard in her destiny? It was dangerous, but these were dangerous circumstances. Wizardry was heresy, or so they taught now, but she and other elders could remember a day when priestess and wizard worked side by side.

I miss the old days, when a mate was a mate. Where are you now, Valedd, my sweet one?

-32-

WHILE GUDRUN and Six Stix acted friendly enough, another part of their minds was aware of this unpleasant fact. A spell is, after all, only a spell and although a creature may be subdued by it, there is a certain part of the mind that can never be fully controlled. In the dimness of the dungeon cell, their smiles were false.

As Polah watched the formerly hostile fighters gaze at each other with tenderness, even she was aware of a great rage boiling beneath the surface. Ignoring Embaza's presence within her mind, she got up and knelt beside Gudrun and Six Stix. Although they had eyes only for each other, Polah made them pay attention to her by tapping them on the arms. She said to the General, "Why were you fighting him?"

The dwarf blushed and smiled a crooked grin. "He killed my two younger sisters." The sweetness of her voice was macabre. "I was right behind them and saw him strike them down. The vision of their deaths will never leave me."

Polah looked at Six Stix. He was nodding, an idiot's smile on his face. "Yes," he said agreeably, "I did well. They were coming at me and I struck them down with my axes. They were dwarves of Estenhame, reputed to be ferocious fighters. I was warned not to give them a chance to strike at me, even though they were armed only with tusk knives."

Gudrun cocked her head to one side, as if perplexed. "I never knew that our small village had such a widespread reputation."

"To be sure," Six Stix gushed, "you women of Estenhame have been the meat of legends for many generations. All know the story of the sword you carry, and its maker." He grimaced and touched the indigo scar along his cheek, a mute testament.

It was Polah's turn to look confused. "What story?"

"My great grandmother Dragonbane—."

"The famous one," said Six Stix.

"Yes, it was forged in her day." Gudrun smiled with pride and reached for her scabbard. Remembering where the weapon was, her brown eyes became sad.

"There, there," said Six Stix, patting her on the back. "I know how hard it is. I've lost two."

Polah shook her head. *Is this what magic is for?* She continued to ignore the wizard's presence within her, hoping he would leave her alone. She noticed that the pain in her back no longer bothered her. She was healing at last.

Tiala was crouching in the corner of the room, humming to herself. Polah paused, considering where she could be of most help, then approached the unconscious Obsidian. She held her hand over her mouth as she made her way over the offal. She squatted beside him and looked at his face, remembering the brave way he had leapt into the room, displaying such speed and grace. He, too, had come to save the Alvarran. They had something in common.

Don't touch him, said Embaza.

Disobeying, Polah reached out and grasped Obsidian's large, callused hand with her small one.

The monk's eyes flew open and his hand closed painfully around her wrist. His accusatory stare pinned Polah like a moth. Then he recognized her, released her hand and said, "What is your name? And who is that presence within you?"

She blinked. *How does he know?* She answered, "I'm Polah, and—I am sorry for disturbing you."

Obsidian waited, his face composed and gentle.

Polah whispered, "My companion is a wizard. He means well. He, too, was fighting Prince Mischa."

"I remember him a little. Where is he?"

"I don't know," Polah said. "But I'm sure he's alive."

Obsidian's senses took in the malodorous cell, the conditions of his companions, and the horrible sounds of the other inmates. He moved his arm and pain stabbed him in the back. "How was I wounded?"

Polah frowned. "Mischa had a sharp, toy-sized weapon. While you were attacking the giant, he threw it at you. The Alvarran bound your wound with cloth from her own garments. There she is." She pointed at the dark elf. "Her name is Tiala."

Obsidian caught his breath and looked, but saw only a crouching figure hiding behind her long, black hair.

"Who are you and what is your calling?" Polah asked.

His eyes still fastened on Tiala, he answered, "I am Obsidian. I used to be a miner; now I am a monk." He had never seen a dark elf before this one. A childhood tale came to mind of a dark elf who kidnapped babies and sold them to the trolls. He shook his head. Master Inota taught, "Superstition is the religion of the fearful, and doom is their sacrament."

He glanced around the cell and noticed Six Stix and Gudrun, then tried to get up. Groaning, he sank back.

"You're not yet healed," said Polah, easing him to a sitting position. "We must both save our strength. I, too, am wounded." She didn't want to elaborate on her battle with the great owl.

"Let me see," said Obsidian, a respect for all living things radiating from him. Polah marveled to herself. She had always lived by a code of aloneness, yet as her animal intuition grew, so did her courage around people. *This man can be trusted.*

She lifted her tunic and made a tent with her hands, gently peeling the cloth of her under-tunic away from the six long scratches raked into her back. They were beginning to scab over, and the red weals looked tender to the touch, but Obsidian saw no sign of infection. "You're healing well."

"What about you?" Polah said, shaking her head over his objections. "No need to be so self sufficient. That's my domain." She laughed, and Obsidian wondered at the edge of bitterness in her voice.

The harem had been his first intimate experience with women since childhood. His high ideals were still shaken. *She seems a mysterious person, but I feel no malice in her.* He turned and steeled himself to her ministrations.

Polah winced at the deep stab wound in the middle of his back. Dried blood and filth encrusted it. The strip of cloth that Tiala had applied was ruined now. Polah looked around. There was nothing clean in the cell, and no water for washing. The best thing might be to cover it up again, although the bandage was ruined.

Using her sharp teeth, she tore a strip from her own under-tunic, which was cleaner, and bound his back, though it would only wrap once. She tied a knot, careful not to tie it too tight. She tried again to impart some of her healing ability to another, but it did not seem to have any effect. She was so intent on her task, she almost missed Embaza's voice.

Sweesoki Nasa. Anzin Turala. Azwin Zia. She knew it was a healing spell. Her nostrils dilated, and the words undulated in her mind like wind flowing through her fur…fur… As she bound Obsidian's back, she sank into the total calm that warned of transformation.

She hurried, fingers moving faster, plaiting the words of the spell into the skein of cloth, tying off the end and biting it with her teeth.

Obsidian turned to thank her and cried out.

Where the woman had been was a fox: large, feral, her shining coat the color of torchlight. She paced back and forth, tongue out, sharp teeth glinting white.

The monk glanced around in confusion, then he remembered. Polah—the fox-woman who fought in the arena. Everyone had been talking about her. *She's as big as a great wolf.* In pain, he crouched and watched as the whimpering fox tried to cover her ear with one black paw. *The noise is hurting her.*

Gudrun and Six Stix shrank back as Polah paced the floor. The General whispered, "That's an enchanter," in a voice that betrayed a deep mistrust of the abnormal.

Six Stix recognized the fox-woman, both from the hallway earlier and from the tales of other fighters. *So, this is the great Polah, who saved the life of the Sargothian.* Had that been the same wizard in the chamber above? Probably. She looked dangerous. He wasn't sure if he wanted such an ally. *Where will she hunt? What will she hunt?*

Polah was hungry. Her keen eyes discerned rats and mice hovering in the shadows of the cell where others saw only lumps of greasy cloth or balls of dust. But the fox part of Polah was still new. The woman part was strong and experienced, and had a mind of its own.

The fox's senses were overcome by the wailing of the other inmates, and she whined at the pain piercing her ears. Her wild eyes darted around, seeing the concern and fright of the others, all except Tiala who was bent over in the same position of torment.

Without thought, Polah was drawn to Tiala, just as she felt rather than heard Embaza's presence within her. His words melted into her mind without clear form, and yet she understood them. He could do no magic upon her, but he could do magic *through* her. She was learning. She went to Tiala and laid her muzzle on the elf's shoulder.

Tiala reached up to stroke Polah's nose. The sounds of suffering formed a wall around them, agony their bond. "How will I ever sing again if the sound doesn't stop?" she asked, raising her head and peering at the fox through a curtain of hair. "You understand this, don't you, Polah? How can I help you?"

The feral eyes implored her, then the fox gave an angry bark. It would not be long before Polah would be driven mad by the noise. A far-off voice in Polah's mind said, *It is only pain, little fox.* But she did not heed it.

Tiala tensed at the hackles rising on the fox's back. With fumbling fingers, she tore strips of cloth from her tunic. The fox bared her teeth, but Tiala bit her lip and tucked a piece of cloth into the fox's left ear, bringing Polah immediate relief.

Obsidian came closer when he realized Tiala had attained a rapport with the fox. He watched Polah let the dark elf place a ball of cloth into her right ear also. Tiala's own pain was forgotten. The fox's nose was cold on her hand, then Polah nudged her fingers up to her lips.

Tiala winced at the thought of trying to compete with the insane cries of despair that lapped like waves at her consciousness, but an ancient healing tune rose from her throat unbidden, as if imprinted on her genes, in a language she neither understood nor questioned. Perhaps some instinct urged her to heal her own agony as well.

Was it her imagination or did the voices hesitate? Were they softer, less menacing? As indeed, the wailing ceased, Tiala's sweet, resonant voice sang the ancient melody that seemed to brighten the gloomy corners of the cell.

She continued to sing, gazing at Obsidian and Polah, who stared transfixed with ecstasy. She recognized Obsidian as her newest champion, attracted to his alien good looks, his pale skin, long lock of hair and deep brown eyes. The last note of her song fading throughout the dungeon, she smiled, her white teeth dazzling even in the dim light.

"Princess Tiala, I am Obsidian," he said abruptly. "I was sent here by my teachers, the high monks. I don't know why Mischa has made himself your enemy, but I offer you my protection."

Tiala had once heard of monks—superior fighters, if she recalled. This one looked strong. She sighed, tired of telling her story. "Thank you, Obsidian. But know that it is a road filled with peril. Whatever happens, we have no choice but to escape from here."

Obsidian nodded. Tiala noticed that he looked at the fox with wariness.

"The enchanter has pledged herself to me, also," said Tiala.

She stroked Polah's fur and said to Obsidian, "Don't be afraid of her. We have shape-changers in my country. Not only foxes, but wolves, rabbits, and even birds. We'll travel to Alvarra as soon as we can leave this place." She glanced at Gudrun. *There's the real problem. Her kind can't abide enchanters. Forging this alliance and holding it together will not be easy.*

"What is it like—Alvarra?" he asked.

"A sweet land of caves, deep underground," Tiala said. Her eyes seemed suddenly bottomless and filled with yearning.

Obsidian was not fond of caves, too well reminded of his enslavement in the mines. "I live in a monastery," he said, "as safe as a fortress. It lies in an oasis, a neutral place where the Prince cannot—or dare not—harm you. I promise you sanctuary if we can get you there. It is but a few days travel from here."

Tiala brightened. "Thank you, Obsidian. It might be the wisest course. I won't forget your help." Her beauty was all the more extraordinary when contrasted with the squalor of the cell. Obsidian was uplifted by it as if she had been a distant mountain enshrouded by mist, or a rippling lake.

Self-conscious now, Obsidian looked around, perplexed to find Six Stix sitting in quiet conversation with the dwarf. *The last I remember, those two were at each other's throats.* He called out, "Six, you must meet Princess Tiala."

"Must I? It wasn't my idea to rescue her." *You are quite a beauty, my dark sister,* thought Six Stix. *But I am weary of beauty.* A tingling in his scalp announced that the spell was beginning to wear off. He flexed his fingers and looked to the General. She seemed restless, too, eyes pinned on the fox, fists clenched.

Obsidian said to Six Stix, "I thought we were agreed."

"It's all right," said Tiala, "we're tired, and whatever our differences, we're in the same predicament now."

"True," said Six Stix and then pointed at Polah. "But what of her?" The astute expression on the fox's face disconcerted Six Stix. She had clearly understood every word.

Gudrun warned, "My lady, Tiala, you don't know anything about this animal. Such creatures may turn on their friends—even their brothers and sisters."

This is going to require delicacy, thought Tiala, searching for the right words.

Obsidian said passionately, "Whatever you think of her, she was a woman earlier. She bound my wounds and spoke in a kind voice. And she, too, is wounded. I say we trust her."

Tiala nodded, but Six Stix said, "I never trust anyone until I have fought with them." He glanced at the General and recognized his old enemy. The spell had worn off completely now. Yet, he also harbored a new respect. He knew things about her now that he had not known before. He rubbed the old scar that etched its deep blue furrow down his cheek, and moved away to join Obsidian and Tiala.

The fox continued to stare curiously after the blue elf, but otherwise seemed comfortable. *She is no ordinary animal,* thought Six Stix. *I wonder if it is pleasant to be so wild and strong.*

"Come now, General, you're not afraid of a fellow woman," said Tiala.

Gudrun did indeed want to come closer. *What's the matter with me? Am I really afraid?* she wondered. She looked at Six Stix as if truly seeing him for the first time. *My beloved sisters. Kindness that comes from a spell is false,* she reminded herself. *I'll take care of him later.* Out of the corner of her eye, she caught the fox's keen gaze directed at her and she faced Tiala, then folded her arms. "I'll protect you, my Lady, but I'll keep my own company."

The fox growled, and Gudrun tensed.

"Thank you, General," said Tiala and took Polah's sooty paw into her own night-black hand. "Of course, you're upset," she said to the fox, "first you are wounded, then your friend, the wizard dies."

Polah barked and Obsidian said, "She thinks the wizard is alive."

"I saw him fall," Tiala said. "The Sargothian was a true warrior and a brave elf."

The fox rose up on her hind legs, placing her dirty forepaws on Tiala's shoulders. The General lunged and grabbed two fistfuls of the fox's fur. Polah whirled out of Gudrun's grasp and bared her teeth, falling onto all fours.

"Enough," yelled Tiala. "General, we can't give in to personal grudges or misunderstandings. Stop before you are hurt—or you hurt someone else."

All were struck by the stern note in her voice. *She has great presence,* thought Six Stix. For the briefest instant, he regretted renouncing his own opportunity at rulership. But that was another story, and long ago. He assumed his brother was ruling quite happily at Cern Keep, and all had forgotten the rash young warrior who wanted to go to battle and find his fortune.

"General," Tiala said softly, "Polah was not trying to hurt me."

Indeed, the fox acted docile now, her intelligent eyes gleaming in the darkness of the cell.

"Speak to us of whatever troubles you, General," Tiala said, and then looked to each of the others. "Only as a group will we escape this horrid place."

Gudrun was ashamed. *What are my problems compared with hers? She is menaced by her own flesh and blood.* She knelt before Tiala. "My lady," she said, then raised her eyes, "Tiala...forgive me. My prejudices are based on rumors and legends." She looked at Polah with ill-concealed fear. A childhood nightmare brushed her mind. "Have you truly pledged yourself to Tiala's protection?"

The fox's eyes flashed fierce in a blink, and Gudrun sighed. "As woman, I will deal with you as woman, and as fox...as fox. Perhaps in this way, I will come to accept. But I cannot promise it."

"Nor I," said Six Stix and the General looked at him in surprise. To Tiala, he said, "Princess, I am Sixtrulinderan Stixan, who renounced Cern Keep to fight for King Derenheart." His gaze wandered over the kneeling dwarf and back to the crouching Tiala. "This day I bury past hatreds. I did many things in battle that I would not do in peace. I pity those who died at my hands." He looked directly at Gudrun. "Let us be battle-mates in a worthy cause."

Warily, the dwarf made a fist and touched her heart. "Well said, Lord Stixan of Cern. I am a daughter of Estenhame, and I, too, will try to bury the past."

Obsidian felt a great surge of pride in his friend.

Tiala broke the spell. Hands on her hips, she stood up and said, "If we're going to get out of here, let's get started."

"Yes," said Gudrun and began to draw with her stubby finger in the slime-covered floor. Six Stix squatted beside her and watched a map take form.

Polah stood alone, staring at the rats and mice in the corners of the cell.

-33-

PRINCE MISCHA sat in his aerie, looking out over the empty arena. *All is going well,* he reflected, *and soon I will bend the Princess to my will. I always find their weaknesses. And the shape-changer—what a magnificent creature. But oh, so dangerous.*

He chuckled. *When the others hear that I have these two powerful women in my harem, the tribes will all pay honor to me. Grandfather will eat his words.* He reached for the silver flute and turned it over in his palm. *I wonder what these runes stand for. Two I recognize…a ward for thieves…and that one is a true note sigil, the commonest of bardic runes. But these others…they must tell of infinite longevity.*

He blew over the holes, causing a slight shimmer of sound in the room. A shiver went up his back and another feeling that shocked him beyond breath—as if someone plucked his skin and threatened to shake his body from it. He set the flute down on the ledge by the window and glanced at it sideways.

The arena was dark in the eerie pre-dawn hour. The Prince smiled a wicked grin. *Today will be very special. Very special indeed…I must make sure that my instructions are followed to the letter.*

He leaned back in his chair and folded his arms. The plain gold ring caused an itch on his left index finger. "Stay quiet, my friend," he whispered, "There'll be plenty of work for you today." Anticipation made his heart beat faster, swelling him with confidence.

"Wait until Grandfather hears of this. First I destroyed that weakling, Embaza, with my magic powers," he boasted to an unseen audience. The sudden memory of the giant toppling the wizard with a blow to the neck, he dismissed as a mirage.

"Then I put a stop to that meddling monk." He laughed, remembering Obsidian's great size, and tossed the blood-stained letter opener on the table to his right. "Most effective—I'll have to remember that."

-34-

In Mischa's dungeon, Polah lingered in the shadows, very much aware of all that occurred. She sensed the link with Embaza becoming weaker and weaker, uncertain if she should be worried or pleased.

The uneasy truce that Tiala had welded between Gudrun and Six Stix still held. The echoes of the dark elf's song seemed to drift among the cobwebs in the ceiling, imparting shreds of strength to the group. Now, in the dungeon, Tiala leaned over Six Stix, a hand on his good shoulder, studying Gudrun's crude map. She hummed a bar of the ancient melody, oblivious to the effect this had on her companions.

Gudrun said, "I haven't been in every part of the Manor, but I think this is a hidden exit used only by Mischa's spies. I propose we try it. All the others will be heavily guarded."

Obsidian gazed at the soft planes of Tiala's face, drinking in the sight like a tonic. *She has a way of communicating that makes everyone trust her, even the fox.*

Six Stix stole a glance at the black-haired songstress, in spite of his determination to resist her charms. The perfume of her sweat tickled his nostrils.

Gudrun thought, *If only I had her beauty, my troops would have prevailed on the Hindrous Plains, and even the elves would have sung my name.*

At Six Stix's urging, Obsidian related the details of their previous escape from the dungeons. Gudrun and Tiala encouraged the monk to try the door of their cell.

Obsidian got to his feet and, tossing his hairlock behind him, attempted to draw on his reserves of calm. He thought, *This fetid place is no meditation room. But, remember, the Tuval mine was no garden, either.*

He went to examine the stout door made of iron. The barred window at the top would be large enough only for someone's head, if it were open. He studied the door hinges to see if they could be dislodged. Bronze pins as large as his fist were secured by over-leaves of hammered bronze, forged in the shape of claws. "Such fine work for a dungeon," he marveled, then said to the others, "Look at this. "

They crowded around. Polah reared on her hind legs and braced her forepaws against the door. Then Gudrun gasped and touched a finger to a cleft in the bronze claw. "The mark of the beast," she said breathlessly.

"What do you mean?" asked Tiala.

"My people leave signs for each other," Gudrun replied, "in case we find ourselves in dire circumstances. It's well known we have a tendency to drink, and quick tempers. And if we meet one who calls us ugly—or short—we'll fight to save our honor." She glanced at Six Stix. "We often find ourselves in jails."

Gudrun peered at the bronze fittings in the dim light. "But where's the eye?" she muttered. "Every beast has an eye…"

Obsidian, standing nearest, strained to look but saw nothing in the metalwork resembling an eye.

Gudrun's roving fingers located a round protuberance on the lower edge of the barred window. Standing on tiptoe, she wiped off the thick layer of grime to reveal a small brass knob with an iron dot in the middle. "All I have to do is push this…" She could barely reach it.

Obsidian said, "Here, I'll do it." But Gudrun shook her head and motioned everyone back. "It needs a dwarf."

Trading skeptical glances, they obeyed, and Gudrun stood on tiptoe once again. With great effort, she managed to push the knob with her thumb, and the iron door creaked open an inch.

There was relieved laughter from the others, and Gudrun let out her breath and bent to rest, hands on her knees. "Thank the Gods of the Forge," she said.

Obsidian stepped forward and wrested the heavy, iron door farther open, and they squeezed out of the cell, first Tiala, then Six Stix, then Gudrun. Polah sniffed about the opening, then came through. Gudrun was uneasy; it was hard to imagine that the great fox had ever been a woman.

The monk looked at the walls for keys to the other cells, but all he saw was the blank gray stone, singed with torch fire. The other inmates of this hell-hole would have to stay.

"Come on," Tiala whispered.

There was no further conversation once Tiala motioned for silence. She crouched and moved along the wall beneath the barred windows of the other cells, making her way toward the stairway. Whether due to her playing or some unspoken dungeon routine, the time for bedlam had passed, and quiet now emanated from the inmates, except for an occasional moan or grumbled oath.

The small group managed to reach the circular staircase without incident. A feeble light wavered from a torch a few feet up the stairs, and they ascended single-file behind Tiala.

Around the corner, the dark elf stopped and shook her head. She pointed, and Six Stix, who was close behind her, was the first to look. Barring their passage was a thick iron gate, carved in the shape of two cave lions with open jaws. On the left side was a large brass bell.

Tiala beckoned to Gudrun, who came forward and examined the gate, but she shook her head. "Not dwarven made."

Six Stix ran his hands over the round iron lock. "Doesn't seem too difficult." He turned to his companions and said, "I need a wire. Do any of you have a bit of metal?"

Tiala looked hopefully to the others, but little had been left to them by the Prince's guards. Then she remembered the extra set of harp strings.

Turning her back on everyone, she worked the thin leather case loose from her bodice, then separated a single coiled metal filament from its fourteen brethren. When she spun around to offer the wire to Six Stix, he gave her a delighted wide-eyed grin and, without a single word, bent to his work.

Obsidian guarded the stairway while the others hovered behind Six Stix. The blue elf's sure fingers worked the wire around and around in the lock until there was a sharp click, but nothing happened. He examined the mutilated wire and frowned. "No good," he muttered under his breath.

"What?" asked Tiala. "Is my harp string ruined in vain?"

"Well," he said with reluctance, "sometimes a lock will be set to a certain combination. Even if you have the right key, it won't work without pressure from the other side." They looked ruefully at the bell.

"This is ridiculous," said Tiala, anger sparkling in the depths of her eyes. "Why should the Prince have such an elaborate security procedure? He has a legion of giants to guard him."

"He didn't invent it," Gudrun said. "It's rumored that this was the idea of someone higher up."

"Higher up?"

Gudrun shrugged. "The King of the Desert—the Patriarch himself— Mischa's grandfather."

Six Stix reached with both hands for the wooden clapper in the brass bell. A sharp tug freed it from its socket. He grinned. "There's no love lost between those two, I can tell you."

"That may be good to remember," said Tiala.

Gudrun said, "What do we try now, my Lady?"

Tiala beckoned to Obsidian. "We can pull together on the door. General, you stand guard." Gudrun moved down the stairs to switch places.

Obsidian grabbed the bars of the gate. "I can do this alone. Stand back."

Tiala shook her head. "Don't be an idiot."

Six Stix touched her arm. "He can do it. Watch." Tiala gave him a cryptic look, folded her arms and stepped back.

Obsidian planted his feet apart, knees slightly bent, and went into deep meditation. As his breathing became more and more regular, he imagined he could hear the evening bell, see the sunset and the hawks flying in the distance. When at last, a mountain lark sailed into his vision, he opened his brown eyes and gazed with serenity at the keyhole between the cave lions' jaws.

Grasping the sides of the lock where the lions' noses touched, he heaved against the ironwork as hard as he could, leaning back until his body was almost perpendicular. The gate as yet wouldn't budge.

Six Stix restrained an urge to prevent the monk from falling.

With a sudden crash, the iron doors parted, then fell off their hinges. The prisoners in the cells below resumed their caterwauling.

Obsidian held onto the bars like a monkey, shielding the others from the impact. The wound in his back reopened.

Now that there was no reason for stealth, they clambered to his assistance, and together lifted the gate pinning Obsidian's body. Tiala put her left shoulder under the monk's right armpit, and Six Stix took the other side. They helped him up the stairs, both pressing on his bandage to stop the bleeding.

As the fox climbed, her animal senses alerted her to danger, one she might've faced before. More than ever, she wished for Embaza's presence. Her hackles rose. *Something unnatural...* She bared her teeth and pushed past Gudrun, who was in the lead.

On the landing, a dark shape waited, tall and thin as a sapling. Polah growled, but then, without warning, the menace swooped down over Tiala, wholly obscuring her form.

The shape shimmered once and faded, leaving an echo of a laugh. Tiala lay on the floor.

Without Tiala's support, Obsidian sagged and fell to one knee. Polah whimpered, licking Tiala's face, but the dark elf was still, save for the slight rise and fall of her breast. Six Stix gritted his teeth, trying to secure Obsidian's bandage. The loss of Tiala had unbalanced them all.

Then Gudrun hoisted Tiala's inert body over her shoulder. She spoke matter-of-factly to Polah. "Scout ahead, shape-changer. Whatever that thing was, it's gone now, but you're the only one who's armed." A sneer creeping into her voice, she asked, "How does it feel to be bodyguard to a monk, Lord Stixan?"

"I've had easier details," he said, hoisting his burden once again, one arm pressed to the wound in Obsidian's back.

Polah looked behind her, trying to sense whether the supernatural presence was truly gone. For now, it seemed to be, but she remained vigilant, and loped to the top of the stairs.

Two corridors crossed here, leading in four directions. Many doors. The area appeared unused, smelled dark and stale. She waited for the others, and Gudrun choose the corridor on the right.

Six Stix said, "I'm worried. We should have been challenged by now. Somehow, it's been too easy."

Gudrun was chagrined. *I should have noticed. Where are the guards? I know Mischa's security, and it's never this lax.* She snapped at Six Stix, "It hasn't been easy for the Alvarran. What would you call that thing we met? Maybe Mischa has found something better than the usual guards. Careful not to get too cocky, elf."

Six Stix grimaced. "Careful, yourself, my bearded beauty."

Gudrun pursed her lips. Perhaps she should have killed him already and gotten it over with. She could never trust him. This train of thought led her to glance at Polah. *I don't trust that one either, but she's more effective now that the wizard is dead. What did he have over her, I wonder?* An unbidden sympathy for the fox-woman rose within the dwarf. *The wizard's death must have wounded her deeply. All the better; it was an unnatural attachment.*

Polah stared at the dwarf, her luminous black eyes hooded with disdain.

Gudrun gave a dignified snort and turned away. *Let her think I trust her,* she thought. *I've been in worse danger than this.*

Besides, she had enough to do just carrying Tiala. The elf's skin looked grayish and Gudrun pinched her cheek, but there was no response.

Six Stix said, "You can't continue to carry her."

"I will if I must," replied Gudrun.

Six Stix frowned at the incipient dawn just visible through a crack in the wall.

-35-

ON HIS way down the stairs, Embaza had found several wall niches, dusty and cobwebbed, where the Prince's minions could wait in ambush in troubled times or perhaps fire crossbows through the narrow windows should the Manor ever come under siege.

In one of these niches Embaza took shelter when he sensed the mind bond with Polah. He wanted a safe place to concentrate his mental powers, and the niche was better than the open stairway. This part of the Manor appeared to be deserted for now, and he wrapped himself in his gray cloak and leaned against the wall in the corner so that unless one were diligently searching for him, he might remain unnoticed.

As he proceeded to guide Polah in the healing and pacifying of her fellows, he had a new suspicion about his unusual connection with her. When he realized she had changed into fox-form, the impression was confirmed. *When she is in animal shape, our bond is weakened.* With this insight came another. *When I use magic, she becomes pliant and feeble. We must learn how to balance these qualities in each other and use the strength of the other at the proper time. She must learn to be a conduit, and I must learn to read her emotions.*

His vision of her cell grew more and more dim, until the bond between them was merely a faint stirring in his nether brain. He peered up and down the stairway, and when satisfied, came out of the niche and proceeded once again down the steps. But his mind was not satisfied; in fact, he was very disturbed by the implications of his connection with Polah. The more he thought about it, the less sense it made.

All along I've assumed that someone was working on us from afar, using magic to manipulate our movements. I've sensed a larger malevolence than Mischa. Maybe even Tiala's brother, Dekhalis. He reached a landing flanked by corridors right and left. A few feet away, the stairs continued. After checking the hallways, he resumed his downward course.

What if I'm wrong? What if it isn't the machination of some evil being? What if we merely have a bond? Such partnerships are rare among magic-users but not unknown. This explanation upset his independence of spirit while at the same time stirring his passion. A tremor lifted the hairs on the back of his neck. He felt someone eavesdropping on his thoughts. *Not Polah…Someone else.*

The wizard closed his eyes. He disliked being out of control, and probed his entire range of psychic ability for any unfamiliar entity, finding nothing more than a remnant of esper.

At this moment of focused introversion the Patriarch rounded the corner. "You, there," barked Rearguard.

Embaza narrowed his green eyes, berating himself for being sloppy. Had there been footsteps? Upon seeing only a wizened gnomad with a long beard and a leather apron, the wizard relaxed. "Yes?" he said.

"I recognize you, young fellow. You're the Sargothian, Embaza, a coward who employs a necklace against his foes instead of true steel."

Embaza examined his fingernails. "I have encountered prejudice in my time, but rarely such bitterness. What is it that has soured you so on magic, my small acquaintance?"

Rearguard rose to his full height of two feet, eleven inches. "Magic has ruined many a man, even in my own family. But I have come to the conclusion that one must fight magic with magic. So, it is with chagrin that I request your services—magician." The epithet was loaded with scorn.

"I am intrigued, good sir," replied Embaza, ignoring the insult, "but unfortunately, I have urgent business elsewhere. I am sorry for your family problems, but I am not for hire."

"Is that so?" the gnome said, snapping his fingers. The stairway filled with soldiers armed with swords, crossbows, spears and daggers. Most of them were human, although some were giant-sized, and a good many were gnomads with weather-hardened faces.

Embaza shook his head. "I might have expected this. Things are never easy for a man of power." He scraped his pocket, hoping for a crumb of sleeping dust. It seemed a hundred years ago that he had possessed such things. He was too tired to use the necklace.

The gnomad squinted, sensing the menace about to confront him. "Before we allow this to get nasty, you might at least hear my proposal."

"As I said, I'm in a bit of a hurry." Embaza pressed his back to the wall so that he could see the troops from both directions on the stairs.

Rearguard gave a signal, and, with lightning speed, two of the soldiers hurled their spears at Embaza.

The metal tips pierced the walls on either side of the wizard's neck at the instant he sketched a pattern in the air. Rearguard nimbly dodged aside, and behind him, a giant tumbled down the stairs.

Embaza's hands continued to move, to weave the air, as he mumbled under his breath.

The gnomad considered Embaza's cool countenance and said, "I see I have chosen well, wizard. Know you then that I am the true master of this keep. My name is Rearguard and the Prince is my grandson."

Embaza's eyebrows rose in astonishment. He moved forward of the spears at his neck to give a slight bow. "Forgive me, Patriarch, I had no idea I was addressing the King of the Desert."

Mollified, the gnome blew his nose on a yellow pocket handkerchief. He gestured to the stone floor. "Let's be seated and discuss this like gentlemen…that is, if you can forestall that pressing business you mentioned."

"Well," said Embaza, "if you promise to be quick." He fished a bit of wax from a pocket his robe to shape as he listened to the gnome.

No sooner had the Patriarch seated himself than he launched into a litany of complaints regarding his rheumatism. Embaza restrained his temper, and when the gnomad finally drew a breath to continue, he said, "Your Highness, I do have pressing business elsewhere, and, to be honest, your ailment doesn't sound life threatening."

Rearguard squinted and stroked his beard. "You young people are all alike—no sense of proportion. What could be more important than the well-being of your elder?"

Embaza leaned forward. "The lives of my friends. I am on my way to rescue them from your dungeon."

"My grandson's dungeon," lied the gnome.

Embaza hiked his brows. "I don't care whose it is. You spoke of a proposal?"

Rearguard replied, "Mischa put your friends where they are. You have no love for my grandson, do you?"

"I admit that."

"Good." The gnome smiled, his blue eyes twinkling. "I have a job for you. How would you like to teach him a lesson—about magic?"

Embaza was instantly alert. "Yes?"

"Show him what a real wizard can do. Take away his toys and trinkets if you fancy them. But—don't hurt him too much—only teach him. How about it?"

"If you will let me rescue my friends first, I'd be delighted."

"No, no," said the gnome. "I want nothing to do with your personal problems. That's a matter between you and my grandson."

"Then, your Highness, we are at an impasse." Embaza's voice was cold. "Let me take my leave."

Rearguard stroked his beard. "Not so fast." He produced a smooth piece of ivory from an apron pocket, which he offered to Embaza. Shaped like a large coin, the disc was etched with a peculiar drawing.

"What's this?" he asked.

"A token. You'll find it very useful anywhere in my realm." He laughed, his teeth discolored with age. "If you are able to escape Mischa's little fiefdom."

If I refuse, my life won't be worth this token. Embaza said, "I accept. Now how will I find the Prince?"

Rearguard glanced at the giants and crooked his finger at the wizard. "Lean down." He whispered the directions into Embaza's tufted ear.

Barely controlling his impatience, the wizard bowed to the gnome.

This gesture pleased the old man for he nodded to his guards to make way for Embaza. Then he clasped his hands behind his back and rocked, smiling, as he watched the wizard descend the stairs. In a few moments, he was chuckling to himself, his rheumatism gone.

-36-

IN A dark room in the northern tower of the Manor, a hooded figure sat crouched over a large globe of smoky crystal. An oversized leather sack rested on the floor nearby. Otherwise, the room appeared to be in disuse. Cobwebs hung from the ceiling, shrouding the room as well as the already shrouded figure. The lustrous globe was larger than a human head and shone obscurely, yet when the hooded creature rubbed it, colors and figures took shape within the crystal.

A desert hawk cried out from a distant dune, and the figure jerked his head toward the window. As he did, the heavy hood fell, exposing a bald head with skin as white as chalk. His mouth was opened in a grimace and showed large crooked teeth, broken and yellowed. His eyes were dark slits, squinting in the dim reflection of the sunlight. When he blinked, the eyes glowed red.

The albino hid once again beneath the hood and returned his attention to the globe.

As the shapes coalesced in the orb, one image resolved itself—the face of a handsome dark elf. On his head was a crown of brilliant citrine, glistening like a fiery halo. Then, from the crystal, the dark elf's clear voice echoed into the room.

"Well, Morbigon, I see you received the orb I sent to you. No doubt you have the locket as well. Have you succeeded in destroying the Usurper?"

"Not yet, Master," said the hooded figure, his voice quavering, "b-but I have located her—she will attempt to escape through a tunnel beneath the Manor." His hand drew the locket from a thong around his neck. "You see, Master?"

"And what of the creatures from the phantom realm? Have you summoned them?"

"Yes, Master. They were killed in battle with the Usurper's allies, but they did perform one task for you—they killed the Mistress of Loote, the healer Zelwyn."

"Excellent, but that is not our chief aim. If you don't eliminate the Usurper this time—you'll find it difficult to come home again, Morbigon." The handsome face radiated a dazzling but cruel smile as the albino hunched deeper into himself, trembling.

"Yes, Your Highness," he said in a sepulchral tone.

There was a swirl of color as the figure in the globe receded.

The albino reached out with gnarled fingers and gasped, then cried, "Wait, your Highness. When I've succeeded—you won't forget your promise? You won't forget—the Wand of Disguise?"

The elf responded with a malicious laugh and whispered, "You'll find I can be very generous to a wizard who pleases me."

The colors in the globe faded to black. *Wizard, yes. That's what I am. That's indeed what I am. Who needs that school of tyrannical old witches—what do they know?*

The sly figure lifted the crystal and nestled it on his lap. Then he took a heavy gray cloth from the sack. After he had swaddled the globe in fold after gray fold, he put the bundle into the bag, arranging the other items around it.

He had carefully hoarded magic objects, including an elderberry wand and a birch-wood wand covered with runic writing. He had also acquired a rune-chased silver goblet, a handful of gold coins embossed with the shapes of hawks, desert lions and deer among others that were ancient, bearing the elemental symbols of fire and water. He grinned. *The King will reward me when he sees the money I've earned from for favors to the Prince. This will pay his new army. One of these alone is worth a hundred luaavh. Then, with the Wand*

145

of Disguise, I'll teach those witches a thing or two.

Morbigon mumbled three words and waved his hands over the bag, which shriveled to the size and shape of a walnut that he thrust into a pouch inside his robe. *Dekhalis might be powerful in his own way, but he does not know the true enemy.*

If I can kill Embaza, then the Nightwing's daughter will be no match for my magic. But where is this upworld wizard? Morbigon had probed the tunnels and found no trace of him. Yet he had caught a brief taste of his power. The albino shuddered to think of it.

Morbigon hurried out of the room, paused to check the hallway, then shuffled down the corridor to a dark stairway. There was another phantom to be summoned.

-37-

OBSIDIAN AWOKE feeling renewed and glad that his wound had stopped bleeding. He insisted on carrying Tiala, thus relieving Gudrun of her burden. A few moments later, Tiala stirred.

"How do you feel, Princess?" asked Obsidian.

"Hungry." She longed for the food that had been in her waist pack. "I hope the Prince finds my food as bitter as I find his."

Still in fox form, Polah's stomach growled for a tasty scrap of mouse, and this hunger strengthened her animal side. Obsidian felt around in his waist sash only to learn that the giants had missed nothing.

The distant sounds of marching reached their ears. Gudrun whispered, "It's the hour before dawn, time for the exercise of Mischa's house guards. They'll drill for about an hour outside while it's still cool. It will be easier for us to escape."

Tiala nodded.

"Come on," said the dwarf and led them from the room into the corridor, then to the north a few yards until they came to a crude stairway leading down.

"Where does that go?" asked Six Stix.

Gudrun pointed her skimpy beard. "The south gate—I think. This part of the Manor is rarely used. It passes under the sewer." There were groans from the others.

Obsidian swallowed. *Tunnels?*

"What wouldn't I give for a wizard light," muttered Six Stix as the party made their way into darker and darker gloom. "I wish we hadn't lost the

Sargothian."

Once again, the fox whined. The corridors, if they could be called that, were little more than gouged-out cavities in the flinty rock. One moment, there was room for four abreast, and the next, a passage barely wide enough to squeeze through. More than once, the elf scraped his skin on a jagged edge of rock. His chin bled in a steady trickle that he absently wiped with one hand.

An occasional wall sconce yielded a wan illumination, barely enough to spy the refuse and the occasional rodent sharing the passageway.

Obsidian said, "I know little of magic, but it seems to me stealth and perseverance are what we need now." He felt a large rat brush his foot, and automatically stepped wide.

Tiala's clear voice echoed off the stone. "I, for one, prefer the darkness."

Polah moved ahead into the inky blackness, her inscrutable, black eyes shining like disembodied orbs as she gazed back at her companions.

The dwarf chuckled. "I, too, my Lady. In fact, I am beginning to feel quite at home. Besides, it's much cooler down here."

"Well," said Six Stix, "I still think it would be easier if I could see better."

Gudrun snorted, enjoying her superiority over the elf. It restored her good humor. Feeling magnanimous, she said to Tiala, "My lady, in your travel-gear, did you bring any phosphor-stone?"

"No, it never occurred to me that I would need light in the upworld. I suppose I was naive."

"Well, what about a magic ring? Don't all you dark elves carry such things?"

They had reached a very wide clearing in the rock with a slanted overhang like a tilted shelf that Tiala climbed up on, bunching her divided skirt to one side to keep from slipping. "I might as well explain something to all of you before we go any farther." She whispered after she realized what an echo her voice produced in this hollow chamber.

The others rested against the cool walls, all except the fox, who stood panting.

"When my sister died, we went into mourning. It's a tradition that when someone dies in the royal family, no one can use magic or weapons until three moons have passed. My brother will take advantage of this time to lay traps for me."

"But how do you know the moon's changes when you live underground?" asked Six Stix.

"There are many signs. The most obvious is a small mushroom called a moonteller that turns silver at the full moon. And, of course, the level of water in the various lakes and rivers. Our worlds are connected in many ways." Tiala raised her chin. "Then there are the more subtle—fertility cycles."

Six Stix smirked. "So, you brought nothing, no weapons or magic protection?"

She said, "I took a desperate risk, I know—maybe I was wrong..." Her voice broke. "But I had lost a sister, we were in danger, and there was no time to waste."

"We should go on," said Obsidian. "I care little for magic. As far as I'm concerned, the natural world is all we need, and where secrecy is uncovered, magic no longer exists."

Tiala said wistfully, "My sister Eleppon would agree with you."

Just then, Polah gave a soft growl, and they heard a rustling in the distance. Tiala was alert. In moments, the unmistakable tramp of feet echoed from somewhere not far behind them, although the source was unclear.

Gudrun closed her eyes and placed her hand against the stone wall. She concentrated and tried to regain her sense of direction. *East, I think.*

She glanced at Six Stix. He, too, was staring at the passageway as if he could determine their location by will alone. *He's picturing my map,* thought Gudrun. She remembered who he had been, the leader of an elite troop. *He was a general, too.* She stared at him in the darkness, then looked away.

Tiala slipped from her perch. Beckoning to the others, she followed Polah who was already exploring the hallway ahead. Gudrun caught up to Tiala, with Six Stix and Obsidian close behind her, feeling their way by touching the walls.

The pitted stone floor was uneven and treacherous, and the darkness continued to hamper their movements. Six Stix mentally swore. He suggested Obsidian switch places with him so he could be at the rear.

As they continued through the narrow passage, the noise of tramping feet grew louder. The ceiling became so cramped that the five of them had to crawl. The closer the noise, the lower the ceiling became.

Finally, they came to a point where they could go no further, and they lay motionless for a moment or two, catching their breaths. The heavy steps thundered from nearby. Then they heard a voice that rattled like gravel in a cup. "Halt! The culprits are nearby. I can smell them."

"Yes, sir." The marching stopped.

"Start digging," came the command.

A small rock dislodged above Polah's head and struck her nose. She felt a tickling sensation and realized it was her own blood. An unnatural calm stole over her, and she thought, *Oh no. Not now.*

While the others listened with strict attention to the digging above them, Polah was aware only of her own dilemma. As her fur turned to skin, even though she tried to relax and endure the transformation, she moaned with distress.

Behind her, Tiala hissed, "Polah, are you all right?"

"No," replied the fox-woman.

"Oh, rat piss," muttered Gudrun. "Let them know we're down here, why don't you?"

"Sssh," Tiala said. "Polah's changed again. Help me get my cloak off." It was indeed difficult in the cramped space, but with Gudrun's help, Tiala managed to wriggle out of the travel-cloak. Polah wrapped herself in its thick warmth.

"My lady," whispered the fox-woman, "I pray you never run out of extra garments."

At that moment, a chink of air and light showed through the rock above Obsidian's head. He squirmed to one side as a bulging eye filled the space, looking around, and a voice growled, "Captain, I smell them, but I don't see them."

"Keep digging," came the gruff reply.

Meanwhile, Six Stix found a shard of rock dislodged by the vibrations on the ceiling. He noted with satisfaction that it was quite sharp on one end. *If he shows his eye again, I'll poke it out.*

Just then, the ceiling over Obsidian gave way, the monk electing to lie still while above him guttural shouts of victory erupted. Six Stix and Gudrun squeezed back into the shadows on either side.

A large, hairy boot landed in the rubble, just missing Obsidian's thigh, and Six Stix saw his opportunity. Viciously, he drove the shard into the intruder's instep, and with a howl, the fiend retreated. In moments, the opening swarmed with giants.

Six Stix grabbed a fistful of stones in each hand and threw them into the faces of the nearest giants. Roars of pain were followed by a spate of filthy oaths. A spear landed inches away from the elf's chest, but to his dismay, one of the giants crushed it with his boot. More oaths poured forth.

Gudrun placed a well-aimed foot in the groin of the stooping giant, and shouted, "Nice way to talk around a lady." The giant recovered himself and lunged at her with a wicked-looking scimitar.

Like a whirlwind, the monk emerged from the rubble in a blur of motion that knocked three giants backwards onto the sharp stones. To the giants, his pale skin and dust-covered garments made him look like a supernatural fiend.

"Demon!" bellowed the captain. "Run!" The troop clambered all over each other in their haste to get away. The sound of their booted retreat continued for several seconds.

Obsidian brushed the dust from his eyelashes and bent to help Gudrun to her feet. She grabbed his forearms and grinned. "Nice work. I like your style."

Six Stix lay back laughing. "Did you see their faces?"

Tiala peered out of the rubble where she and Polah had been trapped. "Help us out, will you? I can hardly breathe in here."

Gudrun grabbed her hand and hauled her up, then Polah followed, clutching the dull green cloak around her and coughing stone dust from her lungs. "We can't go any farther this way. It's blocked," she said.

They all looked about them at the jagged hole created by the collapse of the tunnel ceiling.

"Well," said Obsidian, "they must have come from somewhere. Let's follow the giants."

Six Stix led the others in the direction that the giants had gone, thankful that with more light for the time being he could at least see where to place his feet.

This brief respite from the dark was succeeded by a deeper blackness and the increasingly noxious odor of sewage one level beneath them. The General moved to the front to guide the party, all silent as they picked their way. Tiala was at home in the darkness, and she guided Six Stix and Obsidian by gently tapping their arms.

All at once, a breeze of fresh air from ahead warmed Gudrun's cheek. The others felt it too, and they moved faster. Tiala pushed her way to the front of the group, tired of being a follower. She led with sure-footed grace, thankful for her dragon skin boots and her long sleeve which she pressed over her nostrils against the smell.

When she stopped suddenly, Gudrun stumbled into her.

Six Stix swore as his nose bumped into Obsidian's back.

"Do you see something on the ceiling ahead of us?" Tiala asked.

Gudrun peered up to a dark mass—and it was moving. "Spiders," she whispered.

The dark elf nodded. "In Alvarra, cave spiders are common. All we need is a shield to pass under them."

"No, my Lady, these are bigger. Look."

The walls and floor appeared to be swarming black liquid.

Six Stix asked, "Why have we stopped?"

Tiala squawked at a nip to her leg, then jumped over a patch of spiders. More were dropping, as large as dogs.

"Run!" said Gudrun, grabbing her hand and sprinting ahead. Obsidian hoisted Polah onto his shoulders and raced forward blindly along a path thick with the angry arachnids. Six Stix followed, cursing and slapping spiders from his leggings.

Gudrun pressed toward the archway ahead. One by one, they all hurried after her. Tiala's left leg throbbed, and she stumbled, gritting her teeth.

When they reached the archway, the corridor branched in two directions. The smell of sewage was still strong.

Tiala said, "Which way, General?"

Before Gudrun could answer, there was the unmistakable chittering of rats from the pathway to the right. Polah could not help remembering Anebra's fatal bite from the giant rat in the arena. It seemed like ages ago. As the noise of the rats grew louder, Gudrun hurried to the left, closely followed by the others. She thought, *I hate not having a choice.*

Six Stix wondered, *Are we being herded like sheep? Perhaps this dwarf is leading us to her master.*

Before long, the ground began to slope upward, and the desert heat penetrated their garments.

Obsidian noticed the dark elf limping. "Stop," he said to the others, "there's something wrong with the Princess."

"I'm fine," she said, leaning one arm on the wall of the corridor as she stumbled along.

"No, you're not," said Gudrun, "Let's see that leg you're favoring."

Tiala allowed her to examine the spider bite, and the dwarf said, "It's swollen, but not hot."

"You see?" said Tiala. "There's nothing you can do. We must go on."

Obsidian reached into a hidden pocket of his robe and brought out a handful of herbs. He chose a broad leaf and handed it to Tiala. "If you chew on this, it will help. Don't eat it all at once. It'll make you dizzy."

Tiala wrinkled her nose at the smell, but did as he suggested. In a few moments, she was surprised to find that the pain had subsided.

For nearly an hour, Gudrun rushed them through a maze of twisting and turning corridors that sloped upward, then downward, then straight again. Just when it seemed that they were hopelessly lost, they saw what looked like a large pool up ahead.

A torch flickered on the wall above it, and Six Stix said to Obsidian, "Finally, a light."

When they reached what they had all thought was a pool, they realized with dismay that it was, instead, an open pit.

"We've got to cross that?" asked Polah. She wished she were in fox form.

Six Stix estimated the distance and shrugged. "We can do it," he said. There was a broad landing on the other side, which would make jumping much easier.

Obsidian shook his head. "Look, Six, the Princess can hardly walk, much less jump a chasm like that. And Polah hasn't the stride."

Six Stix looked at Tiala, who was leaning against the wall, her eyes closed. Her dark skin seemed pale. "Well, what do you suggest?" asked the blue elf.

"I'll carry them," answered the monk. Before anyone could protest, he had shouldered Polah and taken a running start. The others held their breaths while Obsidian leapt the chasm and deposited the astonished Polah on the other side.

As he set her down, the wound in his back began to throb. Ignoring this discomfort, Obsidian took another running start and leapt back across the divide. With a polite bow, he hoisted Tiala and repeated his graceful leap, depositing her next to Polah.

Watching the monk, Gudrun cursed her lack of acrobatic skill. Her strength had always been more sheer endurance than agility. Annoyed with herself, she allowed Obsidian to ferry her across. However, she had enough experience to know that the youth was in a great deal of pain. "Better chew on some leaves yourself, lad," she said, hopping from his arms.

Six Stix insisted on making the leap himself, but as his feet reached the opposite side, there was a rumbling sound behind him.

Obsidian froze, having heard that sound before. *Cave-in.*

The tunnel behind them collapsed, doubling the size of the chasm. Now it was impossible to turn back. They looked at each other and continued onward, still covering their noses from the stench. Once again, Gudrun had misgivings. *Another incident decides our path.*

As the coolness of the corridors gave way to heat, Gudrun realized they were near the outer wall of the Manor. Although she had never been in these passages before, she knew there had to be a large exit door. Fourteen feet high, it should be carved with animals. She thought she remembered one of the doors having wild elk carved in it—or maybe wolves.

To her relief, she did see an ornate wooden door up ahead. "At last," she said. "That's the door to the south gate or I'm not the General."

The others hurried to the doorway, and Gudrun pulled the handle at the side where the unmistakable figure of a wild elk was carved. With a scraping sound, the door opened, and a single ray of light pierced the gloom of the hallway. Tiala shrank back, covering her face.

Then they heard it. Cheering.

-38-

Rough hands yanked her through the door, and a deep voice rose above the noise of the crowd. "Welcome, General." Gudrun's eyes widened at the sight before her. The arena was much as she remembered it, with one significant difference. The pit was surrounded by a thick ring of giants in Mischa's purple livery, each with his hands folded around a barbed spear.

As the dwarf was recognized and greeted by many in the audience, hope strengthened her heart. "My friends," she cried out, searching the crowd for familiar faces. Two of the guards ushered Six Stix, Tiala, Obsidian and Polah into the arena.

Tiala blinked at the brightness and her ears throbbed at the insults hurled her way. Through the tiny, slotted windows at the top of the arena, the morning sunlight beamed down. One ray slanted into the pit like a sword.

Polah was numbed by her own defenselessness. The last time she had stood here, she had experienced a rite of passage. What would it be this time? She hugged the green cloak around her nakedness and prayed for a miracle.

Six Stix swaggered around the pit, eyeing the guards with distaste. He tripped over a stick, or so he thought, and in bending down, discovered a javelin. Rather a nice one, at that. *Wait a minute. That's mine!*

The others made similar discoveries. Before long, Obsidian had strapped his butterfly knives gently onto his wounded back. Six Stix recovered both of his swords and two of his daggers. Even Polah found a sharpened tusk knife, similar to the hunting knife she had carried.

Gudrun looked for her sword with only a faint hope, and found instead a broadsword of dwarven make, quite stunning, but not as old.

Polah hefted the tusk knife, and clutched the cloak tighter with the other hand. *What's going on?* The giants had not moved.

A white-robed announcer on the platform above held the huge horn to his lips. "And now…" he began.

A lull in the shouting as the spectators waited for an introduction. "Are those champions fighting the Prince's own guards?"

"Where did that dark one come from?"

"The seven hells, no doubt."

Terror at the fear and hatred pouring from the audience prickled Tiala's skin. She shrank from the ray of sunlight that nearly touched her foot, but one of the hulking guards shoved her into the center of the pit. Off balance, she stumbled and dropped to one hand to right herself, her fingers striking something sharp. She looked down and gasped at a familiar poppy painted on wood.

My harp. She dug the instrument from the sand, aghast at the possibility that it might be ruined, but only one of the fifteen strings was broken. In her overwhelming relief, she barely heard the announcer continue.

"Today, the Prince has arranged a very special exhibition. Not only do we welcome back our favorite General…" Cheering swelled to drown him out and he shouted to be heard.

"Some of you will recognize two of our newest champions, Six Stix, the elven warrior, and Obsidian, novice of the east." He waited until the spattering of cheers subsided. "And perhaps you will remember our esteemed new hero, Polah, who can turn herself into a ferocious beast."

The crowd was beside itself in expressing its excitement. Indeed, many had witnessed the shape-changer's transformation, their blood lust whetted for this contest, whatever it might turn out to be.

"But for a special surprise…" cried the announcer, expertly teasing and cajoling the giddy crowd, "the unexpected…" The spectators stamped their feet in rhythm, indicating their impatience.

"…the capture of a dark elf…trapped in her filthy lair…by our great Prince…her accomplices, escaping." Most of this was drowned out by the hysterical roar of the populace, their childhood fears ignited by the announcer's speech.

The General raised her new sword above her head and shouted to the onlookers, "It's a lie. Don't listen to him." She put her arm around Tiala, and although the dark elf was taller, it was a most protective gesture. Polah, too, moved to Tiala's side.

However, these actions achieved the very opposite of the desired effect. Now convinced that the former heroes were indeed evil, many spectators got to their feet, hurling food and any other item they could get their hands on at the dark elf and her would-be protectors.

Obsidian and Six Stix caught some of this debris and flung it back at the crowd, but it was useless. Eventually, members of the crowd tired of the game, or ran out of missiles.

Meanwhile, the announcer had attempted to conclude his introduction. "For your entertainment, they will now fight each other—or die at the hands of the Manor guards, the dreaded…" He was never allowed to finish, and after a few attempts, finally threw up his hands and stepped down from the platform.

The entire audience was on its feet, stamping and shouting at the group in the pit. "Kill the traitors, kill the beast, kill the dark one, kill, kill…"

Gudrun clutched Tiala's arm and hollered, "I've never seen them this worked up."

Tiala's eyes filled with tears of fear and rage. "How can they be so blind, so brutish?" she yelled.

Polah watched Tiala in mute understanding. She knew.

Obsidian bowed his head in shame, remembering the stories his mother had told him about dark elves.

"My Lady," shouted Gudrun, "Mischa would have circulated rumors about us before this farce even began. He was always good at that." She spat on the sandy floor. "Coward."

Six Stix edged nearer to the dwarf, "I thought you knew where you were going, bitch. The south gate, is it?"

"You call me that again, and I swear I'll take this opportunity to carve out your tongue," she bellowed.

"Stop it," cried Tiala.

Obsidian, who had been scanning the crowd in the hope that another monk might be there, turned at the sound of her voice, and grabbed the dwarf and blue elf by one arm. They squirmed within his painful grip. "Look around you," he said tersely. "None of us will leave this pit alive if we don't work together."

Perched in his aerie, Mischa pounded his fists on the ledge with excitement. "Yes," he said to himself, fingering his gold ring while he waited. In a moment, he would make that monk's back ooze with blood...and then...

He slipped the ring off and set it beside a line of others on his ledge. What fun it would be to use them, one by one.

At a noise behind, he turned in his chair, startled to see the gray-cloaked Embaza holding a familiar object in his hand.

"You," cried the Prince and jumped up, reaching to a shelf for his wand of bonewood.

"Ah, yes, it is I," said the wizard pleasantly, "and I have a special treat for you, my host." He twirled the demongaze ever so slowly and watched Mischa writhe in pain until he sat down violently, his blue eyes glazed and hollow. The bonewood wand dangled uselessly from the Prince's hand.

"I understand that your secret desire is to be a wizard," Embaza said. "And your first lesson will be how to use this sphere of pain. You see, the more slowly it turns, the longer you will last. Now, what else do we have here?" He noticed various artifacts lying about the room, some of which were quite familiar. He took a step forward, and as he did so, his glance drifted to the window overlooking the arena.

Distracted, he stopped twirling the demongaze, and the Prince clutched his own neck, gasping for breath.

Mischa pointed the wand at Embaza, but nothing happened. His hand trembled as he cried, "Why aren't you shriveling into a lizard?"

Embaza laughed softly and said, "Because you're holding that wand all wrong, dear Prince. Shall I show you the proper way?"

Mischa scowled with rage and hurled the wand to a corner.

Embaza raised the demongaze above the Prince's head and twirled the instrument of pain once again. "I see you've arranged yet another spectacle without sport. You'd better start explaining."

Mischa gripped his chair with whitened knuckles and snarled, "They'll fight each other to the death, unless of course, my guards kill them first. Those barbed spears they carry? Each is tipped with a slow acting poison. I'm not heartless, you know. I gave the dark one her chance. Is it my fault that she spurned my favors?" Spite shone in the tormented eyes, and loathing twisted Embaza's gut.

He looked to the ledge where Mischa kept his favorite magic items. *Is there something here that I can use?* Another wand caught his interest. If he could decipher those runes, he would know...

Embaza glanced at the Prince and thought, *I must be done with this noisome pest.* He spun the demongaze faster, but a sudden noise at the doorway made him turn. His eyes widened at what he saw, and he clutched his necklace.

In spite of his pain, the Prince managed to croak, "Morbigon, help me."

In the doorway stood a figure robed in black. His unnaturally pale hands were moving in the air as he chanted in a hideous voice, *"Gor Nee Izgot Zhoido..."*

Embaza's vision glazed over into a black fog. *A blindness spell. Child's play.* He chanted a counter spell. *"Namue Ay, Namue Ziay."*

Even through his haze of pain, in spite of his pretensions, the Prince was fascinated. He knew a real contest of magic when he saw one. As his strength returned, he reached for the demongaze. But his movement alerted Embaza and the wizard twirled the artifact again, forcing Mischa to retract his hand and curse the torment.

In the arena, the five companions had moved to stand back to back, squaring off against the hostile audience and the ring of guards. This, however, had little success, for one of the giants stepped forward and prodded Tiala with the butt of his spear. The giant next to him poked Six Stix with the business end of his weapon. The elf felt a sharp sting, and a small bead of blood welled from his punctured triceps.

"Fight, you two," ordered the first giant, "or you're dead."

Tiala held up her harp. "I'm not even armed."

The giant crossed his arms and scowled at her. "Use your powers, evil one."

Now, both giants aimed their weapons at her breast, while Six Stix swallowed and hissed at Tiala, "Be brave. We'll stall them."

He circled Tiala and lunged at her with his sword, until he sliced a piece of fabric from her sleeve. "Point your fingernails at me," he whispered. "Now frown at me. Growl!"

The crowd roared its approval, and the giants rested their weapons. Six Stix was in top form as he demonstrated at least twenty-five sword positions. Tiala, too, displayed some of the technique for which she was envied in Alvarra.

Even without a weapon, she turned and twisted so expertly that Six Stix never touched her or the harp.

The blue elf was beginning to get warmed up, and spurred on by the crowd, he performed a daring move that happened to be one of his trademarks: a leaping turn in mid-air, the sword curled around his body, followed by a thrust at the opponent at the moment of descent. Unfortunately, he stumbled on the landing, unexpectedly dizzy, and nearly buried his sword in the sand floor of the pit.

Tiala reached out to help him instead of taking the opportunity to scratch out his eyes. The audience hurled obscenities at the mock fighters, and the giants closed the ring menacingly.

Polah clutched Obsidian and cried, "Do something."

The monk reacted with wild leaps and acrobatic somersaults. For a moment, the audience and giants alike were distracted. His expert display reminded Polah of the way he had first sailed into Tiala's room to rescue her.

Obsidian's grace and power were indeed thrilling to watch, but as he feinted at his various companions, the encrusted wound in his back reopened. With a faked hand chop at Six Stix and a feather kick at Tiala's cheek that ruffled her ear hairs, he dropped to his hands and knees. The pain was impossible to ignore and it was all he could do to keep from fainting.

Polah squeezed her eyes shut and balled her fists. *Change, damn you, change. Come on, fox. Where are you?* But it was no use. She couldn't call the animal within her and tears stung her eyes.

The General continued to pound reason mixed with insults at the crowd, thinking, *someone must believe me.* Had all her admirers vanished? "Can't you see the truth, you ignorant pigs? The Prince has lied to you. It's nothing but a wicked show." She dodged a piece of breadfruit sailing at her nose.

One of the men in the front row leered at her and yelled, "So, dance for us, then, dolly. Show us a leg."

"Yeah, give us a real show," shouted another. The audience stamped its feet as more took up the cry.

Two of the giants even grinned, showing their blackened front teeth. They advanced upon Gudrun with their barbed weapons. She recognized the faint yellow discoloration of the metal tip. *Poison.*

"Fine," shouted Gudrun, shaking a defiant fist at them. She did a jig, one hand on her hip, the other raised above her head and called to Tiala, "Play for them, my Lady."

Tiala watched in wonder as the dwarf jumped clumsily around. She brought her harp into position. *If this is my dying day, at least I'll honor it with music.*

There weren't many songs that she could play on a travel-harp with only fourteen strings. But she remembered an old one, a very simple tune that was one of her favorites. With a lump in her throat, she pressed her fingers to the strings, and plucked the melody, seemingly out of thin air.

The nearest onlookers took up the cadence and stamped in rhythm, laughing at the dwarf's antics. Gudrun, pleased with her ruse, shouted to Tiala, "Keep playing, my Lady. Louder."

Tiala replied, "I can do even better." She sang in a strong, clear voice, putting her very heart and soul into what might be her last song: "Oh, gather round, ye maidens dark, and listen to my tale, of the poor, beloved son of Lark and the fairy of Bluegrotto Vale…"

Everyone in Alvarra knew the old ballad that told of the doomed love affair between a fairy and a Prince, son of the Nightwing Lark. But, of course, it was new to this audience, and, captivated by the beauty of Tiala's voice and fervent spirit, they strained to hear the words in spite of themselves.

"Shut up," one poked his neighbor.

"She sings so fair," said another.

And truly, she did sing fair. Soon, the entire hall was hushed as the sweet sounds of Tiala's voice penetrated the very shadows while her nimble fingers danced over the harp strings. Gudrun stood with her sword resting before her and strove not to cry.

Meanwhile, in the aerie, Embaza's troubles had multiplied. The new magic user was full of tricks and cast a bewildering number of spells, most of them poorly. But even an inept magic user was more than Embaza wanted to deal with at the moment.

Worse, the albino and the Prince had gained an understanding. The albino addressed him, "I will tell my master of your loyalty in the face of his enemies."

The Prince croaked, "I care nothing for your master. Only get rid of this devil for me, and I'll pay you twice the wealth he promised you."

The albino laughed. "You don't realize what you're saying. Lord King Dekhalis will make you a magic ruler, and all who are loyal to him will learn to be wizards." The Prince's ears perked up, but he lacked the strength to speak. *If only this fiend would stop twirling the sphere. Imagine. Using my own power against me. He's going to be sorry.*

Embaza could see that his foes were tiring, and he strove to overcome his own despair and exhaustion. Forcing his mind to concentrate, he began to chant.

The Prince could barely keep his eyes open. Morbigon was on his knees, groping in his pocket. With a cry of victory, the albino's hand closed around a walnut shaped object.

Embaza's piercing eyes bored into him and a cold dread seeped through the albino wizard. The light from the necklace was withering his very brain. His fingers opened and the nut-shaped object rolled to the middle of the floor.

"No," Morbigon howled and lunged after it, but Embaza quickly stooped to get it.

The elf laughed. "So, this is your source of power, my fellow practitioner," he taunted in a voice now hoarse from spell casting. He blew softly on the nut and it swelled to the shape and size of a large, brown sack, the contents of which the wizard dumped to the floor.

Seeing his last hope dashed, the Prince slumped into unconsciousness.

Without a focus, Embaza knew the power of the demongaze would begin to drain. He dropped the object into his pocket and relaxed his arm, now numb with fatique.

On his knees, Morbigon clasped his hands and entreated Embaza, "Have mercy, brother wizard. Do not kill me."

Embaza answered, "You give me little choice, but I'll ask you anyway, why should I spare your life?"

The albino's reddish eyes glowed. "I can lead you to immense authority. You are a great wizard, but you can be even greater."

"Greater?" asked Embaza, wiping the sweat of his brow with his hand.

"Yes," gushed Morbigon, "my master, Dekhalis seeks men of power for the new world. He will open the treasure vaults of Alvarra to all who follow him. There are riches and magic items of undreamed wonder and magnificence…"

Embaza heard the madness in his voice and shook his head. *If this poor wretch had studied in Sargothas, he might have had a chance. I wonder what has twisted him so.* He kneaded a piece of wax into a rough shape.

"No…" wailed the albino, putting up his hands.

But Embaza smiled with pity. "If your master is so interested in men of power, I'll make sure he hears how well you died." He impaled the waxen figure through the belly with a needle and Morbigon's scream filled the room. One more thrust to the heart and it would be done, but Embaza hesitated. He turned instead to grab two magic items of specific interest from Mischa's ledge—a wand and a ring. He scanned the littered floor for anything that might be of use from Morbigon's bag.

Then he heard her. He turned and looked down into the arena. The crowd was enveloped in a rapt silence as the sound of Tiala's chime-like voice filled the hall. The last stanza of her ballad soared up to him as he took one last look around:

> "…though her sweetheart's face appears in a dream
> only once in a hundred years,
> the Bluegrotto fairy stands waiting beside
> the lake of a thousand tears."

The last note echoed into the arena, and Tiala's eyes opened. She had never felt so cleansed after singing, exhilarated yet enchanted, as if she were coming out of a trance. She saw the giants staring at her with baffled expressions on their faces. The stands were filled with misty-eyed fighters of every description, many of them draped over the sides of the pit.

She grabbed Polah and Obsidian from behind her and herded Six Stix and Gudrun toward the exit on the opposite side. She prayed this door wouldn't lead to a chasm.

The giants guarding the exit stepped back in a daze, half-frightened of this black elf and her voice.

"Demon," they hissed, making signs of warding.

A few moments later, Obsidian collided with Embaza, hurrying down the stairs from above.

-39-

PRINCE MISCHA struggled to open one eye. A shaft of sunlight illuminated a row of bottles on the shelf beside his head. Each was filled with a different grade of sand, an experiment he had worked on many years ago. It had been delightful testing their weights and other properties, but Mischa could not remember what had prompted him to do it; it had been so long since he had cared about anything but magic.

When he could lift his head and move his extremities, he looked around the room. The albino lay just inside the doorway. *It was a mistake to bargain with that weakling. His spells and magic objects did him no good in the end. And what was it he said? His master would reward me. I could probably teach that Dekhalis a thing or two about magic.*

Mischa left his seat to paw through the splash of objects scattered over the floor. The blue wizard had taken something, he was certain. He suffered a moment of fear, lest something of his own might be gone. For several minutes, he couldn't remember exactly what should be there, but upon seeing the flute in his secret drawer, he sighed with relief.

Since the albino wizard appeared to be dead, he searched his garments and spotted a finely wrought chain about the pale throat. Mischa unlooped the locket from Morbigon's neck. It sat in his palm, the lustrous hair within as mysterious as a patch of night. *A wizard's necklace.* Mischa quickly put it on.

Then he caught a faint gleam near the albino's hand. Mischa unwrapped the gray cloth folded around a large crystal globe and knelt, admiring the piece. He failed to notice the slight pulse at the albino's temple.

He scrambled to his feet and peered down into the arena. The crowd had thinned and those who were left milled around, gabbling with each other. In the empty pit, some of his own guards laughed and talked together. The east door of the arena was wide open.

Mischa brushed off his blue silk trousers and green embroidered vest. He groped the ledge for his rings and cursed when he realized one was missing.

"Mischa."

Startled to hear his name, he whirled around, ready to punish whoever dared to address him with such insolence. He was shocked to see the Patriarch, Rearguard, flanked by six of his most trusted guards.

"Grandfather. What a cheerful surprise. I thought you had no interest in the games." Mischa was suddenly embarrassed to realize that Morbigon's body and possessions still littered the floor. *Will they think I was attacked in my own sanctuary?*

Rearguard pointed to a golden goblet lying amid the clutter and said to one of the giants, "Mustadd, bring that cup to me." The titan jumped to follow the gnome's orders, and Rearguard held the goblet up to the beam of sunlight, then turned his gaze on Mischa. "What do you know about this?"

The Prince yanked his vest down over his stomach and replied, "The thief lies before you, Grandfather. I killed him with my magic powers. You see? There's the rest of his loot." He kicked a pile of coins with his foot.

Rearguard laughed, and once he had started, he laughed so hard that he nearly had to sit down.

The Prince nervously stuttered, "W-what's the joke, Grandfather?"

"You didn't fight this man," answered the gnome. "You never fought an honest battle with anyone in your life, magic or otherwise." He stopped laughing and a frown beetled his brow. "In fact, it wouldn't surprise me if he were your own spy. You probably paid him in these goods stolen from your own people."

Mischa's face reddened, and he was speechless. *How did the old goat know?*

Rearguard himself was pained to see that his guess had been correct. "I'll tell you what," he began.

The Prince relaxed. He knew that tone of voice. He would get away with it, as always.

"I'm going to let you have your toys and magic trinkets, since you set such store by them. I'll even let you keep your riches and fine clothes." The gnome snapped his fingers and told his giants, "Gather up his things and put them in that sack there."

"Careful!" Mischa cried, then turned to Rearguard, "Grandfather, they don't have to do that. I can call in my own servants to clean this up."

"Clean up? Of course, we will dispose of this body with the cremation proper to such scum. But first," said the old gnome, looking around, "Nordoom, give me your waterskin and rations." The giant complied without hesitation, and Rearguard handed them to the Prince. "I wouldn't want anyone to call me unfair." He then grinned up at Nordoom. "Now, carry him."

Mischa's protests were futile against the brute strength of the giants and the iron will of the Patriarch. He was carried down to the south gate, the very gate that Gudrun had searched for with such diligence. The giants held him in the doorway, facing the heat of the vast desert.

Mischa squinted against the blinding morning sun that in an hour or two would be directly overhead. "Grandfather, don't do this," he pleaded.

"Now, Mischief," said Rearguard, "I'm sure you'll have no trouble surviving out here—if you remember what I've taught you. Of course, the tribes have fealty to me and I've instructed them not to help you. But after all, you can always call on your magic powers." He laughed and slapped the Prince on the back. "Perhaps, after a few years, when you're accustomed to the gnomadic life, I'll take you back. When you're ready to settle down and respect the old ways, I'll even get you another wife. Maybe two. You'll thank me for this, Grandson."

The Prince was not listening. His mind was quite clear. A catalogue of all the magic items he would need ran through his mind. Unfortunately, most of them were in his treasure vault. But he would survive. *I'll show him who has power.* He kept his mouth a thin line of uncompromising bitterness, refusing to give the old man even the courtesy of a goodbye.

When Rearguard saw that his grandson was being obstinate, he lifted a booted foot and kicked Mischa in the seat of his pants. The Prince stumbled onto all fours in the blazing sand.

"I swear by all that's holy, you're still my chosen heir. May the God of the Desert return you to me," said Rearguard, and the Prince heard the snap of his fingers. The huge, wooden door scraped shut, leaving Mischa no recourse but to open the brown sack and take inventory.

Back in the aerie, Rearguard and his men were not especially shocked when the body of the albino disappeared before their eyes. It was simply more evidence that dabbling in magic was dangerous.

-40-

As soon as Obsidian recognized the wizard, he shouted, "Trust the balance, you're alive. Somehow I knew it would be so."

The two clasped hands, and Embaza said, "Were you all able to escape?"

Obsidian nodded. "Thanks to the dark elf's singing, the guards just stood back and let us pass. I've never heard anything like it—she was wonderful."

"I know," murmured Embaza as Tiala rounded the corner and gave him a radiant smile.

She whirled about and said, "Polah—look who's here."

The fox-woman sprinted up the stairs behind her. When she saw Embaza, her heart leapt into her throat. It occurred to her that she and the wizard had not spoken telepathically since she had been in the dungeon. She smiled shyly and said to Tiala, "I told you."

"Where's the General?" asked Tiala.

"She was right behind me," answered Polah. They all turned as Six Stix appeared, laboring up the stairs. The blue elf was very green in the face, and obviously having trouble walking. He glanced at Embaza and his eyes widened, "The Sargothian. I don't believe—." He stopped to wince at the sudden pain.

Obsidian rushed to his side. "What's wrong?"

"Maybe something I ate," said Six.

The monk helped him up the remaining stairs to join the others on a wide landing before a branching of two staircases.

Six Stix addressed Embaza. "Where were you when we needed you?"

The wizard frowned, ever one to take things literally. "I was seeing about a certain lordling, for one thing. Where are we headed?"

Obsidian said, "We've been following the dwarf. She's led us down so many passages, I'm not sure where we are."

"Where is she?" Tiala asked again.

Polah frowned at Six Stix, "I thought she was in front of you."

Six Stix nodded. "She was, but when I rounded the corner, she had disappeared."

The others stared at him in amazement, and Tiala voiced their thoughts. "But why would she leave us without a word?"

Polah spoke up. "Maybe to get food and water from the kitchens."

As the truth dawned on him, Six Stix felt quite nauseous. He sat down on the landing. "She went to get her sword, the relic of Estenhame."

"By the heart of Miralor—why?" asked Tiala.

Six Stix enjoyed the look of disenchantment on her face, but much as he hated to admit it, the dwarf was a seasoned officer. She wouldn't have abandoned this small party any more than she would a crack troop of warriors. No doubt she knew how well he had studied her map. He said, "It would mean her very life if she left that sword for others to find."

Tiala observed him with interest. "I see."

Polah came forward, still clasping the heavy, green cloak around her. "What should we do now?"

"We can't stay here," answered Tiala. "The Prince and his guards are sure to find us."

Embaza's deep voice rang with authority. "I happen to know that the Prince is quite occupied with family matters."

Six Stix said, "If I remember, a few more turns to the left, and we'll be near the kitchen. We need supplies."

Embaza had moved to Tiala's side, and said, "I think our main problem is time. Every moment we stand here, the sun is rising in the sky."

Tiala swallowed hard and said, "Only the General knows where the stables are and how to get a conveyance. I don't think we can leave without her."

Obsidian was worried about Six Stix. The elf looked extremely weak. He helped Six Stix to his feet and supported him up the left-hand stairway, behind Embaza.

The monk reached into his robe and pulled out more of the herbs he had rolled up in a makeshift cloth bag. He muttered, "Chew this thoroughly. It will help, but you'll feel even weaker when it wears off. Try to conserve your strength."

"What is it?" asked the elf.

"The monks call it 'heal-all,' and it almost does. What happened to you?"

"One of those coward giants nicked me with his barb. Probably poisoned."

Obsidian took a firmer grip on the elf, but the medicine was already taking effect, and Six Stix walked with almost his usual jaunt, shaking off the monk's help.

Embaza watched their progress from the top of the stairs and was relieved to see the elf walking on his own. *Does the monk have a talent for healing?*

Tiala and Polah joined him on the landing, then Six and Obsidian. They could all smell the kitchen. Everyone was quiet as Six Stix came forward and motioned for them to stay back.

Obsidian ignored his warning. Surprised at her own audacity, Polah, too, moved to his side. She was tired of being in the background. Since her shape-changing had deserted her, she wanted to do something useful.

The blue elf led the way to the kitchen, while the other two sauntered behind him, like guests out for a stroll. From the kitchen doorway, Six saw a couple of young gnomes washing dishes. The female scrubbed while the male poured clean sand from a bin next to the sink. Both had to stand on stools to reach.

While Obsidian and Polah watched the hallway, Six Stix put his thumbs in his belt and swaggered into the room, whistling. Both gnomes looked up, then the male frowned and said, "If you've missed the morning meal, it's not our fault. There's nothing left but the scraps, and they're for the children."

The female returned to her scrubbing. "Get out, we have work to do. In a few hours, you can eat again."

Six Stix meandered over to the barrel in the corner, saying, "Oh, I'm not hungry. I'm just bored...and, well...I'd like to sit with you awhile and hear some desert talk. They say you people are just full of good stories." He snagged an overripe plum that had been left on the sideboard, polished it on his jerkin, then popped it into his mouth.

The gnomes looked at each other in exasperation. What the Prince's guests wouldn't think of next.

"Have a heart," pleaded the male, "you're just going to be in the way. We really do have work to do, so be nice and find some other entertainment."

While he talked, Six opened pots and barrels, tasting and sampling this and that. "Well, if you feel that way, I guess I could go out to the stables, or maybe see what the arena has in store today." He was careful that the gnomes didn't see him fill his tunic with foodstuffs. In the back of his mind, he wondered if he might run across some more of that heal-all of Obsidian's.

The elf moved back to the rain-barrel in the corner. The lid was screwed on tightly, and he looked around for a container. With an air of innocence, he asked, "Do you think I could have a drink? I am thirsty."

The female gnome wiped her hands on her apron and hopped down from the stool in front of the sink. "Really," she said huffily, and pushed Six Stix away from the rain-barrel. "You know the rules. You can have all the ale and mead you want. But save the water for emergencies."

Six Stix leaned down and tweaked her nose. "I never obey rules, little lady."

The other gnome jumped down to the floor. "Let go of my sister, you big bully." Six Stix grabbed him by the hair and lifted him a foot off the ground, while his sibling struggled to free her nose from his grasp.

Behind them, Obsidian and Polah went into action. While Polah searched cupboards and cabinets, drawers and broom closets for waterskins, Obsidian worked at the tight lid of the rain barrel until he had wrenched it open. He filled the skins Polah had found hanging in a nook near the pantry, then re-capped the barrel, and both left as quickly as they had come.

Six Stix released the gnomes, ran to the sink for the bin of sand and dumped it all over them. "Oof, sorry," he said and hurried out, motioning the others to retreat. The shouts and commotion in the kitchen trailed them down the stairs.

"What did you do to them?" asked Obsidian. "It's bad enough we had to steal water."

"In a place like this? Probably happens all the time. It's nothing they can't handle," said the elf.

Six Stix moved to the front of the group again. The General's map had been little more than a crude outline requiring his imagination to fill in the details. In truth, he wasn't sure they were even going in the right direction.

But as the air warmed, it was obvious they were nearing the outer walls. Six Stix remained alert for the sounds of guards, or even guests. Who knew what spies the Prince had recruited?

When he heard the tread of boots coming toward them, he gestured the others to a halt. Obsidian squatted to listen, holding his breath. His back ached. Even so, he watched Six Stix with growing concern. *Those herbs won't last much longer.*

Six Stix drew his sword and tested the blade with his finger before creeping toward the corner as the footsteps grew louder. Embaza moved toward him, thinking it was time he took over.

Tiala shouted from behind, "Wait. It's the General." She had listened to those footsteps for too many days not to recognize them now.

The dwarf rounded the corner, brandishing her treasured sword in both hands. The glint of a second sword winked from a new scabbard on her belt. Six Stix smiled. *Never hurts to be too careful.*

The General read the situation at a glance and turned to the blue elf, surprised he was still standing. She was almost sorry the poison hadn't done away with him. She knew the longer they traveled together, the more difficult exacting her revenge would become. "So, you kept out of trouble while I was gone."

"Humph," he grunted and said, "No thanks to you."

The dwarf reached into her pack and tossed a set of clothes to Polah. "Here, girl, try not to lose these." She frowned at Six Stix. "Are you calling me a deserter, you war criminal?"

"Stop," said Embaza. "You can argue later." He held Tiala's cloak like a curtain while Polah dressed in the dwarf's extra set of brown-hued shirt and leggings. Predictably, they were too wide and too short in the sleeves and ankles, but Polah appreciated the hood attached to the collar. It would be useful against the sun. There were no shoes.

For her part, Tiala was relieved to recover her cloak. She pulled Gudrun aside to ask, "Can we get another cart?"

Gudrun shook her head. "Too dangerous. We'll have to risk open country." She patted Tiala's shoulder at the wild-eyed look on the dark elf's face. "We'll take the Prince's own horses, born to the desert and trained for battle. And we'll travel fast. Be brave. You have your champions, my Lady."

As if to challenge her words, they passed a narrow, rectangular window, through which a shaft of sunlight streamed. To Tiala, the sun's glare was an open wound on the side of the wall, and she pressed her fists to her eyes. *I can't do it.*

Embaza folded her cloak around her and whispered, "Stay near me, sister. Try to remain calm."

Tears filled Tiala's eyes. She leaned on Embaza and wrapped the cloak tight, nestling her face into the dark folds of heavy silk. She was glad her Alvarran friends were not here to see her forced to depend on a male, and a wizard at that.

"We're almost to the door," said Gudrun. "There will be guards."

Obsidian felt the promise of the sun's healing rays on his back and shifted his knife harness to one side. Six Stix drew his long sword with a *swish*, and they followed Gudrun to the end of the hallway. Around the corner was a huge arched door made of thick dark wood, carved with desert wolves and encrusted with emeralds.

Standing to one side were four white-turbaned giants, arguing over a flask of ale, their weapons lying uselessly against the wall. "Give it here," said the smallest one, slurring his words. He was just under nine feet tall.

The tallest giant was twelve feet high and almost reached the top of the doorway. He grabbed the flask and flung it at the wall, where it burst and left a bitter-smelling drizzle. "You've had enough, Nob," he roared.

The other two grabbed the taller one by the arms, laughing. "Just because you don't drink, Dunal, don't deprive us of our fun," said the giant in the padded shirt. They wrestled, good-naturedly.

Gudrun held her broadsword in both hands. Six Stix pressed his back against the wall and looked over Gudrun's shoulder to gauge how close they were to the door.

Obsidian did the same on the other side of the short corridor. "Drink will make them easier to fight," he whispered to Polah, just behind him.

The little shape-changer gripped the tusk knife tighter and narrowed her black eyes. *These giants are big, but I'm fast. If I can get the door open, maybe we have a chance to escape.* She mimed a hand signal of herself running, and Gudrun nodded.

Embaza held Tiala, moving her closer to the bright entranceway. This would be a test for them both. He did not feel strong enough to cast any spells yet, but he took a deep breath, gathering his energy.

Tiala hugged her travel harp and squirmed in his arms, panicked by the prospect of the sunlight. Imagination was one thing; reality another. A scream escaped her lips, though she was hardly aware of it.

The tipsy giant named Nob said, "Did you hear a mouse?" He reached behind him for a bone club, and started toward the sound. Tiala huddled in the cloak and held her breath, Embaza shielding her with his body.

Gudrun pointed at Polah, and the shapechanger made a dash for the door. As luck would have it, Polah crossed Nob's path just as the giant stumbled, and although she managed to trip him, he fell clumsily on her leg.

"Get up, pretty girl," he said to Polah, who was groaning with pain.

The other giants sought their weapons along the wall.

Obsidian charged forward and attempted to wrest the club from Nob, while Six Stix and Gudrun readied to meet the giant Braytok, who wore padding and carried a wooden pike.

Tiala squealed at a beam of sunlight, clutching her harp and cloak. The tall giant Dunal smiled and seized a spear. Embaza noticed the fourth giant fitting an arrow to a long bow.

-41-

Six Stix and Gudrun had teamed up on Braytok, who was soon bleeding through several rents in his padded shirt. He brandished his pike, but was no match for them.

Polah was still pinned by Nob, and thrashing this way and that. Obsidian kept trying to find the pressure point at the giant's throat, while ducking heavy blows from the bone club.

Dunal the tallest guard moved back and forth, trying to line Tiala up with his spear, but Embaza kept shifting his body to block.

The fourth giant, Byder, lifted his great bow to fit a long, notched arrow. He drew the string back, bending the massive weapon with a creaking sound.

Embaza saw the arrow whizzing toward his heart, and simultaneously shoved Tiala to one side while leaping to the other, the arrow embedding itself in the wall between the two. Ignoring the familiar throb in his skin from direct exposure to the sun's rays, he desperately groped in a pocket of his saddlebags for the Prince's ring.

Aiming the gold band at his attacker, Embaza intoned, "*Gordsida Waell.*" A simple spell of activation, it might not work if the ring was too powerful. To his delight, however, the giant dropped his bow and clutched his ears.

The wizard rushed forward to snatch a large stone knife from the guard's own scabbard. He held the blade to the giant's belly and yelled to the others, "I'll kill your brother if you don't stop long enough to listen to me."

It was a gamble, but Dunal paused, his spear now pointed at Tiala where she huddled against the wall. Embaza's threat had sounded all too real.

Tiala clutched her travel harp and slid down the sunny wall to curl into a fetal position about the instrument, her skin seemingly afire.

Braytok was busy fending off Gudrun and Six Stix. "I don't care if you are the General," the giant was saying, "I'm going to teach you a lesson you won't forget."

"Leave them alone. Byder's in trouble," shouted Dunal, but Braytok was too embroiled to listen.

Six Stix's sword sang with the whine that pleased his ears, and Gudrun's weapon fought like the ancient blade it was. But Obsidian's match was over.

The smallest of the giants, Nob, lay still, moaning quietly. Polah was seated beside him, her tusk knife nearby. The monk squatted for a moment, catching his breath, his wound excruciatingly painful. Then he helped Polah to her feet, and she winced, reaching for her ribs.

Embaza said to the giant called Byder, "Does this mean anything to you?" The knife still in his right hand, the blade pressuring the giant's abdomen, he reached into his left pocket for the strangely carved ivory coin the Patriarch had given him.

The giant opened his eyes in shock. "Braytok," he shouted. "Dunal—stop brawling. He's got the Seal of the Elder."

In a burst of strength, Braytok wrenched away from his deadly match, flinging Gudrun and Six Stix off like insects. Gudrun fell on her ankle with a sickening sound.

Byder grabbed Embaza's wrist and raised it to display the piece of ivory. Braytok let his sword to his side and glared at the wizard. "Why didn't you say so in the first place?"

As if by magic, the three giants moved to open the massive door, through which the blazing gold of morning poured like honey over the blood and sand on the stone floor.

Embaza swallowed and shielded his eyes with his hands. *Pain is good...*

In the spirit of comrades-at-arms, Six Stix offered his hand to help Gudrun to her feet. The dwarf rubbed her ankle and allowed him to help her up. The ankle hurt, but she could use it. When she saw Tiala, Gudrun hopped over to her with a cry, "My lady."

Byder, Braytok and Dunal stared at the General in bafflement. Why was she speaking that way to a dark elf? Braytok nudged Dunal and whispered, "The dark one must have enchanted her."

Embaza returned the stone knife to Byder, hilt first, and walked over to Tiala and Gudrun.

Tiala squinted up at him, her face wrinkled with pain. Embaza lifted her into his arms, the harp left unnoticed on the floor, and Gudrun tucked the cloak around her. The giants watched, frowning.

Nob stirred and opened his eyes, peering at Tiala, still within Embaza's embrace. Surely, the Prince would grant a reward for her return...and his family could use that reward.

He leapt to his feet and grabbed Obsidian's arm, twisting it behind so swiftly, the monk became his prisoner. "Get the dark one," he said to Braytok.

Braytok took hold of Nob by the back of his vest and wrested him away. "Leave them, Nob. They're under the protection of the Elder." A loud crunch turned everyone's attention to the travel harp, half-obscured by the sand, and squashed now under his foot.

Tiala gazed at the ruined instrument, dismayed to her core. Polah leaned over to snatch her tusk knife and slip it into her waistband.

Nob said, "Even the Patriarch can't deny me my lawful rights." His companions looked perplexed, but Obsidian turned pale.

The giant shook off Braytok's hold and pointed to Tiala. "I claim her by Code of the Desert." He gestured to Embaza and his party. "The rest of you can go, but not her."

Something in Obsidian snapped. Perhaps it was a vision of the cruelty of his wasted childhood or Tiala's stricken form. "I challenge you to single combat," he said in a voice like iron.

Nob squinted down his nose at the monk.

"What's he doing?" whispered Polah to Six Stix. The blue elf shook his head.

Dunal pushed Nob toward the open doors after handing him an elk horn knife, "So be it. We'll stand as witnesses. Good fighting, Nob."

Nob marched into the desert under the keen eyes of his brothers gathered at the exit.

Obsidian started to follow, but Six Stix grabbed him and whispered, "What's going on?"

"This man wants to return Tiala to the Prince," Obsidian answered softly. "By Outlander law, I may challenge him to a fight to the death. No one can interfere."

On the other side of the hallway, Tiala screamed and twisted free, beating her fists on the stone wall. Gudrun grabbed her by the shoulders and clapped a hand over her mouth. "Help me," she said to Embaza, but he stared at her with unseeing eyes, reciting to himself, *Pain is good. If I have pain...*

Tiala acted like someone possessed by demons. As she writhed within Gudrun's grasp, it was all the dwarf could do to keep from being toppled to the ground. She glared at Embaza, who seemed paralyzed, and cried, "What's wrong with you?"

His intense green eyes swiveled and locked onto hers. She was so stunned by the distance of the look, she nearly let go of Tiala.

As if he had awakened from a bad dream, he blinked and said, "Let me help."

Between the two of them, they wrestled Tiala to a patch of shade behind the open door. She heaved and moaned within their hold, clutching her stomach, overcome by a combination of terror and pain.

Embaza gritted his teeth, reminded of his own initiation. He would not wish that ordeal on the foulest demon, yet she would have to go through something similar if she were to survive. With reluctance, he dug the jar of sunbane from his saddlebags. He had hoped to save it for the open desert, but Tiala was getting worse. Her eyes lacked any recognition, and a telltale drop of foam had appeared at the corner of her mouth.

Even so, for a moment, he considered keeping the preparation for himself. *I can handle a few hours, but a whole day in full sunlight? And what then? When the others find I have deceived them?* One look at Tiala's face, and his reservations dissolved like smoke.

He dipped his fingers into the fragrant orange cream and smeared some on her face. "Be still," he ordered.

She sniffed the ointment and closed her eyes; immediately, her breathing eased somewhat.

"What is that stuff?" asked Gudrun, a little weak in the knees now.

"Sunbane," Embaza replied. "A gift from a healer. There isn't much of it and it ought to be kept in a cool place." His hand trembled as he put it back into his saddlebags.

Tiala was standing on her own now. She looked at the other two, a remnant of terror still pooling in the depths of her eyes. She touched her face with wondering fingers. "Did you say a healer gave you this?"

Embaza nodded, knowing what was coming.

"But this is a very rare preparation—I thought it was impossible to get anywhere but in Alvarra."

He shrugged. "I met an old one from your country, dressed in the blue robe of a priestess."

Tiala clutched his arm. "A priestess of Loote. My mother must have sent her. Otherwise, why is she here? I order you to find her."

Embaza frowned. No one ordered a Sargothian wizard.

"My lady," said Gudrun gently, "I think that will have to wait." They looked toward the open hallway, where the floor was still blanketed in a flickering cover of sunlight.

Tiala seemed to shrink.

"Here," said Embaza, and he offered his arm, although it was shaking.

Dunal blocked the exit, the brightness of the desert a sliver of light that shifted with his every movement. Tiala felt nauseous, but she breathed in the fragrance of the sunbane and allowed herself to be led toward the doorway, Gudrun limping along behind.

Embaza eased Tiala to the floor and re-wrapped her cloak around her.

Gudrun shouldered past Dunal to join Six Stix and Polah, who stood to one side of the contest, opposite Braytok and Byder on the other. The space between them was deepening as both Nob and Obsidian displaced a little more sand each time they landed in a new position.

From the doorway, Dunal could see Obsidian from the waist up and Nob from the knees. Neither had thrown a fatal blow, yet there was blood flowing aplenty.

Obsidian's butterfly knives had left Nob's belly a maze of crisscross cuts, while one of the monk's eyes was swollen shut, the skin turning a deep shade of purple. Both fighters had a welter of other wounds encrusted with blood and sand.

Obsidian was angry at himself. He couldn't remember a single posture, nor one technique from his years of study. If his body had not been imprinted with these things, he would have been as helpless as a city dweller. Unaware that he was performing at his all-time best, he let his emotions overcome his reason, sensing from blind instinct that he was out of control. Somewhere deep within him, he knew this was not about Tiala. He had something to prove—to himself, and the others.

He landed a ferocious kick on Nob's left hipbone, sending the giant staggering to one knee.

Not to be outdone, Nob threw his mighty fist once again at Obsidian's swollen right eye, causing blood to gush forth. The giant heaved a huge sigh of relief as Obsidian went down, both hands over his eye, and the butterfly knives slipped to the sand.

However, the pain only fanned the fighter's bravery to a brighter flame and Obsidian leapt into the air, striking wildly at Nob.

Before the giant knew it, he had several broken bones. Like a house of twigs, the youngest giant brother collapsed into the six-foot hole in the sand. Nob's last breath escaped in a sigh.

Obsidian's hands and feet throbbed, and he sheathed his knives. He peered upward, shading his undamaged eye against the sun. Through blue spots of reflected glare, he saw the silhouettes of his friends. Gudrun and Six Stix reached down and helped the exhausted, bleeding monk out of the hole. Polah stood on tiptoe and brushed some of the sand from his swollen eye.

Dizzy, Six Stix staggered in the sunlight. *The herbs are wearing off.* He straightened up to hide his condition from the others and checked his pack to be sure the waterskins were still there.

Braytok and Byder stepped into the pit and lifted Nob's broken body out, laying it on the sand. Dunal moved out into the sunshine at last, and the three of them towered over their slain brother.

Now that the flush of adrenaline had drained away, Obsidian was dismayed by the tide of his elation. He had proved himself, but at what cost? *I have failed as a monk.* He wiped some of the blood oozing yet from injured eye as he approached Braytok, who stood with his arms folded. *I have killed for personal reasons.* Solemnly, the tall youth bowed to the giant and, squinting up at him with his good eye, said, "I am truly sorry."

Braytok was silent, looking down at the sand, but Dunal answered with a clipped politeness, "It was an honorable fight."

Byder stepped forward and handed the elk horn knife to Obsidian. "To revere him, you must accompany us to our village. There we'll bury him and you will place this at his head."

"I can't abandon my companions."

"They are welcome," said Byder, his voice numb with grief. He frowned suddenly. "But you must keep that demon away from us."

Obsidian grunted and said, "She is not a demon. She is merely sick."

"That is your problem," said Dunal.

The monk nodded. *Why not go with them?* he mused. *I have no wish to return to the monastery only to be tossed out in disgrace.* He rejoined his companions just inside the Manor door, gathering their belongings for the journey.

Gudrun handed a wide scarf to Polah. "You can drape this over your head and tie it around your forehead as people do in the desert. Your skin is very fair." Polah thanked her, and quickly bound it into a turban.

Obsidian said to Tiala, "Princess, if you would consent to it, we've been given passage to the camp of the giants. As a matter of honor, I must go and help them bury their brother."

"No," cried Tiala, "We should go to your monastery as planned. I need thick walls around me." She whispered, "I'm afraid…" The brittle facade she had erected crumbled at last and two tears coursed down her velvety face.

Six Stix said, "I don't trust these giants."

"What choice do we have?" said Polah. *There are too many leaders here.*

Embaza looked at the giants waiting in the sunlight, then back at Obsidian's ravaged face, and said, "Why not accept their offer? Who knows what dangers await us on the desert, and the giants may be our shield as long as we have the Patriarch's token. Look at us. We're not at our best."

Gudrun settled the matter. "It's only a day's ride to the camps of this giant's tribe. We cannot make the long trip to the monastery until we've rested. Besides, it's on our way."

Chagrined, Tiala dashed away the tears and hid her face in the hood. From the depths of her soul, she tried to remember that she was the Nightwing's daughter. "Give me more of that salve for my hands and face."

Embaza drew out the unguent and prepared her for the desert ordeal, rubbing the residue on himself as if to clean his hands.

Obsidian said to Gudrun, "General, why are you not affected by the sun as the dark elf is? Your people also live underground, do they not?"

"We dwarves believe that we are protected because we work with metals, which are said to be the children of the sun. Here, you must take a scarf as well. That hair knot is no protection. Embaza, you, too."

When each had wrapped his head with the new turbans, they shared a hurried meal and a few sips of water.

"Save some food for the journey," Six Stix urged.

Braytok and Byder returned, leading ten giant horses, desert bred, judging by their long snouts and spatulate hooves. They laid Nob's body over the largest steed, a dappled gray mare. Dunal gestured to the rest to mount up.

Polah approached the white gelding, who backed away, rolling his eyes and whinnying in protest. "Quiet, now," she murmured, offering him a choice morsel of her precious food. The animal's hunger overcome his fear, and while he chewed, Polah rubbed the velvety muzzle and wondered how she would ever mount this animal. The next instant, an arm snaked around her waist and nearly flung her into the saddle. Dunal shoved the reins at her, pointed to the saddle horn, and she gripped both in her astonishment.

"Too long," the giant remarked, gazing at her foot, and bent to the stirrup, adjusting the fit with the ease of a man born to life on horseback. In no time he had finished with her, and before she could think to thank him, he was off checking girths and adjusting bridles preparatory to departure.

Polah patted the snowy white neck of her horse and prayed their journey would be without incident.

The other horses were matched chestnuts and bays, the braided desert saddles marking them as tribal steeds. Obsidian helped Tiala onto a chestnut mare, and then adjusted the stirrups before taking up reins of his own assignment, a bright bay gelding.

Soon everyone was mounted, including the giants. The sun had reached its zenith, and the horses became restive, awaiting the signal to go.

Leading the dappled gray, Braytok led off toward the north. Nob's body swayed side to side on the mare's broad back. With no outcry from the Manor, no outward notice of their departure, Gudrun said to Braytok, "Prince Mischa does not deserve such loyalty. I will not miss him."

"Nor I, General," he replied.

Crouched over the neck of her chestnut mount, Tiala clutched the saddle horn, the reins looped carelessly about one hand, and held her breath as long as she could. Ironically, the warmth of the sun through the heavy cloak was almost comforting, even while the unmistakable signs of sickness coursed through her blood.

Embaza rode behind to watch her, looking back every few minutes in case they were followed, but he was soon immersed in his own torment. His familiar dance with the Scourge of Elves had begun and already bright colors swam before his eyes. He wrapped his gray cloak around him, chanting the words of power that enabled its unique protection. He took a sip from his waterskin, even though Byder looked at him with scorn. Embaza knew that he and Tiala—if she survived—would run out of water long before the others.

Ahead of him, Tiala's teeth were chattering and her whole body shook as she held onto the pommel for dear life. This unnerved her big chestnut horse, who soon turned skittish and pranced sideways.

Dunal galloped up beside her and, using a hair-switch from his saddle bag, herded the horse back in line, careful not to touch Tiala's robe or booted feet. His sharp eyes picked out the hazy outline of a lone traveler in the distance, zigzagging the desert on foot.

Six Stix also saw the silhouette, but said nothing, resting in the saddle, trying not to be alarmed by the growing lassitude and numbness in his limbs. He was relieved at the protective way the giants flanked the party, though he would wager their concern was mainly for their horses.

Obsidian rode at the rear. Although cut and bruised elsewhere, his eye was losing some of its sting under the healing lamp of sunlight. Would that his spirit could be healed so easily, he thought.

Polah perched on the giant saddle like a small, tenacious bird instead of a fox in woman's form. Her keen eyes ranged over the dunes with the senses of a hawk, alert and appreciative. She thought there was nothing like the desert for beauty. The only one to recognize the identity of the lone figure in the distance, she was glad when Braytok steered the party in the opposite direction.

-42-

Mischa had been walking for what felt like days. His fancy brocaded shoes were already in shreds, and he had tied his green silk vest over his head for a sunshade. After he had cursed his entire family tree, beginning and ending with his grandfather, he added himself to the list, for he was quite lost.

He raised his waterskin to his lips, but it was empty. In his abstraction, he had drunk every drop.

Dejected, he sat down on the hot desert sand to root through the brown sack of treasure and magic items. His hand trembled when it brushed the silver flute.

At last, he happened upon the tarnished metal jug and rubbed it with his sleeve, trying desperately to remember the incantation the magician had given him. *Nabrizo? Narzibo?* It had to be exactly right, or something awful would happen. That much he recalled. He cursed again, this time because he had traded one of his favorite antique screens for it.

Clearing his throat, he uttered what he hoped was the correct phrase. "*Norbizzor.*" If he did it right, the vessel would fill with sweet, spring water. He squinted intensely into the jug for several moments, but nothing happened. Even more despondent now, he watched a hawk circling overhead.

A popping noise from the jug was followed by a sort of gurgling. He reached inside with his finger and touched a cool liquid. Mischa grinned to himself, then giggled. He extracted his wet finger for a look.

"It worked," he cried and shook his fist at the hawk. "It worked, you buzzard."

He sucked his finger and spat onto the sand. Salt water. He jumped to his feet and hurled the metal jug as far as he could fling it. Then, shouldering the brown bag once again, he turned around in a dizzy circle, looking for a landmark of some kind that he could fix on.

In the far distance, he thought he could discern some sort of structure, towers that shimmered in the heat. With a sickening jolt, he recognized the Manor. He had gone in a circle.

With a nauseating pang of regret, he stared longingly at his home. Then, he turned and strode in the opposite direction, painfully aware of the burning sand through his threadbare shoes.

-43-

As the sun's relentless rays bore down on the travelers, Polah made a peak of her hood to shade her nose, and allowed her unfocused eyes to wander over the desert. Her mind drifted far from the group to all the things that had happened to her while at the Manor.

The sun felt good, beating warmth into her tired body like a healer with strong hands. Under its ministrations, she probed deep within herself for the animal awareness she had come to realize was a permanent part of her.

Her eyes drifted to the wizard's back. She spoke his name inside herself, and evoked a complex tapestry of feelings in response. Was he master or friend, protector or threat? A sweetness bubbled up inside her, like a song, that she fought with all her might, striving instead to call forth the anger and resolve that had brought her this far. *I must never allow myself to be caught or captured.* She feared the consequences if she forgot even for a moment that she was fox. Whatever their bond, true friendship was dangerous, the price too dear.

Beside her, Obsidian also pondered his experiences, but for him, everything in life translated into lessons. He kept a vigilant eye over the landscape by reflex, but there was a glint of despair in his deep, brown eyes. *What further lessons can I hope to earn, now, my Masters?* Nob's lifeless body swinging to and fro on the back of the dappled mare haunted his soul like a demon. He could not imagine any lesson that would demand so much of him. *This will always be with me. Even if they kick me out of the monastery. Or perhaps they will let me stay…to sweep the kitchen.*

Then he remembered. *The Princess still needs me. I am strong and I can fight.* He snorted without mirth. *I can kill.* His gaze drifted to the battle-scarred blue elf from whom he had learned much these past few days. *He, too, has killed. What was it he said? 'It must take much to provoke you.'* He snorted again. *All it took was my own pride.* He glanced at the dried blood scabbing the cuts on his forearm and leg, and noted the bruises beginning on his left thigh. Scant punishment for killing a man.

If he had not been so preoccupied, he might have noticed the difficulty Six Stix was having just staying on his mount. The elf had jammed his fingers under the saddle blanket to keep the reins from slipping, and now he was concentrating on maintaining a good grip with his thighs. A numbness seemed to be traveling up his body. He had no feeling below his knees.

When common sense mastered his own pride, Six Stix thought to call Embaza, who was riding ahead, but all that issued from his mouth was a soft croak. A cold wave of fear washed over him.

He turned to the giant, Dunal, riding nearby, and tried to catch the tribesman's eye, which was difficult, since his own face barely reached the giant's breastbone. When at last he won Dunal's attention, the giant grinned and pointed ahead of them.

"Don't look so worried, old soldier. Just a couple more hours, and we'll be there."

Old soldier, indeed, he thought, wishing he had the strength to reply. Six Stix considered the giant and his brothers. No vassals, these. Pride overlay their service to the Prince. They had the freedom to leave on what they considered more pressing business, with no fear of retaliation by their employer. *Interesting. No doubt they've seen a thing or two at the Manor.*

He wished the General had not left the Prince's service. He knew she rode somewhere behind him, prompting a return of the cold fear. This wasn't a good time to be defenseless. Once again he tried to speak, but his voice failed him.

The most he could hope was that the paralysis would not advance quickly. Exhausted, he closed his eyes and let the sun lull him to sleep. Slumped over the saddle, he did not even feel the sweat that dripped down his neck.

For her part, the General was not concerned with Six Stix. She spurred her horse with her heels until she was abreast of Tiala. One glance at her, and the dwarf almost turned her mount and bolted.

The dark elf sat rigid in the saddle, gripping the pommel with hands like stone. Her face was a rictus mask with bulging eyes that rolled in every direction. Her legs clasped the horse with the same tension, and the poor animal tripped and pranced as if its hooves were on fire.

Leaning over, Gudrun pried the reins from Tiala's mindless grip and then patted the skittish horse on the neck. "Quiet, girl," she murmured.

Tiala whipped her head toward the voice like a serpent about to strike. She bared her teeth in a horrible grin and started to hiss.

Gudrun drew back and steeled herself to return the stare. "I know you're hurting, Tiala," she said in measured words that took every ounce of her discipline. "I am not your enemy, remember? Let me help." Instinct told her this was the moment of greatest danger. Tiala would either pass out—or attack.

But the dark elf did something even worse. She showed her face to the sun and cloudless sky, then screamed at the top of her lungs. The bloodcurdling sound carried with it all her rage at the Scourge of Elves—a relentless foe that held the power to reduce all of her kind to helplessness, regardless of age or talent or wealth or position.

As the sound seeped through their skin and into their marrow, her companions froze, posed like a tableau of disaster.

Then horses broke in every direction, driven by such primeval terror that there was no stopping them—nor did anyone try. The distress of a dark elf in extreme sun-sickness was not an experience any of them were prepared for—not even Gudrun, who had rocked the trembling Tiala to sleep on their first trip across the desert.

The dwarf was one of the first to regain control of her horse, and while she urged the animal back toward her mistress, she caught sight of Six Stix lying on the ground, his bay mount nowhere in sight. She smiled despite her concern for the Alvarran, delighted that her old enemy had fallen. "Some warrior," she muttered.

Gudrun dismounted, trusting these desert steeds had been well-trained, and let the reins drop to the sand, effectively ground-tying her horse. She slowly approached Tiala, the dark elf's mount rearing and bucking in a tight circle as if the very devil was on its back.

Just then, Byder galloped past her to a sliding stop, the rain of sand startling

Gudrun. "Hey," she sputtered, rubbing the grit from her eyes. Byder's loud whistle forced her to look up in time to see Tiala clutching the neck of her mount to keep herself from falling and Byder moving close enough to lean over and grab the bridle, bringing the horse's nose to his thigh. He quieted the distressed mare with a series of calm commands while he quickly collected the trailing reins, keeping a suspicious gaze trained on the dark elf throughout the process. Gudrun remembered then that Byder had tended these animals regularly while in service to the Mischa. His whistle had gotten the attention of every horse within earshot.

Tiala's scream had pierced Embaza's soul. He alone heard the sound of his own pain, his first memory of the desert sun. While his horse gathered its strong withers to make a giant-sized leap across the sands, Embaza confronted the vision of his own initiation.

The older wizards had taken him out into the erg, beyond the sight of any tree or building. They had left him blindfolded, with a flask of water and a small stone whistle. "You will forget, Embaza. You will forget everything—your past, your birth, your childhood. The sun will bleach you of all knowledge. But you will have the whistle. Only that can save you. When you have forgotten everything, even your own name, blow on the whistle, and we will come for you. You must forget all but that, little one, otherwise we won't come. Hold onto the whistle." He had been eight years old. By dark-elven reckoning, a newborn, barely able to produce a 'toot' on the rude instrument.

He could not abide those few seconds of Tiala's torment, remembering his own scream and knowing her heart was breaking. He could not let her go through that same agony. With all the prodigious strength of his years, he reined his horse toward the dark elf, alongside her mount under the control of the giant Byder, angling closer to her until their knees almost touched. Close enough that he could smell the terror on her breath. Then, he draped his own magic cloak around her, over her head and about her shoulders, the thick gray cloak that he had been given at his investiture. Woven by the blind women of Sargoth, every thread contained a prayer, every cross-thread a spell.

He fished his dark blue cloak from his saddlebags and wrapped himself in it, clenching his teeth as his body trembled, more in anticipation than in physical reaction to the sunlight. When Tiala bent over and shook with the rhythmic sobbing that signaled relief, Embaza let out his breath in a ragged sigh.

One by one the small party regrouped, Braytok and Dunal watching from a remote dune. Obsidian rode over to talk with them. He had a heated argument with the two, finally persuading them to shelter the entire party, at least overnight at their camp, and they rejoined the others, albeit keeping a safe distance.

Several moments passed before Gudrun remembered seeing Six Stix lying on the sand. She looked around for him, shading her eyes, but did not see him. She noticed a riderless bay nosing Byder, who was leading Tiala's horse.

Polah had noticed, too. "Where's the blue elf?" she called to Obsidian.

The monk swiveled left and right in the saddle, scanning the dunes, and cursed his preoccupation with his own predicament. He kicked his horse in a lope, riding in an ever wider circle, looking for Six Stix. His anger at himself quickly became anxiety for his friend.

In moments, the entire party was searching for the warrior, all except Gudrun, who had taken the reins of Tiala's horse from Byder. Tracks crisscrossed in almost every direction. Eventually, they would find him, Gudrun was certain, but maybe too late.

Polah discovered him disguised by the sand in which he lay, the hilt of his sword glittering in the sun. Brushing sand from his face, she shouted, "Here he is."

Dunal and Braytok effortlessly tossed the unconscious elf over the seat of the saddle just as Obsidian dismounted. He turned Six's head to the right, studying his face with concern. The blue elf was draped across his horse exactly the same as the dead Nob, filling the monk with a nauseating fear.

"What's wrong with him?" asked Embaza. *Now, we'll see what kind of healer you are.*

"I'm not sure," answered Obsidian. "He's too pale for heat stroke. I think it's the poison." He fumbled in his pocket, wishing he had gathered more of the heal-all leaves. *One left, thank the balance.* Then he realized Six Stix could not chew anything. Instead, he inserted his forefinger into the elf's mouth, stretching his lower lip enough to catch the water he dribbled from a hide canteen. Six drooled afterward, then swallowed, but never opened his eyes. Obsidian took the reins of Six's horse from Braytok and dallied them about the saddle horn of his own mount, then clipped the corners of the saddle blanket into a tent over the stricken elf's head to shield his face from the sun. Even in shadow, the indigo scars stood out in high relief.

"I can help," said Embaza in a dry croak, "but not now. Wait until we're at the giant's camp." He tugged the yoke of his saddlebags to make sure they were securely fastened behind the cantle. "Let's go before the sun melts us into the ground." His weak voice cracked on the last few phrases.

Would Six Stix last long enough to make the giants' camp? To avoid dwelling on the fear, Obsidian offered the canteen to the wizard. "Here—I think you need this more than he does."

Grateful, Embaza drank, trying not to reveal the depth of his need. He had used all of his own supply. When he handed the canteen back to Obsidian, Dunal rode up to them, an expression of deep concern on his weathered face.

Addressing Obsidian, he said, "My brothers and I have decided to leave without you unless you can control the evil one."

Before the startled monk could reply, Embaza forced the rising knot of anger back into his stomach and said through clenched teeth, "I assure you that it will not happen again. She is ill—not evil."

"Ill or evil, she's a danger to the horses," said Dunal, frowning.

With a sinking heart, Embaza turned in the saddle and produced the container of sunbane from a pocket of his saddlebags, then said, "This medicine will quiet her."

"As it quieted her before?"

Embaza scowled at the sarcasm. "I have been saving it for the long journey. There will not be enough as it is." He ended the conversation by bringing his horse alongside Tiala, who appeared to be resting, hugging the neck of her mare, her face buried in the thick black mane.

When she turned her head, Embaza winced at her parched and tender skin, her lips cracked and bleeding, her face encrusted with sand. Ever so gently, he brushed her skin clean, and then rubbed the last of the ointment into her exposed face and hands. He wiped the residue of the sunbane over his own dry lips before taking the cloth sash from her waist to wrap her head like a turban, covering as much of her forehead, chin and cheeks as he could. "Keep your head down and your eyes closed," he whispered. "It can only be a few leagues now. If you need me, call. I'll be near."

He saw Dunal in close discussion with the other giants. They nodded to each other and one pointed into the distance. Then there was a piercing call from Byder, who rose in his stirrups and cupped his hand to one ear to catch the low warble of reply about a quarter league to the northeast.

Gudrun rode up next to Obsidian and leaned close to mutter, "Voice of the Desert. The gnomad way of saying 'All is well.'" Obsidian gave her a curt nod out of respect, embroiled in his own concerns for Six Stix.

At Byder's signal, Braytok looped the reins of the dappled gray around his fist and rode to the front of the party once again, leading off to the northwest. Nob's stiffening limbs no longer thrummed the sides of the mare bearing him to his final rest.

Obsidian urged his horse into the procession, leading Six Stix's mount behind. The giants still rode as far as possible from Tiala. A shiver traveled down the monk's spine in recalling her scream of terror. It was hard to reconcile that creature with the beautiful bard. In spite of his promise, he began to have second thoughts about their mission.

-44-

ALTHOUGH PRINCE Mischa had stalked off cursing his fate, his very anger had saved him from despair. While a lesser man might have given up without food or water, Mischa remembered that he was the heir of a mighty warrior with a tribe beyond number.

No matter that he wasn't really a Prince, that his grandfather had given him the title so he might build his estate. He was still the grandson of Rearguard, Patriarch of all the Outland Territory.

His heart burned with fury and revenge. And after he had finished devising every possible death for his elder, he turned his thoughts to the real architect of his situation. *That wizard, Embaza. And those sniveling creatures with him. Oh, yes—they all ought to die for what they have done—especially the wizard.*

Unconsciously, he wrung his hands, plotting a horrible end for his adversary until something shifted in the landscape that bade him look up from his reverie.

Nearly twenty figures were poised on the rise of the dune before him, the nearest with her hands on her hips. Outlined by the sun, he could only see her silhouette, not her face, and experienced as he was in bride-flesh, he immediately approved of her splendid figure.

Overcome with relief, he stumbled toward her, rehearsing a suitable speech. But when he arrived at the bottom of the dune, the sun was no longer in his eyes and his heart sank to his blistered feet. It was the chieftain Amra's third daughter.

Still, he had his pride. He was Prince of the Outland Territories, whether they liked it or not. He came within a few feet of her sparkling blue eyes, more brilliant even than his own.

He nodded as one ruler to another. "Good day, Azali. What a pleasant surprise."

To his dismay, she laughed, showing her perfect white teeth. Shaking her black ringlets, she snapped her fingers, and three tribesmen grabbed Mischa like a large doll and hoisted him onto their shoulders.

"What are you doing?" he shouted. "Put me down or you'll be sorry."

Azali glowered, brandishing a knife that glinted along its edge, reflecting the sun's glare and blinding him for a moment.

"One more word out of you," she said, "and I'll slit your throat like the desert pig you are."

"Hope she does it, too," whispered one of the gnomads to the other.

Mischa hid his outrage behind his well-oiled mask of guile. Even a prisoner might obtain some water. Before he could plan any further, his bearers broke into a run behind the fleet Azali, and he experienced a grudging admiration as the whole group of warriors ran over the sand like deer, led by the lovely maiden dressed in her gauzy costume of deep blue.

At the top of the next rise, a high tremolo from the west stopped Azali. Her warriors lined up behind her to wait while she cupped her hands together and warbled a long, low note.

Mischa started to shout, but one of the gnomads covered his mouth and glared at him.

Satisfied of their safety, Azali led on again until they topped a rise, and the vast tents of Lord Amra's camp spread out before them.

"One, two, three, four..." Mischa's nerves danced in his body, "...twenty-six, twenty-seven..."

He lost count at thirty five, fearing that if he kept counting the tents, he would lose his mind.

*Well, after all, it's one leader to another. One man to another. Surely Amra will see that...*Even so, he worried.

Azali led them to a large tent, then held the flap open while they trooped inside. At her command, the erstwhile Prince was dumped onto the carpeted desert floor like a sack of grain. Seated on cushions nearby were two familiar faces, Azali's younger sisters, Delyra and Saramba.

Mischa gulped.

The tent was full of women, healthy, young, richly dressed. Was this the Chieftain's harem? Continuing his nervous habit, he began to count heads.

Azali clapped her hands. "Leave us," she told her guards.

And Mischa found himself alone with the thirty-four daughters of Lord Amra.

-45-

TWENTY DAYS had come and gone since Ombra's funeral. While Tiala made her way to the monastery over the treacherous desert of the Outland Territories, her sisters sat in the great hall for their evening meal. All except Inuari, who had begged to be left cloistered in her room.

Eleppon and Noth sat side by side at the long polished table before a sumptuous dinner laid out on crystal-edged, onyx dishes. Noth was dressed in a long-sleeved gown of emerald satin that rustled whenever she moved, but Eleppon disdained finery. Her plain, plum-colored tunic, breeches and boots were typical of all her riding uniforms.

The magnificent cave had a high, arched ceiling from which descended massive stalactites fused with stalagmites. The tinkling waterfall of crystal wind chimes lightened the atmosphere.

Noth looked up from her plate and addressed Eleppon's reflection in the mirror across from them, "We should have made her come. Inuari always over-dramatizes these mystical episodes."

Eleppon frowned. "I may be impatient with her, but I don't disrespect her calling. Haven't you ever been touched by the Goddess?"

"Which Goddess?"

"Oh, grow up. It's time you accepted your duty like I have."

"Look, Eleppon," said Noth, narrowing her eyes at a stuffed beetle claw. "I don't give one *z'a* for religion, but if Drimma will grant me revenge, I'll see that our brother never harms another hair of our heads. What's wrong with that? Don't you want to live out your five hundred years?"

"Of course I do, but not if I have to pray to the Goddess of Revenge." Eleppon sulked. She hated arguments. She would rather jump one of her horses across the Chasm of Doom than trade words with Noth.

Spidersilk tapestries and expensive rugs surrounded her. There were easy chairs placed near the stalagmites. On the south wall hung a long tapestry depicting the family history of the Nightwings. The tinkling wind chimes distracted her.

Noth speared a salted grapewing and dipped it in the white sauce. Delicate scents of sage and rosemary tickled her nostrils. "Fine, be relaxed about this if you choose to. You'll probably die first, anyway, since you're older." She snuck an impish glance at her sister.

Eleppon crushed her lime silk napkin and slammed her fist to the table. "For your information, I don't intend to wait my turn." Her face was flushed, and Noth stared at her with curiosity.

"What do you mean?" she asked breathlessly.

"Nothing." Eleppon composed herself and folded her napkin in her lap. She raised a two-pronged silver fork and toyed with the wild rice and rampion soufflé.

Noth turned her chair to face Eleppon. "You're planning something," she said. "You'd better tell me now or I swear I'll interrogate every one of those zealots you ride with."

Eleppon pursed her lips and banged her fork against the china plate. "You would, wouldn't you? All right, but you've got to promise not to tell anyone." She skewered Noth in a penetrating stare. "On your soul as a future Nightwing."

Noth nodded. Secrets were her specialty.

Eleppon looked about the mirrors and crystal chimes lightening the dark corners of the large room. She scanned for prying eyes and ears. To the north were three archways leading to the library, and beyond that, their personal quarters.

Her eyes drifted to the arched south door that permitted only a glimpse of the Great Hall of the Royal City complex. Soft light flowed from two phosphor-stone lamps on tall metal poles carved with flowering nightshade vines. Brilliant silk banners hung around the walls, depicting the shields of the noble families of Alvarra. The black rabbit banner was prominent over the doorway.

Two tall guards in dark blue and black uniforms faced outward, their arms crossed behind them. Though weaponless, they were not called Ladies of Skill for nothing. And yet...

Still searching for a reason on which to base her unrest, Eleppon looked up, squinting at the waterfall of crystal. Like the phosphor-stone lamps, they emitted a soft light, creating shadows that delighted the eye. This was her favorite room in the whole royal complex, but now it felt unsafe.

Noth tapped her on the sleeve. "I promise," she repeated.

Eleppon shook her head and muttered, "Later." She turned to her meal and ate without appreciating the exquisite harmony of flavors.

Noth drank from a blue crystal goblet of sparkling ale and dabbed her mouth with the silk napkin. She caught her sister's eye in the glass. "I've lost my appetite, Eleppon—think I'll go to bed."

Eleppon nodded, "Sleep well." Noth kicked her under the table.

"I know, stupid," Eleppon hissed. "Your room."

Noth pushed her chair back from the table and made her silent, graceful way across the worn carpet. The guard in the hallway turned and nodded, the Nightwing's own cadre, trained from infancy.

Eleppon waited a few minutes, then she, too, left the room, wishing the guards a pleasant sleep.

In Noth's suite, the traps activated on every entrance, the two sisters sat in the middle of the great round bed, and resumed their discussion. The room was companionably dark.

"So?" Noth said, a lilt of excitement edging her voice.

"Calm down, will you?" snapped Eleppon. "This isn't lover's gossip."

"I know, I know, but you're being so mysterious—you're worse than Inuari."

"Well," whispered Eleppon and looked about Noth's crystal collection on the shelf-lined walls. "I and the other senior officers, Calwyn and Kossi—."

Noth pursed her lips and muttered, "Those two snobs."

"Do you want to hear this or not?"

"Sorry."

"We're going to take our horses and our giant ferrets to hunt him—then, when we catch him, we're going to rope and tie him like a wild horse, bring him before the Temple, and demand that he stand trial for treason." She paused to take a breath.

"You're crazy," said Noth. "Even if you're able to catch him—and I'm not saying you can—what good would a trial do? He's already been condemned to the Purple Moors."

"But don't you see? It wasn't a just sentence. The priestesses shouldn't be allowed to decide this. He should be executed, not exiled."

"Now who's revengeful?" Noth pointed an elegant finger at her sister. "Are you so sure he deserves to die?"

"There you go—protecting him, as always." Eleppon flounced off the bed and arranged her breeches over her athletic hips.

Noth slid to the floor and confronted her sister. "Let's get this out in the open right now. You've never trusted me. Admit it."

Eleppon's steady gaze gave nothing away. "What's your point?"

"My life is on the line, too, no matter what the rest of you believe. Dekhalis used me just like he used everyone who cared for him. I saw through his shallow favors. It's just that I feel sorry for him. Does that make me a criminal?"

"You're right. He's got all of us worked up. Anyway, I'm going to meet my lieutenants tonight—and if one word of this gets out—."

"Are you going to tell Inuari?"

She shook her head. "I'm only confiding in you—in case something should happen to me."

Noth grimaced. "I still think you're crazy, but I wish you well. In fact, I may have some ideas of my own."

"This is no time for your tricks, Noth."

"Don't worry," she replied with a secret smile. "Go on, let me get some sleep."

Eleppon straightened her posture and stood at attention, while Noth deactivated traps so her sister could leave. With a fleet look in every direction, Eleppon strode toward her own room.

Alone now, Noth sat cross-legged on her bed and examined her hands, pushing back her cuticles with gentle strokes. *Eleppon is an impetuous fool, and will get herself killed.* She hopped off the bed and went to a brass-bound chest where she traded her satin dress for a fitted, black, one-piece garment that covered her from head to toe, leaving eye and ear holes and tiny openings for breath. She flexed her fingers in the attached gloves, and adjusted the toe guards. A thick pad of leather formed a yoke across her shoulders and neck, and she adjusted this, too.

She coiled a thin, but strong black cloth around her waist, dug down to the bottom of the chest and unfastened the catch on the false bottom. Within the crevice was a thin waist-pouch made of soft, black leather, a small assortment of cloth-wrapped implements inside. She strapped it on, ready now to open any lock that resisted her, and if need be, to place her wall hooks.

With habitual ease, she negotiated and reset the traps at her door. Then she tiptoed into the hallway and flattened against the wall, regulating her breathing. She could feel the probing awareness of the Nightwing's guards even though they were ninety yards removed by walls of stone and rock crystal. In her mind, she pictured a tiny, green fly. By concentrating on the image, she imagined merging with the insect, feeling its proboscis and antennae, tasting and testing the air, aware of layers of particles too small to be seen by elves.

The scrutiny of the guards subsided. Noth continued to navigate the wall in this manner, stopping after a few feet to merge with a scorpion, then a spider, and so on, until she was free of the royal keep. Her sinuous body flitted over the roof tops of the cave complex like a sigh.

At length, she came to an escarpment of slippery jade. First, she pounded a hook securely into a natural indentation with a small, serviceable hammer specific to the purpose and tied her sash to it like a rope, leaving the other end coiled about her waist. Then, she swung down to the ledge of quartz and yanked on the sash to retrieve it.

There was the sudden sound of wings, and Noth ducked just in time to avoid the sharp claws of the furry creature that whizzed by her head. She laughed softly and whispered, "Topi."

The kitten bat circled to land on Noth's shoulder. Smaller, rounder and shorter-lived than an ordinary bat, the kitten was also more intelligent. Topi had been Noth's pet for five years, half its average lifespan.

With Topi on her shoulder, the dark elf felt more secure. She knew the bat's teeth and claws would be her protection in the absence of weapons, even though she didn't expect any trouble.

Fumbling in the hollow of the quartz wall for the familiar vine, she gave it a sharp tug, balancing on her toes. A seamless door opened inward, casting a circle of pale light onto the dark jade ledge. Wind whistled from somewhere high above. Noth entered.

The corridor stretching before her was clear quartz, glistening with an inner light that blinded her for a moment. Topi nestled his head beneath one wing to shut out the glare. As she walked, Noth's penumbral reflection glanced off the sheer walls. This natural corridor was as smooth as time and water could make it, and its crystalline luster needed no other artistry. Dry now, it would remain so until the next big rainstorm. As Noth advanced, she relaxed into a familiar sense of freedom. This was her domain.

After some time, the light faded and the crystal darkened to a soft charcoal. She was nearing the hamlet of Dezu'o. She recognized her mark on the hidden doorway and paused. Would her brother have come here? No, she decided. Too near their mother. Even Dekhalis must fear her powers.

Noth maintained an easy pace as the smoky gray changed again to rose, mottling before running true.

The City of Douvilwe. There was her mark on the door that led to the Thieves Quarters. She hesitated once more. What if she were wrong? She shrugged, and Topi chirped in mild outrage. Stroking the kitten bat's head, Noth made up her mind. If she didn't find Dekhalis here, at least she could rule out one hiding place.

Putting her thumb in an obscure crevice, the door opened, swinging shut behind her with a hollow sound. Here was a corridor of a different character. This elven-made passage was of roughly chiseled limestone. Instead of water-worn rock, the floor was a mass of jagged pebbles. Noth was thankful for the thick leather hide of her soles as she tiptoed along.

After nearly a league of pebbled limestone, Noth heard voices raised in conversation. She hurried to the connecting ledge that spanned the common rooms of Sour's Tavern. This lookout was a good starting place to hear news of Dekhalis. Too high and narrow for ordinary traffic, she had used it often to observe the doings of thieves and rogues who interested her. She crouched on the shadowy ledge and peered below.

The usual crowd of men were talking and laughing on the tavern floor. This was a man's place, free from the prying eyes of their mistresses. Noth knew Dekhalis had a hand in its creation. Sour was an old servant of his, one who had been paid handsomely over the years.

There were usually a few women out for a thrill, but Noth didn't see any now. She listened tensely for Dekhalis's voice, but did not hear it.

Suddenly, Topi screeched, and Noth whirled just in time to see three rough-looking male elves, home-made daggers in hand, two approaching her from one end of the ledge, one from the opposite end. Crude ladders had been erected since she had last been here, and she cursed herself for failing to notice.

Topi hurled his furry body at the nearest assailant, his claws connecting with a grizzled cheek. The elf screamed and dropped his dagger, and the other two lunged at Noth.

With a shrewd glance, she leapt to the crowded floor beneath. A few of the patrons, swollen with drink, blustered at her, but there were others who soon held something more menacing than tankards in their hands.

In little time, she was surrounded by a ring of men, each carrying a home-made knife. One pinioned her arms behind her. Another slapped her soundly across the cheek, then laughed, shocked by his own courage. Noth glared at him.

Topi tacked away from the ledge and circled the dizzying scene below to get a better view of his quarry. There was so much activity around Noth that the kitten bat was undecided whom to attack first. While he circumscribed the room, the outlaws elbowed each other to get a look at the intruder, raising a racket that hurt Topi's ears. Amid jeers and laughter, four of Noth's captors snared an extremity, and swung the struggling elf woman back and forth.

Topi dove for the tallest elf whose shaggy head made a clear target above the others. The needle-sharp claws found their mark, and the elf released Noth's left arm to cover his bleeding scalp with his hands. Again and again, Topi dropped from the sky like an avenging spirit, and blood spurted indiscriminately from eyes and ears. The tavern floor ran scarlet.

A knife whizzed through the air, slicing a piece of fur from Topi's belly. The bat rolled twice in the air and dove for the attacker's armpit, neatly severing the arm. The elf screamed, blood spouted, and Noth was dropped in the resulting commotion.

She scrambled to her feet and sprinted through an opening in the crowd, scattering more than one assailant in her haste to escape. Her arm brushed a row of glasses and sent them smashing to the floor.

Breathing heavily, she pushed through the circular oaken door that led to the back rooms and a hidden passage to the sewers below. With a frightened glance behind, she pressed her mask against her nose and raced toward the stench.

Beyond the doorway, a large shape blocked her path. She leapt to one side, but too late. The dark elf moved out of the shadows and laughed so sharply, it might have been a cough. In the heart-drumming darkness, Noth discerned the edge of a stiletto.

Moments later, Noth was bound face down with catgut cords to a grate over the sewer. Someone grabbed her hair through the cloth hood and wrenched her head back. A cold sliver of steel split her mask from nose to scalp.

His hot breath warmed her cheek, his voice a caress of fire. "Now you are mine, dear sister." He smashed her face into the grate, and she heard bone crack like a dragon's egg before the world went silent.

-46-

INUARI SAT before the mirror of her dressing table, her eyes in a faraway stare. During the past three days, Aunt Jetta had cared for her bodily needs while her soul had traveled with the Goddess Miralor.

Before her studies were even completed, she had been initiated. Her heart glowed with the new feelings of belonging and joy, but she worried. *Am I ready?*

The youngest priestess in Alvarra, her newfound pride paled before the awful responsibility she now carried. She swallowed, sensing the presence of the Goddess within her. Though silent now, the spirit of Miralor hovered, as much a part of her as her skin.

In the mirror, a circlet of braided white silk over her brow crowned Inuari's lovely face. Her robe of dark blue came to a peak at the back of her neck, then fell to a vee in front, the edges decorated with tiny black rabbits. This would be her uniform for the next century, unless she was promoted within the Order.

Inuari blinked as her mirror image suddenly turned cloudy and then disappeared. Jetta had warned her this might happen. She tried to still her breathing, for the slightest movement interfered with the transmission.

Before her was a blurred picture of her sister Noth—screaming.

-47-

EMBAZA FELT as if the sun were shriveling his very soul. Precious fluid drained from his face. Sand was a constant companion, in his clothes, hair, mouth and nose. In his mind's eye, his skin aged swiftly, magically, his bones shrank, and his face withered into a hideous mask. He reached a tremulous finger to the parchment of his burning cheek. A seam split at the touch, revealing a furrow of blood. He began his litany to pain. *Pain is good…* But the life-saving words he embraced as a boy were not enough this time. Panic sliced through him.

Embaza twisted to reach his saddlebags and fumbled open the catch, tearing the skin of his blistered fingers. Frantically, he reached into the bag, feeling the familiar shapes of his craft, as well as the new objects he had gathered in Mischa's aerie.

He glanced around him. Tiala still slept, draped over her horse's neck, exhausted from her ordeal. The cloak and salve had anesthetized her. Later, he would give her some water, but for now, he must concentrate on himself. He looked for the giants. Two brothers rode far behind him, the third in the lead. Embaza was glad they had such an aversion to Tiala. As long as he stayed near her, he would have the privacy he needed.

He wrapped the edges of his robe around his cracked and bleeding fingers, and brought out the arcane objects, one by one. His teeth began to chatter and he anticipated the seizure that would soon wrack his body. He clutched the objects with raw fingers, watched blood ooze from cracked knuckles, and tried to swallow. He nearly dropped the demongaze. *How did I get this?*

His hands trembled. The next items were two dancers, one onyx and one ruby. *Don't remember these either.* He glanced up at the sun, his entire body beginning to shake, his mind caving in, melting, maddened by anguish and pain. An itch began in his belly, churning upward in a spiral. *What now?* Even as he asked, he knew. It burrowed up from within him, the way it had in Tiala. *The scream.*

A light tap on his sleeve carried the force of a hammer.

"Embaza?"

The wizard stared at Polah as if she were a ghost. He appeared to be in an advanced state of sunstroke. How was that possible? Fervently, the fox-woman thrust her waterskin toward him. "Drink," she commanded.

Embaza drank violently, never spilling a drop. Polah had to wrench the waterskin away from him before he drained it all. Tears streamed from the wizard's eyes and he laughed hysterically.

Polah slapped his face, leaving a handprint of blood. "Stop it, Embaza." All the strength left him and he canted to one side. She spurred her horse to him and slipped her arm around his waist. Bracing herself, she shifted his weight and fanned his cracked, oozing cheek with her fingers.

"Embaza," she cried. "Can you hear me? Try to hold on." She stiffened and looked about her for help. The giants rode with their hooded eyes trained on the distance, clothed in self-absorption, or perhaps the scorn of the veteran for the uninitiated. Obsidian dozed in deep meditation, reins looped about the saddle horn, his fair skin shaded by the hood of his gray robe. Gudrun was too far back to see in the shimmering glare.

The fox-woman was afraid, but of what she was not sure. Embaza was shaking head to toe, not violently, but steadily, like a child in some paroxysm of its own. "What is it? A spell that went wrong?" she asked. "If I didn't know better, I'd say you had the dark elf's sickness."

After crisscrossing the reins over the neck of her horse so as not to spook the animal, she gripped the stiff leather neck of the waterskin and splashed the wizard's face. Just as quickly, she brought the waterskin back to her side, out of his reach. The elf swung his head around with a look of such piercing wistfulness that, for a moment, she mistook it for love. This shocked her. *What business have I to think of love at a time like this? Or at any time?* And yet, the laws of her survival didn't seem to matter now. That scared her, too.

As the temporary relief of water soaked into his scorched skin, Embaza croaked, "Polah." She gave him another sip from her waterskin, snatching it away from his clawing hands to keep him from downing it all.

Sounding more like himself, he said, "In my saddlebags," he tapped the pocket nearest her, just behind his thigh, "there's an iron flask." As Polah withdrew her arm from his waist to reach inside, she looked closely at Embaza, and saw what no one else had.

Beneath the dye of his skin, behind the mask of urbanity and calm superiority, there lay the dark-elven heritage. She had rebelled against the fear and mistrust others took for granted. For her, a dark elf was just another pariah like herself.

"You've lied to us," she whispered, handing him the flask, and Embaza heard recognition beneath her words, the shared burden of one who carried secrets in her blood.

His dark green eyes were slitted as pain returned, but he managed to sit upright to unstop the metal flask. He brought the container to his lips, then paused to look at her, seeing only shadows in the sun's glare. "Don't be frightened by what happens," he said so softly she strained to hear. "I am near, little flower." He downed the contents and tossed the flask to the burning sand. Polah nearly toppled off the horse in her surprise. The wizard had vanished, leaving an empty saddle.

There were shouts from the giants, Byder and Dunal, who both galloped toward her. Obsidian jerked awake. Polah leaned over to snatch a single rein of Embaza's horse, the end of which she coiled tightly about the saddle horn with her small, capable hands.

In a clear, lilting voice, she cried for all to hear, "The wizard has retired to commune with his masters. He will be back by nightfall." Tingling with excitement at her ingenuity, she lifted her chin and ignored the giants' superstitious reaction, as if a companion disappearing was the most natural thing in the world.

Gudrun's mind chewed on what she had witnessed. "Magic," she muttered to herself, and spat a lingering bit of sand onto the ground. "Well, at least things are never dull with a wizard around." She spurred her horse into a trot and caught up to Polah. "So," she said in a hearty, friendly tone, "you had a little disagreement, and he went off mad?"

Polah forced a rueful smile. "He's always been a mysterious sort. Who knows what really motivates him?" That much, at least, was true.

"Well," said Gudrun, eyeing Polah's limp waterskin, "it wouldn't be the first time a fight broke out over water in this desert. If it gets too bad, you can have some of mine." The dwarf reached into her jerkin for a twist of dried mutton, and bit down on it.

Polah found herself unable to take her eyes off the meat and something in her belly churned.

Gudrun chuckled, "Take my advice, girl, chew a little of this several times a day. The sun can make it hard to eat, you know." The dwarf turned to look at the horizon, where a lone buzzard sailed in perfect rings.

The fox in Polah cried out for dominance, while her human consciousness hung on by a shred. This was not the time or place to shape-change.

Beside her, Gudrun had drifted into her own thoughts, still watching the horizon. Polah followed the dwarf's line of vision, and she, too, was lulled by the buzzard's graceful sweep across the windless sky. In that instant, she realized hunger was the trigger that awakened the fox within her.

Hunger. She looked at Gudrun with gratitude. Her advice was wise. She would eat a little at a time and keep the animal at bay. She tore a small piece of mutton from her waist pack, hoping it would not be salty. She brushed the sand off of it, and began to chew. She had almost no water left.

Gudrun reined in her horse until she was trailing behind once more. For the next several leagues, the travelers plodded on, until in the wash of a sunset of lavender, silver-blue, pink and gold they arrived at the camp of the Blacktooth giants. A series of distinctive warbles met them, although the scouts were never visible.

Over the rise of a dune lay the shadowed camp, protected by mountains of sand all around. The muted colors of the tents reflected the loveliness of the sunset, and they spread out across the valley like a multi-colored quilt. To the weary travelers, the sight was as refreshing as the water it promised. The horses easily found the diagonal track in the shadowed dune, and dipped their bodies into its embrace.

As they drew closer, individual decorations on each tent emerged, the once-bright, embroidered images of animals and plants. Curious toddlers the size of colts poked their noses from looming doorways, then disappeared. The spicy smell of food tantalized them, and the horses snorted at the drop in temperature, eager for their long awaited drink and dinner.

Two young men rushed over with flasks of water which they shared around—and a third watered the horses.

Gudrun dismounted and clumped over to gather Tiala from her horse, not trusting the giants. The dark elf still slept with the heaviness of an exhausted child. Gudrun dripped water onto her lips, and hoisted her over her shoulder, then Byder escorted them toward a row of tents near the eastern outskirts of camp. An arabesque of wind chimes serenaded them along their way.

Very concerned about Six Stix, Obsidian moved to lift him from the horse, and Braytok joined him. Together they carried the warrior to one of the small tents in the makeshift village. The tribesman addressed the monk. "Young warrior, it is time for you to meet our Headman and prepare to observe the rites." He gestured at a large tent in the center of the encampment.

While other tribesmen led the horses away, Obsidian called to Polah and said, "Find Embaza. He must help Six. I'll try to be back soon."

"Wait," Polah began, but Obsidian was urged along by Dunal, Byder and Braytok as they led Nob's horse toward the center of the encampment. Polah looked uncertainly at the ashen face of the blue elf. She doubted Embaza—or anyone—could help him if he were truly poisoned.

"General," she called, "Where are you going?"

Gudrun nodded toward a large tent. "Our hosts say this is where we will sleep." She waited for Polah and said in a low voice, "We must hide Tiala's identity. I don't think it will help her cause if they know she is a ruler. They have peculiar ideas about the place of women."

"Would they attack her?" Polah asked.

"Not without the Patriarch's permission. But they are a superstitious lot, and have no liking for dark elves."

Polah's brow furrowed. "Do you think Mischa will have a price on our heads?"

"Let's count on it," said Gudrun with her usual pessimism. Then she remembered. "Didn't the wizard say the Prince was taken care of? We never heard the whole of that, did we?"

Polah recalled the single figure she had seen walking on the horizon early that day. "I saw him. He's out here traveling in the desert—by himself."

"Impossible. Mischa never travels alone, not without hordes of guards and servants."

"I know what I saw."

Gudrun combed the sand from her beard with her fingers. "Well, that's a puzzle, all right." She was rankled by the fox-woman's keen senses, like an unfair advantage in battle. And, thanks to the healing abilities of shape-changers, her milky skin was fresh and moist, while Gudrun's felt like leather. *How can I treat her as a human when she doesn't act like one?*

-48-

OBSIDIAN DISCOVERED that the funeral rites of one culture were not much different from another. Allowing for tongues and traditions, the spirit remained the same, to say farewell to the friend or loved one, and to wish an honorable entry into the afterlife, if such existed.

He envied the brotherly sentiment the giants shared with one another. Even in the monastery, there had been nothing quite like this. The monks had always shown respect and gentility—even kindness, but his life there had lacked the warmth of this tribe.

He suffered the giants' back-slapping with good nature, ignoring the painful throb of his old wound, and when the jewel-studded goblet was passed around, he drank with the rest of them, though he detested the taste of fermented goat's milk.

He allowed himself to join the traditional line dance that snaked around the burial spot, his tongue stumbling over the words of unfamiliar songs, mispronouncing their names.

The giants had a bit of trouble with his name, too, and soon nicknamed him Ob.

At long last, it was his turn to speak a few words to the departed giant. Braytok touched his shoulder, and said, "Say your farewells to the one whose name was Nob." The giant indicated the foot of the mounded grave.

As required, Obsidian laid Nob's elkhorn knife at the warrior's feet, and cleared his throat. He didn't know where the words would come from, but he closed his eyes and conjured up his last image of Nob alive.

"Today we met, and today we said goodbye. You fought with the skill and courage of a sand dragon." He looked around, and the weathered faces regarded him with understanding. Firelight flickered over their simple, honest expressions, and he felt encouraged.

"I salute you, Nob. I am ashamed that I was chosen to end your life. I wish it had been someone else. I have never killed before—."

He was startled by the sudden intake of breath of many of those around him, but then continued. "I did not enjoy it." He hesitated again, filled with an emotion he could not name. "I wish you speedy entrance into the home of the gods." He stopped, self-conscious, and could not move. He prayed someone else would speak.

Braytok clapped him on the shoulder. "Thank you, Brother Ob." He unsheathed a large, sharp knife and turned to Obsidian. The monk had a sickening feeling in the pit of his stomach.

The other giants gathered around, and the one called Braytok spoke again, in a slow deep voice, as if in ritual, "Would you be one of us?"

Obsidian trembled inwardly, but answered, "Yes."

"Where would you be marked?" asked Braytok.

Obsidian looked around the giants, but their faces yielded no answers. Their blackened front teeth took on a new meaning. It wasn't a fate he would choose.

"Where would you be marked?" repeated Braytok, sternly.

Obsidian was confused. *The masters say it is sacrilege to deface the body.* His skin was parched by the sun and a bit red in places, and he winced at the thought of the knife. Then he knew. He lifted his heel, and an old white scar showed slick in the firelight. There was a murmur of disapproval from the giants, and Braytok stooped down, his large hand cradling Obsidian's foot. He scowled at the monk.

"If we mark you here, you will not be able to fight," he said.

On impulse, the monk lifted his sleeve and touched the fleshy part above the left elbow. He had already defied his masters. "Here, then," said Obsidian, "where all will see it and know my loyalty."

"Well said," Braytok replied.

Swiftly, he sliced a half-moon into the monk's arm, sending a line of pain all the way up into his armpit and shoulder. *Strange how nerves are joined,* he thought, disassociating mind from body in the way he had been taught.

"Join us," chorused the giants as each came forward and touched Obsidian as the ritual demanded, either shaking his hand or patting his shoulder. One giant stamped the blood that had dripped to the sand, creating a large hole with his foot. Displaying a gap-toothed grin, he said, "Join us, Ob."

Braytok used a waterskin to wash the monk's arm, then unwound a strip of the ever-present turban from his own head and washed that, too. After his arm was bound, Obsidian walked with the others from the tent, the clenching of his jaw the only clue to what had taken place.

He was touched by the acceptance of these rough men who towered over him. In one night, he had received more outward affection than the monks had shown him in years of devotion.

For the first time that day, he experienced a surge of hope. He was committed to his path. There was no going back. He knew he must face his punishment at the monastery. *But what can they do to me that is worse than banishment? At least, now I have some place to go.* The pain in his arm was reassuring.

He and Braytok had left the tent with Dunal and Byder. The sky was dark now and the moon rose over the ridge. It was just past full, yet its light was obscured by the many flickering campfires dotting the valley of the giants. Obsidian wondered if his companions sat around one of these fires. His sense of direction was confused.

"Where are my other friends?" he asked.

"There, Brother Ob," said Braytok, pointing to two large tents a few yards to the east.

"Is there a healer in your camp who could help the blue warrior? He has a strong poison in his blood and we have no medicine for it."

Braytok nodded. "Go to him—I'll send the shaman."

When Obsidian reached the tents, he found Tiala and Gudrun in the first. The dwarf had built up a small fire that gave a cheery light to the homely walls. Tiala's dreamy face was almost restored to its natural beauty in the reflected firelight, as she lounged on the woven carpet, her mind far away.

"Where's Six Stix?" asked the monk.

Gudrun raised a scowling face. "In the other tent." She glanced at her mistress. "Desert dwellers have a prohibition against female warriors."

"And Polah?"

Gudrun shrugged. "Gone. If you know what's good for you, you'll abide by the customs and leave us, too."

Obsidian looked puzzled. There was much to be learned about his new brothers, but he was one of them now. He wouldn't be bullied. He asked Tiala, "How are you feeling, Princess?"

The dark elf lifted her fine head and stared at him with an almost unnerving gaze. "The night brings me comfort." She listened, trance-like, to the tinkling of the wind chimes from another tent. "Thank you," she said.

Obsidian felt unwelcome, though uncertain why, and he hurried into the other tent, where he soon discovered the blue elf was not alone. A gnomad sat next to him.

The monk was surprised. This was the first gnome he had seen in the giants' camp. "Who are you—one of the tribe, too?" he asked.

The gnome stood up. "I am bound to the tribe by marriage." At the look on Obsidian's face, he cackled and said, "My wife is human." He sketched a pleasing female silhouette with his hands. "Her sister married one of the Headman's sons, poor thing." With a comical grimace, he half-whispered, "He's a big brute, but kind as rain." He brushed off his dun-colored trousers and gave a kind of salute to Obsidian. "I'm off, then. He's lying comfortable. Don't know whether you ought to order a healing or a burial."

Obsidian said, "Aren't you the healer?" But the gnome slipped under the tent flap and disappeared into the darkness, running with a fleet, animal grace.

"I'll be damned," muttered the monk. His gaze darted about the tent, as if his old masters had heard him. Then he moved to Six Stix and put his ear above the elf's nose and mouth. He felt a wisp of breath on his cheek.

He took the last of the heal-all from his pouch and chewed it thoroughly, rolled it into a paste with his saliva and pressed the wad onto the elf's tongue. With a pang of loneliness, he sat back on his heels and stirred the small fire the gnome had built. This was not the comradely blaze he had wished for.

-49-

BEYOND THE tents, a large fox sniffed the air and avoided the campfires, searching the dunes for more mice. Nearly sated now, her hunt was winding down. She let a kangaroo rat pass by without a qualm.

A familiar smell reached her nose, and she turned to the east. Seated on a nearby ridge, arms clasped around his knees, was Embaza. They stared at each other, surrounded by the soft darkness and the smiling moon. "Hello, little flower," he said.

With a sensation of complete naturalness, Polah's womanhood emerged. Fur and claw were forgotten, and with glorious exhilaration, she welcomed transformation like a rebirth of her true self. She was not ashamed of her nakedness. And more, she exulted in her new mastery.

Your shape-changing is getting easier. Embaza's voice echoed in her mind.

She climbed the cool sand dune until she was kneeling before Embaza. Smiling, she reached her arms beneath his cloak and into the front of his robe. She imagined the blackness of his skin under her hands, and it was like embracing the night. Breathing ecstasy into her parched lungs, Polah welcomed Embaza's arms around her, and the two rolled down the hill of sand.

Beneath the shelter of his cloak, Embaza and Polah mated, entering one vision that stretched in a timeless vortex. When the stars had all appeared to emblazon the darkness, they spread the cloak beneath them. Embaza kissed the tears from the corners of her mouth, and Polah breathed in the salt fragrance of his skin. They had tasted each other, and yet an ocean of enchantment and mystery lay waiting to engulf them.

Across this sea, Embaza and Polah stared at each other, knowing they would have no peace until they had explored it. A shooting star streaked across the sky.

Polah touched Embaza's cheek. She had learned a little elven in her few years of schooling and she used it now. "Pain is no longer your friend."

Embaza's smile transformed his face, and he had never seemed so handsome. "You have taught me well," he said.

-50-

GUDRUN POKED unnecessarily at the flames, stabbing the coals with a long stick. She and Tiala huddled over the small fire, two small shadows in the center of the huge tent. "Men," muttered the dwarf.

"You sound like an Alvarran." Tiala combed her tangled black hair with her fingers.

"Alvarra. You don't even have men anymore," grumbled Gudrun.

"They suit us," Tiala retorted. "After hundreds of years of peace, one grows used to gentle company. But these giants are barbarians. My blood boils at the way they treat us—especially me. As if I were unclean. Look at this tent. This threadbare rug and a few sticks."

Gudrun did not bother to reply. She saw nothing wrong with the homely quarters. Desert wolves bayed in the distance.

Tiala sighed, too exhausted to be angry for long. "In a way, I'm glad they left us to ourselves." She raised her eyes to the top of the tent, where the stars beamed through the opening. Their brilliance frightened her, like tiny suns that might grow into Scourges. "I've tried to play the part of a docile upworlder, but it seems an empty role. All that's required is beauty or brawn. No fire or brilliance."

Gudrun wondered if the elf knew what a snob she was. Did she think all females were superior, or just Alvarran ones? The dwarf played with the binding on her oxhide sheath, distracted by the sheen of her blade winking in the firelight. She glanced at Tiala. The dark elf's beauty annoyed her. "Am I not a woman too?" she said, chin held high.

"Of course you are," replied Tiala, her green eyes shining.

Gudrun leaned back on her elbows and stared up at the stars. "I haven't thought about it much. All my life, I've commanded men, cajoled them, inspired them, fought beside them, gotten drunk with them." She turned on her side and traced the pattern of the rug with her stubby forefinger. "Once I even loved one." She glanced at the elf, shyly.

Tiala's steady gaze was disconcerting. "Yes, they can be sweet and inventive. Some are quite intelligent, even exciting." Her eyes glazed with memory. "They're so sensitive. They're not in command of their emotions. And yet, sometimes I think it's their imperfection that endears them to us." She chuckled. "Without them, who would we rule?"

Gudrun frowned. The elf's philosophy was wrong somewhere, but how could she explain? "In my land, things aren't so simple. Your world revolves around women. Your men hang about like shadows in the corners—seen and not heard. But in Tskurl, there's equality. Men can aspire to be captains and healers, lawmakers, teachers, whatever women can do. Why should there be such a difference? In my own village, the priest is male."

"I could never submit my soul to the care of a man." Tiala rose and began to pace around the fire. "Do you see what can happen? Look at the society here. Somehow, they've let the men have a little power, and now the women are parceled off into tents on the outskirts of everything." Her cheekbones glinted like black steel in the firelight.

Gudrun laughed. "It's all for show, my Lady. Under the covers, it's quite a different story. I'll wager a man here lays his head on some woman's strong lap and tells her all his troubles while she soothes his body and soul. It's just the warrior's life. I've done it myself."

Tiala pursed her lips. "Well, I haven't, even when I was a soldier." She thought a moment. "Look at Embaza. There's a man who has too much power."

"What do you mean? He seems all right—for an intellectual. He's certainly been kind to you."

"And why not? He's like all the others. He's curious about me. He sees in me the roots of his own destiny, as all elves do. I can spot them a league away. We get such pilgrims often. And unlike the so-called wise men of Sargothas, our priestesses use the sap of the body and speak to the earth itself. They don't play with wands like children, or dishonor death by disappearing. What dignity is there in that?"

She forgot Gudrun was there, as she bit her lip with unacknowledged envy. "How *did* he disappear?" she muttered.

But Gudrun had heard more than she cared to. "And what if he had been born in your land?" she asked. "Would you have let him rise? Or would he have been the lapdog for some priestess, brewing her evening tonics or ironing her robes?"

Tiala lifted an eyebrow at the veracity of the image. "Even among women, only a few rise to prominence. He's still only a man."

"You'd be surprised," whispered Gudrun. Turning her back, she curled up and half-closed her eyes. "Better get some rest while it's cool. In a few hours it will be morning again and we'll have to find a place to hide you from the sun."

Tiala sighed again. She hated being dependent on others. She moved back to the fire and wrapped Embaza's cloak around her. Lying on her back, she let her gaze travel to the sky with its scattering of stars—mysterious lights she had only known in legend. Although her body was tired, she felt weary in some deeper way. She was very far from home and tired of pretending to be a simple traveler in a hostile land.

She murmured, "You didn't bring me the Glammalee, did you, Gudrun? You promised."

"No, Tiala," answered the dwarf, already half asleep, "If I had your voice, I wouldn't worry about a flute. Go to sleep."

Tiala couldn't help it. It was the one area of her life where she doubted herself. Gudrun hadn't heard the *deep* music. She didn't know what a real bard was. Tiala blinked several times, striving for control. *I miss my home.*

She heard the enchantress, Polah, creep into the tent and slip into her clothes. The shape-changer nestled between the two women, and Tiala welcomed her warmth. *If only these were my sisters safe beside me.*

A tendril of fear floated into her consciousness as she thought of her quest. *Tomorrow, it will start again—the Scourge, the pain. And the closer I get to home, the weaker I will be, easy prey for Dekhalis.* In answer, an old memory surfaced.

She had been a frightened child, about to attend her first party of state. Standing next to the Nightwing, neatly coifed, dressed in a black velvet bodysuit, Tiala had looked into the huge drawing room, overwhelmed by the crowding of color, movement and noise. With the strange clarity of the very young, she had felt the mantle of rulership falling upon her shoulders and grabbed her mother's hand so tightly that it hurt.

Gently, her mother had told her, "You will play many roles in your lifetime, little Tiala. In each situation, find the one where you learn the most. That is the secret to being a good ruler." She had brushed a stray hair from Tiala's dark forehead and smiled. "Now, it is our secret, eh?"

The more Tiala reflected on this remembrance, the braver she felt. *The role I know least about is that of the bard. So why not start living it?* Her eyes shone with excitement. *This could be the greatest adventure of my life. I should be collecting tales and stories. That's what bards do, isn't it? If I'm to become one, I must make songs about my experiences—even my terror.* She shivered. *How many dark elves have known the Scourge-madness?*

-51-

In the tent nearby, Obsidian had finished giving Six Stix the healing leaf when there was a shuffling outside and the flap was pulled back by a strange-looking being. He was a giant, nearly eleven feet tall, dressed in a ragged robe of dingy cloth, and an equally-dingy turban. Obsidian was repelled at first by the pitted face and lopsided eye. A few graying whiskers were sprinkled in no regular pattern, and three brownish teeth decorated the grimace that might have been a smile. But the giant exuded a calm that reminded the monk of his master Tolimane.

The visitor's gaze found the patient by the fire in the center of the tent, and Obsidian moved aside to let the giant take his place. Six Stix's face seemed as lifeless as a mask in the flickering light.

Briskly, the healer went to work, setting his huge deerskin sack down beside him and brushing off the sand. To Obsidian's dismay, the giant drew out a razor-thin dagger that glistened in the firelight. "What are you going to do with that?" he demanded.

The shaman mumbled, "I must discover the nature of his illness," and to the monk's horror, he sliced into Six Stix's thumb and put it into his own mouth. He then spat blood into the sand and pinched the elf's thumb until it seemed to disappear between the giant's vast fingers.

Obsidian watched in wonder. He had never seen a healer who worked with such vigor.

When the cut stopped bleeding, the giant removed a small brazier from his bag and filled it with glowing sticks from the fire, then sifted pieces of aromatic herbs into the embers. He fanned this smoke around the elf's body with his hands. The excess wafted out from the top of the tent into the night air.

Then the healer leaned down and whispered something to Six Stix. It looked to Obsidian as if he blew his own breath into the warrior's nose and mouth. Was it his imagination or did the elf sigh?

The healer unstopped a pottery flask, then beckoned to Obsidian and whispered, "There are strong forces working against me. Hold his head while I pour this liquid down his throat." The monk obeyed while the giant poured a whitish fluid from the flask into Six's mouth. Most of it dribbled down the elf's cheeks, soaking the carpet.

Obsidian felt a little foolish. *Was the old man a faker?*

Struggling to his elbows, Six Stix spouted a stream of white liquid over the healer's face. "What are you trying to do—poison me?" cried the elf.

The healer snapped, "Hold him." As Six Stix thrashed under the monk, the giant poured the last of the liquid down the elf's throat, then held his chin and nose with his huge hands until the warrior finally swallowed.

"You're cured," said the healer and turned to put his things back in the bag.

Six Stix fought to rise, and Obsidian had to sit on him to keep him from attacking the giant. "It's good to see you acting like your old self again," he said.

Six Stix gasped for breath as the blood rushed to his head.

The shaman rolled to his knees, then leaned closer to peer at Obsidian's wounded left eye, pinning the skin back on either side. Obsidian held his breath, but allowed the healer to palpate the skin gently. "You'll be all right," rasped the giant. "But be warned, both of you. There is an evil one who can attack from far away."

"I've heard that before," groused the elf.

As the healer prepared to leave, Obsidian said to him, "My companion would like to give you something for your trouble. Will you accept a gift?"

Six Stix gaped in outrage, then said, "*His* trouble? The fellow nearly killed me. You take one wooden talent, and I'll—"

"Shut up, Six," said Obsidian, but by then the old healer was gone. He wondered if his new status as tribesman had brought them special favor, or whether the tribe was always so generous with its guests. He supposed the code of healers was the same everywhere. Amazed at the swiftness of Six's recovery, the monk wished he had thought to ask the giant how to brew that cure for poison.

Indeed, coming to himself again, Six Stix looked around. "Where are we?" he asked, checking for his weapons.

"At the giants' camp," answered Obsidian.

In the darkness outside the tent, Polah slipped from Embaza's embrace after indicating the tent where he should rejoin the other men.

Reluctant to end the moment, Embaza wrestled with his thoughts. *If I had not met Polah, I would still be a friendless outlaw. With her, I am real for the first time.* He looked at the shimmering sky, drunk with its beauty. *And I feel—joy.* He almost laughed out loud. *So, why am I afraid to show my true self to the others?*

Finally, he lifted the flap and ducked inside the tent, tossing his saddlebags onto the sandy floor.

"You're back," Obsidian cried.

"And you're not dead," Embaza said to Six Stix.

Obsidian gave a brief account of the healer's visit, then hesitated to ask about Embaza's disappearance. "Come have some food and water. The giants have been generous."

Six Stix said, "I'm glad to see you, wizard."

Embaza walked to the fire and threw back his hood. "I have something to say."

Obsidian looked up with interest. Embaza sat down next to Six Stix and folded his dark hands in his lap. He looked at Six Stix with piercing eyes, and the warrior saw a new strangeness in them.

"I'm a dark elf," the wizard said, and waited for their reaction.

Six Stix frowned. "You're joking."

Obsidian shifted his position for a better look at Embaza's face. "I knew something was wrong with you out there. You were strung as tight as a drum. I thought it was some magical thing."

"Not magic," said Embaza. "Forgive me, but I have traveled for years as a blue elf, and the disguise has been useful."

"Humph. No doubt," said Six. "I will say I've never had much respect for you dark elves. After all, you deserted us in the wars and left us to fight your battles for you."

"Hold on, now," said Embaza, showing them his palm. "I am Sargothian, too, remember. We sent our wizards onto the battlefields in great number—and bled the same blood as yours."

Six Stix rubbed his chin, as if to dispel the scenes of carnage such talk invoked. "If you're a dark elf, what were you doing with the Sargothians? I thought they shunned the dark race."

"I was the first." His shuttered face belied the pride in his voice, pain etched in the lines of his cheeks.

How many masks this wizard has, thought Obsidian.

Embaza stared at the fire. "All I know is that my father's name was Valedd. He was a powerful wizard, they say—before such arts were banned in Alvarra."

"Banned?" said Obsidian. "The Princess says it is the land of magic."

"Only if you're a priestess," he replied with a trace of bitterness. "It seems my father made some enemies."

"What happened to him?"

"Dead," his gaze drifted to a sliver of black peeping through the tent flap, "or so they told me. Before he died, he had me kidnapped and transported to the Towers of Sargoth to learn the arts, so that the craft would not be lost to our kind forever."

"Who was your mother?" asked the monk.

"Who knows? My memory is stripped of her—and of my homeland. The wizards made sure of that. I know only what they told me." His voice was as bitter as old tree bark.

Six Stix cocked his head. "Perhaps your father is still alive."

"No. They say he was ancient when he sired me. Even if he had left Alvarra and lived elsewhere, he would be in his grave by now." He scooped some sand from around the fire pit and let it sift through his fingers. It was like the ashes of his own memory. He brushed his hands and got up, signaling an end to the conversation.

The other two looked at each other, then Six arranged his pack like a pillow and lay his head down. In truth, he knew the healer had saved his life, but sleep was the true medicine after such an ordeal. *A strange business to be healed,* he thought, remembering some of the men he'd seen come to life on the battlefield. He felt the pins and needles in his arms and legs, and flexed his fingers. If he knew healers, that drink had contained a tonic that soon would wear off. He closed his eyes.

But Obsidian could not sleep for his worry. He got up and went over to the door of the tent where Embaza stood looking out at the stars and the lustrous moon.

"I attended Nob's funeral," said the monk.

Embaza did not move, wishing instead to see another shooting star.

"They made me a tribesman," continued Obsidian.

Embaza rubbed the ivory token Rearguard had given him between his thumb and finger. "We are doubly protected, then."

"But what of your safety? Tomorrow, we should buy horses and a wagon from the giants. If my status isn't enough, our friend over there has money. You and the Princess need protection from the sun." The monk hesitated. "Unless you plan to disappear again."

He smiled ruefully. "My disappearance was a miracle. The flask contained a liquid that could be used only once. I was lucky it didn't increase my size or turn me into a melonfish."

"My teacher says desperation is the first condition for a miracle."

Embaza turned to look him in the eyes. Obsidian imagined he saw haunted shapes peering out at him. "Have you ever been to the very edges of yourself and looked into the void?" asked the wizard.

"Yes," said Obsidian, remembering his fight with Nob. He swallowed and asked, "Have you ever killed?"

Embaza shivered at a sudden chill. "Sometimes it is the only way."

"Yet each man must choose his own way," said Obsidian, quoting his teachers again, sad that the phrase that once gave him solace now mocked him. *A true monk would have avoided bloodshed even if it meant giving his life.*

The wizard laid a hand on the monk's shoulder. "Come and rest. There will be only one way in the morning—the way to Alvarra."

-52-

HOURS LATER, knowing he ought to be asleep, Embaza was too elated by his newfound feelings to rest. Before the delicate colors of dawn suffused the sky, he shuffled to the doorway of the tent, searching the darkness. The distant moon was a pale emblem that floated far above him.

A rustle nearby startled him. A lithe form melted in and out of the darkness. For a moment, he thought it a phantom and regretted not killing the albino. Had he not been so enchanted by the music from the arena, he would never have spared him. Then he realized the phantom was only Tiala. "How are you feeling this night?" he asked.

"I am fine," she answered. "But tomorrow is another day." She glanced at the moon, trying not to be mesmerized by its beauty. She knew it was already waning. "We need to make plans."

"Where are the others?" asked Embaza, with a sudden desire to see Polah.

"Sleeping." Tiala felt unprotected even under the stars and reached for the tent flap. "I have rested well, for now."

"Come in," said Embaza and gestured toward the dying fire.

The two took seats on the carpet, not far from the sleeping monk.

On the other side of the fire, Six Stix lay with his eyes closed, awakened by their entrance. The habits of the warrior were too old to break. Still weak, he slipped in and out of consciousness, ever on guard. If the conversation were interesting, maybe he would join them.

"I might as well tell you what I've already explained to the others," said Embaza, an edge to his voice.

Tiala looked at him with the barest raising of her eyebrows. A presentiment of danger started a dull pain throbbing in her midsection. "Tell me."

"I, too, am of your race," the wizard said, his green eyes burning with the adrenaline of self-revelation.

Six Stix smiled to himself.

Tiala stared at the wizard. "How familiar you looked to me—from the very first." She turned her gaze to the tent wall. *An Alvarran man.* She was deeply confused by how much she looked down upon him now that she knew he was dark-elven. As a Sargothian, she had respected him. *Is it true what Gudrun says? Have we created an unjust society?*

For a moment, she had a vision of what it must have been like for her brilliant little brother to contemplate a life of useless intellectual play. The implications seemed overwhelming, until her mind erected a barrier against them. She looked back at Embaza. "Who is your mother?"

He shrugged awkwardly. "I am a man without family, without country, without memory." A familiar anger brooded in his chest. "Yet I am of your blood. I, too, suffer unless I travel under the moon and stars—or the protection of a strong wagon. I've already discussed this with the monk. While the rest of us are sleeping, he will buy horses and a conveyance."

"We must wait until the Scourge has fallen before we move," said Tiala, answering a sudden need to establish her authority. "How did you disguise your skin?"

"With a common clothing dye. Very strong, but it fades eventually. It offers no protection from the sun." He rubbed a small circle from one cheekbone with his thumb, chafing the skin until it shone a dusky black.

Tiala bit her lower lip and clasped her arms, oblivious to the pain of her nails goring the skin. There *was* something else. "In the dark like this, you resemble my brother. It's really uncanny."

"You're just homesick," Embaza said sourly. "Don't make more of it."

In the silence that followed, Six Stix grew jealous of the intimacy the dark elves now shared. *Not long ago, Embaza was my brother. And the Princess was just a beautiful woman from another land.* An unreasonable anger itched in his breast. *What do I care? She's a woman, and not to be trusted. And yet, such a voice, such eyes.* He had a sickening feeling of recognition. *You idiot, this is no time to fall in love.* He strove to mimic the regular breathing of a sleeper.

Obsidian was roused from a dream by the authority in Tiala's voice. He opened his right eye. The left one, still healing, was melted shut by sleep. "You shouldn't be in our tent, Princess," he said.

"I couldn't sleep," she said. *Just try to command me.*

Six Stix announced himself, unable to keep silent any longer, "Welcome to our fire, Lady." He didn't know what else to say, almost wishing the dwarf were here. She, at least, was no stranger to the rough customs and plain speech of battle-mates.

Sensing his discomfort, though ignorant of the cause, Obsidian hailed his friend. "Morning, Six." He grinned at Tiala. "Your champion is not easily beaten, Princess. Do you see how Lord Stixan prevails?"

"I expected nothing less," she said sweetly, unaware that the blue elf had been poisoned on her behalf. She prepared to leave, having no desire to be part of anyone's morning ablutions. She flicked another look at Embaza as if she needed to confirm his identity. She also wanted time to think. Forgotten were her dreams of gathering material for songs.

As she turned to go, Embaza said, "We'll come for you when everything is ready."

But she had a last thought. "When you get supplies, ask for a musical instrument. Not a harp this time." She looked at their faces, surprised by the avid interest of the blue elf, and fastened her gaze on him. "Something perhaps a child would play—nothing too precious."

He blushed and the famous dimple flashed in his cheek. "I'll take care of it," he said.

When she was gone, the three discussed preparations for the journey—deciding the number of mounts, type of cart best suited, amount of stores, and so on. An urgency was in the air, but Six Stix found his mind straying to the instrument he might get for the Nightwing's daughter.

Tiala reached the woman's tent to find Polah and Gudrun already risen, and she briefed them on the plans, adding, "Embaza has revealed to me that he is a dark elf. It has complicated things, but when we reach Alvarra, it might be useful."

Before the others could comment, Tiala sank to the floor, looking very weak.

Gudrun urged, "Get some rest while you still have shelter. You'll need all you can."

Tiala wrapped herself in Embaza's cloak with a twinge of guilt and fell into a deep sleep almost immediately.

Polah was restless, and said to the dwarf, "I want to do some exploring. How about you?"

"First I must stop by the men's tent and give my regards to Embaza. After all, someone should welcome him to the fellowship of the underground. Then, maybe I'll join you," said Gudrun. She was also curious about Six Stix, but mentioned nothing of this to Polah. The girl seemed lost in her own world. Just as well.

They exited the tent together. A few of the giants were moving around in the stir of morning chores. It was difficult at first for Polah and Gudrun to adjust their perspective to the grand scale of these creatures.

"Excuse me," said a voice from above. Shading her eyes, the General looked up to the giant guarding their tent. The guard stooped, curious about the strange dwarf dressed in manly fighting clothes.

"Where are you going?" he asked.

Gudrun pointed to the tent. "Our companion has not been well and sleeps now. We are going to stretch our legs."

"All right," said the giant, although he seemed uncertain. "If you're sure the dark one is asleep."

"Yes, but don't uncover her face or awaken her," said Gudrun, "she has an illness that is affected by sunlight." She saw a look of fear pass over the tribesman's face and added, "It's not catching."

Not a bit reassured, the giant nodded, thinking he would be the toast of the tribe when they learned he alone had guarded the evil one. He peeped briefly into the tent, then resumed his watchful stance, shoulders squared and eyes alert.

Polah felt shy now that the sun was coming up. Why were things so often different in the daylight? For some reason, she didn't feel ready to face Embaza so soon. She said to Gudrun, "I'll meet you by that stall over there. You see those women setting up their loom?"

Gudrun stood on tiptoe, but could not see them. "Don't be long. One of us should stay near Tiala in case that giant gets ideas." She watched Polah saunter out of sight, then approached the other tent and cleared her throat.

Obsidian's face appeared, sunburned but rested.

"I'm still sore from the saddle, how about you?" She sidled in and peered around, looking for Embaza. He nodded to her from his seat on the rug. Out of the corner of her eye, Gudrun saw Six Stix bending over his pack near the back of the tent, and looking extremely healthy for a dying man.

Noting her glance, Obsidian said, "He took a blow from a poisoned lance, you remember. In the arena, while some of us were dancing." *Let her chew on that,* he thought.

She raised a frown to him, looking like the general she was. "Humph." She ignored Six Stix's stare and said to Obsidian, "How far is it to this monastery of yours?"

"The caravan route from here generally takes three days. The giants trade with the monks from time to time and have made the journey often."

Embaza broke his silence. "Tiala and I can't travel through the burning desert for three days without shelter," he said.

"There is no other way," said Gudrun.

"Not true," said Obsidian matter-of-factly. "The giants tell me there is another way, a straighter path that takes only a day or so at most."

Gudrun shook her head. "Out of the question."

"Is there something wrong with it?" asked Embaza.

"We have to cross quake-sand," said Gudrun. "By the gods, it's too dangerous."

"How much?" asked Six Stix. "In patches or a mass?"

The monk squatted and traced a circle around the campfire. His tangled hairlock flopped in his face and he brushed it back. "Imagine that is the size of the area we have to cross." He pointed to the stub of a half burned stick approximately as long as his thumb that protruded from the ashes. "Imagine this is the camp we're in now."

All were quiet. Then Embaza said, "I've never actually seen quake-sand. Tell me more." He had always made it a point to travel in covered caravans where the safest routes were a matter of course.

"It's a kind of spontaneous thing that creates huge sinkholes sucking down everything in their path," said Obsidian.

"You can't even get a horse across it," Gudrun said, "let alone a wagon."

"A few have done it," said Six Stix.

"More have died," she muttered.

"Braytok says bandits do it all the time," Obsidian said. "The sinkholes have nothing to do with weight. It's in the timing."

Hmm, thought Six Stix, *bandits do lots of things...all the time.*

Gudrun snorted. "Rumors. You believe these giants?"

"It's not the first I've heard of it," said Obsidian. "There are specially trained horses—."

"We're riding the giants' own mounts," Gudrun replied.

"I agree," said Six Stix. "These horses are as tough as any I've ridden into battle."

Embaza said, "What causes the sinkholes?"

"No one knows," said Obsidian. "The monks think it was the result of too much mining in the old days. Of course, you'll find the usual superstitions about ghosts and demons if you ask the gnomads."

Gudrun laughed uneasily. Obsidian had never lived underground with dwarves who ascribed every natural disaster to dark-elven magic.

"Well, I'm for trying the short cut," said Six Stix.

"Me, too," Obsidian said.

Gudrun scowled. "You're both crazy."

Embaza glanced at each of them, a solemn expression on his handsome face, then he nodded and walked over to his saddlebags, where he bent and sorted through his belongings, reapplying blue dye to his cheekbone.

Obsidian and Six Stix turned to similar tasks.

Gudrun recognized the usual behavior of men when faced with danger. They took refuge in the most humble and familiar of chores.

"Embaza," she said to the wizard. He twisted around, and she admired the graceful silhouette he presented even in the ordinary activity of packing.

The dwarf stumped over to him, hands behind her back. Making sure no one else was looking, she thrust her fist, clapped it to her breast, then turned the palm outward. "Sign of the deepworld dwarves," she said. "If you're ever in Tskurl, ask for the tribe of Gudrun of Estenhame."

Embaza was taken aback by this mark of esteem from so unexpected a source. "Thank you," he said, embarrassed that he had no family name to give in return.

But Gudrun did not require it. Pleased with herself, she hailed Obsidian. "Let me know when you're ready to brace the tarp on the wagon for my Lady and the wizard here. I've done this before, remember." With another sidelong glance at Six Stix, she ducked out of the tent.

"Now, where did that shape-changer go?" She had a sudden yearning for her disciplined life at the Manor and the hours she spent with her troops. By this time, she had usually drilled with them for an hour. From what she could see, there'd be no place for a martial woman here. Ah, well, things changed. That was the one thing she could always count on. And when confronted with a new situation, she always managed to find the good in it. Why not take the opportunity to get another nap? She paused before entering the woman's tent to note the sun's first rays peeping over the horizon.

She frowned, thinking of the journey ahead. *How will they manage? Tiala and that wizard cooped up in the same box under one cloak—and both of them haughty as elves!* She chuckled to herself and hooked her thumbs in her belt. *Them with their beauty and arcane knowledge. Thank the gods I'm not cursed with such problems.*

-53-

A DARK shape hovered over the tent, questing, tasting the air. It appeared to be a very large buzzard, but the giant guarding the tent shivered every time its shadow touched him. The demon's doing, no doubt about it. He would report this to the tribe. These visitors were not welcome here, blood brother or not.

-54-

MISCHA HAD already spent one day and night in Lord Amra's camp, and had yet to see a single man. He half-remembered being given food and drink, although both were laced with a bitter-tasting drug that left him feeling extremely odd. Male-blossom, they had called it. He remembered a sea of female faces. And laughter.

First, the maidens had stripped him of his pack and clothing—with none of the gentle treatment he was accustomed to in his harem. He blushed with anger at the memory of his naked helplessness. His limbs ached and his neck was sore. His skin felt clammy. He couldn't get comfortable.

He was kneeling, hands bound to his feet behind him. Both his legs and feet had fallen asleep. He splayed his thighs and his limp organ flopped like a pale fish onto the stained rug. His back hurt. But that wasn't the worst of it.

He wished he had been prepared. He could have woven pieces of strangleberry vine into his hair like a gnomad assassin and killed a daughter or two while they slept. Or he could have hidden a splinter of wood under his skin and skewered them with it. That would have solved some problems for Lord Amra.

His mind was filled with murderous thoughts as he sat in the middle of the lavish tent, surrounded by silken pillows and embroidered wall hangings. They hadn't even given him a cushion to sit on. He glowered at the shapeless lumps of girls having their afternoon naps. Their innocent snores were irritating, but he wished they would sleep forever.

For hours at a time, they had taunted and teased him. Thirty-four healthy, lusty maidens. Once it would have been a delight. Now, he thought if he heard another high pitched, girlish giggle, he would scream.

Azali was the worst, strutting around him, tapping him here and there, squeezing, pinching, calling him names. She had labeled him weak and spineless. *If only I had my bag of magic tools. I'd turn her into a whining creature even her father wouldn't recognize.*

He had long since abandoned the struggle against the bonds of triple-stranded silk that cut his soft skin mercilessly.

The colors of the setting sun suffused the sides of the tent, dappling them with pale gold. Rivulets of sweat and semen had dried on his body. Performing in the heat had been most disagreeable, but at least it had been warm. Mischa's teeth began to chatter in anticipation of the approaching darkness. Last night, they had not covered him and he had almost welcomed the attentions of his tormentors just to have the warmth of their flesh upon him.

Some of the lord's daughters had tired of the game, but they would be back in the evening. They had a special occasion planned for their guest.

Mischa counted the maidens lying around him in an attempt to calm himself. They looked so innocent, sleeping on their egret feather pillows. Seventeen…eighteen…had he missed that fat one in the corner? He wondered where the rest were, and counted again, although his nerves were far past soothing. Still eighteen. They were all beautiful, fat and thin, young and old. It hardly mattered now. If they had their way, it would never matter again.

He struggled against his bonds, rudely reminded that this caused more pain. He thought of the girls' assault on him. His mind fastened upon Delyra, the fifteen-year old with the hazelnut eyes. Instead of poking or prodding, she had stroked his shoulder with her soft, golden hands, and kissed his jaw with the gentleness of a fawn.

One of her older sisters had laughed and pointed at his swollen organ. "The sun rises for you, Delyra."

Of all of them, he thought she had enjoyed him the most. He hadn't minded her attentions, either. At least the first time.

His skin crawled as he recalled the clapping, giggling maidens. The vision of Azali grinning from her seat in the corner and fingering one of her knives had been enough to squelch the strongest of male desires.

But it had been the mischievous Saramba who had given him a taste of what was really in store for him. He cowed before the encroaching shadows. Would the sun set so soon?

Saramba had taken off that beguiling necklace of silver scimitars and dangled it in front of his face. The perfection of the matched rubies had teased him with their beauty.

"Want it, my Prince?" she had inquired, smelling of tangerine and cinnamon. Mischa had felt a thread of hope stretch upward like the flame of a candle.

The lady had wrapped the necklace around his testicles, staring at him with intelligent black eyes. He had needed an iron will not to fall into those depths, and her bell-like laugh was piercing. "If you're good, I'll let you have it." Her meaning had been as double edged as the scimitars that bit into his tender flesh.

Azali had orchestrated the rest, through the night, and into the next day. The supple maidens had become more and more acrobatic. Over and over, they had taken their turns with him, some of them showing a sadistic creativity he might have enjoyed in other circumstances.

He thought with bitterness that in the old days when his appetites were more unschooled, he had found delight in women. A certain amount of pain was interesting, if mixed liberally with pleasure, but not an end in itself.

When it was obvious to all but his stubborn grandfather that Mischa could not sire a child, his appetite had twisted. Bride after bride was procured and none of them satisfied him. Some brought exotic toys and others knew techniques to stir the imagination of the blankest idiot, but Mischa soon learned that he could have fun with other people's feelings. Cruelty became his passion, where another might turn to ale or the smoke of sweet-flowers.

Eventually, he went too far and killed a lovely child of thirteen. His grandfather had hushed it up, forgiving him the way parents sometimes did, fooling himself that Mischief had not known what he was doing. Feigning remorse, Mischa had buried the whip along with the discarded bride, resolving to be more discreet.

After that, the Prince had turned his interests to the arena, where he could play with emotion on a bigger scale. And magic had become his mistress.

Even so, he found it interesting that women still desired him. Some of these maidens had admitted their enjoyment. He thought of Delyra again. *A nice piece of bride flesh. Maybe I should have bought her when I had the chance.*

He would have been relieved when Azali had clapped her hands and said, "Enough sport." But his keen ears were too well attuned to the game of intimidation. She was the only one who had not taken her pleasure with him. And she had made it clear, at least to Mischa, that she did not intend to.

Some of the girls had paired off, sharing many a pointed witticism at his expense, judging from the renewed giggling that scraped his nerves raw. Azali had let him dangle in suspense. He seethed with frustration and dread, remembering.

The diminutive beauty had tossed her black curls and made her pronouncement. In a characteristic pose, feet wide, hands on hips, she had crowed, "Prince Mischa, I hope you enjoyed our little fun today. You have had the benefit of not one or two, nor even three, but—." She'd looked around the room at the upturned, pampered faces, "How many?"

Several guesses had been called out before she had held up her hand and let the laughter subside, saying, "Well, I think we'll all agree that you made an entertaining pet. Right, sisters?"

Mischa's brain had turned to ice. He was a master at holding his temper when he had to. He had perfected it in many a battle of wills with his grandfather, Rearguard.

"So," Azali said, "it seems you passed the test. We'll keep you." There had been an excited wave of giggling.

"There is one thing, though." She had looked down at him where he knelt on the ruined rug and her gaze had held remarkable pity.

Mischa felt a sliver of fear slide down his spine as he recalled her words.

"You'll have to be gelded. Tonight. We can't have our pets straying off, now, can we?" Azali had looked down at him without a flicker of emotion.

213

The word *pet* soured his belly like rancid meat. Somehow, Mischa had held his rage and fear at bay. He was in real trouble now. The time for playing was over. Even if his grandfather came to save him it would be too late.

Like a man in a dream, he had watched the ladies prepare for their afternoon naps, as if nothing had happened, as if the whole world hadn't split apart.

While he had been remembering all of this, trying to muster every trick and scheme he could devise, he had failed to notice the setting sun. The tent walls had suffused with gold and mounted to a bright orange that matched his rage, before melting to a soft gray. Even though he had been watching for it, he was horrified when he realized it was dark. Goosebumps popped out all over him.

Soon, the servants would bring in the evening repast. Would they feed him a last meal, like a condemned man—or would they starve him like an animal? He swallowed and tugged on his bloody bonds. *I must escape.*

He looked up as he felt something wet on his face. A rainstorm? Such a rarity in the desert, the distraction might buy him more time. A scattering of stars wavered through the top of the tent, and Mischa realized with a shock that he was seeing them through his own tears. *So it has come to this,* he thought with bitterness. He felt his strength drain away.

Suddenly, a gentle hand clasped his wrist and sweet breath warmed his neck. "Sssh," said Delyra of the plump figure and tawny curls. "I'll free you if you take me with you."

His skin prickled with hope. He twisted his head around and implored her with his eyes.

Quickly, she snipped his bonds with a tiny pair of scissors, and he nearly fainted at the pain in his hands. "My feet…" he whispered, and she cut them free as well. Then she wrapped her arms around him, her youthful sweetness filling his nostrils.

"We must hurry," he coaxed, taking the scissors from her.

She thrust a pair of ballooned desert pants and a homespun tunic into his hands.

The clothing was cut wide, but both trousers and tunic were inches too short, and Mischa yanked the hem down with irritation. In one trouser pocket, he found a length of cloth that he recognized as a turban. He had never tied one without the help of servants and handed it to Delyra who stood on tiptoes to wrap it around his head.

She, too, was dressed in rustic, sand-colored pants and tunic, her hair hidden beneath a turban, and her feet wrapped in soft, hide boots.

"What about slippers?" he asked.

She shook her head. "I couldn't find any big enough." She smiled, showing a bewitching dimple.

For a split second, Mischa almost smiled back, then he grabbed her hand. "Come on."

He and Delyra stepped over her snoring sisters, and she put her finger to her lips and peeped out the doorway. The moon was just rising, and the campfires sent their fragrant smoke into the night.

"Where's my bag?" asked Mischa, counting the tents and horses, the campfires.

Delyra pointed to a small tent nearby. "Wait here," she whispered.

In a few moments, she returned, her arms full, and the Prince grabbed his sack with greedy hands. It was quite a bit lighter than before. He looked at the moon's position and calculated, struggling to recall his grandfather's teaching. He wanted to get as far from the Manor as possible. He turned and strode off to the east.

Delyra hurried after him, "Slow down," she hissed, and clutched at his shirt tail.

Mischa stopped and turned.

"Isn't this exciting?" she said.

She carried two waterskins plus a bag that smelled of sweetmeats, and now he smiled. He drank a long swig of water before continuing his flight.

As the two companions rounded the crest of the dune, they saw a large wagon in the distance, flanked by four huge horses. Mischa could not tell by their moonlit silhouettes what tribe they represented, but he didn't think they were gnomads and they certainly weren't giants. If they were traveling merchants, it might be safer to shelter with them. Their tracks would hide his footprints.

He remembered the buzzards, and peered at the gnomad girl. Did she really know what she was getting into? She was definitely going to slow him down. Maybe he could sell her. He smiled again. With money, he could buy his way out of the desert and find that magical king, Dekhalis. Now, there was a man of power who could help him take revenge on Embaza.

His spirits lifting, he set a bristling pace, Delyra skipping double time behind him, borne along by her own exuberance. It would be hours before she would begin to complain and weaken.

I can be patient, thought Mischa.

-55-

As IT happened, Mischa was mistaken about Delyra's stamina. After his ordeal at the camp, he was exhausted long before she. To add to this, the sand was rubbing his bare feet raw. Delyra had made herself useful, if not indispensable, by fashioning wrapped coverings for his sore wrists and swollen feet from her own waist sash. But the material wore thin after a few leagues.

In the end, Mischa gave up trying to catch the wagon. It kept disappearing over the next dune just as he glimpsed the other travelers in the faint moonlight. It was nearly midnight when his ill temper finally erupted and he told Delyra they would have to make camp.

"But we can move so much more quickly in the darkness," she said. "The sand will be cool on your feet."

"Be quiet. Can't you see I'm in need of rest?"

The wretched girl found herself quite unable to console her new lover. She rushed around, trying to make him as comfortable as possible, and this seemed to irritate him more. She finally moved off to make preparations for sleep, tears stinging her eyes.

As the moon swam in the pitch black sky, the canopy of stars made a comforting blanket that turned the surrounding hills into mounds of molten silver. The air had grown cool.

Absurdly, Mischa's spirits soared. Delyra sat opposite him, her arms wrapped around her legs, chin on her knees, drawing pictures in the sand.

Mischa peered at her over the creditable thicket that was crackling companionably, surprised at her resourcefulness. They had not passed any trees or bushes on their journey. She must have carried the sticks in her bag, along with the food.

He began to open his sack, then hesitated. Delyra was still tracing patterns in the sand and hadn't looked up, fearing his temper. He decided this was an appropriate time to impress her with his magical powers.

He opened the bag and probed its contents, ostentatiously bringing out one item after another, hoping to arouse her interest. Sure enough, she soon lifted her pretty face and watched, but warily. She had been taught to respect magic.

When Mischa produced the smoky crystal globe, Delyra said, "Oooh," her hazelnut eyes alight at the pretty bauble. The fire's glow flickered across its surface, sending prismatic shadows dancing over the sand.

"You like this, eh?" Mischa laughed sardonically and laid it at his feet.

Delyra moved to kneel next to him, her hand resting on his thigh. With a deferential gaze, she asked, "What is it?"

Mischa did not reveal his ignorance. Instead, he picked up the crystal and polished it with his sleeve. There was a stirring in the depths of the glassy surface and he tossed it back onto the sand.

As the gnomad and her presumed swain watched, the image of a handsome dark elf wearing an exquisite citrine crown appeared.

Delyra gasped and cried, "An evil one." She scurried over the pile of sticks and then lay flat behind them, peeping through her splayed fingers.

The figure in the globe did not see her, and at first did not see Mischa clearly. "Morbigon?" asked the sultry voice emanating from the crystal.

Delyra froze, her starkest terrors confirmed. The one in the glass was speaking an evil tongue.

Even Mischa was taken aback, but he was also intrigued. At first, he thought the figure looked suspiciously like that wizard, Embaza. But this was clearly a dark elf, not a blue one. And, more importantly, what did he want?

Calculating quickly, he decided the truth was best. He spoke in elven. "Morbigon is dead. I am Prince Mischa of the Outland Territories…and who are you?"

The image in the globe had flashing green eyes whose cold fire burned through the Prince. "I see you have the locket. He must be dead, indeed."

"Yes, I am its master now," Mischa replied.

The dark elf paused to stare, then burst into laughter.

At the presumed insult, Mischa sat up straight and said, "Be careful. I am a powerful wizard."

"Oh, is that what you are?" said the dark elf when next he could speak. His engaging smile was utterly disarming. "Then you are of use to me, wizard, and you will be generously rewarded for your service. The locket will draw you to the Usurper."

"Who?"

"The dark elf who calls herself Tiala," said the handsome elven lord in the glass.

Of course, thought Mischa. *This is Tiala's enemy, and therefore, my friend.* "It will be my pleasure to destroy her," he said, "but who do I serve?"

"I am Dekhalis, Lord King of Alvarra. When you succeed, I will grant you wishes and make you rich."

Mischa gloated, rubbing his hands. This was more like it. He glanced at Delyra, who was still peeking at him through her fingers.

She shared the usual fear of dark elves and to speak with one in a magical globe was unthinkable. Yet, a part of her thrilled to the forbidden freedom of being in the company of this powerful wizard, who could commune with the lord of demons himself. Surely it was not taboo if one was with a master.

The image in the globe faded, and with it, Dekhalis's voice. "I will contact you again tomorrow. Be ready to report, wizard Mischa."

Mischa put the orb back into the sack with a feeling of barely contained jubilation. At last, he had the ally he needed to take revenge on his enemies. Although tired, a feverish energy took hold of him.

He squeezed the locket into his palm and barked at Delyra, "Come on, girl, make me some shoes. I must travel while the moon is high."

Delyra jumped up and rooted through her pack for some cloth, only too happy to put as much distance as possible between herself and her father's horses. When morning came, and Lord Amra discovered she had gone...would Azali tell him right away? The girl glanced at the Prince, wondering why her father hadn't dealt with him personally. It had been a strange treat for the girls to have a prisoner to do with as they pleased. She frowned. *It's a good thing I rescued him. They didn't know he was a dangerous wizard.* Would there be some way to forestall her father when he found them? Or would she have to choose between them?

-56-

FOR THE party of travelers bound for Alvarra, the dry desert air filled their lungs, and they could almost taste the endless stretch of moon-drenched sand. High dunes rose on either side of the worn track which disappeared and reappeared as they rode. A buzzard cried a warning from time to time, yet never came into view.

The horses sensed the tension and danced nervously—especially the two harnessed to the heavy wagon. No casual glance could discern that the conveyance held Embaza and Tiala in its dark embrace. Gudrun and Obsidian rode at the head of the party, leading the team. Polah and Six Stix brought up the rear.

It was a measure of the giants' respect for Gudrun that, female or not, she was saluted on her way out by those who had served under her at the Manor. Obsidian received his own share of farewells, with many a fist clasped in parting.

Six Stix accepted his relatively unimportant status with good grace. The blue elf never failed to wonder at the legends he'd spawned. However, it was still a rare being—elf or dwarf—who recognized him as the leader of the renowned elite guard. He rather enjoyed the anonymity.

Polah had only one thought in mind: Embaza. Over and over, she tried to recapture the rapport of the night before, but handicapped as she was by need, the tenuous threads of intimacy were not to be grasped. Ironically, when she gave up and let her gaze drift to the horizon, she suddenly felt so close to him that tears welled in her black eyes and she could almost bathe in his peculiar aroma. Willingly, she would have crawled into that scent and dissolved.

Embaza, too, gained strength from their union. In the frightening confines of the wagon bed covered by low wood braces peaked under a tarp so thick no sunlight could penetrate, that sweet knowledge was like an anchor-point in a sea of madness. While Tiala sat hunched over her knees, enveloped in the gray cloak, Embaza lounged against the wall of the wagon, propped on his elbow, his long legs stretched out before him. The thick rugs that covered the floor boards did little to cushion the rough passage. Not a chink of moonlight penetrated the thick side boards, yet the dark elves' eyes were soon accustomed to the darkness, and they could see each other's dim forms.

Embaza sought no reference point in the future; only today needed his attention. It was a discipline for which he was especially qualified, since he had already learned to live without a past.

But Tiala found her vision continually striving to anchor itself to a world where safety and order reigned. She knew she was becoming unhinged by this state of constant insecurity. Yet her physical frailty now offered her no resource from which to fashion a more reasonable future. She made no sound, but tears coursed down her face as she buried her dark fists in the cloak.

Embaza held out his hand to her, and she grasped it gladly.

"How do you stand it?" Tiala wailed.

"I made a bargain with pain, a pact of friendship..." He stopped, thinking of Polah.

Tiala shook her head, a gray form in the drizzle of darkness. "I mean—how do you stand the uncertainty? You're so calm."

Embaza shivered. "I am not always. And you will be so again."

His certainty penetrated where logic could not. After a few moments, Tiala slipped into a half-sleep, her body eager for the nourishment of rest. In this state, her mind was especially clear, and she let herself focus on her companion, Embaza. He was handsome—but proud. She would have to teach him the ways of Alvarra before he got into serious trouble. Yet, when she was around him, she didn't always feel like a ruler.

A warmth stole over her that had nothing to do with the desert. Tentatively, she turned on her side and stretched out her legs, so that her left foot touched Embaza's thigh. "I could teach you some Alvarran traditions," she murmured.

Taking his lack of response for acquiescence, Tiala smiled to herself. *Now, this is the way a proper Alvarran man should behave.* She gracefully rolled toward him and sought the mound of his sex with her soft hand.

Embaza sat up so quickly that he hit his head on the roof of the wagon. "Please do not take this course," he said, his tone unmistakably cold.

Tiala was shocked. She had never been rebuffed before and didn't know what was expected of her in such a situation. She said, with as much dignity as possible, "If we were in Alvarra, you would pay dearly for this." She rolled to the far wall.

Embaza snorted, "I am not subject to your rules. Or your whims."

"Do you realize," Tiala said through clenched teeth, "you are dark-elven and I am your ruler now? No longer can you hide behind your towers of Sargoth."

Embaza snorted. "You don't frighten me with your airs of domination. I'll match my powers with yours any time. In Alvarra, you'll need my protection more than ever."

"You'll do no magic in Alvarra," commanded Tiala. "You're a dark elf—and as such, you are in mourning. In fact, if I were as strict as I should be, you could do no magic here, either."

In answer, Embaza chanted, *"Norozaa Minne..."* Before Tiala could respond to this new offense, her eyelids became heavy. She was soon fast asleep, curled into a fetal position.

He cursed to himself. He should not have used his power so impulsively. That was a powerful spell. He was rested now, but who could tell when he would have the chance again to gather strength? The altercation with Tiala had obscured his sense of time. He had no way of knowing if they could cross the quake-sand.

Also, there was something else, a shadow, a feeling of dread he associated with Morbigon. He had felt it more than once since they'd left the Manor. Once again, he regretted not killing the albino.

This woman had too much power over him. He was not himself and it angered him. Tiala had no idea how close he had been to responding to her overture. Though her beauty and voice were bewitching enough, it was her courage that touched him. He thought any dark-elven male would feel so. Were it not for Polah...

He closed his eyes, letting her soft presence move within him. He refused to consider the consequences of their mating. There were other, more immediate, dangers to confront.

How will you fare, little fox? He considered their experience of the night before. Perhaps it was not just hunger, but any raw, instinctual emotion that triggered Polah's transformation. He would have to discuss it with her.

Polah herself was deeply engaged in conversation with Six Stix, with whom she had not had much opportunity to talk. For his part, he was both intrigued and flattered by the attention. He had never known a shape-changer before.

"Why haven't we seen you change your form since the tunnels?" he asked.

Polah shrugged. "I'm not sure, myself. It comes and goes." She did not mention that she had hunted in fox form the night before.

"Don't you worry now that we're in the desert? As a fox, you might not fare too well out here."

Her face grew earnest. "I think you're wrong—the red fox is very adaptable. There's plenty to eat if you know where to look. After all, my worst enemy is man."

Six Stix laughed. "Indeed."

Polah basked in the feeling of acceptance. "All of us have our secrets, I suppose, but I've been curious about you. You never talk about your homeland the way Tiala does. Even Obsidian seems to miss the mountains he ran away from."

Six Stix sighed, half expecting the question. "I suppose you heard them call me Lord Stixan?"

She nodded.

"Well, I gave it all up. A keep and lands create a bundle of worries and duties. It wasn't the life for me. But I do miss my homeland. The woods of Graymere are beyond lovely. Maybe that's why I don't speak of them."

They were both quiet for several moments, the elf's blue eyes dark with memories. Tactfully, Polah changed the subject. "What do you know of the quake-sand?"

"Not much, except that only bandits have crossed it successfully—who knows how often? But then, we have a wizard along."

"You put great stock in him," said Polah.

"Don't you?"

"Of course," she said, blushing.

Six Stix smiled. "I have great faith in wizards. Especially the wizards of Sargothas. They have one quality I've always tried to instill in my troops—they don't allow mistakes."

Polah's stomach knotted. Would they consider her alliance with Embaza a mistake? What if she were to apply for membership, to study and become a wizard? After all, Embaza said she had magic powers. Would they tolerate her kind? She doubted it.

Six Stix took her silence for a desire to end the conversation. He brushed the sand from his lips and whistled a tune.

Up ahead, Gudrun recognized the elven war song. Unsettled by it, she turned her attention to the monk at her side. "The giants took you into their tribe, didn't they?"

Obsidian was startled at her perception. "How did you know?"

"It was obvious, the way they saluted you. All desert folk know those signs. Besides, you're favoring your left arm. I'll wager you have a new tattoo there."

Obsidian was reminded of his resolve to give more respect to the dwarf. "How do the giants fit into the picture out here? They seem so plentiful—and yet they were in awe of Embaza's little token from the gnome."

Gudrun chuckled. "That's a long story, but the fact is, they're outnumbered. By the thousands, I'd say. There's a saying—the Patriarch's seed grew more flowers in the desert than the sweetwater cactus."

Obsidian waited for Gudrun to stop laughing and asked, "Then, what does it mean to have his token?"

"It means we can go anywhere we please, as long as we behave ourselves—and you have a special standing as a member of your new tribe."

"I owe them much," said Obsidian, grateful that the thought was finally spoken.

"They are a proud people, but who knows what obligations the giants may have to the Patriarch and the Brotherhood of Gnomads? It's quite a complicated business, and you should be glad you are going back to your monastery."

Obsidian was quiet. This was one subject he wanted to avoid. He sank his chin into his chest as if napping and tried to guess the weight of the turban on his forehead. Gathering the scant facts he knew about quake-sand, he allowed his thoughts to gestate.

Progress was steady and the party continued through the night, unaware they had left wagon tracks and hoofprints that could be followed.

At the first sign of dawn on the horizon, Gudrun raised her hand and said, "Halt." She and Obsidian reined in the wagon team, while Polah and Six Stix rode to the front to parley. The shadow of the buzzard fell over them like a shroud.

"It's not wise to stop so soon," said Six Stix. "The sun's barely peeping over the rise."

Gudrun answered, "The quake-sand isn't far. If we don't give the horses some rest, they won't have the strength to cross it—if they have a chance at all."

Polah's stomach grumbled. It had been more than a whole day since she had remembered to nibble on the food from her pack. She felt the tremors in her belly that preceded transformation.

Six Stix cocked his head. "I say we go on—until the quake-sand is in sight. Then we rest." He gestured to the horizon. "Why wait?"

Polah jumped down from her horse and began to tear off her clothes. Startled, the others looked at her in astonishment.

"Get her horse," yelled Gudrun, and Obsidian reacted swiftly.

While Polah's mount reared, then whinnied in fear, the monk closed the distance and grabbed the reins. With some difficulty, he managed to quiet the animal and tether it to a wheel of the wagon.

Meanwhile, Six Stix had dismounted and was approaching Polah. "What is it, girl—the change?" He retrieved her discarded clothing.

With a wild look around, she said in a strangled, guttural voice, "I'll come back…as soon as I can."

In moments, her small body enlarged, grew fur and fangs, and the others barely had a glimpse of the brush of her tail as she disappeared over the shadowed dunes to the west.

-57-

ELEPPON DENSHADIEL sat astride her favorite horse, a pale white beast bred on the slopes of crystal where few other animals lived. Like all of her breed, Zola was one of the most sure-footed mounts imaginable.

Eleppon patted Zola's silky neck as they overlooked the escarpment of purple lichen spanning the chasm below. On the other side lay a tanglewood, a maze of trails and turnings that provided endless sport for the Swift Legion, Eleppon's cadre of horsewomen. She nudged Zola with her left foot, and the horse made her way down the rocky trail that led to the chasm itself. Together, they wove through the brush like a melting shadow in the gloom from the cavern ceiling high overhead.

The elf's eyes searched carefully for the puffballs of acid and the occasional serpent, but Zola was a master at the game, placing her hooves like a dancer until at last she gained the plain itself and broke into a gallop.

Eleppon's rose-colored tunic billowed out in the exhilarating breeze, her hair swept back in tangles. This was what she lived for. Her head cleared as her body melded with Zola's in the familiar rocking motion that seemed to etch its way deep into her bones.

The opening to the tanglewood was not evident to the uninitiated, but to Zola it was a homing beacon. She ducked her head while Eleppon flattened herself to the horse's back and buried her face in Zola's silky mane. They negotiated one turn after another, with so many changes in stride and footing that Eleppon lost track of them.

About halfway through the tanglewood, a clearing appeared like a mysterious surprise. Zola stopped just at the edge to graze on the tender shoots of wild black lettuce, a weed that strengthened her night vision, although it made the horse's eyes more vulnerable sunlight. Such a horse would never survive in the surface lands.

Eleppon slid down and flipped the saddle blanket to the other side, to give Zola a chance to dry off. The horse nickered her thanks.

Parting the branches, the dark elf ducked through the undergrowth into the clearing itself, where three large cairns were placed at odd angles.

These old burial mounds had long since yielded their secrets, and Eleppon favored them as places to hold council with the other members of her fellowship. She leaned against a flat stone and plucked a sweet cherry from a low branch. Several cherries later, she was greeted by the sound of hooves on the opposite side of the clearing.

She tiptoed back to Zola, stroking the animal's neck. The horse sensed her master's nervousness and gave a defiant whinny. Eleppon put her thumbs together and blew. The sound of a snowy owl pierced the clearing.

She was answered by identical whistles, and Eleppon smiled, skipping to greet her fellow officers, Calwyn and Kossi. They, too, wore the short tunics and breeches of their craft, Calwyn in dark gray, and Kossi in silvery blue.

The two newcomers left their horses to graze, then flopped onto the grass.

Calwyn was even taller than Eleppon, though thinner, with a hawkish, unlovely face.

By contrast, the willowy Kossi had eyes an unusual shade of lime green and skin that was the coveted true black of the legendary fairies. It was whispered that she was part fairy herself.

Eleppon only saw them as her lieutenants—loyal, dependable, the best of the Swift Legion. Looks meant nothing. When all else failed her, they would not. She retrieved a parchment map from an inside pocket of her tunic and spread it on the ground, then pushed up her sleeves. They all bent over it, intent on the lines and characters in Eleppon's bold, squarish hand.

Calwyn said, "Eleppon, why did you mark the Hub?"

"The last time I went there, the thieves had taken it over," said Kossi.

Eleppon sat up. "But, don't you see? It's the perfect place to attack. They'll be too busy picking pockets to put up a defense."

"You may be right," mused Calwyn, "but what happens when your brother brings in reinforcements? The Hub's the most accessible area of Douvilwe city. What good are horses against outlaws with swords?"

"All right, so I haven't thought it through." Eleppon shrugged and smiled. "That's why I called a council."

Calwyn closed her eyes, thinking.

Kossi frowned. "It's not going to work."

Eleppon protested, but Calwyn shook her head. "She's right, we can't attack him at the Hub." She held up her hand. "Let me think."

While Calwyn sat back to pluck at the grass, the other two studied the map.

Abruptly, Kossi smiled, her eyes agleam. "I have an idea," she whispered. With a squared nail she pointed to Goz'u Way, a broad boulevard that once snaked its patrician path through the city—now a locus of conflict between marauding bandits and placid citizens trying to observe mourning.

"It's here that we strike—not all at once, but in bands, a few here, a few there, just to shake him up a bit, try to draw him out in the open. Then—." She made a slicing gesture across her throat.

Calwyn gasped in horror.

"We can't," said Eleppon. "For starters, we're in mourning."

But Kossi shrugged. "We've got to neutralize him, Eleppon, or what's the point of going in there? Oh—I know, I know, the mourning, the penance—the terrible sin. But think—will the High Priestess punish us when our actions have brought peace to this troubled land? When our actions have saved generations of Nightwings—blessed ones—unborn?"

Calwyn looked to Eleppon for guidance.

Eleppon had doubts. *I will be a Nightwing some day. She speaks lightly of it, but I cannot do this thing.* She shook her head and stood up, yanking her tunic over her hips. "No. I must take responsibility for my station and meet my brother in single combat. Without weapons, so as not to dishonor tradition." She gazed down at Kossi's shuttered face. "I have to agree with you, though, I will be more likely to find him by your methods."

She dropped to one knee and looked at them both with eagerness. "How practiced are you with a rope?" This elicited grins from the other two and soon all three had regained their optimism.

Only later, when the last flutter of Eleppon's rose tunic disappeared up the escarpment, did Kossi whisper to Calwyn, "My sister in arms, whatever new madness our liege is planning, we must pledge to be her shield. Are you with me?"

Calwyn tipped her head back and her nostrils flared. "Though we risk the Lake of All Souls, my friend." She held out her left arm, and Kossi clasped it to seal the agreement.

-58-

THE DESERT sun emblazoned its sovereignty over all that crawled beneath it. For the dark elves in the wagon, the Scourge was showing its true nature. It was apparent to the others that they would make little progress if they did not rest in the shade and conserve their water. Their resources included two tents, extra clothing, blankets and medical supplies, in addition to the food and water they had procured from the giants. Six Stix had been surprisingly generous with his money. Obsidian was glad to see that pragmatism had won over avarice.

When they had erected the dun-colored tents on slender poles, the travelers stowed the other supplies inside and prepared to rest until afternoon. The wagon was shielded by the heavier of the two tents, and the tarp covering the bed had been raised to let Tiala and Embaza breathe more naturally. Even in the semi-darkness, the heat was oppressive.

Six Stix lay near the flap of the tent and squinted one eye at the bright landscape. Though not a flicker of an animal appeared, he sensed life teeming in the sunshine and wondered what Polah would find to eat. Desert mice? Rabbits? Maybe insects?

He also sensed the General's watchful eyes and knew better than to fall asleep until she did. Whatever protestations of truce she had sworn back at the Manor, he felt the lingering malevolence of her attitude and wondered what he could do about it. Obsidian's watch was first, then his.

As he pondered these things, a faint piping melody from inside the wagon reached his ears. A sinuous tune, it made its way from note to note, then expanded into a major chord, reminding him of sunrise after a rain.

Tiala. His heart melted at the evocative melody. He closed his eyes, remembering his first sight of the pipes in the old minstrel's tent. He had known they were for her. Made of ox-bone, smooth as silk, they were laced together with melted gut, their tongues delicately placed. The price the old man had asked for them was ridiculous—a hundred gold pieces. With some persistent haggling, he ended up paying only thirty. But the delight on Tiala's face when she saw them made the sacrifice worth it. *Ah, lady, how you bewitch my soul.*

Obsidian, too, remembered the dwarf's grudge as he watched her irritably thump the pack beneath her head. He sat in a meditative pose, just out of the sunlight, arms folded in his lap, his sore right eye at half-mast. The wound in his back felt much better today. He could move from side to side without pain. His tribal mark also gave him no trouble.

Actually, Gudrun was unconcerned with Six Stix at that moment. Instead, she was gauging the trials ahead of them. She had heard plenty of stories about quake-sand and none of them were encouraging. She was ready to die, but were the others? And what about Tiala's cause? She sought refuge in sleep, knowing that later she could not.

By the time the pipes fell silent, only Obsidian was awake. Embaza had rolled toward the wall of the wagon bed and sought the healing sleep that would renew his powers. Even Tiala dozed, having calmed herself with the music. In her sleep, her hands cradled the pipes to her bosom.

Obsidian's practiced gaze floated over the desert, mastering the art of focusing and unfocusing on one spot, then another. It was the best way to avoid being tricked by the monotonous glare into seeing imaginary vistas.

Thus, when the fox appeared, he knew it was not a mirage. He waited until he was sure this large creature was indeed their friend, and took the opportunity to memorize various details of her appearance—the slightest limp of her left hind leg, the hint of white fluff at her throat, the thinning of hair on the ridge of her back, and as she neared, the unmistakable expression in her glistening black eyes.

He went into the tent, then reappeared with her bundle of clothing. Polah stopped just outside and panted, regarding Obsidian with a steady gaze. He dropped the bundle and withdrew.

After a few moments, Polah stepped into the tent, clad once more in hooded shirt and sand-colored leggings. She took a long drink from one of the waterskins, then joined Obsidian in the shadow of the tent flap. Without preamble, she whispered, "Bad news. We're being followed."

"Not the giants—?" asked Obsidian, voicing his fear that a favor might be due.

"No, it's our old friend, Prince Mischa—and he has a gnomad girl with him. Desert bred, by her skin and clothing."

"Are they armed?"

She snorted. "They act like lovers out for a stroll."

"We can handle them."

She shook her head. "There's more. I heard an army coming this way, not far behind them."

Obsidian frowned, looking at the sleeping Gudrun and Six Stix. Whose army was following them? "We haven't had much rest. I doubt we could fight off even Mischa in our present state."

Polah nodded.

"You check on the ones in the wagon while I wake these two. Then we've got to get these tents down—fast." Obsidian knew the dubious honor of rousing Six Stix and Gudrun, whose instincts when awakened were not disposed to be friendly. The monk was wise enough to stand back.

Polah lifted a corner of the tarp and whispered to the dark elves in the wagon bed, "We have to move on. Mischa is behind us, and he's followed by an army."

Embaza groaned, unable to sleep in the searing heat. He mumbled a phrase and shook Tiala, who awoke with sand in her nostrils.

In a few moments, the various supplies and tents were stowed in their respective compartments on both sides of the wagon. The horses neighed and stamped in protest against working in the heat, but were too well-trained to balk. With a glance behind him, Six Stix vaulted into the saddle and grabbed one of the lead ropes to start the harnessed team. As the wagon wheels began to turn, Obsidian followed suit, taking the second lead to the team while Polah and Gudrun rode just ahead.

Six Stix squinted over at the monk, who looked at ease on the large, oat-colored mare. The elf admired Obsidian's lithe physique. He knew the monk's strength came from a source other than muscle. Despite the wounds Obsidian had suffered this past week, he looked sturdy enough now.

"I would have bet my best dagger that we'd seen the last of the Prince," said the blue elf.

"Apparently, so would Embaza," the monk replied. "Polah says he seemed ill when he heard why we're leaving so soon."

"He's in no shape for a battle, that's for sure. Too bad," mused Six Stix.

"Why?" asked the monk.

"Wizards are powerful allies in war. It brings out something special in them. Not violence, exactly, but just as deadly."

Obsidian was chilled by the thought of more death and killing. Why must there always be this paradox to disturb the beauty and serenity of life?

Six Stix noticed the monk's shiver and looked sternly ahead. "For all your skill in combat, I would not want you at my back."

Obsidian was startled. "I'd protect you with my life, Six. Do you accuse me of cowardice?"

"You have fine principles, my friend, but they don't fill your belly when you're hungry and they wouldn't have saved your skin from that giant."

Obsidian recognized the logic behind the words, but his beliefs ran too deep to accept it. He bowed his head, disturbed that the elf could think so poorly of him.

A rumbling noise like thunder stopped the horses in their tracks. Obsidian tightened his reins and redoubled his hold on the lead rope to the team. The monk was reminded of the mountains where he was raised. Thunder and sheet lightning were a northern child's lullabies, but there was no sign of storm in the desert sky.

Although the animals were trained to suffer the rigors of battle, Six Stix and Gudrun were barely able to calm their mounts, the team becoming more and more agitated as the noise continued. Polah's horse skittered sideways, and she clutched the saddle horn, gripping tightly with her knees.

"Quake-sand," whispered Obsidian. No memory could have prepared him for this. It was always different. He tried to remember the strategies so clear the night before, but his mind was wiped clean by the foreboding sound.

Inside the wagon, Tiala and Embaza heard the muffled noise and stared across the pale gloom at each other.

Embaza was once again chilled by something else out there—more than the sand, more than the blazing sun.

The booming sounds came at the party from all sides. As avalanches started on the dunes and trembling earthquakes shook the sand beneath their feet, the horses reared and bolted in every direction, tossing riders like insects, Six Stix the only one to keep his seat. Desperately, he urged his reluctant mount toward the wagon, mere feet away when the harness snapped, freeing the thrashing team, and leaving the wagon sliding into the opening maw in the sand.

With a swoop, he grabbed a loose end of the harness upon alighting the ground, his horse eager to join the others receding in the distance. "Help me," he cried. "Tiala and Embaza are still inside."

Polah scrambled to her feet, brushing the grit out of her eyes.

The wagon had mired down in the sand, and Obsidian leapt up and hoisted part of the harness over his shoulder, then heaved against the drag of the sand. Slowly the wheels inched forward. "Keep it moving," he shouted.

Six Stix and Gudrun strained at the other side, and with all three pulling together, the wagon began to roll more easily. Polah took the fourth corner.

Inside, Tiala and Embaza maintained a rigid silence, wondering what events could match the terrible things they heard and felt.

As the agitation of the quake-sand increased, a wind came up out of the east. Obsidian freed a hand briefly to tug his turban over his face against the rain of sand. Gudrun and Six Stix squinted their eyes and lowered their heads like bulls. Polah's turban flew off and wild, red hair whipped around her face, as much a nuisance as the sand. At times, she held onto the wagon for support, pushing when she felt there was no danger of slipping under the large wheels.

Their progress was serpentine, since every time they tried to avoid the area of greatest turbulence, the intensity shifted in another direction. It was hard to know whether they were making any progress or merely following an endless circle.

Suddenly, Obsidian yelled, "Look out, it's—." The rest of his words were drowned by the hideous boom. In front of them, a huge sinkhole appeared where a moment before, the sand had been level.

Six Stix and Obsidian struggled to keep from the wagon from pushing them forward. "Turn it," yelled Six Stix, as it listed away from him.

But it was no good. They froze in horror as the back of the wagon slipped around and began to slide into the huge hole. The straps of the harness grew taut, jerking them forward a step at a time.

Six Stix looped as much as harness as he could muster around his hands three times and dug in his heels, the sand up to his knees. Obsidian, with all his strength, bent his body like a bow—so far back that he was nearly lying flat—as he tried to keep the wagon from falling into the sinkhole.

Tears mixed with sharp grains of sand stung Polah's eyes, and she screamed to be heard above the roaring wind. "Embaza. Get out of the wagon!"

Gudrun was already fighting her way through the waist-high sand toward the wagon, but just at the edge of the hole, the ground gave way beneath her, and her squat body was nearly buried.

Tossing the harness aside, Six Stix lunged for her and came up with two fistfuls of grizzled hair. With a heave, he jerked the sputtering dwarf out of the deadly sand. She rolled away, spitting sand between curses.

The wagon now half buried, Six Stix left Gudrun's side and collected a big bite of the harness in his fist again. He towed with all his might while Gudrun waded into the swirling hole and pried loose corner of the tarp covering the wagon bed. The sand dragged at her body, and the sucking noise filled her with a familiar terror that only made her all the more determined.

"Out—both of you!" she cried, just before the sand sucked her down again.

This time, it was Polah who saw the indentation where Gudrun had fallen, and she knelt there, digging her fingers into the sand for the dwarf's coarse curls, which she yanked until the dwarf re-emerged.

"I'm going to have no hair left," Gudrun sputtered between gasps for air.

Meanwhile, the tarp flew back and a blanketed figure rose straight up out of the wagon. Embaza could be heard over the booming sand. "Take her."

Obsidian, locked in a fierce battle to forestall the slide, yelled to Six Stix, "You get her—I'm holding the wagon."

The elf then pulled himself hand-over-hand along the traces, the sand waist high at the wagon bed, where he took Tiala's cloaked body into his arms and then raised her high over the voracious maw of the sinkhole.

From somewhere above, the buzzard's shadow covered the dark elf, then dived toward the cloaked figure surrounded by the swirling sand. Burying his beak in the folds of the cloak, he opened a tear in the thick garment, then climbed back into the sandstorm.

Tiala screamed with fear, her body growing cold as ice, even in the desert heat. The others thought it was the sun-sickness and endured her cries.

Embaza, looking like a scarecrow, vaulted over the side of the wagon and landed beyond the others, obscured by the raining curtain of sand. He had sensed the buzzard's presence, and only now knew what it was. He raised his hands toward the sand-choked sky, and began to chant, *"Gondromin... gondromin bafrakcisdin..."*

Tiala whimpered, and Six Stix shouted, "Spells won't work with quake-sand, Embaza. Run to safety."

The buzzard hovered, as if gathering for a new strike, as Six Stix sank deeper and deeper into the sand.

Still dragging the wagon by the harness, Obsidian was blinded by grit in his eyes, yet he remained deep in the meditative state from which he drew his strength.

Over the din, Gudrun hollered, "Obsidian—they're out. Let the wagon go—."

"Let go," echoed Polah.

As the hungry sinkhole received its quarry, the sand began to circulate like a giant whirlpool, threatening to suck everything within its reach down with it. The others scrambled for a foothold, like waves running uphill.

Just as it seemed they would all be drowned, the hole was gone, and there were only serpentine lines to indicate anything had occurred, much less the extraordinary violence. The buzzard took this moment to plummet toward the dark figure in the cloak.

Embaza had fallen to his knees, his voice barely a dry croak, his eyes sealed shut by grains of sand, yet he continued chanting, arms raised, fingers pointed toward the sinister bird.

The others stared at him in wonder, and then looking up, saw the phantom headed straight for Tiala's breast. Obsidian and Gudrun raced to her defense. Feathers flew in all directions, blood mingling with the rain of sand. Amidst the chanting of Embaza's spell, Gudrun skewered the creature with her sword, then flung the feathered corpse to the sand, where it sizzled in the sunlight and evaporated like a pool of acid.

Embaza collapsed, his arms clasped around him. The party looked at each other as the wind subsided. One by one, they checked for breaks and bruises, brushing off and spitting out the sand.

Tiala lay on her side, quivering beneath Embaza's gray cloak. A few feet away, Embaza huddled, unprotected in his dark blue robe. His teeth chattered, his eyes as frenetic as the quake-sand while he mourned the loss of his saddlebags.

Gudrun felt gritty and bruised all over, but she patted the tearful Polah on the shoulder. "That was a brave thing you did. Thanks to you, I'm alive."

Polah gave a shaky laugh in acknowledgement.

Obsidian felt an ache in his muscles that would take hours to mend. His mind was foggy as he strove to bring his companions back into focus.

They had lost most of their belongings, the waterskins and food in the wagon. Even their personal packs had been lost to the sand. A few tremors still rippled sporadically.

Gudrun looked behind them. "We could go now, while it's quiet..." Her gaze roamed about the scene. "Where's—?"

"Six Stix?" cried Polah, and dropped to her knees to dig frenziedly in the sand. Obsidian hurried over to help her. Polah shut her eyes to concentrate as she groped in a circle. Obsidian found Six's knapsack and he struggled to wrestle it to the surface.

Gudrun watched the others, wanting to help, but couldn't bring herself to move, as if she had invisible bands around her body. *My enemy is destroyed and yet I feel no triumph.* She could not get the image out of her mind of the blue elf holding Tiala over his head. Then she remembered him jerking her free of the sand by her hair.

She plunged her arms deep into the sand, until her chin lay on the top. Her vision was so near the ground that she could see the quake-sand making sporadic leaps in pools across the territory. Her arms and fingers tingled with vibrations from the sand. Was it gathering for another storm? How could something so mobile be firm enough to walk on? She recalled Obsidian saying no one knew how the sinkholes worked.

Taking a chance, she shut her eyes, held her breath, and dove under the surface. She could feel the grit in her nose and ears, but somehow she was able to move like a swimmer. She kicked her feet, feeling her way, until she bumped the solid form of the elf. Grabbing his jerkin with both hands, she doubled her body like a jackknife, willing herself the strength to bring them both to the air.

Obsidian's strong hands reached down, catching hold of her waist, and between the two of them, they brought Six Stix up again. The elf's face was nearly unrecognizable, his eyes and nose caked with sand. Frantically, they cleaned him off. He choked out a breath, and then lay still.

Gudrun spat sand out of her own mouth, then thumped his chest and put her ear to his throat, but the elf was still. "Wake up, damn you," she cried. "I didn't go to all this trouble for you to die now."

Obsidian took over, and he and Gudrun took turns blowing air into the elf's mouth, while repeatedly thumping his chest.

Polah let out a wail that was more fox than woman. The sound seemed to express the feeling of the whole group.

Embaza began to laugh in hysterical counterpoint that tore at Obsidian's heart. The monk rose up and slapped him, then said, "Pull yourself together."

The wizard stared without comprehension, shaking like a frightened child. From a deep pocket in his robe, he cupped a waxen figure, held it to his breast and rocked back and forth, tears streaming down his face.

Obsidian walked over where Tiala lay curled, shivering but quiet under the cloak. He put his hand on her shoulder, noticing the cloth was soaking wet with perspiration. "Steady, now, Princess, you'll be all right." He closed his eyes, trying to communicate a tranquillity through his touch. It did seem to help, and as her trembling subsided, the vibrations of the sand around them became more noticeable.

Polah found the one waterskin they still possessed—in Six Stix's knapsack. She took it to Embaza, and oblivious to all but the water, he drank greedily, moaning piteously when Polah jerked it away from him. She kissed him on the cheek and whispered, "We must move on, now. Come on." Gently, she helped him up. She could not tell if he understood or even recognized her.

Seeing Polah and Embaza getting ready to move, Obsidian gathered Tiala into his arms, cradling her head on his shoulder. She whimpered, but made no other protest. He called to Gudrun, "General, the sand's jumping faster—can you carry Six?"

The General muttered, "I'm not giving up on you, elf." More than once, she had imagined a whisper of breath from his nostrils. With a grunt, she hoisted Six Stix over her shoulder, then leaned over for the pack, slinging it over her other shoulder. She wiped a stream of perspiration off her nose. Her boots covered with sand, she slogged along, careful to avoid the patches of agitation. "You're right," she yelled to Obsidian, "hurry."

The monk set a rigorous pace, choosing a path through the drumming sand the best he could. The others had no choice but to follow, and did their utmost to keep up with him. Embaza was completely dependent on Polah, who urged him every step of the way, "Come on, Embaza, this way, now—put your foot there. That's good."

Gudrun made heavy weather with her cargo, but gritting her teeth, she doggedly kept up. The wind was rising again, and small eddies of sand blew her cheeks raw. She kept having to spit out sand as she walked. One thing, at least—although the sun was nearing its zenith, none of them noticed it now. The sand storm would soon completely obscure it.

They walked, ran, stumbled, and ran again, as Obsidian's course zigzagged across the great expanse. Sinkholes appeared to the left and right of them, but the monk seemed to have an uncanny ability to anticipate and avoid them. By the time they reached the other side of the vast area, they were all nearly blinded by a combination of sand and perspiration.

Obsidian dropped to his knees, cradling Tiala, and gave thanks to the Master of All.

Polah came behind, leading Embaza by the hand. The wizard's skin was horrible to see: discolored, dry as a bone and pitted as a walnut. His green eyes lacked recognition, though determination flickered yet in their depths. By contrast, the shape-changer's face was radiant with purpose and affection. Seeing her, Obsidian felt an absurd happiness tinged by jealousy for her state of grace.

Last, through a foggy curtain of sand, the dwarf appeared, still shouldering her burden. She dropped the pack to the ground, then thumped the elf on the back a couple of times and tossed him down. She studied him a moment, combing the sand out of her beard.

When Obsidian rose to his feet. Gudrun placed her hands on her hips and announced, "Lord Stixan lives."

Sure enough, the elf raised his head, shading his eyes with one hand, and looked up at her. "General," he croaked, "You're a fine lass, and no mistake about it."

-59-

MISCHA AND Delyra were alarmed at the sight of the large, red fox that stood on the ridge, watching them with disdain. But Delyra said, "Prince, why don't you kill that fox with your dagger, and we'll have it for dinner?"

Mischa's face showed both amazement and disgust. "I'm no common hunter. Besides, that's no common fox."

"Why not?"

"She's enchanted." The Prince was pleased by the flicker of fear in Delyra's eyes. "If you ate of her, you would be enchanted, too."

Delyra swallowed nervously and said, "Can we stop for awhile?" The talk about eating had made her hungry.

The Prince was glad to rest, his feet a mass of blisters. He took a long draught from a waterskin, and Delyra curled up in his lap like a desert hare. Absently, the Prince stroked the pretty, tawny curls that peeped out of her turban. At least she was company. He, too, curled up, shading his face with the sack, and napped.

Soon after the fox disappeared, they continued following the faint wagon tracks. It was not long before they came down the slope toward the tract of quake-sand. There was not a sound now, and three buzzards circled overhead.

Delyra had never seen the fabled quake-sand, but had heard all the stories of its treachery. "The wagon couldn't have crossed that," she said.

As if to underscore her words, they saw the scattered hoof prints of horses, leading off to the north and south. The wagon tracks ended ominously, a few feet further ahead. The Prince frowned. He had never paid enough attention to matters outside the Manor. His scouts and spies reported what he told them to report, and no more. He wished now that he had taken more of an interest in this part of his domain.

"Something happened here...are they dead?" He scratched his head, excited by the idea of his enemies buried in sand.

"Maybe they rode off on the horses," Delyra suggested.

"Possibly," replied the Prince. He had an urge to look into the globe and speak with the dark-elven king, Dekhalis. Unconsciously, he sensed the urge was unnatural. He snapped at Delyra, "Why don't you do something helpful?"

"Don't yell at me. It's not my fault."

"Yes, it is. Your people travel everywhere." He swung his arm in an arc. "What is this place?"

She quailed before him. "It's c-called quake-sand." She gulped. "It's dangerous."

"Any idiot can see that," he roared. The sand answered him. Mischa's head jerked around, as one area after another began to thrum in the great expanse, and a wind came up out of nowhere.

Delyra clutched his hand with both of hers. "It's starting. Run!" They ran—not toward the little storm—but back the way they had come. No sooner had they reached the rise of the hill when they saw Lord Amra's troops bearing down upon them from the horizon.

"Oh, no! It's Father," shrieked Delyra.

"Do you think I'm blind? Do you think I'm stupid?" shouted the Prince, turning back toward the quaking sand.

"Wait," shouted Delyra. "You can't go in there—you'll die."

"Shut up."

"Don't leave me," she wailed.

But the Prince decided to cut his losses. Heedless of the whipping wind or the mysterious drumming of the sand, he raced across the pitching landscape, leaping like a kangaroo rat.

In spite of herself, Delyra caught her breath in the middle of a sob and watched until his dancing form was obscured by the whirlwind. In a few minutes, her father appeared on his glistening, dappled gray stallion. He barely glanced at the treacherous tract of quake-sand, and silenced the queries of his men with a curt wave of an arm.

Delyra could smell the horse's sweat as its great chest heaved. She looked up and winced at Amra's angry face.

"I see you've been discarded," he said. Predictably, she burst into tears. Amra gestured to a tall gnome nearby. "Get her—gently." The lieutenant leaned down, lifted her easily and settled her in front of him. Lord Amra gave the signal to the others, and in moments, they were thundering toward camp.

Prince Mischa did not hear the company ride off, nor did he feel the trembling of the ground from their hooves. He was completely occupied by the booming sand all around him. When he saw the first sinkhole appear, he yelped and realized he might be about to die. It was a shocking thought, one that had never seemed so plausible.

Filled with dread at the surety of his imminent demise, he ran like a daredevil, without strategy or system, not caring where he put his feet. When the sand opened before him, he leapt over it, landing to the right. Zigzagging to the left, he sped by another sinkhole. Somehow, by pure chance, he avoided every snare the sand set for him.

When his feet touched solid ground at last, it was almost an anti-climax. He bent over, panting, hands on his thighs, and later turned to survey the turbulent scene behind him. Three buzzards circled high above like sentinels.

He brushed the remaining sand out of his eyes. Wispy hair escaping from the edge of the turban was bleached almost white by the sun. His sack still hung—by some miracle—across his chest, the drawstrings hopelessly tangled. He could not remember paying it any attention after the first sink hole.

He shaded his eyes and peered at the new horizon. The shape and substance of some structure appeared—not the Manor this time. He saw the beginnings of vegetation, too, and some scraggly trees a little farther off. Was that where the dark one went? Surely, the fox was with her, too. Good. He wanted them all together when he destroyed her.

The urge to speak with the orb overwhelmed him. He sat down, opened the sack, and looked at the crystal. It winked at him, beckoning. He rubbed it on his sleeve and settled it in the sand, waiting for the dark king to appear.

Dekhalis was not wearing the crown this time. He had a thick shock of black hair that stood high on his head, and his large ears lay on either side. The chiseled eyebrows rose in peaks over smoldering eyes. He lifted his finger to stroke the large spider sitting on the back of his hand.

"Well, Mischa, my henchman, what have you to report? Have you found the Usurper?"

The Prince wondered again how much of the truth to tell. "Yes, Lord," he said finally.

"Lord King," Dekhalis corrected. "Have you destroyed her?"

"Not yet," answered Mischa, "but I will. I want to be sure she is with her friends. I have my own score to settle with them."

Dekhalis's eyes flashed. "*Your* score? Don't trifle with me, Mischa. Remember, you carry the fate of an entire country on your shoulders. You want to live, don't you?"

"Yes, Lord King," the Prince heard himself say. He was appalled. *What's happening to my independence? I've never been subservient to anyone.*

But the elf narrowed his eyes, and the corners of his mouth turned up in a wicked smile. "I will contact you tomorrow—and I expect to hear that Tiala is dead."

The colors in the globe swirled and disappeared once again. Drained of energy, Mischa put the artifact back in the sack with eager fingers and wished he had never seen the cursed object. His grandfather's words came back to him. *Magic is a cruel master, Mischief.* He suffered a pang of regret. Rearguard was his closest relative. *Why didn't I listen to the old man?*

With a sigh, he fished in his bag until he found the waterskin he had stolen from Delyra. He drank from it gratefully, but saved enough for another hour. He was learning.

-60-

IT WAS not much farther to the monastery from the quake-sand, and the six travelers made their way toward it as quickly as possible. With Polah's help, Embaza was able to walk, though he stumbled often and begged for water long after the last drop was gone. Gudrun and Six Stix, if not the greatest of friends, at least had no lack of topics to argue about.

Obsidian carried Tiala without complaint, glad to have her welfare to distract him from his fate once the masters heard his story. Soon, he was able to see the spires and domes of the Temple-City gleaming in the sun.

The straggling vegetation that dotted the edge of the Outlands began to give way to the oasis. All of the party had sand in their eyes, their nostrils, and every part of their garments. They had seen nothing except sand for so long, it was hard to imagine any relief.

The buildings of the monastery were constructed from gray fieldstone, and a wide street meandered in a gentle incline through it, passing under archways and terraces. Trees thrived in every corner and flowers decorated the variegated stone walls. On one side of the tall entrance gate, there was an orchard of pear trees, and on the other, an olive grove.

Obsidian recognized the song of a thrush from a nearby pear tree. No matter what was in store for him, at least he was home.

The distant figures of monks could be seen tending their gardens and strolling along the stone walls. In the orchard, a young monk was standing on a wooden ladder, gathering pears into a basket. He was barefooted and dressed in a long, brown tunic with a belt of plain linen. When he noticed the strange group of visitors, he climbed down and walked to the gate to meet them. He had a hairlock like Obsidian's.

Obsidian recognized his rival, Keth. They had vied for every honor from the beginning, each testing and challenging the other, until Obsidian's triumph had won him the right to prove himself in the Prince's arena. Keth had been at pains to hide his jealousy.

Why him? Obsidian groaned to himself. He resolved not to divulge his shame before this monk. He'd wait until he stood before the High Abbot himself.

"Keth," he hailed, and the young monk approached, smiling warmly, to clasp Obsidian's forearm in ritual greeting.

"Welcome, brother," he said. "You look worn—and who are your companions?" He glanced with curiosity at the cloaked bundle in Obsidian's arms, then scanned the group, frowning when he noticed Embaza's withered countenance. He shyly avoided the eyes of the women.

"I'll get water," said Keth, and he ran back toward the well, where a windlass hung next to a large pail. When they reached the gate, he met them with the dripping refreshment. He unwrapped his belt, dipped it in the water and patted Embaza's parched face. The dark elf screamed with pain.

Keth drew back, glancing at Obsidian, who said, "Just help me get them inside."

A light breeze fiddled with the leaves of the orchard, and the tops of the olive trees sighed, as the party wound its way into the fastness of the monastery.

The cold stone was a shock after the hot desert, and they could feel their body temperatures drop almost immediately. Keth led them down a long corridor to the guest rooms. The party could see plain but comfortable quarters beyond each doorway they passed.

Keth said, "Take whatever room you wish. We rarely have visitors. Each room has a pitcher of water which you may refill from the pump in the courtyard."

Polah helped Embaza into one of the first rooms along the way, and Gudrun chose another soon after, but Six Stix followed Obsidian and Keth who entered a large sitting room opening into a bed chamber. Obsidian laid Tiala on the bed, then parted the hood of her cloak, revealing her terrified face.

Six Stix said, "Is she all right?"

"Yes," Obsidian said. "Just weak."

"Who is she?" asked Keth.

"The reason we're all here," he replied. "She is Tiala, a princess."

At the sound of her name, Tiala's eyes cleared, and she recognized Obsidian and Six Stix. "I need water," she rasped, and Keth reached the pitcher first, while Obsidian held the glass.

When she had drunk her fill, she collapsed into sleep, as if tranquilized. Obsidian whispered to Keth, "Her kind is sun-sensitive to the point of madness. She must rest now."

Keth gripped Obsidian's arm and murmured, "I'm glad you survived the test." He looked as if he wanted to say more, but for the presence of Six Stix, who gazed fixedly at Tiala's dark beauty against the white spread. Keth said, "I'll bring food later," and left the room.

Six Stix tore his gaze away from Tiala and asked Obsidian, "Want to bunk together?"

Obsidian shook his head.

"I'll not disturb your meditations, if that's what you're thinking," the elf said with a chuckle.

"Don't be offended, Six, but I need time to myself." He spread his arms. "Take any room you wish. I won't be far."

With a shrug, Six Stix moved down the hall to the next doorway, shifted the curtain, and liked what he saw. He crossed to a linen-covered bed, and next to it, a basin with a pitcher of water on a one-drawer nightstand near a reed wardrobe on the same wall. A simple rug of homespun at the foot of the bed stopped before a doorway that opened onto a small terrace and a grand view of the orchards. He sat down on the firm mattress, and took off one of his boots, emptying a stream of sand onto the rug. With naught but a curtain for a doorway, he supposed thievery was unimaginable here.

Polah had led Embaza to a room completely shaded from the sun. Just as Keth promised, a cool pitcher of water sat in a basin on a small table near the bed, and she prepared to wash him. "My poor brave fool," she murmured, prying the melted wax from his hands. A long time passed before the sense returned to his eyes, and longer yet before his hands stopped shaking.

Gudrun had chosen a room that opened onto a garden of bright red blooms she had never seen before, though Keth called them poppies. Ignoring the pleasant furnishings, she entered the garden and bent down to touch a red-orange petal with her grimy finger. She chuckled when a small white butterfly flitted away.

-61-

EMBAZA LAY on his side with Polah curled behind him. Her warmth soothed his abraded nerves, and he drifted into a deep landscape of dreams. At first, there was nothing but his dream-body floating like a feather in a velvety darkness.

Ahead of him blossomed a blue light. He thought it strange that it did not hurt his eyes. Then a voice, soft as moth's wing but compelling as the wind: "Embaza, wizard of Sargoth, son of Alvarra."

He asked, "Who's there?" but his question was without sound, as if the light absorbed it at the very source.

"I am your Nightwing." The blue light glowed, and a radiant form appeared within it, the lithe silhouette of a woman.

Embaza's dream-body felt more solid now. He looked down to velvety blackness, but he could also sense the boundaries of himself. In the place where he thought his heart to be, a faint blue light stirred.

"What does it mean?" he asked, feeling like a child, an apprentice in the Towers of Sargoth, at his first lesson.

"I do not know," said the Nightwing, but the uncertainty didn't disturb the serenity in the timbre or tone of her beautiful voice. It was enough to know that there was an answer, somewhere. Her next question shocked him.

"I sense that Tiala is distressed by you. Why?"

The light in his chest streaked pink, then red. In his mind, he formed an answer that seemed to emanate from his feelings. It was wholly without words, inchoate, yet clear enough for the Nightwing's understanding.

Her form developed edges, became crystalline, her light sparkling like stars. "You have had an interesting upbringing for a dark-elven male. You will be a challenge to all that is Alvarra. You know that wizardry is forbidden here—even when we are not in mourning?"

He had not.

"My daughter is wiser than I thought. She did not tell you everything, so you would not be hobbled by the restraints of culture."

He laughed. "It was an oversight, I assure you. She has already forbidden me to use my powers in your realm."

"There is something wrong—I can feel it."

He was helpless to stop the flood of remembrance as he watched the light in his heart change to bright red.

"My daughter offered herself to you. And you...spurned her. Why?" There was the merest hint of anger in her tone; perhaps he imagined it.

His heart found words. "I love another," he said, and the light in his body turned to yellow and gold, with flecks of silver.

"Be careful. Tiala's pride will heal, but she is not used to being denied." The edges of the Nightwing's blue light softened again. "You remind me of her. Your spirit is strong and you have a formidable talent."

He quested toward her. "How can you know these things?"

"I am old."

Embaza felt his dream-body waver, the light winking in and out. After the first fright, he sensed an emerging trust like the bud of a new plant.

The Nightwing moved within the globe of light, her body shifting shape so swiftly and into so many different forms, he was unable to follow them. One of the forms was a fox-woman.

"Your mate is unusual, too. She has the power of a tiger-leopard, although she is untrained." Once again, he imagined a thread of anger in her voice, but her next words charged through him like arrows.

"When you meet Dekhalis, it will be on a battlefield of his choosing. You will have no choice but to use magic. Both of you."

Both of you. His dream-body swam in the nothingness, buoyed only by the light.

"You have my blessing and that of each of my priestesses. I will decree it.

Tell my daughter."

"Why can't you tell her?"

"Goodbye, Embaza." The light flickered and died, and in spite of his best efforts, his consciousness faded with it. Soon, he was in a deep, dreamless slumber.

-62-

Obsidian looked for Keth in the hallway, but the monk had gone. His other companions had settled themselves, so he made his way up the curving stairway that led to his old room. He paused, then pushed through the curtain in the doorway.

He wasn't sure what he had expected. The room was exactly as he had left it. Always a place of peace and satisfaction, it gave him that now, despite his troubles.

To Obsidian, the nicest thing about the room was its proximity to the herb gardens. His was one of six identical rooms that faced the inner courtyard. Each of them had one wall that was open to the garden, with only a low stone facing about a foot high to mark the boundary.

All the furniture was built into the walls or floor. His bed was a single slab of stone, covered by a mattress stuffed with rosemary needles and sage. A smooth block of stone in the middle of the floor functioned as both writing desk and dining table. A thick mat of woven reeds was covered by a square of yak hide. He knelt on it now and contemplated the room, drinking in the smell and feel of it. A single drape of homespun cloth covered a closet cut into the wall. Through the cloth, he could see his robes, undisturbed.

From the garden, the aromas of mint, thyme, hyssop, coriander, sage and others wafted in on the breeze. The familiar nectar blotted out thought. He drank a deep breath and suffered an overwhelming homesickness that brought tears to his eyes. However could he have thought it easy to leave this? He had been a fool at the camp of the giants, imagining he could be happy with his new tribe. Even the warmth of their fellowship did not give him this sense of well-being. *If only I still deserved it. Well, I will have Tiala's quest to occupy me now.*

Abruptly, he stripped to the skin and walked into the garden. At the center was a hexagonal fountain where the monks bathed in the ever-renewing water of the oasis. Through an elegant, uncomplicated system of natural porous rock and diatomaceous soil, the water cleaned itself on its journey into the earth and back again.

Obsidian washed his body of the accumulated dirt and blood, gratified by the sting of the cool water on his cuts and bruises. He had never felt so alive.

He sat on the edge of the fountain and watched the garden as bees visited the purple blooms of sage, and butterflies the clematis vines. He looked up past several stories of nested gardens to the highest terrace where a cloud of bougainvillea spilled in the sunlight.

When he was dry once again, he returned to his room and drew aside the curtain of his closet. There were five robes here in the colors of the desert: sand, blue sky, night, stone, hawk. He chose sand, the most humble shade, a color in which a man might hide.

He looked at the bed with fleeting desire, knowing it would do his body good. But it was his soul he had to attend to now; he could put it off no longer.

Dread hardened the lines of his face as he belted the robe with a plain thong from the closet, and then left the sanctuary of his room.

He was a little surprised that he had not seen any of the other monks— neither in the halls nor in the complex that faced the herb gardens. Some would be studying at this hour, others at their chores. Where were the rest?

He ascended the circular stairs to the next floor, then walked past the chambers of several monks who were his seniors. Some of his teachers lived here, but no one was in sight.

He reached the next set of stairs and ascended these. Again, he passed room after room without seeing a soul. A feeling of disquiet fluttered in his solar plexus.

At the end of a long hall, he ascended three steps and found himself in the upper reaches of the monastery. Here were the rooms of the High Abbot, and those special, reclusive masters who were sworn to solitude. He always felt a tingling in his scalp in this part of the cloister. Nearly everyone did.

He walked with utter silence, at least he prayed to do so. There was no transgression more humiliating than awakening one of the hermits. To his relief, he passed all seven of their entrances with no incident, and came at last to the great circular doorway that led to the High Abbot Umsel's receiving room.

The symbol of the circle was said to be the most perfect of subjects for meditation. It signified all things and yet also housed the void. He took the opportunity to study it now, willing his knees to stop trembling, pushing his breath into his lower belly as he had been taught. When he had recovered a measure of calm, he reached forward and grasped the two metal handles to open the double doors.

At that instant, the High Abbot announced, "Enter, Obsidian, novice from the northern lands."

Obsidian paled, blinded by a ray of sunlight beaming through the enormous circular window on the opposite wall. The trembling in his solar plexus returned, worse than before. He could see only the silhouette of the High Abbot, seated in front of the eight-petaled flower that formed the window. The sunlight turned the petals gold and white, bathing the High Abbot in a pale aura.

Despite his agitation, Obsidian forced himself to walk with measured steps, proud and dignified as a monk should be, yet the terrible effervescence inside him threatened to erupt. He tried to focus on the smooth, polished boards beneath his feet.

He had gone a few steps when he heard breathing on either side. He felt and smelled the bodies of men. As his eyes became accustomed to the light, he saw rows of his brothers seated in two lines on either side of the chamber. They were in ceremony.

His shock was like a spoon stirring the already dangerous foment within him. He forced himself to breathe deeply, counting each breath.

When he reached the High Abbot, he sank to his knees and sat on his heels, hands folded. He stared into the deep brown eyes that peered at him from folds of doughy, yellowed skin. The old man's hairlock was a wisp of white threads.

"You have completed your journey." The lugubrious voice was that of a man in his prime, and Obsidian marveled at the amount of air the High Abbot could fit into his narrow chest and belly. His body appeared weightless on the thin, blue cushion.

"You know all, Eminence."

Umsel indicated the acolytes and monks on either side. "They do not."

Obsidian swallowed. *Must I expose my shame before all of them?*

Umsel's brown eyes contained a nod.

"I had to kill a man."

"Why did you *have* to do this thing?" The High Abbot's smile was avuncular.

Obsidian's eyes smarted with tears. "I forgot everything I'd been taught—I acted from instinct."

"And what instinct was that?"

"Only the instinct of self-preservation, Eminence." Obsidian looked down.

The High Abbot turned his head to look at one of Obsidian's teachers—the Master Tolimane. The tall, thin monk rose to his feet to stand like a sapling in a thick gray robe. His hairlock, once black, was now gray, reaching almost to his knees.

"Did you teach him all that you knew, Tolimane?"

"Yes, Eminence," said the Master.

"Sit down," said Umsel. One by one, he called on Obsidian's teachers, asking them the same question. Each of them answered in the affirmative.

Obsidian wondered if at any moment the very floor in the sunlit chamber might open and swallow him so that he would never be seen again.

At last, the High Abbot regarded him with somber eyes. "Your teachers gave you all the learning they could impart, all the wisdom at their command. But it was up to you to do the rest. Control in the face of death is more than a supreme art, it is a highly personal matter."

"I know, Eminence," Obsidian whispered.

Umsel shook his head. "My son, if they could have taught you this control, they would have. I would have. But until that time, we must live like men."

Obsidian stared at the High Abbot, uncomprehending.

The old man's face broke into a rubbery network of smiles. "From this day onward, you are a full monk. You have passed your first test, Obsidian."

The youth gazed with astonishment and clasped his hands together, bowing his head. He would have to ponder this. "Thank you, Eminence."

"Yes," Umsel nodded. "Now, we will discuss your fellow travelers and their destination."

Obsidian felt abashed. He had been so busy with his own worries, he had forgotten all about Tiala.

"I know of your promise to the dark elf," said the High Abbot, always one to cut to the root of matters, "and your reasons for wanting to aid her. I would like to tell you about mine."

"Yours?"

"I have never visited the deepworld. The countries of Alvarra and Tskurl are known to us, but there is much to learn from them. Humans are not generally welcome there, and especially not men. A male society such as ours is unknown to them."

One of the other monks rose. He was wearing a sky blue robe, belted loosely over his muscled body. The High Abbot addressed him, "Speak, Jeon."

"Eminence, I have made a study of these Alvarrans and request permission to speak with the dark ones. Will you hold council with them?"

"It is my intention."

"Then, it would be well to choose a darkened room and provide them with plenty of sweet water. Isn't it so, Obsidian?" The monk nodded.

"Thank you," said the High Abbot, having heard nothing he did not already know. "Sit down, Jeon." He smiled. *Such an enthusiastic response from Jeon,* he thought.

"Take your place, Obsidian," said Umsel. "We will now say a mantra of thanks to the Master of All for bringing you home safely."

There was a murmur in the large chamber that sounded like wind in the grass. The words were old and sonorous, punctuated by the soughing breath of the men as they sank their consciousness deep into themselves, no more heeding the room or each other.

When Obsidian opened his eyes, the acolytes and monks had left. Eleven of the masters had remained with the High Abbot Umsel.

"Obsidian," said the High Abbot, "we come now to the most serious of subjects."

Obsidian felt the hairs on the back of his neck stir and suppressed a shudder. Perhaps, after all…

"You were inducted into the tribe of the Blacktooth giants."

"Yes, Eminence," said Obsidian.

"And you have given your word to the dark elf that you will help her as well."

"I have," he replied.

"You do not see any difficulty with these promises?"

The monk looked down at his hands, still clasped before him.

"You will meditate on this conundrum until daybreak, Obsidian."

"Yes, Eminence."

"Then visit me in my study, will you?"

"Yes, I will."

"And Obsidian…"

"Yes, Eminence?"

"I'm proud of you."

-63-

WHEN TIALA awoke, the waning moon was high above her, still pregnant with spectral light, but she did not see it nor the glittering stars. The room where her companions had left her was dark, save for one sliver of moonlight coming through the crack in the doorway. Her sensitive eyes noticed it immediately.

She had had a nightmare, in which she had been standing with Embaza on an escarpment of crystal near her room in the Royal City—a secret place she only brought her favorites. As she had gazed into his eyes, he had embraced her, his strong arms enfolding her, his lips warm with fire. But ecstasy had changed to terror, as his hands had encircled her neck, and the handsome face was not Embaza's—but that of her brother Dekhalis.

She sat up, trying to throw off a wave of disquiet. Leaving the cloak on the bed, she eased to her feet. Her body ached throughout and sand abraded every crevice. She longed for the waterfall in the Royal City, but thinking of home made her remember the dream, and she became angry. Embaza's arrogance could be a problem. He had a lot to learn. She looked forward to getting him underground, where he would see the way men should behave. *If I am not a mindless victim of the Scourge of Elves by then.* She touched the crack where her bottom lip had split in the heat. It stung from her salty fingers.

Someone had refilled the pitcher, and the cool sweetness of the water tasted wonderful, but there wasn't enough for a bath. After washing her face and hands, and drying off with a mint-scented towel, she felt better. She was as comfortable in the darkness as a human would have been in the light, and it did not take her long to explore her room.

Besides the bed and wash-stand, there was a small bureau filled with linens and a wardrobe which contained three long robes and a belt of yak hide. With an exclamation of delight, she chose one of the robes and flung it on the bed. It was wonderful to relieve herself of her gritty, travel-stained garments, and the soft, white cotton felt cool against her skin. She wrapped the belt around her waist, then rolled her other garments into a ball on the pillow.

She started to put on the cloak again, then dropped it with disgust, and chin high, opened the door to the garden. Apprehension dissolved at the fairy-like beauty of the scene before her. Hollyhocks and gardenias, lilacs, lilies, persimmon bushes, snowdrops…she had never seen so many different kinds of flowers, flowers that even the Royal Gardener couldn't grow.

There was a wide stone bench in the middle with curved, rayed pathways leading in eight directions. Tiala meandered down one of the pathways, stooping to smell and touch the petals and leaves as she went. The bench felt cold through the thin cotton robe, but she hardly noticed. The moonlight threaded its way through the floral profusion, making a cross-path of its own.

Closing her eyes, the dark elf began to sing. The garden seemed to impart a magical ability, after the rigors of her journey. Words flowed through her mind like a cascade of harmonies, then issued from her lips of their own accord.

She sang of her peril, her tangled fear, her journey to the Manor, the enforced patience of her vigil. Rising and walking along the serpentine paths, she sang of the gathering of her champions, then their imprisonment and their flight through the tunnels, only to arrive in the arena. Raising her arms to the moon, she opened her heart and poured out her exultation at discovering that she was a bard.

As her voice grew in volume, it remained as silken as thread, yet the lightest of sleepers had awakened, and many a monk lay entranced, listening to the clarion liquid tones below. Some of them had not heard a woman's voice since babyhood, let alone an elven one. By the time Tiala's lyric had come to the crossing of the quake-sand, the High Abbot himself was awake.

Embaza was close enough to discern her words, and he was impressed with her rendition of their adventures. Her rhyme schemes were inspired, her ingenuity shone through every line. And yet, a part of him resisted the charm of her phrasing, guarding himself against her passion.

He looked around, wondering where Polah had gone. He realized it had been hours since her warmth had kept him company. No doubt she was hunting. He, too, climbed out of bed and sought the doorway leading to the garden.

He was glad Polah had discovered how to regulate her shape-changing. It simplified matters—no fear of transformation while they mated. He hoped she had the sense to prevent a pregnancy. If not, what was it—ginger root? This plant brought on the cramps. *The smell of the flowers must be addling my brain. I know nothing of medicines.* A ray of moonlight fell onto his shoulder, and he stepped instinctively away, blinking at the shadows.

Gudrun stood on the opposite side of the garden, watching Embaza, glad he had not noticed her. She leaned against a tall cedar, stripped down to her linens, her bodice unlaced, picking her teeth with a vine stem. She welcomed the uninterrupted opportunity to listen to Tiala's singing, and she let the tears fall without shame. Here, she was not on guard; there was no need to pretend a sternness she did not feel.

Obsidian had fallen asleep still seated in meditation. Upon awakening, he thought at first that he was in paradise. He chuckled to himself, remembering that this was what Six Stix had said when he had awakened in the Prince's harem. It seemed a lifetime ago. From this distance, he could not make out the words, and Tiala's song could almost have been the rise and fall of a desert flute had he not known her voice so well. Soon, he drifted back to sleep, as if an angel had sent him a lullaby.

Even Polah, perched on a distant ridge, could hear Tiala. She bayed, throwing her head back like a wolf, and was answered by some creatures far away. She loped toward the monastery, seeking the relative safety of the orchard. The field mice had been tasty after the last two nights of insects. She would save the baby rabbit for tomorrow. The music emanating from the monastery had a strange effect upon her, reminding her in some visceral way of her human roots.

Of all Tiala's companions, it was Six Stix who was most affected, partly because his room was immediately next to hers. His keen elven senses were also so attuned to her voice that at the first sound of her humming, he was awake. He lay for a few moments on his elbows, transfixed. Then he threw off the coverlet, grabbed a gray robe from the wardrobe and crept to the doorway of the garden. Unlike Gudrun and Embaza, he did not venture outside—for an obvious reason. The dark elf was standing not six yards away, her face uplifted to the sky.

The path of moonlight illumined the tips of the flowers, transforming them into sparkling fairies of white light. Tiala's profile was immensely delicate and winsome in their reflection. He imagined her body entwined with his, but he could not move. Both her ballad and her presence paralyzed him.

As Tiala ended her song, a flock of birds in the trees set up a concatenation of applause. The moonlight limned her dark body under the white robe. She wanted to remain in the spell of her own making, the last chords of her ballad echoing in her mind, but she was exhausted.

Six Stix saw her body sway, and rapidly reached her side. Without a word, he lifted her into his arms. Unprotesting, Tiala lay against him. The slender strength of her body emboldened his desire.

"Tiala," he whispered.

The dark elf opened heavy-lidded eyes. She saw the naked hunger in his face and laughed, not cruelly but with tired affection. "At least you have a man's normal appetites."

The indigo scar along his cheek writhed with passion at her words and she saw that she would have to make a decision. "Put me down," she ordered.

He frowned, but complied, setting her on her feet with a sigh of resignation. "Another time, perhaps," he whispered.

She chuckled. "Perhaps. There are many who would covet a night in the arms of a future Nightwing."

He turned to go, but she said, "Come, I have a need to talk." He followed her to her room, and she climbed onto the bed.

Tiala stretched out her legs and tossed her head. Her emerald eyes glowed with purpose. "Are you pledged to me?"

Six Stix sat down at the end of the bed. He shook his head as if she were a child who had asked about the moon. "How can you doubt me?" As if by accident his hand brushed her ankle, and she did not move away.

They were interrupted by a polite knock on the wall outside Tiala's doorway. She started, realizing she had felt relaxed for the first time since she had left home. "Who's there?" she asked imperiously.

"The High Abbot sent me. He thought you might wish an audience while it is still hours before sunrise."

Tiala's face underwent a transformation. "I am not accustomed to being interrupted in the middle of —." She glanced at Six Stix, who was shaking his head, finger to his lips. "In the middle of my rest," she finished.

"Very well. I am sorry to disturb you," said the deferential voice.

Six Stix said, "You were a little hard on the poor fellow."

"Do you think so?" she said.

The haughty look on her face surprised him. "He was only carrying out orders."

"Then his superior should have known better." She shifted her hips to draw her feet up beside her.

Six Stix shook his head. "This is a monastery where men like Obsidian are proud to be insensitive to the needs of the flesh."

"What a ridiculous idea." She turned away from Six Stix to gaze at the garden. "Humans live such short lives. Why waste a man's child-rearing years, the years of greatest sensitivity and pleasure?"

"I agree," Six Stix whispered, his voice like dried leaves in the wind. He felt an unbearable tenderness for this elf woman, this exotic flower in a cruel land. He loosened the belt of his robe.

Although tempted by the look of longing in his eyes, Tiala's apprehension returned. *This is not time for the oblivion of pleasure.* She turned and slid off the bed. "Let's see what this Abbot wants."

"As you wish," he said, gruffly.

Tiala smiled. Men were like children, their minds as pliant as their bodies. She remembered Embaza's rejection, but then censored the thought. *After all, he's a transplanted Alvarran—a flawed and perverted individual. Probably a deficient lover as well.* But this excursion into fantasy failed to assuage her doubts completely, especially when she recalled his comment about her lack of subtlety.

Six Stix misread her expression and said, "Don't be worried, Tiala Denshadiel. You'll be getting home soon."

She gave him a grateful smile. "Come on, Stixan."

Although the messenger was long-gone, the monastery was easily navigated. Each floor was designed around four separate courtyards, and eventually, the stairs led no higher. Tiala and Six Stix assumed that this would be the High Abbot's floor, and they proceeded to the circular double-doors, but there was no sign of him, even in his receiving room. They decided to return down the opposite stairs.

As they did so, they passed an open doorway through which came the strong aroma of oleander. Six Stix stopped to investigate, and Tiala recognized the decoction.

"That's minaxis, a medicine we use in Alvarra."

"What's it for?"

"Headache. And in large quantities, poison to kitchen spiders." She had no wish to be reminded of the sly interest her brother had shown in the death throes of the kitchen spider. "Leave it," she urged.

The blue elf resisted her and, instead, peered inside. In the middle of the wall to his right an old man stirred a cauldron with a long-handled metal spatula. The thready flame under the black pot illuminated his aged yellow face and wispy white hairlock.

"Come in," he said with a toothless smile. He laid the spatula on the waist-high stone hearth and wiped his hands on his apron.

Irritated that Six Stix had not obeyed, Tiala shoved him aside to precede him into the room.

Larger than it had appeared from the hallway, the room must have been used for instruction, since there were stools piled atop one another on the far wall. On the left, three arched doorways led to a courtyard. "We're looking for the High Abbot," she said to the old man. "Who are you?"

"My name is Umsel. I am a gardener," he said. Underneath his apron stained red with oleander juice, he wore only a plain robe, so faded it might once have been yellow. He gestured toward the yak-hide stools, and Six Stix brought one for each of them.

Tiala sat, poised to leave at any moment. Through the arched doorways, the smell of the flowers intermingled with the simmering oleander. The familiar scent was most unwelcome, and she covered her nose against the mesmerizing humidity.

Six Stix said, "Your home is more impressive than Obsidian described it." The old man nodded, and the blue elf strolled across the room. "I'm curious about something, Umsel. The monks' fighting prowess. Particularly, what Obsidian called pressure points."

"Ah, yes," said Umsel.

Six Stix observed the old man's crafty silence. *Then, it's true. There are such points.*

The smell made Tiala more and more irritable, and her face was taut in the wan firelight. She rose to her feet. "A messenger came to my room earlier. If the High Abbot wishes to see me, I—."

"Didn't your mother teach you any manners?"

"What?" Tiala was shocked. No one spoke of the Nightwing like that.

"Or are you perhaps anxious because the sun will soon be rising?"

"That is no business of yours."

A soft tapping drew their attention to the doorway, and a young boy with the short hairlock of a new acolyte bowed to the old man. "Those you summoned are here, Eminence."

Tiala crossed her arms and paced with furious steps.

"Show them in, Gort," said Umsel, "then take the cauldron off the flame before you leave. Good lad."

The boy leapt to the task and departed while into the room came Embaza, followed by Obsidian and another monk whom the old man addressed as Jeon. Both Obsidian and Jeon were dressed in pale blue robes, whereas Embaza wore a clean white one with green medallions embroidered on the sleeves.

Six Stix noticed Obsidian's look of health and confidence. He gallantly hurried to help them with stools from the pile against the wall.

Tiala ignored Umsel with a contemptuous silence, but she looked directly at Jeon and bestowed a charming smile that brought a blush to the young man's face.

Tiala gave Umsel a curt nod, as a monarch to her vassal. "I see you enjoy playing games, Abbot."

"Life is the only game," he answered.

-64-

WHEN THEY were all seated, the High Abbot said, "I am sorry to bring you here so early. I had planned to wait until you were more rested. However, it is not every day our humble monastery is blessed by the presence of a bard." He smiled at Tiala. "We were much moved by your talent and your tale."

She lifted her chin. "Song is my way of finding relief. I'm gratified that you found favor with it."

Jeon noticed Tiala trembling and quietly got up to close the doors to the courtyard. "Thank you, Jeon," said the Abbot. The room was pleasantly dim, illuminated only by the thin flame that still flickered on the hearth.

"And you," Umsel said to Embaza, "it is also rare that we entertain a wizard of Sargoth."

Tiala glanced at Embaza. His skin was completely black now, shining with health, and only a trace of the blue dye was left in the creases of his eyelids. His eyes, though half closed, seemed calm. He had plaited his long, black hair back into a single braid. It was thick, like her brother's, but the resemblance was not so great now that she saw him in profile.

Embaza said, "I have been to many places, High Abbot, but rarely any so harmonious."

Six Stix saw Tiala admiring the wizard, and he was hurt but philosophical. After all, they were two of a kind. He doubted Embaza returned her interest. The old campaigner smiled with the confidence of experience. She'd come around.

Jeon cleared his throat. "Eminence, I would like to ask the dark ones some questions." He blushed again, with a side-glance at Tiala.

She pursed her lips.

"Certainly," answered Umsel.

Jeon rose and said to Tiala and Embaza, "Honored guests, I have studied your race for many years. At least—it would be many years by our reckoning."

Embaza's handsome face was closed. He said, "I, too, have studied my race. But I feel compelled to admit that I have never been a full citizen of Alvarra. I consider myself a Sargothian."

Jeon was taken aback. "I mean no insult, but tell me, were you exiled?"

"In a way," replied Embaza.

Tiala faced Jeon. "Direct your questions to me, why don't you?" The charm in her tone melted the youth's diffidence.

"Of course. Sorry, na'a Nightwing," he said, blushing a third time.

"Ah, you are familiar with our etiquette," said Tiala, her face lighting with pleasure.

"Was my pronunciation correct?" asked Jeon.

"Nearly perfect."

He spread his hands. "May I ask a personal question, na'a Nightwing?"

"If you wish."

"I have found nothing written about the marriage customs of the royal family." His blush deepened.

"Well, there have been arranged marriages, although, of course, it's always prudent to choose with the heart, too. Elopement is not uncommon. Secrecy adds spice, don't you think?"

The monk looked even more flustered.

"When it comes to love and sex," she said, "we are as ordinary as the next Alvarran. We put off the duties of marriage as long as possible. Surely, you, too, find it normal to taste many dishes while you're young."

Jeon swallowed, clearly embarrassed, and stammered, "The first hundred years or so?"

"What's wrong with that?" asked Tiala. She appealed to the High Abbot. "Obsidian has told me a little of your customs—your vows of celibacy—but it cannot mean no one ever strays from the rules."

The old man shook his head. "To stray from the rules on this point is to demonstrate an unwillingness to be a monk. It calls into question the most fundamental principle of our order…self-reliance."

"And the women in your order accept this principle also?"

He shook his head.

"The priestesses are not celibate, then?"

"There are no priestesses," murmured Obsidian. She stared at him, then frowned, whether in disbelief or disapproval he could not tell.

Jeon knelt before her. "Forgive my brother Obsidian—he should not have put it so tactlessly."

"Don't cater to her," said Umsel, gesturing for Jeon to return to his stool. To Tiala, he said, "This is an all-male society, a difficult thing for you to accept, I know, but you must realize—it is not easy for some of us to accept you, either. If you want our help, you must be patient with us."

Tiala said, "What do you expect to gain by cutting yourself off from the wisdom and guidance of your mothers and foremothers?"

"Serenity," said Umsel.

Embaza interrupted to say, "I have no memory of Alvarra, and am at a slight disadvantage in this discussion. However, I think we would be better served if we talked more to the point."

"Go on, please," said Umsel.

"Tiala here, whatever you may think of her prejudices, is the only hope for her people against a rival who will stop at nothing to destroy her." There was a pause as everyone digested this.

Jeon said, "Doesn't the Nightwing have an army?"

Tiala answered, "The army is only a defensive force—maybe a hundred at most. A handful of officers like me and my sister Eleppon, a battalion or two, and the Nightwing's own Ladies of Skill—the elite guards. That's all we have. For most people, combat is dangerous. It twists the soul. And only the specially trained may use weapons."

"The specially trained?" asked Obsidian.

Umsel explained, "The Nightwing holds trials each year and invites a few children to enter training. They come to live in the Royal City and learn the arts and mysteries of life and death. Some go on to become healers; others enter the army. A few return to their towns and villages to serve as peacekeepers."

Tiala's eyebrows rose. "You are extremely well informed, High Abbot."

"This is very similar to our ways at the monastery," Umsel replied. "Only a few are chosen for the fighting arts."

Embaza said, "You've left out one important factor." He turned his gaze to Tiala. "What about Dekhalis's assassins? You've said they steal and make their own weapons, hide in the back alleys of the larger cities, or hunt in bands, preying on the villages and farms of the cultivated lands."

Tiala nodded. "We've always had a few outlaws. Now they follow Dekhalis. He must have planned this for years, to be so organized."

Jeon frowned. "But what of the common man? If they aren't used to power and don't know the first thing about combat, how are they suddenly turned into soldiers who fashion their own weapons?"

"We never heeded the signs until it was too late."

"I have new information which may give us some hope," said Embaza. "I was visited last night by the Nightwing."

Tiala gasped. "Impossible."

"In a dream," he explained.

"You're mistaken," she said, deeply jealous.

Umsel said, "It is not the first time she has been inside these walls."

Tiala's eyes widened and Jeon realized she trembled in fury, not fear.

Embaza felt the sting of her anger, but ignored it to address the Abbot. "The Nightwing told me she was sending a decree to all her Orders—that I was to be allowed the use of magic while I was in Alvarra."

Tiala rose as if propelled by force, fists clenched, and stalked over to the wall beside the hearth. Gripping the stone with her fingers, she stilled her breathing. *I must exercise patience.* She spun around, and said, "That's a lie, Embaza. How dare you slander my mother? She has never flaunted custom. We're in mourning, and all such arts are forbidden."

Embaza went to her and said, "Tiala, calm yourself. You're being childish."

"Childish, am I? You would do anything to further your own ends. You're afraid of what will happen if you can't use your tricks."

He frowned dangerously, looking so much like Dekhalis that Tiala took a deep breath and closed her eyes. Umsel had also risen to his feet.

Tiala felt a touch on her sleeve and turned to the old man, his face suddenly as ageless as that of the High Priestess in Alvarra.

"Na'a Nightwing, come sit down. I am sorry to have been so hard on you." He led her to the stool once again. "You are far from home and everything is very different—and, no doubt, frightening." She started to protest and he patted her hand. "Don't deny it."

Tiala looked at him with suspicion. A man. A surface man…and a celibate. Her face showed her confusion.

Umsel continued, "Embaza—a dark elf himself—gave you the cloak that saved your life, did he not? While he suffered in torment and terror, you were comforted."

She stared at the Abbot, her face a mask.

"And the old warrior here nearly gave his life in your service."

She looked at Six Stix, her eyebrows lifted, as if asking forgiveness. She blinked back a tear of shame.

"Do you wish to elaborate on the superiority of the female species?" asked Umsel.

Tiala's voice shook with icy formality, "Forgive me, High Abbot, if the manners my mother taught me are different from yours. I must admit, I've never been in a council where a man was in charge."

"Would you feel more comfortable if your female companions—Polah Fennwarren and Gudrun of Estenhame—were summoned?"

"You've no right to use the dwarf's personal name," she snapped. "She'll be insulted that you announced it for all to hear."

"She will forgive my ignorance," said Umsel with unruffled politeness.

Tiala's voice was like tempered steel. "And will I?"

Both monks in the room became increasingly nervous with this exchange. Obsidian entreated, "Princess, no one is trying to dishonor you."

Rising to his feet, Jeon said, "She is an Alvarran monarch, the proudest of creatures. She should be surrounded by servants—and guards."

Tiala rolled her eyes upward, her breast heaving. "First I am a 'dark one'—now I am a 'creature.' We are talking about fundamental principles—not trappings of monarchy." She pointed to Embaza. "Do you recognize my status as your sovereign?"

He shrugged noncommittally.

"It's apparent to me that you have no memory of your homeland, and to cover this deficiency, you insist on fabricating a relationship with my mother."

He crossed his arms, and a nerve jumped beside his mouth. "Suit yourself."

During this exchange, Umsel had sat, eyes half-closed, his breathing as soft and regular as if he were napping. Suddenly he looked around and fastened his eyes on Obsidian. "Perhaps you've thought over the problem I posed for you."

The monk was surprised; why was the old man bringing up a private matter here? "Yes, Eminence. I have pondered it thoroughly."

"And what have you decided?" asked Umsel.

Obsidian looked at Tiala with the open-faced conviction reserved for the innocent. "I, too, have been studying. I have learned that in Alvarra, I would be called 'Diahrmidar.' Isn't that so?"

"Yes," said Tiala. "It is an old name, reflecting our respect for the smooth, black rock that the earth has used to carve Alvarran cities."

"To further the knowledge of my Order, and to fulfill the meaning of my name, I rededicate myself to your cause, Princess Tiala."

"Na'a Nightwing," corrected Jeon.

Tiala said, "No, Jeon. To Obsidian I will always be…Princess." She touched the youth's shoulder. "Thank you, champion."

Umsel said, "And what of the noble Embaza? Was his sacrifice of no value?"

The two dark elves stared at each other, and a palpable taste seemed to linger in the air. "I do not wish to leave without you," she said.

Embaza heard the truth in her voice. "We will mend our differences, my sister."

At the word 'sister' Tiala's eyes widened. She remembered her nightmare, him turning into Dekhalis, his cold hands on her throat.

Umsel said, "Yes, make peace, you two. The Nightwing did indeed visit

255

your dream, wizard, as she visited mine before you arrived. We are old friends, Avenwyndar and I." The Abbot ignored Tiala's gasp.

She stared at both of them and licked her lips. The cut on her lower lip stung anew. "My mother has not visited me since I left." Her tone was transparent, a mix of anger, hurt and bewilderment.

Embaza eyes were grave. "Perhaps she is protecting you. Your brother is using some kind of magic artifact to communicate with his minions. I met one of them at the Manor, an albino named Morbigon. I sense that we will meet again. He sent foul creatures that attacked Polah and me—and you, remember?"

"But then, why would Mother take a chance contacting you?"

"She must have a good reason," answered Umsel. "My friend, you need to learn a little trust."

Tiala leaned forward, looking deeply into the old man's eyes. "You know, High Abbot? I like you. You're an interesting man and a worthy opponent. What a consort you'd have made."

He chuckled. "Would that I were younger."

Six Stix smirked. This wench was full of surprises.

The Abbot turned to him and said, "Be careful you don't gorge yourself on whims while destiny goes hungry, Lord Stixan. Your brother is not suited to rule Cern Keep."

Six Stix's blue skin turned almost purple, but he cleared his throat. "Thank you for the advice, Abbot, but I have business elsewhere."

Tiala took the blue elf's arm. "He's coming with me. There will be no lack of destiny in Alvarra, I assure you."

Umsel moved to the stone hearth. "Good luck. Send word to me before you leave." Although he appeared to be speaking to Tiala, each of the others felt the Abbot's words personally.

The party headed for the door, led by Jeon. In the hallway Keth appeared, quite out of breath. He gave a quick nod to Obsidian, entered quickly, and announced, "Eminence, there's trouble."

The old man looked up. "What is it, Keth?"

"The grandson of the Patriarch of the Desert—Prince Mischa, at our very gates. He is asking a lot of questions about our guests."

"Give him the rooms by the mimosa garden."

"But, Eminence, you know his reputation," said Keth.

"He seeks sanctuary. We cannot turn him away. Invite him to have dinner with me here, in my study."

Embaza said, "Abbot, he is dangerous and carries magic with him always. No doubt, he has some device that has caused him to follow us. Yet he has no real understanding of such things."

The Abbot nodded. "Ignorance is always dangerous. Leave him to me."

While the others filed out, Umsel stopped Obsidian. "My son."

The young monk looked into the kindly eyes that held so many surprises. He had been granted few private audiences with the Abbot. The last had been in early childhood.

Umsel gestured toward the courtyard, and Obsidian opened the doors and followed the Abbot out into the incipient dawn. There were no flowers on the thorn bushes, but clumps of thistle imparted a downy beauty in the wan light. "How does it feel to be a full monk?"

"To be rewarded simply for surviving—I still find it hard to believe, Eminence. Perhaps it is a dream from which I will awaken."

Umsel sat on a stone bench in the middle of the courtyard and invited the monk to join him. The Abbot leaned over and brushed a hoary thistle top with his fingers. "In time, you will come to regard yourself as no less important than this plant here." He straightened. "Tell me more about your pledge to the aristocrat."

"Eminence, it was not a rash decision. At least, not this time." Obsidian noticed with chagrin the Abbot's smile. "I believe that my destiny lies in Alvarra. It's a cause worthy of my training."

Umsel folded his hands inside his robe. "And what of the Blacktooth Tribe?"

"My bonding with them was tied up in the rigors of the moment. I had no other choice." He paused. "That they treated me with kindness and respect was good fortune."

"Fortune?"

"Sorry, Abbot. I mean, I did not ask for it. I was accepted into the tribe, and I made peace with that fact, and with whatever obligations it might include."

Umsel was quiet for a minute before he spoke, adding to Obsidian's discomfort. "When you speak of destiny, imagine that a small bird has landed on your shoulder. You did not call it and you do not speak its language. But it is imperative that you form some sort of understanding with it, or it will fly away."

Obsidian breathed the fragrance of thistle and briar in this rather austere garden.

The Abbot continued. "You speak of obligation, but do you not see that it may go both ways?"

"Yes, Eminence, I think I understand. If I take all that has happened into myself and tie each event onto my path with soft knots, then in the end, I will have a strong but flexible rope."

"Well said," said Umsel, "but do not tie the knots too tightly. A rope is not a bird. What did Tolimane teach you about quests?"

Obsidian thought a moment, feeling more at ease. "He said that one always has a personal reason beyond the collective goal."

"And what is yours, my young monk?"

Obsidian raised his chin. A ghostly thought was suddenly plain. "To face my fear of caves."

The old Abbot smiled, and his face shone in the pale thorn garden, awash with the pallid light of dawn. "You are young."

Obsidian gave him a quizzical look.

"You will have all the more time to teach others when your travels are over," said the Abbot.

"I will still be too young to teach."

The old man's eyes bored into Obsidian's. "What does old age have to do with wisdom? Do you think that is my secret? If so, I would sooner be an elf or a gnome."

Obsidian realized the Abbot was waiting for him to comment. "So, as humans we can only rely on experience?"

"Yes, experience is our greatest teacher. I never cease to court her favor, while others take her for granted. I have observed that you do the same." He slipped his hands out of his sleeves and flexed his fingers. "Leave me now. I must prepare to meet the Prince."

Obsidian rose, bowed, and left the thorn garden, glowing with the peculiar euphoria that followed an audience with the High Abbot Umsel.

Part Two

Prologue

Archives of Alvarra

History of the Siadhin Lords

In the reign of the High King Vandor, the Siadhin Lords were charged with the task of building a Library of Magic. They assembled their priest-magicians and the sounds of the pens of scribes were heard through every bell in the dark-elven cities. The Siadhin Lord Ryddys was most assiduous in his efforts to gather lore, and his four sons scoured the country for artifacts and men of knowledge.

By the end of his cycle, the Library became so renowned that wizards from far and wide came to Alvarra to learn at the citadel of magic. It was thus that treasured books were copied by the men of the surface, and the famed Towers of Sargothas were built beside the great Sargoth Sea. It was thus, too, that the surface people developed their superstitions about the magic of the dark elves.

Even in the time of the Nightwings, the Library is consulted by the Priestesses of Miralor and Drimma, as well as the lesser orders. However, it is a little known fact that many of the old books were looted by consorts of the Nightwings, who, having access to special favors, kept them as personal treasures.

Thus some of the oldest lore of Alvarra now resides in the Merimn'a among the outcast wizards and other outlaws. High Priestess Kalista has said that such books are better forgotten, since they were crafted in the time when men ruled Alvarra and are not suitable for the service of Miralor. However, it is argued by the Drimman Priestess Theowla Twomothers that these books should be returned to the Library where their knowledge can be used again.

Time is a firefly that never glows in the same place twice.
—Alvarran proverb.

-1-

WHEN POLAH AWOKE, she reached for Embaza, but her hand found only the muslin sheet. She squinted into the bright courtyard and tiptoed into the adjoining rooms, but he was not there either. "How long have I slept?" she mumbled, quickly throwing water on her face from the basin on the dresser. Her clothes had been cleaned and pressed during the night, and she was grateful for the impeccable hospitality of the monks. She wondered if they knew she was a shape-changer and if, like Obsidian, they were all untainted by superstition.

Finding a coarse brush on the bureau, she attacked her tangled thicket of red hair. By the time all of the knots were out, she was impatient to join her companions.

She had satisfied her hunger on the dunes in the night and felt refreshed at the memory of hunting in the moonlight. However, the smell of food promised company, and possibly she would find Embaza at table, so she let her nose lead the way.

A few doors down the hall, she found a hearty repast laid out on a long wooden table. She was surprised to see the General was the sole diner.

The dwarf seemed to have taken some pains with her appearance. Her gray-brown curls were still damp, and her beard was combed. Her brown eyes sparkled with the light that followed a good sleep. She wore her own clothing and, like Polah's, it had been cleaned during the night.

Gudrun smiled good-naturedly, but Polah was conscious, as always, of a certain lack of warmth toward her. Resolutely, Polah took a chair on the opposite side of the table. "Good morning, General. You look rested."

With a nod of mild appreciation, Gudrun returned to her porridge.

Elbows on the table, Polah leaned her chin on her hands, "You don't like me much, do you?" Once the words were out, she had butterflies in her stomach, but tried to ignore them. It would be better to know.

The General swallowed, wiped her mouth with her napkin and set down her spoon. She gave Polah a measured look, and from a small tankard of milk, drank a long draught.

Polah waited, watching carefully for any change of expression that might be a clue to the dwarf's thoughts. With a sinking feeling, she realized the General might not answer. Polah wondered what she was supposed to do next. She didn't have much experience with this sort of confrontation.

She was saved further confusion by Gudrun, who said, "I'm afraid you'll attack me some night in my sleep."

Polah stiffened, balling her fists in rage that had brewed a long time. Her anger was out of proportion to the dwarf's statement, but it wasn't often she had the chance to answer her detractors. "That's unfair," she said, intending her response to sound dignified, but managing little more than a growl.

Gudrun locked eyes with the shape-changer, and by habit adopted the soothing tone she often used with her troops. "Now, now, I was joking. Eat some of this loaf while it's still hot."

Polah's glazed eyes focused without recognition on the thick slabs of whole-grain bread piled before her. Her mind was paralyzed with the intensity of her emotions. The unnatural silence was broken by Gudrun's noisy eating.

It was upon this provocative scene that their companions entered. Tiala's skin glistened in the wan light. She was relieved that this room did not receive direct sunlight. Embaza wore a black robe threaded with gold, which he had found laid out on his bed that morning.

Even Six Stix looked like his former self. The blue elf walked in with his usual swagger and took a seat as far away from Gudrun as possible.

As a former resident of the monastery, Obsidian was quite comfortable in his monk's robe, his hairlock still wet from his morning bath in the fountain. He sensed the tension between Polah and Gudrun. Once everyone was seated, he said, "Tell us about Alvarra, Princess. What should we expect?"

Tiala's lilting voice betrayed the strain of urgency beneath. "The deep world will be dark and cold compared to this place. There is but one entrance to Alvarra, and that ancient portal is usually guarded by peacekeepers. They will want to know who you are and your intentions. My face is not well-known in the uplands and dressed as I am, I can claim to be a forager. Some brave souls still gather herbs from the upworld."

Gudrun gulped a morsel of bread, and said, "Your brother may have posted his own sentries there."

"Yes," said Tiala nervously. "We'll have to stay in character—just visitors. I wish I knew exactly what he is planning." She glanced at Embaza, and he raised his eyebrows. "Do you have the ability to farsee?"

The wizard grimaced. "Curse the desert. That was one of the scrolls I lost."

Tiala's anger flared. "You and your scraps of parchment. My priestesses at home travel worlds of dream and shadow." She took a quick sip of water from the earthenware goblet at her hand and looked up at the stricken faces around her with a pang of guilt.

"Never mind," she said with a sigh. "The first part of Alvarra is a warren of shops and taverns where visitors come to trade. Mostly elves." She glanced at Gudrun. "Of course, citizens of Tskurl are free to travel anywhere." Neither of them mentioned that dwarves rarely did.

Six Stix asked, "How will we find your brother?"

"My mother the Nightwing will know. We'll go straight through my secret tunnels until we reach the Royal City. It would be too dangerous elsewhere. Not only are visitors strongly discouraged, but there is much chaos by now if I know Dekhalis." The dark elf spooned a thick glob of honey onto her bread.

There was a tense silence as the others tried to imagine the ordeal ahead.

Six Stix asked, "Who are these peacekeepers you mentioned?"

Tiala dabbed a drop of honey from a corner of her mouth. "Elite troops, trained by the Nightwing's own guards. The Ladies of Skill. They could be of great help to us."

"But they are in mourning," said Gudrun. Her hand unconsciously went to the hilt of her blade.

Tiala grimaced. "Believe me, they are trained not to be hampered by a little thing like a lack of weapons. Although against a poisoned blade…"

Obsidian paused to take a deep breath. He had been ravenous and totally engaged in shoveling the familiar, hearty food into his mouth. "Maybe the High Abbot will allow me to train you in some of our weaponless forms."

Tiala frowned. "We have little time, but do what you can."

Six Stix's pointed ears flecked outward and the indigo scar crinkled with his smile. "That's what I've been waiting to hear. I'm getting soft, traveling with the likes of you." He winked at Gudrun, whose eyes widened before she scowled and ducked her head, pretending great interest in her porridge.

Polah asked the monk, "What's happened to you? You seem so much more cheerful."

Obsidian was caught with a mouthful of porridge, but Six Stix laughed, "What did you expect? A night with a tribe of barbarian giants, a trek across an erg of quake-sand—."

"It wasn't an erg. And that's not what I'm talking about," she insisted.

Obsidian could not stifle a grin of pride. "I was given my full investiture as a monk. I passed the first test."

Embaza had been brooding quietly. Now he said, "Our teachers throw us to the mercy of the world, never lifting a finger to help. Do you not feel betrayed that you were sent by yours on such a senseless quest?"

"Why should I? Life is a bowl of wisdom. Either I eat it or push it away. Ultimately, it is my own choice." Obsidian shrugged and took another bite of porridge.

Embaza leaned forward. "But the whole matter was of their devising—not fate's. Can you not see that?"

Obsidian put down his spoon. "Tell me. What do you consider to be the ultimate test of character?"

Embaza allowed a brief silence before he said, "How one greets the unknown."

The monk smiled as if the answer pleased him. "And do you not trust anyone besides yourself?"

Embaza answered without delay. "No one."

Polah looked up. *Not even me?*

Obsidian said, "My teachers were wise to withhold the ultimate nature of the test from me. I have profited by that wisdom. Perhaps you misjudge your own teachers, Embaza."

The wizard's voice was dry with sarcasm. "There is nothing they can do for me now." But he wondered, remembering his moment of doubt in the arena, faced with the arcane threat of the sand demon. *There are always more secrets and new levels of mastery.* He changed the subject, turning aside to Polah, whose plate was full. "Aren't you eating?"

She dabbed at her mouth with the coarse napkin to cover her embarrassment. She wished he hadn't brought it up. "I'm just taking my time."

On the other side of the table, Tiala and Gudrun were bent over a piece of sun-bleached cloth. Tiala pointed with her long, sensitive fingers, guiding Gudrun's stubby ones. The dwarf's map-making ability was uncanny, considering her gnarled, battle-scarred digits. On the homespun napkin, with a soft piece of black stone from the garden, she had drawn a detailed map of the entry passages to Alvarra and Tskurl, the main tunnel leading to the cultivated farmlands of the dark elves, and under Tiala's tutelage, further canals and tunnels leading to the major cities below.

Gudrun said, "What will we do for money in the underground? Won't we have to convert everything into *luaavh* if we go in disguise?"

Six Stix's ears perked up. "Lua? What's that?"

Tiala said, "One silver piece. Literally, *luaavh* means Moon's Tears. In Alvarra, we're on a silver standard. Everything composed of silver is more valuable, all the way down to gold at the bottom of the scale."

The blue elf said, bemused, "And how does silver convert to gold, then?"

"One *luaavh* equals…oh, one thousand *z'a*—gold pieces. It depends on where the *z'a* was mined. The gold of the Merimn'a is a little more valuable—not as flashy—say, eight hundred to one." She shrugged. " But gold is very soft, really a rather worthless metal."

Six Stix remained quiet, calculating. Unwittingly, the dark elf had opened a whole new avenue of conjecture for him.

Polah asked, "Where do you think Prince Mischa is?"

Obsidian said, "If I know the High Abbot, he's put the Prince in the most luxurious and closely guarded room in the monastery."

Something lurked in the back of Embaza's mind, but its disturbing nature refused to come to the surface. He changed the subject. "What is this drink?"

"Yak's milk. You may have seen the herds on the hillside behind the monastery. We raise them for their silky hides and milk, and they are useful in the fields."

"Do you think we might use them for mounts?" Tiala asked. "Are they strong beasts?"

Polah laughed nervously, her pointed teeth somehow atavistic. "I used to ride them when I was a child on my father's farm. They were ten times as big as I was."

Obsidian said, "I'll ask the High Abbot. He holds open council each evening, before sparring practice. He likes to free his mind before physical exertion."

"You're joking," said Six Stix.

"Not at all. Come and see for yourself," said the monk. "You're all welcome. That is, if we're staying."

Heads turned toward Tiala, and she sighed. "One more day might make us stronger."

Gudrun nodded. "Very wise, my Lady."

-2-

PREPARATION FOR their journey was a simple matter, since none of them had many belongings.

Umsel had opened the monastery stores to them. They now had medicinals, food and water to replace that which had been buried in the sand.

Once again, the wizard lamented the loss of his precious saddle bags. He didn't even have his dagger. The memory of some spells remained, and he realized that if nothing else, his teachers had given him the keys to calm himself when those around him were panicking. He spent several hours in meditation, and Polah had to find company elsewhere.

She walked down a corridor with no particular goal in mind. As she walked, she pondered whether to tell Embaza about the growing intensity of her fox-senses and the premonition that something magical was occurring within her. She felt as if there were a profound evolution hanging over her, like an incipient storm. She missed the narcotic balm of his presence as she prowled the halls aimlessly, carrying her shoes in her hands.

Somehow, she had lost her way, and found herself in a part of the complex that seemed less austere. The walls were painted with thick coats of white-wash and the floors were polished. An occasional curtain decorated the stark passageways. Her sensitive nostrils filled with the luxurious scent of lilies and mimosa. Was this an especially sacred part of the monastery? She was suddenly alert, her senses primed. She wondered what the penalty was for trespassing here.

She turned to leave when she heard a voice she knew, somewhat thin and petulant, from the end of the hall, behind a curtained doorway. Holding her breath, she tiptoed in bare feet toward the sound.

At the edge of the curtain, she paused, trying to gauge whether the speaker was facing her. When she determined it was safe, she peeked inside the bright, inviting room.

Even from the back, she recognized the flaxen-haired Prince Mischa. He sat cross-legged on a cushion, facing a richly scented garden of mimosa, speaking to someone just out of her view. She found the cloying sweetness of the flowers nauseating, but she stayed to listen, flattening herself against the doorway as she peered in.

"Yes, Master, the locket has guided me well. This is the last refuge between the Outland Territory and the Great Forest."

Who is he talking to? The open courtyard absorbed the sound of his words, but the Prince suddenly raised his voice.

"I am s-sorry, Lord, but how can I destroy her here? This is a stronghold of fighting monks. Believe me, I've seen them in action."

The voice that answered was louder and scathing in its indifference: "I have no time for simpletons or cowards."

Polah could not discern the rest, but felt the scrape of that cold voice down her back. She heard the clink of objects. The Prince seemed to be fumbling around, looking for something.

"This little thing? This is the Bihillit Seed?"

Polah heard a murmured answer.

"As you command, I will use this to send her to you."

Polah gasped, and strained to hear more, but the silken voice must have cautioned him to be quiet, because the Prince continued in a whisper. Even with her keen senses, she could not discern any more of the conversation.

When she saw him prepare to get up, she sprinted back down the hall, her bare feet making soft thuds on the stone floor. She kept running until she found a familiar passageway, then paused to catch her breath before dashing to the door of the rooms she shared with Embaza. She was aware of the shimmer of a spell in the air, but she barely noticed it. Belatedly, it dawned on her that Embaza must have cast a protective ward on the doors.

She ignored the sizzling sound as she turned the knob, enduring the pain as her delicate skin exploded into blisters. Panting, she burst into the room. "He has a magic seed or something —to send Tiala to her brother..."

Embaza strove to bring his consciousness back to the room. His cat-like eyes opened to slits. "Slow down and start again."

When she had explained what she had seen, Embaza knew his fears were confirmed. "The Prince is in league with the demon himself. He must be using an artifact. He was probably speaking to a *sending*—or some other manifestation of Dekhalis's. You were right to interrupt me, little flower."

"Don't call me that," exploded Polah, suddenly aware of the pain that wracked her body. "I braved this—this agony to come to you." She laughed on a sob. "Don't ever call me that."

Embaza rose and embraced her. At his touch, her pain subsided, slipping off her shoulders like a gown. "Sssh, Polah. I'm sorry, love."

Huge tears formed in her eyes. Her life had contained so little love, she was never prepared for it.

"Come," said Embaza. "I'll need your help. We'll plan a surprise for the Prince—and his master."

-3-

GUDRUN LOOKED forward to watching the High Abbot spar with the young monks. She suspected he was every bit as good as Obsidian had promised.

Six Stix was more skeptical. He had seen the ravages that old age could do to a fighter. There was a limit to what one could do to preserve his muscle and sinew. Six had hoped to spend the afternoon persuading the lovely Tiala of the many benefits of his ardor, but the dark elf was nowhere to be found.

When one of Umsel's messengers stopped Tiala in the hallway, asking if she wanted anything, she requested a quiet place to think. The boy led her to a narrow room, facing a long courtyard, protected by the shadows of eaves. She thanked him and breathed a sigh of relief to be alone. She suddenly realized how much she had needed this.

Afternoon approached, and on a curious impulse, Tiala drew back the curtain to see the shadows brushing over the garden. The immensity of her ordeal washed over her, and exhaustion slowed her breathing. She was too tired to be afraid, even of the sunlight. She realized it would never have such a grip on her again. It was a familiar nuisance, a known force, but no longer an evil one.

She clenched her fingers and flexed her arms to stretch the stiff muscles. She sympathized with Six Stix. It wasn't good to let oneself get out of practice. She identified within herself the cocoon of resolve that had been coiling itself for weeks. The politics and petty concerns of the others faded from her mind. Whatever their reasons for aiding her, she was on her own in a real, spiritual way that none of them really comprehended—not even Embaza.

She smiled. For all her rancor at his rejection, she felt closer to him than to the others. Embaza was of her blood. She must teach him what it meant to be a dark elf, and—she could admit it to herself—he could teach her, too. A picture of the High Abbot flitted across her mind.

She was eager to encounter him again and rather hoped he would be bested by one of his own monks. She wished there was some way she could show him what a real fighter could do. Her own elite guards were easily as graceful as Obsidian and twice as ruthless.

As it turned out, none of them was prepared for what occurred, not even Obsidian, who had seen Umsel in action.

-4-

MISCHA AWOKE to darkness, and for a moment, could not remember where he was. Then, the vaguely familiar shapes of table, pillow and curtain became discernible in the pall of evening. He lurched to his knees, rubbing his eyes. His head felt heavy. How long had he slept?

Next to his rumpled couch, a curve of dull crystal peeped from under its dusk-colored shroud. Seeing it, Mischa's blue eyes glowed feverishly.

His hand slipped into his right pocket and extracted a hideous, dung-like nugget that nestled in his palm. *The Bihillit Seed.* He shivered, remembering Dekhalis's words: "To activate the Seed, wet it and place it on the ground near her. When it begins to grow, make a swift exit. Whatever you do, don't extract it before it roots."

The Prince swallowed, remembering his next question: "What are its effects—Lord King?" It still rankled him to use such a title even in private. Dekhalis had impaled him with his wide, luminous eyes. "It is better you don't know."

A booming gong halted his uneasy reverie. Its sonorous clarity sliced through the evening quiet, wiping the wrinkles from his brow and scattering his fears to the winds.

He thrust the wizened seed back into his pocket and adjusted the new clothing provided by the monks. The homespun pants and tunic were of poor quality, but at least they fit, and now he had desert slippers made of softened leather. He cradled the orb with as much tenderness as a mother with a newborn babe and held it to his breast for a moment before placing it into his sack.

He smoothed back his straggling, blond hair, hefted the bag over his shoulder and took a last look around, eyes blazing with the fire in his belly. He strode down the corridor in the direction of the reverberations.

Two monks appeared behind him, and more came from side passages as he walked. Since he had no reason to believe otherwise, he assumed that they, too, were following the summons of the gong. Mischa waved his hand and smiled with the aplomb of habit. Charm curled from the corners of his mouth. Even in the plain, brown clothing, his squat figure exuded an aura of wealth and authority.

All ears were filled with the deep ringing clarion, and when it stopped, the monastery vibrated with echoes. As Mischa walked, more monks entered the hallway ahead of him. He followed them through an arched doorway into a large, octagonal inner courtyard lit by candles in parchment lanterns. Pools of overlapping colored light danced over sand and stone benches.

He noticed the sheen of sweat on the arms of a nearby monk, and his educated nostrils detected a familiar tang—the adrenaline of combat. He nearly fainted with excitement. This was *their* arena.

Mischa strained to see amid the towering humans. There were eight identical archways, through which a steady stream of monks entered. Peering ahead, he caught sight of a circular area in the center of the courtyard, flanked by stone benches. Rayed pathways led from each entrance. His hand crept to the locket, where it seemed to burn his skin.

He pushed through the throng of men to get a seat near the center.

Suddenly, he found himself face to face with a handsome young monk, who squatted in the aisle next to him. The youth brushed his dark hairlock away from his unlined face and said with utmost respect, "Excuse me, your Lordship, but I must ask you to leave your bag at the door."

273

The Prince's eyes flickered with annoyance as he strove to mask his alarm. "Nonsense. I can't possibly let this out of my possession." His hand tightened on the neck of the sack.

The youth blushed. "There will be no harm—believe me, it's only a formality."

The Prince scowled. "And if I refuse?"

"Is there a problem, Farr?" said a deep voice.

Mischa and Farr looked up at the smiling face of an older monk whose hairlock was tinged with iron. He was dressed in a knee-length, dark blue tunic, belted by a leather thong. His hands were clasped before him, and Mischa could feel an air of stubbornness radiating from the corded body.

The Prince's eyes narrowed. "I demand to know why I am being singled out in this way. I wish to see the High Abbot to protest this treatment."

The older monk gestured for Farr to rise and said, "I am Master Riddel, the High Abbot's emissary. He expressly hoped that you would attend our evening ceremony, but if you don't wish to, that is certainly your privilege as an honored guest."

Mischa knew he had been outwitted. With as much good grace as he could muster, he handed the sack to the acolyte.

"Careful," he snapped, "there are things in there that might bite you." He was pleased by the apprehension in Farr's eyes.

Master Riddel escorted him to a seat on the front row of benches, where no one else's head would block his view. The Prince gave his curt thanks, and Riddel withdrew to a seat several rows behind him.

Mischa resisted the urge to finger the seed in his pocket. No room for mistakes now. These monks were too observant.

Prompted by an obscure impulse, Mischa looked up and gaped in amazement. The immense dome of dark blue sky sprinkled with evening stars presided overhead. The desert wind was still and the cool air was fragrant with the redolence of the coming night. For a moment, he regretted the overbearing architecture of his own arena. The blossom-like lanterns cast their pale light around the edges of the courtyard as more and more people came in, but the center of the area remained in semi-darkness.

The Prince was so occupied by his own thoughts he did not notice the dark-elven beauty and her party, led by Obsidian, who ushered them to seats on the opposite side, near the front row.

It was only when four torch-bearing monks came to stand at equal points around the circle that the Prince was given a clear view of his enemies. Embaza, then Tiala, Six Stix, that traitor the General, and Obsidian. All of them here—in one place. He could hardly contain his elation—or his fears.

Mischa caught Tiala's eyes across the circle. He leered as the dark elf gave a start, then nudged Embaza at her side, but the wizard was already quite aware of Mischa, and the Prince felt Embaza's eyes upon him like twin coals of blackness. Once again, he resisted the urge to touch the Bihillit Seed.

The locket burned like fire now, and he pressed the cloth of his tunic between it and his skin as sweat danced on his brow. As always, he sensed the powerful draw of the magic in the artifacts he carried, and was both wary of and attracted to these forces beyond his control. He jerked as the huge gong sounded.

The monk seated to his right must have noticed his discomfiture, for he explained, "The gong rings to remind us of our duty in life. That's why it is placed on the north side of the courtyard." Mischa looked at him, nonplussed, but the monk had turned his attention back to the center, where the High Abbot beamed at the assembly. Mischa had not seen him enter.

"I am a window on this wondrous world," said the High Abbot, opening his arms and pivoting around, his intense, brown eyes lighting on one face after another. His thin, white hairlock shone in the torchlight and his seamed face stood out in high relief. His body seemed to disappear under the robe of inky black.

Mischa shrank at the light in those eyes as they rested on him briefly.

The monks murmured their reply in unison: "My body is a gateway to truth." Umsel then bowed to all, and each of them bowed in turn.

Another monk in a white robe came forward and poured a line of glistening mica into a grooved circle around the ring. As he retreated back into the crowd, the High Abbot intoned, "Within the circle, there is power." And the answer came, "Only within the circle."

Then Umsel unbelted his robe, letting it fall to the sand. A young acolyte pushed forward and gathered it up in an easy motion, racing to the opposite side of the circle.

Beneath the doughy, wrinkled skin, the High Abbot's body rippled with well-tended muscularity. In his short, black breeches and tunic, he moved with the fluid grace of a much younger man, but Mischa had seen too many fighters, including monks, to be impressed by appearances.

Umsel called out, "Nessim," and clapped his hands twice.

A tall, thin monk came forward from one of the rear benches, striding confidently toward the center, his long hairlock as black as a raven's wing. His beaked face was determined, and Nessim bowed to the High Abbot. The gong sounded again, and to his own shame, Mischa flinched.

Nessim adjusted his pale blue breeches, tucking up the sides to give more freedom to his legs. Mischa enjoyed watching Tiala and Gudrun for their reaction, knowing they would be at pains to show no interest in this manly act. He suddenly remembered the fox-woman. Where was she? A hint of warning teased his mind like an itch in a place he couldn't scratch.

The two combatants circled each other slowly three times before either made an attack. Nessim struck first, his fist aimed squarely at the High Abbot's midsection. It was unclear to Mischa exactly what Umsel did to parry this move, but in another moment, Nessim was flung behind the Abbot to land rudely on the sand. The stricken monk raised his head, leaning his weight on his forearm, and Mischa got a clear sight of the monk's chagrin as he pulled his arm back across the silvery line of mica.

Nimbly, Nessim clambered to his feet, turned and bowed to the High Abbot. Umsel smiled, returning the bow. Then the old monk raised his hands and began a series of slow, hypnotic movements. Nessim mimicked his style, and the two opponents circled each other, hands writhing like snakes.

And like a snake, Umsel struck with just the forefingers of one hand, landing a sure blow to Nessim's collarbone. The young monk staggered back a few feet, but did not fall.

Nessim looked behind him, but he was still within the circle. Gathering himself quickly, he jumped in a dazzling somersault over Umsel's head, landing a shoulder jab with his foot that knocked the old man off balance.

For a moment, Umsel swayed like a tree in the breeze, then he chuckled, giving Mischa the impression that the High Abbot could have easily deflected the blow.

Nessim turned, and seeing the High Abbot's position unchanged, bowed again. Mischa detected a sly smile lurking at the corners of Nessim's mouth, as he tucked and rolled across the floor, leaping to his feet as he came up, and in another graceful motion, landed with his hands on Umsel's shoulders.

As Nessim's kicking feet soared upward, his whole weight descended on the ancient monk, but Umsel squatted and then uprooted himself—again, like a tree—and in the process, Nessim's body was hurled to the ground with great force. This time, he landed fully outside the silver circle.

Umsel stood with folded arms as the young monk struggled to his feet, gasping for breath. With a reddened face, Nessim clasped his hands and bowed for the last time that evening, then left the center of the courtyard.

Unlike in Mischa's arena, there was no applause, just a few murmurs of respectful comment. The gong sounded again, but now Mischa was prepared for it. He leaned back and thrust his hands into his pockets, attempting an insouciance he did not feel. He didn't want to miss his chance to use the Seed against the dark elf—and yet, it was many years since he had enjoyed the luxury of a front row seat in such a contest.

He did not have long to wait. In the wake of the gong's booming baritone, Umsel called out, "Inota," and there was a gasp from several of the monks behind Mischa. This must be someone special, he thought. *Just as I suspected.*

This is the real battle. The other one was a warm-up.

The monk who came to stand before Umsel was seasoned, his yellow tunic stained with age, his legs and forearms puckered with old scars. To the delight of the Prince, a young acolyte hurried forward to hand the newcomer a large, bronze saber with a curving blade.

Umsel smiled, bowed and said, "Master Inota, I am honored."

Inota's shaggy eyebrows curved upwards, his long, heavy mustache twitched. "It is I who am honored, Sage," he said.

The High Abbot began to circle. "Sage, is it? Now, you flatter me."

"Not at all," said Inota, as he matched Umsel's movements, hand and foot.

They moved like mirror images, or like insects on the face of a mirror, giving the impression of more men than appeared to the eye. Umsel turned a full circle, threading his steps intricately, leaving no telltale footprint.

While Inota mirrored him step for step, he said, "You are in fine form tonight, Eminence."

The High Abbot answered with two handsprings, and once again, Inota followed, a half-second behind. His saber grazed the sand, leaving a thin line six inches long.

"Is it heavy?" teased Umsel.

Inota shrugged and whirled the saber around his head three times, then let it fly in Umsel's direction.

The High Abbot leapt four feet into the air, his toes so close to the saber that for a moment, it appeared to Mischa that the old man was riding upon it. When his feet touched down, there was a dark blur of motion between his legs, and Master Inota came up hard with his fist.

Mischa winced, shutting his eyes for a moment, but when he opened them, it was Inota who was pinned to the sand, the High Abbot's thumbs applying pressure to the monk's windpipe.

"Do you concede the contest for this evening, Inota?" There was a grunted reply, unintelligible.

Umsel giggled with what seemed to Mischa childish delight, as he jumped off Inota's body and did a somersault.

Old habits die hard, and Mischa had interfered in many a contest. As unprincipled as he was about some things, he still disliked an uneven battle. Without thinking, he took the Bihillit Seed from his pocket, and cupping it in his hands, he spat on it and tossed it into the center of the circle.

The monks on either side of him jumped up immediately, and one of them was inches away from the missile, which immediately grew roots that plunged deep into the sand. With the speed of a diving hawk, Umsel uprooted it, even as the plant sent a dark green vine to encircle his left thigh. Flames of crackling red lightning tinged the air, and Umsel screamed, "Don't touch it—you'll be burned." Seed and stalk kept growing, as Umsel wrestled with it. "Stand back. I'm going to—"

Whatever he had been about to do, he would never do. A loud explosion filled the courtyard with dark smoke. Everywhere the shouts and choking obscured clear-headed thought and action. For once, Mischa's short stature was an asset. He crouched down and gulped for breath.

In the din, Mischa recognized Embaza yelling, "Let me through. Let me through." The Prince ducked back into the crowd and grabbed the nearest monk. "Where's my sack? My treasure? I must have it—now!"

The monk shook him off, choking, a dazed and helpless expression on his face. Mischa sprinted through the weave of robed and bare legs to the nearest doorway. He found the pile of bags stowed neatly in a corner inside the courtyard and pawed through them, frantically, locating his own by feel. He plunged his hands into it, rooting around until he was sure the orb was there.

He snatched up the sack and turned to face a tall shape lunging in his direction. Mischa's attempt to dart around it was fouled by a long, black robe. Strong hands gripped him, and he squirmed, biting the dark fingers with his teeth, but the figure did not let go, and a familiar voice said, "Now, I've got you, you devil."

In desperation, Mischa reached into the sack, and grabbed the first item that came to his hand. A slender birchwood wand, it was surely one of Morbigon's things he had never seen before. He squinted at the runes and shouted, *"Tuska Nomus,"* sloppily mispronouncing the arcane words.

Embaza's robe was suddenly aflame. The dark elf screamed, and releasing his quarry, tucked and rolled across the sand. When he stopped at last to catch his breath, his tattered robe was smoldering, and Mischa had disappeared, along with the half-charred wand.

From the shouts of the monks behind him, so had Umsel.

The wizard wiped his brow with disgust. His plan had failed. He looked around for Polah, but did not see her. *Why have you let me down, little fox?*

From a nearby archway, a familiar musk aroma wafted through the smoke. "Polah?" he called. He hurried to the corridor just in time to lose sight of the fox.

He raced to catch her and, rounding the corner, found Polah pacing and growling before a dark alcove.

As he approached, he saw that she had trapped the Prince, who was holding a blackened wand in his hand, a brown sack at his feet. Embaza sprinted forward. *Polah, be careful.*

She barked out of fear and excitement.

The Prince brandished the wand. "Don't come any closer, or I'll destroy you both."

Out of the corner of his eye, Embaza saw that something else had rolled out of the sack. He smiled, fished a piece of wax from a pocket of his robe and began to shape it. "Remember this, Prince?"

Mischa started, *"Tuska…"* Then he remembered only too well how the rats had died in the arena. What was the rest of the spell? Part of the words had been obscured beneath the charred half of the wand.

Slowly, he stooped to retrieve his bag, never taking his eyes off Embaza. He flattened himself against the wall and sidled toward the corner. *A lion that escapes the snare lives to fight another day.* He streaked down the corridor.

Polah growled and gathered herself to follow, but Embaza grabbed a hank of her fur in his fist to hold her back.

On the floor of the alcove lay an orb of dull gray crystal. To Embaza's senses, it gave off an eldritch power unlike anything he had ever known. He coveted the object and was not ashamed to admit it. *No need to follow him now. We've pulled his fangs.*

He sensed her relief. Near the orb was the piece of rag which had covered it. He snatched away the cloth and rolled the crystal toward him, but when he did so, something moved beneath the murky surface.

Embaza cautioned her, *Don't look into the orb. Stand guard.* Quickly, he sketched a protective ward in the air and mumbled a brief phrase. The fox stood her ground.

Colors swirled in the crystal, and Embaza could feel his heart beating as a face appeared—a face almost identical to his own. At first, he thought he was looking into a mirror, but the handsome face in the crystal was as astonished as he and underwent a series of transformations.

Finally, the elf in the globe wore a crafty look and said in the Terargian tongue, "You magicians are always trying to impersonate me, but it will do no good. I've changed my mind about waiting. By the time you arrive, all of Tiala's sisters will be dead."

Dekhalis's image was replaced by a dark letter "X" on a latticework frame. Embaza frowned in confusion. Then, the grisly details emerged.

A tiny, dark-elven woman wearing a black velvet tunic and hose was tied to a trellis in a dark, stone chamber, and her lovely face was streaked with tears as she writhed in vain. The sound of diabolical laughter echoed from the orb, as the colors gave way to the opaque and innocent glass.

When Mischa discovered that the orb was not in the bag, he cursed himself and all his relations. Grabbing the charred wand, he raced back, repeating, *"Tuska,"* over and over under his breath. Although he searched the corridor, there was no sign of the wizard or the great fox. In rage, he broke the wand in half and tossed the pieces away.

-5-

ALL THROUGH the night, the monks searched for Umsel and just before sunrise the long horns finally blew their sad notes throughout the monastery that Obsidian recognized as the lament for the dead. He felt the terrible loss, and tried to master his feelings. When he had dressed and made his way down-stairs, he found Tiala and Gudrun eating a hearty breakfast in preparation for their departure.

The night before, Embaza had startled the others with his disclosure of the elf in the orb. If it was indeed Dekhalis, there was every reason to hasten to Alvarra. Embaza had also warned there might be more behind Mischa's attack upon Umsel than the influence of the artifact. Some mind had enhanced it. He was reminded of the albino wizard Morbigon, whom he had defeated but not killed. The dark elves had rested in the shade long enough.

They had immediately gone to inform their hosts of the danger. Even the monks had urged them to leave. Master Tolimane said, "The sooner you are away from here, the easier it will be to quiet the others. We need to mourn the loss of our High Abbot and return to normalcy."

Obsidian had objected. "But Master, what about Prince Mischa? It was our fault that he came here."

Inota answered, "We will deal with the Prince. His family has a long history of negotiations with us. We can remind him of that. Umsel would have wanted you to help the dark lady and her sisters."

"Go, and serenity be with you," Master Riddel added.

Suddenly, the young monk, Jeon, had thrust forward, dressed in the same traveling garb as Obsidian: gray short robe and leggings, belted with a black sash. "Masters, let me go, too—please. There was no sign of the High Abbot's body. What if he was not destroyed? The wizard believes he may be alive. Someone should search for him."

This request had received a dismissal by Master Tolimane. "Whatever happened, we must assume that Umsel is lost to us. This quest is not yours, Jeon," he added, kindly.

Riddel then asked the other Masters, "Do we mourn his loss, or are we eager to see who Umsel has named as successor?"

Inota folded his arms. "We will not open the sealed documents of office until a decent span of time has passed."

"Jeon," Tolimane said, "we must accept the proof of our senses. The High Abbot Umsel is gone. His body was probably destroyed in the explosion."

"We know how you feel," Riddel sympathized.

Under protest, Jeon had finally been persuaded to stay. Obsidian clasped arms with him in goodbye and said with a challenging glance at his masters, "I agree with you, Jeon. If he is alive, I will find him."

Master Inota's mustache had twitched with scorn, "Are you an expert on magical explosions now, Obsidian?"

"No, Master Inota, I am a monk," he answered, with a bow.

This time, no one had contradicted him.

-6-

Now, OBSIDIAN rode behind Gudrun, who was a study in brown as she guided them along the path, her yak content to pick his way through the sparse, sandy forest, stopping occasionally to nibble at a clump of bracken. The mistletoe that quivered on the sinewy ironwood trees would soon yield a profusion of pulpy, white berries. She had spent so much time in the desert, she had lost track of the seasons and was eager to be home in Tskurl, where she could enjoy the signs of spring, the gathering of moisture on the cavern walls, and the mating scent of moths.

The trees were spaced widely, and the yak's horns could easily pass, but Gudrun knew the forest would eventually become dense. She allowed Obsidian to catch up to her and said, "What will we do with the yaks when the trees become thicker?"

"At dawn, Master Ewan will blow the great horn and they'll return."

"Then, we'll have to go on foot. It's nearly two days travel from here," said Gudrun, speaking to herself. "The Alvarrans will have to rest from the sun-sickness, too."

Six Stix proved to be as good with yaks as he had been with horses. Although the sturdy animals were not built for speed, the blue elf patted his mount and urged it on with soft, clicking sounds. The yaks had plodded unprotesting through the night and most of the morning. Now, the light of mid-afternoon scattered through the leaves of the tall, ironwood trees.

Tiala crouched behind Six Stix, her arms around his waist. In a frenzy of controlled impatience, Tiala had lost her temper more than once during their preparations. Embaza's ensorcelled cloak was tucked around her, and with new resolve, she gritted her teeth and listened to the soothing sounds of the many birds that inhabited the forest.

Embaza rode last, tied securely to his mount. Half asleep, he was shaded by the canopy overhead except for an occasional shaft of sunlight that penetrated the dome.

Obsidian took a deep breath. He was still angry at his masters. Embaza's words about the folly of trusting teachers rankled even more. "He's nothing but an intellectual—what does he know of character?" The monk was unaware that he had spoken aloud.

"Embaza?" asked Gudrun, with a glance behind at the dozing wizard.

Obsidian blinked, embarrassed. "Remember his answer to my question about the greatest challenge?"

"How one greets the unknown," quoted Gudrun.

Obsidian's words tripped to catch up with his thoughts, "Yes, and has he not faced death and survived because of his training? Yet Embaza repudiates his own teachers, saying they can teach him nothing. How can he be so arrogant?"

"Did you ever ask him what his teachers did to make him so bitter?"

Obsidian shook his head. "Wisdom comes with pain. We all know that. Our teachers invest themselves in us at great sacrifice."

"Something is troubling you, Obsidian," said the dwarf.

He seemed unaware of her. "How much of them do I carry around inside of me? They are more than my teachers—they're my family."

"You and Embaza are a lot alike, I think," she said. "I'm worried about him. What do you know of his constitution?"

Obsidian glanced behind him. The skin of the wizard's face was drawn and his body seemed wasted as he slumped in the black robe covering his borrowed leggings and shirt. The dark elf appeared to be sleeping, or in a daydream. His slippered feet dangled from the sides of the yak.

"Six says the wizard can fight when he has to—he's resourceful and strong," said Obsidian in reply to her question. "He saw him practice at the Manor. It's hard to believe that now."

"No," said Gudrun, "I've seen many a dark elf in the sun but none who has endured it so long—and survived."

They were both quiet, recalling Tiala's scream in the open desert.

Behind them, Embaza was plagued by more than the Scourge of Elves. Impervious to the rocking motion of the yak, the blistering of his skin beneath the pools of sunlight that lapped through the trees, and his mounting thirst, the wizard's attention was centered on the orb of power within his pack. Even with his eyes squeezed shut, he could see it—a grayish ball of sickly light that threatened to blot out rational thought.

Through the haze of corrupted magic, his anger bubbled like a fistula—at Mischa, the arrogant Dekhalis, Tiala and her superior ways, Obsidian's pious smugness, and himself for being attracted by the artifact. *I should have known its power.* With a wrench, he opened his eyes to the sunlight, his fellow riders silhouetted ahead of him. He sought blindly for relief, as his mind probed each shape before him. *Polah—flower of my heart…Help me…give me strength… Where are you?* Then his eye fastened on Tiala, covered with his own cloak. *If I could have it back…*

Embaza's plea sent a tremor of fear through Polah's solar plexus, but she did not realize its source. Was some magical enemy preparing to attack them again? She sensed a weakness in Embaza's mind that would cause trouble for them all. Perhaps she should warn him, but she was so tired. The night had been bad enough, having to steal away from the group like an outlaw so she could hunt. The more nocturnal she became, the more she craved sleep during the day.

A few times, she had heard a voice in her mind—in fact, several voices, but none was Embaza's. They had sounded like—foxes. This made her even more fearful. *What do they want with me?*

She longed to confide in Embaza, but he had acted so strangely ever since he'd taken that orb. Jealousy stabbed her. *He's forgotten me—and our love. All he cares about is the dark elf and her sisters.* She glanced around guiltily and sure enough, Embaza was staring straight at Tiala. Polah felt alone in a way she had never been before.

Six Stix nodded to her. "Glad to be moving again?"

The enchantress cocked one leg on the yak's broad back to sit sideways. She resembled a compact amber bird with flaming hair. "I guess so."

The blue elf nudged his yak to catch up to her. "I admire your pluck, you know." He lowered his voice. "What's it like being allied with a wizard?"

She blushed. "It's all right." She started to change the subject, but something in the elf's indigo-scarred face emboldened her. "Actually, it's pretty scary."

He gave a grim smile. "You'll do fine." He scratched the yak between the ears. "Too bad we can't go any faster. Maybe we'd be better off if we could *all* change into animals."

Polah's ears pricked up. "And what form would you choose?"

"Sand dragon." He made a clawing gesture in the air, contorting his face in a snarl. Like Gudrun, he wore a homespun shirt, leather jerkin and trousers tucked into leather boots scored by the desert to a dull sheen.

Polah gave a sardonic laugh, half amused, half sympathetic. It made her uneasy. It was one thing to be a shape-changer, but never had it occurred to her that she might meet Alvarran enchanters who assumed other forms. She would have to remember to ask Tiala if there were cave dragons or manticores or giant spiders. She unslung her leg and faced forward, leaving Six Stix to his own thoughts.

Behind him, Tiala asked, "How far have we gone?"

Six Stix patted the hand that clutched his waist. "We're making progress. Try to rest."

The dark elf closed her eyes, leaning her face against Six Stix's broad back. Under the jerkin, his thin shirt was damp with sweat, and the prosaic smell reassured her. Despite her resolve, she was frightened, and she was ashamed to recall the way she had acted in the monastery. *I allowed myself to become angry—at Umsel—Embaza—even my mother. This is not behavior worthy of a Nightwing.* She was losing control of the group, and she sensed new anxieties in all of them.

Embaza's tidings of doom had amplified her problems. Noth—the description was clear—tied to a sewer grate. And where were Inuari and Eleppon? She balled her fists, her arms wrapped yet about Six Stix's waist. The Orb of Wonder, a sacred relic of Alvarra…here, in the upworld. She was still angry at Embaza for refusing to let her carry it, no matter if she was a future Nightwing. His patient explanation of the dangers had been infuriating. Wait until she had her priestesses with her.

Like a dark flower in her black silk travel ensemble, she nestled under the heavy gray cloak and, worn out by the unfamiliar strain of terror and grief, fell into a deep slumber.

Polah soon drifted into sleep, too, succumbing at last to the demands of her animal nature. In her dreams, a strange band of multi-colored foxes surrounded her, sniffing and whispering, enveloping her in a net of fellowship as dense as night and as soft as fog. Meanwhile, other nightmarish figures gathered like crows upon a dead body.

-7-

WHEN MISCHA escaped out of a window and sprinted for the open desert, two monks watched him until he was out of sight. If he was going home, there was no further threat to their brother, Obsidian. They reported immediately to the masters, who convened a formal council in Umsel's receiving room.

As the eldest, Tolimane addressed the monks assembled in the chamber, but no one sat on the cushion before the eight-petaled window. "I know you will join me in wishing an end to our ill fortune," he said.

Someone muttered, "If such exists."

Tolimane ignored the rebuke. "It is natural to want to revenge ourselves for the violent death of our beloved High Abbot." He allowed quiet to descend. "But this is not our way. The power that rules our lives also rules our enemy's. Let us have faith in it."

Master Riddel got to his feet and raised his eyebrows in silent entreaty. Tolimane gestured for him to speak.

"We've always survived by staying aloof from the world," said Riddel, "But, if we do not act, what will prevent this madman from coming back?"

A balding monk stood, quietly, with folded hands. He was short and ruddy-faced.

"Master Ewan," said Tolimane.

"We know nothing of his motives. What if he brings an army? At dawn, I will blow the great horn to call the herd. Why not send a messenger to the Manor and inform the Patriarch?"

Master Inota rose and was recognized, his heavy mustache bristling with energy. "The High Abbot would say that the Master of All speaks to men who close their eyes and breathe deeply." He waited for dissent, but there was none, and he sat down.

Tolimane sighed. "It is agreed, then. Let us meditate on this and meet again on the new moon." As if by silent signal, the monks rose to their feet and filed out.

-8-

Prince Mischa was no fool. Once he was sure he was not being followed, he doubled back on his trail and swiftly found the prints the yaks' large hooves left in the sand. When he discovered a black silk thread caught in a cluster of mistletoe, the locket grew warm against his neck.

He was nearly a day behind, but that was good. He didn't want to let the fox catch his scent. He frowned. *I must have the orb—and kill that Sargothian.* One after another, his thoughts ranged over the members of the wizard's party. Elaborate death fantasies eased the weariness of his muscles as he hurried to keep up with them. He imagined a band of desert wolves tearing them from limb to limb as he picked his way from shadow to shadow through the trees.

-9-

Tiala awoke to the distant sound of a horn. Her sensitive ears vibrated with the deep, even tones, and she visualized a monk blowing into a yak horn, or at least some kind of bone.

Gudrun slid off her mount. She was joined by the others in relinquishing the docile animals after gathering their packs and waterskins for the long journey on foot.

Obsidian untied Embaza and eased him to his feet. "Can you walk?" he asked, remembering Gudrun say she'd never seen a dark elf survive the sun this long.

The wizard nodded, but his eyes were haunted. He leaned heavily on the monk's arm for support.

"This way," said the dwarf, shouldering her duffel. Her eyes twinkled in the last orange gleam of the sunset. The others followed, Tiala holding Six Stix's arm, more for companionship than weakness. She already felt better after her rest, with the prospect of night coming on.

Six Stix asked Gudrun, "How far do you think we'll get tonight?"

"There's a hut a few hours away where we may shelter. It was empty the first time we crossed."

Well rested, and glad to be back in her human form, Polah had moved to Embaza's side, alarmed by his feverish, distracted countenance. She said to Obsidian, "For his sake, I wish we could travel all night."

"He's too weak," said Obsidian.

Embaza shook off Obsidian's arm and stumbled. "Nonsense. I'm stronger than any of you." His face seemed withered in the gloaming.

Obsidian gently grasped his arm again. "No one means you insult."

Suddenly, Polah froze in her tracks. "Hush…someone's following us."

A twig crackled underfoot, and they all stopped, listening. There was only the quiet breathing of the evening around them. Gudrun knelt and put her ear to the ground.

At length, she got up and brushed off her knees. "You're getting spooked, Polah. It's as silent as a tomb."

The fox-woman scanned the trees, but the others shrugged and followed Gudrun deeper into the forest. Obsidian hesitated. He tended to trust Polah's senses. At a prickling along his neck, he wondered if it was intuition or merely his own fear.

-10-

Mischa was alarmed by the sounding of a horn and ducked behind a tree. Was it a signal? Had he been seen?

It was nearly nightfall when he heard the plodding sounds of the yaks approaching. He looked around for somewhere to hide, but the trees provided the sole cover, so he climbed one of them with great difficulty, then realized he had left his sack below and had to scramble down again.

He was no athlete, and his hands and feet were soon scraped by the coarse bark of the scraggly trees. When he regained his perch, he rooted in his bag for something he could use against his enemies. *This is the moment when I can annihilate them.* All fantasies were gone as his hand closed over the prism of glass he had used on his grandfather. It seemed like a year ago.

A fever swelled in his brain—*I must get that orb back.*

When he saw the riderless yaks munching their leisurely way in his direction, he was filled with disgust, and swore loudly. He jumped down from the tree and took a sip from his waterskin, then looked ruefully at the patchy scrub grass. If the yaks could eat it...

It occurred to him that he was beginning to act like an animal, and he drew himself up to his full height, adjusting the simple brown tunic over his pudgy hips. "I may be hungry, but I'm still the Prince of the Outland Territories," he stated to a placid yak staring at him with gentle eyes.

He rummaged in his bag, looking for the food he had packed. Instead, his hand came up with a small vial of a thick, pinkish liquid. Mischa couldn't read the faded script straggling down one side. He uncorked the vial, getting an acrid whiff. Good. It was still potent.

He muttered, "Now, what did that fellow say to do?" He touched a drop to his tongue. A surge of energy flowed all through him that was soon gone, leaving him weak-kneed. He peered at the writing on the vial. He recalled something about a word of power...

"Oh, well," he said finally and took a generous sip, then wiped his mouth with his hand. In moments, his blood fairly danced in his body. "I feel like I could run all night." Hoisting his sack, he took off at a steady lope, threading his way past the yaks and through the trees.

Behind him a dark shape lumbered unnoticed, in and out of the shadows.

-11-

By DUSK, everyone was out of sorts—particularly with Polah. They had stopped so many times at her urging that their nerves were abraded nearly to hysteria. Disgusted, the fox-woman had dropped back as far as she could from the group.

Under the last of the unpredictable golden beams that flickered in and out of the ironwood trees, Tiala felt like a battered doll in the hands of a thoughtless child. Embaza fared even worse, his face hardened into a mask of withering scorn for all his companions, as Obsidian half-carried him. The dark elf had finished all the water in his watersack, and carried his new travel pack over his shoulder.

At the entrance to a small clearing, Gudrun slowed her footsteps.

"General," Obsidian called softly, "are we near the hut yet?"

The dwarf grunted. "Maybe we've passed it. It's hard to tell. We didn't come this way before." Choosing a level spot, she put down her belongings and went off to gather a pile of twigs for a fire.

The waning moon was descending and the sun just peeping up when Mischa smelled the faint cookfire up ahead. Satisfied that his quarry had stopped, he curled up around a nearby tree, covering himself with his sack. In the dim light, he resembled a brown clump of roots. *First, I'll rest, then I'll sneak up and kill them all.* His limbs relaxed as the potion began to wear off. Sleep came over him like a drug.

While they made camp, Six Stix grumbled. "You're lost, aren't you?"

The dwarf bristled. "Do you want to keep your tongue, elf?"

"It's worth a finger or two," he countered.

Embaza's strangled howl cut short the budding confrontation. All eyes fastened on the dark elf as he dropped to hands and knees, then clawed at his throat. Obsidian fumbled at his waterskin, trying to get the catch open. Embaza seized it and ripped the tough leather with his teeth, ignoring the catch. The water gushed over him and he gulped at it like a Sargothian sea lion, wasting all but a few mouthfuls.

Six Stix rushed up with his own waterskin, and together with Obsidian, they wrestled the wizard onto his back, then propped up his head. "There, now. Swallow carefully," said the blue elf to the sputtering Embaza. The wizard's sharp nails dug painfully into the monk's forearms as the water finally found its way down his throat.

Polah came to help, her belly clenching, while Gudrun stayed at a safe distance.

When the wizard had quieted, Obsidian appealed to Tiala, "Princess—na'a Nightwing? Embaza needs his cloak."

Six Stix put an arm around her protectively. "She needs it more."

Embaza glared at Tiala as if he could rend the cloak from her with his eyes. A trickle of foam appeared at the corner of his mouth. His mind reeled at the vision of a dark elf wielding a huge sickle—a dark elf who looked uncannily similar to himself.

"Look at him," said Obsidian and turned all eyes to Embaza's ravaged face.

In the wan firelight, the dark elf's skin was ghostly gray. His eyes rolled to the back of his head, and Obsidian instinctively covered Embaza's mouth with his hand, anticipating the scream.

The pain in Polah's stomach intensified. *Embaza, beware the phantoms!*

She collapsed in a heap, drifting into a half-conscious state in which she saw invisible combatants like wraiths surrounding the wizard.

Embaza wrenched out and upward, tossing the monk and blue elf to either side. As he streaked toward Tiala, he saw not the familiar bard, but a hag with the face of a devil. Behind her a dark shape loomed, and another figure lurched from the bushes to hover over her.

At first, Tiala thought, *He's afraid of me.* But, to her astonishment, he brought both hands to her neck and began to squeeze. *The dream.* She scratched his hands with her waxy, black nails, twisted out of his reach and shoved the cloak in his face, but he batted it aside like a moth.

As Tiala sprinted away, Six Stix ran to see what happened to Polah. She was unconscious, her face set in a grimace of pain. Obsidian and Gudrun were flanking Embaza, and Six Stix joined them to make a circle, closing in on the wizard as he hopped up and down like a kangaroo rat, swinging his arms wildly as if he were under attack from a demon he alone could see.

Tiala took a running leap and pounced, digging her fingernails into Embaza's neck, gouging half-moon cuts that filled with blood. He roared, dumping her to the ground, then threw himself on top of her. The two rolled over and over, a turmoil of biting, scratching fury. As soon as one would get a good hold, the other would scramble to their feet, only to wheel and attack again.

Gudrun held up the fallen cloak, planning to drop it on them, while Obsidian tried to get close enough to use a pressure point that would stun without causing serious damage.

Six Stix caught hold of Tiala's jerkin, but Embaza bit him on the wrist, and the blue elf landed an indignant kick before jumping clear. "Some allies. This is a disaster," he grumbled, trying to hide how alarmed he was at the insanity raging in Embaza's eyes. The blue elf had seen that look before in the eyes of battle-weary youths.

Gudrun said, "No. A disaster would be doing this in Alvarra." She remembered the journey with Tiala across the desert. "This is sun-sickness. Let them fight it out. We'll give the cloak to the loser."

Obsidian refused to give up and circled about the two combatants, impressed with Tiala's wrestling ability, and genuinely appalled at the wizard's madness. *I can't let him kill her.*

Although Embaza rained a series of punishing blows to Tiala's ribs, she used her arms like a vise, trapping his head and squeezing with all her might. They rolled into a tangle of creosote bushes that partially obscured them from view.

It seemed that whatever phantoms had surrounded Embaza, now they were fighting in league with him, or inside of him. All his energies were directed toward destroying Tiala.

Obsidian leapt to one side of the briar bush and saw that Tiala's foot had caught in a loop of strangleberry vine hanging from the limb of a tree. The more she thrashed, the tighter it became. In another moment, she was suspended twenty feet in the air, impotently punching and kicking.

Embaza immediately plunged into the bramble bushes and began to climb the tree.

A menacing figure loomed from the shadows, and Tiala ceased her struggle. The newcomer was twelve feet tall, dressed in the hide armor of the desert, and carrying a barbed spear that glinted in the sputtering firelight. He grinned, revealing two blackened front teeth.

Obsidian stared with astonishment. "Braytok—what are you doing here?"

"Brother Ob," said the giant, clasping his fist to his breast. He gave a warble, and five more tribesmen came into view. They parted in two lines, and a headman entered the clearing, wearing a white turban embroidered with the universal symbol for water.

This giant was larger than the others, though his muscles were slack with age and his mustache bleached white. He looked around at the strange group: the battle-scarred blue elf, the sunburned monk, the homely-looking dwarf and the prone figure of the red-headed woman.

All eyes turned to the wizard climbing the tree, and the dark elf dangling there by one foot.

The giant clasped his fist in ritual greeting and addressed Obsidian. "We wanted to be certain that you were safe. We were told by the shaman that a demon was following you."

Obsidian's mouth nearly dropped open. "Thank you—sir." How did one address a headman anyway?

The headman pointed, and Braytok strode into the brambles, threw his curved knife into the air, and deftly sliced through the strangleberry vine. Tiala plummeted into his arms.

"Aya," howled a voice that seemed tinged with madness. Down from the tree, and through the tangled briar, bounded Embaza. Though half as tall as Braytok, he seemed to cast a longer shadow. He raised his arms and faced the giants, with an eerie wail, *"Andikita..."*

The headman clapped his hands to his ears and dropped to his knees. A black smoke rose out of the ground in front of him.

"Zeeona..."

Another giant screamed in agony, while out of the smoke, a hideous demon took shape before all. It was a hunchback, skin covered with boils and four eyes blazing flames. Embaza tasted its slavering hunger, inwardly appalled at this apparition, but could not force himself to stop chanting. *"Ziama..."*

The demon produced a wand that flared lightning as he touched each giant. One by one, they fell, accompanied by a crackling, sulphuric sizzle. Each time the wand cracked, the skin of Embaza's fingers burned so fiercely, tears blinded his eyes. And still he could not stop chanting.

Tiala had covered her head with her arms, shutting her eyes; terror filled her soul; she sensed the presence of her brother and retched convulsively, oblivious to the pain in her ribs.

Polah, rousing at last, was alarmed by the vision of a rabbit with its throat cut. She squeezed her hands together, willing herself to transform. *Change, damn you. Now.* With a sickening jolt, she realized the rabbit represented herself. Like the others, she was caught in a web of evil.

Obsidian's innocence was buffeted by a malevolence so powerful it paralyzed his will. He imagined looking into his own soul and it rotting like a corpse.

Gudrun had never been so terrified of magic. More horrible than her worst nightmare, she fainted, nearly falling on her sword.

Six Stix alone was still standing. He had started to hum the moment Embaza began the spell. Even when the evil creature emerged from the smoke, he kept his eyes open.

"Ennia Bisch-Ogon..."

The wizard droned on, crooning his fearsome lullaby to the distant moon, painfully aware of the mayhem he was causing. Then he spoke another power word: *"Reenamon Afarr-zeno.* Show yourself!"

The foul shape that had hovered in the air for so long resolved into a hooded robe and folds of water-soaked cloth from which Morbigon the albino emerged. In mortal terror, he cowered in the shadow of the demon Embaza had summoned.

With a crackling of lightning, the demon fell upon Morbigon. A burst of greenish flame ignited the wizard. His scream echoed about the ironwood forest, as his body disintegrated slowly, each fleshy piece dissolving into a pool of blood where once his feet had been.

His work finished, the demon shriveled into the smoke like a sprite returning to his bottle.

Embaza was silent. His companions were stricken—Tiala retching on the ground, Gudrun unconscious, Obsidian on his knees in pain, Polah coiled into herself like a rope. Six Stix, still standing, wore the slack-jawed expression of exhaustion. The seven giants lay in deathly stillness.

The wizard sucked on his charred fingers and swayed, eyes bulging at a vision only he saw—the demon plucking out his heart and holding it with dripping hands. "What have I done?" he whispered, then crumpled to the ground.

-12-

MISCHA RUBBED his eyes and listened to one insect call another. The moon was high, but the night was all black. *How long have I lain here? I didn't intend to fall asleep.* In the sudden dread that his enemies had left him, he quietly scrambled to his feet, grabbed his sack and crept toward the clearing.

He looked for the campfire, but it had smoldered out. His eyes skittered this way and that, noticing several large shapes sprawled in the darkness.

His senses reeled—a scouting party of Blacktooth giants. He tiptoed closer. *Two of them my own guards. What are they doing here? And what is that awful smell?*

A little farther away, he recognized the familiar forms of Embaza, Tiala, Six Stix. His hand closed on the prism and he looked with satisfaction at the well-kept weapons on the bodies of the giants. Now, he would get the orb. He took a step toward Embaza.

Just then, a woman began to cry with a longing that pierced the night. Clutching his sack, the Prince's eyes swiveled across the clearing, to a figure on her hands and knees, wild hair hanging down. His blood ran cold—*the fox-woman.* Panic seized him and, forgoing stealth, he sprinted out of sight.

Between sobs, Polah lifted her head and listened. *So, the Prince still follows. Perhaps now they will believe me.* She growled in anticipation, strength flowing into her forearms, silky fur along her hind legs, a thick brush of tail emerging, ears pointing upwards. She snapped her teeth and her eyes glazed gold in the darkness. *Time to hunt.*

Mischa had gone but a few yards before feeling the sibilant menace of the fox behind him. In his haste, he blundered into a thicket, and thorns ripped his arms and legs, confounding his sense of direction even more. He heard the panting creature, knew her anticipation, and a peal of fear rang through him.

Polah sensed another presence in her mind once again. *Was it—? No, not Embaza.* Layers of human and animal instinct merged with one purpose.

Mischa raised his hands in self defense, as the spectre of death loomed above him. Eyes squeezed shut, he waited for the inevitable. But to his amazement, nothing happened. He peeped out, gingerly.

The giant fox was immobile, paralyzed in the very act of springing off her powerful hind legs. Her eyes shone with fear. Mischa's disbelief changed to elation as he realized he was still holding the prism.

As Polah's fox-self slipped away, a welter of emotions dizzied her. In a moment, her body had returned to human form.

The Prince looked at her with steely, blue eyes, reveling in his power, leering at her nakedness. "So, now you know who is your master," he rasped.

The redhead's stare radiated defiance.

"Oh, yes—you thought it was that magician, Embaza." He felt her withdraw, as if troubled. Eagerly, he pursued the clue. "But perhaps he has changed toward you—?"

She looked down.

"Ah," he exulted, "and why? Because he has a new mistress—."

Her eyes flashed up again.

Mischa was dumbfounded at his own good fortune. Had he stumbled onto a new piece of information? "This mistress is a pretty little moon of gray glass, a thing of such wonderful power, no student of the magic arts can resist it."

Polah's eyes shone with glazed fascination.

Mischa snapped his fingers and said, "You will bring me the orb. Then the Sargothian will be yours." He paused to think, then added, "And do not hunt me in this form again."

He held the prism in front of her nose and said, "You will forget this confrontation as soon as I am gone." He snapped his fingers again. Then he extricated himself from the thorn bush, ripping his breeches and receiving a long scratch down one thigh for his impatience. Cursing with renewed self-esteem, he stumped through the underbrush, looking back over his shoulder until he was out of sight. In his haste, the prism rolled unnoticed into the obscurity of the thicket.

Polah shook her head in confusion. *Where am I?* She barely had time to wonder before her hunger reasserted itself. A musk-mouse wriggled under the root of a tree, pinned by the fox-woman's glowing eyes.

-13-

WHEN POLAH re-entered the clearing, dawn was still an hour hence. A slight eastern breeze ruffled her fur and teased the leaves of the ironwood trees, with their shaggy capes of mistletoe.

It seemed to Polah that each time she transformed, the mysterious process was becoming easier; what pain still attended the change was less frightening. Her clothes were where she had left them, strewn about the campsite.

The picture spread before her was a depressing one. The smell of death was nauseating. By contrast, birdsong surrounded her in the pre-dawn magic of the forest. A mourning dove's plaintive lament contrasted with the cheerful twittering of songbirds. She gathered twigs from a nearby creosote bush and built up the fire again. Her companions would be hungry. Her dual nature definitely had its advantages, and she appreciated the vigor of her animal constitution.

One by one, the others awoke—first Obsidian, then Six Stix, then Gudrun. The dark elves still slept, their faces hidden beneath their arms like children.

Polah's glance at Embaza filled her with a turbulence of conflicting thoughts and emotions. Her lover, teacher, partner in magic—was he evil? Suddenly, she dropped the sticks for the fire and shouldered past Six Stix, who was coming toward her. He turned and caught her arm. "Where are you going in such a hurry?" he asked, his voice gruff with sleep.

"To Embaza—."

"Let him sleep," Six ordered. His grip was implacable. "The wizard is going to be a problem—we need to discuss it."

Polah tried to wrench herself free, but he led her to the fire, where she squatted impatiently.

Gudrun frowned into the flames, as she stroked her beard free of dirt. She looked up to Obsidian, returning from the bushes where he had relieved himself.

Soon, the four were scrutinizing each other with intensity.

Gudrun said, "I say we tie up the wizard and leave him here."

"Are you crazy?" said Polah, balling her hands into fists.

Obsidian merely frowned.

"Listen to me," said Six Stix, startling Polah with his authoritative tone. Obsidian watched him intently, thinking, *This is the real Six Stix.*

The dwarf grumbled.

"We all disapprove of what he did." Six scanned each face. "But think what the Sargothian is capable of. He is still our greatest asset."

Obsidian and Gudrun both began to talk at once, and Six Stix stopped them with an upraised hand and said, "General?"

Gudrun stood up, making her the tallest for once, and hooked her thumbs in her belt. "One doesn't carry a live coal in one's bosom. How can we trust him?"

Polah blurted, "But we could restrain him somehow—bind his hands."

Gudrun frowned. "I'm not such a fool to think I can control a wizard." She sat down.

Six Stix gestured to the monk. "Obsidian?"

The youth's voice quavered with emotion, each word an effort. "They came to help. And he killed them all."

An uncomfortable silence ensued, while Obsidian wrestled with his anger. He challenged Six Stix in a look. "They were misguided—true—but they called me brother. I can't forget that."

"What do you feel you must do—as a brother?"

The word had many connotations, and the monk considered them. Finally, an idea took root, and his anger ebbed. "If he shows remorse, I'll offer him my friendship." He blushed. "It's what they did for me."

Polah had been thinking. Now she was bursting to speak, and Six Stix nodded to her. She jumped up, twisting her hands in agitation. "You don't understand." Tears sprang into her eyes. "He is doomed."

"What do you mean?" asked Gudrun.

"He's being controlled by the orb he took from Mischa."

Obsidian raised his eyebrows. "How?"

"It's linked somehow to Dekhalis." She was poised to run.

Six Stix didn't like the gleam in her eye. Gudrun drew her sword, and the fox-woman stared at the weapon.

"Come," said the dwarf, "we'll get the orb, then tie him up."

"What then?" asked Six as he followed Polah and Gudrun.

"We'll decide that later. It's best to deal with magic quickly—before it has a chance to gather allies," said Gudrun.

Embaza lay a few yards from Tiala. His new travel pack was partially buried under him, and in his sleep, he shielded it with one arm.

Polah crouched down to reach for it just as the dwarven sword sang through the air, slicing it open. The contents spilled onto the ground, and the orb rolled toward them with a wicked gleam. Polah snatched it up with a gasp of triumph, as Embaza lurched to one elbow, blinking.

In a flash, the fox-woman sped into the forest, followed closely by Six Stix and Gudrun. Obsidian knelt, noting the lines of strain around the wizard's tormented eyes.

Anxiety and anger flared in Embaza's face as he saw his ruined pack, and noted the missing orb, but when his glance fell on the giants, his whole body seemed to deflate. He said, "I'm going to be sick," and was as good as his word.

Obsidian remained silent and offered Embaza water to wash his face. The wizard gave Obsidian a look of naked despair and whispered, "I am no longer a wizard."

"What are you then?"

"A necromancer."

"What is that?"

"One who does magic for magic's sake, without regard to the consequences." He looked morosely at the charred and swollen form of Braytok, grotesque in his death throes. "Forgive me," he whispered.

The monk sighed deeply and sat back on his heels. "Forgive yourself, brother. You were influenced by another."

Embaza shook his head. "It was still my fault." He gazed again at the ruined pack. "Where is the orb? It is evil."

"The others will make sure it is never used again." Obsidian felt inadequate to comfort the dark elf and watched him gather his meager possessions into the pack as if they belonged to another. Embaza's hands trembled and he clasped them together.

"What's wrong?" asked the monk.

"I should do a spell of weaving—but I'm afraid. The cursed object still haunts me. And something more—the mind that is using it."

Obsidian swallowed; the fear was contagious, but he kept his voice level. "I am here. I will protect you."

Embaza took a deep breath and sat up straight. His handsome face was haughty for a moment, then he closed his eyes. "If by doing this, I succumb to evil, you must kill me." Flexing his smooth, dark hands, he intoned, *"Wishna Amunda'illo Millaz."*

They both watched the edges of the ripped bag. Even the forest was hushed in anticipation.

Embaza repeated the spell three times to no effect. The sun was peeping through the ironwood trees, and the trembling in his hands worsened. Suddenly, he was not sure those were the correct words.

Obsidian said, "There, there." Not knowing how to comfort, his eyes searched the ground. "I wish we had a needle."

Embaza began to laugh—a grim, almost hysterical sound. He slid one of the needles from the inside pocket of his robe and handed it to Obsidian, who threaded it with a thin strip of hide.

When the monk had taken the last stitch in Embaza's bag, he rose and walked toward Braytok's body. He said, "There is no one left in their tribe to perform the proper rites now." He turned to the wizard. "Will you be my witness?"

Embaza slowly got to his feet, as if doing so took great effort.

Obsidian folded his hands and squared his shoulders, looking up at the ironwood trees. "I knew Braytok. He was the brother of Byder and Dunal—and Nob, whom I killed in fair contest. The headman I never knew, but he was a brave tribesman and wise leader who brought them through many seasons."

Obsidian's words floated over the clearing, as Embaza stood still, flinching at the occasional rustle of mistletoe. A lone songbird added an accompaniment to the solemn occasion.

"Now, we must bury them," said Obsidian. "But how?"

Embaza whispered, "Maybe..."

"What?"

"I could try the spell of disappearing. I used in the desert." *If I can even remember it.*

Obsidian stared at the wizard. If the spell of mending had not worked, there seemed no point in a second futile exercise, but he said nothing.

Embaza murmured, *"Insagramo Mesaweea Echzawmbus Dayad…"* The headman's body shimmered for a moment, then dissipated, leaving only an imprint in the soft earth.

Embaza swallowed with tentative relief, and sweat beaded his forehead. He continued repeating the phrase until the only body in the clearing was Tiala's, curled inside the dirty cloak that had once been gray.

A sigh escaped the wizard and he sank to his knees. For a terrible moment, he considered suicide, but thought instead, *I have pledged my aid to the dark elf. At least, my death should mean something.* Nervously, he fingered the necklace hidden beneath his robe. Now his sole link to the powers he had once possessed, it might be too dangerous for him to use.

Obsidian patted the wizard on the shoulder, and pondered the mysteries of destiny. He did not understand magic, but he did know what happened to those who misused power.

-14-

POLAH WAS not sure where she was going. She knew she had to find Prince Mischa. Then he could take the orb, and Embaza would be safe.

But Gudrun and Six Stix were right behind the enchantress. She heard their belabored breathing, the thump of their footfalls, and something in her fox-memory stirred. The smell of men hunting her, their slavering dogs, panting. Before she knew what had happened, she had dropped to all fours and begun to change. The orb was forgotten.

Six Stix scooped up the artifact, retracting his arm to hurl it away, but Gudrun cried, "Wait. Put it on that rock over there—the flat one." She gripped her sword, the hilt throbbing in her hands as its will pulsed through her.

With a grin, the elf complied, and Gudrun took aim. Six Stix envied the way the rune-wrought blade pierced the heart of the artifact. They shielded their eyes from the small chips of crystal that flew in every direction. In moments, the orb was a memory, and an indescribable wail tapered to a whisper in the forest stillness.

Six Stix looked around for Polah, but there was no sign of her amid the rustling mantles of mistletoe. He gathered her clothes and said, "She'll find her way back."

Gudrun was not listening, but staring in horror at her sword. Her arm tingled with sharp needles, yet worse than any pain, an ugly black scar was etched down the length of her blade, intersecting the once-graceful runes. Her movements slowed by a leaden regret, she sheathed her weapon, then shook her arm hard, seeking the pain, while angry tears sprang to her eyes.

From his vantage point in the branches of an ironwood tree, Prince Mischa saw the fox-woman's failure and the dwarf's destruction of the orb with her magical sword. He seethed with rage, as he watched his link with Dekhalis severed. He was all the more determined to follow his enemies until he saw a way to defeat them. Perhaps he could yet win the gratitude of this foreign king. He watched Gudrun's swagger as she disappeared into the forest. *You'll be sorry you crossed me, dwarven pig.*

-15-

As THE Nightwing Avenwyndar lay dying, she had fallen into an impenetrable silence. Fearing the worst, the senior priestesses of each order were maintaining a dedicated vigil around the huge seashell bed.

The High Priestess Kalista ignored the teardrop that inched down her cheek. With prodigious effort, she probed the corners of her mind for any sign of her old friend. Finally, exhausted by the tedious process, she said to the priestess Lowanda, "Read something from the archives, it will help to quiet our thoughts."

The circumspect Lowanda got up and crossed to the wall, opening a hidden panel with the ease of habit. Inside were the sacred volumes of Alvarran lore. The fragrance of pressed wood filled her nostrils. She hesitated, her fingers roaming the venerated tomes, stopping at a thin green leather volume whose binding was not as worn as the others.

She drew it out and read the gold letters on the cover: *The Consecration.* Well, why not? These were troubled times.

The Priestess Evendove of the Sisters of Loote was also present. She whispered to Kalista, "Has anyone seen the sacred pet?"

Kalista shook her head. The Nightwing's black rabbit had been missing for twenty-two bells. Another bad omen. There had been many of late.

Lowanda began to read, her aged voice still sweet:

"I, Seran of Sonner do hereby proclaim obedience to the Great Goddess, Miralor, and having held council with Her on the crystal moors, do testify that the daughters of Alvarra will take office. Henceforth, it is we who shall rule the beloved land.

"*In obedience to the edicts of my Goddess, Miralor has named me Nightwing. Hereafter, that shall be my title. But I shall also bear the name my mother gave me, thus I shall be Nightwing Seran.*

"The hero Flickerel speaks.

"*I, Flickerel, whose mother was Goodroot and whose father was Mannet, do recognize you as the true ruler of Alvarra, Nightwing Seran. As your first act, I propose that we make a list of all those men who oppressed us for these many centuries. And that each name on this list be inscribed in the blood of his accuser.*

"*I, Flickerel do also request, in the name of the Goddess Drimma, that when any daughters of Alvarra accuse one man of such criminal acts against women, that he shall be executed. We must cleanse our land of men who would sully our new order with their foul deeds.*

"The new Nightwing speaks.

"*Our new order is dedicated to the Great Goddess Miralor, first and last. Although it is true that Drimma, Goddess of Retribution, has served our cause well, She is for endings, not beginnings.*

"*I, the first Nightwing, command that we put away our weapons and build a new society. We will have our own temples, schools and houses of law, and we will institute an order of peace-keepers who will have my authority to dispel intruders and criminals.*

"*I, Nightwing Seran, order that a great house be erected to each goddess and god—even Myrrhspell, consort to Miralor and God of the wizards. I will listen to your objections later, sisters.*"

Kalista rasped, "Pass that part, Lowanda. Read us the accounts of high deeds that will inspire us in our trouble." She was too polite to comment that her uneducated ancestor's attempts at formality sounded stilted and unnatural. These were women of action, not words.

Lowanda scanned ahead to a passage entitled, "Insurrection at Inkro."

"*Then came a group of Women to rescue a hundred daughters of Alvarra from the slave pens of the one called the Brute, Mandrake of Inkro in the City of Douvilwe. Some say their screams were like ravens and owls, as with knives made from the sharpened bones of their own dead, the daughters broke in and killed the Brute. Then they freed their sisters, many of whom were covered with sores and the scars of beatings, many diseased and all thin to the point of emaciation.*

"*Caring not for their brazen acts, they carried Mandrake's head on a long pole through the streets of Douvilwe, inciting the outrage of the city's rulers. The High Council sent its troops against them, and a bloody battle occurred, winding through the city's passageways, all the way to the Great House of Douvilwe where the High Council itself was in session.*"

As the priestesses listened to the recounting of their history, hearts stirred with passion—and compassion—for those women of long ago. They pictured their ancestors, wives and daughters who knew only labor, barred from military training and unschooled in domination, yearning for freedom, taking their unsuspecting oppressors by surprise with their tools and homemade weapons.

It had been one of the great elven miracles, the Insurrection at Inkro, and all that followed. In the next three days, as news had spread, there were uprisings throughout the land. The ruling class had never considered the folly of breeding so many women, as their desire for more and more slaves had risen. This greed was their undoing.

As Lowanda read, the priestesses quivered with empathy for the brave hero Seran as she faced the High Council in the Great House, delivering her final speech to the captured assembly:

"From this day forward, no man will rule in Alvarra. Your destiny will be to serve women.

"But we will not follow your example. We will not withhold our compassion. We will not enslave you. We will not beat you, or rape you, or terrorize you in the very streets. We will not oppress you and slay your hope. We will not bind your soul with iron bands.

"Under the Sisterhood of Miralor, you will become productive citizens. And one day, perhaps you will stand with us and with the guidance of our Great Mother, help to determine the future of Alvarra."

Lowanda stopped, too moved to continue. *Seran the Dreamer,* they called her in the history books.

"That is enough," said Kalista. "If our dear Avenwyndar could speak, she would no doubt remind us that history often repeats itself. Let us hope that it does not."

-16-

DEKHALIS HAD taken the risk of returning to his bedroom in the Royal City. It was imperative that he discover who had the orb. One who could impersonate him might be a powerful ally—if he could be turned to the cause. *That shouldn't be too difficult. The man is sure to be Alvarran. All know an illusion must have basis in reality, and he simulates my face too well.*

When he had recovered the mirror from its hiding place in the chimney, Dekhalis knelt with it in his lap. This time, he did not put on the citrine crown. He schooled his thoughts, trying to achieve a calm he had never really possessed. He hated being out of control. It was easier to control everyone else instead.

He held the mirror before him, and as always, his image was soon replaced by the familiar swirl of colors. For a moment, he saw a strange scene—a wooded place but nothing else. Not the face of that groveling gnomad, nor the impersonator. Who had the orb, then?

Dekhalis watched as a macabre wail emanated from the artifact. Suddenly, there was an explosion in the mirror, throwing him backwards, and he hit his head on the stone hearth of the fireplace. He had the sensation of being whirled into the center of a maelstrom. His stomach churned, and he felt his very grip on his identity slipping away. He lost consciousness.

When he opened his eyes again, the room had stopped spinning. He had no idea how much time had passed. He sat up, rubbing the swollen knot on his head, possessed by a new fury. He looked at the silver frame still clutched in his hand. The glass had shattered, littering the area and his body with a fine shower of sparkling debris.

He flung the frame into the fireplace, and leapt to his feet, shaking the glass from his clothing. His eyes flicked angrily around the room, wishing a victim were at hand to soothe his rage.

He hoisted himself gracefully through the roof and scampered into the boughs of the cedar-birch, climbing upward. He had no patience for tunnels now.

-17-

WHEN GUDRUN and Six Stix returned to camp, Obsidian and Embaza were sitting by the fire's remains, chewing dried mutton.

They sauntered to the campfire and squatted down. The wizard's face was composed, but his trembling hands were disconcerting. The sun had passed its zenith, and Embaza sat in the shade of the ironwood tree, but looked ghastly.

Six Stix said, "What happened to the giants?"

Obsidian glanced at the wizard and replied, "Embaza helped me dispose of them."

"My last act of magic," he said, his dejection palpable. "I have lost my power."

"Is that true?" asked Six Stix, frowning.

The wizard's face was more eloquent than words.

"He lost his scrolls and has little memory of spells," explained Obsidian.

Gudrun smiled at the dark elf. "You're one of us, then. Better to depend on steel than spells, I say. Give him your dagger, Stix."

Six Stix recoiled. "Mine?"

"Oh, rat piss," she said irritably and pulled a small dirk from her boot, which she handed, hilt first, to Embaza.

He reached for it, but his hands shook uncontrollably and he clasped his fists together in frustration.

"Later, perhaps," she said, returning the dagger to her boot.

They shared some of the dried mutton and passed around a waterskin, Embaza already beginning to show the signs of thirst that would intensify throughout the day.

"Where is that damned hut you said we'd find?" Six Stix snapped.

"It's too late for that now," said Gudrun. "If we leave soon, by nightfall, we'll be in the underground."

Obsidian shivered. *Caves.*

Embaza spoke at last. "I want to be gone from this accursed forest." He searched the faces of the others. "Where's Polah?"

"Don't worry," said Six Stix. "She always returns."

Embaza did worry, but his mind felt clogged with obscure images that reeked of the grave. He thought, *I've lost my powers—and probably her, too.*

Obsidian and Gudrun rose to their feet and went to Tiala.

"I hate to awaken you," murmured the dwarf, gently shaking the dark elf's shoulder.

Tiala sat up, clutching the cloak, and blinked at the bright sunlight filtering through the canopy of leaves. "I wish our way did not lie in the Scourge's path," she whispered.

Obsidian helped her up and quickly explained the situation. She took one look at Embaza's dejected form, and her heart melted. He would do no evil in Alvarra, not now.

She walked over to him and placed her slim, dark hand on his shoulder. "You have suffered much. I'll not add to it." Tenderly, she placed the cloak around his shoulders.

"Thank you," he replied, unable to meet her eyes.

Six Stix gazed at her beauty, remembering the feel of her in his arms that night at the monastery.

When Tiala had eaten the homely food and slaked her thirst, she, too, asked, "Where is Polah?"

Gudrun answered, "She disappeared when we destroyed the orb."

Embaza's stomach knotted. "How did you destroy it?"

"With this," she said, bringing her sword an inch out of its scabbard. The runic silver gleamed. She let it slide back into the sheath without exposing the blackened scar.

Tiala looked at them with alarm. "Embaza, was this the orb in which you saw my brother?" He nodded and she continued, "That object has been in my family for eons. It should have been returned to the archives. Besides, how will we learn what has happened to my sisters?"

Embaza's hands clenched the edges of his cloak. "Surely you saw the evil force within it—it was a growing, living seed. And it was getting stronger."

"My priestesses would have cleansed it and used it for good."

"Impossible."

"Nothing is impossible to those wielders of Alvarran earth magic, my friend. Even your talents cannot compare..." She stopped at his look of despair.

"Please, Princess," said Obsidian. "We must find Polah and go on."

"Right," she said. While Six Stix and the monk scouted for the fox-woman, the other three broke camp. Embaza was too quiet, Gudrun too loud.

Ironically, Polah entered camp soon after the two went looking for her. She remained aloof from Embaza, afraid to test their intimacy in the wake of all that had happened. Tiala took the girl aside. "Be gentle with him. The evil has drained him of power."

Polah shook her off. "I don't need you to tell me that." His presence within her was a mute lump of misery. "What do you know of his feelings?"

"He is an elf."

Polah stared at Tiala. "What difference does that make?"

"It is a harmony. There is magic in our blood. He will heal."

The fox-woman wished she had not asked. "That's no answer. He's hurting."

"Perhaps you're not as close to him as you think."

"You cannot understand our bond."

Tiala said, "If you've become lovers, it's nothing to me." *No doubt he'll tire of you when you've begun to show your age.*

"As you say," said Polah, lifting her chin.

Tiala shrugged and walked away.

Polah looked after her, anger a thorn in her belly, then glanced at the others. None of them understood. She was a fool to think she could make friends with them. As for Embaza, he still needed her. Now more than ever.

She crossed the clearing to where he stood, gazing through the trees at his own visions. Rising on tiptoe, she handed him his pack, gently adjusting the strap over his shoulder. He looked down at her with a tormented expression.

When they were ready to go, Six Stix said, "From now on, let's be more careful. Who knows how many traps are in these woods?"

Polah walked to the front. "I could scout ahead."

"This way," Gudrun said, pointing.

As they walked, Six Stix was touched by the way Tiala and Embaza shared the dirty gray cloak between them. But he wondered. If Embaza still had his powers, would she be so generous? He told Obsidian, "You know, the wonderful thing about traveling is that you meet so many people."

"Yes, but someday you'll have to go home. Didn't the High Abbot say something about your brother not ruling well?"

"Oh, that. The estate practically runs itself," replied the elf with a laugh.

The two remained silent, each wrapped in his own thoughts. All of them pondered the hazards that lay ahead, their fears lulled by the eerie beauty of the forest. As the trees became more numerous, the canopy of shade provided a welcome change, especially for the dark elves. Tiala listened with longing to the nuances of the bird calls, wishing her heart was not so encumbered.

They passed the deserted hut not a league from camp. Gudrun snorted in disgust, and Polah said, "Sssh. Stop." All were still. "We have to go around this area." She motioned them on.

One after another, she found—and avoided—five deadly traps, all showing signs of recent construction. The most gruesome was a pit of scorpions. The party's nervousness increased, and Polah was startled more than once by a rustling in the bushes. Upon investigation, there was a scattering of rabbit tracks and a peculiar scent that Polah alone seemed to notice. She filed away the knowledge that her sense of smell was becoming more acute over time.

The fox-woman barely noticed her companions, and for long moments, she felt alone. Embaza's presence seemed more and more distant now. And yet, she still had the sense of something growing within her—as if others lurked on the periphery of her mind.

Finally, the woods ended. She stepped from the shade into bright sunshine—a plain of stubby grass, dotted with sheer, slanted rocks and bushes of bracken. Gudrun motioned to Polah to wait near the treeline.

When the others had caught up, the dwarf announced, "This will be dangerous. At the entrance, we'll have to get by the guards—some of them will surely belong to Dekhalis, is that not so?"

Tiala said, "Yes."

"There's not another way in?" asked Six Stix.

The dark elf shook her head.

Obsidian looked at Embaza. The despondent wizard seemed more hindrance than help.

Tiala cleared her throat, shrinking back against the trees. "I'm quick on my feet, and I can act as a decoy while the rest of you sneak in. The guards may have orders to capture me, but Dekhalis won't know or care about a ragged bunch of visitors from other worlds."

"I wouldn't be too sure about what he knows—or wants," said Embaza. "Besides, he's seen my face." He suddenly had an idea. "He does resemble me, but how much?"

Tiala looked at his parched, wrinkled skin, his dirty robe and threadbare slippers. "I don't know—if your hair were shorter and you had better clothes...of course, you're taller. But you could pass for Dekhalis—there's a definite resemblance. Your voice is very similar, though your accent will be wrong."

"And does the whole world speak Terrargian—even there?" asked Six Stix.

"No." A smile creased her face, transforming it for an instant.

Gudrun snorted. "Dark-elven, the oldest elven in the world. There are times when even I don't understand it. And every dark elf living seems to have a different pronunciation."

"You're right," said Tiala, brightening. "Alvarrans are eccentric. We invent new dialects to amuse ourselves. My brother especially."

Embaza nodded, and said in dark-elven, "At Sargothas, we learned that all words have power. I have a good command of the language, although I've not had much occasion to use it."

Tiala frowned. "My brother speaks in classical tones and with a haughty air. But you might fool those who aren't close to him."

Polah glanced anxiously at Obsidian. She had barely understood any of Embaza's words. The monk shrugged. Polah wet one of her sleeves and dabbed the wizard's face, washing off a layer of dust. Even this slight amount of liquid restored some of the elasticity to his skin. "Shall I cut your hair?" She drew her sharpened tusk knife.

"I'd better do it," said Tiala, gently taking the knife from Polah.

Embaza knelt and sat on his heels, while Tiala loosened his braid and carefully trimmed his long, blue-black hair. Gently, she fluffed the hairs in his tufted ears.

Polah turned her back, and contemplated the ironwood trees rather than watch Tiala cut the hair she had touched with such rapture.

Gudrun broke her silence. "Are there no dissenters, my Lady? Surely not every man would turn against the Nightwing."

"If we run into friends, we'll just switch places. Embaza—as Dekhalis—will be *our* prisoner."

Gudrun laughed. "I'd better lead, then. The daughters of Tskurl go where they please."

"The Prince still follows us," Polah hissed.

Six Stix groaned. "We have more danger ahead than behind, I'll wager."

Just then, a black rabbit poked her nose out of the undergrowth. Polah held her breath in kinship with the animal.

The rabbit scurried out of sight, and Gudrun said, "Let's go."

She led them over the rocks in the blazing sunshine, Embaza and Tiala huddled together under the cloak. Gudrun stopped at one large stone partially hidden by a thick hedge of bracken. She parted the branches, revealing a steep flight of stairs curling down into darkness.

A whiff of cold air tickled Tiala's nose like a promise.

Gudrun whispered, "I'll go first." Her sturdy form disappeared into the dark.

In a few moments, the dwarf poked her head out and said, "It's a bad sign. There's not a guard in sight. Be careful."

Embaza and Tiala followed her, then Polah. Again, the fox-woman identified the musky smell of the black rabbit.

Unlike the dark elves and the dwarf, Six Stix and Obsidian could see little in the dark. They groped along the coarse rock walls, placing their feet with care on the worn, stone steps. Obsidian tried to push away the feeling of entering a tomb.

He counted as he descended—11, 12, 13…No one passed them on the stairs, not even rats. This added to his sense of oppression as the cold darkness burdened his heart like a stone weight.

Six Stix was wary, frustrated with the helplessness of being in the dark, but he felt an unmistakable tingle along his sword arm as he anticipated the inevitable battles ahead.

Tiala and Gudrun were elated at being near home. With each footfall of their descent, Tiala's steps lightened. The cool air soothed her fevered skin, and her hair began to spring up with the breath of the caves, instead of lying limply along her scalp. Even the fluff that lined her tapered ears stood out, as the sensitive hairs filtered the echoes.

Embaza was surprised by an unexpected sense of homecoming. More than just the healing effects of being out of the sun, for the first time since he had destroyed the giants, hope surged within him. He could feel the magic all around, welling up from the very stones. Maybe Tiala was right—anything was possible here.

For Polah, the passage downward was like a dream. She felt more and more disembodied from her fellows. Magic was around her—and in her. She could not have told whether she was woman or fox anymore. Her body seemed an afterthought, her name unimportant. She knew without a doubt that there were shape-changers here. There were foxes. As her feral eyes pierced the darkness, she drank in the drab surroundings with eagerness and anticipation.

At long last, they reached bottom of the stairway. A torch flickered weakly on one wall, showing a crude, convoluted stone tunnel that curved out of sight.

Embaza whispered, "Where's the beauty you promised me?"

Tiala chided him, saying, "We're not in Alvarra yet. Remember to speak in dark-elven. I can't keep reminding you."

As they continued down the corridor, the walls grew more refined. Gudrun pointed proudly and said, "Dwarven-made."

Obsidian noted with dismay that the floor sloped ever downward.

They turned a corner, and the tunnel spiraled like a birth canal, every surface beveled by the dwarves to a pleasing softness. Ancient bronze runes had been set into the floor long ago, worn almost unreadable by the passage of booted feet.

Tiala was thrilled to be home despite the circumstances. A shadowy figure emerged from a hidden passageway behind her. Polah gave a sharp cry as she saw a thick arm close about Tiala's neck. The meaty hand held a needle-sharp dagger just under her chin. Her eyes widened, sending a silent entreaty to Embaza.

The wizard growled in clear dark-elven, "You there—hold her steady."

-18-

OF THE two largest cities in Alvarra, Douvilwe had been more fortunate than the capital, Renradel. Many of the common areas, or free caves, had been untouched by the riots, most notably the city's fabled arboretum.

This lush park was contained beneath a vaulted crystal ceiling that stretched more than five leagues and, at times, glowed like a false sun, waxing and waning as if mimicking the day and night cycles of the surfacelands. Some old timers claimed the illumination itself was a magical gift of the fairies of old, but no one really questioned it.

Centuries past, the master gardener of that time had planted every possible tree thought of as exotic in Alvarra. It was said the Nightwing Nubria had added her own special earth magic to attract the birds and butterflies.

Huge cottonwoods abounded, hawthorns crowned with pink and white flowers, stately ash and rowan trees, sugar maples and cedar-birch, fragrant balsam, green-leafed beech. Oaks and willows were planted near the center of the arboretum, and in the pride of place grew an enormous, spreading fig called the Wellambtree, the only one of its kind.

This legendary tree bore a fruit whose milk was said to confer immortal sleep. To many long-lived elves, death was a blessing, but the figs were rarely plucked.

The arboretum was inhabited by hundreds of fireflies who sought the nectar of its flowering trees. The greenish tinge of their luminescence matched the glow of dark-elven eyes. The tiny lamps flashed on and off, like the joyous play of children.

But there would be no play on this occasion. A ring of male guards surrounded the arboretum to prevent the entry of common citizens. The guards wore the rakish clothing adopted by the Swords of Siadhin. Their tight suits were in bright colors, some adorned with mirrors that blinded the eye with every move. They carried crude weapons, mostly home-made bonewood knives with lovingly carved handles.

Dekhalis himself was present, garbed in one of his dyed bat-leather suits, this one in brilliant blue. It fit like his skin, and featured laced leggings and a vest of the same color. He strutted into the center of the arboretum where workers were building a large platform around the wide Wellambtree. In his hands, he toyed with a moonteller mushroom. Its once-silver skin had dulled to gray. "Hurry up," he snapped.

Iridescent green poles had been placed around the platform. Wychwood, they were called, but in fact they were foxfire, the luminous fungus of decaying wood. In such profusion, they produced a garish light, especially as the illumination of the crystal ceiling had begun to wane. Pale green moths fluttered nearby, their papery wings transparent in the glow. In the trees, dark blue butterflies with gold-spotted wings congregated as if they, too, were waiting for a sign. Their exotic aroma permeated the area, irritating Dekhalis.

A few of his followers stood nearby, but Dekhalis' closest henchmen, the dreaded spidermen, were absent. From the tallest branch a night owl cried "Tu-hu, tu-hu," and Dekhalis looked up, further annoyed. He crushed the moonteller, and the ruined pulp fell to the ground with a musky fragrance. "Almost moon-dark and still my sisters stand in my way."

Drawing out a moleskin slingshot, he fitted a flat, white stone into the pocket, his eyes narrowed on the space above the owl's keen beak. Her head had swiveled all the way around on her neck to look at him. Holding his breath, he drew back the sling, locking eyes with the owl in a test of wills. Then, he let go.

Her talons left the branch just as the missile whizzed beneath it. The glossy brown-and-white bird settled back onto her perch, as if nothing had happened.

Dekhalis put the slingshot back into his pocket and bent down nonchalantly to tighten the lace of the leggings over his left shin. From a hidden pocket in the leggings, he withdrew a long piece of strangleberry vine, with two leaden weights at each end. As he straightened up again, he hurled the cord toward the top of the tree with a flick of his wrist.

The owl never knew what hit her. When her lifeless body reached the ground, Dekhalis knelt down and plucked the two largest feathers from the wing, brushing off the ends. He added one of the feathers to the contents of a pouch beneath his vest.

Those around him watched, enthralled. The laced leggings of his red suit left open circles along his shins and thighs. Pouches and pockets were hidden throughout the costume. He had been known to carry everything from rabbit poison to snow-bear claws, and he was expert at using them in creative ways.

Among his followers was one dark-elven woman, small and round-faced, with long, thick hair bound with strips of black leather. Her natural beauty was marred by a furtive look of pure malice. She wore an iridescent body suit that fit her athletic form like a glove. It was pebbled in shades of blue that shimmered when she walked. Her bound breasts and traditional weapons sash were the only clues to her calling. She had the tough bare feet of a mountain climber.

Dekhalis beckoned to her now, saying, "Owla." She moved lightly to his side and stroked his muscled stomach with a proprietary purr. He handed her the owl feather. When she smiled, her eyes turned up at the corners.

He admired her exotic face; it might have been used as the mold for a mask of classic evil.

"Thank you, Lord King," she said, her voice husky with intimacy.

Dekhalis turned from Owla's distracting presence. "Where are the Pretenders?" he asked one rustic-looking lieutenant whose outfit was a deep purple that matched the brilliant lichen on the oaks.

The lieutenant pointed toward the perimeter, eyebrows raised in relish. Owla's delicate mouth quivered at the corners, and she puckered it in a mocking kiss at the guard.

From the edge of the park, where creeping perennials lined the pathways in starry blossoms, three more guards approached, carrying a struggling Noth between them. Hands and feet tied, she was gagged with her own black velvet belt. She squirmed with reflexive anger that had lost its immediacy. Her eyes were ringed with exhaustion. The bridge of her delicate nose was broken, a knot already forming between the purple circles under her eyes.

Behind her, two more of the Swords of Siadhin led Inuari, gagged and blindfolded, her wrists tied behind her back. When terror slowed her steps, a third guard prodded her from behind with a wooden stake, and she stumbled forward again. Her new blue robe was torn and stained, and the small black rabbits embroidered in the vee-neck seemed twisted in torment. The white silk circlet was gone from her brow.

Dekhalis moved close to Noth and smirked. "Traitor," he hissed. Seeing how the madness was devouring him, she strove to hide all emotion from her face.

The guards forced Inuari to stand beside them. The priestess remained erect, sniffing the air for familiar signs. From behind her blindfold, she sensed that she was in the arboretum, and yet, the sweet "Tu-hu" of the owl no longer sounded from the Wellambtree. *Oh, Miralor,* she prayed, *help me.*

Fireflies thronged about her, circling her face and body with a sheath of ghostly light. "Look," cried some of the guards, frightened by the earth magic of the priestess.

"Enough of your tricks," said Dekhalis, cuffing his sister across the face. She nearly swallowed the gag, falling backward, as the guards let go of her. She lay helplessly winded on the dark grass, wondering what had happened.

Dekhalis turned away, bored. "Defenseless slug." He appreciated the frightened expressions of some of his followers. "See that she stays this way. I want her rested for the ceremony."

Noth kept her face deadpan. *Ceremony?* She looked at the female henchman, Owla. She knew that one. Her real name was Theowla Twomothers. Daughter of a warrior, carried from one barracks to another, she had grown up to be a formidable fighter—one who enjoyed killing. She had been in the royal guard until she was passed over as leader of the cadre. Ambition was a poison that seemed to have driven her into Dekhalis's arms.

Noth had lost the thread of Dekhalis's conversation—until she heard a name that sent a tremor down her spine.

"In a little while, we will invoke the aid of our ally, the Goddess of Retribution. Drimma has come to me in dreams. She has promised me that she finds great favor in her cause. But we must be willing to earn her aid." Dekhalis's voice was as smooth as cat fur.

Inuari had also been listening, and her blood curdled at the very idea of a Festival of Drimma in this sacred grove.

"Since the beginning of time, Drimma has battled her sister, Miralor. Now she has asked us to deliver one of Miralor's favorites to her." There was a hush over the crowd. "At next bell, we'll sacrifice a priestess to ensure our success. I will relinquish my own sister to the Goddess." Dekhalis's silken voice was taut as a bowstring, trembling with feigned emotion.

Inuari's body became rigid with fear. She thought, *Mother, where are you? Why have I heard nothing from your priestesses? Are you dying at last? Oh, blessed Miralor, not now.*

Suddenly, there was a shout from the perimeter. "Master! Horses approaching."

Dekhalis raced to the edge of the arboretum. The Swift Legion had been an annoyance, stampeding through parts of the cities where he was reputed to be visiting. He had been fortunate enough to duck out of sight each time, relying on the maze of tunnels to stay out of their way.

This time, he had planned an end to the game. As he saw his sister Eleppon and her lieutenants charging down the escarpment of red crystal overlooking the park, his heart leapt in his breast. *She has taken the bait.*

First the fairy-blooded Kossi on her gray mare, then homely Calwyn on the bay. Last, Eleppon on Zola, the mare's pale coat the color of moonlight. Behind them, ten more riders, all wearing the dark blue costume Eleppon had popularized—the divided skirt, soft boots and long-sleeved tunic. Each rider carried ropes of silk-vine, the stuff of breeders—gentle enough not to cut the flesh, but strong enough to stay a horse in flight.

One by one, they leapt the precipice, forming a neat, serpentine line, the obvious intent to encircle Dekhalis and his entourage. Kossi sat lightly, black skin stretched over glistening cheeks, lime-colored eyes agleam with purpose. The tall Calwyn came right behind, her thin frame bent like a reed so that her hawkish nose lay pasted to her horse's mane.

Suddenly, the gray stumbled with a whinny of alarm. Kossi's mount crumple beneath her, and looking down, she saw the sharpened stake protruding from the mare's breastbone. She jumped off just in time to avoid being trampled by Calwyn's bay.

Calwyn was not so lucky. As the bay went down, she fell beneath it, lost in the crush of the stricken animals. Both horses screamed in agony, impaled on stakes tipped with poison.

Eleppon, horror-stricken at the loss of Calwyn and the slaughter of the innocent beasts, steered her panicky steed to one side, ululating a fierce war cry. Her rope sang in the air as she whirled it above her head.

Dekhalis took from his waist a curved piece of lemon-wood with a slotted hole in the middle. He pushed his henchmen in front of him, then darted behind a goodroot tree, taking aim on his sister. The weapon sailed true, slicing Eleppon on the left temple. Blood spurted as she dropped like a stone, landing on her left arm. Unconscious, she was spared the snap and pain of the breaking bone, but Zola kept going, heading straight for Dekhalis.

In moments, Kossi had leapt to Zola's back, hands knotted in the white mane. The horse continued to plow forward with foaming jowls and rolling eyes. Kossi took up the ululating cry where Eleppon had left off.

At every attempt to assist, the ten hand-picked riders and their mounts were cut down by implanted stakes. Without rope or plan, unaware that she was all alone, Kossi stuck onto Zola's back like a fly, hurtling toward her quarry.

Dekhalis leapt from a deep squat and caught the lowest branches of the Wellambtree. Swinging his feet upward, he gained the safety of the limbs just as Kossi sailed beneath.

Undaunted, the horsewoman wheeled to make another pass, but Dekhalis snatched a miniature crossbow from his vest, and aiming it easily from the comfort of his perch, released a crimson-tipped bolt. It grazed Kossi's cheek, whizzing by to imbed itself in Zola's rump.

Kossi thought, *He's missed us.* Zola raced toward him like an arrow. As they neared the limb where the madman clung, the beast's forelegs went down, then her hind legs, and with a great sigh, she was still. Kossi barely had time to wonder what had happened as she, too, was stricken by the poison.

Dekhalis dropped to the ground, kicked Kossi's numbed body away from him, and started giving orders: "Get ropes and haul the carrion away." His followers sprang into action. "You—get back to work on that platform. I want everything ready before the worshippers arrive."

As if on cue, a group of musicians could be seen trudging up the steep incline of basalt to the south. They carried the curved horns, log drums and bladder drums traditional to the Goddess Drimma. Behind them came a small group of males, one leading a white goat, another carrying a silver basin. Others behind them held bouquets of deadly nightshade. Dekhalis noted with satisfaction that a few of them were female.

Owla sidled up to him. "You were magnificent," she whispered. Although the thousand implanted stakes had been her idea, she knew the wisdom of giving him the credit. When he made her his queen, she would have her revenge upon Tiala and all the others who had disregarded her.

-19-

Tiala squirmed in the vise-like grip of the hooded dark elf, while Embaza barked orders in the unaccustomed tongue. Reluctantly, the brigand released her and bowed before Embaza, croaking, "Master Dekhalis?"

"Take off your hood," demanded the wizard, attempting to pattern his voice on his one brief conversation with Dekhalis.

Apparently, it was sufficient, for the dark elf complied, and Tiala gasped, "Jos." He was an old servant of Dekhalis's, a hulking, dull-witted fellow who would do anything her brother asked of him. She gave thanks he was not clever enough to be suspicious. He was dressed in a tight-fitting suit of green and yellow, and Tiala had never seen him in anything except a simple black robe, as befitted an Alvarran man.

"Quiet, slut," ordered Embaza, raising his hand as if to strike her. When she cowed convincingly, he turned to the minion. "You—guard this passage. Make sure we are not followed."

"Yes, Lord King," the dark elf said, remembering the new title. He hesitated, blinking his eyes at the strangers with his master and the royal sister.

"Well?" snapped Embaza.

"What about the others, Lord King? They await your signal to move." He gestured vaguely to the right, at an unremarkable stone wall.

Embaza held his breath, thinking fast. Was there a secret passage behind it? A passage that hid an army? "Do you challenge me, Jos?"

"N-no, Master. It's just—"

Embaza scowled. "Speak."

"Your delegation—to the surface."

Embaza noted the way Jos cringed in terror. *What a monster this Dekhalis must be.* The wizard stepped into the shadows, smirking as he imagined his counterpart would do. "When I have gone, give the signal. If they are so eager to search for enemies, let them." Inspiration leapt to his tongue. "Tell them if they don't find any enemies, they will be cast out of my kingdom." He added, "Remind them that I like my prisoners alive."

The old servant bowed, his face suffused with relief. "Thank you, Master." He replaced the yellow hood through which his green eyes peeped.

Embaza added, "And, Jos, don't mention my other captives," he indicated Gudrun, Polah, Six Stix and Obsidian with a wave of his hand, "I want them to be a surprise."

The dark elf nodded his shrouded head, his assent muffled. He touched a spot on the stone wall beside him and slipped through the shadow of a door. In moments, the wall was unbroken as before.

Relieved, Embaza leaned against the wall. Tiala squeezed his arm in reassurance. "Quick thinking," she whispered.

Gudrun ran her hands over the stone admiringly, and Six Stix said, "Don't tell me—dwarven-made."

Tiala put a finger to her lips and pointed into the darkness. The party moved toward the flickering light at the end of the passage, their steps whispering on the smooth floor. The tunnel seemed to move in and out, as the light glimmered. Six Stix and Obsidian could see a mere handspan ahead of them, and a deepening sense of oppression slowed their steps.

As Gudrun had said, the tunnel that connected the nations of Alvarra and Tskurl was of dwarven construction. This was not for lack of skilled artisans in Alvarra, but the result of an altercation with a dragon. Although the elven priestesses had finished him off, a Tskurl'an warrior had struck the first blow. Thus, the dwarves had the honor of completing the tunnel in their own fashion.

At the crossroads, the two massive doors led to the respective countries of dwarf and elf, but here the resemblance ended.

The Tskurl'an door was made of rich, stained walnut, its surface covered with inlaid silver runes the size of a fingernail. The ancient script caused a mixture of emotions in all who saw it: a proud awe to those of Tskurl, a thrill of mystery to travelers from other lands, and discomfort to Alvarrans, who were reminded of an alien culture that was as old or older than their own.

In contrast, a little farther on, the circular Alvarran entrance was a paean to simplicity. The graceful curve of smooth teakwood showed no seam, and there were no runes to advertise the dark-elven realm. Beneath the sill flowed a stream of clear water that disappeared into the rock on either side. A humid, floral scent escaped into the cool hallway.

With a wistful glance at the ornate, walnut door, Gudrun turned to face the teakwood entrance and its rippling water beneath. She looked at the others.

Six Stix suggested, "Why not let Embaza go first? It seems that only Dekhalis may pass here." Tiala agreed.

Embaza moved forward, but Polah stood in the way, transfixed. What was that horrible green light around the door? Didn't the others see it? In moments, she had taken on her fox form and was snarling viciously.

Gudrun drew her sword with a shriek of metal. "I told you so," she muttered tersely.

"Wait, General," said Embaza and narrowed his eyes at Polah. *What's wrong?*

The fox growled deep in her throat, and Gudrun stepped back, giving her clear access to the door. Polah leapt at it, and the momentum of her huge body bowed the door inward slightly. Through a horizontal crack in the middle, a flurry of crystalline arrows whizzed through the air, just missing Tiala and bouncing impotently off the far wall.

The tips of the arrows dripped with a dark red substance. Tiala caught her breath, and Gudrun whispered, "Your brother's work?"

"Yes," said Tiala. She acknowledged the fox-woman with a nod of thanks.

Hastily, Gudrun hid her ruined sword in the ox-hide scabbard before the others could remark upon it. Embaza, whose eyes missed nothing in the dark, filed the knowledge away in his growing catalogue of depressing facts connected with magic. As an afterthought, Gudrun retrieved the shape-changer's clothes from the floor, and stowed them in her own pack.

Tiala showed Embaza an indentation in the door, and he put his hand into the crevice and yanked. He stepped aside cautiously, but no more traps were activated. The door swung open, revealing a scene of startling contrast to the austere stone passage.

Two flowering trees entwined before the doorway, creating a circle of pale yellow blossoms that arched over their heads. The translucent petals also embroidered the ground in a fragrant carpet. Beyond the door, fragile shafts of sunlight filtered down from the upper reaches of the immense cavern. The drip-drip of water caressed the echoing silence of the grotto.

Obsidian caught his breath. "I can't go in there," he gasped softly. To his dismay, the light seemed to emphasize the darkness. A flurry of bats rushed by him on their way to the dark forest that hovered beyond. He felt the breeze on his face, but the bats never touched him.

Six Stix was suddenly at his side, his hand on Obsidian's arm. "Easy, now. We'll go in together."

They followed the others through the fluttering circle of petals and into a cavern whose walls glittered faintly with crystal. They could hear the trickling stream that meandered to the left. Though hidden from the eyes of Obsidian and Six Stix who were still unused to the darkness, the others were dazzled by the flowers, trees and natural formations in the rock around them. Glistening stalagmites and stalactites interspersed the lush vegetation like sentinels from another world. Velvety white roseglove bushes created a meandering path, their fallen petals giving off an intoxicating fragrance as they were crushed underfoot.

A soft chorus of strings issued from nearby.

"The breath of Miralor," whispered Embaza, wondering where he got such ideas.

Tiala gasped. *Harp-trees.* She strained to get a glimpse of them, but their path led straight ahead, into the highlands, where they might lose themselves in the crowd of upworlders come to visit fabled Alvarra. If all went well, she'd lead her party to her secret tunnels.

Polah stiffened and growled at a shadow on the wall to the right. Before the others could react, the fox lunged, tearing at something in her massive jaws. When she stepped aside, they saw a red-and-white garbed assassin, his garrote limp in one hand. Blood flowed from the gaping hole in his neck, as he lay sprawled against the velvety rock. Gudrun rolled him on his stomach, confiscated his daggers, and hid the warm corpse in the shadows.

"Come," Tiala said urgently, "there may be more." She led the way with determination, and they followed, faintly accompanied by the harp-trees.

As the walls of the passage began to narrow, Obsidian's breathing grew more labored. He hadn't the heart to appreciate the chips of mica and crystal that embellished the gray stone, or the flowers of white fungus that grew in the cracks. Darkness still prevailed, and with every step, he became more frightened. He tried to recall some wise quotation from his teachers, but all he could remember were Embaza's words: "How one greets the unknown is the greatest test of character."

Six Stix stumbled along beside Obsidian, hampered also by the darkness. The elf's presence did much to fortify the monk, and he matched his friend's footsteps as closely as possible. As they penetrated deeper into the chambers, an occasional spray of fireflies punctuated the gloom. Although this lifted their spirits, the illumination did little to help them get their bearings.

On the wall a little gray bat hung upside down, enshrouded in slumber. Tiala ran the tip of her forefinger gently along its back, and it stirred in its sleep. The fur was soft and velvety. She remembered her great-grandmother tell of the gray robe of bat fur worn by the last High King.

From the interior of the forest, they heard the voice of a hermit thrush. Once again, the corridor opened up to a vista of loveliness. The path of stone gave way to soft earth, and the ground dipped beneath them into a wooded area. The goodroot trees were similar to oaks, but their leaves were broader, and instead of acorns, they hosted velvety buds of violet fungus. Shrubs of soft leaves and flowers grew in abundance, almost disguising the pathway.

A flood of gauzy moths descended from a mingus tree, with its fan-shaped leaves. A group of brown bats flew by through the dark. All around was the fresh smell of the dripping water, the coolness of the night and the perfume of the washed flowers.

Tiala beckoned to Polah to precede them as she looked up fearfully at the treetops. The cavern ceiling was somewhere in the darkness, far above. It would be child's play to hide assassins in the trees. Would such men be affected by music? She berated herself for not asking the monks to give her some sort of instrument, having lost the ox-bone pipes to the sand. A raven called from one of the treetops. She replied, automatically mimicking the sound. A childish game, perhaps, but one that always gave her courage.

Embaza brushed his hand against the violet goodroot bud. *This must be gathered before it blossoms, or it will lose its potency,* he thought, again startled by this unforeseen knowledge.

Tiala's gaze met Polah's, and the fox's luminous black eyes were alive with wonder, even as her nose scented danger.

"Yes, enchantress," whispered Tiala. "Isn't my land beautiful?" As if to challenge this statement, two dark-elven men fell from the goodroot tree, barring her way.

"Who trespasses here?" one barked, as Tiala shrank back. Embaza noticed they were dressed in colorful body suits like the one Jos had worn. He thought of his own dusty robes with dismay. From out of the forest, a dozen more men emerged. All carried weapons.

Masking his fear, Embaza stepped forward. "What seems to be the problem?"

"Lord King," said one.

"Give the password," said another, shouldering his way to the front.

-20-

"How DARE you?" challenged Embaza, shading his voice with the utmost contempt.

"You said to beware of impostors, Master," answered the outspoken one. He carried a barbed spear that Tiala recognized as an uprooted fence-pike. Their tight clothes unnerved her—a red one with blue circles, another of iridescent orange.

Embaza snapped his fingers at Polah and crooned wickedly, "Come here, my pet." *Sorry, Polah.*

With a meaningful growl, she emerged from the shadows, and the minions gaped at the ferocious animal. Still, the one with the fence pike held his ground. He had seen with his own eyes the penalty for slipshod behavior. He waved his weapon around at the others and said, "Who are the intruders, Lord King?" He sneered at Obsidian's pale skin.

Six Stix gripped Tiala by the shoulders and thrust her forward. Speaking in halting dark-elven, he said, "Surely you recognize the Usurper, the tyrant's second daughter, Tiala Denshadiel?"

"As you say, Lord King," said the rebel, covering his shock. He shot a nervous glance at Tiala. None of his companions would look her in the eyes.

She lifted her chin, recognizing the dialect of a city dweller. These were not farmers. They might even be educated. She wondered how many citizens of the towns and cities Dekhalis had poisoned with his ambitions.

Embaza said, "As you see, we have allies from every quarter. Here is a lord from the woods of Graymere, who commands a great army of his own."

The rebel looked with suspicion at the blue elf's battle-scarred face. "If he's a lord, I'm the Nightwing's rabbit." He brandished his weapon at Tiala. "There's no doubt about her, though." The barbed spear rested just below her chin. "Should I kill the Usurper now?"

Gudrun's hand tightened on the hilt of her sword. "Let me, Master. You promised." The rebels looked confused.

Embaza said, "Not now."

"What claim do these outsiders have on you? What have you promised them?" challenged one of the others, stepping forward. He waved a curved sword, and Tiala again recognized a home-made weapon—probably part of a door-frame.

"Yes," said another, as he crowded closer, brandishing a stone chisel. "We champion your cause, Lord Dekhalis, but do they?"

Embaza's glared at the speaker as he pondered the situation. *I must gain the upper hand, here.*

"I would never hurt you," cried Tiala, squirming in Six Stix' grasp. "You are my people."

Embaza pointed to Obsidian, "Silence her."

The monk didn't understand the dark-elven phrase, and Gudrun whispered,

"Silence Tiala."

Obsidian pinned Tiala's arms from behind, and whispered directly in her ear, "Fall when I touch you." He jabbed Tiala's neck with his finger, and she fell to the ground.

The rebels gasped at this obvious show of prowess. With a flourish, Embaza seized the advantage. "You see what allies I have brought you? Support for our cause is even growing in Tskurl, is it not, General?"

Gudrun spat at Tiala's prone form, and when she spoke, the authority in her voice made Embaza proud. "All Nightwings are thieves. The trade agreement you've proposed will be a great improvement."

"Our plans advance," Embaza gloated, rubbing his hands together. He seemed to tower over them as he summoned all his wit and charisma.

Most of the rebels retreated into cautious compliance. They bowed to the false Dekhalis, and one said, "We stand ready to obey your commands, Lord."

"Lord King," corrected Embaza.

"Long live King Dekhalis," called one elf.

"Long live the Swords of Siadhin," said another.

But the brash, young rebel persisted. "You still haven't given the password, Lord Dekhalis."

Embaza grabbed a piece of wax from his sleeve, kneading it quickly. It was the first magic he had ever learned; he prayed it would work. Polah crept to his side. The rebel stepped back, but did not lower his weapon.

Embaza's silence created disquiet in the ranks of the Swords of Siadhin. They pressed closer to their brother, waiting for his answer.

The erstwhile wizard pulled one of his needles from his sleeve, all the while fixing his eyes upon the handsome, young elf before him. When he spoke, his voice nearly mimicked Dekhalis's completely, accent and all. "The last person who challenged my authority died like this." He inserted the tip of the needle into the center of the wax.

The rebel doubled over in pain, and his companions retreated in fear, mumbling under their breaths. Some had not seen Dekhalis in action; all knew his reputation. No one had seen him do this before, nor had anyone spoken of a great fox beside him.

With renewed confidence, Embaza replaced the wax and needle in the depths of his robe. He folded his arms, glowered at his henchmen and his eyes roamed over them until they fastened on a tall, thin elf with a long forelock. "Come here," said the wizard.

The rebel stepped forward, tucking his bear-claw hammer into his belt.

Casually, Embaza flipped the ice-blue necklace from beneath his robe and riveted his eyes on the elf. "I gave you the password earlier, did I not?"

The henchman gulped. "Yes, Master," he said, nodding vigorously. A wave of murmured surprise erupted from the other Swords of Siadhin. The thin one's teeth chattered, hands shook. "You did." He could not take his eyes from the glittering necklace.

"Well?" said Embaza, blistering rage teasing the edges of his voice.

The tall elf fell to his knees, clasping Embaza by the legs, "I'm sorry—forgive me, Lord King. Do not kill me, please. Truly, you gave the password."

Polah growled, nuzzling Embaza's side. This further terrified the rebels. Embaza looked at her, and she blinked back at him with dark, liquid eyes.

He pointed a long finger. "Lead us to the next sentry post so that all may share my victory." The henchman scrambled up and pushed his way to the front of the other lieutenants. They avoided the body of the stricken Sword of Siadhin lying conspicuously in the middle of the pathway.

Obsidian lifted Tiala's limp form, and hoisted it over one shoulder. He was glad to have something to do. His eyes were becoming more accustomed to the darkness, but he was still apprehensive.

Six Stix said, gruffly, "Careful with her."

Gudrun kept her hand on the hilt of her sword, but they were not challenged again. In fact, there was very little traffic.

Peering from beneath her hair, Tiala noticed this, too, and was worried. They passed the traditional sentry posts—empty. No one trod the narrow corridors except her new friends and the brightly-clothed escorts with their chiseled elven faces and long-limbed grace. At least, she might be safe from assassins, for now. They passed arched doorways of natural stone that led to other parts of the highlands, but there was no sign of visitors.

Polah padded along, watching the rebels keenly. With her new sensitivity, their auras were hideous and they exuded a nauseating smell. She growled, and the Swords of Siadhin glanced back at her nervously.

Good, thought Embaza, *let them learn to fear you.*

With a *cling!,* Gudrun unsheathed her sword, its silver edge suddenly illuminated by the eerie glow of a firefly. Embaza regretted his behavior at the campsite, wishing he had taken the dagger Gudrun offered. He gestured to Six Stix to draw his sword, and the blue elf did so.

When they came to a stellate branching of pathways, some of the rebels gaped at Gudrun's miraculous sword with the deep scar of pitch, while others were fascinated by Six Stix's sword and Obsidian's unusual knives.

Stark envy plastered their faces, and one dropped back to walk beside Embaza. Lowering his voice, he said, "Master, why can we not confiscate the priestess' treasure—or at least break into the storerooms of the City? And why have you allowed these upworlders to keep their weapons?"

"You dare to question me? I told you," Embaza said, improvising hurriedly, "be patient. I will give you weapons that make these look like toys." The elf gave Embaza a suspicious look, but nodded and went forward once again.

Polah sniffed around, and the hackles on her neck rose. Without being aware of it, she had assumed the attitude of the hunt. Some of the pathways showed the wear of constant traffic and a melange of exotic visitors; others were dusty and dank, and Polah inhaled the deep coolness of an underground far more vast than she had imagined. Hunger gnawed at her, but she knew it would help her stay in fox-form.

Their guides chose one of the least traveled corridors. The fox pricked her ears and Gudrun frowned at a burst of laughter from up ahead. Embaza tensed and raised his eyebrows at Gudrun, who whispered, "Tavern." A flurry of startled bats flew by, causing a rush of cool air.

As the party turned a corner, two dark-elven males stumbled out into the passageway ahead of them, vaguely limned by a wan phosphor-stone globe that hung from the ceiling. Bluish light spilled from an open doorway. One laughing elf slapped the other on the back.

The Swords of Siadhin ignored the two drunks, and led with impassive faces. Gudrun was instantly alert. She reasoned the highlands of Alvarra could hold many dangers, especially if Tiala was recognized. The dogged purpose in the rebels' postures worried her as well. She dropped back and partially covered Tiala's face with a corner of the gray robe.

As they passed the tavern, one rowdy elf pointed at Polah. "Look at the big fox," he shouted to his friend. The other elf covered his mouth and guffawed, then cried, "Woof woof."

Polah swished her tail, and with the grace of her kind, moved toward them, her nose turning up at the sickly smell of fermented huckleberries. Pointed teeth gleamed from her muzzle. The two elves scurried back into the doorway, closing the heavy oaken door.

The weak illumination of the phosphor-stone lent a surreal glow to the corridor, which branched again in several directions. Obsidian felt a wave of panic boil up through his chest and into his throat, as he realized he would never remember all the turns. He could still see only a hand's breadth ahead of him. "Where are we?" he squeaked, then cleared his throat with embarrassment.

Six Stix muttered, "Don't worry about it. If we're successful, we'll be mobbed with potential consorts."

Obsidian grinned. "Always thinking about the ladies," he chided, his voice still shaky.

Six Stix glanced at Tiala and he sensed a smile beneath her hooded face.

Their escort chose the pathway to the left. Three of them dropped back and surrounded their master, separating him from his strange companions.

-21-

MISCHA HAD quite a bit of trouble finding the entrance to the underground. From his vantage point, he had taken careful note of the exact rock, and waited patiently a goodly span of time before creeping up to it. However, try as he might, he could not find the opening.

He wasted precious minutes running from rock to rock, swearing with vexation, until he was hopelessly confused. For the next half hour or so, he alternated between cursing and stomping around, and trying this or that rock once again. The locket no longer warmed his skin, and he was afraid he was losing precious time.

At one interval, he rooted around in his sack for something that might be of help. His cursing grew more pronounced upon realizing just how few items were left: an elderwood wand, a scroll (which he could not read), a flask that contained some noxious-smelling liquid—and the flute the dark elf had called the Glammalee. He shuddered at the sight of it, and withdrew his hand.

He hated to use any of the items, but he finally decided on the wand. *After all, it'll be no good to me if I can't find Dekhalis.*

He flexed the smooth branch of elderwood in his pudgy hands and looked at it in bewilderment. The body was free of markings. He had not noticed that before. He pursed his lips, thinking, *If I am to be a wizard, I must take risks.* He surveyed the area. Gripping the wand with both hands, he pointed it at the rocks and turned in a circle. The wand trembled, or perhaps that was just his own hands shaking.

There must be some word to release the power. He closed his eyes and tried to conjure up the nonsense-sounds he had heard wizards use. *"Mimbus Zeon Dwill…"*

The wand quivered violently, encouraging Mischa to repeat the phrase again. *"Mimbus Zeon Dwill."* There was a rumbling beneath his feet, and before his eyes, a hooded figure emerged from beneath one of the rocks. More creatures followed.

Mischa's whole body was trembling so that he could hardly keep his grasp on the wand. Of its own volition, the wand pointed itself at the hooded figures that poured out of the ground. Mischa felt queasy, and his legs went out from under him. He landed on his well-padded rump, waving the slim branch of elderwood in every direction.

A fissure suddenly opened up in one of the rocks nearby, and a violet light poured forth. Mischa stared with fascination at the phenomenon. The wand throbbed in his hands, and he wrenched his attention back toward the group of hooded figures still coming from below. With a start, he realized they were dark elves; through their hoods, he saw the tips of their large, pointed ears. He scrambled to his feet, marshalling his dignity, and with some difficulty, thrust the wand under his arm.

Cautiously, he approached the band of brightly-garbed creatures. He knew enough dark-elven from his studies at the Manor to make himself understood. "Stay where you are," he ordered, "or I'll annihilate you." He noticed that they carried crudely-made weapons, and wondered briefly why they weren't forged. Nervously, he counted an even dozen hooded elves.

"Who are you?" demanded the apparent leader of the group in a crude dialect of the dark-elven tongue. The elves seemed unsure of themselves, as if they were unused to the surface.

"I am a wizard of Sargoth—my name is Mischa—Mischa the Great," said the Prince, speaking in high elven, a language few elves even used. *Try that on, you haughty insect.*

The elf was handsome, with long, pointed ears and a high-bridged nose. "Show us some magic, then, if you are a real wizard."

Mischa was tempted for a moment to draw out the flute, but remembered what Tiala had said about it being a precious dark-elven relic. Besides, he still recalled the sound of that first note—and his fear.

Instead, he pointed the elderwood wand at a nearby rock, and said, "*Grimmus Nimbus Beenew.*" Nothing happened.

The elves edged nearer, seemingly unafraid, which bothered Mischa. He pointed the wand again and uttered a new phrase, "*Pordish Pazouna Ravree.*"

This time, the rock began to turn green, and a weird smell emanated from it—rather like a rotting heap of vegetation. The elves made noises of disgust as they recoiled from the foul-smelling phenomenon.

Mischa replaced the wand under his arm, planted his feet securely and stood as tall as he could. "I hope you're satisfied with this small display. I don't want to endanger any of you without cause."

The lead elf said, "You appear to be a wizard, but we'll leave that to our Master to decide."

Mischa said, "And who is that?"

"Lord King Dekhalis, the all-powerful. True ruler of Alvarra."

"Ah, just the one I'm looking for. Lead me to him."

Another elf cautioned, "He doesn't seem like the kind of enemy our Lord King meant."

Mischa gave a grim parody of a laugh. "Enemies? You're looking for them? No doubt, they've already passed through your incompetent fingers."

The head elf loomed over him, a black shadow of menace. "You can see them with your wizardry?"

"Not at the moment," Mischa, said, then hastened to add, "but there is another wizard—a false one who is trying to kill your master."

"A likely story," cried one.

"We must have proof," said their leader. "Our Master's orders were to bring back our enemies—not an outland wizard no one has ever heard of—begging your pardon, Mischa the Great."

"You must know that in the realm of the invisible, proof is hard to obtain," said Mischa, wearing his most menacing expression.

Still skeptical, the elves seemed torn, until their leader decided the matter. "Let's go and give him to Dekhalis. He said to bring a prisoner, and this one should satisfy him. At least, he's a wizard."

Mischa noticed how they shrank from the sunlight, even in the forest. He suspected that many in the party were beginning to show the first signs of sun-sickness. Some were frothing at the mouth beneath their bright hoods. Others were gritting their teeth or rolling their eyes.

They were not far from the entrance when the first elf succumbed, falling to the ground, arms and legs kicking wildly.

"Do something, Great Mischa," cried an elf.

"If you are truly great—help him," demanded another.

With rising dread, Mischa pulled the bottle from his pack. It smelled horrible, like most medicines. Avoiding the convulsing limbs, he snatched the stricken elf's hood free of his head and poured a drop of the noxious liquid in the vicinity of the fellow's mouth. When he saw the elf swallow, he jumped back to watch.

There appeared to be no effect. The elf continued to writhe on the ground in obvious agony. Then, suddenly, his face went rigid. His eyes nearly popped out of his head. He looked around at the others, a stark terror on his face, before he just as abruptly closed his eyes and lay still.

"You've killed him," cried the leader of the elves. Two of the party grabbed Mischa, pinning his arms, while a third reached from behind and grasped him by his hair.

"Wait—" began Mischa.

Just then, the stricken elf got his feet gracefully, easily, dusting off his yellow body suit. He rubbed his mouth and looked at the Prince. "Phfew—that stuff is strong," he said.

Mischa was released, a dozen elves crowding him now. "Give me some."

"No, me!"

"Let me have it."

Mischa passed the bottle to the elven leader, with a warning. "Only a drop, mind you—more is quite dangerous. Careful, now. That's right..." One by one the elves drank of the foul-tasting liquid. When it finally came back to Mischa, the bottle was empty.

The leader said to one of his companions. "Go to our Master, and tell him we have found no enemies. We are returning with an ally, a great wizard who has medicine against the Scourge."

Mischa was impressed with himself. Things were going splendidly. Not only would he vanquish his enemies, but he was going to the fabled Alvarra at last. What better place to find new toys?

-22-

DEKHALIS CURSED to himself. *Where's the orb? Who is this wizard?—are there two? Or—is he so powerful that he can be in two places at once? I'll have to get someone I can trust. That means the Merimn'a. What a nuisance.* In moments he had made a summons, and a voice said, "Yes, Master?"

"Zagadon, bring me a new wizard—from the Merimn'a."

"The forbidden realm?" quailed the other.

"Yes. Tell him he will need my good will in future—and hurry."

"Yes, Master."

The slender Owla sidled up to him with a languid grace that belied her tension. "What is it, my love?" She stroked his ear, and Dekhalis was annoyed by the answering tingle in his groin.

With a grimace, he shook her off, grasping her forearm tightly. "Owla," he said tersely, "go and torment Noth. Be useful."

"No," she said, pouting, "I don't feel like it." She tilted her face, prettily.

Dekhalis scowled at her. "You forget yourself. Consorts can be discarded—you're not my queen yet."

She raised one eyebrow, undaunted. "'Khalis," she said, her voice a caress and a promise, "you know my skills are irreplaceable." Her compelling eyes locked with his before she jauntily looked away.

Dekhalis's face was a distant mask. "I'd like to see you try them on one of my spidermen."

Owla hid her fear of the inner circle with a shrug. "If you like, though the prospect bores me. Your sisters promise more sport." She sauntered off, her spare frame a hymn to the iron discipline of daily training.

Dekhalis watched her go, relishing the fear she had revealed. *She is so easy to manipulate. They all are, when you know where to squeeze.*

While Eleppon lay unconscious and Inuari battled blindfolded terror on the makeshift scaffold, Noth had regained enough of her wits to scheme. She was tied to a broad-limbed mingus tree, her arms and legs numb from their bonds, but her mind was no longer dulled by the pain. When she saw Owla coming toward her, she thought, *Oh, Scourge. I need time to think.*

As if she had heard, the dark beauty folded her arms, and her slanted eyes bored into Noth's bruised, impassive face with its swollen nose.

"So, you'd rather not talk with me, eh, little sister? Indeed yes, we'll be like sisters when I am queen. That is, if you're still alive." She enjoyed the slight pursing of the lips that betokened Noth's anger. "Still not ready to talk with your brother? He wants to know where Tiala is." Owla looked back over her shoulder and whispered, "Although, just between you and me, I don't think you know, do you? But we won't tell him that. No," her face became sly, "I'll protect you from him. And you can give me something in return, little sister."

Noth wished she could retch in the other's face. She tried to focus on a spot halfway down Owla's nose to calm herself.

"Just tell me where the Nightwing keeps her long-life potions—the ones that maintain her beauty."

Noth burst out laughing and said, "Is that all you really want, you vain idiot? Do you enjoy being controlled by a *man?*"

Owla's face turned deep purple with rage. She pivoted on her heel, spitting her reply over her shoulder. "You're dead."

Noth swallowed, watching Owla cross to the scaffold where Inuari was tied. *So much for planning, stupid dolt,* she berated herself. Tears sprang to her eyes. *Damn my temper.* She was glad that Owla hadn't seen her tears.

Inuari sensed Owla's hateful presence even through her blindfold. She knew the kind of playmates Dekhalis had, but she never stopped hoping he would reform. This new evidence of his nature hurt worse than the vine that clawed at her wrists.

Owla put her face next to Inuari's ear and whispered, "Hello, witch." She plucked at Inuari's sleeve and laughed when the priestess flinched.

Inuari breathed in the ordinary smell of forest mold and lichen, and it gave her courage.

Owla paced up and down, arms behind her back. "Perhaps we should be kinder to you," said the assassin, her voice as silky as down. Gently, she removed the gag from Inuari's mouth. Inuari felt a twinge of hope, as she gingerly moved her jaw in a painful circle.

Owla continued, "You have a special relationship with Miralor. After all, she may not want you to be sacrificed. If you pray to her, she might grant you a landslide, or a raging river, or maybe a cave-in…"

Inuari tensed. "Surely you know—Theowla Twomothers—that the Great One does not answer such requests. Nor would I ask."

"Oh, is that so?" Owla's tone was suddenly like a shard of ice. "I didn't realize you were so helpless." Her long fingers toyed with the fabric at Inuari's neck, and fear licked the young priestess as her bodice was ripped downward.

In the next moment, a cold sensation crept into her neck, and she realized Owla had laid a metal instrument against her skin. At a stab of pain, she felt the wetness of her own blood. Owla's laughter was hideously cruel.

"Oops, did I slip? Sorry," she said, pocketing the knife.

Blood trickled into the hollow between Inuari's bared breasts, and she squirmed, wanting to scratch. This only tightened the strangleberry vine at her wrists. Owla's receding footsteps echoed, strangely loud in her ears. The pulses at Inuari's temples throbbed with the pain of concentration. "Miralor," she prayed, "just once—" She stopped, suddenly afraid, and from somewhere nearby, heard her brother's voice.

"You were supposed to torture them. So, why aren't they screaming?"

-23-

WHILE OBSIDIAN threaded his way through the darkness, fighting his fear of caves, guilt jabbed Tiala as she rode like a sack of meal on his shoulder. She could no longer fend off visions of her three sisters. *I should be in their place—I'm the one he wants. Why ever did I leave them?* She considered her new champions. A blue elf and human—bumbling and blind in the dark; a disabled wizard; an enchantress who had not yet learned control. *Ironic that a dwarf should be my most trusted companion.*

Suddenly, she heard the music of a singing harp—the forty-eight-stringed instrument that presaged a bard of renown—and all other thoughts were driven from her mind. There were a mere handful in Alvarra who could play such a harp. One of them she knew well—Selisor, her first music teacher, in whom she had confided her desire to become a bard.

While Tiala strained for recognition of those beloved hands, she remembered another bard who played the singing harp. A self-taught outlaw—a man—and a good friend of her brother's. She felt a sinking despair. Qwodor. *Oh, Miralor, let it not be him.*

She had been a mere fifty when this elf had tried to court her. In the way of young beauties, she had spurned him without a qualm. He had also been envious of the talent he had seen in the young bard, and had spread gossip about her at every opportunity.

She was sick to death of mistrust and danger. Alvarra was not made for such complications. It was a world of magic and miracle, majesty and mystery.

The Goddess spoke in the heartbeat of the earth. Did the others feel it? Could they hear it? There was more than her own blood beating in her long, graceful ears. The singing harp produced the sound of a host of instruments to the experienced listener. In spite of her knowledge, she found it hard not to imagine a full orchestra, with chalumeau, cithara, khamango, nanga, sarangi and other stringed instruments.

Although she could not say it, Polah did feel a heartbeat beneath her sensitive paws, had felt it from the first moment. She panted softly, keenly aware of the resonating sounds ahead. The velvety darkness seemed to caress her fur, and the fireflies were a mild nuisance. The smells of damp earth that emanated from below tickled her nostrils again. Her awareness heightened each time she caught that scent, as if it carried the knowledge of her entire past, present and future. She wanted to drink it like an elixir. The music seemed to heighten this desire.

Embaza slung his arm about her neck, ruffling her fur. "Polah," was all he said. In his voice dwelt a cavern of desire, catching on a note of sadness and loss. He was submerged beneath the feelings.

The chamber filled with shimmering harmonies, swelling with overtures of ecstasy and peace. Gudrun and Obsidian stopped, and Tiala held her breath. Embaza began to speak, then stood dazed, without his usual protections.

Polah's hunger intensified. Bemused by the spectral symphony, she never noticed the gaping hole in the ground beside her foot, and in an instant, she had stumbled into it, and fallen out of sight. Embaza was too rapt to notice.

Even the Swords of Siadhin were subdued, and swayed in rhythm, standing in clumps at the head and foot of the party.

Six Stix was dimly aware of the music. By some obscure instinct, he had immediately begun to hum. When he realized the others had stopped moving, he shook Obsidian's arm, "Hey, wake up," but the monk did not respond. With mounting dread, Six Stix tried to rouse Gudrun and Tiala. The wizard, too, was staring stupidly at the woods ahead. The fox-woman had disappeared.

Without torch or even moonlight, he had only the intermittent glow of the fireflies to guide him. Six Stix headed toward the sound of the music, humming an intricate tune in which he tried to remember all the parts simultaneously. He moved with the silence of a blue-corps leader, betraying no hint of heavy boot or armor. His humming might have been the buzzing of an insect.

When he reached the edge of the glen where the harpist played, not a glimmer of light appeared. The trees formed a dense canopy over the bard, and all Six Stix could see was a faint shimmer in the air. He continued to hum, sword gripped with both hands. The others remained enthralled, even the Swords of Siadhim.

Out of nowhere, something knocked Six Stix on the chest. He stumbled, swinging his blade wildly. He swore loudly, on a note, still humming. He saw nothing. But he detected a kind of 'feel' to the air—something almost tangible. It was only music. *Music.* He slashed toward the shape of the note, thinking it was madness.

By some miracle, his sword connected. Whatever he had hit, a chord emanated from it, threaded with melodies that multiplied in harmony, coming at him in waves. He sang out loud, heart and soul engaged in the most unusual battle of his career.

Another swath of raw music tangled with his sword, clawed up his arm, seeking his throat. He severed it with his blade, gaining confidence now, as his ruby-throated weapon began to whine a sharp-edged song of its own. Indeed, the opposing symphony dwindled to a few thin notes.

Six Stix worked with determination, whittling away at the strange adversary, never catching a glimpse of the wielder of the harp. He had never battled in full song before, and his baritone voice nearly gave out more than once. His breath was ragged when he delivered the final blow to the harpist. An eerie stillness followed, broken only by the thud of a body falling heavily.

Ironically, it was at this moment that a group of fireflies showed themselves, or perhaps the music had mysteriously doused their winking lamps. In the ghostly light, Six Stix glimpsed a dark-elven male dressed in a lilac tabard over a blood-red, fitted suit.

The singing harp loomed over him like a sentinel. Seven feet tall, its dark, burlwood stem was glossy with the bard's sweat—or was it blood? The strings seemed to breathe with pain. Six Stix reached out his hand to still them, then drew back. A sound startled him from behind, and he turned, gripping his sword. *Guards.* Quickly, he moved behind a tree, melting into its lichen-covered bark, nostrils filled with the moldy perfume.

He closed his eyes and the footsteps of the rebels vibrated beneath his feet. He heard one mutter, "Where did the fox go?"

"Dekhalis won't like it if we've lost it," the other hissed.

Embaza's voice rang out, and Six Stix almost didn't recognize him from the Alvarran dialect. "Fan out. Search quickly. I want the fox found."

There was a flurry of movement, then Tiala's voice whispered, "Six Stix—."

"Sssh," said the blue elf, as he walked with his new sound-sense toward her voice. He clasped her in his arms. "Dark girl," he murmured against her hair.

"Thank Miralor you're safe," she said softly. Six Stix was elated at this sign of her affection.

Tiala's eyes pierced the glade, alighting on the singing harp. She gave a wrenching cry and bounded toward it, leaving Six Stix standing. "Wait," he said, but the dark elf stepped daintily over Qwodor's body and faced the harp. She held up her smooth palms a hair's breadth from the strings, as if she could thus commune with the instrument. Tears in her eyes, she dropped her arms with a sigh and turned to the others. "It's ruined. Hopelessly out of tune." She wept, and Six Stix came forward to comfort her.

She turned on him, frowning. "What did you do to it?"

He put his arm around her waist. "Not now. We must keep moving. And where's Polah?"

Tiala started to object, then turned away from the harp, slipping free of Six Stix' embrace.

With a sense of triumph, Gudrun said, "Seems we're always asking about Polah."

Embaza sent a tendril of thought toward the part of Polah that resided in his mental recesses. *Polah?* There was no answer. An image of her slim body falling down a hole appeared to him. "Seems she was carried to the underground by a different route."

Gudrun stared at him, and Embaza brought his fingers to his temples as if they ached. He could not explain, and felt suddenly deflated. A cricket sounded nearby, answered by a frog. Was it morning or evening here? He supposed he would get used to it if he stayed underground long enough. *The arboretum keeps both day and night in tune...* He sighed, dropped his hands to his sides, and shook his head to clear his mind. Where were these errant thoughts coming from?

Gudrun said, "I don't like this—magic. My lady, is this a common occurrence around here, or more of your brother's tricks?"

"Dekhalis seems to bring out the worst in people." Tiala looked down at the body. "Another strange costume."

"Yes, I noticed that, too," said Six Stix. "Embaza needs such a garment to complete his disguise." Just then, a bell sounded in the distance. The forest seemed hushed as the tolling repeated nine times.

"Hurry," urged Tiala. She and Embaza stripped the lifeless bard and covered him with the wizard's robe. In moments, the false Dekhalis wore the garish red body suit and lofted his pack over his shoulder. "How do I look?" he asked, jauntily.

Tiala shook her head. "Ridiculous."

"No," said Gudrun, "you look just like the others." As if in answer, they heard the men returning.

Embaza shouted an order. "Stay here until you find the fox, or you will feel my displeasure."

"This way," hissed Tiala, and the party hurried after her into the darkness ahead. Where no path was visible, she plunged into the bushes, counseling them to try and leave no trace of their passing. Eventually, the path widened slightly, appearing to be an animal trail for deer or antelope.

As they ran through the seemingly endless forest that co-existed with ancient stalagmites, their nostrils filled with the smell of sticky sap from the thick evergreens. Insects bowed their guttural notes to the distant ceiling, and curtains of fireflies and moths shifted across their path. A song sparrow seemed to follow them, fluttering from tree to tree, as the forest became denser.

Tiala looked up every few moments, alert for more assassins. Gudrun watched the ground for traps and grumbled once again that Polah ought to be with them. She noticed the small hoofprints of under-deer and the occasional mouse.

Obsidian grew increasingly uneasy. Feathery evergreen branches kept swatting him in the face until he fanned his hands before him. It increased his sensation of blindness. "Where are we?" he asked.

"In the animal preserve—it protects the cultivated lands," said Tiala.

"Does anyone live here?" asked Six Stix.

"Just animals and birds."

"Sssh," said Gudrun. "We may be followed."

They moved quickly along the deer track. At the rear, Six Stix listened for sounds of pursuit, but heard none. Obsidian whispered, "Six—can you see anything?"

"A little, but better yet, I hear little," replied Six Stix. "I'd feel better still if we knew where Polah was."

Embaza said, "She's safe. We must hurry." In the back of his mind, he had his own worries about her, but sternly reminded himself he must not be distracted.

Through the copse, they saw a small clearing, filled with huge standing stones tilted at odd angles. Tiala darted forward, and the others followed. She knelt before a large obelisk of basalt, and dug until she found a slim piece of silver shaped like a teardrop. Scrambling up, she inserted it into a hidden indentation in the center of the plinth of rock. A crack opened and a gust of cold air slapped her face. Tiala yanked both sides of the stone to widen the crack, revealing a stairway of translucent, green stone. "Follow me."

Gudrun quickly obeyed, then Embaza, Obsidian and Six Stix. Tiala stood on the landing, waiting for them to pass. She then pushed the edges of the stone back together and pocketed the key.

Hearing the scrape of stone close them off, Embaza made one more attempt to contact Polah. Again, he received that faint sense of reassurance.

The stairs continued down for about sixty feet. At the bottom, they entered a cavern, damp and cold, with a ceiling seven feet high. Obsidian instinctively stooped, unaware of the space above him.

The walls were entirely made of green quartz. A light emanated from the stone, and for the first time, the monk could see clearly. He bent over, hands on his knees, breathing deeply. Gudrun frowned. "Cave fear," she pronounced, her voice echoing hollowly in the cavern.

Tiala said, "No time for weakness. Take heart, Obsidian," and led the way into the cavern, and down the passage beyond. Light played inside the crystal, casting eerie beams like sentient webs over their bodies as they passed. Embaza's red suit turned sepia-colored in the greenish glow. A few yards ahead, the corridor turned, smoothly, like a worm.

-24-

WHEN THEY had walked about half a league, the ceiling arched upward, while the floor carried them ever downward at a gradual decline. Six Stix was increasingly uncomfortable, as the temperature dropped. His skin broke out in goosebumps, and he could hear Obsidian's teeth chattering.

Even Gudrun shivered. The caves of Tskurl were much nearer the surface. "I'd heard it was cold down here." She wondered if her ancestors had mined these caves.

"Is this typical?" asked Embaza, although he already felt his blood racing, excited by the climate.

With a shrug, Tiala passed the cloak back to him, but he shook his head. "I'll get used to it." He passed it to Gudrun.

The dwarf wrapped it around her for a moment, enjoying its warmth, then sighed and handed it off to Obsidian. "Here, human, maybe this will stop your teeth. They're getting on my nerves."

Embaza said, "Too bad this bard had no weapons. It would be better for me to carry something, especially as I am impersonating Dekhalis."

Tiala said, "Let's not start this argument again, Embaza. You may be impersonating Dekhalis, but you're not him. You're in mourning, like all dark elves."

Embaza was silent. He had no intention of obeying the rules. At the earliest chance, he would obtain a weapon. His eyes discerned a clear, star-shaped protrusion on the crystal wall. It was double the size of his fingertip. As he walked, he saw more and more of them.

"What are these?" asked Gudrun, who had noticed them, too.

Tiala pried one off the wall with a popping noise and held it up. "Stoneflower. It has suckers, see?" She chewed on the edge of it. "Mmm, sweet. Here," she handed Gudrun the rest.

The dwarf smacked her lips. "Delicious." Soon they had all sampled the stoneflowers, and the taste of the food lifted their spirits.

Obsidian asked, "Is it an animal?"

"No," said Tiala. "Fungus."

The monk's stomach was queasy.

The corridor turned again, and Tiala gasped. A few feet ahead, a pile of green crystal rocks the size of her fist littered the pathway. Beyond them was a huge mound of large, quartz boulders. Their faceted edges gleamed at her like a dare. She looked down at her hands, wishing she had gloves and digging tools.

Gudrun came forward with the obvious intention of moving the rocks.

"Wait," said Tiala. "They're very sharp."

The dwarf pursed her lips and rolled one of the smaller boulders off the pile. "Ouch," she cried, sucking her finger where a cut had immediately opened. She wrapped the hem of her tunic over her fist and rolled another boulder off the pile.

Six Stix came up to help her, and soon they all went to work, protecting their hands as well as possible. It was not long before they realized they would make little headway. For all they knew, the pile was endless.

One by one, they sat down to rest on the greenish floor, all except Gudrun, who paced back and forth. Obsidian broke the silence. "How often do you have a cave-in such as this, Princess?"

Tiala said, "Rarely. Very rarely. These caverns are thousands of years old." She touched the wall. "Beyond this are layers and layers of rock."

Obsidian swallowed, oppressed by the image.

"So, what could cause it?" asked Six Stix.

"Maybe a severe rainstorm high above—occasionally, the rivers rise, and we get a few tremors. Caverns fill and we have to drain them. But the rainy season isn't due for another moon." She twisted a lock of her hair. "Or a really serious eruption—when the Earth Mother rumbles in her sleep. But that won't happen for at least another five hundred aeons."

Obsidian sat in mute terror. For a moment, they were all silent.

"Now, what?" asked Gudrun.

Tiala sighed. "The canal is probably the safest. We'll have to buy or steal a boat." She looked at Embaza. "Or get one by subterfuge."

Embaza realized he had left his needles and wax in his robe. He resented the fact that this would have pleased Tiala.

"What canal is this?" asked Gudrun.

"You saw the start of it at the entrance, remember?" Tiala began placing small rocks in a pattern. "It connects us here—and flows through the cultivated lands—into a series of locks." She made a fan of seven larger stones. "Each of the locks leads to a different city." She pointed to the third stone. "Douvilwe sits above my family's compound. We'll go there."

"Then, what?" said the dwarf, remembering accounts of other Tskurl'an travelers. She didn't expect a warm reception.

"Guards unload the boats at the checkpoints. Only merchants travel these canals. Ordinary citizens go by foot or horse."

"Why?" asked Embaza.

"Safety," she said. "The canal is treacherous, filled with whirlpools and cross-currents. Even large fish. Pilots have to be trained—in navigation, water craft, boat making, and thoroughly tested before they take one journey on the river."

"You've had this training?" asked Six Stix, impressed.

"No," said Tiala, scowling at Gudrun's snort of disgust. "I've studied, though. I've read about the canal and seen drawings of the water creatures. It is part of a ruler's education." She looked down and fiddled with a stone. "Besides, I was interested."

Embaza said, "What happens at the checkpoints?"

"In ordinary times, we would have to show our passes. Each merchant has to carry an official paper that lists her cargo."

"Again, women?" complained Six Stix. He chuckled at Tiala's stern face. "Easy, lass, no insult meant. It's just hard for an old elf to adjust, that's all." His hand rested on his sword hilt, an unconscious gesture of assertion that was not lost on Tiala.

"The big problem is finding a convincing reason why Dekhalis would be carrying visitors from other lands. This seems too unpredictable, even for him. I can't seem to think, I'm so tired. I must rest a bit." She looked around. "At least we appear to be safe here."

"My lady," said Gudrun, kneeling awkwardly on the floor, "tell us the old tale."

"What do you mean?"

"You know—why Alvarran women rule with such an iron hand."

"Surely you're taught this in your schools," said the dark elf. The men held their tongues, curious.

Gudrun shook her head. "We study our own history. It's enough, believe me."

"Well," said Tiala, leaning on one elbow and stretching out her legs, "it's no mystery, really. In ancient times, men took power over women, fighting among themselves for who would rule. As time went by, they became more and more brutish, until women were treated like animals." She looked around her captive audience. "Worse. We were beaten, enslaved, and grew old before our time working the mines and farms, and raising our young." She paused,

333

imagining her ancestors, always awed by the courage they must have had.

"Finally, in desperation, we committed acts of violence to take control over the men. To save ourselves—and them—from a doomed future." She traced the outline of a rabbit with her forefinger on the floor. "Because of man's tendency toward violence, our grandmothers deemed them too unstable to rule; thus they became the governed." She looked up, and defiance flashed from her eyes. "But we rule with compassion."

Obsidian sensed a partial untruth, unsure how to address it. Six Stix grunted with disagreement. He had seen how men could be changed. Embaza was lost in thought, thinking of Dekhalis.

Gudrun said, "No—there is little difference between men and women. By my beard, men are flesh and bone, are they not? They fight and work and love. They struggle and hope and doubt, as we do. In Tskurl, we live in harmony with each other."

Six Stix laughed. "Quite an exaggeration, my old foe. The bickering among dwarves is legendary."

Gudrun's voice grew hard. "Let us not start an old argument."

Embaza ended the discussion with a challenge to Tiala. "Perhaps it is no longer fear of man that perpetuates your world, but fear of the effect they could have on you."

Tiala stared at him, struck by his words. She said, "I need rest, and so do you. No more talk." She leaned her back up against the cavern wall and closed her eyes.

-25-

Mischa could hardly contain his excitement: an armed escort. And here was the legendary Alvarra, that place of mystery and rumor. He forced himself not to make the sign of warding he had seen demonstrated by others in his keep.

He would have liked a more leisurely passage, however. Surely there were magic items he could purchase in the underground, but it was all he could do to keep up with the long-legged elves. Besides, his night-sense had never been particularly good, and he could see only the colors and large shapes of trees and crystal formations.

The elves had shown a certain amount of curiosity about his appearance, one of them gingerly touching his flaxen hair to see whether it was real or not. He had put a stop to this by reminding them that he was a wizard. *It's convenient being a man of wisdom.*

As it happened, they passed the same tavern where Polah had frightened the two dark elves. The door was open, and Mischa gave a longing glance at the warm interior. "Why not let me have a drink?" he asked. "Aren't you thirsty?"

The leader of the party shook his head. "We're on duty."

"Well, I'm not," he snapped, unused to being denied his whims. The guard prepared to argue, but the Prince forestalled him. "Don't cross me. I'd like not to turn you into a snake." With that, Mischa stepped into the tavern, leaving the disgruntled guard outside with the rest of his escort.

The cavern was dimly lit by the iridescent green of wychwood lamps. Three dark-elven patrons sat at a white marble table to the left. Otherwise, the tavern was inhabited only by a barkeep behind a curve of polished rhodochrosite.

Mischa admired the way the architects had enhanced the natural form of the cavern rather than concealing it. He thought the arched ceiling would promote lofty thoughts and the curve of the walls would contribute to a delightful feeling of intoxication. He stepped up to the rosy-hued bar, his nose barely reaching the top. Clearing his throat, he said, "I want ale."

The dark-elven tavern master was a scrawny-looking woman dressed in a body suit of lemon yellow. Her face was pinched and sour—until she smiled. Then, the creases at the corners of her eyes and mouth lent an air of compassion to her visage. She thought she had seen it all. "It's nearly ten bells, you know. I'll be closing up soon."

"I'm a paying customer."

The barkeep smiled now at the half-gnome's haughty airs. "Ale, eh? We have groundmint, sassafras, strawberry, kumquat, sweet potato, spiced onion, beet, straw beetle, hemp root, witch vine." She paused for breath. "Let's see …marigold, bitterrose, sorghum, maple, dream vine, snow radish, rhubarb, licorice root and…oh yes, nightshade honey."

Mischa was impressed. "Maple," he ordered and reached in his sack, then remembered he had no money. All that remained were the empty bottle, the cryptic scroll, the flute and the elderwood wand. Mischa withdrew the bottle, and after the barkeep had set a glass of cool maple beer before him, he surreptitiously poured an inch of the liquid into the bottle.

The barkeep told him, "That will be five *luaavh*." Mischa did not answer and the dark elf's face grew sardonic once more. "That's silver pieces."

The Prince jutted his chin and said, "I could pay in silver, but I have something worth far more." He plunked the bottle down on the polished bar.

The dark elf raised an eyebrow. In her job, she often acquired valuable items and this had the look of something magical. "What is it?"

"Remedy for the sun-sickness," said Mischa proudly.

The elf shrugged. She'd heard that claim before, but it would be easy to sell. "Good for one ale, I suppose," and pocketed the bottle.

Mischa scowled and started to reply, but was suddenly aware of someone crowding him. "What else do you have in the bag, little man?" a slurred voice asked. Mischa looked up to see a tall dark elf with the coarsened features of a hard drinker. The elf's nose was veined and she had two ugly rips in her pointed ears.

Mischa downed half his drink before he answered. "I am a wizard of Sargoth. Out of my way."

"Not so fast," said the elf, and her grasp on Mischa's arm was painful.

"Let go of me—you'll be sorry," he said. He tried to gather his wits, but his head felt soggy. *Damn the ale.*

The elf laughed and lifted Mischa like a doll. In seconds, the Prince was suspended by his heels, while the objects in his bag tumbled out onto the stone floor. Mischa watched in horror as the wand and scroll fell in opposite directions. The flute rolled to a stop by the bar. Lastly, the elf dropped Mischa on his head. The Prince yowled with pain, holding his crown with both hands.

The barkeep came around to intervene, and she shoved the brute aside. "You've caused enough trouble, Garla."

The taller elf was surly. "I want to see the magic toys."

"Sit down. I'll bring you a raven pie," said the barkeep.

Apparently, this was a prospect that dwarfed all others, for the hulking Garla shuffled docilely to a seat at the marble table. Her companions were steeped in narcotic slumber, their glasses long since drained.

The barkeep helped Mischa to his feet, then noticed the silver flute. She leaned down and retrieved it. The instrument tingled in her hands, and she looked at Mischa. "What's this?" Something elusive tugged at her memory from her school years.

The Prince stood up, still rubbing the knot on his head. "None of your business," he said and made a grab for the flute.

The barkeep held it over her head. "I saved your life. What's that worth to you?"

"Ha," cried Mischa, "I could cook that Garla with one stroke of my wand."

"All right," said the elf, amused by this boastful fellow. Mischa opened his sack, and the elf dropped the flute into it with a twinge of misgiving. She had no use for it, after all, not being a musician. But the wand was something else. "I'll trade it for this," she said, snapping up the elderwood switch.

"No," said Mischa. "Much too dangerous." He held the bag open.

The barkeep smiled and shook her head. "I'll keep it safe for you. Who knows? You might run into another bully."

Mischa glared. That wand was the best weapon he had ever had. "Give it back or you'll be sorry."

But the bartender ignored him and walked away with the wand. Mischa's head ached, and he still felt a bit dizzy from the soporific ale. With a glance at the group of elves snoring in the corner, he stooped and grabbed the scroll. It, too, went into his sack. He stumped up to the bar once again, and pounded his fist on the wood.

"I want my wand back—it's your last chance."

The bartender spun around to face him, and said, "You still here? If you don't behave yourself, I'll have to throw you out. And from the looks of you, that wouldn't be too hard." She laughed.

Mischa drew out the scroll, and bluffing, pretended to read it. *"Ama Wamma...Benooma ..."* Even to his ears, the words sounded silly. *The ale must be addling my brains.*

The bartender laughed again, louder this time.

At a tap on his shoulder, Mischa turned to see one of the guards behind him. He said, "That barkeep has taken my wand. Get it back for me."

The guard murmured, "Excuse me, Mischa the Great, but it is dangerous to keep the Lord King waiting."

"First, my wand," ordered Mischa.

The guard grabbed for the wand, and he and the barkeep struggled for a few moments, until the wand split into two pieces. The guard dropped his piece, but the barkeep squealed and fell on the floor, clutching the other half in her charred hands. The guard drew back in horror.

With a scowl, Mischa thrust the scroll back into his sack, which he slung over his shoulder before stomping out the door, the guard a step behind.

After the miasma of the tavern, the cool air of the corridor revitalized his senses. The restless guards leapt to their feet and ushered him down the pathway. Mischa trotted along, already irritable. "Slow down."

"We've already lost enough time," said the leader.

Mischa grumbled and plodded along, soon bewitched in spite of his discomfort by the strange topography along the way. He had never imagined such an eerie landscape. The stalactites hovered above, glistening with crystal tears that pierced the darkness like stars, accompanied by the scents of the trees. As they proceeded, trees loomed around them like shadow guardians, their musk sweetening the air.

Suddenly, the leader stopped to cry out, and the guards crowded around a large harp and something dark on the ground. Mischa thought at first that it was the corpse of a giant. When he came nearer, he saw the near-naked body of a dark elf, his face covered with a familiar black robe.

Mischa knelt to turn the cuff back on the left sleeve, exposing several long needles threaded into it. "You see? Here's proof," he crowed. "The evil wizard did this. He uses needles to kill his enemies."

-26-

As the harp music faded away, the fox was alarmed to find herself in a cold, damp cavern that smelled of animal musk. She hardly remembered her fall or how long it had lasted. She had no broken bones, but her knees were sore.

The scent was both disturbing and exciting. Polah looked around wildly, already missing her companions. Her fur rippled with cold. She knew she was deep underground.

As her eyes adjusted to the dark, she noticed the imprint of foxes on the walls, a flickering glow of blue and purple. She blinked. Was it a mirage or real? Moving cautiously toward the images, her hunger returned, and she whimpered at the pain in her belly. Had that been an answering whine or an echo? She stopped, fur on end, ears pricked forward.

A cool draft ruffled her neck from a passage ahead, carrying an even stronger smell of musk. She padded toward it, hunger gnawing at her with each step. The stone was damp under her black-socked paws, and she shivered again. When she reached the passage, they came from every direction.

The foxes were of all descriptions, from red to silver-gray to inky black. Some were mere cubs; some were larger than Polah. She counted over twenty.

Enchanters. She was too excited to realize she had formed the word in her mind.

Yes, sister. Welcome to Comrhae Deip.

Polah's head swiveled around, looking for the speaker. *How did I get here? Am I still in Alvarra? Where's Embaza—and Tiala?*

The foxes moved closer to her, and she sensed laughter. *One question at a time.*

Polah found the next voice subtly different from the other. *Look at her. She's hungry.* A black fox dropped a piece of meat in front of her, a tender tidbit of burrowing rodent. Polah ate greedily, without embarrassment, memorizing the scent of the vixen who had shared her meal.

The food did much to improve both her disposition and her senses. She felt a new fluidity within her. Elated, she tried to communicate this to the foxes.

Yes, said a voice, *you are maturing fast. You can already see the true aspect of things. There will be other faculties, too. Be glad you're a fox enchanter, and not a bird or spider. You'll know true power.*

Polah followed the pack deeper and deeper into the cavern. The draft of air came from a flue, she discovered. There were more of these openings along the way, but she couldn't tell if they were natural or elven-made. She felt quite safe here, as if time were suspended. Yet, her fleeting moments of worry about Embaza increased. *Strange,* she thought, *that I should be more concerned for him than for myself. Is this what it is to love?*

Yes, but it's more than love. It's blood-bond. Old, old magic—from long ago. You and he have mated before. Ah, you knew it. You felt it. You should be proud. It's as rare as a butterfly in the Merimn'a.

As their bodies flowed over an outcropping of stone, the fox fur ran together like one variegated pelt. Polah melted into the unity of the Comrhae. From this perspective, the nuances of each voice absorbed her, as she listened to the wisdom of her companions.

I did feel these things. Somehow I knew. But how—why? I don't understand. Her paws were stiff from the unaccustomed cold, and she trotted to keep warm.

Ah, the ageless question. Who knows why? None of us. Yet, we all ask of our origins. That is why we band into Comrhaes, so we can draw on each other's strength—and wisdom. Our Comrhae is called Deip ... The word is foreign to you? It means 'fox enchanter' in your language.

Polah heard the rushing of water nearby. It reminded her of the river near her father's farm—a lifetime away, now. As the pack led her ever downward, the sound grew louder.

Eventually, the path disclosed a ledge that opened to a huge cavern. Before them was a waterfall crashing into an underground pool lit from beneath by luminescent stones that made the surface shimmer in the darkness. The foxes descended to the rocks and drank from the clear, sparkling water.

Polah joined them. As she quenched her thirst, a desire for human form stole over her, and a small still voice within whispered of the delights of ten-fingered abilities and the curious power of human frailty.

In wonderment, she sensed a sympathetic wave rippling through the Comrhae. Along with her, the enchanters underwent their transformations, appearing at last in dark-elven form. *How is this possible?* she asked, swept along like sea foam, her body altering with ease.

A tall dark elf with long, silky hair like Tiala's gazed at her with liquid green eyes. "You are one of us now. When we are together, the power is magnified." It took Polah a moment to adjust her ears to the elegant Alvarran dialect. She still had difficulty understanding.

Another dark elf chimed in, "We act as one in harmony with the Mother of All."

Polah noticed that there were both dark-elven men and women here. The children had jumped into the pool to play, splashing each other. Their laughter merged with the rushing water of the falls. Her nakedness felt natural, although she was still cold. The other enchanters didn't appear troubled by either the chill or shyness. Their acceptance of her was interesting, too. Why weren't they more curious? Was there some sort of instant fellowship among enchanters that transcended differences of race and gender?

She sent a tendril of thought toward the woman next to her. *Do you always go around without clothes?* The woman ignored her, and Polah realized the powers of telepathy did not extend beyond fox form. Thoughts of sex and telepathy reminded her of Embaza. She suddenly missed him with an intensity that turned her stomach to water. Her teeth began to chatter.

Now, the dark-elven woman noticed her distress. "How stupid of us. Binaer, bring Polah a suit of clothing." A young man got up and walked toward a small cave behind them. An older dark-elven woman came to her and began to comb Polah's tangled red hair with a smooth piece of black wood that had two curved prongs.

Polah's elven bore the heavy accent of the schoolroom. "How did you know my name?"

The older woman answered as she plied the comb, "We first learned of your existence when you were not far from our world. We tried to contact you. Since then, we've been following your progress."

Polah remembered the strange voices she had heard in the ironwood forest. "Yes, I felt and—and heard you, but I didn't know who you were."

Binaer returned and handed Polah a pair of pants and shirt made of a soft, green quilted material. She put them on, gratefully. The pants had a cleverly woven waistband that fitted to her slender form.

"My name is Swano'dar," said the enchanter with the comb, "and this is Zie. Binaer is her son." She began to introduce the others, but Polah soon lost track of the names.

"I am called Polah Fennwarren."

"Come," said Swano'dar. She motioned to the other enchanters. "Let's show Polah our home."

The shape-changers rose with the same unity that had characterized them as a pack, yet individual personalities were gradually emerging. Polah also noticed the harmony between male and female; there was no trace of Tiala's superior attitude here. Pride surged within her and a thrill of belonging that she had felt only once before—with Embaza. She numbed the ache of yearning for him by concentrating on the rocks under her bare feet.

They did not have far to go. Swano'dar led them directly to the waterfall. Polah was a bit frightened. "I can't swim," she told Zie.

"Don't worry, you won't have to." Sure enough, the path of stone led behind the thundering sheet of water. The sparkling curtain sprayed drops onto the enchanters as they passed. An owl hooted from some hidden perch far above. Behind the waterfall was another cave, into which Swano'dar disappeared.

Polah followed the others, glad to be on smooth stone once again. The acoustics were so pure that when someone cleared his throat, the echo continued for several moments. It encouraged them to whisper, even the enchanters, who were used to it. Polah looked nervously at the men in the group and murmured, "Zie, do all of your men support Tiala's cause?"

"Every one," replied the elf with passion. "We may have sympathy for the men, but not for Dekhalis. We cannot be fooled about a person's true intentions. If only we knew what he is planning. Do you have news of him?"

"All I know is what Tiala told us. We were on our way into a city called Duveel."

"Douvilwe. Perhaps we should join her there."

"But how did I get here?" asked Polah again. "The last thing I remember was harp music."

"It could be many things. Perhaps the harpist was a magician. Perhaps someone transported you with a crystal. Or maybe you're going through the rites of passage."

"What's that?" Polah asked, but Zie had moved ahead.

Binaer had taken her place in the conversation, his baritone voice a contrast with his youthful face. "The rites affect everyone differently. Some have wonderful visions or hear the voices of trees. Others have mysterious blackouts. They're walking in one place, and suddenly they awaken in another. Perhaps that happened to you."

"Perhaps," she said doubtfully. "But it seems a great coincidence that I should find myself here—with you."

"Not at all," said Binaer, chuckling. "This cavern is enchanted in such a way that certain travelers are drawn here. No one fully understands why. It has always been so, since the first enchanter of Comrhae Diep."

Either the cavern was getting warmer, or Polah was becoming used to the climate. Her clothing was faintly damp with sweat by the time they reached the interior. She saw a glow that she thought at first was firelight—but there was no smoky smell. As she came closer, she recognized a large phosphor-stone globe on the stone floor.

Swano'dar's voice echoed loudly in the cavern. "Here, you must rest."

Polah peered ahead, and said, "Thank you."

"Do you have any other questions? This might be our last opportunity to talk," said Zie. Quietly, a few of the enchanters left, bidding Polah a good sleep.

"Tiala explained a few things to me," Polah said. "But I admit I still don't understand how one disgruntled lord could make so much trouble in a world where the males don't even own land."

A thin elf woman named Nefra said, "We've grown soft—25 hundred years of Nightwings and peace have made us so. We're a people who have put killing behind us. Even enchanters such as yourself, when in animal form, are inhibited from hunting. For many, it's the hardest part of the initiation."

"When Dekhalis began his reign of terror, we were unprepared," said Swano'dar.

Binaer said, "Until recently, my cousin lived in the small village of Ginma, where he brewed the ales for upland taverns. Then murders started, and his village began to live in fear. They tell me there has been rioting and looting in the cities. Even in Ginma, bands of outlaws spilled barrels of precious ale in the free tunnels. Afterward, these Swords of Siadhin appeared. He went to one of the meetings. It was filled with men with cruel eyes."

"What was the meeting about?" asked Polah, rubbing her arms, suddenly cold again.

"That the Nightwing was the cause of all the trouble, that she was a tyrant. They called Tiala the Usurper. Some brave men tried to speak otherwise, but they were thrown out."

Nefra nodded. "Dekhalis sends his assassins before him to stir up trouble, then he comes and uses his charisma to recruit new followers, while those who are still loyal to the Nightwing are helpless."

Zie said, "But we have one advantage over our brothers and sisters in mourning." She held up her hands, and her nails gleamed in the light.

Polah's face became crafty. "Where is the one place Dekhalis is afraid to go—the holiest place?"

"The Royal City," supplied Binaer.

"Then that should be our destination," said Polah.

"Even if the guards let us in, what good will it do?" asked Nefra. "Why be in the one place that he is not?"

"Perhaps the Nightwing will know where Dekhalis is. She'll guide us to him," said Zie.

"Then we'll fight," said a dark-elven man, his mouth set in a grim line.

"Tooth and claw," said Binaer, grinning. His face was cadaverous in the glow of the phosphor-stone lamp at his feet.

-27-

IT WAS quick work to backtrack to the secret entrance. Tiala scouted for signs of pursuit, but all was quiet. "It worries me that we aren't being followed," she told Six Stix as she led the way through the tunnel to the ferry docks.

Surprisingly, it was Obsidian who confirmed this. "It's too quiet. Like the desert just before a sandstorm." He was red-faced, Six Stix noticed, and not just from exertion. The monk's silent battle with fear was far from over.

"Reminds me of the tunnels in the Manor," grumbled Gudrun. She expected the docks to be similar to those in Tskurl, a hustle and bustle of activity. The two countries shared commerce on the canals leading from the deepworld river called Everandiel by the elves and Riannach by the dwarves. However, such was not the case.

Tiala and Gudrun flattened themselves against the wall and peered out around the corner.

The long stone dock was nearly deserted. Four small, narrow barges were moored by guide ropes. Three of the barges were tied together. The canal lapped peacefully against the sides of the gray-black cavern leading deep into the heart of the mountain.

A brightly garbed male elf leaned against the guard shack, whittling a piece of wormwood, while a single phosphor-stone lamp swung on a pole above his head. It cast an aqua reflection into the water from the elf's body suit. There was something of the laborer about him, and he appeared to be past middle age, the tips of his ear-tufts frosted white.

Tiala gestured for Embaza to join her. He had straggled behind, searching both physically and mentally for signs of Polah. He was enduring the hundred deaths of the lovelorn, fearing one moment she had left him because he was powerless—and the next that she had been wounded by some mysterious foe.

"Embaza, it's time for you to take over," said Tiala.

"It may be a trap," said Gudrun. "Something about this looks staged."

"We have to take the chance," said Tiala. "Six Stix?"

"I agree."

"Can you see well enough to steal a boat?"

"I could do it with my eyes closed." The blue elf rubbed his hands together, elated at the prospect of action.

Obsidian clenched and released his fists, concealing his nervousness as best he could.

"Embaza," whispered Tiala, "remember your accent. Haughty. Remember?" He nodded, adjusting the sleeves of the red body suit.

Tiala walked out of earshot and squeezed Six Stix's arm. "I am glad you came," she murmured.

The blue elf raised his eyebrows.

Embaza, seeing he had a moment alone, asked Gudrun, "Do you still have that dagger you offered me?"

She handed it to him with a grin, hilt first.

Embaza polished the blade on his sleeve, then tucked it into his belt. He gave his pack to Obsidian, whose fingers shook. His cave fear had grown worse, and it was all he could do to keep his teeth from chattering.

With studied elegance, Embaza sauntered to the dock, hailing the man as he approached. "I need a boat, brother."

Tiala exulted. His voice had contained just the right note of command and indifference.

The dark elf at the dock snapped to attention, pocketed the knife, and dropped the wormwood he had been carving. He clasped his hands in the sign of victory. "Yes, Lord Dekhalis. Halroc at your service." He glanced furtively at Embaza as he untied the hawser to the flat-bottomed boat behind him.

Embaza casually inspected the craft. He had some experience with boats, though he wished he had paid more attention to the comings and goings on the Sargothian Sea. The barge was small, presumably for carrying cargo, not passengers. The seats were for the eight oarsmen except for one padded seat at the helm. He'd never seen oars like these. They were short, spatulate paddles—probably for navigation, he decided, noting the swift downstream current. Strips of wychwood were embedded down the center of each oar and along the rudder. Embaza's sharp eyes noticed new zigzag scratches as if someone had tried to obliterate the glowing substance.

"Why is this post unguarded?" Embaza said in reproach, dropping back into character.

"I don't know, Lord King," said the man, fumbling with the tow line.

Embaza read a certain strain in the elf's behavior. "You seem nervous, Halroc. Are you hiding something from me?"

"N-no, my Lord King," stammered the elf, gulping several times.

Embaza drew himself up, cracked his knuckles and lifted his eyebrows. "If I find out you're lying…"

The elf said hastily, "I don't like to bother you with this, Master. At first bell we received a large shipment of bitterrose ale from upriver, but it was tainted."

"Tainted? How?"

"When we opened the barrels, they were filled with vinegar. That's why the dock is deserted, Master. The others returned with the shipment to find out what happened. They left me here to stand guard." As if to underline this, he pulled out his knife again.

Obsidian shifted his weight from one foot to the other.

Embaza looked askance at Halroc. There was still a mystery here; he could swear the fellow was holding something back. Was he Dekhalis's man—or one of the Nightwing's loyalists? He posed a test. "We need a navigator. Are you skilled with boats?"

Halroc's eyes widened, then darted side to side. He took a step backward. "W-wouldn't it be better if I stayed to guard the docks?"

Embaza ignored the question and called out, "Bring me the prisoner." He paced up and down, while Gudrun swaggered up to the dock, followed by Obsidian and Six Stix who pretended to drag Tiala between them. The bard appeared to be unconscious, and Embaza suppressed a smile at her subterfuge.

The unfortunate ferryman twisted his hands around the hawser. "M-my Lord?"

Embaza scowled. "Meet your cargo, Halroc." He gestured towards Six Stix and Obsidian. "And you two—meet your new navigator." He gave a short laugh.

The miserable Halroc found small solace in the fact that he could see better than the two strange henchmen. They were large, well-muscled, and carried real weapons. While Six Stix and Obsidian blinked under the wan lamplight, Halroc dropped the fat rope, slipped behind Embaza and pressed his knife point to the small of the wizard's back.

"Release the na'a Nightwing," he ordered, "or your leader dies."

Tiala jerked free, extending her arms to him. "Halroc, don't."

He hesitated long enough for Embaza to twist around and disarm him. "Have no fear," the wizard said kindly. "I am not Dekhalis." He offered the knife to the boatman, hilt-first.

Halroc stared at him in utter amazement. "What magic is this?" he whispered.

"No magic. He is not my brother, my vigilant friend," said Tiala, her voice ringing with pride. "I had not dared to hope for such supporters."

"Oh, my Liege," cried Halroc, dropping to one knee. "There are many more of us. Not all believe in this conspiracy of the Swords of Siadhin. We are faithful to the Nightwing."

She said, more sternly, "What were you going to do with that knife?"

Halroc glanced at the blade still in Embaza's hand, then said, "You can't expect us to sit still while Dekhalis's band of cutthroats roam the country. They have weapons, na'a Nightwing."

Tiala raised her chin. "Weapons can be broken. Sacred tradition must not. If our people endure, it must be because we are worthy."

Halroc frowned for a moment, then sighed. Embaza slipped the knife into his sleeve.

Quickly, Tiala made introductions, and Halroc accepted the strangers with the open-mindedness becoming a middle-aged dark elf.

"Will you take us down river?" she asked.

"Gladly," said Halroc, lurching to his feet. He indicated the narrow barge.

345

"Careful getting in." He handed Embaza the hawser, then helped Obsidian and Six Stix to their places at the oars and showed Tiala and Gudrun to theirs. Then he took the helm, and Embaza leapt in and cast off the rope.

The subterranean current was fast-paced, and the barge sped silently over the surface of the river. The only sounds were drops of water striking the surface of the river with notes whose echoes were magnified by the walls of stone.

The tunnel leading deep into the mountain seemed to Obsidian like the maw of death itself, and the black water a river of blood. He suddenly noticed something was missing, and then realized it was the occasional swarm of bats. A small, fluting wind rushed by his face. Without the phosphor-stone globes or fireflies to light the darkness, he was totally blind.

They passed through a kind of loose mist, innumerable droplets of water drifting in the air. Six Stix looked to the sides of the river where water-carved stone was sculpted into shapes in which an active imagination could see faces and animals. He fancied there was movement in the shadows.

Gudrun closed her eyes. She had avoided watercraft all her life, as did many dwarves. She had never been particularly ashamed of the fact that boats made her queasy; now, however, she was reluctant to expose that weakness to the others. She gripped the sides of her seat in an effort to calm her stomach.

At the helm, Halroc steered with effortless habit, and the barge glided along, entering a tranquil pool where the river widened. Tiala breathed in the cool air of the Everandiel. She watched the snow-white catfish playing beneath the surface. Their swimming made patterns that reminded her of music—swelling into a bellows shape, then narrowing again.

Halroc nodded over the rudder, and Gudrun wondered how anyone could nap under these circumstances. More nauseated by the second, she was the first to notice the barge dancing around in an alarming way. "Halroc," she called, "make it stop."

The helmsman didn't move.

"Obsidian, help him," she said.

The monk felt for Halroc, and made a sickening discovery: a slender dart in the dark elf's back. Leaning closer, he detected an acrid smell.

"He's dead. Killed by a poison dart."

"Let me see," said Tiala, crawling to the helm. The needle-like projectile was unfamiliar, but the poison was not.

They all looked around at the cavern walls rising on either side, and Six Stix asked, "Has anyone ever piloted a boat like this?" He swatted a pale, little fungus gnat away from his face as a ghostly swarm gathered around them. The subterranean passage was damp, dark and silent.

No one replied. Tiala took the rudder, gently moving Halroc's body to one side. "I know how—in theory."

It was at that moment Gudrun chose to retch over the side, and thereby saved their lives. Through watered eyes, she saw a dark shape. "In the water," she cried, drawing her sword.

The huge snake grazed the hull as it undulated beneath them. Its green diamond-backed scales stood out in relief from the darker black that predominated along its twenty-five foot length. At the opposite side of the boat, Six Stix unsheathed his broadsword, and squinting his eyes at the murky depths, thrust it blindly into the water.

Tiala hollered, "Help—Six Stix," as she strove to hold the helm steady. The barge canted dangerously, and the serpent came back for another pass. Though he could not see, Obsidian's sharp ears heard something striking the wood planking. The same sharp smell of poison reached his nostrils. "Get down," he shouted.

Suddenly, there were missiles flying from every direction. The flat craft pitched from side to side in the heaving river. Obsidian felt a dart pass directly through his hairlock. Tiala screamed again, as she and Six Stix lost control and the barge flipped with inexorable force, dumping all of them into the cold water. Halroc's body sank immediately, an easy meal for the great snake, which followed him to the bottom.

Gudrun spluttered, crying out, "I can't swim," and Embaza grabbed her, tucking her into the crook of his left arm, while he clenched the submerged lip of the hull with his right hand. Tiala, too, had managed to make a handhold of an empty oarlock, and the three sailed forward into the shivering gloom of the mountain, until the *plop* of falling darts no longer echoed behind them.

"Six Stix?" called Tiala, her voice rebounding off the stone walls. "Obsidian?"

Embaza spat a mouthful of water as Gudrun's thrashing nearly dunked him for the third time. Something batted hard against his leg, and he flinched, anticipating the return of the snake. But a black, curly head appeared, haloed by spraying droplets of water.

"Six Stix," exclaimed Embaza.

"No. It's Bilbok the River God." The blue elf grabbed the side of the boat. "Where's Obsidian?"

Embaza shook his head. The blue elf peered into the darkness, "You can see in this murk. You find him." He eyed Gudrun with distaste. "I'll take her."

"Hands off," said Gudrun.

Embaza ignored both, looking around with keen eyes. "There," he said, pointing upstream to a bobbing shape behind them.

Six Stix followed Embaza's finger and dove in. By the time he reached Obsidian, he was nearly exhausted from battling the current. The monk was flailing about under an overhanging rock he had tried to grasp several times, but his hand kept slipping. Now he was hysterical with panic, and nearly drowned Six Stix in the elf's attempts at rescue.

Finally, however, the old warrior soothed the monk's fears long enough to stop him from kicking. Resolutely, Six Stix rallied his aching muscles and hoisted Obsidian to his back. He called out to Embaza to guide him with his voice, but the downstream current did most of the work. Obsidian held on to the elf's shoulders, choking for breath, arms clasped around his neck, barely aware of the powerful tide that pulled them toward the capsized barge.

-28-

Noth found that if she stayed very still, the strangleberry vine eased to a comfortable tightness. She concentrated on breathing deeply and slowly, and the resulting calm filled her with new purpose.

With the silken slipperiness of a snake, her hands ever so slowly shed their bonds. It took all her control to keep her breathing regulated, what with the adrenaline charging through her.

As blood flowed back into her fingers, she winced at the pain. Gritting her teeth, she kept her focus on her breathing.

Hooding her eyes as if she were half asleep, she looked around and what she saw made her heart beat faster. Inuari—breast bared, blindfolded, bound to a scaffold, Eleppon—lying forgotten on the grass, while the Swords of Siadhin stepped over her prone form as if she were a boulder in their path, and Dekhalis—leaning against the trunk of a goodroot tree, and fondling one of his daggers.

Her stomach lurched as he stared at her. She willed herself not to move, knowing it was her only means of deterring his interest. They had once been so close. She would have bet she knew him even better than their own mother did.

But his gaze did not waver, and she had the impression he was looking straight through her. Or—was it someone behind her? Cold hands on her arms shocked her. *Spidermen.*

Two dark elves yanked her from the mingus tree with a steely grip, dragging her despite her resistance to the spot where her brother waited.

He stared at her, and for one moment, Noth saw a spark of the old affection in his eyes. Or perhaps she imagined it. The next moment, it was gone, and she held her breath in growing dread.

He laid the flat of his dagger to her left cheek, forcing her head to the right, face to face with one of her captors, a dark elf with a wicked grin and eyes that drained the warmth from her body.

"Welcome to the company of spiders, *dear* sister," said Dekhalis. He waited for fear to take hold of her dainty, battered face, then smiled. "You tried to escape. We punish those who try to leave us, don't we, Xiak?"

"Assuredly, Lord Dekhalis." His voice held a frigid note of authority, as he continued to leer at Noth.

"And you, Toadh, what do you think?"

"She's your sister, my Lord King," replied the chuckling spiderman on her other side. He brushed his unkempt hair back with a coarse hand. He was tall and muscular in a bright teal body suit with swirls of gold.

Dekhalis laughed, a sound as macabre and half-beautiful as the rattling of golden chains in Douvilwe Prison.

Noth's tears blurred her vision as she looked at this brother she no longer recognized. "'Khalis," she implored.

He glanced at her with contempt. "Rape her, Toadh," he ordered the spiderman.

A sword of ice coursed down Noth's spine. She vowed to remain calm. Not a flicker of emotion showed as she glared at the roughly handsome Toadh. But when she was actually stripped and lying on the ground, a primitive panic began to stir.

Then the spiderman was upon her, inside her. As he tore down her outer resolve, pounding, beating her, the soft beauty of her inner core was ripped open. She screamed with an outrage that would have made her ancestors proud.

Hearing Noth's shrieks, Inuari screamed too, not knowing why, but infected by her sister's fear. Owla laughed, bounded up to the stage, and kicked the priestess viciously in the ribs. Inuari jackknifed sideways, straining painfully against the ropes that bound her to the scaffold. Owla laughed again and stuffed another rag into Inuari's mouth.

By the time the fifth spiderman had taken a turn, Noth was moaning in torment, her body like that of a stranger's. She whimpered and prayed, then begged. She imagined she was nothing more than a shapeless mass of pulp—and wished it were so. She implored the incoherent earth to suck her down into its safe, black core, but there was no way to run and nowhere to hide.

Noth's screaming had penetrated Eleppon's penumbral stupor as nothing else could. Like a slug inching across a rock face, the stricken horsewoman gradually raised her knees up to her chest and cradled her injured arm.

All but the outermost guards thronged to catch the exotic thrill of a royal rape—if not actually to participate. Even Owla hovered on the edge of the group, curious to see what torments were in store for her old rival's sister. She grew hot at the scene unfolding before her. It had been weeks since Dekhalis had touched her, and she missed him with increasing hunger.

349

Owla was not disappointed by the show. The delicate creature bled most beautifully, her face twisted in a mask of agony, her pathetic moans music to Owla's ears.

The spiderman Xiak leaned over Noth, pinning her arms, ignoring her writhing, clawing resistance. "Little sneak, I've seen you creep around the city. Not so fine, now, are we?" His taunt was barely audible above the excited jeers of the knot of cheering spectators.

Suddenly, blood blossomed at the back of his head. Onlookers glanced about, puzzled. What had happened? Xiak released Noth's arms, and reached behind him to snatch at the furry ball that flew away just in time.

The kitten bat circled again, while Noth's benumbed fingers scratched the spiderman's face. Another Sword of Siadhin stepped forward and grasped Noth by the hair.

She opened her eyes just as blood surged into her extremities resulting in a tingling adrenaline of power.

"Topi," she cried, struggling with the Sword of Siadhin yanking her hair, while the dazed Xiak remained astride her defiled body.

The bat answered swiftly with claws and teeth. The Sword of Siadhin fell to his knees, hands clapped to his bleeding eyes. Topi climbed away and prepared to make another strike.

Dekhalis shoved Xiak off Noth and kicked his sister hard in the waist. "Nobody touch her," he ordered. "She's mine." In various states of undress, the spidermen drew their weapons and waited.

Noth rolled to her side, immersed in supreme pain, then saw her brother draw a vial from his inner vest, into which he dipped a needle-thin stiletto.

Topi reappeared, taking aim and flying straight for Dekhalis. "Topi—no," screeched Noth.

With a diabolic flick of the wrist, Dekhalis sliced a tiny piece of flesh from the kitten's throat. She screamed and tore his right ear as she sailed by.

In calm fury, he waited, knife in hand. With amazing speed, Topi wheeled in full flight and rocketed toward him. She almost reached him, almost peeled the skin of his chest to reveal his heart, but the venom of a slime-root spider was a particularly fast-acting poison. Dekhalis had perhaps the only pair in captivity, the yellow ones that turned pale white in the rainy season.

Through a haze of tears, Noth watched Dekhalis grind his foot into the helpless creature, and heard the crack of the small backbone. A hard knot of anger congealed in her belly. She spat a clot of blood from her mouth, and touched her tongue to the place where she had bitten through her own lip. "Fine. Good work, brother," she said.

With the infinite grace and spirit of a goddess, Noth brushed the sodden mass of hair out of her eyes. The men sighed collectively, watching her rise slowly from the flattened grass, her spindly legs adorned with rivulets of blood and semen, her torso glistening with sweat and sticky fluids. She was magnificent, a dark angel made of mist, not mere flesh and blood.

Dekhalis's cold eyes bored into her, a bee with his stinger, seeking the soft vulnerability of the rose, angered at finding none. Unblinking, he began to remove his clothes. Owla gaped in horror.

"No," whispered Noth, as despair claimed her at last.

Swords of Siadhin around him froze. Two of the spidermen roused from their shock and grabbed her by the arms, forcing her to the ground, holding her down for their leader to deflower once again. However, some of the Swords of Siadhin were not all sure about this. They traded frowns amongst themselves, sharing a queasy feeling in the pit of their stomachs. Was this what the new reign was all about? Were they expected to rape their own sisters?

One whispered to his neighbor, "He must hate women even more than I do," and laughed uncertainly.

Theowla Twomothers was not about to see her lover waste his seed on another woman. Not when she had waited so long. While Dekhalis displayed the flawless body he had molded for just this sort of occasion, Owla drew a spongy piece of white fungus shaped like a half-moon from her waist sash. She had soaked the fungus in treespider venom for several days, then dried it in her own conservatory. She knew its power.

Owla shoved her way through the spidermen, and threw herself on the ground beside the fallen Noth. She avoided Dekhalis's eyes, as he stood astride his sister. "Take this—it will dull the pain," she urged, holding the fungus to Noth's mouth. But the captive thrashed her head from side to side, lips squeezed together. Noth's eyes flashed a hatred that bordered on madness, and she spat at Owla, splashing the lovely skin with blood.

Dekhalis grabbed Owla's wrist, his fingers and knuckles as smooth as black stone. While the assassin's eyes brimmed up at him with passion, anger, grief and pain, he leaned down and kissed her hard on the mouth. With his other hand, he gently drew his razor-sharp stiletto across her throat.

Her head rolled back, blood spurting over the ring of guards hiding the scene from other spectators. "Remove her," Dekhalis shouted to the men nearby. He took a lingering look at Owla's body, and a shudder seized him, though he appeared unconscious of it.

Then, with precise and brutal purpose, he entered Noth's body, concentrating all his rage and hatred upon his helpless target. The Swords of Siadhin were too shocked to utter a protest. Some grimaced and turned away. Others gritted their teeth, trying not to be sick. Mutual glances of disgust hinted at burgeoning rebellion.

When their leader was through with her, Noth never moved, save for the slight heaving of her breast. Dekhalis signaled his spidermen and they dragged her body under a nearby willow tree. The unconscious Noth was unaware of their reluctance and shame.

Dekhalis put his body suit back on, as if donning another mask, while the stunned and silent crowd dispersed. Around the park, preparations for the festival were proceeding.

Musicians were gathering near the platform, and food stalls were being set up, while delicacies were laid out on long tables.

Dekhalis sauntered over to Owla's body where the Swords of Siadhin had dumped it, behind a table piled with fruit. He squatted down, and with the same stiletto that had taken her life, he sliced a lock of her hair, twirled it around his finger and sniffed its perfume.

He looked up as a tall dark elf approached. This man was not dressed in a bright body suit, but wore a gown of crimson. His hair was stark white. Then Dekhalis remembered. *The wizard I ordered—from the Merimn'a.*

-29-

POLAH HAD found the shape-changers' lair inviting, with its pervasive smells of fox. Here and there a tuft of fur was embedded into a bed quilt or hand towel. She marveled at the ease with which they seemed to live with their duality.

Now in dark-elven form, the members of the Comrhae broke up into smaller groups, fourteen of them making preparations for the journey ahead. They dressed, ate, and rested themselves for the battle ahead.

Accompanied by the chittering of bats, Polah followed the Comrhae along the arduous trail to the Royal City, through a maze of passageways, up rock faces, and across subterranean streams that chilled them to the bone. Polah found her night vision, though by the fourth time they had stopped to rest, the shape-changer was exhausted. By her reckoning, they had walked for eight hours.

The path had narrowed to a mere thin trail, bounded by high, fragrant evergreen bushes. In the distance, they heard a bell ring four times.

Polah said, "I keep hearing bells. It is a signal?"

An old elven man named Inkharg chuckled, "Time-keepers. Fourth bell is midday meal, though we don't pay much attention to all that in the Comrhae. Time's for the city bred."

Swano'dar added, "There are bells for meals, for prayers, for shop-keeping, for visiting, for dying, for being born, for spirit travel—."

"Spirit travel?"

"When the spirits walk freely. Timid people stay indoors, thieves and ruffians may take their chances."

Polah raised her eyebrows.

As they rounded a corner, Polah skirted a ridge of dark root jutting from the rocks as the path rose upward. Then Nefra stopped and dug from under a boulder a small bundle of woven material tied by a red string. She moved a bush aside with her foot and revealed the intricately-carved obsidian statue of a black rabbit.

"Shrine of Miralor," she explained to Polah. "There is always a bundle of food here for the traveler. You take it."

Polah swallowed. "Is there water?"

"Here." Nefra bent down, and from another part of the bushes, retrieved a silver flask filled with spring water. When all were refreshed, the pack moved on.

In surprisingly little time, they reached the luminous gates of the Royal City. Polah studied the high, crystalline double doors. Worn with time, they were covered with markings she knew to be runes, although she couldn't read them.

The larger runes were made of clear quartz, forming warped, transparent windows. Through them, she thought she saw a figure move, then a stern, female voice from behind the door asked, "Who's there?"

Swano'dar answered, as the senior member of the party. "The people of Comrhae Deip. I am the Comrhae Mother, Swano'dar."

"What is your business in the Royal City?"

"We come in peace, to visit the Temple of Miralor and ask for the prayers of the High Priestess."

There was a long silence before the reply, less stern in tone. "You may enter, fox-people. How many are you?"

"Fourteen." Swano'dar put her finger to her lips. No use announcing their visitor until they were inside the City.

The crystalline doors opened to about two dozen tall, well-muscled women. Their glossy top-knots and loose garments of pale yellow reminded Polah of Obsidian. They carried themselves with the ease and confidence of athletes, and as expected, wore no weapons.

Around them rose a cavern of light green stone, marbled with threads of gold and smooth with age. Fashioned by the hands of ancient elves in the shape of a huge flower, its "petals" curved down to the floor, where the palest green was sculpted into palm-shaped leaves. At the back of the cavern was a circular door made of aged, black wood.

The captain of the guards eyed Polah with her pale skin and red hair, then quietly approached the fox-woman. The guard was a head taller, in the prime of youth, her arched eyebrows like silken feathers over brilliant green eyes. Around her waist she wore a silver belt with a rabbit-shaped buckle. "We allow very few foreigners to enter the City, Comrhae Mother, and certainly not during mourning," she said to Swano'dar.

Zie took Polah's hand. "I will claim responsibility for her, Lady of Skill."

"She is an upworld enchanter—our blood-sister—come to join us, Lady of Skill," said Binaer, out of turn.

The guard frowned at Binaer and spoke to Zie. "Have you tested her?"

Polah looked from one to another, confused. *Tested?*

Zie put her hands on Binaer's shoulders. "Yes, Lady of Skill. The fox-woman is not a creature of forbidden magic. She is an ordinary enchanter."

"Very well," said the guard. "But we will search her. She is human."

Two guards quickly patted Polah down, while their leader waited.

The Ladies of Skill flanked the group, forcing the fox-people to walk two-by-two. They entered the cavern, and were ushered through the round black door into a dark passageway, made even darker when the door was closed. Their muffled footsteps echoed companionably.

Three-quarters of a league of straight passageway led to a second circular door. This, too, was opened silently by one of the Ladies of Skill.

Through the door they could see a pattern of flickering light on the floor. Its source was a lantern filled with fireflies hanging high above in a nest of honeysuckle. The tiny insects flitted in and out of the metalwork openings, attracted by the nectar.

Ten arched doorways radiated from the entrance. The Ladies of Skill fanned out across all the doorways save one, the sixth. The captain gestured for Swano'dar to come forward and said, "As leader of Comrhae Deip, you will come with me to request an audience."

"Will the others stay here?"

The captain nodded. "If the priestess consents, the women can come also."

Swano'dar said, "Distinctions of rank are for elves—not foxes."

The guard folded her arms. "Tell that to the High Priestess. You're in the Royal City now."

While the others waited for Swano'dar and the captain to return, Polah did all she could to put the guards at ease. She asked polite questions and allowed the enchanters to translate when she had difficulty in understanding.

By the time Swano'dar returned, Polah had learned a few more dark-elven phrases that might prove useful.

The High Priestess Kalista accompanied the Comrhae Mother and the

Lady of Skill. Kalista had no need of a cane, and could have navigated these halls in her sleep. It was presumed that she would do just that someday, as her predecessors had done. When she reached the hallway, her eyes widened, and from beneath the folds of wrinkled black skin, they were twin orbs of glittering emerald that disconcerted more than one member of the Comrhae, and even the guards.

Polah was transfixed by those eyes, and found herself in awe of the ancient elven woman. In the dimness of the firefly lamp, Kalista's face was a map etched with experience.

Polah could smell the gardenia-scented water Kalista had splashed on her face. Her once-velvet robe was so old that the nap had worn off, and black threads showed patches of skin at her shoulders and knees. The white silk unicorn embroidered on her collar was her only sign of rank.

"Miralor welcomes you," said the High Priestess in her ageless voice. The enchanters bowed, and Polah followed suit.

Kalista folded her wrinkled hands into the sleeves of her robe. "Your Comrhae Mother tells me you seek the Nightwing's counsel in defeating the royal son, Dekhalis. One will be as difficult as the other. The Nightwing Avenwyndar's thoughts have turned inward. Events outside have ceased to interest her, and as her servants, we cannot disturb her."

"Could you intercede for us, Your Reverence? We placed so much hope on her guidance," said Swano'dar.

The priestess gave a deep sigh. "The Nightwing is unreachable, whether you are friend, sister or servant, or all three, as I am. She is dying." She lowered her eyes, but not before they reflected her pain.

"Is there nothing she can do?" asked Polah. "Can't we even see her?"

"No, child," said the priestess. "What is your name?"

Polah brushed her red hair back from her face. "I am Polah, your Reverence."

The High Priestess closed her eyes and said, "You are anchored in each other like ships in the Sargothian Sea."

"How do you—," Polah started, then blushed.

"I cannot say more," Kalista replied and her eyes bored into Polah's with a knowledge that frightened the fox-woman into silence.

"Thank you, your Reverence. We'll find Dekhalis ourselves—or he'll find us," said Swano'dar, her face resolute in the pale green glow of the firefly lamp.

"Miralor's blessings go with you," said Kalista. She glanced at Polah, "And my blessings, too." With a graceful turn, she disappeared down the corridor from which she had come.

The Ladies of Skill then led them through the last archway to the right, and down another dark corridor that ended at a portico of curved white marble overlooking ten steps leading to a garden of thistles. The area was illumined by another firefly lamp. Pink flowers embroidered a path through the root-wrought earth, until they meandered out of sight.

"Where are we, Lady of Skill?" asked Swano'dar.

The captain pointed. "Through there, you'll find the guest house where you may rest. Duty forbids me from taking you further. However, I'll send two of my Ladies—and a map that you may use." Her lips formed a thin line.

"Thank you, good sister," said Swano'dar, and they clasped hands.

At the stroke of the sixth bell, the group was rested, and as promised, two of the Ladies of Skill appeared. Instead of the yellow pants and shirts, they wore black, the color reserved for the humblest and the highest, the most popular color of the city-dweller. Their pants and shirts denoted their rank as females, and they carried a map of Douvilwe and its surrounding towns.

"This is the nearest city," one explained. "Dekhalis has been seen there often." She handed the map to Swano'dar.

The other Lady of Skill nodded and pointed to a dot on the map. "The High Priestess could not speak of it—or would not—but today there is a feast of Drimma, the evil one, in the Douvilwe Arboretum. We've just heard. Dekhalis is sure to be there."

When the Lady had left, Swano'dar said, "As Comrhae Mother, I urge you all to be careful, especially of the children. This battle will be no hunting party. We'll not change shape until we reach the park. Agreed?"

Members of the pack nodded. Polah swallowed, hoping her new mastery would hold. Under her façade, she was deeply troubled. *You are anchored in each other like ships in the Sargothian Sea...* What had the old Priestess meant?

-30-

Six Stix reached the capsized boat at last. Holding on with one hand, he rubbed his aching neck muscles with the other. Obsidian let go of Six Stix and splashed awkwardly, struggling to keep his head above water.

"Don't panic, lad," advised the blue elf. "You can float if you trust a bit."

It sounded good in theory, but Obsidian wasn't able to put the wisdom into practice. Gripping an empty oarlock with all his strength, he soon had the broken craft rocking dangerously. His butterfly knives dragged upon the harness at his back. Gudrun, who was terrified of drowning, shouted at the hapless monk, "Are you trying to kill me?"

Six Stix and Embaza managed to wrest the monk's hands free of the vessel and kept him bobbing between them until he had regained some confidence. The current slowed as the river narrowed, and Tiala blinked at the six arcs of light ahead. She couldn't remember which of the locks led into Douvilwe. Ruling family did not travel the river. They used the secret tunnels.

"Embaza," she whispered hoarsely, "can you help me steer this thing? I want to try for that third lock."

With the wizard's help, the disabled craft gradually eased toward the third lock, a shallow cavern lit by the predictable phosphor-stone lamp.

Dark elves with impassive faces lounged against both sides of the canal, watching as the survivors straggled along. The motley group clung to various points along the sides of the exposed hull, shivering and quiet. In spite of this uninspiring welcome, when they reached the landing, strong hands reeled them in, and brandy was passed around. Apparently, victims of the river were treated with respect, no matter who they might turn out to be.

At first, Embaza and Tiala were ignored, while Gudrun, Obsidian and Six Stix garnered more than their fair share of curious stares.

Once again, Embaza made a convincing Dekhalis, explaining with plausibility his unusual allies. However, when he saw the looks these elves gave Tiala, he regretted the decision to use her real identity.

"So, that's the Usurper, is it?" one said, elbowing the man next to him in the ribs.

Embaza cursed himself. He had lost the dagger and other supplies to the river. Now, he had only his wits. "Give me your weapon, brother," he ordered one of the guards, a small, wiry elf with a tuft of curls around his ears. The man handed him a half-sword made of crudely forged bronze. Embaza hefted the heavy blade with confidence, slicing the air with short, diagonal strokes. He was gratified at the admiring looks of the men.

"We need dry clothes," he said, "and an escort into Douvilwe."

"It will be an honor, Lord Dekhalis," said one of the men, snapping his fingers. All but two of the dock hands sprang down from their perches on the ledge by the wall.

"Here is your escort, Lord King," said the leader.

Embaza led them all into the small, wooden guard house. Food and dry clothing were brought in, and when the guards had left, the two women retired to the privacy of a second, smaller room at the back.

Embaza donned a new, bright blue body suit with flamboyant cut-outs along the sides, knowing instinctively it was right for Dekhalis. In some strange way, the more he impersonated this twisted elf, the more he understood him. While his own psyche was at its lowest ebb, he imagined his enemy to be gloating with pride, a fantasy that threatened his better judgement.

Six Stix and Obsidian were given similar garments, hoping the garish clothing would make them less conspicuous to the rank and file of Dekhalis's minions. If ever there was a time for anonymity, this was it.

Obsidian held the bright green outfit to his chest. "This is too small. It'll be restrictive," he said.

Remembering Tiala's counsel, Embaza whispered, "Do whatever you're told. Few visitors get this far down, and those who do are probably kept on a taut rope."

A wave of nausea engulfed Obsidian. All he heard were the words "...this far down." He reluctantly donned the body suit, then gently tore the seams at the sides to allow him more mobility. He winced as he settled the wet leather harness over his new clothes. The butterfly knives had fared well, but he almost wished he didn't have to carry them. In this new garment, he felt doubly hampered.

Meanwhile, Six Stix was glad of the form-fitting clothes, vain enough to appreciate the way the lavender complimented his dark blue eyes. However, he refused to give up his leather boots. They would dry out, same as his scabbard. Like Gudrun's, his swords had escaped drowning.

Gudrun was given a plain set of brown clothing that might have belonged to some chunky dark elf during her child-bearing years. The sleeves were a little long, but the outfit was very similar to her own water-logged clothes.

Tiala was not so lucky. Her black silk pants and shirt clung to her body, and she dripped, clasping her arms around her, while the others got into their clothes. Finally, she went back into the main room of the guard house. "What about me?" she asked Embaza. "I have nothing dry to wear."

He strode out to the jetty and ordered another set of clothes for Tiala. "I refuse to carry the baggage dripping wet," he explained.

The men crowded around the doorway, to get a glimpse of the royal she-demon, as they called her. Staying in character, Embaza folded his arms and scowled at Tiala.

She flipped her sodden hair over her shoulder and stood shaking, lips turning purple, chin high, eyes flashing. One of the dark elves tossed a bundle of clothing into the room, where it fell at her feet. She plucked it up and started to retreat to the back room. This caused an outcry and catcalls among the guards.

"Where're you going?"

"Let's see what a Nightwing is made of."

Embaza realized he must take control of the situation. He put a hand across the door, barring entry, frowned at Tiala and said, "Undress."

She drew a breath and gritted her teeth, anger boiling into her chest. She remembered the way Embaza had rebuffed her advances in the carriage on the desert. *So, you want to play villain, do you? I'll make you sorry you didn't take me when you had the chance.* Slowly, without a hint of embarrassment or awkwardness, she disrobed, her sleek body causing more than one dark-elven man to sigh in lustful admiration. Six Stix clenched his fists, while Embaza struck an indifferent pose.

Tiala's eyes flashed angrily at Embaza, as she nearly forgot he was not her brother Dekhalis. With a grudging respect, she realized he was playing his part well.

When she had donned the coarse white robe, she tore a strip from the hem and wound it about her waist twice, binding the garment to her slender form. Somehow, she didn't present the stricken image the men had expected. This disappointment aroused a seed of outrage in them, and one stepped forward with a raised fist.

Sensing the tide, Embaza roughly grabbed Tiala's arm and said, "All right, worm, get in the back room where you belong." The men drifted away, joking loudly, their pride salvaged.

When the door was closed again, Embaza rounded up the small band, and they ate and drank hurriedly. The simple food tasted delicious, though it was just potato bread and fermented soup. The bitter, orange-flavored brandy warmed their blood, and the party was ready to face whatever came next. "Embaza, remember, there's no need for you to carry that weapon. We're in mourning," said Tiala. *I'll show you who's in control.*

"Dekhalis cares nothing for your laws—why do you even bother?"

"Because you are not Dekhalis. You are my subject," she answered, coolly.

"Don't wear me out with your scruples," he said. "Right now, we've got to stay alive. Wouldn't you agree that's the main objective?"

"No. I am still ruler of Alvarra." She folded her arms. "I am responsible for your spiritual welfare, and I say you must put down the sword."

Gudrun said, "My lady, listen to Embaza. Let us fight for you. You came on this quest to find champions. Have you forgotten?"

"Come, lass," said Six Stix, "my brother, Embaza, has proven his worth in battle. Why waste it?"

"After all, he can't use spells…" Obsidian chimed in, with a sympathetic glance at Embaza.

Tiala shook her head. "Some things are worth dying for."

"Yes, but this isn't one of them," said Six Stix firmly. "I say he keeps his weapon. When our enemies are defeated, then you can put him in jail if you like."

Tiala fumed, muttering, "You can be sure I will."

The wizard had not altered his stance, as he looked down on the haughty beauty, his nostrils widening with unexpressed anger. "You still haven't figured out what's going on with your own people, have you?"

"What are you talking about?" she snapped.

Guessing she was still hurt that he had forced her to disrobe before the men, he decided not to press the issue. "Never mind," he said, gathering his things together. "Let's get out of here. We've got to find your brother before he kills again."

Tiala had much to ponder as the group was escorted by two-dozen armed elves to the City of Douvilwe. She watched the guards disarm several ingenious traps, the worst of them a noose of copper wire.

When they reached the huge double doors of the blue crystal gates of Douvilwe, Embaza regarded the rune-work with a thrill. What artisans they were, these Alvarrans. *My people.* A voice called out from behind the door, "Who's there?"

"I, Dekhalis," answered the wizard.

"I must ask you for the password, by your own orders, Lord Dekhalis."

Embaza snapped his fingers, and one of his guards immediately replied, "Rozadon's beard." Embaza smiled as the gates drew open and he gestured for some of the dark elves to precede him, as if desiring an escort. With any luck, they would lead him directly to Dekhalis.

Tiala thought, *So, Dekhalis is using his father's name as a password. If I didn't know better, I'd think he has some family feeling, after all.* She expected to see signs of her brother, but when she entered the city, she was unprepared for the extent of his influence.

The name Douvilwe meant literally "City of Wonder." Although not many surface dwellers ever came down so far, Alvarran farmers enjoyed a frequent change of scene from their orchards and vineyards here.

The streets through the high-ceilinged caverns were made of bright feldspar, and were normally swept each day before the courts opened at second bell. The caves that formed the Houses of Law were located in the far western side of the city. Douvilw'ans were used to seeing graceful pathways marked with hand-worked signs in stone. Visitors were easily identified by the fact that they were looking down. City-dwellers were more apt to be admiring the caged birds, ferns, wind-chimes and sculptures that ornamented their route. However, this was not the Douvilwe she had known.

First, there was the stench. The rotting corpses of rats littered the feldspar walkways, interspersed with the wreckage of personal belongings. Dead birds lay at the bottoms of vine-work cages. Crippled sculptures, broken lamps and wind-chimes bore the signs of wanton destruction. Handbills bearing Dekhalis's handsome image were plastered everywhere.

Although Six Stix and Obsidian could smell the odious perfume of decay,

Embaza and even Gudrun were shocked by the sights that met their eyes. Tiala stumbled, her eyes blinded by tears at the destruction.

Their escorts seemed uncomfortable also. When the guards still hadn't moved, Embaza realized they were waiting for him to give a destination. *Curse my haste, why didn't I foresee this?*

Tiala realized this, too. *Where would Dekhalis go? Like a spider…to the center of the web. The center of Douvilwe—the Arboretum. But how do I tell the wizard without giving anything away?*

Embaza was about to choose a direction at random, if only to play for time, when that voice issued forth in his mind. *The Arboretum keeps day and night in tune.* He shook his head. Was his mind playing tricks again? He had been having strange intuitions all along, but nothing so clear as this. Then he knew. *Polah.* Both love and hope coursed through his being and Embaza cried, "The Arboretum," with such enthusiasm that some of the guards looked at him with surprise.

No one was more surprised than Tiala. *How did he know?* A guard shoved her roughly, and she almost tripped over a child's doll, a representation of the Nightwing. She picked it up, clutching it to her chest. The left arm dangled by a thread, but in the tiny hand was an even smaller black rabbit.

One of the guards laughed. "Keep it as a souvenir of your reign, for it'll be all that's left of you Nightwings."

Tears filled Tiala's eyes, sorrow swelling her heart like a river unbound. *Please help me, Mother.* There was no answer, and despair opened a flood gate in her mind. *What if she dies before I reach her bedside? I'm not ready to be Nightwing.*

Six Stix and Obsidian remained quiet as they traversed the city. Six scooped up the occasional gold piece left by the looters. The dark-elven escorts shook their heads in wry amusement at his interest in the worthless metal.

Gudrun found herself the object of interest as well. Prejudice against dwarves in elven villages and towns had been an accepted fact for centuries, and Gudrun tried to ignore the nervous stares.

Her mother, Niërssa, had visited Douvilwe long ago and spoken many times of the rotten treatment she had received there. "My girl, a dwarven woman is not fit to shine their lanterns. The groundmint ale they served me was water. My bed was full of lumps. And the way they treated your father was shameful."

Gudrun was acutely aware of the black gash along the center of her sword. The weapon was still untested after the rending of the orb. The balance felt odd to her, but it would have to do.

Obsidian cowered under the high-ceilinged caves and gasped for breath. Embaza's chance phrase kept a cadence in his mind: *…this far down…this far* *down.* A laughing guard quipped, "Some ally, eh?" Obsidian felt ashamed and tried to get his fear under control, but deep inside, he knew he had lost his nerve. *Even if I make it as far as the Arboretum, I'll be of no use to Tiala—or anyone.*

As they neared the center of the city, Tiala missed the commerce, courts and sanity that had prevailed. The rhythm of life was absent here.

They passed knots of men dressed in bright body suits, brandishing all manner of crude weapons. Some drew back and eyed the group timidly. It was obvious these men were play-acting at being soldiers. But other groups had the hard, mean eyes of the petty thief and assassin. Their weapons were of quite a different variety.

Tiala quailed at the hatred she saw, even the timid shopkeepers who peeked out of their doorways. *What have we done to deserve this?* she asked herself.

An old man with grizzled beared leaned from a round window and pointed at her. She recognized him as one of the gardeners in the temple of Miralor. He was educated. She lifted her eyes to him in entreaty.

His voice shook. "You Nightwings filled your bellies with the wine of power while the rest of us starved! Now you'll know how it feels to be invisible."

She walked on, eyes trained on Embaza's back. *You tried to tell me.*

-31-

As Mischa's eyes grew accustomed to the light, or rather the lack of it, he began to feel more at home. The place reminded him of the dungeons at the Manor. He tripped over a rock, and one of the elves caught him quickly and set him back on his feet. "Slow down, will you?" he complained.

"No time to stop," answered the elf, and Mischa grunted. He was tired of trying to keep up with the long-legged elves, but they never stopped for long even when they gave in to his need for rest.

In a way, he was grateful. He wanted to catch up to that vile Embaza and his friends. He frowned, recalling the corpse lying by the harp. *The wizard must have used his needles or a spell.* Mischa patted the sack at his side which contained only the scroll and the magic flute. *He'll be sorry he ever tangled with me.*

He looked at the elves around him, feeling more at ease now that they were unhooded. They seemed to be in awe of him, but he trusted no one—not even his supposed ally Dekhalis.

After what seemed an age, he saw a dock up ahead. It was deserted, and the elves grew agitated. Obviously, they had expected to see someone here.

The leader went into the guard house and came out with a map. He gestured to the others, and in no time, Mischa was shoved into one of the boats, and the elves squeezed in beside and around him, taking up the oars.

Mischa found himself the unwilling custodian of one of the dozen oars as well. He gladly would have exchanged places with the helmsman had he known how to navigate. He had heard about boats, but had never seen one—nor even a river, for that matter.

He looked at the dark, rippling water and smelled the cool humidity, heard the slow drip from the walls of the cavern. "It's a good thing I'm a great wizard. You wouldn't dare drown me," he said to the elf next to him. He didn't expect an answer. They had all been fairly silent thus far.

The dark elf surprised him, though, turning to regard him with glowing green eyes. To Mischa, he appeared ageless, his features gray in the dim light. "Can you tell us about this upworld wizard who can kill demons?"

Mischa said, "He's a dark elf, though he sometimes goes around in disguise. He bears a striking resemblance to your master."

"Impossible," said the elf. "No dark elf could survive on the surface for long—not even one with powers."

Mischa laughed with a grudging respect for Embaza. "You don't know this wizard."

The elf at the helm barked, "Row. You act like a bunch of lazy women."

Mischa took up his oar and made a few half-hearted feints at the water. The current seemed to be getting swifter, and the boat was pitching slightly from side to side. "What's happening?" he asked his talkative oar-mate.

"We're out of the shallows now," said the elf. "Coming to the rapids."

"Rapids?"

"Don't worry. The boat is sturdy."

Mischa stuffed his sack into his shirt, carefully tucking it down so it wouldn't get wet. He shivered at the cold penetrating his thin homespun clothes. They were meant for the desert—not this subterranean chill. The bottom of his feet were clammy, and he put one foot in his lap and tried to massage his toes back to warmth. Startled, he looked down: his foot was wet.

"There's a leak," cried Mischa.

Soon, the dark elves made the same discovery and were stuffing pieces of cloth—hoods, belts, gloves—into the cracks along the bottom of the boat and even bailing with their hands. To no avail; they were sinking deeper with every passing moment.

The helmsman shouted, "Do something, Great Mischa. Use your wizardry."

Nothing else could have roused the Prince from his miasma of fear. The hypnotic water seemed to invite him to a dark, mysterious and bottomless death. He wrenched his eyes away from it and opened his sack. Still wary of the flute, his hand went to the scroll and he drew it out. "I can't see," he cried, and one of the dark elves drew a walnut out of his pocket. Unscrewing the two halves, he revealed a piece of phosphor-stone that lit his face from below like a skull.

The glow mesmerized Mischa for a moment, a beacon of hope onto which his spirit latched. The walls of the cavern glowed eerily, like the giant ribs of a whale. Mischa squinted at the scroll and read in sloppy runic, "*Ogon, Ogi...*um, *Mildawizo.*" He took a deep breath, the water lapping at his ankles.

"Nothing's happening," cried an elf.

"How can it if you keep interrupting?" yelled Mischa. He continued to read. "*Isstazarrow. Mildawoosh. Zel. Bing...*" The boat began to rise. "*...Bing,*" he repeated. The boat rose higher. "*Bing,*" he said again, gaining confidence. The hull skimmed the surface of the water now, hovering in the damp cavern.

The elves cheered, and Mischa boldly read on. "*Nizaword muzzawid. Agga.*" The boat hurtled forward, like a speeding firefly, and the elves gripped the sides, their ears flaring backwards in the rush of air.

By the wan light of stone, Mischa saw one wall of the cavern rushing toward them as the river bent on its way. "We're going to crash," yelled the elf at the helm. "How do we steer this thing?"

Mischa gulped and continued to read, "*Nuo chuo...*" A splashing spray of water obscured the light. "*N-nuo...*"

"Do something!" shouted an elf.

"Hurry," cried others, as the wall grew closer. In another moment, the bow would touch.

"*Imma Drana...*uh, *Imma Dranana*—no, *Drananada,*" intoned Mischa. The boat swerved abruptly, skirting the wall like a breeze, and the leader sighed deeply in relief. The elves cheered their new wizard once again.

The Prince rose to his feet, enjoying the illusion of height over the elves. He watched the boat follow the edge of the wall, seemingly guided by a kind of radar. "All in a day's work. It is nothing." He made a great show of rolling up the scroll, and holding it with both hands.

At the next turn, the boat slammed the wall with a sickening thud, and splintered to pieces, all except for the one portion of wood planking upon which Mischa stood.

The maddened elves fell into the cold water, screaming and splashing. Apparently, not all of them could swim. Fascinated with death, as always, Mischa watched to see what a drowning might be like, disappointed that it was too dark to see much.

Mischa looked at the scroll, feeling a surge of pride once again. "I am a great wizard," he boasted. Recalling a word from the spell, he intoned,

"Drananada." The fragment of wood skated out from under his feet, and dropped him into the cold water.

Three figures waited on the dock with folded arms.

Mischa yelled, "Help!" He barely registered the fact that they, too, carried crude-looking weapons. The stoutest of the three guards stepped forward to snag Mischa by the arms.

"I am Prince Mischa, the famous wizard. Take me to King Dekhalis—." In the distance, he heard the splash of swimmers. "And hurry."

"Not so fast, you little runt," said the guard. "By our Master's orders, no one enters the locks of Douvilwe without a pass. Not even a friend of the Lord King's."

"No doubt he left you behind for a reason," quipped another.

Mischa struggled to open his scroll, but the guard ripped it from his grasp and flung it aside. "No, you don't."

"Wait," the Prince wailed, watching the scroll sail into the rapid current and disappear under the water.

He was hoisted unceremoniously over the shoulder of the stout guard, who said, "I'll take him to the city. They'll know what to do with a foreigner."

The second guard said, "Don't be long."

"I'll be as speedy as a black cat in heat."

The third laughed.

Too tired to struggle, Mischa found it was a bumpy ride away from the locks, and he could see nothing. He shivered in the thin, wet muslin clothing. Every time he grumbled about the lost scroll, the guard whacked him on his calves and rump. "Ow! Where are you taking me?"

"To the prison, of course. Where else?"

"But—but I have news for the Lord King Dekhalis."

"What news?"

"There's a false wizard who is out to kill him—he's already wiped out a tribe of giants who were coming to join you."

"Now, this sounds interesting," said the guard. "Perhaps I should take you to Lord King Dekhalis," he stopped to shift his unwilling burden to the opposite shoulder, "I'll go back to the checkpoint and consult the captain."

"You don't need him," urged Mischa, a self-proclaimed expert in the manipulation of underlings. "You're smart enough to make the decision yourself,"

"I suppose so," said the guard. Independence was like a new drug. The more, the better.

"Set me down then."

"Why should I?"

"I need your help to find Dekhalis. Besides, I have neither the desire nor the energy to run."

The guard roughly set Mischa on his feet and asked, "What's your name, wizard? What else can you do besides raise objects and fall in the water?"

"I am Prince Mischa the Great, to be exact." The Prince adjusted his tunic, disdaining to answer the second question. He was surprised that his clothes fit looser than he remembered. Suddenly hungry, he said. "Do you have anything to eat—er…?"

"Sabel." The guard reached into his pocket for a wizened piece of dark fruit. "Help yourself."

Mischa sniffed the unfamiliar piece of produce before biting into the tough skin. It smelled slightly bitter. He was thus pleasantly amazed at the burst of heavenly flavor filling his mouth from the sweet pulp within. "Sabel, eh? I feel better already." He skipped to keep up with the guard's stride. His clothes had dried a bit, and the food warmed him.

Ahead, he saw the now familiar phosphor globes with relief. *Finally—to see again.* A huge gate stood before them, made entirely of fine, blue quartz, through which a plethora of shapes wove back and forth in a sea of color. Mischa felt a thrill unrelated to his quest. "Is this the gate of Douvilwe?"

"That it is," said the smiling guard. He knocked and a voice asked him for the password. He drew his wooden knife meaningfully across his throat and frowned a warning at Mischa, who shook his head, one finger to his lips.

"Rozadon's beard," replied the elf, and the double doors opened to reveal the spoiled splendor and stench that had once been called the City of Wonder.

-32-

THE CRIMSON-robed wizard who confronted Dekhalis was ancient, but he had an air of grace and youth. In a scabbard at his side was a splendid sword that glowed with a pale yellow light.

Dekhalis's eyes gleamed with envy. He would require that sword as a tribute as soon as the opportunity presented itself. He bowed slightly, as one did with wizards. Their well-known ego was such a bore, he thought. "Whom do I have the honor of addressing?"

"I am Rozadon," replied the old dark elf, twitching his white eyebrows expressively.

For once, Dekhalis was dumbfounded—and immediately suspicious. Guile swelled his thoughts. Sneering, he said, "My father's name was Rozadon. But I have no father."

The wizard's eyes blazed with fire. "I have come from the depths to aid you in your cause. I am proud of you, son."

Still frowning and suspicious, Dekhalis said, "I do not want your help."

"But it was you that called me. You have need of your old father, whether you know it or not."

Dekhalis felt an unaccustomed softness, and banished it from his heart. "In Drimma's honor, I will sacrifice a priestess of Miralor in the Nightwing's own arboretum. I'm sure the Goddess of Revenge would approve." He narrowed his eyes at the old man. "Do you?"

The wizard shrugged and hiked an eyebrow. "I'm not superstitious. Who's the priestess? Some old bat who has wronged you, my son?"

Dekhalis laughed, wickedly. "See for yourself." He pointed to the stage, where a dozen or more guards had been stationed about the helpless prisoner, where she hung, bound and blindfolded on the scaffold. Fear of the powers of Miralor's own persisted, especially in a place where Drimma would be served.

Rozadon frowned. "What is this nonsense? She's a baby who wouldn't swat an earwig if it bit her."

Dekhalis laughed, delighted by the analogy, then changed the subject. "The Nightwing is dying." He watched his father closely for further signs of weakness.

Rozadon sighed. He had been fond of Avenwyndar, even as he had hated her for shackling his ambitions. "I assumed she died years ago. To those of us below, it means little who rules here."

Dekhalis squeezed the old man's shoulder. He had no choice but to trust him. He needed a wizard. "It will matter now, Father. When I am Lord King, I'll give you power over the underworld. The whole Merimn'a will be your kingdom."

"Well," said Rozadon, "it's a beginning. But I won't have a part in the death of that young girl."

Dekhalis propelled the wizard by the elbow toward the stage, avoiding the cluster of phosphor-stone lamps. "Surely, you won't deprive us of our sport."

Rozadon jerked his arm free to stop and look at his son. "I remember even as a baby, you tore the wings off of small birds."

"If you want to save her, find a way to neutralize her powers. I'll not have my own father turned against me."

Rozadon looked up at the young priestess. "She has a certain look." He turned around, and for the first time, noticed Eleppon's broken body. Why was she not being seen to? He stiffened and said, "My son, I can be of no use to you."

"Is that so?" replied Dekhalis, and with a *cling!*, wrenched the wizard's sword right out of its scabbard.

Rozadon gasped. "No. That's the sword of..."

"What?" asked Dekhalis, holding the blade under Rozadon's chin. "Answer me."

"Kill me if you dare."

"I should kill you for being such a weakling, for leaving me to be raised in my mother's house. Why don't you save yourself with your magic, Father?"

Rozadon laughed darkly and said, "You know nothing of magic, you misguided—."

Dekhalis drew blood under Rozadon's chin. "If you won't save yourself, then try to save my sister." He glanced at Inuari in her torn blue gown.

The old wizard shuddered. There was no doubt his son was mad. "Give me room."

Dekhalis backpedaled a step and bowed with a grandiose mockery. Rozadon flexed his hands, then brought them close together, palms parallel and facing each other. A thin, pinkish light crackled in the small space between them. Swords of Siadhin watched, pride mingling with their fear.

The sword in Dekhalis's hand tingled, and he gripped the silver hilt tighter. The hairs on his neck stirred, and he clenched his jaw.

Rozadon said softly, *"Memnose,"* and the pink light arced from his hands to encircle Inuari's body. The priestess cried out once through her gag before being encased in a sheath of pink light that held her fast.

Rozadon turned to Dekhalis, his hands at his sides. "Give me the sword, son," he said, quietly. "I promise I will leave peaceably."

Dekhalis laughed. The weapon was still tingling. Now, he was sure. This was a sword forged for the Siadhin Lords themselves, maybe the last one in existence. "This is a sword of power. It should belong to me."

Rozadon shook his head. "It can only bring you harm. You are not conditioned to it. At least let me help you." He stepped forward, hand out, and two spidermen stepped out of the shadows, ready to intervene.

"You'll do nothing except stand beside me and follow orders like my other soldiers." Dekhalis snapped his fingers. "You are less to me than one of my spidermen." He sneered. "As long as you obey orders, my sister Inuari will stay in the prison you have made for her." He pointed to the cocoon of light on the stage.

Rozadon bowed his head in shame. His wizardry was not equal to the task before him. It had taken years to learn the one spell he had used today. Wizardry was an outlawed art, thanks to Avenwyndar. Old anger burned within him like dragon's bile. He stepped back. "So be it." Still, he eyed the sword. *Poor Dekhalis.* The weapon had a mind of its own, and would easily turn on its wielder if those minds differed.

Meanwhile, the spidermen ushered new warriors into the park, making sure a ring of guards still protected the five leagues of vegetation forming the perimeter. Swords of Siadhin from all the boroughs and neighboring towns had been alerted. They streamed in, not wanting to be left out of anything as important as this meeting. Many had never heard Dekhalis in person and came with all the expectancy of first love.

Although the bells had not rung, the waning glow of the arboretum's crystal ceiling signaled the approaching festival. Even the birds were silent.

Tables had been laid out under the hawthorn and cottonwood trees. Pink and white flowers littered the ground. A spiderman walked by and casually snagged a hawk's egg, which he broke with the tip of his stiletto. He sucked the yolk from it, then carelessly tossed the shell away.

Only the fireflies seemed oblivious to the difference in atmosphere as they flickered on and off. The rowans stood like mute sentinels at the edge of the park, as if aghast at the evil scene they must witness. The Wellambtree endured, forgotten, where it had rooted from the beginning of time, in the center. Its massive, ivy-covered limbs spread above them, while all around the trunks of oaks and mingus, goodroot and cottonwoods were splotched with the colors of brilliant lichens.

Once again, Inuari thought of the owl and missed her song. Though immobilized in the light of a spell, she felt no pain, and was thankful that she could still hear.

Dekhalis whispered in Rozadon's ear, "Perhaps you'd like to preside over the ceremony. We have no priestess of Drimma today."

The old man sighed, wondering if it was useless to protest. "I'd rather you chose someone else. It's not my province." To his surprise, his son conceded this point. Dekhalis turned to one of the spidermen, and said, "Bring Drimma's Consort."

A white-robed dark elf approached the stage, carrying a basket of poppies and white lichen, which he spread along his path as he came. Around his neck was an amulet made of sardonyx and bloodstone, depicting the symbolic mating of two lizards with elven faces. In Alvarran mythology, this was the symbol for retribution.

Two young children walked on either side of the so-called priest, each with a small forked spear. Dekhalis noticed with approval that the children were both male, a further departure from tradition.

The priest mounted the stage, where another table had been set with the customary implements of the ceremony: horn, cup, bowl and knife. When the children had been seated beside the table, he brought the ornate, wild bull's horn to his mouth. His amplified voice was loud and somewhat reedy.

"Celebrants. We assemble as in times of yore at moon-dark. Our Lady Drimma, twin sister of Ordella, favors not elven law, but the higher law of the unseen."

There were murmurs of assent from many in the park, as the fireflies winked in and out, illuminating faces of determination and hope.

The priest continued, "Let us now implore Her for the revenge we deserve. Is that not what we seek?"

An excited response and vigorous applause answered him.

Dekhalis knew the value of melding old customs with new. Before long, the people would be ready for a male god. Perhaps a revival of Myrrhspell, the Consort of Miralor, or better yet, Kiraloko, God of Mischief.

Just then, the pink light around Inuari began to waver. The priestess felt a weakening in the shield and she strained against her bonds.

Dekhalis barked at his father, "Keep her still or I will hang her as I promised."

The wizard held his hands up once again and, with great effort, renewed the spell. "I cannot hold it so long, son," he said. "My power comes from the sword."

Dekhalis eyed the beautiful blade. Now that it was in his grasp, he felt its power, too. He was reluctant to part with it. Ignoring his father's protest, he bounded upon the stage and took the bull's horn from the white-robed priest.

In a voice that rang with confidence, he announced, "Men of Alvarra! You will soon be liberated. Today marks my victory—and the victory of all of you. Even my own father, the great Rozadon, has returned from the Merimn'a to join us. During my reign, you will see many more men of worth freed to assume power in the land."

Dekhalis had to stop until the cheering subsided. However, there was one area of the park where a different kind of noise continued. He leaned down to ask one of the Swords of Siadhin near the stage, "What's going on over there?"

A shout came from the perimeter. "Enchanters of Comrhae Deip."

"To arms!" shouted Dekhalis. He was startled by a flapping of wings above him, but it was merely a black-crowned heron, on its way to the marshy edge of the pond. "Drimma be with us," he yelled, holding high the sword of the Siadhin Lord.

He dropped the horn on the table and leapt down from the stage. "Careful," warned Rozadon. "The sword must not be wielded."

But Dekhalis heeded nothing. He strode swiftly toward the commotion, pushing one elf after another out of his way. Spidermen attached themselves to him as he passed, forming a wedge of protection, but he seemed oblivious, as he made his way toward the pack of ferocious foxes attacking the guards on the perimeter.

Vastly outnumbered, the fox-people had resigned themselves to the fact that they would battle to the death, if necessary. They had taken sides, and their instincts were not fettered by the chains of nonviolence. They knew, with saddened hearts, that they had an advantage over their milder fellow citizens, and they used it to the full.

Other enchanters of Alvarra had joined the battle as well. There were raven enchanters, the small pack of dark wolves, and the two cave bears out of hibernation. The foxes were the most numerous.

By contrast, some of the Swords of Siadhin were armed with little more than thorn-like darts.

Polah fought for Tiala, but also for Embaza. Ripping with teeth and claws, she defeated the first three Swords of Siadhin who came at her with their sharpened stakes and knives.

It was not long, however, before the enchanters faced more formidable opponents—the spidermen. Armed with well-made weapons and trained from childhood, a new, fiercer battle ensued. Polah was alarmed to see the young Binaer go down, but she could not stop to help him.

As the eldest, Swano'dar directed the Comrhae from behind, seeing gaps in their defenses and sending thought-messages where needed. At her signal, Nefra sprang to aid the aged Inkharg, who was trying to throw a spiderman off his back. Polah had no difficulty receiving and responding to the Comrhae Mother's messages.

When Dekhalis reached the area where the foxes battled his spidermen, he was distracted by another disturbance. Through the perimeter on the other side came a motley group of foreigners, in whose midst was a woman dressed in a white robe.

He grinned from ear to ear. "Ah, Tiala," Dekhalis said, gripping the sword more tightly. "I knew you would come...but who is *that?*"

Embaza was dressed in a blue body-suit identical to Dekhalis's own, and many observers thought he was a magical duplicate. Uncertain how to react, they made way for him as he passed.

Dekhalis felt an unaccustomed emotion, and identified it as fear. He shouted, "Where's Rozadon? I need a wizard. Now." He vaulted onto the shoulders of the nearest spiderman and crowed, "I am your leader. My enemy the Nightwing has sent a demon to frighten us." He pointed at Embaza. "Kill him."

Embaza yelled, "Cut down that imposter before he destroys you all."

Now, Dekhalis noticed the retinue of Swords of Siadhin with Embaza. They were armed and fighting with their crude weapons—his own followers—protecting this demon! He quickly surveyed the rest of the park.

All over the Arboretum, a fierce battle was raging. He saw three forces ranged against him—first, the foxes, then this strange dark elf and his minions.

And now, it seemed, there was a small army of dark-elven men from the other side of the park. He thought he heard one cry, "Long live the Nightwing."

Dekhalis shouted, "Father. Help me." This time he sounded sincere.

-33-

WHEN HE heard his son's impassioned call, Rozadon felt a stirring of blood bond. He sped to Dekhalis's side and noticed immediately that the sword had begun its work.

Dekhalis, too, felt its power. The hilt glowed within his grip, and before he could stop it, the sharp blade had sliced the neck of the nearest spiderman. Toadh's head toppled to the ground, rolled up to Rozadon's feet, and then the body followed, as Dekhalis leapt to the ground, staring at the sword with a mixture of fascination and distaste. Still, he clenched it before him.

Rozadon extended his hand. "Give me the sword, Dekhalis. It will destroy you."

Dekhalis felt the weapon's tingle again, and again the strange glow in the hilt almost burned the palms of hands. "It's mine," he shouted.

"It's not yours, my son," said Rozadon. As if to prove this fact, the sword once again swung of its own accord, slicing the midsection of another spiderman. With a horrible howl, Xiak clutched his stomach and fell.

At last, Dekhalis dropped the sword, and Rozadon rushed forward to snatch it from the ground. "Now, show me your enemies," he said to his son.

"There." Dekhalis pointed toward a crowd of fighters, his graceful forefinger indicating Embaza and his retinue.

Rozadon surged toward the tall, dark elf so like his offspring, plowing his way through other fighters without receiving a scratch, but before he could reach Embaza, he was met by Gudrun and Six Stix.

Gudrun's blade, scarred by its experience with one magic adversary, was thirsty for more. In her hands, it sang and glowed with its own silvery light. Six Stix's sword also came alive, the ruby hilt radiant with inner fire.

Those around them backed away from the shimmering contest of the three magical blades. "Beware my edge," said Rozadon, "lest it send you to the limbo of the damned."

"I see you have a tongue," said Six Stix. "Perhaps I'll cut it out." As he worked, Gudrun thrust and parried right beside him.

This was necessary, they found. The wizard's blade was, indeed, too strong for one alone to counter. It overpowered both the dwarf and blue elf with ease, and they found themselves pushed back, skirmishing with spidermen and their whetted swords as well as Rozadon and his blade.

Gudrun felt a difference in her sword that at first she could not understand. The old familiar heft was gone, the balance changed. But the black scar down the middle came to life in an emerald light seething along its seam that temporarily blinded Rozadon.

He held a hand up to his eyes, his sword arm trembled, and yet the Siadhin Lord's blade fought on as if it needed no help.

Six Stix hummed for all he was worth, but it did no good. Gudrun thought it was for the benefit of morale, and joined him. This infuriated Rozadon, whose face twisted in fury, but still, his sword fought on.

Behind them, Embaza had retreated to a spot of relative safety. He coveted the magic in the swords, and once again, cursed himself for losing his powers. He hefted the crude, bronze half-sword and moved forward to use it. However, the sight of the white starflowers on the ground beneath his feet caught and held his gaze, and he felt hypnotized, the sword hanging limply in his hands.

The dark elves around him cried out, "Lord Dekhalis, what's wrong?" The Swords of Siadhin formed a circle around him.

For Embaza, time stood still. He smelled the sweet, innocent fragrance of the little flowers and suddenly remembered his childhood as if it had been yesterday. He knew where he was, and who he was. He remembered—everything. He knew his father, his mother, and the long line of dark elves stretching backward through time.

He knew why the Nightwing had come into his dream. The weapon fell from his hand.

With new eyes, he looked around him, and his gaze lit on Rozadon's magical blade flashing back and forth almost of its own accord. More forgotten lore surfaced in his mind. His teachers had been honorable, after all. He sent them silent thanks.

"I am Embaza, eldest son of the Nightwing Avenwyndar, and citizen of Alvarra. I am in mourning," he announced in a voice that rose above the din of battle. To the consternation of those around him, he pointed at Dekhalis, "My brother is evil. He must be stopped before he leads you down a path of even greater evil."

Tiala, standing inside her ring of protectors, stared in shock.

The Swords of Siadhin near Embaza froze with indecision. They had long resented Dekhalis's cruelty, and new hope stirred within them. Perhaps this brother would make a better King.

Rozadon shouted, "Impossible. The Nightwing's first son died." He advanced on Embaza, but Gudrun pointed her glowing sword at Rozadon's neck, causing him to focus his attention on her. Six Stix closed in with his ruby-throated blade, and for the first time, Rozadon was on the defensive.

Embaza deftly skirted a table laden with food, as the bleeding carcass of a huge gray fox fell across one end, toppling everything to the ground.

"As you can see, I did not die," said Embaza, using the fallen table as a shield. "I was smuggled into the uplands, into a family of flower-gardeners who supplied the medical college. My father Valedd wanted me to live—and to learn wizardry."

Spurred by rage and jealousy, Rozadon cried, "It is my son who will rule, not you." With a flourish, he swung the sword and said, *"Mizro Zewo Uma."* At a brilliant flash of light, both Gudrun and Six Stix disappeared.

"Where did you send them?" Embaza demanded.

"To the limbo of the damned," said Rozadon.

"Unlikely," he said, "that is an ancient sword you hold. No doubt it thinks you are the Siadhin Lord himself, its first owner. The ancient ones had no knowledge of such realms."

Rozadon swung his sword in an arc around him, keeping all others at bay. "Correct," he said, "but are you man enough to take it from me? Or are you, too, fooled by this league of women with their silly vows of piety and pacifism?"

"I am no fool, but you are no wizard," Embaza said. In his mind, he called a name.

A moment later, Rozadon was siezed with agony. He was horrified to see the shining teeth of a giant red fox embedded in his side. He stared at Embaza, pleading with his eyes. "I wish—" With his last ounce of strength, he willed the sword to cut down his enemy.

The weapon gave off a horrible whine, blazed with golden light, and swung for Polah's head. A hair's breadth from her nose, it hovered, then dropped straight down, burying itself to the hilt in the earth. At the same time, the pink sheath vanished from around Inuari, still bound and blindfolded on the scaffold.

Polah stood over Rozadon's body, her muzzle dripping. A thread seemed to shimmer between her and Embaza.

For one shining moment, the two gazed at one another, but this was their undoing.

Dekhalis lunged for the sword, unsheathed it from the earth, and whirled it over his head, heedless of the pain as the hilt seared his palms. "My brother," he cried, "are you this fox's mate?"

"Behind you," yelled Embaza, and Polah turned as the magical edge bit her neck, pierced her flesh, severing her backbone as she fell.

Embaza's griefstricken howl sent despair through all within earshot. He fell to his knees, hugging himself as if afraid he would fly apart. In his mind, a piece of himself shriveled and disappeared, and terror raked his soul with icy talons. He was oblivious of the battle, but a ring of dark elves had made their decision.

Seven Swords of Siadhin moved in to protect him, shouting, "Long live Lord King Embaza."

At the edge of the arboretum, Obsidian, too, was heartsick. His pride and courage had been on the wane ever since he'd left the ironwood forest. The dull clamor of the battle around him seemed like a dream. At the sound of Embaza's wail, he moaned with anguish, "Oh, Power, forgive me." Words came forth from a childlike part of him he had all but banished. "Help me. Mother of night and the cave. Help this worthless monk, oh Goddess Miralor. I'm so alone," he sobbed. Suddenly, above the howl of grief and the clamor of battle, he heard—or felt—another sound. A heartbeat.

Obsidian pressed his ear to the ground. Sure enough. Tiala had said it, hadn't she? The heartbeat of the earth itself. Miralor had answered. Shakily, he got to his feet and drew his knives, trying to get his bearings.

Meanwhile, Dekhalis advanced toward Embaza, still wielding the magical sword of the dead Siadhin Lords. "Now, brother Embaza, stand with me," said Dekhalis, "or I will dissect you like a spider."

Embaza's eyes flared daggers of pain. "Put down the sword."

"So you can have it? Never. I am Lord King, now."

Embaza thought, *Forgive me, Mother, I must use my magic.* With a wary glance at his evil half-brother, Embaza reached for Polah's still-warm body, burying his fingers in her fur and willing her to return to life. His seven new protectors stood shoulder-to-shoulder like a shield around him. Dekhalis watched with disdain, yet curious about this unnatural mating—and this long-lost brother.

Was it Embaza's imagination or had Polah's neck stopped bleeding? Was she not dead? Feverishly, he pressed his hands to her chest, rewarded by a fragile pulse throbbing beneath his fingers.

A voice appeared in his mind, as pure and sweet as liquid silver. *Help me. Use your power. I need your strength.*

I can't. I have no power.

You can, came the voice, implacable, calm. *Remember—your own words. The magic will choose you because you have opened a place within yourself.*

My love, how I wish it were true. How I wish—. Suddenly he understood Rozadon's last words, "I wish…" What would any wizard wish for? *To learn true magic.*

And he, Embaza, had been given that gift. Tentatively at first, then with more confidence, he sent a tendril of life-giving energy from his mind to Polah's. Seconds later, he saw her body knit together, healing in moments what it would have taken hours to do by herself.

The spidermen watching were still confused. Who was their master? This dazed figure holding the glowing sword? Or the one tending the enchanter?

With lightning speed, and cries of, "Long live Dekhalis," six spidermen attacked and killed four of the dark elves shielding Embaza. As if by magic, more elves replaced them. The battle continued, as confused loyalties caused more mayhem.

Dekhalis rallied, feeling the sword singe his palm. It quivered in his hands, and he realized it wanted to kill again. His heart thrilled with an answering lust, but he did not want to cut down his own men. It was all he could do to hold the sword steady. He gritted his teeth, muttering, "Obey, you demon."

From the perimeter, Obsidian ran forward and opened both eyes as wide as he could on the scene before him. All he saw were battling dark elves among a forest of tall trees. High above was a canopy of glistening rock. Intermittent fireflies and a few phosphor-stone lamps lit the way. He extended his senses to maximum and felt them extend further yet. His hearing became impeccable.

And then, he saw a face he recognized, the High Abbot, Umsel. He shook his head. *Impossible.* But the vision imbued him with new spirit, and fired by the love of the Earth Mother herself, he ran to Embaza's side and fought like a madman.

Many of the spidermen were sure he was a devil, for they had been warned of men with the skin of white worms who fought with the strength of giants. This one had more than strength, though. He had agility, dexterity, and above all, he had the training of the Masters Umsel, Riddel, Inota and Tolimane.

Wary of Embaza's new ally, Dekhalis looked around for another opportunity to gain victory. He saw Tiala standing unarmed in a plain white shift, surrounded by a ring of Swords of Siadhin. *Odd. Why should they protect her?*

When he drew near, they held their crude weapons up to form a shield. "So," he said, "the Faithful," and he laughed. "I had heard of you weaklings. Hoping to be pets of the new Nightwing?" He wielded the sword of the Siadhin Lords more confidently now, letting it fill with passion. It glowed with ancient, yellow light. It would kill again.

One after another, the dark-elven champions were cut down by the magical sword, but as soon as one fell, a new shield-man replaced him. Yet, not one had raised a weapon to strike. At first, Dekhalis was confused, and then he heard his sister's unmistakable voice cry out, "You're in mourning. Remember Ombra. Remember the Nightwing who loves you—as I love you. You are men of Alvarra. You are men of peace."

Dekhalis laughed viciously and swung the sword in a mighty arc, killing the defenseless elves faster than they could be replaced. In the center, Tiala continued her chant of encouragement to her people, her face streaked with tears.

Like a wraith, a small figure moved forward, oblivious of the fighters. Stumbling, her hand closed around a crude dagger, her eyes never leaving the bright blue figure with the shining sword. By some miracle, she slipped between the others, intent upon her prey, until she stood behind his back. She raised the dagger in both hands and prepared to bring it down with all her might.

Perhaps he sensed her. Turning, he showed her his profile, and for a moment, Noth saw the image not of her defiler, but of her childhood playmate. The hesitation was long enough for a spiderman to grab her wrist and twist it until she released her weapon. He hurled her away from him like a broken branch. When she hit the ground, she rolled to her knees, and searched frantically in the grass for another weapon.

Just then, a new voice was heard over the din of battle. A high, petulant voice, but a loud one. "Where is Dekhalis? Where's the Lord King?"

"Who wants to know?" asked a spiderman.

"Make way for the great wizard, Mischa," cried a voice with a decidedly gnomadic accent.

Dekhalis looked up in wonder. "Just what I need. Over here."

Having recognized the odious voice, Embaza groaned and rose to his feet, a head taller than those around him. He saw the Prince advancing with a retinue of guards from the docks. More men had joined them along the way, until the party represented a small army.

Embaza broke through the circle of dark elves, and intersected Mischa's path. As he drew nearer to Dekhalis, something held him from going further. With a rush of understanding, he said, *I'll not leave you, Polah. Keep healing, my love. You are the true magic.*

When Mischa came closer, he saw not one, but two dark elves, dressed in identical blue body suits, their handsome faces both resembling that of the Lord King who had announced himself in the Orb of Wonder.

"Which one of you is Dekhalis?" he asked.

"I am," said Dekhalis. "We met in the orb. This is my evil brother, Embaza. If you're truly a wizard, you should know that." As he spoke, two of his spidermen moved to stand beside him. He felt the sword tingle, but its blood-thirst was satisfied for the moment.

"Great Mischa," Embaza said, "don't be fooled by this trickster. Join me, and take your place at my side." The Swords of Siadhin who overheard moved in to watch.

Confused, Mischa looked from one to the other. It had never occurred to him that Embaza and Dekhalis might be brothers. To him, all dark elves looked more or less alike. Why hadn't he studied the face in the orb more closely?

"Which one of you promised to reward me with magical artifacts?" he asked, seeing no point in mincing words.

"I said I would reward you—if you pleased me," said Dekhalis.

"I'll not waste your time," said Embaza, "I'll teach you *real* magic." He could feel Polah struggling to rise to her feet behind him.

"Are you implying I am not a real wizard?" asked Mischa. He reached into his sack for the flute.

"Stand back," ordered Dekhalis, hefting the magical sword. The spidermen obeyed, instantly. "I'll show you who wields magic." With lightning speed and the expert strokes of a perfect assassin, he slew the last three of Tiala's protectors and held the sword above her head.

Quiet reigned for a horrible moment in the clearing. In desperation, Tiala sent a silent plea to her mother for guidance. She cried, "This is an unfair contest." Her piteous tone plucked the very strings of Mischa's heart like an instrument. He had dabbled in many an unfair battle. The locket around his neck fairly hummed with warmth.

Delyra had been but a gnomad child. But Tiala—dark as night—was as stately and entrancing as his own dead mother. In his hands, he held the last thing of magic he possessed. Drawing himself up to his full two feet, Mischa said, "Let a real wizard save you, Tiala Denshadiel." He put the flute to his lips.

"Not with that," she screamed.

But it was too late. Eyes closed, and with a deep breath, Mischa blew his very soul into the artifact.

The supple notes of the Glammalee drowned all protest and skimmed out onto the air of the Arboretum as if riding on the gossamer wings of dragonflies. Not one ear who heard those notes was spared their effects. Not the dark elves, nor their visitors, not the shape-changers nor the animals in the trees and bushes. Not the insects, nor the birds.

The Earth Mother Herself heard the sound, and the legendary voice of Miralor responded. Just as it was told in the mythologies, there was a rumbling in the earth, very soft at first—barely a loving growl.

But it grew until the high-ceilinged cavern began to quiver. The ground trembled and the tree roots began to loosen.

Chaos ensued as people screamed, running in panic toward the edges of the forest and the tunnels of egress. A silver cloud arose, whirling about the crystalline cavern, and time seemed to stop. The earth shifted, fissures erupted, and ancient stalagmites broke in two.

Alvarrans, animals, insects and plants were gathered into the cloud and hurled in all directions. Stalactites shattered from above, rocks fell, and when it had finished, the cloud dwindled to a thread of silver and disappeared into the earth.

The Arboretum, which had been planted in the time of the Nightwing

Nubria, was littered with the bodies of the living and the dead.

One of those dead was Prince Mischa, who had finally performed true magic, his skull split by a splinter of crystal three times his size.

Near him, the bodies of two handsome dark elves in bright blue body suits lay side by side. One got up. His emerald eyes glistened with tears that might have been despair or grief, as he looked around him, surveying the wreckage. The brilliant colors of lichen and flower petals clung to the landscape like a carpet woven by a mad weaver.

Behind him, a large, red fox rose from the rocks, the gaping wound at her neck still healing. With shaky steps, she walked toward the dark figure, and bared her teeth in a growl.

-34-

THE BLOOD-bond tugged at Polah. *Embaza?* she probed, staring first at the blue-garbed figure before her, and then at the one lying still. *Which is you?*

There was no answer.

Avoiding him, Polah walked carefully over the rocks until she stood over the elf who lay still. His handsome face was streaked with dirt. Bruised and wounded dark-elven fighters and spidermen, bound each to their leaders, staggered nearby, dazed and bewildered. Was all lost? They watched the fox, half-hopeful, half-afraid.

She pushed her muzzle into his neck. There was no pulse. No breath. His smell was foul.

She moved to stand before the tall, dark elf. Her lips pulled back in a snarl, but he showed no fear. *Polah, flower of my heart.*

She sniffed his hand. Tears watered her soft black eyes.

Embaza knelt beside Dekhalis's body and looked at the face of the half-brother he had never known.

All he saw now was a mask of terror and madness. He noticed a shard of crystal embedded in the elf's right ear. Looking more closely, he winced as he saw that Dekhalis's entire body was riddled with slivers of needle-sharp crystal. Deliberately, Embaza pulled the cord from around Dekhalis's neck and pocketed the keys.

Behind him, a voice cried, "Tiala? Six Stix?"

"Obsidian," said Embaza, clasping the monk's arm.

Together with Polah, they searched for survivors, especially for Tiala.

In the once-wonderful park, fallen trees and tumbled blocks of stone and crystal made a nightmarish landscape of phantom shapes that loomed out of the broken earth.

Among the survivors, there were few who had escaped without injury, and fewer still who had the heart for battle. For the remaining spidermen, their leader was dead, destroyed by the Glammalee. Both Swords of Siadhin and Faithful were united in a brotherhood of tragedy.

Embaza and Obsidian lent their hands to help the wounded out of the rubble and from under the fallen trees. Embaza was quick to introduce himself as "The Wizard, Embaza," and he was greeted with a mixture of disbelief, fear, disappointment and hope.

Obsidian's pale skin and hairlock were alien to the dark elves, and the monk still had not had time to master their language, but all understood a helping hand. Polah was happy to see that some of the members of Comrhae Diep were among the living.

-35-

TIALA SEARCHED for her sisters. She tore the hem off the cumbersome white dress and staggered over the rubble. Groping for what was left of the stage, she collided with a dark blue shape and caught her breath. "Inuari."

After Tiala had loosed Inuari's bonds, the priestess buried her face in her sister's shoulder. "Thanks to the Goddess, you're home."

Tiala knotted the torn robe over her sister's bared breasts.

Together, they found Noth lying among the rocks, her face and body a mass of cuts and bruises. When they touched her, she gave a terrified scream and thrashed from side to side. With difficulty, they wrapped her in a tablecloth stained with mistletoe juice.

"It's your sister—Inuari. Don't be afraid." Inuari looked earnestly at Noth, but the terrified eyes seemed to stare right through her.

Embaza caught sight of them, and hurriedly approached. Noth jerked her head and stared at him in stark terror.

"Don't come near us, brother," said Inuari.

Tiala said, "Look closer. This is Embaza, not Dekhalis."

Inuari said breathlessly. "Not—Dekhalis?"

"He is dead," said Embaza.

Noth screamed, a howling, hysterical keening that made them all nearly jump out of their skins.

Inuari slapped her, and Noth gave a sob, as the pain from her broken nose was reanimated. Inuari embraced her, stroking her hair.

Tiala turned to Embaza. "You're sure he's dead?"

He nodded. Tiala's luminous eyes held a terrible sadness, and Embaza said, "You still have me."

She grasped his arms. "Then I wasn't dreaming. You did say—."

"Yes, I am your older brother." He saw Inuari look up with surprise. "My father, Valedd, wanted me to be a man of power, not a jewel for the Nightwing's court."

Tiala's eyes glistened. "Always the philosopher." She brushed a lock of hair from his temple.

Noth stared at him with an unreadable expression. Inuari whispered, "Thanks be to Miralor."

Tiala noticed the monk standing apart and linked arms with him. "My champion, I'm glad you're unhurt."

Obsidian asked, "Have you found Six Stix or the General?"

"They fought brilliantly—together," said Embaza, "against a foe with an ancient weapon. Then they vanished."

Like the High Abbot, thought the monk, remembering his vision.

Tiala said, "I hoped my eyes deceived me."

A dark-elven man touched Tiala's arm and said, "Na'a Nightwing? Your sister Eleppon is hurt."

Quickly, she followed him to the spot where the horsewoman lay against a pile of huge boulders, her leg bent strangely. Her right arm was useless. But she was alive. "Tiala," she croaked.

Tiala brushed the thick mane from Eleppon's forehead. "Oh, how I've missed you." She was afraid to hug the battered body. "We'll go riding again, soon. You'll see." Eleppon smiled, then winced with pain.

Tiala said to the man, "Hurry, bring a healer from the Temple."

"Yes, na'a Nightwing."

"And tell them my brother is dead. Find his body and have it brought to the Royal City."

Eleppon closed her eyes, breathing shallowly. "Dekhalis is dead?"

Tiala held her hand and whispered, "Yes. Sleep now." She looked up and saw that some of the men had ventured nearer. She motioned to them, and two came to her side. "Bring my sisters here, and watch over them, will you?" They nodded, one gulping with evident shame. Their faces were deferent, concerned, yet she remembered the hatred, the resentments that still lurked beneath. They would rise again, if she did not do something.

She rose and brushed off the filthy, once-white garment. She looked around her, gathering impressions. Knots of men milled about the ruined Arboretum amidst the flashing of the fireflies whose greenish lamps were a gentle reminder of peace and normalcy.

Tiala climbed the highest boulder in sight, and her clear, sweet voice rang out: "People of Alvarra." Conversation ceased as the men looked up at their ragged sovereign. Her figure was framed by the remnants of the Wellambtree whose soul ran deep into the earth.

A tall elf whom she recognized as one of the Faithful handed her an item. She looked down and realized it was the horn of Drimma, brought for the ceremony to the Goddess of Revenge. A new crack scored it all around. Gently, she broke it in half and let the pieces fall to the ground.

"Most of you know me. I am Tiala, na'a Nightwing. Soon, my mother will die and I will be your ruler."

There were mutterings among a group of Swords of Siadhin, and one called out, "We will not be your slaves."

"Do you think a woman cannot challenge her own tradition?" she cried, and there was silence.

Tiala's voice carried softly over the crowd, and Embaza marveled at the way she managed to use the echoes in the still magnificent cavern. "Ironic, isn't it? For eons, we Alvarrans lived beneath the earth, driven by our fear of the Scourge to change our world of stone and shadow into a wonder." She spread her arms, and they remembered the way it had been.

"But the spirit of darkness became a spirit of ignorance. All we knew was the language of oppression. Man to woman. Woman to man." She paused, remembering a certain General of Estenhame. "We even tried to dominate our neighbors, the dwarves." She waited for the grumbling to subside.

"And all for fear of a natural force." She paused, and rolled back her sleeve to show her still parched skin. "I have felt the Scourge on my body and in my bones. And I have survived." There were murmurs all over the park. She raised her hand, "And in this new light, I have seen that men are shadows of women, and women reflections of men. We are as equal as two wings on a bat."

A man called out, "Why should we believe you? Dekhalis warned us of your golden tongue."

"Yes," cried another, "Your words are but Scourge-madness. At first bell, you'll forget them."

She paused. "I can understand why you feel embittered. Try not to be prejudiced. We must have faith—and hope—if we are to craft a new future. Once I would have been glad to come home, believing the upworlders to be an abomination. And then I met...my brother." At a ripple of protest, she raised her hands. "My older brother, Embaza." She paused again, then called out, "Come here, Sargothian."

A tall figure climbed the rock to stand beside her, and some recognized him now. This was not Dekhalis, but the stranger who called himself "Wizard."

"Here is a dark elf who grew to manhood," said Tiala, "without having to bear the mantle of brutishness—or frailty." She had them now. "I say it is my brother, Embaza, who should rule."

There was a gasp from the men in the park and then a cheer from a throng of dark-elven men, who were primed for a hero.

Embaza's eyes roamed over the crowd, searching for a sign. From the edge of a clearing, a pitifully small group of changelings were illumined suddenly by the fireflies. Embaza picked out one white form in their midst. He turned to Tiala.

"I have spent my life learning how to become a Sargothian wizard, whereas you have spent your life learning how to become a Nightwing. I think Alvarra has need of both."

"Then I will ask you again someday. Meanwhile, Alvarra will not scorn your magic."

Inuari stepped forward and extended her arms. Her voice quivered with emotion, "You threaten to throw us back into the past, my sister. Have we learned nothing about wizards?" She pulled a broken sword from beneath a rock. "See this? In their ignorance, they could imbue it with powers, but it cannot know the value of life." She tossed it aside. "Real magic lies in the arts of Miralor and Loote."

Embaza said, "You speak truly, sister. But why fear me? Is that not also ignorance? I would rather we learned from each other. In the Towers of Sargoth, where I lived my childhood, I was taught that a man of power is not necessarily a man of violence."

Inuari looked unconvinced, but she pondered his words.

Tiala said, "Truly, Inuari, this man—perhaps any man—is more than we have believed. Embaza understands the value of the life within." She touched his shoulder.

Embaza looked at the upturned faces of the men in the crowd, and discerned the fire still raging beneath the docility. He said, "I, too, have been humbled in the presence of the great Goddess Loote." He was pleased to see Inuari's eyes widen with surprise and he said to Tiala, "May I speak to the men, n'a Nightwing?"

She nodded and stepped back to let him have center stage.

"The reign of Nightwing has brought much that is gentle and good into a violent world, but at what cost to her men? Do you not deserve to know power and grace?" There was a spontaneous burst of applause. Embaza said, "How many of you would follow the ways of magic if there was a school to teach it?"

Above the excited response, Tiala locked eyes with Inuari and said, "It is time." The young priestess folded her hands into her sleeves and bit her lip.

Obsidian followed the speech as best he could. He wished he could have shared this moment with Six Stix and Gudrun. The dwarf would have understood. She had been so afraid of magic, yet she had used it when she had to.

The familiar voice rustled in his mind, like the sound of dry leaves in the wind. *"My son, I see you have made your peace with caves."*

Embaza climbed down from the rock and walked over to join Obsidian, and the men in the crowd parted to let him through.

Tiala continued, "Which of you wishes to join in the renewal of the Arboretum? I need Master Gardeners and designers with fresh vision…" Her words plucked at the hearts of the Alvarrans who moved closer to get a glimpse of the new Nightwing.

When Embaza reached Obsidian, he could see the monk's thoughts plainly written on his face. "It is a mystery how one becomes a man, is it not?"

Obsidian replied, "More than I knew. I will be glad to go back to the monastery."

"It is your home," said Embaza.

"And you—will you stay?"

The wizard didn't answer. He was recalling the ceremony he had attended for Anebra's death, so long ago. What was his destiny now?

Across the park, Polah stood with the enchanters of Comrhae Deip. She had wrapped herself in a green velvet robe from the knapsack of a fallen warrior.

Many of the foxes had not survived the battle with the spidermen. Polah was glad to see Zie, the black vixen who had shared her food that first day. Polah pressed the enchanter's hand.

Zie said, "You belong to the Comrhae now, if you wish."

Polah's eyes fastened on Embaza, standing with Obsidian. When she turned to Zie, her eyes were shining. "We will meet again," she said.

Zie nodded.

Nimbly, Polah navigated the shards of broken crystal, rocks and fallen trees to join Embaza and Obsidian.

Embaza sensed her approach, and turned. "Little flower." He pulled her head against his heart, and she felt it beating even more loudly than her own.

Obsidian smiled a little sadly. Umsel would have enjoyed this. One of his sayings was, "Love is always true."

From her perch on the high rock, Tiala announced, "I give you my promise, people of Alvarra. There will be equality—and peace—in our land. Men, go home to your women and tell them we will make new laws. Tell them to bind your wounds, as I will bind mine. Tell them you were heroes today, fighting for a cause you believed was just. But you will be even greater heroes tomorrow."

One man approached her with something long and silver, wrapped in a tattered cloth. He handed it up to her. It was the Glammalee. Battered and scarred, the runes could still be read in places. She cradled it for a moment, then folded it back into the cloth. Her hands trembled. She looked into the distance where a strand of poplars faced a ruined stone cavern. A small cave-wren sat poised on a high branch, as if waiting for some sign or promise.

Tiala began to sing. It was a simple song, a song that women sang from the beginning of time. It spoke of binding wounds, and coming together in love to do the work of the Goddess. All over the Arboretum, voices rose to join hers, and Alvarra was united again, at least for this moment.

From her perch, Tiala saw a group of dark-elven men dressed in the livery of the Royal City. Two of them carried a stretcher made of white oxhide. Inuari gestured to them, and they moved toward the unconscious Eleppon. A young priestess accompanied them, her face pallid with shock at the throngs of men and the destruction of the Arboretum.

The song finished, Tiala climbed down, and hurried to help. When she drew near, the priestess intercepted her, and whispered, "Your mother, the Nightwing has asked for you."

Tiala took a deep breath. *At last.*

She saw Obsidian approaching with Embaza and Polah. Tiala ran to meet them and clasped the fox-woman's hand. "I won't ask how, just thanks to the Spirit of Night you're alive." She looked at Obsidian and Embaza. "Please—come with me."

-36-

DRAGONFLY NYMPHS and fireflies lighted the way to the Royal City, as Tiala and her sisters hurried to the bedside of their mother, accompanied by the anxious priestess and Tiala's three remaining champions. Behind them, the stricken Eleppon was carried by two strong, dark-elven men in the black robes of the Royal City.

Instead of traveling the tunnel to the outer, crystalline gate through which the enchanters had entered the City, the priestess led them down a side passage ending in a circular door of plain, gray stone. Using a key from the ring in her pocket, she opened it inward, with a scraping echo.

Tiala and the priestess hurried the party down a narrow path through a high cavern. Bunches of purple fern hung over their heads, and fungus-violets nestled between the rocks below, continuing the theme of simplicity. Polah's keen nose sniffed the welcoming perfume. Tiala breathed deeply of the fragrance, her homesickness abating at last.

The path wound its serpentine way to the side gate of the Royal City. A black dove cooed at them from a rock ledge.

At length, the path stopped before three large, moss-covered, stone steps that led up to a great, circular door made of polished, black stone. The door was bisected by a vertical line of molten silver, and to one side hung a weathered bronze bell, entwined with river dragons.

Tiala rang the bell, and a surprisingly delicate chime pealed forth. The priestess pushed on the door, and it opened to a huge, natural cave lit by wychwood lamps on tall metal poles carved with flowering nightshade vines. Colorful silk banners depicting the shields of the noble families of Alvarra hung around the walls from the high ceiling. The Nightwing's banner hung directly over the door, a silk panel of dark blue with a white rabbit leaping in the center.

Three tall dark-elven women came to greet them, each wearing a deep blue body suit emblazoned with a silver rabbit on the breast. They gasped at Tiala, who still wore the grimy piece of white linen that might have once been a dress.

"Na'a Nightwing," said one of the women, dropping to her knee. "Welcome." She kissed Tiala's hand.

"Thank you, Lady of Skill. It's good to be back," said Tiala. "Has Evendove been sent for?"

"She and the other Sisters of Loote have been with the Nightwing for more than sixty tolls of the bell," said the guard.

"My sister Eleppon needs a healer. She is behind us. Make her comfortable and send for Evendove immediately. I speak for my mother in this."

"Consider it done," said the guard.

Past the entrance, the great hall opened up to the collected splendor of generations of Nightwing families. There was hardly time for the newcomers to appreciate the silken tapestries, the velvet-covered chairs and marble tables. Obsidian tiptoed carefully around a pillar of amethyst carved in the shape of a dragon. He regretted the clods of earth he ground into the pale, green spidersilk carpet.

Tiala led them past the satinwood harp dominating the hearth. She ached to touch it. From one of the arched doorways, soft music was already playing. Inuari grabbed her hand. "Look at Noth."

Both sisters stared at Noth, who had lapsed into a menacing silence since they had left the Arboretum. Inuari put her arm around Noth's shoulders, as the stretcher-bearers entered with Eleppon's motionless form. Tiala ran to them, and asked, "How is she?"

The men shook their heads, and she looked at the graying face on the stretcher. Putting her cheek down to Eleppon's mouth, she felt the cold, marble lips.

"No," she screamed, her fists clenched. "No."

Inuari shook with silent sobs, while Noth stared at Eleppon, her eyes brimming with one more tragedy.

Heavy-hearted, Tiala joined them again. "Our mother waits."

Her glance caught Embaza's, where he stood near the tall harp. "You must come," she ordered. "You, too, Polah and Obsidian." Her voice trembled with emotion.

They passed from the great hall through a magnificent archway of polished yellow quartz. The music rose in volume, as they continued down a black marble hallway hung with silken banners. Each banner bore the embroidered history of a past Nightwing or priestess.

When they reached the base of the central tower, they crossed a mosaic circle of deep purple tile in the shape of a five-petaled flowering nightshade. Thirty musicians and bards were stationed on tiers of quartz crystal that formed a spiral around the central cone of the tower.

There was a staircase of blue calcite that snaked its way around, and at each stage of the stairway, the instruments created a different balance of sounds.

As she climbed, Tiala identified two travel harps, a chitarrone (large lute), a rack of horn bells, a Tskurl'an wind stick, an onyx flute, kuta (carapace of a giant turtle played with sticks), several timbrels, pipes and rattles, stone drums, goblet drums and a five-stringed, crystal oud. These she passed over quickly, her eyes turning to the bards, who stood in their respective places.

There were four, and each played a different harp. The bard facing east played a twenty-four-stringed talking harp, to the south was a thirty-five-stringed whispering harp, to the west was a forty-eight-stringed singing harp, and last, at the top of the stairs, the rare sixty-three-stringed dreaming harp played by the famous bard, Solange.

Tiala held her breath, memorizing each detail of the rhapsodic melodies. In her entire lifetime, this would never be repeated, until the last moments of her own reign as Nightwing when she would be beyond caring.

At the top of the stairs, a blue-robed priestess rose from her seat by the door. The chair was cut from a solid piece of sapphire, and the priestess had added a plain, gray pillow to the seat to make her vigil more comfortable. She was mature, but not aged, and Tiala did not recognize her. She supposed this was a task that required many shifts.

The priestess bowed and betrayed no shock at the disheveled appearance of the party. She said to Tiala, "The Sisters of Loote have departed—all but one. You must go in alone, na'a Nightwing."

Tiala brushed aside the black velvet curtain, and entered her mother's bedroom. Her hands tightened around the ruined flute in its cloth wrapper. The robed priestess at the door bowed to her, and Tiala moved to stand beside the ancient priestess Kalista, who was seated next to the giant seashell where

Avenwyndar lay. The Nightwing's black rabbit nestled under her quiescent hand.

Tiala squeezed Kalista's shoulder, then hurried to the other side of the bed, sinking into the black velvet chair. With searching eyes, she gazed at what was left of her mother, looking for signs of life in the transparent image that wavered in and out. She could see through the insubstantial skin to the thistledown sheets beneath. Tentatively, Tiala reached out to stroke the rabbit, as she had often seen Avenwyndar do.

Kalista whispered, "Sssh," and closed her eyes.

Tiala did the same. Then, by a miracle, she heard Avenwyndar's voice.

"I am proud of you, daughter. You took the brave and dangerous path. You are a true hero."

Tiala stifled the sudden tears that welled beneath her eyelids.

"Now, you show an even deeper heroism—by creating new traditions."

Tiala held her breath. *Do you approve?* She cracked one eye open.

The image on the bed seemed to smile. "It is the prerogative of a Nightwing."

Tiala spoke aloud, "I have met my older brother."

"Yes…I will see him at last. I will never forgive his father, Valedd, for deceiving me."

Tiala said, "Valedd. You always spoke of him with such tenderness."

"A part of me wishes the same love for you, my daughter, and yet it is a path fraught with peril. Life is a river, reflecting events, and then moving on. Always changing and evolving." The Nightwing's voice stopped as if to gather force. "But there are moments in time that are universal, captured for that instant like a seed under crystal, or a nightingale's song. They have the power to open our hearts, make us see truly, elevating ordinary life to the realms of the fairies, our ancestors."

"I have felt that love, Mother," said Tiala.

"Ah…"

"For music."

"Yes," said Avenwyndar. "You will be the first Nightwing Bard. It makes my old heart happy. I see that the Glammalee has been retrieved from where Miralor buried it."

"It is ruined," said Tiala, holding it before her.

"Not so," said the Nightwing. "I have been told that you alone can play it as it should be played."

"Told by whom?" asked Tiala.

There was no answer.

Tiala opened her eyes and saw no change in Avenwyndar's figure, unless perhaps it was even more transparent than before. Now, she could not stop the tears. *How will I rule without you? I'm not ready.*

Kalista said, "Your mother is tired now. Go and bring your sister Noth."

"But—." Tiala stopped, a weight in her heart, her hands clenched. She gazed at her mother's diaphanous form, closed her eyes and sent a flood of love to the fading Nightwing.

A soft voice entered her mind like a cloud. "Seek me in your heart, child, for there I will be." Tiala's hands unclenched and she arose.

When she had left, Inuari led Noth to stand by the bed. Kalista winced at the look in Noth's hollow eyes. She put out a withered hand and got to her feet, easing Noth into the other chair.

Again the voice emanated from the mist. "Noth, my daughter. I know of your despair." From within the depths of her misery, Noth felt her mother's presence shake her like thunder. Dry-eyed, she held onto the moment.

"The mantle of experience sits on your shoulders, while your peers hide under their cloak of childhood. Your heart is pierced with a dagger of vengeance. Give yourself a second life, my darling."

Noth slowly turned her head at the soft touch on her shoulder. The robed priestess of Loote had crept forward with a goblet in her hand. A dragon chased its tail around the precious silver, cooling the dark purple liquid within.

The healer said, "Drink of the flower of forgetfulness. Drink and be made new, daughter of Nightwing."

Noth recognized the rare liquid from the Purple Moor of Forgetfulness, the poppy that annihilated the past. A deep sigh welled up in her, the burden of her experience already lighter. She reached out and took the goblet, while a curious lethargy took hold of her. Time seemed to stop as the events of her life unraveled within her. She closed her eyes and savored the highlights of her hundred and eleven years.

When she came to the confrontation with Dekhalis, she gripped the goblet with both hands, trembling. Tears coursed down her face, a grimace contorting her delicate features. "Topi," she sobbed, and the goblet tipped.

The healer took it from her hands and stepped back.

Noth created a layered web of echoes in the hollow cavern. Her wails turned to screams, and then to sobs again. The other women waited, eyes closed, as the anguished sounds evoked their own fears.

Finally, Noth gave a long, shuddering sigh and opened her eyes. The Nightwing's still form was barely visible on the down coverlet.

"I am sorry, Mother. I want…to remember…those I've loved." Her statement sliced through the cobwebs of grief like a shaft of moonlight. "Even Dekhalis." Her voice wavered on his name, but did not break. Fresh tears welled into her eyes.

"My daughter, you have reached a maturity that others may dream of. I myself do not know if I would have made such a choice. The path of wisdom is not easy, but I think you will never regret it. You will be one of the great Nightwings, as free from vengeance as I have been bound by it."

Noth hid her face in the folds of the tablecloth, and the bitter scent of mistletoe filled her nostrils. Her heart felt eased for the first time since Ombra's funeral. A spark had fled from her eyes, but they were calm now.

Kalista took her arm and beckoned to Inuari, who was poised by the door.

"I love you, Mother," said Noth.

"Be at peace, daughter," came the soft reply.

Inuari rushed to the bed, clasping the edge of the seashell and laying her head by her mother's side.

"My daughter, Inuari. Like me, you follow in Miralor's footsteps. In time, you will see with Miralor's own eyes. I wish I could be with you." Inuari felt Kalista's presence behind her, not as a teacher but as a second mother.

"Be kind to Noth, my daughter, and do not quarrel. You are the two sides of a single coin. It is not necessary for you to see the same viewpoint."

Kalista came around the bed and helped Inuari to her feet. "She grows tired."

Inuari reached out her slim hand and touched the Nightwing's barely discernible shoulder. It felt like a cloud, and she whispered, "I'll miss you, Mother."

The compassionate voice reached out to her. "I'll be near. The Land of the Dead is not so far away, you know. You have but to call for me."

Inuari looked upon her mother for the last time and stroked the black rabbit with her grimy hand. The animal's fur rippled and it gazed up at her with eyes that seemed to glow with Avenwyndar's own knowledge. Inuari gently reached the tip of her finger to stroke its nose.

Kalista said, "Go now. She must speak with her son."

Noth and Inuari left the room, to be greeted by Tiala, who clasped Noth's hand and looked searchingly at both her sisters.

"She asked for you...Embaza," said Inuari shyly.

The wizard eyes widened, and he entered the dim chamber. Seeing the priestess Kalista seated beside an empty bed, Embaza thought at first she was the Nightwing.

Kalista gave a crooked smile and indicated the bed, where a thin shadow remained. He sat down on the velvet chair.

Avenwyndar's voice came, a bit stronger than before. "My son, welcome home."

Embaza swallowed and closed his eyes. "It is good to see you, Mother."

Kalista felt a shiver up her spine at the density of feeling in the room. Not another word was spoken. When Embaza opened his eyes, a pale, indigo flower lay on the thistledown sheets, and the shadow was no more. He smelled the flower's sweet essence, and heard a gasp behind him.

"What is it?" asked Embaza, with a foreknowing.

Kalista said, "It's a true-blood blossom, the token he gave her so many times."

"Who?"

"Valedd," whispered Kalista.

My father.

The healer by the door stepped into the hallway and beckoned to Tiala, who was standing with Polah and Obsidian. The old woman knelt and said, "Nightwing Tiala, your long day has begun."

Tiala's green eyes glistened with emotion and she helped the healer to her feet, then turned to Polah and Obsidian. "My dear friends, I am sorry. My mother wanted to express her gratitude, but her time was short."

"It's all right," said Polah, squeezing Tiala's arm.

Obsidian smiled and nodded. Tiala adjusted his butterfly knives and said, "Of all who mourn, Obsidian, you alone will be allowed to carry weapons, in honor of your dedication. It was you who taught me what a man of peace really is."

To Polah, she said, "I am filled with joy that my brother has found a true love—something I may yet find myself."

When Embaza re-entered the hallway, he heard Tiala's clear voice, as she stood on the balcony overlooking the majestic cavern of crystal.

"Let the lore books state that in my reign as Nightwing, there was a place for men of power and greatness. Let them say 'Alvarra is forgiven in the Realms of the Wise.'"

But Embaza did not hear the rest. To the delight of the priestess in the sapphire chair, he took Polah into his arms and kissed her, engraving his love forever upon her heart.

-37-

THE FOLLOWING day, in a vast cavern leagues below the earth's surface, eighty-nine dark elves, one human and one shape-changer were assembled for the funerals of the Nightwing Avenwyndar, her third daughter Eleppon, and her youngest son, Dekhalis. Like dark statues beside the shimmering Lake of All Souls, their faces were illuminated by the flickering blue light of the phosphorescent water. The dripping of stalactites echoed in the immense chamber. All wore the sacred black of the Nightwing, supreme ruler of Alvarra, land of the dark elves.

On a high rock on the banks of the lake stood the Nightwing Tiala, her spidersilk gown glittering with gossamer threads of silver. As each of the crystal caskets was lowered into the bottomless Lake of All Souls, the seven highest bards in the land played "The Endless Dream." The eighth place was empty and one crystal dreaming harp was still.

Embaza, Inuari and Noth were on Tiala's right. Inuari glanced with awe at the tall Embaza. He looked quite regal in the black velvet robe he had found among his father's things. Inuari tossed a pink starflower into the shimmering water, and the others followed suit.

On Tiala's left, Obsidian and Polah marveled at the events that had brought them there. The monk closed his eyes and added a silent prayer for the High Abbot, Umsel, the dashing Six Stix and the brave Gudrun, though a secret part of him hoped they were alive.

Tiala looked up at the ceiling of the cavern, from which descended the thrice-woven silken rope that encircled the third crystal casket, containing the body of Dekhalis. She tossed her last starflowers into the lake and watched as the delicate petals formed a perfect star before they floated away and sank.

Then she made her way to the empty dreaming harp. The whisper-soft strings quivered with a life of their own before she even touched them. She could feel their breath, and a shiver played up her back. Gently, she placed her fingers against the silkwood. Solange had cautioned her, "You don't have to actually play it, Nightwing. Only touch it, get acquainted with it. Nothing more is expected." The cavern seemed out of focus, and Tiala closed her eyes. The harp felt alive. It breathed.

One by one, her fingers found the notes, and an ecstasy she had never known possessed her. Her fingers were placed where they belonged, and she was where *she* belonged, in the company of bards. "The Endless Dream," though timeless in sound, was not truly endless. Yet, for Tiala, the memory of those few moments of pure harmony, of glorious fellowship, would never be surpassed.

Above the crowd, a ledge jutted out from the slab of stone, and the High Priestess Kalista stepped onto it. Her stern face was radiant in the reflected light of the lake. As the last rippling notes fell from the dreaming harps, all eyes lifted to her shadowy figure. The quiet resonated with the dripping water, and the crone waited until the echoes filled the cavern. When she spoke, her voice was strong.

"The time of mourning is at hand." There was a murmur of assent from the people, and several priestesses echoed her words. The High Priestess tossed a last starflower into the lake and said, "Our beloved Nightwing has descended. And to accompany her, she has brought her daughter Eleppon and her son Dekhalis. Name them with your wishes."

"For Avenwyndar...for Eleppon," murmured the crowd. "For Dekhalis," murmured a few.

Kalista finished, "We send them wise counsel and profound love as they join their revered ancestors. May they be happy in the deeper life."

Again, there was only the sound of dripping water until the silence was pierced by a deep melancholy bell, whose somber tones echoed mournfully through the cavern. Each tufted ear reverberated with the sound, as did the entire country of Alvarra, from the depths of the Royal City to the grotto of the poorest farmer above.

The priestess said, "The death bell has rung from the Temple of Miralor, and all over Alvarra, emissaries of the Goddess will now gather our possessions of power. Thus, we put ourselves at Her mercy, knowing that life and death are in Her hands. You may approach, Appointed One."

One figure entered the cavern from the far exit. She wore a robe of bright red and a matching mask, and carried a large toad-skin bag. She made one pass among the celebrants, but few had anything left to relinquish.

After the ceremony, the new Nightwing found a quiet moment to leave the confines of her rooms. She slipped away down a secret tunnel that led to a large rock near the ocean of the Merimn'a. The sound of distant waves pleased her, and she pulled out the Glammalee. Hesitantly, she put it to her lips and blew, thinking of her own father, who had never known the freedom he deserved simply because he was a man. In her heart, she embraced all the Alvarran males who had ever suffered at the hands of the Nightwings. And the music issuing from the flute soothed the minds of all who heard it, in the lands above, and in the dark worlds below.

In the bushes nearby, a black rabbit hovered, her nose twitching in the cavern's breeze.

-38-

FAR BELOW Alvarra, the darkness was palpable. Not a particle of light defiled the inky velvet of the nether cave. Here, a sensitive one might hear the ancient voices of dwarves who had once called themselves Alvarrans. Long before the elves took possession of the land above, the "little people" mined for silver, gold and precious jewels. Their haunting cries of woe still seemed to echo in the chambers. As if its work was finished, the rushing waters of the

Merimn'a, the underground sea, had receded from the caverns.

However, into this sanctuary of time and nature, an alien voice was raised—and swore.

"Didn't have the sense to bring a single torch, did you, my bearded beauty?"

About the Author

A writer, artist and traveler, Stirling Davenport has spent most of her life doing various day jobs to support her writing and painting. In 2005, she volunteered for one year in northern India, teaching art to Tibetan refugee children and filming a documentary about the exile experience. A student of Buddhism, she has made seven trips to Tibet. In India, she learned to play the Tibetan dranyen (stringed instrument).

But writing will always be her first calling. While *The Nighwing's Quest* is her first published novel, Stirling Davenport's extensive publishing credits include poetry and numerous short stories in the science fiction, fantasy, horror and mainstream genres.

She has a son and granddaughter, and currently resides in upstate New York.

Lightning Source UK Ltd.
Milton Keynes UK
05 November 2009

145873UK00002B/5/P